I0612922

To Steal a Sea

BY

SIMON D REAGAN

Reagan Publishing, London.

Published by Reagan Publishing.

ISBN 978-0-9575267-0-9   Paperback format

ISBN 0-9575267-0-9   eBook-Kindle format

To Steal a Sea

To my Daughter

It is said that the brilliance of angels' wings is enhanced by the darkness brought into this world by monsters. In bright daylight they would move among us unnoticed: it is the contrast which makes them visible. There are some who'll say after my death that I did indeed provide this contrast, that in life I was truly a wicked man: I say to you, my daughter, that this was never true. Love of one's nation transcends all other considerations: it focuses the mind and the soul, sloughing away trivial and superficial needs. You grew to know me through your childhood, but also through my more recent schemes and dreams, and now you despise me: this troubles me, but I make no apology for having done what I knew was right. I made only one mistake in a lifetime of sacrifice and unquestioning commitment, one extinguished soul, and you will learn of this in my final testimony.

My time is short, measured in the weight of scribbles of lawyers, the last grains of sand passing through the neck of an hourglass. Arrangements have been made. Perhaps you'll remember me with horror, wondering how your love could have been so misplaced, but I am a product of events which took place so very long ago. The monster you discovered was created in killing fields more terrible than you could ever imagine, but in the midst of which I remained a loyal servant. I leave this, my apologia pro vita sua, the justification of my life's work, that in death you might know me better. In error I sought absolution through you for a single sin which expanded infinitely to fill an empty universe. You failed me, but in truth perhaps it could never have been any other way. Some sins are beyond redemption.

PART ONE

A Loyal Servant

Chapter One

The first time I killed a man was late on a hazy afternoon in September. I remember the day, the hour, the minute, the second; even now, sometimes, when I close my eyes I recall the shades of light through my eyelids, and breathe in the mustiness of stale air again. Involuntary mental revisiting of the scene of a first crime briefly heightens the senses, gently disturbing the emotional dullness which has been laid down like coral throughout the intervening years. Although hundreds more would follow, none mattered to me or disturbed my peace of mind; it's always the first which truly counts, providing the reference point in one's life. Everything is measured from that fracture in time, the break point between innocence and darkness, the great leap into the void. After the first dozen the rest became a blur. That autumnal day was so beautiful, so perfect, with a chill in the air that, since then, I've forever associated with the first bullet, that unique moment of loss of the soul's innocence.

For several hours I'd lain on the floor of the derelict building, peeping out through the smashed glass still clinging to the window frame. The dampness in the building quickly soaked through my clothes; a chill seeped into my tight lungs. But I couldn't cough: I couldn't even puff out a wisp of condensation to confirm that I was still alive.

It's strange what your mind's eye registers from that first time. I remember the slow plop, plop, plop of water falling from icicles in the smashed shell of a house in which I lay stiff like a corpse. Plop went the seconds, the minutes, the hours, but my own heartbeat seemed to keep better time. I remember looking up to the sky and seeing the gentle, cold glow of the falling sun, knowing that today was the last day someone as yet unidentified and forever afterwards unknown to me would gaze upon the Earth.

I was desperate for a cigarette to force warmth into my struggling lungs, but this would have to wait until after the kill. I listened for a sound, any sound, but heard nothing apart from the gentle, paced inhalations of my companion gazing out from another window along the wall. We didn't speak; there was no need for words. Neither did we exchange glances, since this was a time for solitude. He'd trained me diligently and heartlessly so that now as we lay in the filth we'd moved beyond the point of words. Until that afternoon I'd been an innocent, in deed if not in mind. The moment of truth had arrived.

In the distance I began to hear the crunching of heavy footsteps on pristine snow. My companion tapped the soft wood of the rotting sill to draw my attention to the tiny figure which had appeared at the end of the street, but I was already calmly aware of its presence. My heartbeat didn't even catch up with the drops of water, maintaining its slow gentle rhythm. A thickening of spit in my mouth was the only physical response to the uniqueness of the occasion, to the sense of terrible expectancy.

When I reflect upon that first killing in my lonely moments, it surprises me that of all the hundreds that were to follow, this was somehow the calmest. Slowly the little figure became larger and larger as he strode with determination through the snow, still bright despite the gently fading light. I rested my rifle on the sill, with just the tip balancing half an inch outside the frame. I snuggled by head against the ice cold steel barrel and looked out through the cross hairs. He was tall - about six foot five, with a swarthy, unshaven face. How standards had fallen! Occasionally he glanced from left to right, mainly into the shadows: the last place where people like us can be seen, trained at concealment, wearing darkness like a cloak. He was chewing on something: it looked like bitter fruit, and the irregular clenching of his teeth hinted at its fetidness and his disgust with its taste. He wore a heavy greatcoat, with once-shiny buttons done up to the chin. He was about twenty one, fit and strong at one time in his life perhaps, but now not so full of youthful confidence. Extreme situations empty a man's soul, sucking out youth from the marrow. And then all that remains is the husk, gnawed by fear, self doubt and self loathing.

I wondered momentarily why he was alone. But these, of course, were times of chaos and organizational breakdown, when bonds of order, discipline and friendship disintegrated like wet paper. In his hand he carried a large container, probably a water bottle, maybe just for himself, maybe for others. To kill a water bearer, now that was a prize! He came into range and for a while I just watched. He was nobody's son, husband, or lover: just a target like the countless rats and dogs I'd slaughtered during the past few months, skinned and eaten to keep me alive.

I watched him with detached curiosity, I can put it no other way. He picked up one foot, put it down, then the other, and so on, and in this way a living object slowly manoeuvered itself across the field of vision. He lifted his hand to scratch his mouth then moved it back again. It was like watching a mechanical toy, or perhaps I just wanted to perceive him that way. I was fascinated! Then I heard my mentor tap again as he too looked out on the scene. Without drawing back his sleeve he tapped his wrist. Now was the time. I looked back at my quarry and lined him up in the cross hairs. Not positioned face-on, I knew this would have to be a side shot - less clean and the impact less immediate. He'd stopped to pick residual fruit skin from between his stained teeth; now his temple appeared to be within touching distance. I took aim, then pulled the trigger.

It's said you don't hear the sound of the bullet that kills you, but I believed then that for a split second he was aware of my presence. I can recall the brief, hesitant straying of his eyes in my direction as I squeezed and perhaps that look of knowingness on his face should have haunted me ever since. But it only did so for a short while. Perhaps the soul I once had, which was troubled by such feelings, died soon afterwards. Living amongst corpses affects men in different ways; some become angry, some resigned, some just cold. The coldness at the core of my being proved positively advantageous, steadying my hand when reaping lives; warmth engenders hesitancy, a primordial compassion which detracts from clarity of purpose.

The sound of the shot ricocheted off the walls of surrounding buildings and for a moment I was afraid others might come running. But no-one came. Perhaps he'd been alone after all. Or perhaps there was nobody with the will or the care to come to a comrade's aid. The bullet struck exactly where I had intended, the temple on the left side of the skull. His head seemed to pop and a jet of blood burst forth as the body crumpled into a grey heap of flesh, bone, and patched greatcoat. It twitched once and then was still. Where he lay on the perfect whiteness it looked as if the ground itself was bleeding: a trickle of red quickly spread.

He was dead. He was my first. I looked across to my mentor. Our eyes met, but he didn't smile. He returned his gaze to the now blood-soaked scene and safe in the knowledge that nobody had heard the shot, he lined up the water bottle and fired. It jumped into the air then landed, bursting out its precious contents. I was surprised; I'd been taught that water bottles should be filled from stagnant pools and then left to tempt the weary, the weak, and the desperate. After the frostbite and the days of hunger, dysentery hastens the demise of the soul, if not the flesh. But this was my first time, and neither of us had enthusiasm to spite, to go down into the street to hasten the suffering of further victims who'd come later upon the scene, long after we'd gone. Instead we continued observing the street below, in total silence. As I lay in the semi-darkness I berated myself for sensing a need for praise, for some acknowledgment of my first success. Was I expecting approval or congratulations for having just blown a man's head off? Perhaps I was, but I was young and he was older, wiser: an 'old head' from the Party's earlier glory days; the days when they had fought for power and won the final victory though brutal doggedness, after years of struggles across our country against the Whites, the foreigners and anyone else who stood in their way.

He saw the future in me, when young men through force of circumstance would go out and kill and kill again, then return home to an untroubled sleep. This was the end of humanity; the genesis of a brutal universe.

After the first blooding, some men experience elation at their apparent power over life and death, while for others it's the beginning of a lifetime of self-disgust. The reality is that there's no single universal emotional response: some take pleasure while others bend then break under the weight of guilt at what they've done. A reaction on my part would have presupposed the infringement of some internal set of spiritual values, the spinning of the needle of a moral compass, but I possessed neither. My soul was already under siege in the eighteen months I had spent in the wastelands of Stalingrad. I felt little emotional reaction. Some sadness, but no regret. Mainly just an awareness of the dampness seeping through my clothes and a fleeting reproach that I'd not gone down into the street to strip the corpse of that warm greatcoat.

Within an hour three men appeared at the end of the street, walking in our direction. We both watched through our sights but these were not fresh targets. They passed safely past our vantage point. Their clothes were filthy and they strode along without as much as a glance into the shadows between the broken blast-blackened teeth lining either side of the street. One of the three was probably drunk, taking long gulps from the vodka bottle clutched in his right hand. Suddenly they spotted the body and their confidence evaporated.

I continued watching through the cross hairs as they crept towards the body. Although they squinted briefly in our direction, it was clear that we remained undetected. Besides, they probably assumed that the person responsible for the death was a 'comrade'. The drunk threw away his empty bottle and drew a long curved knife from inside his overcoat. I saw the knife gently glint in the fading evening sun as he crouched alongside the body. He hacked off the ears and nose of the young body lying in the snow, casting them aside into the gloom. I wondered whether the body was still warm. After rifling the pockets of the dead man, taking a photograph from his inside pocket and pinning it to the front of his greatcoat, the three wandered off; they'd not in all likelihood live to see their families again. These were the 'proud heroes of the Motherland', Stalin's fodder - born into squalor, forced into battle at gunpoint and slaughtered in their millions.

And the young man I'd killed with a single bullet would also, of course, never see his family again. He lay filthily dead in Stalingrad's vast, ruined slaughterhouse, a body still loved by his family who would probably never find out what had happened to him, a soldier lauded by a nation too afraid to face the truth that the war was slipping away. The strength and glory of a young man in his prime had now become the desecrated heap of an earless corpse.

Nighttime arrived bringing the familiar coldness which squeezed one's lungs and froze the body's essential fluids. My mentor and I spoke, whispered, in the darkness and dampness of the windowless room which had been our home for the past week. We didn't speak of the killing, but instead about his work as a Party Commissar. He'd survived the murders and persecutions, the Great Purge instigated by our Leader, 'The Great Bastard', during the past decade (he couldn't bring himself to speak Stalin's name: his hatred for the Georgian was too much). But with the end of the Ribbentrop-Molotov Pact which gave each side time to prepare for war, he'd left his rural base and headed for the front line.

The idea of taking me with him was his boss's suggestion, a fat, indolent high-flying Party apparatchik who lacked the guts to put his own life on the line in this struggle to the death. My mentor had been a teacher, and in the darkness he'd recite Pushkin and Fet. He wanted to keep our morale strong, to keep alight the struggling flame of recollection of prior existence: it would guide him back to his former life when the war finally ended, if it ever ended. This was the routine for future nights: one killing, two killings, a dozen killings during the day, and then poetry later, just before broken sleep. I remember those nights with perfect clarity: I still hear his voice in my dreams, recounting stories of innocence and struggle.

The following day was uneventful. We watched as a group of twenty thickly-clad skeletons entered the street, marching to nowhere, coming from nowhere. Although we didn't know it yet, by now the paralysis at the heart of the German High Command was complete; its sole aim was now to survive, to hold out for the arrival of Field Marshall Erich von Manstein's 4th Panzer Army. The relief expedition eventually reached within thirty miles of Stalingrad but then, on 27th December 1942, the Red Army halted it. Faced with the prospect of encirclement, von Manstein would turn back and flee, cursed by his Fuhrer in Berlin, damned in the annals of history. Paulus's proud 6th Army would be left to its fate, dependent upon the ability of its scouts to find rotting scraps or carcasses of recently dead animals, in and around buildings long since destroyed by their own artillery. When a man is hungry, truly hungry, he'll eat anything, even the bodies of his enemies. And for a while, he'll leave the bodies of his own side alone, at least until desperation eventually gets the better of him.

When the group came across the mutilated body, howls of anger and hatred resounded off the smashed buildings. I watched through the sight and saw a young man kneel beside the corpse and detach the photograph from the now-soaking overcoat. He was about the same age, his face as death-white as the body alongside which he crouched. He was crying, but the air's cold was so intense that not even a tear could escape his eyes. Fleetingly I was struck by the awfulness of what I'd done, but the spasm passed. We would let these people, the walking dead, pass by unharmed. Besides, we knew we'd catch up with them in a few days' time, after they'd divided into smaller groups. Then they'd be easier to pick off, one by one. They left the body where it had fallen, without the token gesture of an improvised burial; it would only be dug up again by the rabid dogs now roaming the ruined streets. After gazing in open fear at the surrounding buildings, perhaps looking for the glimpse of sunlight on a rifle sight, they moved on again. Their pace quickened from a natural fear of snipers lurking in the shadows.

In the final week's occupation of our allocated sector of the city we moved to a building on the opposite side of the street. This suited me: the building from which we had spied, whilst affording an excellent vantage point from which both ends of the street could be watched, was infested with rats which scurried over my body as I restlessly slept each night. Whether it was the harmless but unsettling scratching at my clothes, or the fear of not being able to move whilst a rat ran over my face lest I draw attention of soldiers in the street below, I cannot say, but the rats troubled me. Our new 'home' was much the same, although the rats didn't arrive until the final few days before we left the city. By this time I'd dispatched another nine of the enemy, or was it a dozen? I forget. All of them were cleanly taken out with a single bullet to the front of the head. Each fresh kill helped sap their collective will, a sense of hopelessness trickling drop by drop into the exhausted, frightened enemy mass. Deserters were still being shot when caught: it was an easier and nobler way to die to simply stand in open ground and hope that we were nearby. To be executed as a coward remained the ultimate fear: in contrast, we offered a quick and honorable exit from the madness of the situation. In another time Comrade Khrushchev, our 'peasant president', would observe that if nuclear conflict ever broke out, 'even the living would envy the dead'; no better description could be applied to the closing months of the siege of Stalingrad.

A group of four soldiers came into view; I knew that this was a small enough unit to be picked off, one by one and in quick succession. I slowly raised my rifle, gently resting it on the windowsill. I began lining up the cross hairs, but my mentor tapped on the soggy wood to gain my attention. He held up one hand, with two fingers uncurled. He looked at me and I nodded; Albert and Franz would make it back to their unit this evening, but not the others. But then he tapped again, just as I was realigning the hairs. This time he pointed at his leg; I didn't understand, so he signed the strategy again. He drew his hand across his throat, and then waved to indicate that death was not to be the outcome this time. Again he tapped his leg, and then I nodded. I understood.

We both took aim and then gently pulled the triggers, almost simultaneously. Two men fell to the ground, writhing in agony as single bullets struck each kneecap. We then began firing randomly and without any particular target in mind, careful not to hit either of the two now crouching beside their comrades. They began firing towards our building but without a clear target in view. As they fired, they dragged at the collars of the greatcoats of their fallen brothers who were already screaming in pain, reaching the relative safety of the building adjoining the one we'd previously occupied.

Now it was our turn to leave; we scampered through smashed walls between each house in the decaying bombed-out street, making good our escape. We now assumed the characteristics of the rats which had previously so disturbed my dreams. Within an hour we had left the city, heading for the next 'turkey shoot'. As for Klaus and Dieter, they'd probably return to base with the help of their comrades who would have half dragged, half piggy-backed them through the snow for half an hour. Their wretched deaths were close at hand; their legs would soon become infected, and within a couple of days they would be dead. Their demands upon the dwindling resources of their unit would be high, their moans contributing in that drip, drip way, to further erosion of morale of the rest of the unit. Our goal was achieved; this time two wounded soldiers had been more effective than four dead bodies found in the snow with bullets through their heads.

In the final weeks before Paulus's inevitable defeat, all sniper units received new, more terrifying, instructions from Moscow. By this time the desperation in Stalingrad was immeasurable, not just amongst the occupiers but also the locals. Now they too were to be terrorised, but by their own folk. Any sign of weakness, surrender or thought of fleeing was to be punished without mercy. They'd become hostages in their own city. Comrade Stalin had decreed that he'd see them all slaughtered before his own city be conquered or evacuated. Months of carnage, famine and squalor had left an air of death so thick it could be weighed. There were unburied, naked bodies everywhere, like so many bleached white branches washed up on a dreamscape's beach in a strange land. The freezing temperatures helped postpone putrefaction; bodies heaped like small crowds gathered in wait for trams which would never arrive. The rabid dogs which once howled at the moon, bringing further terror to our unwelcome guests, had disappeared, eaten by the troglodytes now occupying this city of death. I recall staring into the face of a German soldier just before I stripped him to replace my saturated clothes; his eyes were wide open and he sat in the doorway of a bombed-out tailor's shop. He still wore his helmet, and his polished buttons hinted at the fastidiousness which once characterised his army. His eyelashes, eyebrows and stubble were peppered with the dry snow which blew around the city like sand across a desert, forming huge white dunes in courtyards and doorways. Soon this corpse would transmute into something completely different: a naked white heap slumped in a doorway, a ghostly apparition.

I crouched beside him and for several minutes just stared into his face. I'd never been so close to a German before! I wanted to touch his face with my naked fingers, to feel the smoothness of his icy skin. In all of this death and mayhem some human contact, even with a corpse, would have helped me, would have made me aware of my own mortality, reminded me that I was still alive. I now inhabited a twilight world flickering between the living and the dead: a strange creature which scoured the Earth, gathering souls by day, gnawing on the rotting flesh of animals at night. I took off my glove and placed my fingers against his pure white complexion. I tried to close his eyes but the lids had frozen wide open. The child in me wondered how he'd ever be able to sleep if he couldn't close his eyes, those deep blue marbles which gazed past me into the distance. I gently brushed the white dust from his face and pushed the straggly blond hair off his forehead.

My fingers began to ache with the cold and suddenly I snapped back to reality. I quickly set about my purpose, stripping the corpse and gathering its clothes into my canvas rucksack. I rifled through the pockets and came across a photograph of a young, smiling uniformed man holding a baby, standing alongside a beautiful woman who'd smiled at the man behind the box camera and now gazed at me. For a second I was there, alongside the family in that studio, perhaps in Berlin one afternoon a lifetime ago. I gently folded the photograph, prized open the young man's frozen jaw, placed that most valuable of belongings into his mouth, then snapped the jaw closed again. There it would be safe, retained forever by the person who valued it above life itself. I stood up, glanced around and left.

Several days later we received further orders from Moscow. Morale amongst the local population was near collapse. Food had run out, and the failure of water systems meant that death from dysentery as well as starvation was widespread. The smell of death was everywhere as the bloated bodies piled high in doorways, alleyways, and in open fields, popped, releasing pent-up gasses into the cold air. There was now an imminent danger that the Soviet state would be attacked by its own people.

White flags were beginning to flutter outside houses, proclaiming 'Welcome to our German guests'. Shopkeepers were fraternising with the enemy in some parts of the city, inviting soldiers to help themselves to whatever was available. In this way they might save the building and possibly their own families from destruction. We were ordered to combat such defeatism by unleashing a terror which matched or exceeded that inflicted by the invaders. Anyone found with a white flag was to be shot on the spot. Shops displaying any sign of capitulation were to have their occupants dragged out, summarily shot, and their premises torched. It was through such brutality that the city's population would be kept in place, cowed and deterred from turning on the Party.

Within the first three days of receiving the new order we executed thirty townsfolk, some from a distance, others at close range and usually in their own homes after kicking in front doors or simply peppering shots through front windows. As NKVD we'd received extensive training, but it was our comrades who put this into effect with boundless brutality.

We co-ordinated our strategy with Party officials in Moscow. I found their relish in giving orders and demanding their implementation to be unsettling, despite the fact that my own head count had probably long since exceeded most of theirs. The city's inhabitants who survived the earlier German onslaught now experienced a greater evil from their own 'protectors'. Bodies were left where they fell. Collaborators and suspected sympathisers were executed without mercy, their bodies hung upside down from makeshift gibbets outside the tiny hovels which they and their families had somehow been subsisting in.

One smoky evening I was making my way silently, carefully, along a snow-choked side street, my rifle swaying by my side, pistol tucked into the inner pocket of my bloodstained German trenchcoat. Although 'Moscow Protocol' required sniper units to patrol in twos, I was alone as my mentor was measuring out distances, vantage points and shooting ranges in a nearby street along which a small unit would soon pass.

The prospect of lying in another rancid bombed-out building, motionless for hours on end, neither depressed nor excited me: I'd become indifferent to the terribleness of my existence and habitat. My purpose was simple enough: the defence of my country and the exacting of terrible revenge upon the invaders. During these days of slaughter I swept through the ranks of the German semi-dead like a reaper swishing his scythe as he zig zags through a corn field. Swish, swish, swish, pop, pop, pop, go the heads. I'd heard from comrades that a local storekeeper had hung a white flag from his upstairs window: now I was heading in his direction to put down this futile act of insurrection. Why couldn't he hold fast as our Glorious Army had done in Leningrad in June '42? None of them had returned, and now our city was infested with human rats, betraying the heroes through their desperation to cling on to things which simply didn't matter.

When I arrived at the store I was struck by a contrast: although the buildings on either side had been bomb-blasted beyond recognition (as had been nearly every other building in the street), this store retained a semblance, albeit a tenuous one, of incongruous normality. Two of the front window panes were still intact, whilst the third had shards which clung to a smashed frame. I'd been correctly informed: hanging from the first floor window of this three storey building was a soiled white flag - a bedsheet - proclaiming in German the owner's welcome to the 'guests'. The words scrawled on the sheet were difficult to read, most likely written by an unsteady hand.

I peered into the darkness of the ground floor room, picking out outlines of unidentifiable shapes scattered randomly across the floor. Pieces of furniture, broken chairs, boxes and other debris would have to be navigated in order to pass through to the inner rooms and then up to the higher floors. Apart from the familiar sound of the scurrying of rodents there was no other indication of life in the building. I kicked in the feeble front door; both it and the frame collapsed inwards without resistance, dampness muffling the splintering of the wood.

My pistol had found its way into my right hand without conscious thought on my part, and I kicked my way through the rubbish, the relics of previous generations, emboldened by a bloodlust now coursing through my veins. I had come to collect a life, and would not leave empty-handed. Knowing by animal instinct that there was no-one hiding in the shadows, I made my way to the staircase leading up from the rubbish-strewn anteroom. Half of the stairs were smashed so I proceeded gingerly, silently, to the first floor.

On the first floor I was faced with a choice. There were four doors, three wide open, the fourth at the end of the landing, slightly ajar. A flickering light visible through the crack between the door and the frame was the first sign of life, heightening my senses and quickening my heartbeat. Like a somnambulist I drifted towards the room, holding my breath while steadying the freezing weapon to which the skin on my fingers was now sticking. I pushed at the door with my index finger then passed into the dimly-lit room.

A candle flickered on a mantelpiece immediately in front of me; to its left was a small vase overflowing with decayed stems of geraniums collected during the summer. To its right I could make out the outline of an elephant with sharp protruding tusks, incongruous even at that distance. Above the mantelpiece, an icon of the Madonna and Child. To my right a large table, at its centre a samovar which returned distorted flashes of light thrown at it by the candle on the mantelpiece. A movement to my left drew my attention to a large bed, apparently heaped with blankets and rags. Slowly, silently, the bedclothes were pushed away by the bed's ancient occupant. I took aim and waited.

The elderly man gently lifted his left leg over the side of the bed, and then the right, then, having placed both feet on the floor, uncurled himself like some unwinding caterpillar. We shared the same height but he was skeletally thin, with a distended and death-white face. He wore a rotted greatcoat which appeared not to have been removed for months. His sallow cheeks had long since collapsed, his eyes barely visible, having dropped back into their bony sockets. I caught sight of the deep cracks on either side of his tight, small mouth, and surmised that it had been weeks, maybe months, since he'd last eaten a meal of any substance. He upturned his hands as he raised his arms towards me, showing his blackened palms in a gesture of passivity. Lowering his arms to his sides, he slowly rolled his tongue in his mouth to summon up sufficient moisture to facilitate speech. He began to speak in broken German. Realising I'd not understood his words, and perhaps believing that this was due to the strained and rasping tone in which they'd been spoken, he repeated himself. I felt anger because of an awareness that his visible helplessness and wretchedness had triggered an emotional response in me. I wanted to leave immediately, to run as far away as possible to a darkened place where the numbness of my soul could be restored. But instead I stayed.

'I am Petr Damyanovitch of the NKVD Stalingrad. We know you've been supporting the Enemy and I'm here to order you stop or face the consequences. Do you have anything to say?' The old man hobbled towards me and then almost falling forward, clasped at me. I stood motionless for seconds, not knowing what to do or say. And then he spoke, this time in Russian, the language I'd used in addressing him. This time his diction was clear and precise. 'Welcome, Petr Damyanovitch. Welcome to my home. I've waited so long to see a comrade, to speak in my own tongue. But nobody came, not until now. You are most welcome'.

I didn't know what to say, how to respond. Not wanting to engage in conversation which might humanise the situation, I returned to my initial enquiry. 'Why have you been inviting the Enemy into your home? Why have you broken the Party's rules which everyone in this city must obey?' The old man looked at me without fear and then clearing his throat, spoke again. 'I'll tell you why, but not yet. Just a while, just a few minutes, and I will tell you. I will tell you everything. But first you must hear me. And if I tell you what you want to know, you must grant a request. And for your promise to make binding the agreement between us, I'll make a gift to you. Do you promise?' He grabbed at my arm; there was urgency in his hoarse voice. 'Do you promise?' he repeated. I could have shot him there and then, ransacked his house and taken anything of value: we both knew he was in no position to bargain. But in those milliseconds I made a fundamental error. The cardinal rule of my training had been broken: that common humanity should never cloud one's judgment before a kill.

'I'll hear you out old man, and give you that promise. Now, speak'. The mention of a gift had not even registered with me. After all, what could he give from the junk and debris of his lost years, now heaped in small piles about this room? Slowly he scuffled across the darkened room towards a dilapidated desk. Two questions flickered across my mind: first, what would I do if he was to take out a gun from the desk and second, would I be able to shoot him dead without some intervening moment of fatal hesitation? I reckoned my reflexes would be faster than his: it would probably be me that left the room, after I'd rifled it of course. If he broke my trust in this way, then I'd leave his body to the rats without as much as a second thought.

He opened the flap of the desk and after bringing out a piece of card he returned to where I'd remained standing. He held the photograph up to my face. Three young men smiled out from the yellowing picture, all proudly attired in Tsarist uniforms. 'Boris, Georg, Vaslav, my three sons'. I looked at the faces, then back at him. 'They all died in Siberia on the same day, the same hour: 25th November 1919. Proud soldiers in the White Army, servants of the Tsar, killed by the Communists. I died on that day too'.

He paused, his mind drifting away to years long passed, to a place of mental sanctuary from this hell he now inhabited. He remembered their childhoods, summer afternoons in the mountains, walks by rivers with his wife; images rushed across the mental plain like gossamer on the wind. He gazed at the picture: the pride of early parenthood never fades, despite an ageing body and the onset of cynicism. Soon it would be time to leave it all behind, to escape the filth and the fear. 'Three months ago my wife left this place to pray at a church across the Volga. Her name was Katarina. I loved her and she loved me in return. She was the mother of my three beautiful sons. But I'll never see her again. I'll never see any of them again. Tell me young man, do I have the right to cry?'

During the past months I'd immersed myself in death, putting out of mind the suffering and despair of those left behind to grieve in the wake of my actions. This old man, this husk, was causing unwelcome moments of reflection, and for this I was beginning to hate him. I looked into his eyes, without a sign of emotion. 'Few choose their time to die. It is the

Motherland alone which endures. Now, again, to the reason I'm here. What do you say in defence to the charge of treachery? Why have you collaborated with the Enemy?' He smiled and the candle flames danced in the stillness of the damp room, touched by a gentle puff of air seeping in through an unseen crack in the fabric of the building. 'At ten o'clock every morning, if you look out from that window, you can see a German runner cross that piece of ground on his way to deliver orders from Paulus to General Hoth on the other side of the city. I get out of bed each day at that time just to watch him, sneaking across the horizon. And he never knows he's being watched. How could he?' My visit had been worthwhile. I'd contact base in the evening; the runner would be captured by NKVD tomorrow, taken to a basement, interrogated, then his battered corpse left to bring further terror to the hearts of the invaders.

He slid open the sodden frame of the window from which he spied on the soldier and lifted a bundle of rags, perched upon the sill just below the window, inside. Clutching the bundle in his hands, he looked at me again. 'Your promise, will you still honour it? Are you ready to grant my request?' I confess that I was interested in the contents of the rags. 'Yes'. A single word of absolute commitment, but I'd decided to spare his life anyway, so the favour I felt sure he was about to ask had already been granted. So many times I'd been offered money, valuables, even gold, to spare the lives of traitors who begged for mercy. But this was different. This man had pride, a history, a face, and three sons who I now knew. Three sons, and a wife who'd never return.

'This is for you'. He passed over the rags and as I peeled them apart with my filthy fingers a beautiful item revealed itself. I was holding a golden carriage, aboard which was a perfect turquoise egg caged in a golden carapace. The carriage was drawn by four exquisitely rendered horses, decked out in the old Tsar's livery. The phaeton was encrusted with stones, probably diamonds. I gently broke open the egg to find another smaller carriage mounted within. I gasped, my breath crystalising in the chilled air. The old man spoke again. 'You're right my friend, it's made of purest gold, given to me for safekeeping by a member of the Tsar's household in 1917. But he never returned to collect it, and now it's yours. Will you take it?' I felt a strong urge to have it, to hold it, to tuck it into my rucksack and keep it close. I couldn't reply since I wasn't proud to take the gift. This was the paradox of the killer of dozens: now too

ashamed to utter words of gratitude to an ancient man too weak to protest even if he'd wanted to. Had I now become just another looter, a bullying thief? In my mind I reassured myself that his gift had been
voluntarily given, but then remembered that I'd promised a favour. To
grant this now would make everything right, restoring my 'nobleness'.
I slowly and slyly undid the fasteners on my rucksack and gently slid the
shimmering object inside. The deed was done, the gift accepted: now to
my side of the bargain, sparing a life to seal the contract between us.

'Old man, I'm ready to honour your request, but first tell me why
you invited the Enemy into your home. Tell me before we come to my
side of our bargain'. For a fleeting moment the old man looked pleased
as I took his sole possession of value in a world blackened with decay and
corruption. I saw him smile as the carriage slipped surreptitiously into
my bag, catching sight of him in the corner of my slyly narrowed and
guilty eye. The old man turned his gaze away from me and suddenly
started to shuffle towards the far end of the room. I heard the gentle
muffled footsteps as he drifted away towards the cracked window. He
stopped and his translucent hopeless eyes stared out over pale blue snow-
fields past the neighbouring ruins. I wanted to hurry him, and get back
to base.

He wearily drew in his breath and began to speak, barely audible but
with underlying resoluteness. 'My family's gone. My friends are dead.
This place where I've lived for so many years and which has seen laughter
and happiness is now my tomb. A cold place of darkness and half-remem-
bered voices, whispering to me in my loneliness'. He didn't even turn to
me, looking instead past his own reflection and out towards the distant
horizon. 'I've nothing left to live for, but still I linger here as everything
falls and decays around me'. He turned back to me, his eyes piercing me.
'I invited the Enemy into my home because they'd have freed me. But
they never came. They never came to my rescue, to release me, to free my
soul. And yet in all this madness my faith prevents me from delivering
myself. But now you are here, and I have your promise'. My throat tightened and my lungs shuddered as the purpose assigned to me dawned. So
many, many deaths during the past handful of months and yet at the
prospect of this one simple, solitary execution a hesitation, although no
more than that, seized me.

'You my young friend, will be my angel of death. We have a bargain, and now I call upon you to honour it'. He turned back to the window, straightening up now like an old soldier vainly trying to raise to attention a tired and broken body. 'God of Mercy hear my prayer. Into your hands I place my soul. Agnus Dei qui tollis peccata mundi: dona nobis pacem'. He raised his hand and crossed himself.

I drew my pistol and walked quickly across the room. I placed it to the back of his head. I pulled the trigger. A red mist filled the room. The body fell. I left. The first day of my fifteenth year of life drew to a close.

Chapter Two

The true value of peace can only be measured against the ferocity of the war which precedes it. This simple truth only a soldier can know. And what is war? A unique event in the lives of men when ideologies, hatreds, concepts of race and nationhood are crystallised, sharpened, and used as justification for slaughter. A time when power is pressed into the hands of men eagerly awaiting a fleeting moment to make a mark in human history, delegated downwards by opposing leaders to trusted underlings, trickling down structures like honey dripping down the side of a tree. Power over others, the ability to order and direct one's own side or to decide who amongst the enemy taken prisoner should live or die, is sweeter than honey, an intoxicant on the lips of favoured sons. But the wiser soldier, however high in rank, knows that power is ultimately illusory, fleeting; either it is torn from one's grasp in the field at that serene moment of defeat, or simply withdrawn by a capricious master in punishment of something judged to be an error.

From a distance I watched an old, broken man struggling to maintain his stature and dignity whilst his world crashed down about him. Once, perhaps as recently as a month ago, his greatcoat fitted him well: now it enveloped his racked body like a loose shroud about a corpse. The previous day he'd been elevated to the highest of ranks, Field Marshal, by a vengeful overlord in Berlin, despite the reality that the army he commanded, the glorious 6th, was now in tatters. The promotion was a sly deception; no Field Marshal had ever surrendered on the field of battle so if he was to be the first, his name would echo in infamy down through future generations.

But the kesselring had held; Von Mannestein failed to break through the encirclement of Von Paulus's 6th, now trapped in the ruins of Stalingrad, to save the remnants of a broken army. Every man makes many mistakes during his lifetime, but there's always one, a single decision, a sin of omission or commission, which towers above all others. An error, a diamond sparkling in the debris, that one can point at and know for eternity to be the fulcrum about which the remainder of one's life turned before spinning off to destruction. Mine turned out later, simply to stay too long in an insignificant German village, Nemmersdorf; his was to decide to stand and fight and not break out from the kesselring closing in around his men. But the order from Berlin had been unqualified: the last life was to be offered up if not in victory, then in a blood-soaked crescendo of defeat which in time would become the stuff of legend. This man, Von Paulus, this brilliant tactician, had hesitated, and when the time of inevitable surrender arrived, and of his final disobedience and treachery, tens of thousands more young men lay dead and naked in the snow-choked streets of a bled-white city.

I looked on as Von Paulus listened closely to the translator carefully relaying the terms of surrender from our brilliant, ambitious, psychopathic leader, General Vasily Ivanovich Chuikov. I heard none of the words; proximity to the discussions was denied because of my age, lack of rank and insignificance at this moment in history. Momentarily I was amused to observe that this high commander of a hitherto invincible army had a nervous twitch, a spasm in his face, which added to the pathos of the spectacle. He tried to maintain his pride, the unique aura of military arrogance that characterised and protected military tacticians of his rank, but was undermined by this tick as he listened to the victor's demands. Now he was a captive of the much-feared 'untermenschen': they had utterly triumphed and all he could do, this man who days earlier commanded the fate of hundreds of thousands of walking dead, was to listen, nod, and shiver. His humiliation was complete. He bowed his head to Chuikov, they shook hands, and then he left.

Chuikov and his officers moved away in the opposite direction; the formal discussions at an end, the 6th Army, or what was left of it, was to lay down its arms and pass over into our custody. Later I learnt assurances had been given on our part that prisoners would be dealt with fairly; sickness, particularly frostbite and dysentery, would be treated and all would be returned to Germany when the war was ended. Everyone without exception knew this to be a lie - empty words uttered to satisfy the war etiquette expectations of a wider international audience. Von Paulus had lost one hundred and fifty thousand of the German Army's finest during the siege, with a further ninety one thousand now passing across to us. Of those who entered into our 'care', only five thousand would eventually return home, a decade after the end of the war, the balance dying in freezing obscurity, buried in heaps in unmarked graves. Our losses, the defending soldiers and civilians of Stalingrad, came to half a million; taking account of this discrepancy in the balance sheet of death, who could criticise our refusal to show mercy or honour promises made at the moment of victory?

A few days after the 6th's final capitulation and humiliation, I watched as an endless crocodile of thousands of the damned and the wretched twisted its way out of the killing fields of Stalingrad. These were our prisoners, but as to what should be done with them, nobody seemed to know or care. They were to be marched through the snow to some distant place far away, hopefully obliging their captors by dying to the last man along the journey. From my vantage point on a snowy hill overlooking the scene I watched as an army of huddled skeletons dragged themselves into the distance. Sleeves of greatcoats hung loose by sides, arms missing through frostbite and gangrene. Improvised crutches supported lopsided bodies of one-legged prisoners, their unblinking eyes set in coal black sockets peering out from behind rags that gave no protection from the terrifying cold. Strangely, although the column comprised thousands, there was not a sound in the air, apart from the crunching of toeless boots on fresh snow. Not a word was spoken, not by them or by the soldiers escorting them like cattle along the route.

Although I observed at some distance away from the column, occasionally a gentle breeze passed over the scene and drifted all the way up to my look-out point. The smell of gangrenous decay, of filth, of death, caused me to press sleeve across nose and mouth. Stalingrad had been a butcher's block: now the abattoir was disgorging its product. There's only one thing worse than death to a defeated soldier, and that is to survive; it's the utter powerlessness, the depthless shame, and the fear of the caprices of one's captors that terrifies the soul, inculcating a desperate desire to be dispatched. It's the unbearable weight of sadness of remembering one's family, knowing that they still long for your safe return, which tears at your heart; this, combined with terror generated by the thought that in time they too may meet with the same fate destiny has determined for you.

As the column passed below, meandering into the distance and eventually out of sight, I loaded my rifle. It was early morning and the light was perfect for my purpose. As I lay on the ground I feared the effect of the cold on my undernourished body should I remain there, supine in the snow, for the length of time my commander had instructed the previous night. I took aim and within half an hour twenty bodies lay either side of the column. By the end of the morning I'd dropped a further thirty: all perfect head shots, instantaneous death. But I was becoming tired; focused concentration through a rifle sight over hours exhausts the mind, draining the body of its natural reserves. And if your bones are already too close to the skin, lacking a protective layer of fat, then to lie on the iron-cold ground for hour after hour, occasionally breaking away from the task at hand to remove ice from your freezing face, it's easy to become dulled, and lose awareness of your physical frailty.

My commander's order had been a simple one: I was to execute captives attempting to break away from the column. After a handful had been shot the rest would follow the barked instructions of their drivers like docile cattle: fear would keep them obediently in line. The reality was that we were few in number, a fraction of the number of those to be driven; if we lost control during the journey then chaos would ensue, enemy combatants would escape, perhaps killing their guards and re-arming themselves in the process. Random shootings of those straying too far from the column would serve to deter, to extinguish any glimmer of hope remaining in the desperation of their predicament.

But my masters had failed to appreciate the choice that my presence on the hilltop now presented to those trudging into oblivion: either they could continue along the path we had in mind for them, to be worked to death in some slave camp on the purgatorial outskirts of humanity, or they could run, run free, to be reunited with those with whom they'd served, those they loved. A living death or a second's snuffing out of a flickering flame. Now I noticed how, as each new target struggled away from his comrades, he'd look up to the hilltop where I lay, pause, and then move a little quicker, as far as frozen and broken limbs permitted. They knew I was there, they knew my exact position, and now they sought to offer themselves up to me, to make my task as easy as possible. Cripples, the blind, and the frostbitten; I made no distinction. I dispatched them all, and my soul, for I believe I had one at that time, didn't even pause for breath, for doubt. As the bodies mounted I'd only interrupt my enterprise to reload, to replenish from the heap of magazines I'd brought with me up the hill. I was the bringer of death, the freer of souls: my gift was received with gratitude by those to whom I gave it, without reproach, without malice.

I watched as an ancient young man sloped away from the column, passing by the nearest guard who didn't attempt to obstruct his escape. I lowered my gaze and peered through the sight, readying myself for the kill. But he wasn't running, and his pace didn't quicken at all. When he was a distance from the column he stopped and turned towards me, looking up the hill. Through the sight I looked at his face, his bleach-white haggard face: it was contorted, tears coursing down through filth. He reached into his pocket and brought out something, a scrap of paper. He held it out in front of him, thrusting it in my direction. I knew, as I struggled to focus on it even with youthful eyes and the assistance of the very best of British rifle lenses, that it would be a photograph of a loved one, his most treasured possession in this world of grief.

He screamed and cried like a madman, his body convulsed as though in a fit. I heard his words- the acoustics of that empty snow-cloaked environment were so perfect- but could not understand them. I knew, though, what he craved from me. I looked again through the sight, lined up the cross hairs, and then fired. He fell to the floor, dead. Vicariously I felt his sense of relief, of freedom, in that fragment of time when the soul tears itself from the racked body of an exhausted soldier, passing upwards into the stratosphere and above the devastated world from which it has escaped.

I sat back in the snow and bit into a huge, juicy apple. Its sweetness was sharpened by the freezing air. In the world I inhabited basic sensations such as taste, touch, even a finger placed upon another's dead flesh, become beautiful, summoning up fragments of a past remembered life like sparks rising from a bonfire. I allowed the juice to trickle down my chin then wiped it away quickly lest it freeze on my face and pull away skin. In Stalingrad in 1943, despite the legends later, Russian bodies, too, were gnawed at by the extreme cold, that huge invisible rat, although good clothing supplied by our factories in the East, essentials for an ice-bound environment like thermal ware and snow shoes, went some way to helping us avoid the frostbite which ravaged our enemies. But even so, the simplest of functions like taking a piss had to be approached with strategic planning; fluid leaving one's body could freeze before touching the ground, snapping off one's vitals if one was not quick enough to take preventative measures.

Earlier that day I'd been drinking from my flask but in a moment of urgency-a soldier had drifted too far away from the column- I spilt some of its contents over my right hand. Fearing the cold, I'd quickly replaced it into the glove, raised the rifle and then dispatched the escapee. Hours passed, and with the need for renewed concentration I'd instantly forgotten about the insignificant incident. But later I felt a sensation in my fingers, numbness, a strange unresponsiveness to orders from my brain to bend, to straighten, to tighten. Despite the worsening cold I took off my glove, even if just for a matter of seconds, to rub some warmth into my joints. I pulled at the glove and heard a sound, an unfamiliar and barely audible crack, like the crack of a twig snapped from a tree by a truanting schoolboy. The glove slid off, the tips of two of my fingers remaining within it. I stared at my mutilated right hand, two digits now strangely invisible below the joint. I felt no pain, and momentarily gazed in surprise at where my fingertips usually were. And then came horror. In a panic I turned inside out the glove, and from within the wet circulation-constricting material tumbled out two pieces of flesh upon bone which looked like stubby chunks sculpted from blackened parsnip. Although the mutilation of my body was slight compared with the legless and armless captives passing below, this was scarce consolation. I placed the tips in my pocket and headed off down the hill.

The attention I eventually received was cursory, my mutilation, my war trophy, insignificant compared to those of my comrades. I was ordered to place both hands into a large bowl of warm water, holding them there until sensation (and a great deal of pain) returned. This, combined with rudimentary bandages, was the extent of the care I received. My commander approached as I sipped a warmed vodka, keeping my damaged hand still in its glove. He smiled and asked about my injury, feigning sympathy when I explained how it had happened. He asked whether I'd kept the tips, knowing well enough from thousands of similar incidents the answer that would be given. I withdrew the tips from my pocket; he held out his hand and I placed them into his palm, wondering why he'd want to inspect them. He looked down at them, smiled, and then threw them into the fire in front of us. I watched as the flames licked at them, crackling and hissing as flesh peeled from bone. He laughed as I stood, mesmerised; flesh was nothing- only the spirit endured. Such a 'keepsake' was unhealthy: I'd thank him in time for what he'd done. He walked off, knowing it was too late to fish out the charred remains.

One of the most memorable and unique experiences in war is crashing through open fields sitting astride the gun turret of an enormous tank. You lumber, or hurtle, for mile after mile, laying waste to everything and everyone before you. The roaring of the engine, the stench of fumes, the shaking that penetrates to the very core of your being until your heart synchronises its beat with the vibration. You feel insignificant as the massive metal beast flattens its way across the landscape; fields of unharvested wheat (of course, no one remains to harvest the crop) all falling under the massive treads. I remember lifting my face to the sky and opening my mouth to catch freezing, thirst-quenching raindrops: I felt more alive then than I've ever done since. There was nothing on Earth or above it, no hand of man or intervention by God, to obstruct us or challenge our simple purpose. We were heading for the heart of the Reich and there we'd tear it out. There we'd bring terror and death to those who'd murdered and butchered their way across our own land. In Berlin we would avenge our blood-soaked nation. In Berlin we would justify their fears.

I was once asked by an underling during a violent interrogation in the Ljubianka (I think it was in '68 but the year's not important), when my soul had died. He was young, and appalled by what he'd witnessed; youth is entitled to its fleeting naivety, its sweet innocence, and for this reason I was willing to overlook his impertinence. It was a strange question in the circumstance, but a simple one: what had created the 'soulless monster' he believed me to be? After washing my smoking blood-caked hands, and after reflecting upon the question, I replied. 'In Stalingrad in 1943 my soul started to wither in the cold and the horror. In Nemmersdorf in 1944 it died'. He didn't press for explanation: there are desolate places in a man of my generation's past into which youth knows by instinct not to trespass. The prisoner lived to be interrogated another day: my concentration had been broken.

Chapter Three

In November 1943, as part of the Soviet offensive to dislodge Generalfeldmarschall Erich Von Manstein's 4th Panzergruppe Sud and the Sixteenth, Seventeenth and Eighteenth Armies from the Ukraine and Poland, the 3rd Guards Tank Army (to which I was now attached) reached Kiev, under the leadership of Pavel Rybalko. Von Manstein had been pushed back, waiting in vain for reinforcement by the 40th and 48th Panzer Corps. But everyone, on both sides, knew that the war, at least on the Eastern Front, was hurtling towards its apocalyptic conclusion. Words alone cannot describe our elation, our sense of overwhelming pride, at passing unopposed through the streets of Kiev on the 3rd of November, even though we knew our presence might be temporary if the enemy were to be reinforced by a redeployment of fresh divisions.

Shortly after our arrival at a suburb called Syrets, we came upon a large ravine known locally as Babi Yar. The name of this place was unknown to the outside world, cherished only by those who knew of its beauty or who tended graves in its nearby nondescript small Jewish cemetery. I stood at the edge of the vast enclosed space and closed my eyes. Military triumph, or at least the prospect of its imminent accomplishment, forces one to pause, to stop, listen, breathe the air deeply, see patterns of dancing light through closed-tight lids, and listen for sounds of distant, unintelligible voices. All is then impressed accurately upon the inward eye of mental record, to be summoned up again and again during the decades of tedium of later life when expectations encapsulated in that moment standing atop the world are never quite lived up to, when disappointment becomes engrained in the soul, seeping in like rain into fetid cloth.

I listened and could hear comrades labouring in the black lake of soil below: I looked but couldn't discern the purpose of their activity. There was a sound of metal upon stone and earth: I looked again, but this time closely, and saw that they were digging in the dirt. Apart from the incongruous sound of spade slicing through soil, there was a deathly silence in the ravine: now even my comrades had fallen silent as they went about their task. I walked, ran, slid down the steep slope leading into the ravine. When I reached the floor I noticed how little of it was covered by grass: this was in fact a vast sea of broken black earth, across which rivulets of water meandered, trickling down from the other side of the small canyon. I approached the commander of the unit of soldiers who were now diligently, silently digging through the dirt. I asked him what they were doing. He stared back but his eyes were dull. 'Go and find out for yourself'. Still confused, I trudged off and made my way to the first digger.

Soldiers were randomly spread out throughout the ravine, but there was no sense of collective endeavour, as each worked alone in his allotted plot of land. I started to speak to the first man I came to, but he didn't respond, not even looking up, but instead continued shoveling, by now standing up to his waist in a black hole. I spoke again; perhaps he hadn't heard me or was still unaware of my presence. Again he ignored me, not even looking up from the small pit in which he worked. Suddenly a shovel-load of earth landed at my feet; it had not been deliberately targeted but fell around me, caking my shoes and trousers. I looked down and saw hundreds of specks of white in the dirt. I bent down and immediately realised what I was standing in: dozens of fragments of bone and teeth. Another load landed, this time comprising larger pieces of bone including pieces of smashed skulls.

I gasped as I stepped back from the grave and looked up at the dozen or so other soldiers working throughout the ravine. Each stood at varying depths in pits, all with large piles of earth and bone and remnants of clothing heaped alongside. This was a vast graveyard, an enormous killing field that ran the full length and breadth of this desolate place. As I looked at the men toiling down deep into the soil it was apparent that there was layer upon layer of compressed remains, ending at a depth which the diggers were yet to reach. Here there had been a systematic slaughter and a neatness in burying the evidence of which only the Nazis were capable. Momentarily I became lightheaded as I looked into the distance and contemplated the extent of the carnage, knowing that beneath where I stood were the remains of countless more victims. The ravine floor wasn't grassed over, and the topsoil revealed at the rim of the pits indicated that the ground had recently been broken up, churned, and then compacted down again, probably with bulldozers. We knew from discoveries of earlier slaughters by the SS Einsatzgruppe in the East that as the German Army had been pushed back, so they became obsessed with leaving no evidence of their atrocities. Bodies had been exhumed, burnt, and the ashes and fragments scattered over as wide an area as possible. But in this place the murdering had been committed on an industrial scale: tens of thousands had tumbled down the sides of the ravine, already dead or perhaps still alive as they fell.

I walked back to the commander, delegated by higher authority with the task of overseeing the investigation of this vast graveyard. He knew that I now understood why the name Babi Yar would be remembered forever, whatever the war's outcome. He moved his hand in a motion from one side of the ravine to the other; information had been brought by the few prisoners who'd managed to escape to the Red Army that in this place in September '41 over thirty thousand Jews had been slaughtered, along with a further seventy thousand Russian prisoners, Ukrainians and Gypsies executed in the next few months. As the Nazi dream of an empire in the East faded, they'd used slave labour from the camp at Syrets to dig up the bodies here in Babi Yar, burning them by the thousand on huge pyres made from flagstones taken from the local cemetery, and then scattered the remains throughout the ravine. I asked him if he knew what had happened to the slave labourers who had exhumed, burned and grinded down the evidence of the slaughter. He pointed to the far side of the ravine where no soldier had yet been deployed: I was to dig into the soil, and when and if remains were found, at that point mechanical equipment would be brought in to take over the task.

My concern was a simple one. Elsewhere in the ravine the Nazis, with customary thoroughness, would have ensured that evidence was broken down into its smallest constituent parts: decomposed bodies decimated then bone reduced to layers of dust and fragments between compacted sand. But for those who'd exhumed at gunpoint there would have been no-one willing to dispose of their bodies with similar efficiency. The prospect of searching for these recent victims mildly unsettled me; our estimate was that three hundred or more corpses lay just below the surface, pressed down by tractors into the stratum of chalky dust that remained of the hundred thousand dead.

I asked to be found other work instead, perhaps with units moving through the city seeking out snipers left behind by the retreating enemy. I'd know where to find them if they remained, what vantage points they'd prefer, how they could be dislodged and brought out into the open to be dealt with. The commander looked at me impassively, recognising my reluctance. He spoke quietly. 'We need evidence of what's been done here. Our allies won't accept unsupported allegations of so-called sly and lying Slavs: they see us the same way our enemy does. Dirty Untermenschen, not to be trusted. You must take this'. He pushed forward the large spade. I hesitated to accept it, foolishly questioning him again. Were there not others who knew better what to look for? He stared at me and then screamed in my face. 'You dare question my orders? You'll do as I say. Our comrades lie in the filth here. If they're not found by us, they'll stay here unmourned and unremembered for eternity. You'll dig in the earth until you free them. For as long as it takes'. He then drew closer, whispering but furious. 'And if there's goodness in you, if there's a soul behind those assassin's eyes, today it will be driven out and killed. Then you'll be ready'. I took the spade and ran to the far side of the ravine; none of the toilers looked up from their pits as I passed.

I broke through the topsoil easily; tractors ordered by SS Standartenfuhrer Blobel had simply pushed the earth forward without attempting to compress it down as had been done in earlier years when the strategy to conceal had not been so urgent. The coldness of the place combined with the physical exertion of digging made breathing difficult. My hand ached in the glove: I knew my severed fingers were now bleeding from the dark stain seeping through the thick material. But I had to complete the task set by the commander before the land began to freeze again with the coming of night.

Soon I was standing in a large plot of open earth, wider and longer than those nearby. A fog descended, swirling about the ravine then settling like cotton wool into the pit I'd excavated. I pulled my greatcoat about me. The cold permeated my bones but I was determined to continue wielding the spade into the dark earth now barely visible in the fog and gathering gloom. I gazed around the ravine but could see nothing nor hear a single voice in the vast cobweb pressed down by a falling sky. Only the echoing of steel on stone and broken bone. Suddenly my spade hit something, causing a muffled clanking noise which ricocheted off the surrounding sides of the enclosed space. I looked closer, bending and peering through the settled fog. Beneath me and to my right a skeletal hand poked through the surface, as if reaching up to be helped out from the earth. Briefly I stepped backwards, repulsed by what had been revealed, then returned to my task. I dug a little further around the arm, soon uncovering more of the corpse which had been flung into the ground, then forced down under the weight of a tractor while still, perhaps, holding a few gasps of life left within it.

I put my spade aside and gently pulled at the arm; a greater part of the torso came into view, still wearing the tatters of the familiar striped uniform of the local prison camp in Syrets. Realising the body was still intact I decided to leave it and switch to the other side of the pit. Again my spade hit bone: another half body emerged above the surface, a skull grimacing as if startled at being hauled out of the darkness and into the half-light of the late afternoon. To pull at the body or dig around it any further would be to risk damaging the evidence, incurring my commander's wrath. I gently leaned the exposed part of the clothed skeleton against the side of the pit; it stared back at me and for a second I waited for it to say something, to speak of crimes and horrors I couldn't begin to contemplate. It of course remained silent, and I reverted to my task once again. Within the next half hour I unearthed a dozen more bodies; most had the same striped uniform, some the apparel of our comrades. I was now surrounded by an otherworldly audience, all gazing at me through the fog, whispering and staring at each other through empty sockets.

I climbed out of the pit; beneath my feet other skeletons no doubt lay, and my continuing presence felt vaguely disrespectful. I walked back to the commander who stood at the head of the ravine, receiving reports from the vague somnambulists wandering back and forth from their individual pits, their own entry points into the hell beneath the soil. I reported my findings, explaining that there were probably many bodies, perhaps a few dozen, perhaps even more, buried beneath the plot where I'd been working but that, just as one skeleton was revealed, so another would break through the surface, attached, fused, with the remains of another victim. He nodded his understanding, his face remaining expressionless. I was ordered to return to the plot, and within minutes mechanical equipment was brought alongside. The driver dismounted and began attaching ropes around the exposed torsos. He approached the task slowly, diligently, respectfully. When the cat's cradle was in place he climbed back into the vehicle and started up the engine. The ropes stretched up, tightened, and then began to pull up that which lay below the surface. At first a few came up, attached to them others. And then more, all fused with each other. The space adjacent to the pit began to tremble: suddenly bunches of entangled skeletons, some naked, some still clothed, began to come into view, erupting slowly from the earth, disgorged from deep beneath the pit I'd worked in, but also from further afield, from beyond my line of vision. I watched at what the earth was giving up; here were the last victims of the final days of Nazi infestation of this once beautiful place.

It quickly became apparent that one vehicle would be insufficient for the task: the evidence of hurried slaughter was greater even than the stoic commander had envisaged. Other vehicles were brought up, my commander now closely supervising the efforts of those redeployed from other parts of this mass grave. I sat on the edge of the pit, watching corpses being hauled from the ground about me like some huge interconnected crop being torn from the earth. I looked around and when it appeared that sufficient fog was enveloping me I placed my face in my hands and wept. It was the first time I could ever remember having cried, and I'd never do so again. I raged at the war, at the world, and although I grieved for those now rising, silently, from the earth, my anger burst forth from a deeper wellspring. Perhaps, too, it was simply the eventual outpouring of despair and disgust at everything I had seen and experienced (yes, and done) since my country had been invaded.

Staring out across the ravine I contemplated the mindset of those who had committed such barbarities. They were devoid of humanity - monstrous representatives of an insane nation, its leaders obsessed with deluded notions of racial purity. Every killer, every murderer, needs an excuse, some grain of self-justification. As I contemplated the hundreds who'd died at my own hands I realised that the need to justify actions to myself no longer existed; I'd stepped beyond normal moral codes and had become a killing machine with no need for a reason for the work I efficiently carried out, like an automaton of death. As the legions of souls of the dead emerged from the fog and crowded in around me, I couldn't tell which victims were mine and which were those of the enemy. Could it be that I was the greater monster? I watched as the smallest speck on the horizon, my remaining humanity, flickered then disappeared.

I stood to my feet: meting out revenge upon those guilty of making me what I'd become would be terrible and unforgiving, executed with the clarity of purest amorality. Fleetingly I contemplated the possibility that in truth no-one was to blame for what I was, and that perhaps I'd been born without a soul. No - I'd not question myself further. Others were to blame, or at least this would be the darkened prism through which I'd track the hazy light of self-justification drifting across endless battlefields of death and slaughter. The commander suddenly stepped out of the fog and stood in front of me. He said nothing. I held up a clenched fist and forced earth and dust through my fingers; I stared at him and my anger and hatred made him momentarily pause. He spoke quietly. 'Now you're ready. Now you understand what has to be done'. He returned to the supervision of the collection, collation and documentation of the evidence: pieces of clothing, estimates of scale of the atrocity calculated from a million fragments of bone and a million more handfuls of dust. And, weeks later, when all had at least been attempted, that which remained was restored to the earth. I heard prayers spoken, picked up by the wind and scattered to the four corners of the Earth. I said nothing. It was time to leave.

Chapter Four

After the liberation of Kiev I was summoned back to Moscow; servants of the NKVD were accustomed to frequent redeployment to new units and the places of greatest need, wherever those might be. To my surprise I, along with several others, was called to attend the Ljubianka. Some of my colleagues visibly shook as we were driven in an open-top wagon; to be summoned in this way usually meant one had failed to please one's masters and that death before a firing squad was just a few breaths away. For myself I didn't care; I'd given a good account of myself in Stalingrad, but if this was not sufficient then those whose commands I'd followed to the letter would simply have to do their worst. Besides, after the countless killings I had perpetrated and witnessed over the past year, and after Babi Yar, my own life, and the lives of others, no longer seemed to have any value.

We entered the headquarters and were directed to an ante-room where we waited in silence. I was the first to be called in, and momentarily my heart started to beat more quickly, a thick syrupy spit of fear forming in my mouth. I entered the room and was surprised to be met by the man who had controlled and directed my destiny since Stalingrad. Lavrentiy Pavlovich Beria, trusted confidante of the Great Bastard, stood in front of me. His little piggy eyes squinted out from behind nondescript large, round glasses, his balding head sweating slightly; he looked like a headmaster or petty local council official but, of course, he was much, much more than that. His brutality and deviousness had become the stuff of legend since appointment as Head of the NKVD in November 1938, rooted in part in the ruthless efficiency with which he'd purged then executed half the Organisation's personnel on taking charge of it.

I looked at Lavrentiy Pavlovich and felt an instant affinity. He embraced me then smiled and shook my hand. I'd been summoned for two reasons. Firstly, in official Party recognition of my valour in the battle of Stalingrad, I was to be awarded the Red Banner. My division, the Soviet 76th under Voroshilov's leadership, had also been recognised for its service during Operation Uranus's encirclement of the 6th and 4th Panzer Armies. Our loyalty to the Motherland at Stalingrad was to be acknowledged with the award of the Order of Lenin, while the Red Banner was for my personal endeavours. I was also to receive the Distinguished Sniper medal. He pinned the pieces of cheap painted metal to my jacket, and then shook my hand again.

The second reason was to inform me that I was to be attached to General Chernyakhovsky's 3rd Belorussian Front during the coming push to Germany. We were to enter the enemy's territory through East Prussia and our instructions were to leave not a blade of grass standing; death and destruction was to be unleashed upon the civilian population and in so doing, quicken surrender by those still holding out in Berlin. As I'd done in Stalingrad and the Ukrainian campaign, I was to keep a record of the names of any and all persons, particularly those of higher rank, who showed any trace of disrespect for either the Leader or the Party, who questioned any order sent from Moscow, or who showed any other hint, however minor, of disloyalty. Depending on the magnitude of the crime, such persons should either be executed in the field, or be noted, and dealt with after the war. The Party's future depended upon the unquestioning obedience of its servants and my first loyalty was to the Party rather than to the unit to which I happened to be attached.

To Beria, I was of miniscule insignificance in the grand scheme of things; just a young man with a sharp eye who was capable of killing at a great distance. But above all things he was a planner, a long term strategist, who aspired to hold even greater power than he currently possessed; a power which was already considerable. To achieve this goal he needed loyal creatures for the time when the real conflict would begin, after the war had ended. He needed servants whose first loyalty would be to him, then to the Party, and only then the country. He'd heard reports of my 'kill count' and concluded that it was impressive for someone so young. And to pay him his due, he'd done more and continued to do more than anyone else, more even than the Great Bastard, to militarise the nation and cast off the nascent defeatism that clung to the generals during the early days of the war (I'd heard whispers that, almost to a man, they'd been executed).

For such a man to spare a few minutes to pin a medal to my shirt was honour indeed. I felt fleetingly proud and then condemned myself for this futile emotion. My admiration for the psychopath reinforced, I left the room. At a minimal cost his goal had been accomplished: he had ownership of another willing creature for the post-war settling of scores. Of the other dozen who'd attended that morning, nine lay in unmarked graves around the city before the day was out. I knew that two had made mistakes in the battlefield, holding back from easy kills when their targets were perfectly in view. Compassion can create such uncertainty, and cause hesitance in the trigger finger. As for the others, a vague impression of suspected disloyalty had been sufficient to seal their fates.

Operation Bagration started on June 22nd 1944, and Lvov-Sandomierz a little later, on 17th July. Both marked the start of our push to drive the enemy from the occupied territories. A huge red wave was now poised to break across the continent, drowning everyone and everything that stood in our way. In Bagration we fielded one hundred and twenty divisions of troops, numbering one million two hundred thousand men, against the enemy's eight hundred thousand demoralized troops. The outcome was the liberation of Byelorussia and the territories occupied since 1941; the cost to the enemy was three hundred thousand dead, two hundred and fifty thousand wounded, and one hundred and twenty thousand captured. Our losses in the campaign were insignificant by comparison - sixty thousand dead, and one hundred and ten thousand wounded.

Poland east of the Vistula was retaken, and then our push into East Prussia began. Lvov-Sandomierz was part of the coordinated strategy, its goal to push the enemy from the Ukraine and Eastern Poland. By the time I joined up with General Chernyakhovsky's 3rd Byelorussian regiment, he'd already entered German territory, pushing into East Prussia. Everyone knew of my record at Stalingrad, of the medals I had been awarded for my service to the Motherland, and for this I was respected. However, my association with Beria and his NKVD was also known, and because of that, I detected deep suspicion, even detestation.

In accordance with Party protocol I presented myself to the General. It was a brief, cursory meeting: there was a deep-rooted suspicion of Party interlopers within the military, rightly concluding that the purpose of such 'travelling companions' was to spy on leaders and report back to Moscow. He was courteous towards me but with an unmistakable disdain. I was struck by his youth: he was the youngest ever Soviet General of the Red Army, a quietly spoken man of great physical strength, military brilliance and, more importantly, charisma. It was the first and last time I'd speak with him: less than a year later in what was at that time East Prussian Konigsberg he died in battle, before reaching his fortieth birthday. For the moment though, I was given my deployment instructions by one of the General's underlings and within a day I had joined up with a unit already in occupation of a small, inconsequential East Prussian village, Nemmersdorf.

The following day I was taken to a point just outside the village and left, alone. I was to walk the short distance and report to the commander of the 25th Guards Tank Unit which had just secured the area. With rifle over my shoulder and heavy rucksack on my back, I started off. It was a perfect late October afternoon with a cloudless sky, crisp, cold air, and rural quiet. I looked into the distance and could make out the banks of the Agrappa river, a feature in the landscape I could use to fix my bearings. I suddenly noticed figures on the river banks dancing, running, pulling at each other as though in a game. I took out the rifle sight from my bag and placed it to my eye. They were not soldiers - they were in civilian clothing - but what they were doing, running along the river bank? Looking again through the sight I realised who they were, and their purpose. These were the German inhabitants of Nemmersdorf, its grandparents, sons, daughters, and children: all were tied together in familial groups with rope which they themselves had tied, binding one member's hands to those of the next. Their intention and mental processes were entirely rational, the scene itself worthy of a tragi-comedy acted out by inmates of an asylum.

I watched as one group stood on the bank, hesitated, and then leapt into the water. It was evident that they'd weighted themselves, probably with rocks, from the quickness with which they sank out of view. Another group approached the bank. One of the party appeared to have a change of mind, tugging at the rope that bound her to the next in the link. But this resistance was to no avail, and as the first in line plunged into deep water so others were pulled in behind him, the reluctant infant daughter struggling for seconds to raise her head into the air, then disappearing. I watched the suicides continue. Their fear of death was trumped by their fear of the savages from the East who'd arrived to wreak unspeakable Slav barbarism

upon them and their ancient village. I should have felt ashamed but I'd waded through too many mud-clogged death pits, seen too many headless corpses, to feel sympathy for anyone, neither the guilty nor the innocent, the young nor the old. I pulled out a carrot from my rucksack, ate it, watched for a short while longer, then strolled off towards the village.

By the time I reached the outskirts of Nemmersdorf the village was in darkness. As I walked along the main road I saw bodies propped like dolls on either side, carefully spaced at regular intervals. I looked at each as I passed: the fortunate ones had been shot in the head whilst others had been murdered in more brutal fashion. As I approached the centre of the village the smell of death grew stronger. Bodies were scattered everywhere, lacking the methodical neatness which had guided the killers during their endeavours on the outskirts. I passed by a large barn and on its door a naked man was attached, dead, nailed in cruciform. A new kind of carnage was everywhere and I wondered whether in fact I'd died earlier that day and was now commencing my assured journey down to Hell.

Soon I came across troops of the 25th; there were half a dozen of them and they were drunk, laughing, staggering, wailing like madmen. They'd have killed me too if it hadn't been for the papers provided by Chernyakhovsky's assistant; only one of their number was capable of reading and on seeing the General's name he patted me on the back then forced a bottle of vodka to my lips. Not wanting to offend I took a large mouthful then pushed the bottle away. The party wandered off in search of other victims: their bloodlust was unmistakable. It would not be sated in one night.

After a further quarter hour of reconnoitering and by now mildly unsettled by the totality of the massacre that had taken place throughout the past day, I arrived at the village church. I stood outside in the blackness of a bitter October night, perfectly still, listening for any sound of life in the immediate vicinity. The bodies I'd passed, littered throughout the village, often forming small mounds, didn't give rise to any sympathy or emotional reflection within me; these people, the dead, had happily supported the thousand year Reich when it was in its ascendancy, when it was winning. But now that it was on the receiving end of brutality their flopped-open jaws and gazing eyes seemed to want, to expect, absolution. I could not forgive, could never forgive, and if I could deny to them peace in their journey into whatever afterlife there might be, then I'd do it. They'd brought down this hell upon themselves: just as Sodom and Gomorrah had been destroyed, so Germany would be trampled beneath the feet of our huge regiments.

My thoughts returned to Babi Yar, my hatred inflamed by mental images of layer upon layer of innocent Soviet dead. In the scales of retribution a few dozen victims stacked in heaps in a small German village that nobody had even heard of was simply *nothing* when weighed against the atrocities committed across our own land. Illogical and unfocused anger at this imbalance forced its way out from the core of my being, as it often did in such fleeting seconds of musing. I remembered the promise I'd made, to avenge without mercy, whilst toiling through the iron earth of the great pit at Babi Yar. Just then, I heard murmurings from within the church. I carefully pushed open the great oak door and walked inside.

The church was full of villagers, young and old, but there was no priest standing at the altar. Most had their heads bowed; many were on their knees in the pews. As the heavy door opened a noisy deluge of leaves blew in. Everyone turned to look for the cause of the disturbance and when they saw me standing at the closed door, their terror was absolute and tangible. As the younger members of the congregation caught sight of the rifle hanging from my shoulder they started to scream, setting off wider panic within the church. I screamed at them to stop, to be silent, but truthfully I wanted the manifestation of their fear to continue. And then the blood red mist of rage that had blotted out my vision in Stalingrad and Kiev descended again - the cloying fog of madness that numbs then vitiates any remnant of humanity.

My heartbeat quickened and my breathing spun out of control as the cacophony reverberated off the cold stone walls: I felt the need, and had the power, to silence them. I took my rifle from my shoulder and began to fire, first a few rounds directed at specific targets and then mindlessly, almost randomly, firing off bullets in every direction. I walked slowly towards the altar, reloading as I went, shooting dead those still moving between the pews, those whom I'd missed. By the time I reached the front of the church silence had fallen. Trails of blue smoke drifted up towards the vaulted ceiling; holy faces gazed down from walls at the atrocity committed before their eyes but their demeanour didn't change, despite fragments of childlike expectation within me that it would. As I passed I saw a child slip slowly from a pew, coming to rest in propped up position upon the floor. I walked over to her but as she expelled her last gasps of breath I didn't know what to do. I picked her up and held her, shaking her briefly as if this would be sufficient to shock her back to life. The futile effort failed; I gently pushed the shock of black hair off her porcelain-white face and then replaced her in the pew. It seemed that she was wearing a poppy, blood-red, on her white dress: I watched as it blossomed, and then turned away.

I became aware of the presence of two young, severely undernourished men, hiding behind a pillar at the far end. I ran towards them, reloading again. As they saw me approach they stepped out from the darkness: they were wearing the familiar tattered uniforms of the camps. So many times I'd pulled such decayed material from the earth, usually wrapped around skeletons, that I immediately knew them not to be Germans or even inhabitants of this village. They raised their hands and I lowered my rifle: I didn't want them to be afraid. I saluted, the instinctive gesture when one soldier meets another deemed friendly off the battlefield.

In a dazed state after the act I'd just carried out I gave my name and the name of the unit, the 2nd Guards Tank Corps of the 11th Guards Army, 3rd Belorussian Front, to which I was attached. These were the first sane words I'd spoken since entering the village and then the church and despite their insignificance, they broke the roaring silence that follows in the wake of atrocities. They stared at me and then at the bodies sprawled amongst the pews, in the aisle, and at the altar: they trembled with fear as they replied. Polish Jews, they'd escaped weeks earlier from Gross Rosen camp, a satellite of Sachsenhausen. Since their escape they'd traveled, sometimes with a sense of direction but more usually haphazardly, with the sole purposes of avoiding recapture and returning to their homeland. They slept by day, usually in derelict barns. By night they'd traveled on foot but sometimes as concealed 'passengers' in the haywains of farmers who asked no questions: sympathisers with ancestral links to the Old Country.

The men had reached Nemmersdorf the day before I did and hidden in the church since their arrival, fearful that German troops were still in the area. Villagers using the church knew of their presence but were too concerned for their own survival to question those who now shared this holy space with them. They intended to resume their journey later that night. I offered my hand, and they were perturbed by its disfigurement, the missing finger tips, but quickly grasped it, recognising it as a sign not of friendship but of empathy, kinship and most importantly, a signal they were not going to be slaughtered that night. Stepping over the bodies strewn about them they made their way to the huge door at the back of the church. In the blink of an eye the two escapees, the only witnesses in the world to my crime, disappeared into the darkness.

This deed, this war crime, had eclipsed the dead star of my humanity: I knew things could never be the same again. I would never recover, not completely anyway, from this night of slaughter of the innocents, of a child. I stepped out into the freezing night. I replaced my rucksack onto my back but for the first time it felt heavy, a burden. Taking it off again I rummaged through it to find anything that could be discarded; more space would soon be needed to accommodate the larger quantities of ammunition that would be taken to Berlin. I took out the precious stones-encrusted golden carriage taken from the old man in the derelict building in Stalingrad months earlier. I turned it over in my hands; it was as beautiful as it had been when he took it out from the filthy bundle of rags and handed it over to me. It sparkled and gleamed in the moonlight. But I could no longer keep it with me; it was too heavy, and there was the risk that it would be taken from me while I slept by a comrade who'd drunk too much, possessed a rifle, and wanted it for himself. I looked around for a safe place but could see none. And then I noticed somewhere no-one would look, where it could remain safe for a lifetime if need be.

I walked over to the small graveyard alongside the church and with all my strength pushed off the solid granite lid from a raised grave. Peering inside I could see a coffin: the cracks in the panels caused by expansion and contraction over years of hot summers and frozen winters suggested that this was an old grave. The space was dry, dusty, and almost airtight. I leaned over the edge and carefully lowered the carriage to rest alongside the coffin then heaved the solid top stone back into place.

Chapter Five

1945 was both the best and the worst year of my life. The best because the war was won: the worst because it had come to an end. The proclaimed clash of ideologies was drawing to a close, although of course history was merely witnessing a realignment of forces in preparation for the next conflict. But the Great Patriotic War, *Velikaya Otechestvennaya Voyna*, was ebbing towards its bloody conclusion.

On April 19th 1945 I stood on the Seelow Heights, the 'Gates to Berlin', an area of low rolling hills ninety kilometres east of the city. After four days of fighting and over thirty thousand dead on our side, twelve thousand on theirs, we finally broke through the crumbling German lines, seizing the vantage point from which we'd rain hell down on the inhabitants of a dying city. Apart from their dogged fighting spirit, inspired by fear for the survival of their nation, there was no means by which they could match the strength of force which we were able to commit to the battle. On our side were General Zhukov and an army of two and a half million soldiers; on their side, the brilliant but belatedly arrived strategist, General Gotthard Heinrici, defensively deploying a desperate army exceeded ten to one by its enemy.

I knew of Heinrici. I'd been briefed at NKVD Control during my earlier recall to Moscow, now probably knowing more about the enemy generals than the men leading our own armies. Heinrici was an enigma to us - a talented man, highly religious and married to a so-called half-Jew, his military career had flourished despite his refusal to join the Nazi Party. Know your enemy so that you are better able to predict his next move: this was what I'd been taught, and yet in our efforts to evaluate Heinrici we'd been unable to gain access to his mind, to calculate how he'd respond to our onslaught. War brings forth such men: they interest me during moments of reflection when military tacticians wave arms across maps, forgetting the truth that the greatest of wars, the mightiest of armies, can be lost, defeated, by the irrationality, unpredictability and capriciousness of, for want of a better term, 'unusual men'.

Zhukov himself, one of our greatest ever generals, was affected by base human emotions: stubbornness and a lust for glory. When the Great Bastard, Comrade Stalin, believed the pace of our campaign was decelerating, he 'quickened' his general not by a threat of execution but instead by permitting General Konev, Zhukov's only rival, to bring forward his tanks to bear down on Berlin. Zhukov, faced with the possibility that the final prize might be denied him at the very last moment, redoubled his efforts, making mistakes and sacrificing more lives than he should have done along the way.

Beria personally ordered me before I left Moscow: 'Send me news, but not of war and ammunition supplies and the bravery of soldiers in the field. I know of all such matters. They are unimportant. Tell me instead about the human frailties and fears, the weaknesses of those who cross themselves before going into battle. *Tell me the names of men who eat alone*'. He knew that wars are won and lost through idiosyncrasies, flaws, and the unexpected, simple errors of men.

By the simple laws of attrition we could not be resisted, and on the 19th April Zhukov's 1st Belorussian Front, the army to which I was now assigned, seized the Seelow Heights. I gazed into the darkness: our enemy lay prostrate in the distance, waiting for Doomsday. Wave after wave of Katyushas scored the black sky, showering down upon a civilian population and defence force trembling in a fire-ravaged city, cowering in its ruins, in its cellars and bunkers. I looked on as my comrades danced in the darkness. Reflections of bright tails of rockets flashed in excited eyes and as they leapt up and down in the night's blackness, they resembled ancient spirits summoned up from Hell, relishing the imminent harvesting of souls. Katyushas left Earth in vast numbers, arching up into the smoke-choked night sky. So many were their number that often they criss-crossed each other's paths, colliding sometimes, creating temporary nebula of bright light. The sound was deafening, a deep whooshing that made your organs vibrate, shaking every atom in your body.

As I gazed upwards I witnessed for a few fleeting seconds in the heavy smoke Satan rise up, towering miles into the atmosphere, horns protruding from his vast head, the bright trails of the Katyushas luminous borders to a vast black cloak. He reached across the darkness, extending his arms towards doomed Berlin, embracing it in its terror and trepidation. As he fell to Earth in clouds of smoke and ordinance, I gasped at the scene; this was the end of days, the final hours of humanity, as the conflict roared towards its conclusion in a crescendo of fiery death and destruction.

Four days later Berlin was encircled. Of course there were mistakes, and with usual diligence I reported these back to Moscow. Comrade Stalin's plan to pitch two egotistical generals at each other's throats and in so doing quicken a competitive race to Berlin almost backfired in the closing hours of the encirclement. Zhukov and Konev struggled not just with the enemy but with each other, the priority of each to secure that unique place in military history: the first to enter the city.

There were errors of strategy: highways into Berlin were used unnecessarily by our troops and tank divisions - for there were alternative routes - bearing the full brunt of ferocity and fanaticism of the city's defenders. And in the blackness of the night such was the absence of coordination between the two competing generals that the density of fired rockets sometimes rained down upon our own troops instead of striking the enemy.

At the height of the conflict Konev alleged that a thousand of his men were dying each day, not in combat with the enemy but instead because of a simple refusal by his rival, Zhukov, to redeploy his forces' artillery. Thirty thousand of ours died at Seelow, twelve thousand of theirs. But nobody seemed to care: provided their suffering came close to ours, then this was all that mattered. We had the numbers and provided there was some proportionality between the deaths on our side compared with those on theirs, then by simple arithmetic we'd have a vast army still standing in the field when their very last man or boy finally dropped to the ground. Beria, of course, remained unconcerned by the casualties we were sustaining: all that mattered was the taking of the city ahead of the Americans.

Ultimately it would be Zhukov and not Konev who seized the victor's crown, taking the city whilst his rival battled through the remaining lines of defence on the outskirts. Stalin had been correct: the personal animosity between the two had spurred them on to fulfil his strong desire to capture Berlin ahead of our so-called allies. Ultimately it was he and not they who'd been the real victor and it would be for him and not them to claim the spoils of the war's outcome in the months, years and decades that followed.

For five hours I lay in the shell of a bombed-out building overlooking one of the main thoroughfares leading into central Berlin. I watched as wave upon wave of our tanks trundled along, followed by the thousands of Red Army troops now pouring into the city, washing around its squares and hidden streets like some mighty wave bursting through a battered and broken dam. Mechanical noise was everywhere, interspersed with machine gun fire and muffled booms of incendiary devices thrown into crowded cellars whose occupants refused to give themselves up when ordered to do so (always in Russian, of course).

A dank, heavy atmosphere of fear and primitive foreboding was omnipresent: the city's inhabitants now waited to be slaughtered, like so many penned sheep, hoping that death, when it came, would be quick. Many took their own lives; as I looked down the main thoroughfare I counted but then gave up as a pointless exercise the number of those hurling themselves from top floors of collapsing buildings. The road itself was marked its entire length with scarlet splashes and puddles visible from afar to the naked eye; broken and lifeless bodies, although some still twitching, lay everywhere.

I saw old men walk calmly out from their homes, as if walking out into a sunny day, and then slash their wrists with knives or shards of glass, falling to the ground where their life blood gushed into the gutters. Their hopeful calculation was that if their bodies lay on the ground outside a dwelling, the assumption might then be made that no-one else remained alive within it, and in this way wives and families could survive for another day.

As dusk fell small groups of old men began traversing the road, moving out from bomb-blasted buildings where they'd hidden during the daylight hours. Their greatcoats, torn remnants from earlier victorious years, now hung enormous about their skeletal bodies. The Fatherland was now calling upon the Volkssturm, the Home Guard, to join the battle, to fight to the death against the invaders from the East. Civilisation and the purity of the blood had to be defended to the last man, woman and child; all had to die if the alternative was the triumph of the Untermenschen over the Aryan race. I watched as they sneaked about in the half-light, scuttling between buildings and alleyways, occasionally joined by children clad in the soiled and torn uniforms of the Hitler Youth.

Images of bodies lying between pews flashed across my mind's eye, the coolness of a child's last breath on my face: Nemmersdorf's haunting of my soul had begun. I placed my rifle on the ground, shaking my head to forget my monstrous deed. For a while I succeeded. Suddenly my attention was drawn to a large open-topped army truck careering into the street. I instantly recognised it as one of ours but still, I picked up my rifle and gazed through the sight: I could hear laughter and screams, and was curious. Four soldiers sat two by two either side of the truck, recognisable from their uniforms as belonging to Zhukov's 1st Belarusian Front. Lying across the floor between them three women, screaming in terror as their captors laughed hysterically, pouring vodka over their half-naked bodies. The soldiers' intentions were obvious enough: mass rape was by now a principal instrument of fear and humiliation and was being widely unleashed upon the city's defenceless inhabitants. Our generals knew, Stalin knew, but in those closing days it was not for them to intercede between soldiers and what they regarded as the spoils of war. They'd marched across a continent, unearthed pits in which the carcasses of their countrymen had been shoveled by the hundreds of thousands, and yet still obeyed orders from the Party and a leader whom they respected but despised. Here in this dying city they would not be denied their entitlement to wreak vengeance upon those seen as responsible for their loss of innocence. And our generals, knowing it wise not to intervene between a pack of wild dogs and a cornered quarry, stood aside, at least for now. Later, after killings and rapes numbering into the tens of thousands at the very least, discipline would be restored; but for now, anarchy was everywhere.

I felt neither sympathy nor sadness for those soon to be violated by my drunken, ignorant comrades, baying like rabid animals as their captives pleaded for their lives in an incomprehensible language. I gazed up into a beautiful sky, the burnt embers of setting sun firing the deepest blue: the barbarism in the street below was incongruous. Our enemy called us Untermenschen: now, as we hurtled downwards into the blackest pits of our souls, we proved ourselves worthy of the name. But killing, whether in time of war or peace, should never be for pleasure or an emotional spasm disguised as vengeance or retribution.

Nemmersdorf had been my aberration from this rule: the speck of an island, the craggy rock of guilt, in the otherwise placid sea of my consciousness. Without a higher purpose - loyalty to country or party or political ideology - noble assassins become baser creatures, satisfying a futile blood lust. My comrades in the street below were not standard bearers in a conflict of philosophies but were instead simple criminals. I lowered my head and gazed again through the sight. Three bullets left my rifle in quick succession; two soldiers somersaulted backwards off the truck, the force of the bullets removing their heads in the process. The third target, struck off-centre, slumped dead to the floor. With another bullet fired at an angle through the windscreen the driver too had been dispatched. The lorry crashed through a smashed storefront; when it came to a halt the three captives leapt to their freedom, running in different directions like mice escaping an open cage. They'd survived for another day, but probably only until another group of comrades got their hands on them.

The days and nights following our entry into central Berlin were featureless for me: I lost count of the numbers I dispatched through the deadly focus of my cross hairs, always at a distance. It might have been dozens or hundreds, but I didn't keep count. Quieter moments were spent shooting cats and dogs, honing my skills as one of the finest snipers in the ranks of the Red Army. Surprisingly, humans presented less of a challenge: they lacked the agility of these animals as they sneaked between shattered buildings. Their weary movements were slow and their attempts at concealment pathetic. There were also many times when I aimed my rifle at those participating in the onslaught against the Nazi empire but who in doing so exhibited much of its vileness and contempt for life. As I slaughtered them like so many rats, I reflected upon the grand paradox of it all: that I, the killer of children, should dare to ascend the moral high ground to condemn those so lacking in intelligence that they could never have been expected to know better.

By the close of April 1945 I could move relatively freely during daylight hours, such was our dominance of the city and its environs. Now, instead of skulking in shells of buildings and waiting at the side of bomb-blasted window frames for targets to emerge from the shadows, I was able to walk along side streets, mindful of the remnants of SS foreigner brigades who were still present in the city, fanatically devoted to a moribund dream. Our troops and tanks were omnipresent, moving with ease along the city's main thoroughfares.

General Rokossovsky's 2nd Belorussian Front, Zhukov's 1st Belorussian Front, and the 'late comer', Konev's 1st Ukrainian Front with two and a half million men between them, flooded the heart of the dead empire. One sunny, perfect afternoon, I observed one of Zhukov's units dispatch a group of about twenty Hitler Youth boys. After they'd disappeared from sight I stepped out into the open ground of Wilhemstrasse, one of the main conduits for tanks which now rumbled incessantly, night and day, throughout the city. I approached the heap of bodies, still warm but none moving. After identifying one which in its life had had a physical frame similar to mine I dragged it out from the heap, quickly stripping off the greatcoat that enveloped the bones within. I took off my wet and torn outer clothing and threw it away. Later, a pocket knife would be used to slash off the Nazi insignia from the lapels; for now I'd just have to hope that none from my own side came across me, for no explanation would be accepted. I pulled it about me: it was a perfect fit, no doubt stolen from another corpse by its now dead owner.

Three days later, on 30th April 1945, I stood outside the Reichstag, gazing up at its huge columns. A cool breeze blew up from nowhere and then disappeared just as quickly. Despite the sound of distant gunfire and screams, there was a strange unwelcome sense of an ending of things, of the beginning of repairing of tears in the fabric of history as the world begins to come together again, to reform itself after years of cataclysm. Damned are the peacemakers, I thought, for they shall bring uncertainty through their good endeavours.

I knew from word passed among our men that we were close to taking the Reichstag so had hung back near it in order to witness the event for myself. I didn't have to wait long, and as I looked up I saw a soldier stumbling on the rooftop, partially concealed in the darkness. He unfurled a flag, the glorious red victory flag of our triumphant Soviet Union. I looked down at the watch on my wrist, torn from a corpse a few days earlier; as ten o'clock passed, roughly as my sources had predicted, the red flag now billowed out on the wind, heralding the arrival of a new balance of power in the world.

Meliton Kantaria, a sergeant in the 150th Rifle Division of the 3rd Army of the 1st Byelorussian Front (his identity became well known later in our country), screamed and laughed and cried in the darkness; here was the only moment in his life that would ever matter and if he'd tumbled off and died, plummeting through the darkness to his death in the street below, he'd have welcomed it in his final breath. Nothing could ever subsequently match this fragment in time, no medals, births, or marriages of his sons and daughters. Nothing could ever exist to equal the intensity of emotion he must have experienced in standing on top of the world, triumphant against our country's mortal enemy. He would live, subsist, for nearly another fifty years, feted for the iconic image presented to the world in that brief handful of minutes. And yet throughout those decades his unfulfilled expectations, his failed dreams of greatness, gnawed at his soul like a rat at a bone. When I met him decades later, in Moscow in 1993, just a month before his death, he was alone and seemed embittered; he had been driven from his home in Abkhazia by a petty secessionist war. I told him how I'd watched him, seen him drunk on the unique and perfect sweetness of that earlier moment: he said he wished I'd killed him and in so doing, stopped the moment passing. It seems the awfulness of defeat, which I had also witnessed when it engulfed our enemies in Stalingrad, was matched only by the emptiness of victory. As I watched him swagger and shake his fist at the world that night I was engulfed by feelings of resignation and unfathomable grief. My sense of purpose was drifting out like the ebb of the tide.

Chapter Six

That night, February 28th 1953, I stood in the corner of the cold room, concealed in the gloom out of the reach of the dim lighting, watching and waiting. The old man lay on the bed, breathing heavily and irregularly; occasionally his body twitched with involuntary spasms. The air was stale and dank, and there was silence, and darkness like tar not wholly attributable to the heavy curtains blocking out all but the smallest flecks of starlight. I remained motionless although I instinctively knew that he, despite his deeply unconscious state, was aware of my presence.

Once his hand had emerged from beneath the heavy blankets, flopped to the side of the bed but then raised itself, pointing precisely in my direction and then falling again. I said nothing, although there was much I wanted to say. To tell him of my unquestioning loyalty, of the sacrifice of my soul; and he would have understood, he would have respected me. But I'd been ordered to remain silent and keep guard. If anyone should come to assist him I was to execute them without enquiry, dispatched with a slash of a blade across the throat. And if he was to show signs of wakening from his drug-induced slumber, I was simply to press a pillow across his nose and mouth, holding it there until he breathed no more. But otherwise this was not a task with which I'd been entrusted; at my hands the execution would have been efficient and immediate, but Beria had reserved to himself this right, entirely for ignoble reasons.

After an hour the door was gently pushed open. Another guard entered, taking up position in the corner of the room closest to the bed. He too stood and waited. I watched his silhouette as first his hands started to shake, mildly and then erratically to such extent that he had to clasp them together to hold them still. His head also trembled and as the tremor began to take hold of the rest of his body he leaned back against the wall, pressing his head against it to keep it still. I could smell fear and the odour of involuntarily released urine on military fatigues.

Ivan Vassilievich Khrustalev, Stalin's most trusted guard, waited in the darkness, no doubt hoping that at this late hour in the conspiracy he'd be relieved of his imminent role in history. After a further quarter of an hour, which passed interminably, the door opened again. This time, a short man with gimlet eyes and spectacles perched on the end of his nose tip-toed in. I recognised his ovoid, partially bald head as he gingerly, fearfully, made his way over to the bed. He looked in my direction and then towards Khrustalev, now shaking uncontrollably like a madman. He stared down at the motionless body and, seeing the absence of movement, became emboldened, standing up to his full height instead of the creeping stoop with which he'd entered the room.

The prone body started to writhe, an involuntary spasm brought on by the drugs and warfarin administered earlier that evening. Beria fell to the floor in terror, remaining there until the body was still again. I watched as his head re-emerged above the side of the bed. My contempt for the coward was reinforced: despite his victim's near-catatonic and helpless state, he still hesitated to strike, to bring death quickly to a dying man. Realising that his fears were groundless and that the old man was now physically unable to protect himself or retaliate, he stood up. Starostin, Tukov and Lozgachev had long since left for the night; nobody would now intervene to save him or provide witness testimony at any later trial.

Beria started to rant, screaming at the barely alive form lying still in the darkness. He cursed him, spitting, swearing and gesturing at him with his hand. His pent-up hatred poured out as he spun about the bed like a dervish. I looked on impassively as the surreal scene played out for several minutes. And then he stopped with the same abruptness with which he'd started. I could see his outline in the darkness, catching his breath. He beckoned towards the terrified man standing nearby; at first he stood as though his feet were nailed to the floor. Beria summoned him again, but this time more urgently. Khrustalev emerged from the shadows; withdrawing the syringe from an inner pocket, he handed it to Beria.

The killer with the physical demeanour and drab attire of a village teacher tilted the old man's head to one side and gently pushed the needle into one of the main arteries leading into the neck. He then returned the head to its previous position, turned to one side. For a while he stood at the bedside and Khrustalev withdrew again into the shadows. Eventually with strenuous effort the two hauled the body off the bed, dropping it like a sack of rubbish to the floor. Beria took the victim's pocket watch from the side table, wound it forward and then smashed it, bending its arms to a time when all of us would be safely elsewhere with unbreakable alibis. He dropped it and it landed alongside the body's still slightly twitching hand.

Only a few hours earlier Khrushchev, Bulganin, Malenkov and the coward Beria (my patron) had sat with the man who was now dying, toasting his successes and feting his political skills and wisdom; sycophants, all of them. I'd been invited there, to stand in silence at a respectful distance, partaking in neither the feasting nor the conversation. I watched as my master smiled and cursed with the man from whom he derived his power and protection. Everyone present knew of my reputation as Beria's acolyte, his creature and homunculi tasked with the more risky and difficult assassinations of the regime's opponents. None of them respected me. They knew of my war record of course, but it was the unquestioning obedience to such a fawning little man that raised in their minds the wisdom or otherwise of allowing me to remain alive.

When the old man tottered out of the room to relieve himself against the wall outside, they'd plotted openly and without fear. He was to be killed - had to be killed - before he plunged us into another war, this time with a power which couldn't be defeated, such was the economic and military might of the United States of America. They whispered amongst themselves about his madness, and the as yet unspoken fear of the imminent wave of anti-Semitic attacks it was believed he would soon unleash across the country. Indeed they knew as did I of the concentration camps hurriedly being constructed in quiet rural areas, out of sight, and out of knowledge of the many Jews now occupying positions of influence in the Politburo and the wider Party.

His paranoia now threatened to destroy all that had been achieved. It was Beria who emptied the sachet of fine white powder into his Majari before he returned. The others looked away as he tapped the small envelope over the glass, believing that by not seeing the act they'd have a defence should the conspiracy go horribly wrong. And yet we all acquiesced in Beria's treachery, they from ambition and fear, I for a nobler reason they wouldn't have understood even if I'd chosen to explain it to them. I feared for the survival of our ideology and, far, far more importantly, I feared that the destruction of the nation was close at hand. They knew I'd heard their every word and yet this didn't trouble them, such was their certainty of my loyalty to Beria. Perhaps they also believed it would be unwise for me to report their conspiracy lest I too be executed in the purge which would inevitably follow.

Within quarter of an hour of drinking his wine, Stalin stood up and then stumbled, steadying himself by grabbing Khrushchev's arm. His eyes rolled as he raised his hands to his head. He cursed us and embraced us, then ordered us to leave. As Khrushchev passed by he looked into my eyes. It was the first time that evening he'd acknowledged my presence. He winked at me as if to say 'now is the time, and you are part of this'. I looked away; his physical diminutiveness, his moon-shaped face, thick lips and fleshy ears, splashes of wine and food down the front of his suit, indicated a man of no consequence, a fool. I looked down at him, at his fat, dumpy body and ill-fitting suit straining at the seams, and couldn't conceal my contempt. And yet instead of provoking his anger, he laughed loudly in his usual earthy peasant manner. My contempt seemed to amuse him; he embraced me and then left.

Later, at half past four in the morning, I left with Beria. Comrade Stalin had already retired; he'd be alone in his dacha for the remainder of the night. For the Leader to be unprotected in this way, left alone and in no fit state, was indeed a tribute to the meticulousness of the planning done by Beria and his 'silent partners' in the conspiracy. I drove him to MVD headquarters and his parting instruction was clear and precise: I was to return immediately to the dacha, wait in Stalin's room, and ensure that nobody who entered left alive. He was evidently confident that by now Stalin would be unconscious, unguarded, and unable to protect himself or call for help.

I arrived at the dacha at five o'clock, entered the room and found him spread out upon the bed, as Beria had envisaged. I took up my position in the far corner of the room and waited. With Stalin now permanently incapacitated it would be only a matter of time before death took him. In the hours that followed, the Politburo's principal members - Khrushchev, Bulganin, Malenkov and of course Beria - were called by the newly arrived guards who now feared for his health. Their concerns were dismissed and it would be many hours before medical help was summoned.

The tiny chance of survival after the lethal injection earlier that morning had vanished in the hours which followed; hours in which, perhaps, some drug could have been administered to offset the effects of the warfarin. Five days later, by March 5th 1953, he was pronounced dead.

The days following Stalin's death witnessed an orderly reconstruction of government and Politburo when the opposite might have been expected. The death of tyrants is almost invariably followed by bloodletting and purges on a grand scale as those who've waited long in the shadows step out to seize power. But this was not to be the case, as Malenkov was installed as Prime Minister, Beria Deputy First Minister, and the oaf Khrushchev became Party First Secretary. In reality Malenkov was simply a useful tool or perhaps the fool of another. True power rested in the hands of Comrade Beria, head of the KGB and the man whom Stalin had come to loathe in the days, weeks and months preceding his assassination. Within weeks of the transition of power I'd been promoted within the KGB, favoured by Beria as a trusted and efficient dispatcher of those who might oppose the new order. Beria continued to accrete to himself the power he'd so craved but had been denied by Stalin, first by merging ministries and then by consolidation of his power in the Party. Apart from Malenkov, there appeared to be nobody able or willing to obstruct his ascendancy. Neither Beria nor I had paid much attention to Khrushchev, the poorly educated peasant from the Ukraine, and this was to prove a fatal mistake. By the end of the year Beria had been executed for treason on Khrushchev's orders; the Party First Secretary snatched the prize, removing the one remaining obstacle in his own path to power.

The day following my patron's execution I was summoned to Khrushchev's dacha. All knew of my association with the now-dead former head of the KGB, and for this reason alone I anticipated an immediate and violent death. I'd likely be arrested upon arrival and taken to local woods where I'd be shot in the back of the head then buried deep beneath the roots of some vast and ancient tree, there to rot and gently return to the soil. I'd done the same myself to others so many times before, and knew well the tight schedule that had to be followed. A show trial was unnecessary for someone without public status and besides, I knew too much - I knew about the conspiracy to assassinate the Great Bastard- and if this was known, it could prove fatal to the career prospects of those now rising swiftly to power.

The prospect of death neither unsettled me nor caused the slightest frisson of fear; in these postwar years, in my darker moments I'd come to believe the better years had passed, and with them the best opportunities to influence the course of history. Now there was only compromise with pygmies: nothing to believe in or die for. Perhaps now was a good time to die before everything I'd lived for, killed for, was reduced, through moral and ideological decay, to dust.

I arrived at the dacha shortly after two o'clock and was escorted through to a large room at the rear of the building. I entered to find the First Secretary seated at a small table. In front of him was a plate bearing the carcass of a large chicken. He was feasting on its parts, tearing off a leg as I approached. Two of his shirt buttons were undone, revealing a glimpse of his large white belly. He continued eating as I approached. The late afternoon sunlight entering the room was reflected off the fat smothered about his mouth as he continued gorging, licking his lips. How he still relished simple peasant pleasures, even though he now occupied the highest point in the country's political hierarchy. And yet to equate a peasant's upbringing with a simple mind was to vastly underestimate the cunning of this man, wise enough to wait in the shadows whilst adversaries squabbled over power, destroying themselves in the process.

He looked at me and threw a large stripped bone down onto the plate. 'Please, sit'. He gestured toward the rudimentary wooden chair opposite, drawing his shirt sleeve across his mouth before continuing. 'Your patron Comrade Beria was executed yesterday. My advisors say I should order the same for you today. No point in killing the snake, only to leave its offspring to cause problems later. Are they right?'

I paused before replying, continuing to look directly into his eyes. 'Mr. First Secretary, this is a decision only you can make. I've served the Party well in war and peace. My loyalty has only ever been to the nation, not to individuals who've held power at brief moments in its history. If this is not enough then so be it. The Party has invested power in you to decide my fate. I'm ready and not afraid'. He smiled at my confrontational tone. 'You justify yourself well, but some say you're just a killer without the principles you claim to have. Beria spoke highly of you and for this reason alone I should call upon the comrades waiting outside to eliminate you now. I wonder, what is the best course of action to take here, for the good of the Party?' I realised he was pressing me to explain myself, to provide him with reason for sparing me when all common sense and impartial advice seemed to suggest otherwise. 'I've never killed without reason and justification'. (I hesitated, waiting for the all-too familiar images from Nemmersdorf to pass: this was, of course, a lie). 'I never blindly accepted Comrade Beria's orders: where they were clearly contrary to the Soviet Union's interests, I cautioned him to pause and reflect, and he was wise enough to do this most of the time. I've made mistakes, but everything I've done has been for the wellbeing of the State and of the Revolution. There will always be innocent victims amongst the guilty, but the ends justify the means'.

He interrupted: 'You mention the State's wellbeing, and you have made your own decisions on what that wellbeing was, isn't that so? If you thought I was a threat to that wellbeing, what would you do? Would you line up your rifle sight against me?' I looked at him but didn't speak. He nodded: he knew the answer. He picked up a hunk of meat and whilst appearing to concentrate on tearing it apart, I knew his thoughts were focused on me. When he'd finished he delicately wiped his short fat fingers in a small napkin.

'Comrade Damyanovitch, I've decided to let you live. There will be no execution; not today, anyway. Your first loyalty must be to the Party because it is the Party alone which represents and protects the interests of the State. And since I am Party First Secretary you will owe your allegiance to me and me alone. Do you understand? Do you accept my terms for allowing you to live today?' If he was expecting words of gratitude or sycophancy then he was mistaken. 'Yes, Comrade Khrushchev, I understand and of course I accept your terms. I'll continue to serve and protect the State'. He interrupted: 'And the Party'. I continued, 'And the Party as long as it continues to do the same'.

He knew the response not to be clever equivocation on my part, and momentarily this made him uncomfortable. 'Then I think we now know each other better. We'll speak again soon. You may go now'. My dismissal was peremptory, made with the directness and simplicity of words of a man perfectly at ease with the absolute power he wielded over the lives of millions. I left without the feelings of elation or gratitude which I knew would normally be experienced by someone whose life, having hung in the balance, had just been spared.

Chapter Seven

It's a paradox that the more we proselytise our propaganda to the masses, the greater the risk that we come to believe it ourselves. Since I was a child I had been indoctrinated with hostility towards the United States in general, and its capitalist leaders in particular. I'd never been in close proximity to this 'alien race', and for this reason had no means of confirming the truth or otherwise of what I'd been told. This was to change after eight years of unquestioning obedience to Khrushchev. In June 1961 he ordered that I accompany him on an overseas diplomatic mission.

I'd traveled abroad before; during these years, of course, this was one of the privileges of rank in the KGB. 'True believers always return home—where else would they go?', he'd observed when questioned about the relatively high degree of freedom accorded me. By this time the First Secretary trusted me implicitly, or at least to a greater extent than he did the other Party apparatchiks who competed for his favour. I was to accompany him as part of his entourage to Vienna where an informal summit was to be held to reduce tension which had been escalating between the two Great Powers during the past few years.

For Khrushchev, apart from the mundane protocols and niceties of international diplomacy (for which he had little understanding or enthusiasm) it was an opportunity to indulge in the pleasures and luxuries of the West: excesses he so frequently condemned in his speeches at home, but which he secretly wallowed in during his trips abroad. This hypocrisy was a product of the peasant inheritance within him; the ability to condemn and crave in equal measure. During our delegation's first night in the Austrian capital I lightly chastised him for his ideological shallowness; he smiled at the condemnation like some guilty schoolboy brazen in his truanting. I respected him for his cunning, for his quick mind and ability to outmanoeuvre opponents (who were, intellectually, his superiors) by a substantial margin. In recent years I'd almost come to like him. His ability to keep his mind free of dogma whilst simultaneously articulating the platitudes of the Party in an earthy language which the masses both understood and accepted, endowed him with a level of pragmatism which his predecessors had lacked. His fleshy face, his expansive suits and his earthy and offensive observations and rants softened the reality that he was indeed a formidable adversary to those at home and abroad who were seeking to undermine the political system he served.

Shortly after our people arrived at the ornate Viennese hall where discussions were to be held, the Americans walked in. We had of course been seated on opposite sides of the huge table by our Austrian hosts, a reflection of our entrenched positions on a range of international conflicts. Kennedy walked over to the First Secretary and shook his hand. The contrast between the two could not have been starker. Comrade Khrushchev was short in stature, thick-set with a white complexion made more striking by his baldness. Kennedy was tall and slender, naturally holding himself with patrician poise; his face was tanned by the sunshine of his home state, his attire perfect. He had an almost tangible aura of natural authority. Khrushchev never possessed this quality but to his credit, had nevertheless made his way to the same position in the hierarchy of power.

I watched for signs of condescension on the part of the charismatic American but saw none. Instead, his gestures evidenced an understanding that this was a meeting of equals, despite the reality of the economic and military imbalance between our two countries. Although their words were translated, there appeared a vague amity between them as they laughed and exchanged self-deprecating observations. I was introduced to the President and we shook hands; his grip was strong but his skin was soft to the touch. This was not a man who'd ever laboured for a living.

Within half an hour of the commencement of talks the lower-ranking officials on both sides, including myself, left for an ante room. There we were to wait while our masters discussed more sensitive issues. Soon, I decided to leave; I'd return within a few hours, taking advantage of this rare 'idle time' to walk around a city I'd not seen before either in peace or war. Upon leaving the building I noticed I'd been followed out by another participant from the American side. He walked briskly behind me and when he'd caught up, took my arm. 'Excuse me sir. It's Mr. Damyanovitch, yes? Petr Damyanovitch?' I turned around, somewhat defensively; in a thousand and one other situations I'd have expected a gun or a knife to have been revealed at this moment.

'Yes, I'm Petr Damyanovitch. And you are....?' I immediately recognised him from the morning's summit, but couldn't recall his name. 'Sorry to accost you on the street like this, Petr - you don't mind if I call you Petr do you? You see, when I saw you leaving the conference room I knew this would be our only chance to talk before we go home. I'd really like it if we could talk for a while. I'm reckoning on going back in within a couple of hours, so if you're willing, can we walk together?' He was about five years older than me, with an accent fundamentally different from both Kennedy and for that matter all the other attendees on the American side. It was almost as if they were from different countries, although it was obvious he was American. I wondered whether I was about to be offered some inducement, financial or otherwise, to betray my country. It would be amusing to see how the terms were put, even though they would be entirely rejected at the end.

'Yes, it would be a pleasure to walk with you, but, unfortunately, I've forgotten your name'. I held out my hand and he took it. 'I'm Carter Buckmaster, one of the legal advisors traveling with the President. Although I'm with the State Department I also have a small law practice in Tennessee'. I smiled; his manner was open and genuine, his demeanour, as far as one can ever tell of these things, honest and at ease with the world. For the following hour we walked through the city, admiring its architecture, occasionally stopping at pavement cafes, talking about the prospects for success at the summit. We both agreed that, given the many points of conflict between our two leaders, a useful compromise was unlikely. The sticking point, of course, would be East Germany. Put simply, Khrushchev wanted to recognise the state through a peace treaty, whereas Kennedy opposed this, seeing it as a device with which pressure could be exerted over West Germany. Buckmaster envisaged that while the summit probably wouldn't collapse, neither side would leave satisfied.

'There's a particular reason why I wanted to speak with you, Petr. The White House believes that at these times of heightened tension there's always the risk that one side will miscalculate, the other misinterpret, and we'll end up with a conflagration which none of us want. Wars often start more by accident than design. For this reason it's important to have as many formal and informal channels of communication between both sides as possible - this is the way to prevent the mist of war rolling in. We know about your position in the KGB and your closeness to First Secretary Khrushchev. He trusts you. The White House wants you and I to be in touch, informally and without commitment or expectation on either side, as a channel through which concerns or feelings of threat can be transmitted easily and quickly between our two governments. The President wants a continuing dialogue, government to government, embassy to embassy, academic to academic, so that the silence which precedes the breaking out of war can be avoided'. He had said all this in a measured, unhurried tone, and with a continuing friendly smile.

We came to a halt beneath the Anchor Clock in the Hoher Markt: I gazed up at its gaudy Art Nouveau design as the figure of Joseph Haydn walked out across the bridge. Tourists also stared up, clicking their cameras. I turned to him and gave my reply. 'Yes Carter, I will do this. I will do it because I believe it's in the interests of my country to avoid any misunderstandings. Of course, I'll inform the First Secretary of your approach and this conversation after our return to Moscow. It's important for my personal position and for my safety that my role be transparent from the start. And if, in future, our leaders use us to communicate their concerns to each other instead of immediately resorting to conflict, then we'll be providing a service to them and the wider world. Assuming that Mr. Khrushchev agrees, I'll be in contact with you as soon as I can'. This was the first day of our association, initially based on patriotism and good sense on both sides, and later, increasingly, based on mutual respect and a friendship which would deepen and hold fast for the next forty years. We shook hands on it in a quiet corner of a small Viennese square.

We returned to the conference room, resuming our positions at opposite ends of the table. Kennedy re-entered at the same time, having taken his fourth break of the past few hours. The atmosphere was relaxed. As delegates took their seats Khrushchev looked at him and then turned to the translator. He spoke, and the translator looked visibly shocked but I was unsurprised: I knew how he liked to offend and catch people off-guard with earthy language.

The translator paused before addressing Kennedy. 'The First Secretary wants to know....' He looked across at Khrushchev who gestured him continue. 'The First Secretary wants to know why you Americans have such weak bladders- why you need to urinate so frequently'. Khrushchev leaned forward and tapped the table: his knowledge of English was greater than he wanted known. 'I said piss. Why the need to piss so frequently?' The American delegates looked shocked, offended. I smiled at this typical uncouthness. Kennedy smiled broadly before responding. 'If Russian dicks weren't so small and tight, then perhaps my friend would also be willing to relieve himself - take a piss - as often as we who are better blessed sitting opposite'.

The translator looked mortified as he wondered where to begin but Khrushchev had instantly understood the retort and roared with laughter. To have his offensiveness reciprocated with such an insult delighted him. But he also knew from our intelligence in the States about the President's poor health, of the drugs he was routinely obliged to take for his back pain, and of course of his long-standing kidney problems - hence the more frequent breaks than was normal for a man of his age. Khrushchev had exploited this knowledge, but in a harmless way. Both men had the measure of each other and observers would later correctly suggest that they almost liked each other, while at the same time being constantly frustrated by what each man perceived as the other's intransigence.

When Kennedy broached the subject of East Germany the summit entered the history books as a failure. The First Secretary insisted that he would sign a peace agreement with the new state, turning over control of roads and air routes and in turn obstructing essential supply lines into West Germany. His face turned bright red, and his tone and gestures were excited. 'Force will be met with force. If the US wants war, that's your problem. It's up to the US to decide whether there will be war or peace'. His volatile outburst evidenced his lack of understanding of the finer points of the diplomatic game. Kennedy responded firmly; in his demeanour I saw a man willing to take the world to war again (a war we Soviets would surely lose) if American economic or ideological interests were challenged.

'Then, sir, there will be a war. It will be a cold, long winter' Shortly afterwards the summit ended, with each leader underestimating and slightly misjudging the other, and any new era of rapprochement remaining tantalisingly out of reach. Within two and a half years Kennedy would be dead. Khrushchev would remain in power for a further three years, deposed by Brezhnev in 1964 after his failure over Cuba, and poor harvests and weak industrial modernization at home. I remained loyal to him until his last day in power.

During these years Buckmaster and I fulfilled our role as conduits between the exasperated leaders contributing, albeit in a small way, to the maintenance of peace at a time when the odds favoured war.

Chapter Eight

Entering Wenceslas Square on the night of 20th August 1968 standing atop a massive lumbering tank stirred distant memories in me of better, simpler times. Of course we were part of a huge convoy all heading for the same rendezvous and purpose but the feeling of absolute power, of being masters of the Earth, was just as potent, just as unique, as it had been last time, twenty three years before. Then, we'd crashed through the barricades clogging the streets of Berlin, forcing our way along the arteries and eventually into the heart of the dying Reich.

This time the circumstances were different. Instead of being faced with fanatical soldiers driven mad by years of Nazi propaganda, we were confronted by fellow Slav civilians, by young and old alike, who were cursing us in the streets. I closed my eyes as we smashed our way through, the deafening roar of the engine, the smell of burning diesel, rousing sensations of our past victory. The sense of imminent violence excited me and I hated myself for this base instinct in this wholly different circumstance. Just as in Berlin, I wanted to roll over the bodies, to send crowds scuttling off in fear for their lives, but here I knew our opponents were not so neatly definable as the 'enemy'.

How to justify to myself the killing of the young and the innocent caught up in the conflagration was something I knew I'd have to return to in later years. But that night was not a time for self-doubt; we'd arrived in the country for a reason, for a simple task. The so-called 'Prague Spring', led by the naïve and factious Dubcek, had to be crushed and its leaders taken back to Moscow. If this meant loss of life, even on a considerable scale, then this would be a price worth paying to restore order. Czechoslovakia would recover in time: this challenge to our authority, the confusion and ambivalence under Dubcek, were not to be countenanced. We'd come to restore order and discipline, but also to prevent this wellspring of so-called liberalisation, of chaos, from trickling then flooding across into neighbouring states.

I stood with head and shoulders above the hatch, passing crowds; many swore as we trundled through the darkness, others simply wept. But what was the 'freedom', which these Czechs wanted? The right to challenge and tear down authority then put in its place a simplistic set of values founded upon 'autonomy of the individual' at the expense of all else? To sacrifice the oneness of society in the pursuit of selfish goals? I regretted many of the killings of innocent Czechs - those on our side who indulged in excessive violence I dispatched with my pistol and left in the gutter as I had done in Berlin and elsewhere- but the basic justification of our endeavour, our noble cause, I didn't for a second question. We had right on our side, and the dim need to find morality in my actions, with all its implications of self-confounding uncertainty and nebulous subjectivity, never clouded my sense of duty and loyalty to the State. Without such single-mindedness, without such sacrifices and yes, butchery, Berlin would never have been won. But the years since then had been mired in a thousand compromises, serving a motley bunch of lying and dissembling apparatchiks who squabbled over power like a pack of wild dogs tearing at a carcass. Brezhnev's order to put down the Prague insurgency, his ideological objectivity, had reinvigorated my sense of purpose. I gazed up into the night sky and longed again for the clarity of war without end.

After our tanks and armoured vehicles had taken up strategic positions and the main thoroughfares into and out of the city were secured, we dismounted and fanned out through the Square and the surrounding side streets. Our aims were simple: to disperse the crowds through threats of violence, and to seize the ringleaders. In such moments of chaos the majority of civilians will flee; after protesting they return to their homes to hide in the darkness until order of some kind is restored. In some parts of the city, particularly around the radio station, resistance was more organised although its weaponry was rudimentary. Futile barricades were thrown across many of the smaller side streets behind which small groups of young people sheltered, throwing Molotov cocktails and bricks and whatever else they could lay their hands on.

In the main we responded with exceptional moderation: a bloodbath had been anticipated by the Kremlin, but this simply didn't materialise. President Svoboda continued condemning the occupation as illegal over the air waves, but even this focal point of opposition was soon silenced. I remember walking alone across Wenceslas Square as the crowds rushed past me, twisting off in different directions like shoals of small fish. In their fear they seemed oblivious to my presence; if they'd noticed the military insignia on my greatcoat then perhaps they'd have stopped, the opportunity to kill one of the invaders to be seized without hesitation.

And then I saw them. In one of the Square's far corners I saw two people, a man and a woman, both, probably, in their late twenties. They were embracing each other around a child, all three holding tightly on to each other. From a street nearby a Polish soldier emerged brandishing a Kalashnikov. He started waving it in the air as he ran screaming towards them. Shots rang out as he drew nearer and the three separated, the parents - for I assumed they were the parents- running off down another street to distract his attention away from the child. The strategy was a successful one and he pursued them leaving the child, a little girl, standing alone in a state of dumb terror.

I ran down the side street after the three but by the time I reached the small courtyard it was too late. The soldier stood by the two bodies lying like broken dolls on the ground, single bulletwounds to each of their heads. I walked up to the soldier and shot him between the eyes, leaving him fall alongside his victims. I returned to the Square and found the child still standing in the same place, not even crying, rooted to the ground like a sapling. I looked at her and all I could see was the Nemmersdorf child. I gasped as once again the guilt forced itself into my consciousness. I scooped her up in my arms and without a word between us took her to a nearby armoured truck. I gave my orders: as one of the higher ranking KGB officers present in the battlefield that day, they were obeyed without question.

She was taken to a military helicopter on the outskirts of the city and from there to Moscow. For several months afterwards she remained in an orphanage in the city. I ordered that the administrator keep me informed of her progress on a daily basis, and it quickly became evident she was failing to adjust to the fundamental change in her circumstances. For the first time in my life I was uncertain as to what to do next. Objectively she was nothing to me but subconsciously I felt a responsibility for her wellbeing. My dreams continued to be haunted by Nemmersdorf, exacerbating a sense of guilt which I now transferred to this child. At the end of the third month I ordered the release of the child into my care. Three years later I adopted her. She would be my atonement.

Chapter Nine

For an empire to collapse, first it must rot from within. The process may be a gradual moral or economic decline or it may be swift, perhaps through the damage and destruction of military defeat. Rise, decline and death are all stages in the inevitable processes of empire. And for those who have served the broken state, those left clinging to the wreckage, no hope or sense of purpose remains, no justification for the sacrifices of body and soul and conscience now cursed by shallow men as errors of misspent lives. They become outcasts in their own land, despised and rejected by those they had always protected.

So it was when the state I'd served with my life collapsed into nothing in the blink of an eye. Initially, my hatred for the pygmies who'd brought about our demise knew no boundaries: I would gladly have executed all of them had there only been one brave enough to order it to be done. Terror usually restores order and from this, new beginnings. Concessions and tolerance merely quicken decay.

On the 17th August 1991 I was summoned to KGB Chairman Kryuchkov's office. He said time was short; perhaps it was already too late but he and others planned to remove First Secretary Gorbachev from power the following day, placing him under house arrest at his dacha in the Crimea. I was to await instructions after a State Emergency Committee was established; the purge of so-called reformers which would follow would need to be comprehensive, and in this I was to play a crucial role.

There'd be condemnation from the usual quarters, of course, especially the Americans and their allies, but in time this would subside and eventually things would continue as normal. The Party would survive, and the decline would be halted. I looked at the ageing Politburo member, Andropov's protégé; his voice trembled as he spoke, his self-delusion was obvious to both of us. These were the final days and we knew it. But

I agreed to support the coup, not out of conviction - the slyness of the little men, the conspirators, appalled me - nor from misplaced belief in the prospect of a successful outcome. Instead I'd fight and fail and die for a system now in its death throes but to which I still remained utterly committed. The lack of preparedness, the uncertainty as to how the military and Special Forces would respond to orders to slaughter Muscovites in large numbers if necessary, confirmed in my mind the hopelessness of the endeavour. But standing in Kryuchkov's stuffy office with its drab décor, I kept my thoughts to myself: this was an exercise in Canutean futility which had to play itself out and only then could we survey the debris and make plans to rebuild.

On the 19th the plan was launched. Military vehicles and personnel moved into Moscow, radio stations were closed down: in essence, the usual strategies characteristic of amateur banana republic coups which were doomed to failure. I watched the emergency news bulletin as Gennady Yanayev declared Gorbachev unable 'for health reasons' to continue in his post as President. Yanayev would become acting President, committed to the same reforms, 'Glasnost and Perestroika,' which his deposed predecessor had initiated. The address was unconvincing and stilted, made by a man lacking in ideological backbone and charisma. I knew how Muscovites would react, and within hours my assessment proved correct. As civilians rallied to protect the White House, Commander Yazov, evaluating the potential scale of the slaughter and unsure of the loyalty of foot soldiers or higher command, ordered a withdrawal. By the 21st it was all over; Gorbachev was back in power, the clown Yeltsin was elevated to a status higher than he could ever have imagined, and all the conspirators were placed under arrest, except poor old Boris Pugo, who had the decency to shoot himself in shame. All the rest were prosecuted and imprisoned, only to be released a few years later under amnesties and acquittals. The attempted coup had been an ill-planned fiasco and its failure was well-deserved and predictable. As for my own role, I had not actively engaged in the plot's planning or implementation; instead I waited on the sidelines for its inevitable demise and for instructions which never came.

In the days and weeks which followed I observed, as a passive witness, the disintegration of the Party and the dismemberment of our empire. I was warned that it was only a matter of time before I too was arrested for past crimes against the People (the Party now vanished, was replaced by the ignorant autocracy of the masses). I waited for the midnight knock on the door: echoes from Comrade Stalin's time were everywhere as the new regime looked to avenge itself on its predecessor's supporters.

I remember how in those bewildering, depressing early days, the cleverer former apparatchiks looked to line their pockets with the nation's assets stripped out in auctions which they themselves controlled and manipulated. Corruption was the common currency; these were days for rich pickings. Foreigners participated in the 'great treasure hunt' too, buying up symbols of culture at street hawker prices. This was an orgy of looting that shocked me; the nation was like a drunkard lying in the gutter, his pockets picked by sly and dishonest 'well wishers'. And at the pinnacle of power sat Yeltsin, a jester, a useful fool of the foreign powers who wished above all to see their old enemy brought to its knees and impoverished.

I recall walking along a street in central Moscow and seeing a crowd gathered outside a nondescript building. I stopped to ask what was taking place inside; it was not unusual to see people queuing outside shops or foreign exchange dealers (fearing the domestic currency was about to collapse), but this building had no signage indicating its function. I was told an auction was taking place, and that foreign buyers with suitcases crammed with dollars had flown in to buy up the lots. I entered and sat down and waited, curious to see how this quaint feature of the new capitalism worked. For the next half hour items were brought out and held aloft; bids were made directly by those in the room and also by agents on behalf of anonymous foreign buyers. The frenzy of the bidding was ugly, as the baying crowd scrambled to buy baubles and artworks from the Tsarist years which were now bubbling up to the surface from a thousand secret repositories around the country. Everything was for sale: our culture, our history, our soul.

I believe in fate. If on that day I'd taken my usual route to work, if I'd not passed by that building and been drawn in by idle curiosity, then my life would have followed a different trajectory, towards abject poverty. Lot 303 was brought out and held up to the audience; it glimmered and sparkled beneath the bright lights, drawing gasps from around the room. The perfect pink, gold, and sky-blue Faberge egg with its intricate internal mechanism and studded diamonds had remained hidden in a farm's outhouse since the Revolution, liberated or stolen depending on your perspective of events, by one of the hundreds of thousands of rioters who swarmed through the palaces, looting and destroying, in those early days of anarchy. It had only recently been rediscovered and its true value determined. I gasped at its beauty. And then I remembered. I watched and listened in disbelief as the bidding escalated, first in hundreds of thousands, and then leaping past a million dollars. I left the room without waiting for the final bid; it was time to return to Nemmersdorf, now renamed Mayakovskaya, the location of my spiritual destruction.

I was the only passenger on the flight from the military airbase on the outskirts of Moscow to the Kaliningrad oblast. One of the privileges remaining to me was the power to demand transportation to any part of the country at short notice. I'd retained my rank in the FSB, Yeltin's grand idea for a replacement of the now officially disbanded KGB, although prospects for my long-term survival within the organisation were poor.

At dusk, as the jet gently coasted to a halt on the tarmac, the young pilot looked back at me and asked for further instructions. Looking out over the flat asphalt and distant patches of pine forest, I told him I'd return within three hours; until then he was free to do as he wished. I commandeered a military vehicle and left the base. Within a short time I was driving at high speed through the countryside, recalling an earlier time when I'd made the same journey sitting astride a tank's gun turret. Nothing had changed; this part of the former East Prussia, seized by Stalin from a defeated Germany at the War's end and frozen in time as a side-effect of its military importance, was just as I remembered it, even in its unaltered roads and lanes.

When I reached the edge of Mayakovskaya for the first time in my life I felt a sense of dread. I tried to rationalise the situation, thinking of the purpose of the journey and its importance to my future, but it was difficult to maintain regular breathing or to calm my straining heart. This place held the secret of my soul's death and now circumstances had forced me to return to face it again. I walked into the village; it was pitch black and all I could see were bodies stacked neatly like piles of dolls on either side of the road. A villager greeted me but I ignored him. I passed by a barn; across its huge door I saw again a naked body, nailed in cruciform. A farmer smiled and waved, but by this time I'd left the present. The smell of death and corpses filled my nostrils. I felt nauseous. A group of soldiers staggered towards me, drunk, then vanished into thin air: I knew I was drawing closer.

And then I came again to the church, still standing, rising into the darkness like a focal point in a nightmare. I froze, not wanting to proceed but knowing I had to. I pushed open the door and walked inside: the place was deserted and silent, a candle burning upon the altar. I looked at the row upon row of the faithful, muttering their desperate prayers, crossing themselves as they waited for Armageddon. I stood absolutely still and then heard again the thundering of the rifle, the sound of bullets ricocheting off walls, penetrating soft flesh. I heard the screams, so many screams, and looked up at the walls at the faces staring down upon the war crime being perpetrated in their midst. They were witnesses and had not forgotten with the passing of decades. This was the ultimate blasphemy - the slaughter of innocents in a holy place. I raised my hands to my face as I progressed to the front and then stopped alongside the pew where my soul had died. I looked down and saw the child; I watched myself pick her up and cradle her in my arms, but it was too late. It was always too late. I knew I should weep but was unable to; instead all I could feel was depthless sadness.

I looked past the smoldering bodies and saw the other witnesses; they'd not appeared in the hundreds of dreams since that night, and this was the first time I remembered them. I saw the two Jews peeping out from behind a pillar, their clothes torn and faces wan, and wondered what had happened to them. Perhaps they'd died in the chaos, murdered by remnants of the retreating army. Perhaps instead they'd been killed by our own: a bloodlust doesn't discriminate amongst its victims. I stayed a while longer, sitting in the brooding silence, waiting for the blue smoke drifting upwards to clear. But it didn't - it never does. I wanted to put out the candle but I couldn't bring myself to approach the altar, kept at bay like some wretched spirit from the underworld, frightened of the light, of the presence of a Greater Power in the smallest of things. Instead I left, an unpunished coward.

I pulled closed the heavy wooden door and made my way into the graveyard. There were other graves of course, but I had no difficulty finding the grave I had prised open what felt like a thousand centuries ago. New headstones gleamed in the light; the majority of inscriptions in Cyrillic contrasting with the German engravings on earlier stones. I came to the grave, recognising it immediately after revisiting it hundreds of times since in my dreams, my nightmares. I heaved off the heavy stone: it slid to one side with an ancient grating sound. I leaned in and beside the shattered coffin and broken skeleton the cloth bundle still lay. Hauling it out, I was surprised by the absence of decay. Slowly, carefully, I unwrapped the treasure hidden within the filthy rag; the phaeton with Faberge eggs shone in the moonlight, its gems and diamonds sparkling as I held it up. It was beautiful, much more beautiful than the lot seen at the earlier auction, and by my inexpert eye, likely to be of considerably greater value.

I recalled the emaciated old man whose request I had obliged, and held again his magnificent payment for my service. I wrapped it up, gently placing it into a satchel brought along for the purpose. A short time later I was back at the airbase boarding the same small plane by which I'd arrived.

In the following weeks, with the help and shrewd advice of my friend Carter Buckmaster, the Tennessee lawyer, I set up an offshore company in Cyprus. Through it I was able to sell the Faberge phaeton at auction in St. Petersburg, receiving full payment in US dollars without anybody ever knowing my identity. For a while I kept the proceeds, the few million dollars, with a Geneva-based bank, the account in the name of the Cypriot company in which I was the sole shareholder. But what's the point of wealth if it can't be used? In new Russia's maelstrom of economic chaos it was possible (and with determination, political connections and minimal capital in fact rather easy) to take control of hopelessly undervalued assets. In 1992 I bought a small and insignificant Moscow bank. Within ten years, Moscow Alpha was to become one of Russia's leading finance houses, its reach into the newly independent neighbouring states unparalleled by its lesser domestic competitors.

I had emerged from the chaos as one of the country's new breed of 'oligarchs', with a power and influence greater than I'd ever known in my previous incarnation as a loyal servant of the Party. Now I had the tool with which I planned to avenge myself upon those who'd destroyed my life's work. Now was the time for a mightier empire to rise from the ashes. Now was the time for planning, for utilising capitalism's weapons of conquest - the harnessed forces of the global financial markets. I knew my time had come.

[Notes of Prisoner KT-1370, together with other personal effects, to be forwarded to next of kin. By order of the Governor, HM Prison Brixton, London].

PART TWO

———

Three Friends.

Chapter Ten

'And that, ladies and gentlemen, is the reason why you should elect me to the post of treasurer of this great union; my commitment to financial integrity and transparency means you can rest assured I'll never fail to live up to the trust you place in me'. The main hall of the student union of Caius College, Cambridge, erupted with applause as Saul Quartermain stood resolutely upright at the podium, his hands outstretched, acknowledging the cheering crowd. Towards the rear of the hall he could make out the silhouettes of Adam Creed and Thomas Stoneacre, his friends and accomplices whose strategic planning of his election campaign was about to deliver an historic victory, despite unproven allegations of corruption and bribery by the other candidates. He smiled into the darkness and winked at them, his mischievously twinkling deep blue eyes briefly betraying his satisfaction with a perfectly dominated election. He waited for the applause to subside, swept back his blond hair, and returned to his seat on the platform, alongside his sullen, inevitably defeated rivals. The two figures at the back of the hall slipped away unnoticed, not needing to wait for the final result. Half an hour later he'd been elected as treasurer, taking full responsibility for the union's finances. After shaking hands with the other candidates he left the building, making his way to an Italian restaurant tucked away down one of the warren of back lanes adjoining the university grounds, to meet with his friends and co-conspirators.

Saul Quartermain was in the final year of a banking and finance degree. A highly talented student, he was renowned amongst his contemporaries for three qualities. First and foremost, he had charm and wit and a self-deprecation which endeared him to the opposite sex. Second, he had exceptional intellectual ability which was respected by classmates and lecturers alike. Third and perhaps most important, he had an unshakable commitment to his two friends, Adam Creed and Thomas Stoneacre.

The three were often regarded with suspicion, with some justification given the unsubstantiated rumours which had swirled about them during the last two years concerning gambling in the university halls of residence, and petty criminality including the illegal bootlegging of cigarettes and wine. Conspiracy was their currency and their pleasure, but it was the absolute trust they had in each other which delivered their greatest successes: when they worked as one, they were unbeatable.

Saul arrived at La Trattoria at 9.30 and was welcomed by Mario, the head waiter. 'Good evening, Mr. Quartermain, has your day been a good one?' Saul handed over his overcoat. 'Thanks Mario. Today's been a great day, so please, plenty of your best wine tonight. We have a success to celebrate!' He made his way to the corner table which had become theirs by occupation during the past month, sat down and smiled. Adam took a long draw on his cigarette, looked up at the ceiling and exhaled the smoke slowly; without lowering his eyes, he spoke in his characteristically dry, sarcastic tone. 'It's such a shame when democratic processes are subverted by rogues who'll stop at nothing to win an election, even if that means bribing anyone with a vote, or besmirching an opponent's good name. Where's the honour in winning by fighting dirty? I fear for the future, I really do'. The three erupted into laughter, and so began what they knew would be a perfect evening. Saul turned to Thomas for a practical appraisal of the costs of his election to high office in the union. 'So Thomas, how much did we pay in the end, and are you sure the Cambridge Chronicle can't trace the Hobhouse story back to us?' Thomas placed his thumb to his tongue in true mafia-bookkeeper fashion; 'Payments to floating voters cost us three hundred pounds. An extra two hundred went to the van driver to get a boxload of our opponent's voting papers lost in transit. That makes five. Well spent, I think we'll all agree.'

'On the Hobhouse scoop', chipped in Adam, 'there's no way we can be traced as the source – I didn't have a chance to tell you yet, but I was scrupulously careful. I sent the information about our friend's previous petty theft conviction by post from a box fifty miles away, anonymously of course. The local paper was so unoriginal: they copied my proposed article word for word. But I guess that 'Prospective treasurer convicted thief: union's bank account in safe hands?' did have a certain journalistic flair. I might dabble as a columnist, eh? Anyway, when our good friend Hobhouse started making 'scurrilous and unfounded allegations' about your involvement with the smuggled vino, he sacrificed his right to a fair campaign'. Saul raised his glass and smiled. 'Too true. Let he who is without sin, and all that'.

Thomas, Saul and Adam had known each other for two years, studying at the same university but towards different degrees. Thomas's intention was to take up a training contract with a major firm of accountants in London, subject to his managing a good degree. The only son of a middle class Yorkshire family, his principal long term goal was to return to the North where he dreamed of taking over control of his father's specialist engineering business. In temperament he was noted for his passivity, although his friends knew differently, having witnessed his condemnation of petty cheating by fellow students on his degree course. By way of his Northern Calvinistic roots in general and his father's influence in particular, Thomas had inherited a keen awareness of financial probity which, while playing little part in his daily life at the university, nevertheless lay dormant within his consciousness, momentarily raising itself whenever his brothers in crime advocated commission of an even more daring deception upon the unsuspecting university fraternity. Thomas was there for the ride, for the vicarious excitement, and accordingly his moral pangs over minor acts of criminality were both fleeting and easily controlled. Although he reached the same First Class exam results as Saul and Adam, he'd long since admitted that this was done through hard study rather than natural ability; he was the plodder, the long-distance runner, they were the effortless sprinters.

As the evening wore on, the conversation shifted to a subject which had preoccupied their thoughts over recent months. They were at the start of their final year and all three knew the time was approaching when they'd have to make career decisions which would affect the rest of their lives. There was awareness that while university life had its occasional serious moments, it was nevertheless a time when they could enjoy pleasure without consequence, foolishness and fleeting fun with the women they bedded interspersed with, at least from Saul and Adam's perspectives, short bursts of concentration in pursuit of academic excellence. The 'outside world' of work would probably be different. Adam was the most certain of the three in terms of the path he intended to follow. For the past two years he'd achieved outstanding academic results and was by far the most talented of students in the recent history of the law school.

It didn't matter whether he acted for the defence or the prosecution at the mock trials or moots at the school: he had always won each and every case he fought. However, the admiration which his lecturers held for his ability was tempered by their concern about the perceived arrogance he showed following a victory, and his willingness to test the law, and the morality underpinning it, to its limits. He was the perfect student, apart from this one fundamental character flaw.

'So I guess it's investment banking for you Saul, and law for you, Adam'. Thomas attempted to appear mildly disinterested, but inwardly he hoped they'd simply agree with his observation and then move on to discuss his own career options. Although his medium term goal of taking over his father's business was clear enough, his present difficulty was working out how to get there, and what to do in the meantime to gain experience and become equipped with the knowledge to make a success of it. He needed training in accountancy and finance before he could even begin to plan for succeeding his father as chief executive of Northern Engineering. Saul's reply was uncharacteristically hesitant; 'Although I could walk into any job in the City, I'm not sure I could cope with all that fake 'gentleman's agreement' stuff. I've always wanted to know where the rules of acceptable behaviour are just so as I can enjoy the excitement of breaking them even more'. There was laughter from all three, and raised glasses at this sentiment, even from Thomas, who lacked the daring of his friends.

Saul continued: 'Conformity's just not in my makeup and there's no point in pretending otherwise. How long would it be before I broke the rules - professional, legal, ethical; the whole lot, and landed myself in jail? Handling other people's money; well, do you know of anyone less qualified by temperament than me to take that on? No, I'd rather just have fun, because that's what life's all about.' The other two laughed again, but his concerns struck home for both of them. All three were individualists rather than team players and knew of former students who, despite being exceptionally talented, had failed in various occupations because of an inability to 'fit in' and now drifted around, borrowing from their peers. 'But whatever I do, I'll be the best, and I'll not be hidebound by rules in achieving this'. 'I'll drink to that'. Adam raised his glass, keen to move the conversation along. 'And if you ever need a lawyer, then I'll be your man!' 'I hope it doesn't come to that but... it might, and then you'll be the first person I'll call. And if it's a complex fraud, I'll always have Thomas here to ensure that the accounts are well cooked!'

'So what about you Adam, do you see yourself 'fitting in' with the culture of a large law firm, or would 'professional ethics' get in the way?' Adam smiled: only Thomas could make such a comment, an implicit damning criticism, and get away with it without a fierce retort. 'I'm going to commit myself to a career in the law and I'll be the best, and if necessary I'll break every rule which gets in my way. And I'll break anyone who tries to stop me too. If there's one thing that studying law for the past few years has taught me, it's this: its main function is to protect the weakest from the consequences of their own stupidity, not to provide some idealised set of moral principles with which we should all comply. I love the law and I'll excel at it, but don't expect me to protect those who make their own foolish decisions and then ask others to protect them from the consequences.' Saul and Thomas looked at him with slight surprise: they were familiar with his uncompromising views, they'd heard them before; but they were unsettled by this expression of them, his sharpest yet. They both recognised the emotionless, impassive, fixed stare of those pale grey eyes as he spoke. Sometimes, caught off guard, he hinted at a brooding darkness which was difficult to reconcile with the good humour and cool wit for which he was renowned. All three friends knew that their lives were about to change: suddenly they all felt less secure, less certain of what lay ahead.

The evening drew to a close and the candle at the centre of their table began its last splutters of life. As Saul and Thomas contemplated the journey back to their student flats, Adam's gaze switched from the candle's shrinking pool of light to the doorway on the far side of the restaurant. Saul and Thomas followed his stare to a vision in red moving towards them. Adam gently pushed his chair back and slowly stood to his feet. 'I'm sorry my friends, but I've got to leave you now. Let me know my share of the bill tomorrow, and I'll settle up then.' He stretched out his arm and the woman in the crimson dress walked towards him and took his hand. 'Helena, meet Saul and Thomas, my partners in crime. Saul and Thomas, please meet Helena Scherer, my partner in suffering at the law school.' He gently kissed her lips. Saul and Thomas rose, shook her hand, and then wished them a pleasant evening. After hearing of Saul's election, she passed on warm and sincere congratulations, although it was more than likely that she knew all about the subterfuge by which it had been achieved. The two then left, Adam whispering into Helena's ear as they strolled out into the cold, crisp, autumnal evening air.

Saul and Thomas had seen it all before, of course. Even the silent gesture, the outstretched arm, was familiar, by now rehearsed to a state of 'spontaneous' perfection by Adam. Of the three, Adam was the most successful in terms of his romantic conquests during the past two years. Saul had had his own successes although his preoccupation with more worldly matters, such as making money and the deliberate breaking of university rules for his own gain, brought him in second to Adam. Thomas came in for the bronze medal; time spent labouring for exams combined with an innate suspicion of promiscuity precluded the possibility of his full commitment to this particular game. Adam's philosophy in such matters was a straightforward one, explained to Saul and Thomas on more than one previous occasion. First, he would never make the first move: if a prospective partner approached him with full knowledge of his reputation beforehand, then she could make no allegation of unfaithfulness when later he progressed to his next conquest. Second, he would never feel a sense of guilt, whatever the hurt that he caused upon starting or ending a relationship. Regret, remorse or shame were feelings felt by weaker people who made their choices voluntarily but then expected sympathy when it was all too late. To an outsider, Adam was a paradox: he brought elation and contrition in equal measure. His friends were simply impressed by his coldly efficient way of succeeding in always getting what he wanted.

As the two later made their way back along silent, echoing lanes, they laughed and joked about the events of the first few months of the new academic year. Finally Thomas had his evening's wish to discuss the career choices which were now opening up to him. Saul listened closely to his hopes and fears as he would have done for a brother, if he'd had one. For the first time in the last two years he recognised in Thomas an inner level-headedness absent both in Adam's personality and in his own. Perhaps this was the reason why Thomas was so crucial to the bond between the three of them: he held them together by counterbalancing the unpredictability and volatility of the other two and grounding it in good sense and some semblance of conscience. Saul mused to himself how lectures on mergers and take-overs attended earlier that week could so easily be transposed upon the friendship: the sum of the separate parts being less than the sum of the whole when acting together in unison. As Thomas explained his life ambitions it was clear that in addition to a strong desire for financial success he had a need for inner calm and contentment. Saul had no such ambition, and for the first time in his life he acknowledged this dimension of his character to himself.

Soon the two reached the crossroads where the three always parted company and went their separate ways to their respective flats dotted around town. No sooner had they started to walk off in different directions than Thomas turned and ran after Saul. 'I knew there was something I'd meant to ask you both this evening. Why did we want to win the treasurership of the union anyway?' Saul roared with laughter when he saw the genuine expression of curiosity on his friend's face. 'Do you mean to say that over the past few weeks of planning, door knocking and bribery you didn't even know what it was all for?' Thomas replied: 'I just did it for you, and for the fun of the ride'. Saul replied with a simple but precise statement of his own personal philosophy; 'I wanted it because the university didn't want me to have it. For such a position of responsibility to fall into dubious, unscrupulous hands like my own, that would be the true measure of our success. You know me well enough by now; what I shouldn't have I always want!' Thomas now understood the real challenge the election had presented; he smiled then returned to his journey home. 'And the cash I'll be handling may come in useful too!' shouted a voice from the darkness behind him. Thomas shivered and didn't laugh; was this an end-of-evening joke or was it another, perhaps more dangerous, scheme?

Chapter Eleven

In the months following his election Saul exceeded all expectations by a sensible and successful execution of his role as union treasurer. In addition to raising student membership by twenty five percent, he also convinced several local companies that it would be in their interests to buy advertising space in the union magazine. The union also began selling its own merchandise including shirts, scarves, and sports equipment. Local manufacturers sold their products to the union at discounted prices and the union sold them on to students, complete with the union logo. Saul always took an undeclared percentage from the manufacturers and revelled in the thought that this was both an abuse of his position as treasurer as well as a conflict of interest as chief negotiator with the local suppliers. Commission was always payable in cash and collected by either Adam or Thomas. By the Easter following Saul's election the union's cash balance was at an all time high. A new student minibus was ordered and the union was upgraded to include new pool and snooker tables, with an indoor squash court now a distinct possibility too. Despite this success certain lecturers and a hard core of students were still unwilling to suspend judgment on Saul, suspecting him of improprieties which, while they were as yet unproven, would be in keeping for a student with a history of 'sailing too close to the wind'.

As the successes continued and the number of suppliers to the union multiplied, Saul came to believe that his position as treasurer was unassailable. This belief sowed the seeds of the beginning of his downfall. A local supplier of sports shirts to the union, Granstead Textiles, had recently changed its board of directors after being bought by a rival. The marketing director with whom Saul had originally set up the union contract had been the first of the old board to go, mainly because it was widely known within the company that he'd been involved in paying 'backhanders' to local buyers. The new board wanted to clean things up.

The departing director, a Mr. Albert Simmons, chose to retire on health grounds. The first that Saul heard about the change of company personnel was a telephone call from the new marketing director, Andrew Phelps, in which Saul was invited to the company's offices to discuss the existing arrangements and the new terms which the company wished to propose for doing business with the union.

Saul's first impression of the new marketing director was not a favourable one; the man was a good four inches shorter than Saul, thin, and with a generally unkempt appearance. The two shook hands. 'Mr. Quartermain, or may I call you Saul?' Saul nodded his consent. 'As you know, Granstead Textiles has been supplying sportswear to the union for a number of months now, and I'm reliably informed that you're our principal point of contact'. Saul replied that the union had been dealing with the company for seven months and were looking forward to continuing with the existing contract. But then he detected a change in the tone of the conversation: could it be that Phelps was about to renegotiate the secret commission agreement? For that matter, did he even know about the agreement?

'I'll get straight to the point, Saul. I know everything about your little arrangement with Mr. Simmons and I must say that your abuse of your position at the university disgusts me'. Saul was shocked by the directness; this was his first experience of a confrontation in the 'real world' and he was unprepared to deal with it. 'I'm sorry Andrew, but I think you're mistaken. Every transaction between us has been properly documented, invoices submitted and full payment made on time. I suggest you make enquiries of your accounts department if you have any doubts as to whether or not this has been the case'. Saul knew that this was a weak defence but he didn't quite know what else he could say. 'Don't bluff me, son. I was catching out backhander arrangements like this when you were a schoolboy. Now here's what you're going to do. First, you're going to bring me a full account of everything paid to you by Mr. Simmons throughout this agreement. Second, you'll pay over all of those moneys to me. Third, you will ensure that the unit price you pay to us is increased to bring it into line with the price currently paid by ordinary customers in the high street outlets. Have I made myself clear?'

Saul decided that the time had come to leave: he stood up and started making his way to the door. 'I repeat, we had no such arrangement with

Mr. Simmons, but I'll ensure a full investigation is made into your allegation.' 'You do just that. But you can be sure that if you don't agree to my terms, this will result not just in my reporting the matter to the university, but also to the police. And there's nothing like a criminal record to put off future employers, as you would then find out.' Saul emerged from the building; he was perspiring heavily and his heart was racing, but in a strange way he felt exhilarated. It was the thrill of the chase, the danger which this new situation presented, which excited him in a way which momentarily worried him too. He ran back to the university to find Adam.

Adam had just completed a mock trial involving a complex fraud. Although he'd won the case he had done so on a technicality; the trial 'judge', one of Adam's law professors, had criticised him for his conduct of it, relying on the letter of the law and ignoring its moral foundations in his determination to win. After congratulating Adam on his victory the judge warned him and the wider student audience that law and morality were inseparable and that intellect should not be employed in the subversion of the spirit of the law. The chastisement was wasted; Adam's goal had been to win, whatever the cost and however strident the judge's disapproval. He barely listened to the judge's warning and advice.

Saul met Adam in the union coffee bar. He sat back and blew smoke rings into the air as Saul recounted the morning's events and the demands made by the company's new marketing director. Adam smiled as he listened to the terms. 'If Phelps was so disgusted by our crime, why was he so eager to discuss it with you? If he had the evidence, why didn't he take it to the university? It seems to me that his only concern is to get his snout into the trough. Obviously he doesn't know that blackmail is against the law, and for us to pay him would be against the law too. That just wouldn't do, would it?' He smiled mischievously. Although Saul wanted to go along to the Wednesday meeting it was nevertheless agreed that Adam should go alone; given that both Saul and Adam were considerably taller and physically larger than Phelps, they didn't want to hint at intimidation; not yet, anyway.

Adam arrived at Granstead Textiles on Wednesday morning and was led straight into Phelps's office by his secretary. The thin man looked surprised by this new, unrecognised visitor. 'Good afternoon, Mr. Phelps. My name is Adam Creed and I've come in place of my colleague

Mr. Quartermain who I believe you met earlier this week'. Phelps was outraged. 'Are you telling me that he didn't have the guts to come back today? Who the hell are you?' Adam paused and then replied authoritatively; 'Mr. Quartermain felt that since I'm legal adviser to the union it would be more appropriate that I attend instead. Now, either you can continue the earlier discussion with me or I can leave now and we will wait to see what happens next. What's it to be?' Adam was not even legally qualified but felt that the lie about his position in the union would lend him the necessary legitimacy to bring the tricky negotiations to a satisfactory conclusion.

Phelps sat down again. 'Okay, talk. But any funny business and I'll end this meeting immediately'. 'Saul tells me that you think he's received bribes from your predecessor, Simmons, as a reward for the contracts set up between your company and the university union. Is that correct?' 'You're dead right it is. He's a thief, and if I- I mean, the company- don't get some of the money back, then your friend will be in big trouble'. Adam smiled: this weak man's agenda was becoming obvious. 'Let me tell you what really happened when your predecessor was in office', began Adam, his cold grey eyes fixing Phelps. 'In addition to Mr. Quartermain, there were two other people receiving commission, and one of them is sitting in front of you right now. The arrangement started with the very first sale between your company and the union, and continued until Mr. Simmons's premature retirement.' Phelps began to sweat; in all of the petty, corrupt deals he'd uncovered during the past ten years, none of the perpetrators had been as blatantly proud of their deceit and dishonesty as this hostile, arrogant young man. The usual procedure was that in return for his silence a percentage of the takings would be passed over to him, with nobody being any the wiser. 'Well Mr. Creed, I must admit you've taken me by surprise', said a nervous Phelps understatedly. 'If what you say is true, then I will of course look to you as well to make good the loss which has been suffered by this company'. He feared he was losing control of the game.

'Let me tell you why you're going to drop this demand, Mr. Phelps. As you are no doubt aware, your company was given the contract to supply the union because its prices were significantly lower than those quoted by rival companies. How do you think Mr. Simmons was able to keep prices so low?' In a fit of anger, Phelps decided it was time to go on the offensive; 'Why are you going on about prices? It's got damn all to do with the fact that you've been taking bribes.' Adam ignored the outburst and continued. 'The reason why you were able to give such low prices was that none of the items were charged with sales tax. This fraud will lead to a heavy fine on your company, after its systems and paperwork have been torn apart during the investigation, of course'. Phelps knew that a full inspection could result in some damaging disclosures, since every company in his line of business was driven to break the rules every now and again to win new business. 'Okay, Mr. Creed, I understand your point and I will of course investigate. But even if what you say is true, I can remedy the problem by reimbursing the underpayment. My experience is that provided a company is willing to come clean, Customs is usually reluctant to impose hefty fines. So I'm afraid you'll have to do a little better than that'.

'But I've not finished yet, Mr. Phelps, so I hope you'll hear me out'. Adam spoke softly but there was an unmistakeably threatening undertone in his voice. 'Mr. and Mrs. Simmons are old and fragile, as far as I'm aware, living in blissful retirement at some seaside guesthouse on the coast. Be in no doubt, if I or my friends are put at risk because of your greed and stupidity, I'll ensure they're both brought back here, in the back of a police car, to face the same charges. We are young and we'll survive, one way or another, but they are old and simply won't be able to cope. I promise you, I'll see that they both break like dry twigs in the trial which will follow. And be in no doubt, the damage to your company's reputation will be substantial'. Phelps looked into the emotionless eyes and knew his adversary was not bluffing: he was willing to sacrifice an elderly couple, people he himself knew, and as such he was not a person with whom deals could be made. Whilst Phelps was aware of his own shortcomings, he knew he lacked the indiscriminate viciousness with which he was now being confronted. He was afraid. 'Okay Mr. Creed, you've made your point. Keep the money, but stay away from this company. Our contract ends today. I'll say nothing but I never want to hear from you or your friend again. Now get out'. Adam stood up and made his way to the door. As he left he heard a few words, but did not turn to respond. 'Take care, Mr. Creed. You're a vicious bastard and you're going to get yourself into trouble some day'.

Chapter Twelve

In the following months Saul, Thomas and Adam were invited to attend interviews with companies and firms eager to employ them following their graduations. All three knew they could pick and choose from the best training contracts, and although Saul criticised the 'cattle market' process, none of them could deny that they were flattered by the attention they'd received from leading London law firms, investment banks, and international firms of chartered accountants. They felt that the world was truly their oyster: their talents, combined with a healthy economy, meant that the only difficulty was deciding how to choose between the outstanding career opportunities they were presented with. When tutors were asked to comment upon the character, suitability and honesty of the three (informally, and 'off the record', of course), it didn't seem to trouble the 'talent scouts' that praise of ability and intellect invariably came with significant hints about their exploits, strong wills, and reluctance to play by the rules or abide by the norms of acceptable behaviour. Indeed, some of the recruiters seemed to become even more determined to make breathtaking offers when provided with examples of the suspected but unproven misconduct of the three during their years at university.

Thomas received invitations to interviews from the six largest accountancy firms in London. However, his preference was to take up a training contract with a middle ranking firm, his reasoning being that, since it was not his intention to stay with them for the long term but instead to work at his family's engineering business, he should not take up a position which would demand his every waking hour in return for the quality of the training it would provide. His intention was to qualify as an accountant, work hard and study hard along the way, but also to enjoy life in London. After attending the obligatory interviews, Thomas found himself in the enviable position of holding six offers of training contracts, but also an offer from a middle-sized firm on the outskirts of London.

When Thomas returned home to the family estate, 'Ravens Haven', he was surprised to learn that it was his father's intention to rapidly expand the family business, Northern Engineering Ltd. After the 'welcome home' dinner laid on by his mother Alice, his father Philip left the table and invited Thomas to join him for a walk. Father and son had always found it easy to openly discuss their thoughts, plans, worries and successes with each other; they were close, perhaps partly because Thomas was an only child and had also been a 'late blessing' to the marriage. 'I must admit, Tom, that I've been thinking about changing the direction of the company for several years now, but just haven't got around to doing it because I've been too busy keeping up with the workload from our local clients'. Thomas continued walking with his father, drawing in the scent of the hundreds of roses which crowded the paths around the house and which had been nurtured so carefully by his mother over the years. 'But why is change so necessary now? The company's doing well, your order book is full, and you're sixty eight; perhaps you should be thinking about easing up rather than starting off in new directions'. 'I hear what you say Tom, and you know me well enough to realise that I'm always the last to accept new business ideas and the first to criticise those who try to convince me about new ways of doing things.' A gentle breeze teased the branches of the towering oaks which lined the main paths around the estate and which as a boy Thomas had been reliably informed by his father had been planted as acorns by his great, great grandfather, the company's founder.

Philip Stoneacre, tall, lean, and as always, standing straight as a gun barrel, looked into the distance and continued to set out his hopes for the future of the company. 'If the company is to survive and prosper, it must change, adapt, and reinvent itself to combine traditional skills and new technologies. Let's talk: I'll set out the plans and arrangements I have in mind. I can explain it all to you in more detail when we meet with Morris Hurst tomorrow morning.' By the time the two reached the house Thomas knew of his father's full intentions for the company's future. The two entered the house to be met with the familiar smells of cooking which always filled the house the evening before Thomas returned to university. 'So have you put the world to rights yet?' asked Alice as she dusted flour from her hands. 'I think we have', replied Philip with a smile. That night Thomas slept intermittently, the swirling and conflicting emotions of hope, apprehension and self doubt taking him out onto the balcony outside his bedroom at four o'clock in the morning just to look at the stars and breathe in the cool air.

The following morning Thomas and his father went to the local offices of Hurst, Cook, and Fontleroy, the family firm's accountants. They were met in the reception by Morris Hurst, a short, dapper man with spectacles balanced on the end of his nose. Thomas had met him on several previous occasions and knew that, although the accountant resembled a Dickensian bookkeeper, there was nothing out of date or behind the times about this highly experienced, highly professional corporate advisor. There followed a detailed presentation by Morris of structural changes which would be made to the company over the next few years in preparation for Thomas's assumption of the chairmanship. The accountant explained that while Northern Engineering would continue to do the work it had always done in the United Kingdom, the core of the business would become more focused upon marketing of the company's services and products overseas. The company would prioritise the winning of foreign contracts, particularly in natural resources exploitation, while heavy engineering production would be satisfied by others on behalf of which Northern Engineering would negotiate and share the resulting profits.

The meeting eventually drew to a close and as father and son left the accountant's office, Morris shook the hand of his new client. 'I wish you every success for the future, Thomas. I'm looking forward to working with you after you've finished your professional training, when you take up your new position as company chairman. These are exciting times, and the future belongs to you'.

It was a warm morning when Adam set out on the train journey from Cambridge to London for his interview with the prestigious law firm, Roxburgh Thymes and Partners. The previous evening he had carefully wrapped a dozen small presents he was to take to London, as he'd done every several months for the past five years, placing these in the large canvas bag he took with him whenever he made this trip. Small toy cars, puzzles, packets of sweets: he always managed to find the money for the purchases, but with his share of the proceeds of the recent union bribes he had had a surplus of cash to buy better gifts than usual. As the train chugged through the countryside Adam stared out of the window, preferring to reflect upon a past injustice than to read the legal textbook he'd brought with him for the journey. The trip to London made in secret every few months was always a time for reflection tinged with a bitterness he still held which had not abated with the passing of years.

Eventually the train pulled into King's Cross Station. Adam disembarked and walked quickly to the left luggage office where he deposited his bag. He then took the underground to Temple and from there walked to the offices of Roxburgh Thymes. After an hour of small talk, the five senior partners who'd assembled for the interview confirmed to Adam that the training post was his if he wanted it, but that they'd require a decision within five days. After courteously thanking the partners for their offer, he left the chrome and glass building and emerged into the stale air of a hot afternoon, heading back to King's Cross to collect his canvas bag. His emotions had been on a level plane all day, and he felt no great excitement at the offer he had received.

Later, as he made his way through the crowds, the straps of his canvas bag became damp with the sweat which trickled down from his hand. Within quarter of an hour he'd arrived at his destination; the building never changed, and as he paused at the foot of the steps where he'd cried in the rain sixteen years earlier, he reflected upon the iron which had entered his soul during the intervening years. He'd long since realised that he'd never fathom the mind or the heart of a mother who could desert her child, leaving him to live or die in the dark and the cold of a midwinter's night. He walked up the steps and after entering 'Saint Peter's Refuge for God's Children' he knocked on the first door which he came to. He knew that this was the room of the only person in the world, apart from Saul and Thomas, who had ever truly cared for him, and who had rescued him during his hour of need. 'Come in', came the firm Irish voice from within. Adam pushed open the door and on seeing him Father Stephen Hennessy walked over to shake his hand. 'Adam, good to see you again! You're looking so well. So what brings you to London today? You should have let me know you were coming - I'd have arranged a meal with some of the brothers. You know you're always welcome here'.

Adam smiled. The warmth of the welcome he always received when he returned to his 'first school of life' meant so much to him; although his soul had grown cold over the intervening years, a small flicker of emotion remained, sustained by his continued contact with this modest place of simple grey stone, his home for the ten years following his desertion by his mother and step-father. 'I'm in town today for an interview with a law firm, but I was coming here anyway. The pull of this place is one of my few weak points'. The priest laughed a deep roar of a laugh which always put Adam at ease. 'And the interview, was it successful?' asked the priest, knowing the answer before he'd even asked. Adam casually answered 'Oh, I think so. So what's the news here, Father? Did you get planning permission for the new wing and more to the point, did you raise the money to pay for it?' The priest confirmed that everything had gone according to plan and that work would commence within the next few months. 'And what about you Adam - what news of your studies? Are they still going well? I expect you're coming up to your finals so don't forget, pace yourself and don't forget to rest well and eat properly. Remember, Mens sana in corpore sano!' The priest was the most modest, humble man Adam had ever met, but he also knew that he'd been the youngest qualifying Jesuit of his generation. He'd also achieved a double first in law and the classics at Oxford as a student at Corpus Christi College before the last war.

'I'll be preparing the sacraments in a while, so why don't you accompany me?' The two left the room and made their way to the chapel situated at the heart of the Home. They talked about their lives and the people in them, and laughed about their own day-to-day failings with an openness Adam would never have shown in the outside world. On their way they stopped outside the children's wing, and the priest waited as Adam swept in, with his canvas bag now open and at the ready. The children had long since come to regard Adam as a sort of surrogate Father Christmas, except that he was one who turned up throughout the year, not just in December. The priest looked on as he distributed his gifts among the crowd which had quickly gathered around him. This former resident had a talent for entertaining and for giving genuine attention which was all too often lacking in the 'professional' visitors who attended the Home on a weekly basis, but did so without making the slightest difference to the lives of its inhabitants. The priest mused to himself how threads of sunlight were always more pronounced when set against the darkest of skies. But the coldness and harshness in Adam's soul had grown stronger over the years, and he feared that acts of kindness such as these would soon be outweighed by greater deeds of malice which he suspected were well within the capabilities of this embittered young man.

When the two men entered the chapel, Adam felt at peace in the tranquillity and silence; this hidden place in Adam's past life never changed and nor did he want it ever to do so. The coolness of the sanctuary contrasted so starkly with the heat of the afternoon sun outside that it momentarily took his breath away. 'So how goes the war, my friend? Is the line still holding?' Adam smiled; it had been several years since he and the priest talked of the battle between good and evil raging in every man's soul, but of late he'd come to believe that for him, at least, the battle had long since been decided. The young man whispered, his face pressed into his open palms. 'I'm afraid the line's broken, and the darkness in my soul races like a storm cloud across a summer meadow'. The priest looked at the tormented man sitting alongside; despite his experience in matters of life and faith, he felt powerless to intervene. When academic brilliance, talent and strength of will were turned in one so young to serve the darker side of the soul, it required more than gentle words in a holy place to join the battle and make a difference. 'I look at you, Adam, and see a future of great deeds and even greater self-fulfilment. You can make a difference for good in the world. But all will be lost if you walk away from the struggle which we all must confront. Be strong. Remember God's love for you. Change before it's too late'.

Adam turned to him, his face pale with anger; 'You talk to me of struggle and change but there's no reserve of goodness in the well of my soul which I can draw upon. I feel no love.' The young man's voice began to rise: distant thunder warned of an approaching storm. 'You know all this, but I will tell you again anyway. Today I stood on the same steps where I was dumped like a sack of rubbish sixteen years ago. And after the betrayal my parents simply vanished, never to be seen or heard of again. They were true cowards without any sense of shame or morality. I've nothing to give, but much to take. I wish I could climb the highest mountain and shake my fist at the world. I see hypocrisy and selfishness everywhere'. The angry man's voice resonated off the smooth, cool walls, and the priest feared for his future. 'I understand, my son. You know I do. You know too that you show love and warmth here, to those who need it. It's a far braver and more noble thing to face down evil feelings and let God's love triumph. We'll talk again, but think carefully on my words. Come, walk with me'.

They left and walked out into the arboretum which was enclosed within the Home's grounds. The two friends returned to small talk of university, politics, and the priest's early years as a missionary overseas. It was the last of these which most interested Adam when he'd lived at Saint Peter's, and even now the priest's stories fanned his imagination. The hour passed quickly and soon it was time for Adam to leave for the train back to Cambridge.

❧

The first interview Saul attended was with an investment bank in the heart of the City. Sheldons Bank had been established in 1750 and boasted in its recruitment literature of its association with major turning points in world history during the past three centuries. It had helped finance the Southern States during the American Civil War. One of its early French involvements had been to fund Bonaparte's war with England and Prussia. The literature didn't add, but left its reader to surmise, that despite being on the losing side in each case, the bank had prospered then and since. Saul had been given an interview time by the personnel department, this being 9am sharp. He arrived at the offices at 9.10, deliberately taking a coffee which lasted until that time at a cafe located a stone's throw from the bank. He reported late to the personnel director's office, offering not a word of explanation or apology for his tardiness. It was through such minor discourtesy that he'd test the strength of their interest in him. He was however surprised by the intensity of the interview process to which he was subjected throughout the morning, transported as if along a conveyor belt through the various departments and at each stage assessed by individuals who didn't make their criteria for assessment known. He was further irritated to discover that he was not the only candidate passing through the system, and that if he was to win a place he would have to 'sell' himself along with all the other aspiring applicants.

By the end of the day he was physically and mentally drained. He firmly believed he'd given a good account of himself in both the oral and written tests, but it was the uncertainty of the outcome which created in him a feeling of vulnerability, of fallibility, which he'd not experienced before. At 5pm he was taking a break with the other applicants in the sparsely furnished visitors' reception room when a tannoy crackled out the order; 'Saul Quartermain to room 801, eighth floor'. Was it good news, or bad? He arrived at room 801 several minutes' later, knocked firmly and entered. The room was dimly lit, the furthermost wall made entirely of glass and looking out upon the rows of terminals through which currency dealers conducted transactions across the globe. A physically imposing man whom Saul had neither met nor seen during the day's interviews stood at the glass, gazing into the distance.

After a moment's silence, he spoke. 'Answer me this one question, Mr. Saul Quartermain. Why should Sheldons Bank take on a candidate described in reports by his tutors, those who should know him well, as frivolous, scheming, and not to be trusted?' Bitterness flickered across his heart; he'd been stabbed in the back and the job opportunity he coveted had been lost because of their betrayal. The inquisitor continued. 'Speak to me. Defend yourself if you can'. Saul hesitated: if he was not to be given the job, he was determined to leave with his pride intact. 'I ask for the job because I'm the best candidate for it, by technical ability and depth of knowledge. I demand the job because I am young and hold the future in my hands. I deserve the job because nothing's ever been given to me; I've always had to fight for what I've got, and in life only the strongest should succeed. As for my detractors, perhaps there's truth in their words, but I'll succeed whatever they say, whatever they throw when my back's turned. They can all go to Hell'.

The bank's head of recruitment smiled, knowing that, contrary to the advice of his colleagues, he'd made the correct selection. 'Your results were the best for the group which we've interviewed today, so I guess you're right on your first assumption. You have youth and the changes which are coming to the City will create a new world which your generation will inherit. But I will be direct with you: this false shallowness you show to the world, your contempt for whatever people may think of you, this is your weakness, your Achilles heel, not your strength as you seem to think it. Your time with Sheldons will be prosperous for all of us but take it from me, we'll part company prematurely if this character flaw remains unchecked. But this is not a problem for us today. It just remains for me to say the job's yours if you want it. Do you want it?' Saul responded confidently; 'Yes, I want it, and at this moment in time there's no other job I'd rather have'. 'Then I'll wish you every success with your finals at university, and I look forward to you joining us in a few months' time. Good evening, Mr. Quartermain'. The two shook hands; the only successful candidate that day then left the building. Saul realised he'd won a prestigious training position in investment banking from a man whose name and position he did not know, but whose words both of praise and of warning left him exhilarated and unsettled in equal measure. His hopes for the future soared.

⸺ ❧ ⸺

In accordance with tradition, all graduates at Caius College Cambridge were invited to a succession of summer balls to celebrate the conclusion of their years of study. These were evenings of tuxedos and evening dresses, of horseplay on worn croquet lawns beneath sinking suns, of warm beer laid out on trestles beneath ancient pale canvas marquees. So many goodbyes as bright young things prepared to cross their own personal threshholds into the cut and thrust of a new world harsher than the one they had grown used to and which was now so quickly fading. For those who chose to stop and think amidst the celebrations, the laughter and the exchanging of future addresses, these sunset days of champagne flutes and pale starlit skies would never return. For Adam, Saul and Thomas, these were the final days of irresponsibility, of passion, of basking in the glory of academic achievement. With each new ball there were new partners for the three: confident, pretty, fresh-faced women who had been elusive or evasive during the past three years, but now, in these final hours, chose to accept the charms of their well-dressed suitors.

'So what's it to be? Are we going to stay here for the rest of the evening, or head off to town for a change of scene?' Adam was bored. He'd been rebuffed by Tara Kingsley, a student at the same college destined for great things at the Bar, seemingly guaranteed by the fact that her father was a High Court judge. He'd also been involved in a blazing row with one of his professors. An aged, failed barrister had informed him at the ball, and in front of his fellow students, of a fact of which Adam was already aware: he'd recommended to the partners of Roxburgh Thymes that they should think carefully before offering him a training contract, given the rumours of dishonesty and rule-breaking which had floated around him throughout his time at Cambridge. Adam had loudly dismissed the professor as a failed, envious lawyer but the confrontation had spoiled the evening for him. He stood in front of his friends, impatiently drawing upon a cigarette, urging them to leave before it was too late to gain admission to some of the less salubrious pubs nearby. Reluctantly, the two left with him.

In the couple of hours which followed they visited several of their usual haunts. There, they exchanged telephone numbers and gentle kisses with several graduates who had also tired of the various college balls and had, like the three, sought excitement in the seamier parts of the city. The evening had slowly faded away in the dwindling evening light and into a haze of wistful recollection. Now the three were alone, contemplating a suitable ending to this, the final evening of their university life. La Trattoria would have closed by now so after considering the few other options available, it was decided that the evening required a suitably outlandish ending: they would walk to the local fairground, open till the small hours, and endeavour to try every ride and show still open at that time of night. After a short walk the three arrived at the fair, still in tuxedos and black ties. A colder breeze tugged at the bunting hanging from awning of every side show after the warmth of the earlier day. They sauntered around the stalls, brimming with the exuberance which accompanies youth at moments of greatest success. Prizes won on shooting ranges were given to the handful of giggling girls who seemed to be following them, drawn to the immaculately dressed strangers.

'So come on, you two, what's the dare?' Thomas and Adam knew that the evening was drawing to a close when Saul issued the customary invitation at the end of such celebratory nights. They never reciprocated in kind, but this didn't seem to trouble him; his goal was always to end such a night on a high point, a unique spectacle to mark the occasion. Adam pointed towards a dark corner of the fairground and in the gloom it was just possible to make out the ascending structure of a rollercoaster. The lack of lighting or bunting made the rusted snake vaguely menacing as it reared up into the night sky, only to crash down again to Earth at various points of its body. There'd been a time when it was one of the leading fairground attractions: now it crouched in the darkness, neglected, its fortunes declining in a world grown more sophisticated and more easily bored. Adam was quick to take up the invitation; 'Here's my dare, and let's be having a good show. You see the rollercoaster over there? Here's fifty pounds which says you can't get to the top and tie this balloon'. Adam crumpled the oily note which he'd won earlier that evening in front of Saul's deep blue eyes. Thomas smiled: at long last they'd found a dare which not even Saul, the risk taker, the showman, would ever agree to accept.

'You're on. Make way for the King of Dares'. Taking in his right hand the string to which Adam's red balloon was attached, Saul walked towards the 'Hell Ride', jumped up onto its metal rails, and started up the steep ascent. Adam lit another cigarette; Thomas noticed in the match's glow how his eyes remained impassive and unconcerned despite the danger which he'd introduced into the evening. As Saul proceeded to clamber up and along the tracks, he was struck by how cool the air was compared to when he'd stood on the ground, gazing up into the night sky. Everywhere there was the acrid smell of paint slapped on by fairground workmen over the past few days in a fruitless attempt to conceal the rust and decay. He suddenly thought of his father and wished he'd been there to see the success his only son had achieved. He would have been so proud. The coldness of the night tugged at his lungs as he advanced up the rusting rails. But his father could not be there now, nor for the graduation ceremony, nor for the rest of his life. He reflected upon his father's years of commitment to his employer, an ungrateful City financial institution, and his anger mingled with sadness. First there'd been the suspension. Then the charges: fraud first, then theft, then others to follow. Some true, some entirely untrue. Saul couldn't remember the days of the trial: he'd been too young and had been sent to stay with family friends during those final days.

He reached the top of the rollercoaster, climbing the last section, a 60-degree incline, like an assault course, using his fingers, elbows and knees for support. Briefly standing to his full height he waved to his friends on the ground far below. He laughed aloud as he tied the balloon to the track and quickly kneeled for safety; the dare had been won and his reputation for foolishness, for risk-taking, was intact. But while he laughed and waved tears of sadness began rolling down his face. The last blurred mental image he had of his father was from a hot afternoon in May, all those years ago. The family friends had come to collect him since this was the final week of the trial. While they'd waited in the garden, his father had embraced him, stood back, and then saluted in his usual exaggerated fashion. 'Look after yourself, little man, and remember that your father always loved you'. He'd then walked off into the summer heat haze to find his place to die. The red-top papers later reported that 'a City fraudster' had 'topped' himself, found hanging from a great oak tree before the jury had had the opportunity to make its verdict known. Saul looked up at the stars, all these years later, and wept and then, standing again and stretching his arms out to their full length, hurled himself off the steel structure and into the night sky.

Swirling colours and distant sounds rose up to greet him as he crashed towards Earth, eventually to be engulfed in the deep green sea of the safety barrage strategically placed beneath the structure by the painters who'd laboured so pointlessly in the hot afternoon sun earlier that day. Thomas stood gasping at the edge of the barrage, his heart pumping with fear after his sprint from the distant observation point. He'd watched in horror as his friend had plunged through the air: now he looked on with relief and confusion as Saul clambered off the barrage and onto terra firma. 'You could have been killed, you bloody fool. Just what were you thinking of?' Thomas realised the fall had probably been part of the theatrics of the dare but its danger left him wondering whether Saul, in a moment of madness, had put his life at risk for some other reason.

'You know me, Thomas - anything for a dare, and always a showman. Now, where's my money?' By this time Adam had wandered over to the rollercoaster, lighting up his final cigarette of the evening. 'Bravo, bravo. An excellent show. And now, much as it breaks my heart to part with it, here's your reward'. He passed over the fifty pound note, accepted with a flourish by Saul and then tucked into the top pocket of his tuxedo. Thomas looked at the two and for a fleeting moment he wondered if Adam had known about the safety barrage before the fall. He began to wonder if he really knew his closest friends at all. As the final side show's tarpaulin was rolled up for the night, the three knew it was time to leave the funfair.

Chapter Thirteen

'Let's go over your position again, Mr. Coughlin. According to your version of events, the main reason why Delphi Investment Corporation failed was the general downturn in the economy, and not because of any malpractice on your part. Both you and your company were victims of events beyond your control. Would that be a fair summary of your position?'

The young, combative lawyer Adam Creed sat in silence as Andrew Cannon-Smith QC brought a tense meeting with Silas Coughlin to a close. It had been a fruitless three hours since it was clear that the client, accepted by the law firm Roxburgh Thymes in haste but now regretted at leisure, was unwilling to co-operate with the very people now standing between himself and a seven year jail sentence. He'd met Coughlin more than once before and indeed he was the violent fraudster's first point of contact with his firm.

As the evidence against Coughlin had mounted over the preceding months, Adam couldn't but help admire the man for his coolness under pressure. For the past few hours Cannon-Smith, a leading Queen's Counsel whom the firm frequently instructed, had cross-examined him at length. It was obvious that he detested the client, but Coughlin had stood his ground despite the barely concealed scepticism of the barrister appointed to represent his interests when the case came to court.

'I've told you before but perhaps I need to explain it again in a simpler way, Mr. Cannon-Smith. I was simply doing a job, just as you're doing a job here today. Just as you're subject to the caprices and discourtesies of the solicitors who give you your work, I'm exposed to the greed and selfishness of the institutional investors, the brokers and the banks which give me mine'. Cannon-Smith interrupted; 'You speak as if you're still in business sir, but I must remind you that this is no longer the case.

It's more than your livelihood which is at risk now, and maybe you should reflect upon that fact before our next meeting'.

Coughlin smiled then continued undeterred in his usual matter-of-fact, reasoned mode of delivery. 'Don't talk to me about reality, Mr. Cannon-Smith. It's my business which has been destroyed by those cowboys at the Serious Fraud Office. They were obsessed with breaking me, jealous of our successes. First we had phone taps. Then raids on my offices - always during the day, to maximise bad publicity. Finally they turned up at my house in the early morning. My wife and I were still in bed. They were so thoughtful: they'd even called the papers beforehand to make sure the cameras were rolling when I left my home in handcuffs to be charged.'

'Perhaps we could go over the specifics of the case again, Silas. Only this time, try to explain them from the Prosecution's point of view rather than your own. I'm trying to help you. This is the best way to identify any weaknesses in one's own case'. Coughlin turned away from the fleshy-faced barrister sitting opposite him to look again into the pale grey eyes of the young man whom he'd met during his first 'visit' to the police station. Adam Creed was dressed like a typical lawyer: a dark pinstripe suit, a white silk shirt, and a wine red tie. Maybe his jet black hair was further over the collar than usual for the legal profession, but it would be difficult to draw any conclusions about this young man on the basis of appearance alone. His words were the usual lawyer-speak: application for this and that, orders of the court, discovery of documents, etc, etc, etc. Coughlin had dealt with lawyers before, during the early years of his business when he'd been naive enough to believe that people could be held to their word by legal means alone. He'd soon come to realise that 'alternative' methods of enforcement were invariably more cost-effective. But there was something about this lawyer which set him apart from the others he had known. Was it his casual cigarette smoking, or the way he unbuttoned his collar after becoming visibly bored with the line of questioning pursued by Cannon-Smith? Coughlin looked at him and wondered: could this be the man to tip the scales in his favour?

'OK, let's go back to the link between Delphi and the Gandalph Trust. The Prosecution contends that both of these entities were in fact controlled by you, and you used Gandalph to siphon off the cash assets of Delphi. Was this the case?' 'I've told you before, Adam, there was no link between these two companies. I controlled Delphi in the sense of being the largest shareholder, but I had nothing at all to do with the running, ownership or decision-making processes of Gandalph. When the Prosecution has the courtesy to make full disclosure you'll see that there's no evidence of any link between the two'.

The barrister snapped waspishly. 'You know as well as we do, Mr. Coughlin, that Gandalph is a company registered in Switzerland, and its shares are held by a dummy corporation run out of Panama. *Nobody* knows the true power structure within the company, and you have been either unable or unwilling to give any evidence to rebut the strong likelihood that there was some degree of association, some might say collusion, between Delphi and Gandalph.'

Cannon-Smith had been representing criminals for nearly thirty years but Silas Coughlin came within a category of client for which he had the greatest disdain. He was one of those clever fraudsters who acted without morality and (usually) with violence, never showing any remorse when they were inevitably convicted. From his years of experience in Crown Court trials he'd already estimated that Coughlin would go down for between six to eight years. He felt personally disrespected by the implicit contempt his client showed for the legal process in the manner of his replies. He was also irritated by the rapport which had developed between the younger solicitor and the thick- set man with shovels for hands who smiled at him across the table.

'The ownership of shares in Delphi was properly registered in the company's records. All Delphi's resolutions, including its investment decisions, were also properly recorded and filed with the appropriate authorities. The running of the company was not subject to my exclusive control, although of course I was its chairman. There was an independent board of directors which had the specific responsibility of overseeing all of its activities'. 'Sorry to interrupt, Silas, but as you know, Delphi's board was *not* independent - its members were hand-picked associates of yours!'.

Adam took a final draw on his cigarette before stubbing it out in the throw-away aluminium ashtray. Coughlin hesitated before replying. 'All the board members, apart from Andreas Melas, will give evidence at the trial that they exercised full impartiality at all times in Delphi's decision-making processes'. This was the first time impartiality had been exercised at gunpoint, Cannon-Smith mused to himself. 'With regard to control of the Gandalph Trust I do not have, nor have I ever had, any involvement with this. At no time did I exercise any influence upon the Gandalph board, nor did I personally profit from any financial dealings between Gandalph and Delphi'.

Of course Coughlin was lying, and everyone in the room took this to be an unspoken truth. The Delphi Investment Corporation had purchased bonds from Gandalph at prices which, in each of the three hundred transactions taking place over a three year period, were at premiums varying between twenty and fifty percent above the market price at the time. Adam had no doubt that the client had stashed the excess, the mark-up he creamed off from Delphi, in some Swiss account which he held in the name of Gandalph's dummy Panama-registered corporate shareholder. Gandalph also regularly invoiced Delphi for so-called marketing and consultancy support; another ruse for drawing out capital in an ostensibly legal manner. In this way the Delphi Corporation had been looted, plundered, and deposits made with it by thousands of pensioners transferred to an untraceable account, held by a secret corporation registered in Panama. It had been a clever, merciless, immoral strategy which, with a little more forethought on the client's part, could have remained undetected for who knows how many more years. Adam looked at the client and then at the barrister, and acknowledged to himself that it was the man in the pale blue, ill-fitting fatigues with whom he had the greater empathy.

Whilst Coughlin continued to confront and play with his barrister, he was conscious of being impassively observed by the pale grey eyes of the silent lawyer to his right. This pleased him. He mused to himself: if the lawyer knows I'm guilty, and I've done my level best not to conceal it short of actually confessing to my crimes, then he must be watching me for some other reason. What's he thinking about? Can he be persuaded? Can he be bought? 'Mr. Coughlin, it's been a long morning so I'd like to bring this meeting to an end by asking you again about Andreas Melas. As you're no doubt aware, the Prosecution are keeping this man at a secret location because they fear some harm might come to him if you or your associates are able to contact him. Are they justified in this concern?' What a patronising question, thought both Coughlin and the young lawyer. 'This is just an attempt by the SFO to portray me as a violent man, when nothing could be further from the truth. I trusted

Mr. Melas. I appointed him to the Delphi board and welcomed him into my home on many occasions. When I refused to give him the chairmanship of Delphi, which he craved, he turned on me'.

'Well, Mr. Coughlin, we'll have to see what he says when we get full disclosure. But I can tell you now that, since the Prosecution will be relying on him as their key witness, we can expect his explanation of the course of events leading up to your arrest to be particularly damning. It's unusual in a case like this for a witness to be given round the clock protection unless the evidence he holds is crucial to the Prosecution's case, and he is deemed to be in grave danger. As I say, we'll just have to wait and see'. Mr. Cannon-Smith stood up, walked to the door and knocked firmly. 'Okay officer, we've finished in here now, thank you'. The two men shook hands with their client, then walked out into the natural daylight.

Adam's university friend and ally, Saul Quartermain, had by now received extensive training at the London offices of the niche finance house, Sheldons Bank. His managers had been impressed by how quickly he assimilated the mathematics of the bond markets, and the ease with which he applied this knowledge across the bank's businesses. Such was his confidence in dealing with corporate clients that he was soon given the lead negotiating position in several lucrative hostile takeovers in which the bank was the principal advisor. Saul's confidence soared to new heights. He had the ability, the youth, and the determination to survive and prosper in the brave new post 'Big Bang' world, one in which traders, brokers and bankers were only as good as their last deal.

With an end to the fixed commissions which had brought order and stability to the City for over a century came a new form of aggressive competition: stateless financial institutions vied with each other for bigger slices of a fast growing cake. These were times in which heavy northern accents mingled with home counties tones in dealing rooms large enough to accommodate symphony orchestras. This was the new democracy: a meritocracy in which employees came to believe they'd be judged solely on the basis of their contribution to their employers' profits, and not by the social class from which they came. While the sun shone, Saul was determined to make hay. Unlike his counterparts who relied exclusively upon trading in particular markets such as currencies, commodities or interest rates, he'd been trained in wider business skills. He was an 'all rounder': not only was he fully conversant with the 'buy-sell' world of the traders and sales teams at Sheldons, he also had expertise in the more complex markets of syndicated loans and project finance for deals as diverse as paper mills in Malaysia and Indonesia, hydro-electric dams in Iceland, and oil refineries in the Middle East. Saul's earliest childhood memory was his disappointment and anger after coming second in his school sports day races; he had not come second to anyone since, his competitive spirit driving him to excel in both his professional and personal life. But at the core of this dynamism was another driving force: the anger of a son for a pilloried, ridiculed, and then prosecuted father, driven to suicide by an unforgiving, hypocritical world.

'I just can't quite get my head around it, Saul; what's the difference between being 'long' in the market, and 'short'? I mean, I can understand selling something you've bought, and I can understand somebody agreeing to buy a commodity at some future time. But... I think you're telling me there are two things which can be bought and sold: the commodity itself, like orange juice or oil, and the risk associated with it. So how can these two things be separated from each other, and traded on different markets?' Saul pushed back his hair: it glowed in the bright summer haze, complementing his deep blue eyes which, in turn, matched the blue stripes of his shirt. He grinned and gazed out over the open-air skating rink at which he and Thomas had met for lunch, feeling comfortable in the presence of so many dealers and brokers gulping down Champagne at the rinkside bar. Set in the heart of the City, the rink and winebar were the three friends' favourite meeting place.

He was about to bite into the shiny red apple he'd bought from a barrow boy when he decided better of it; it would provide a useful prop for his impromptu explanation to the quizzical accountant. 'Take this apple. Will you buy it from me today at fifty pence?' 'Yes, I'll buy it from you today if I want to eat it now'. 'Okay. So what if I offer to sell you an apple at sixty pence in one month's time: will you buy it then?' 'Well, that would depend on the price of the same sort of apples for sale from the barrow boy at that time. If he's charging sixty five pence, then I'll buy it from you. But if he's asking fifty five pence, then I'll buy it from him and not from you'. Saul smiled and straightened one side of his red braces. 'And there you have your answer, my friend. There you have the difference between the physicals markets - the apple itself, and the risk markets, the markets of futures and options. If I agree to sell something to you at a certain price at some certain date in the future, that is my risk. My promise to sell at that price gives you the guarantee that, whatever happens in the real market, if there is a surplus or a drought which destroys a crop, you know you can deal at the price which we agreed on the date specified in the futures or options contract. On that date you'll have the choice of either accepting my price, or instead taking the price in the real market at that time. If you go for the latter, you'll let the option expire and just lose your premium. But remember, a futures contract is an obligation to do something, not a choice. This is the difference between it and an option... the right, the choice, is in the hands of the holder as to whether or not it should be exercised'.

During his training with Clements Accountants, Thomas had attended seminars on futures and options, and despite posing the question was slightly irritated that Saul assumed him to be entirely ignorant of the subject. He knew Saul's explanation had been deliberately simplistic; on the other hand, it was nevertheless helpful to clarify things in his mind, avoiding the jargon and maths used at recent seminars provided by the firm. 'Now, if I agree to sell you something such as a currency or a commodity, let's say wheat or oil, at some time in the future at a preagreed price, and I already have a right to it now, then that's taking a long position. If on the other hand I agree to sell you something I don't already own, then that's going short. Short is agreeing to sell something in the future that I don't already own, banking on the price falling by the time I have to buy it to make delivery to you'.

Saul paused. 'Got all that?' His friend nodded with a slight grin. 'OK. But if on the day you decide that you'll buy or sell in the open market and not accept the price which I've offered you, then that is where hedging comes in. I can agree with the market, through buying options, that if necessary I can sell to the market at a pre-agreed price. If the market price has fallen, meaning I'll make a loss in the physicals market, then I can still get a higher price by exercising my option. If there is a higher price in the market, I'll not exercise the option. In other words, the markets provide the means to insure against changes in price at some point in the future. This is what hedging's all about. And this is how real things, such as currencies and commodities, can be separated from their risk, which can itself be separately traded on recognised international exchanges'.

Something in Thomas's earnest, intelligent mind suddenly clicked, and he grasped the main principle underlying risk trading; it was often the case that first he'd learn the technical aspects of a particular subject, but only later would they fall into place when the simplest explanation was given. He drained the last drop of chilled orange juice; it was firm practice not to drink during the lunch hour (unless in the company of a client). Over the years neither Saul nor Adam had ever been able to accurately work out Thomas's intellectual or practical abilities, but they did know him to be hard working and perhaps more straightforward than the two of them. 'Well, Saul, I'd better be getting back now- not all of us can while away the day guzzling Champagne and canapés'. 'Give me a call when you've spoken to Adam about that weekend in Biarritz next month. I called him this morning but he couldn't talk, and I can't call him this afternoon because I'm out at an audit... it's a dirty job but someone's got to do it. See you later'.

Saul watched his friend disappear into the distance. He looked around the rink, and then at the wine bar from which a steady stream of brokers, lawyers, and dealers continued to trickle. He gazed up into the cloudless sky as an aeroplane flew overhead and felt at peace, confident in his abilities and the future. He became aware of a figure skating towards him, and looking down he noticed it was someone from Sheldons, although it was not possible to put a name to the face. Judging by the jeans, it must be his day off. 'It's Saul, Saul Quartermain, isn't it? A bit late to be soaking up the afternoon sun, isn't it?' Saul was irritated that his line of thought had been broken. 'This morning I closed a syndicated $200 million power plant deal for the Thai government after three months' work. If I want to drink myself stupid, then today's a day when I'll be justified in doing so'.

The skater put out his hand. 'We've met before. I'm Nicholas Herschell from Equities, and you're Saul Quartermain from M and A's and Flotations. I remember you from your training with us last year'. Saul smiled, taking the outstretched hand. 'Right name but wrong department. I left Flotations six months ago, and now I'm in Syndications.

So how are things in Equities - still on the bull run, without a bear in sight?' The Head of Equities Trading laughed. 'Things have never been better. Stocks are booming, and the institutional investors just can't get enough of what's on our books. So, my clients are happy and so am I!'.

Saul's thoughts returned to work; he'd better put in an appearance this afternoon despite his success in the morning. He also had to call Adam. 'Well, Nicholas, it's good to see you again. I'd better be getting back now. Keep in touch'. 'Okay, let's do that. How are you fixed for a meal later this week? How about Friday at seven?' Saul wasn't sure he wanted to 'keep in touch', this being his usual semi-polite way of bringing a conversation to a neat end with someone whose potential usefulness didn't exactly spring to mind. But this 'Nicholas' was persistent, and if he wanted to get back to work he'd have to give an answer. 'Friday's fine. Where do you have in mind?' 'Seven o'clock, the India Star, Brick Lane'. 'OK, see you there'. The two shook hands again and then went their separate ways.

When Saul arrived back at his desk he made casual enquiries of his contacts in other departments at Sheldons. It transpired that Nick Herschell was a 'blue blood' equities trader, coming from a titled landowning family in the shires. He was one of the most successful performers in his department as well as being head of it, recently receiving the highest bonus ever awarded by the bank. As Saul sounded out his sources, he became intrigued as to how this trader had achieved such a reputation within such a short period of time - he'd been with Sheldons for just two years - and why he'd been so eager to arrange dinner with someone who was practically a stranger. The cheap, nondescript venue for Friday's meal added further ground for suspicion. But Saul was unprepared at this point in time to attribute his own ethical standards, or more precisely his lack of them, to Herschell; all he could do was wait until Friday when the true purpose of the meeting, if indeed there was one, would be revealed.

Chapter Fourteen

Thomas Stoneacre had graduated top of his year in the end, and then gone to work at Clements Accountants, a medium size London-based firm. Despite the high regard in which he was held by the senior partners, he was bored by the mundane work he was required to do on what seemed to be a daily basis. He was even more unsettled by the excitement his two friends seemed to be enjoying in their chosen careers; it was difficult for him to enthuse about the latest European Union company tax directive when they spoke of billion dollar deals, bonuses and international fraudster clients.

Whenever the three met up after work, Thomas would question them at length about what they'd done or seen that week, but it was rarely the case that his inquisitiveness was reciprocated. Although his working days were taken up at Clements, he'd still managed to find time to take an active part in the development of the family business, which his father continued to expand. Thomas found that an increasing proportion of his weekends and holidays were spent at Northern Engineering Group's main factory in Yorkshire. He was leading a 'double life'; if his employers had known of his involvement with the company, they'd almost certainly have dismissed him, since his contract prohibited involvement with outside businesses.

Thomas's hopes and ambitions for the future had changed the day he'd met the first true love of his life. Chloe Peyton was a barrister in a small chambers located on the outskirts of London. They met when they were both working on a particularly complicated insolvency case. Although they'd been working for different sides - Chloe for HMRC, Thomas for the company defending itself – they'd struck up a friendship from the moment of their first encounter in court. The friendship had developed quickly and despite his commitments at the firm and family business, they were soon spending an increasing amount of time with each other.

This was Thomas's first serious relationship, his first time really smitten. But he also knew that for Chloe, the development of her career at the Bar took precedence over any other considerations. She was ambitious and unwilling to sacrifice her aspirations for marriage and children just yet. It was for this reason that he'd not proposed, mainly out of fear that he'd be rejected, and that such rejection would lead to the unravelling of their relationship. He decided instead to leave it to her to set the pace at which the relationship developed, resolving to avoid all talk of marriage until she was good and ready to commit to him.

On the break they had promised themselves for months, Thomas stood looking out to sea, thinking about how to broach the subject which had been on his mind for the whole of the weekend. They laughed about his ongoing travails with the illiterate and deaf eighty year old chairman of a paper-making company Clements was currently auditing. But Thomas had hired the cottage in Cornwall in the expectation they'd have uninterrupted time in which to discuss the future of their relationship. The weekend was a welcome rest, an escape for both, but the subject Thomas most wished to discuss had not been raised. He felt frustrated, almost tongue-tied and unable to force the issue, apprehensive about pressing his lover on a matter vitally important to him but perhaps of less consequence to her. He felt powerless. But he needed to know her thoughts, and to find out whether she even contemplated a long term future together. The afternoon was drawing to a close and soon it would be time to return to the cottage, pack up the bags, and drive back to London. For the past hour they'd walked arm in arm for miles along a beach teased by the first gentle breezes of autumn. Thomas stared down at his bare feet as they slowly disappeared beneath the sand of the incoming tide, and for a time his mind fell vacant. Sensing that his thoughts were a million miles away, Chloe splashed cold sea water against his knees to regain his attention. He returned his gaze from the distant horizon and looked into her beautiful pale green eyes. 'If we stand here any longer we'll take root!' Chloe's words seemed to be far away against the gentle rush of the incoming waves. Suddenly he took her in his arms and kissed her, a long and thoughtful kiss. 'So what was that for?' asked Chloe, unaccustomed to such spontaneity. 'I want you to know how much I love you, how much I need you, and how much I hope we can be together always'.

The words hadn't come out as planned, but Thomas was happy to have lifted the weekend's conversation to the subject so important to him. She looked into his large questioning eyes and smiled. 'I love you too, Thomas', she whispered. 'I love to wake up beside you in the morning and to see your face before I sleep. I love being with you. But I can't give the commitment you want today. It has to be a 'maybe' for now'. Thomas was about to say that this was enough for the time being, but was silenced when Chloe placed her finger to his lips. He'd failed to get the indication of commitment he wanted, but was content that she was willing to keep an open mind; a 'maybe' was to be preferred to a 'never'.

The low rumble of an approaching storm crept up from the distance. The heavens opened within a minute and heavy droplets of rain began cascading from the grey clouds overhead. As the rain ran down their hair, faces and clothing, they embraced and kissed again, and then started the short run back to the car. As they ran they laughed, exchanging small talk about what the week ahead held for them. They clambered into the car and it was then that Chloe asked the question Thomas had been hoping to avoid. 'We've been with each other for months, Thomas, and yet the two people who are the important part of your life, I haven't even met. I've met your parents, your colleagues at Clements, even your company accountant, but never Saul or Adam. You talk about them so often I feel as though I already know them. When are we going to be introduced?'

Chloe was one of the few, perhaps the only, secret he'd ever kept from his closest friends. But it was not Saul from which he sensed danger: he could be relied upon for brotherly advice and consolation whenever a relationship came to an end. No, it was not Saul whom Thomas feared in matters of the heart. He smiled at Chloe and promised to arrange a dinner some time in the not too distant future, when their busy working schedules permitted. He knew he was postponing the inevitable, and the question now was for how long he could delay it. They returned to the cottage, loaded up the car, and started the long drive back to London.

Chapter Fifteen

The day of Silas Coughlin's bail hearing at the magistrates' court had arrived. Adam agreed with Philip Rothermere, the senior crime partner at the law firm Roxburgh Thymes, that he'd attend the hearing: it would be a formality in which the client would simply pass through this preliminary stage of the criminal process on his way to a full trial at Blackfriars Crown Court. He would, of course, be refused bail, and accordingly this appearance would be over in minutes. In their earlier meeting at Pentonville Prison, Coughlin had joked that, since the sentencing powers of the magistrates were restricted to a maximum of six months' imprisonment, perhaps they should consider electing to be tried in this court, the lowest in the criminal court hierarchy, instead of the Crown Court where the possible jail sentence was considerably higher. Cannon-Smith QC, not amused, reminded Coughlin that, taking into account his previous convictions for assault and embezzlement and the seriousness of the present charges, a Crown Court trial was unavoidable. The granting of bail, he announced dismissively, was not even a remote possibility.

On his arrival at the magistrates, Adam made his way to the cells to which Coughlin had been temporarily transferred before the five minute hearing. His client was sitting at the only table in the cell, resting his head on one elbow whilst puffing on a cigarette he held in the other. He stood up when the solicitor entered the cell and shook his hand with the firmness which Adam had noticed in previous encounters. The client seemed agitated although his outward demeanour was one of calmness and detachment. It was this latter characteristic which irritated Cannon-Smith; clients charged with serious offences were expected to be fearful of the process and respectful of its principal actors, the lawyers. Coughlin appeared unwilling to study his lines for his part in the play which was about to commence, and for this the barrister despised him.

Adam lit up a cigarette and sat down at the only other chair in the small windowless room. He looked at Coughlin across the table and after a few seconds' pause explained the process that would be followed after they'd entered the courtroom. 'This is a minor hearing to decide the issue of bail. As you know, the Prosecution will oppose your freedom pending trial, so I suggest we don't waste time arguing this application. And anyway, the Bench will have tried and convicted you before you even set foot in the courtroom, since that's the general order of things in offences involving breach of trust. So unless you want to instruct me otherwise, I suggest we just sit calm, and get this appearance over and done with as soon as possible'. 'If that's the way you want to play it, Mr. Creed, then I'll follow your advice. I'll just keep my mouth shut, and look on respectfully'. Adam permitted himself a wry grin, stood up and started towards the cell door. 'I'll see you in court then', were the last words he heard as the officer slammed the cell door closed behind him.

Adam entered the court and took his place before the Bench. The Crown Prosecution Service lawyer entered shortly afterwards, his creased three piece suit, scuffed brown shoes, and disorganised files the clearest evidence why a career in the private sector had been closed to him from the day he qualified with some unknown local authority. 'Hi. Roger Pitt, CPS. 'You been waiting long?' Adam shook the outstretched hand, introduced himself and then passed over his card. Pitt looked at the card's inscription. 'Roxburgh Thymes. Now, that's some firm! You must be smart. Me, I just couldn't put up with all the hard work. I went for a quite life'. Adam looked at the overweight thirty-something sitting alongside, and decided not to respond, briefly contemplating in his usual detached way the future of the legal system entrusted to the hands of petty bureaucrats so perfectly typified by the gasping official now slumped beside him. He decided to change the subject; they were, after all, in court to commence a process which could result in a man's imprisonment for a significant number of years.

'Roger, what are your thoughts about this bail application? Are you willing to see my client out pending trial, or are you going to object?' The man in the crumpled blue suit blanched, started to sweat and then wiped his brow with an ancient handkerchief which he took from his inner pocket. 'No, no, no, Adam, I've received strict instructions from the police that I must resist bail. They tell me your client's a real bad'un, to quote them exactly, and it's not for me to question their judgment. I'm just a small cog in the machine'. 'But I thought you people at the CPS were supposed to be independent, to make your own decisions, but now you're telling me that you just do as you're told. Now I'm really shocked'. Pitt missed the sarcasm. 'Anybody who tells you we're independent needs their heads read. We just carry out instructions. To tell you the truth, I haven't even read the files for this case - a few minutes ago I was briefed in the street by the arresting officer. Your client's as guilty as hell and there's no chance of bail'.

Coughlin was lead out into the dock. He looked around the courtroom: he'd been in courts before, but this time felt mildly afraid. This was going to be the big one, the case which could see him put away for more years than he wished to contemplate. He'd done time before, when he was younger and fitter and the sentences had been months rather than years. He looked ahead at the Bench and bit his lip as hatred welled up in his soul. Eventually his gaze came to rest on the only man in the court whom he trusted, whom he believed was not enmeshed in a system which afforded justice to no man. He waited for the play to commence, surveying the opening scene from his own private balcony. 'Mr. Pitt, would you like to start for the Prosecution. Please explain why the defendant is in custody and whether you believe that such further detention is desirable pending trial of this case'. Roger Pitt struggled to his feet. 'The defendant has been charged with fraud. The reason for his current detention is that it is the firm belief of the police that the defendant would interfere with the principal witness in this case who is presently being kept at a safe house. We believe that such risk of interference continues to exist. For this reason we strongly object to the granting of bail'. Coughlin looked on impassively, musing that rarely had he heard such an accurate summary of the truth by a lawyer. 'Mr. Creed. Do you have a submission to make in rebuttal of the Prosecution's objection?' Adam stood to his feet. 'For the present time we'll not be challenging the Prosecution's position. Accordingly we will not be applying for bail at this point in proceedings'. The hearing ended with the defendant formally remanded into custody. Coughlin was returned to the cells pending transportation back to Pentonville.

After the brief hearing Adam revisited his client in the court cells. He was surprised by the extent to which this brief appearance had unsettled

Coughlin, who was on his feet even as he entered the cell. Adam sat down and lit up, expecting his client to do likewise. But instead Coughlin continued to pace around the cell, his anger and frustration hanging like a thick cloud in the small confines of the room. Adam had met with the man on previous occasions and each time he'd appeared calm, astute and without fear. He'd long since accepted Cannon-Smith's observation that this was a 'very clever criminal', but now something had changed. There was something dark and brooding about Coughlin, an air of extreme violence which the young lawyer had not encountered before. In the cold room there was a feeling, almost a presence, of evil. Coughlin continued to walk around the room whilst Adam looked ahead, slowly drawing upon the cigarette. The prisoner was muttering to himself, his punctuated hissing cutting the silence and emptiness of the room. It seemed to Adam that the paced circle was gradually growing smaller and that Coughlin was in fact closing in on him. The whispers gradually became audible.

'That bastard Melas. I should have killed him when I had the chance. Yes, stuck him like a pig. And that would have been his last squeal, yes, his last betrayal'. He glared at Adam as he said this, then laughed to himself, and the laughter was the laughter of a man whose grip on sanity had loosened. Adam was shocked, although his continued draws upon the cigarette would have suggested to a wider audience that he was bored, listening to the same ranting heard in a hundred previous cases. But this was not the case: he feared that the thump, thump, thump of his heart would betray his unease. 'For God's sake, Silas, control yourself before you say something we're both going to regret'. The circle had now collapsed in on Adam, and Coughlin stood immediately alongside his young adviser. Slowly he lowered his head so that his mouth was directly aligned with Adam's ear. The whispering continued while Adam, partly out of fear, partly out of bravado, continued looking straight ahead.

'Do you honestly believe I'm going to entrust my soul to this charade? To lay out my corpse for fancy lawyers in black gowns to feast upon? In life I've been a man more sinned against than sinner, viciousness breathed into me by a world of brittle principles and tuppenny souls'. In the blink of an eye he pulled a small square of white paper from his pocket and pressed it into the lawyer's hand. Adam remained still, not daring to move as Coughlin's huge hand enveloped his own. As his fingers were forced closed around the paper he was struck by his own powerlessness, an emotion not previously experienced. The face was now so near he could see it looming in the corner of his eye. 'Next time we meet you'll let me know your answer'. Coughlin stepped back as Adam finally managed to jerk himself into motion. The unnerved lawyer rose, placed the piece of unread paper into his top pocket, opened the cell door, and walked out of the court, along the corridors and out into the fresh air. This had been a difficult day.

⚬⚬⚬

Saul sauntered along the narrow side street as he approached Brick Lane. It was a warm summer's evening and the breeze wafted a smell of spices and cooking through the air. Instead of returning to his flat in Kensington, Saul had decided to stay on at work to complete the heads of agreement for a merger between two medium sized pharmaceuticals companies. He found this aspect of his work the most tedious, involving preparation of dozens of covenants, pledges and other contractual undertakings, but he had an eye for detail and prided himself on his mastery of this more mundane part of his responsibilities. His technical competence had also been strengthened over the years by the fact that he regularly discussed legal documentation with Adam: his drafting abilities never failed to impress.

As he continued along Brick Lane he was struck by the diversity of the population bustling around the countless takeaways and all night coffee bars; it seemed as though every country in the world was represented by a face. City types in pinstripe suits and designer label ties wove their way between beggars and hawkers, tradesmen and conmen, and ordinary people in their multitudes. Saul melted into the crowd, exhilarated by its vitality and anonymity, and but for his glowing mop of blond hair, would have been invisible to the eyes of the children and the women in burkas peering down into the street from bedsits above shops overlooking the Lane. On arrival at the India Star, he greeted the owner who stood, arms folded, just outside the entrance. Nicholas Herschell had already arrived and stood up to greet him with a handshake. 'Good to see you again, Saul. I hope you didn't have a problem finding this place but it's one of the best Indians in the East End. And I know we'll get some privacy here to talk about things'. Saul's suspicions were not allayed by the greeting but at the same time his curiosity demanded to be satisfied. The two sat down at a table tucked away in a darkened corner of the restaurant like two furtive gangsters plotting their next heist. Throughout the evening they discussed their jobs at Sheldons and their hopes for the future. Saul had gradually talked himself round that perhaps he'd misjudged his colleague, and that in fact the invitation had been made for entirely innocent reasons. The small talk continued, but Saul was becoming disinterested and mildly disappointed. And then, with a handful of well-chosen words, Herschell propelled the evening in the direction which he'd intended from the moment they first spoke at the ice rink the previous week. 'So tell me about this merger you're working on at the moment, Saul. Is it true that Penderfen Chemicals and Forst Pharma are merging, and if so, on what terms?' Saul laughed as he unwrapped the last of the cheap mint chocolates brought with their coffee. 'You nearly caught me out there, Nicholas. You know as well as I do that 'Chinese Walls' can't be breached. 'Deal makers shall not pass on inside information to traders in the same institution', and all that stuff. Remember? Correct me if I'm wrong, but I think there's up to seven years in the slammer waiting for anyone caught fixing the market'.

Herschell smiled as he topped up Saul's coffee. His guest had not left the table, had not stormed out of the restaurant as a previous target had done earlier in the year, and had not demanded a discontinuance of the conversation. Now it was all just a question of price. 'A month ago I got into work early, just in time to meet the office cleaners before they finished their shift. The 'team leader', a lady called Pearl Stanton, was nowhere to be seen and a new guy, Andy Smith, had taken over. I asked about Pearl because we'd started at the bank on the same day, and often exchanged jokes and chit-chat. Andy said she'd retired, but here's the point. Andy is Pearl's nephew. She'd told him she was about to leave and that he should apply for her job before Sheldons got around to advertising it. Although he had some diploma in business studies or something like that, he hadn't worked since leaving college. So here was his golden opportunity, a chance to get in before Joe Public even got to hear about the vacancy. Now you tell me, Saul, why am I telling you this story?'

Saul summoned more coffee. 'I know the point you're making Nicholas; it's a simplistic one. There's a world of difference between inside information which nets *a cleaning job at a bank* and financial information which can be used before it reaches the general markets and make someone hundreds of thousands when they fill out a single buy or sell slip'. Herschell knew he'd won the argument. 'So what you're saying Saul is that it's the amount alone which is the distinguishing factor when it comes to insider dealing. The practice itself only becomes unacceptable when it's the 'yuppies' in the City who benefit. If it's Pearl Stanton passing on information which she alone knows then somehow this is different and morally okay. But in both cases it's the wider public which loses out, even if it's just another unemployed office cleaner who might have got the job if Andy Smith hadn't been so quick in using Pearl's inside information. The truth is that insider dealing goes on all the time. But it's just straightforward envy which leads to you and I being singled out. What we're doing is no different to what's going on in thousands of different situations in every day life'.

Saul listened impassively. The conversation was leading inexorably to an invitation to him to join a criminal conspiracy, and he knew it. He had access to all the corporate deals in the making at Sheldons, and at the same time, Herschell had access to the markets in which this inside information could be exploited to the full. He also had no doubt that his guest was working with others at the bank, and maybe at other banks too, and, indeed, this would explain how he'd been able to consistently outperform his colleagues over a suspiciously prolonged period. Saul had been waiting for this opportunity from the first day he'd joined Sheldons but now that it had finally arrived, he hesitated. The dangers would be immense but the prospect of the thrill of the crime, and of course the opportunity to make vast wealth in very short time, was intoxicating. He would need much more information, of course. He would take his time. 'It's been an interesting evening, Nicholas. I think it's time we should be going'.

The bill was called, arriving upon a small silver-plated platter. Saul placed a handful of notes onto the dish, including a suitably inflated tip. Herschell patted his mouth with a napkin, mildly perplexed by his colleague's sudden desire to bring the evening to a close. 'You should let me pay: it was my invitation, after all'. He'd also brought cash for the evening: to use a credit card would have fixed a time and a date which could prove embarrassing if the meeting had to be denied later. Saul grinned. 'Don't worry about that - you can pay for the next one'. Herschell had been a successful angler for many years; this sport (and of course foxhunting) was part of his traditional upbringing on the ancestral estate in affluent rural England. There was always a unique pleasure in landing a trout at the end of a day spent gently wading in the shadows of a river-bank, but which until that moment had threatened to be time wasted. The dinner guest had been hooked and however he might bob and weave, it would only be a matter of time before he was gently reeled in.

The two employees of Sheldons Bank emerged from the darkness of the India Star and into the colder light of a late summer's evening. 'I need time to think, Nicholas. I'll be in touch when I'm ready'. 'I'll wait to hear from you then, but don't be too long in your thinking'. The aristocrat laughed as he extended his hand. 'I'll think about it, Nicholas, but always be sure that I'll never take a fall for someone else's crime'. The evening over, the two would-be conspirators went their separate ways, through the throng in the street and the neon-lit lonely all-night coffee bars, to their flats at opposite ends of the city.

Chapter Sixteen

As Chloe puckered her lips before applying her lipstick Thomas looked at her in the mirror and gently kissed the nape of her neck. The evening had arrived and with it the meeting he'd tried hard over the past few months to prevent. In celebration of its two hundredth anniversary, Sheldons Bank had arranged a ball at one of the most exclusive hotels in London. Invitations had been issued to the chairmen and directors of leading companies advised by the bank over the years, but also to employees past and present. Higher ranking employees - dealers, traders, and deal makers who'd generated substantial fees over the past year - were all offered tickets. Saul saw the event as an opportunity to introduce his friends to colleagues at the bank. It also presented one of those unique occasions when, to his way of thinking, the three could see for themselves the progress they'd made since leaving university, measured by the glitz and glamour of the circles in which they now moved. Thomas hadn't intended to inform Chloe about the evening, at least not until it had safely passed. But in a moment of carelessness, when pressed about an invitation to the opening night of a musical from a colleague at Chloe's chambers, without thinking he had said he was unable to accept due to a prior engagement. Chloe had been surprised by his furtiveness; it was clear that he'd intended to go to the ball without her, and without her knowledge. She knew that her partner's secrecy would not be for the traditional reason for suspicion in any relationship: he wouldn't have taken another lover, nor did she think he would ever be capable of such deception. No, there had to be a deeper reason for his secrecy, and this intrigued her. She insisted that she should attend the ball, and reluctantly, he'd agreed.

When Thomas told his friends that he'd be bringing his 'new' partner to the evening, they intuitively knew there was something different about Chloe, something which set her apart from other partners to whom he'd introduced them over the years. He'd been hesitant, and the light-heartedness with which he'd approached previous relationships was missing. In their different ways the two concluded that, should this be love, it was the start of a lifetime's happiness for him.

'So, how do I look? Am I acceptable or shall I ring around some of my friends to see who else might be your arm-candy instead?' Thomas looked at the beautiful woman standing in front of him and was momentarily stunned into silence; her deep red dress gently clung to the contours of her perfect figure, her face radiant with health, vitality, and the reflected glow of her attire. Her eyes glinted with excitement; at last, she was to meet the people with whom she felt she'd shared Thomas from the earliest days of their relationship. For several moments Thomas could find no reply to his lover's tease. Taking her gently in his arms, he whispered; 'There can never be anyone else. This evening belongs to you'. She looked at him in his immaculate white tuxedo, black cummerbund and perfectly arranged black tie; she loved him but wished she could love him in the way she knew he loved her. This was the flaw, the intractable problem which wouldn't pass.

Soon a taxi pulled up outside the flat and the two stepped out into the still night air. The driver leaned out of the window and flicked a cigarette stub into the gutter. He looked at the couple, radiant in their youth, as they drifted towards the car. Arm in arm they whispered and laughed to each other as they approached, oblivious to the world around them. 'So where are we going to this evening, good friends?' 'Hotel Excelsior, if you please', replied Thomas, realising that their driver for the evening was not the silent type, but rather the typical 'Cockney cabbie' who never let his passengers get a word in edgeways. His first impression turned out to be correct, and the following twenty minutes with retired boxer Frankie 'The Fists' Malone left the two exhausted of all small talk. But Frankie's banter had placed Thomas in a better frame of mind; for several days he'd worried about the risks the evening presented, and yet deep in his soul he'd also reproached himself for doubting Chloe and mistrusting Adam. He decided he'd try to relax and enjoy the evening, taking pleasure in the company of his two friends, and his beautiful Chloe. By the time the taxi arrived at the Excelsior, Thomas was at ease. The meaningless banter with Frankie and Chloe's gentle whispers and caresses at his ear had combined to make him feel at peace with the world. The faint wisp of doubt dissipated into the cool evening air; he was now ready and confident for the evening ahead.

Arm in arm, the couple walked up the steps into the hotel. As Thomas surveyed the crowd his sight soon alighted upon the familiar mop of blond hair visible at the far side of the room. He kissed Chloe and then slowly but purposefully they made their way past the glamorous, confident guests who now packed the ornate grand halls of the hotel. As soon as Saul saw the approaching couple, he rushed to greet them. 'Thomas! Welcome; glad you could make it. And you must be the mysterious Chloe. No wonder Thomas has been keeping you such a secret. It's great to meet you. Welcome to the Sheldons ball. After this evening you'll never come across a greater concentration of fraudsters, impostors and undetected criminals in one place again, present company excepted, of course!'. Saul winked at her, and spontaneously she began to laugh. 'I'm pleased to meet you, Saul. I've heard so much about you: Thomas talks about you and Adam all the time'.

Just before the couple's arrival, Adam had left Saul to make a telephone call from an upstairs cloakroom. Silas Coughlin's next magistrates' court appearance, his committal to Blackfriars Crown Court, was to take place within the week, and Adam needed to discuss with Cannon-Smith the likely sentence which could be expected if he was eventually convicted. The news was not good for the client. In view of the abuse of a position of trust and the record of violence and intimidation in both this and previous cases, he was looking at a five to eight year jail term. He knew he'd have to make his decision soon. He took out the piece of paper Coughlin had forced into his hand and read the message again. 'Guilty or innocent: does it matter to you? Will you break the bottle and free a genie? If yes, what's your price?'

He returned to the hall, and as he made his way to where he'd left Saul he noticed that Thomas had arrived. But his progress through the crowd came to a halt when he saw the woman on Thomas's arm, her presence and grace setting her apart. He paused, his eyes tracing the outline of her perfect figure, her natural smile, and her sparkling, excited eyes. 'Hi everybody. Sorry Saul, but I couldn't get to the bar so we'll just have to wait for drinks.' Adam looked at Thomas, and then to Chloe.

'How long have you been here, Thomas, and aren't you going to introduce me to your beautiful friend?' Thomas's anxiety briefly resurfaced. 'Chloe, meet Adam Creed, my friend and comrade in war and peace'. Adam was moved by the words but felt his heart quicken as he took Chloe's outstretched hand. 'Delighted to meet you, Chloe. Usually there are no secrets between the three of us, but it's clear tonight that sometimes the rule gets broken.' Chloe smiled, informing Adam that although he knew nothing about her, she'd known plenty about him for some time. Adam was intrigued as to what she may have been told, but also mildly irritated that Thomas had been keeping an important part of his life hidden from his friends. His failure to understand Thomas's reluctance was genuine enough, equalled only by his inability to envisage the concern which had weighed so heavily in Thomas's thoughts over the past while. After further gentle conversation the group drifted into the dining hall, among the glitterati who had chatted, fussed, argued and drunk to excess all evening.

Adam, too, had gone beyond his usual limit of Champagne, but not so far as to lose his sense of occasion or his sharpness of wit. He was happy for Thomas, and looked on at the seemingly perfectly matched couple as they made their way to the table. Fleetingly he reflected upon his own history of one night stands and failed relationships: surely he, too, deserved more from life? But his restlessness and dissatisfaction had never progressed to jealousy, and indeed he was unable to recall a time or a circumstance in which he'd felt envy for anyone else's success. This was one of the rare gifts bestowed by his intellect - a confidence that, if he so wished, he could match and exceed the greatest success achievable by those around him. At the same time he genuinely felt goodwill towards his friend.

Saul had been appointed by Paul Phineus, Chairman of Sheldons Bank, to deal with the planning of the evening. He knew that Adam would be attending the ball alone: his last, brief, relationship had ended a week earlier, and for this reason he'd seated him next to Clarissa Anders, a corporate finance executive from Banque Basle, a major Swiss syndications rival to Sheldons. Saul had known Clarissa for years, and although they were keen business competitors, they'd struck up a close friendship based upon a mutual respect and liking, and professional courtesy. He'd thought for several months that Clarissa's keen intellect, her elegance and quick wit, made her an ideal partner for Adam; accordingly he arranged the seating in the hope that a match would result by the end of the evening. Thomas, of course, was seated next to Chloe, who in turn was seated next to Saul. As the evening progressed, Saul looked around the table at the two couples now absorbed in their own private conversations. Clarissa and Adam spent most of the evening whispering and laughing at what he surmised to be private observations of guests on nearby tables. Thomas and Chloe also appeared to be enjoying the intimacy of their own company.

He looked at his friend and saw contentment in his eyes. He smiled to think that Thomas would perhaps be the first of the three to make the great leap forward into married life, whilst at the same time acknowledging that of the three he'd always been the most stable, the most conventional. Occasionally a conversation would widen to include all five guests seated around the table. It was during these briefest of exchanges that Saul, always alert, noticed the flicker of an expression on Adam's face which betrayed deeper, darker, dangerous thoughts. He hoped he was mistaken and that Clarissa, the deal-maker from Banque Basle with whom Adam had clearly established a warm rapport, would dominate his attentions, even if just for the evening.

Clarissa gazed into Adam's pale grey eyes as he spoke about life at Roxburgh Thymes. His confidence and intensity fascinated her, his jet black hair and brilliant white tuxedo creating a presence, an aura, which distinguished him from the other suitors who'd pursued her throughout the evening. But during the successive dinner courses, as they spoke and argued and laughed with each other, she had the impression that his mind was elsewhere. Although he appeared to be paying her the closest attention, he also seemed to be eavesdropping on another conversation taking place in the background, further along the table. But it was only an impression, and since she was enjoying his company, she decided to ignore this mild impoliteness. 'So tell me, Clarissa, how does a woman cope with City aggression? How does a member of the gentler sex survive in a man's world?' She knew she was being baited and teased, and yet she was happy to play the game. She smiled mischievously. 'But Adam, it's not us who are the gentler sex, it's you men. You're the hunted. Nowadays we occupy plenty of the highest positions in law and finance, and we're not stopping there. Look a little closer. We women have a different skillset – we're more subtle, and without any false modesty, we get what we want more often. Even the revolution in politics was led by a woman'. Adam gazed at her with a deliberately disbelieving expression, hoping to unnerve her or provoke her into an outburst which could then be patronisingly put down to gender. He obliquely cast an eye across her body, gently pushing at her perfectly tight but discreetly cut dress. Yes, in other circumstances she would have been a challenge he'd have welcomed; her keen intellect and striking looks attracted him, and he knew the attraction was mutual.

Suddenly he leaned across and gently kissed her on her cheek, flushed with the heat of the room. With equal swiftness he returned to his previous position. 'Now see what you've made me do! Your assertiveness has made me feel so confused I just had to find some way to re-establish my weak and foolish masculinity. We males are sometimes too obvious in trying to get what – or who – we want'. Clarissa threw her head back and laughed out aloud. 'Well, you've put me back in my place, Adam, no mistake. I'll take your gallantry as a compliment'. His thoughts returned to someone else.

Chapter Seventeen

Adam drove slowly into the car park at Pentonville Prison. The journey from his flat had been emotionally exhausting as he struggled to decide his course of action in the Coughlin case. In essence he faced two alternatives: to help the defendant in a way yet to be revealed but which would be, inevitably, corrupting, or instead to let the wheels of justice grind and turn, eventually producing an outcome that was certain even now, before the court doors opened. He was accustomed to representing villains, clever and stupid alike, but somehow Coughlin was different. Until now he'd approached the criminal fraternity with professional detachment, keeping his distance and never becoming emotionally entangled. But at the heart of this strategy lay a paradox of the iconoclast who longed to test the system, to find the extent to which he could subvert it, whilst at the same time ostensibly committing himself to the traditional behaviour and ethics of the ambitious solicitor, clambering up the greasy pole to partnership. His loathing of the petty hypocrisies of his profession and of the partners at the firm who exemplified them gnawed at him.

He manoeuvered the car between the bright white markings of the prison car park, switched off the engine, closed his eyes and tilted his head back against the headrest. In the silence he could feel the frantic beating of his heart as contemplation of the enormity of what he might be about to do forced its way back into his consciousness. His pale face and the dark circles beneath his eyes were irrefutable testimony to the cross-currents of doubt and uncertainty, conviction and supreme confidence, which had swirled like colliding eddies across the river of the previous sleepless night. Now he had to decide, to commit. Better to be a maker of history than a bystander, he mused to himself in the depths of his doubt. No final decision having been made, he got out, slammed the door more heavily than he would ordinarily have done, and briskly made his way to the small door leading into the prison grounds.

Adam entered the small conference room to find his client seated in the same blue plastic chair on the same side of the room as he had been in at their meeting several weeks earlier. By instinct Coughlin always faced a door whatever the circumstance, always sitting next to a window, even if reinforced with steel bars and without any means of being opened. The difference today was that the podgy-faced barrister wouldn't be attending a meeting in which solicitor and client were simply to discuss court procedures for the trial at Blackfriars Crown Court in twelve days' time.

The prisoner stubbed out his cigarette and placed it with the dozen others which tumbled from the aluminum tray on the table in front of him. Rising to his feet he greeted the solicitor with a broad smile, successfully concealing the anxiety which had disturbed his sleep intermittently for the past week. He was a professional criminal and knew that following conviction for the offences with which he'd been charged the tariff started around seven years and ended at who knows where.

'Hello, Adam. You've been in my thoughts since our last meeting'. Adam shook the outstretched hand, again struck by its size and strength. A mental image of both hands gripping his throat flickered across his consciousness like a comedy sketch: he let out a brief but definite laugh. The two men sat down on opposite sides of the blue formica-topped table. 'I've been thinking about your note, Silas. If I understand you correctly, you want me to subvert the legal system, pervert the course of justice, and breach my code of professional ethics. Would that be a fair summary?' Coughlin leaned back in his chair and pushed his hands through his greasy black hair: had he been mistaken about the young lawyer? Was he wired? But in for a penny, in for a pound; if he was to be convicted of attempting to pervert the course of justice in addition to the current charges, it would be unlikely to make much difference to his final sentence. He pulled his chair nearer to the table and, leaning across, beckoned to Adam to draw closer. The gesture was faintly amusing, as if he was about to whisper a risqué joke. Adam leaned forward; turning his head his ear was aligned with the client's fleshy lips, perfectly positioned to hear the barely audible whisper. 'Mock me, my friend, and you'll be dead before the day's out, do you understand?' Adam recoiled in horror. Coughlin smiled at him, winked, and then placed his index finger to his own lips. 'But talk of... *nastiness* between you and I doesn't seem right. Let's get down to the business of whether you're willing to help me. Will you work for me? If you will, what's your price? I can make it worth your while.' Adam regained his composure, angered both by his client's threat and his own fearful reaction to it. 'Tell me the truth and I mean *all* of it, and then I'll make up my mind'.

Coughlin sighed. 'Fine. Delphi was set up as a financial consultancy to give investors with limited capital opportunities to invest in the 'no risk' UK gilts market. Money flooded in from the nouveau riche, all chasing the trappings of wealth, the fast cars, apartments in Spain, what have you. My colleagues and I ran a number of investment 'roadshows' to market our products. To see so many greedy eyes popping at risk-free returns, well, this was a rush, compensation for sharing the same room, the same air, with these people'. Although he described the essentials of the business in a matter-of-fact way, Adam realised that emotions of envy, loathing, and contempt ran deep. Of even greater concern, Adam reflected, was the reality that he seemed to have much in common in outlook with the villain he soon might conspire with.

'Within a year a large amount of cash had accumulated in Delphi but since this belonged, legally-speaking, to the clients, I couldn't get my hands on it. I had to work out how to siphon off this excess wealth, and of course get away with it. After considering a number of possible schemes I decided to set up the Gandalph Trust. Gandalph was incorporated in Switzerland ostensibly to provide, and I quote from memory from the legalese of the incorporation document, 'marketing advice and consultancy, investment strategies and brokerage services' for UK-based retail financial services providers. Seventy five percent of Delphi's share capital was transferred to Gandalph, making it effectively a subsidiary of a Swiss parent. And since I owned Gandalph through nominee Swiss shareholders, I now controlled Delphi outright. Why was there a need to divide ownership in this way? Well, all transactions between the two had to look legitimate; if there was evidence of fraud on my part then all those UK investors could have come running after me, tracing the money - their money - paid to Gandalph by Delphi. Over time massive dividend payments were made to Gandalph, but since Delphi wasn't making any profits anyway, these payments had to come from its capital base - illegally, of course'.

'It was all about extracting the last drop of cash from Delphi, magicking it across to Gandalph, and then out into the great unknown where not even the very best forensic accountant would be able to find it. To a Panama-registered owner of the shares in Gandalph, which I, of course, controlled. And who was going to complain about the services or products bought by Delphi from Gandalph? I'd appointed the board members and nobody was going to challenge my decisions. All weak and greedy fools. In reality it was all about switching money from one pocket to another in the same coat, because I owned and controlled both pockets... I mean, companies. As for the investors, they just handed over money to Delphi as a long term investment; they'd been assured that government bonds were risk-free, and all they had to do was sit back and wait for the interest to roll in. I doubt if they even read the annual reports, although even if they had it wouldn't have made a difference - those were a pack of lies anyway'. Coughlin smiled as he reflected upon the simplicity of the structure. In the space of ten years he'd progressed from a small-time back street thug for hire, to being one of the most talked about wizards in financial services circles. A few name changes had been necessary along the way, of course, but he was the same man he'd always been, and the greed of individuals willing to suspend caution in the pursuit of riches never changed.

'So, Silas, your financial wizardry made you a fortune, but all of it was held outside the UK in bank accounts in the names of bogus shell corporations. At this point Mr. Melas, your bookkeeper, comes into the picture - the man charged with protecting your secrets and overseeing your empire. Maybe this wasn't one of your better appointments; one you made out of a misplaced trust?' The client smiled; the reality was that he'd appointed Andreas Melas, an extremely competent accountant from Malta, out of an expectation that he'd be committed to him body and soul. He'd come with a glowing recommendation from Coughlin's brother-in-law on the island, and had a reputation for discretion when processing cashflows from dubious origins. There was also a rumour he'd previously acted for high-ranking military figures in the Gadaffi Government but this had never been proven, much to the frustration of investigating officials at the Maltese financial services authority.

'I treated Melas like a brother. I trusted him and gave him a salary beyond his wildest dreams. I saw to it that his sister was given a job with a leading US bank on the island too'. Adam looked into the client's eyes and a sparkle of hatred briefly illuminated his inner thoughts. Adam reflected on the adage that the eyes are indeed the windows into the soul before taking another draw on his cigarette. 'And then one day he got religion. Simple as that. I have to admit that his betrayal, the treachery, was for the noblest of reasons'. Silas laughed as he regained his composure, amused at the paradox that he'd come so far, had evaded the intrusions of investigative authorities around the world for over a decade, only to be caught by the crisis of conscience of an honest man.

'Melas didn't just get religion: this wasn't the main reason he went to Scotland Yard to 'spill the beans' about Gandalph, was it? He had a mental breakdown, didn't he? He was so distressed when Delphi went under, leaving thousands of pensioners facing poverty because their savings had been stolen, that he ended up voluntarily committing himself for six months' psychiatric care. He felt personally responsible for their despair, although perhaps, if he'd been a weaker man, he could have justified his actions to himself by saying he was simply carrying out orders. It was only after this, facing God's judgment, that he decided to leave you. And now he's the leading witness'. 'The only witness' interjected Coughlin. 'Okay then; the only witness standing between you and seven years at Her Majesty's Pleasure'.

The defendant looked up at the clock on the wall behind Adam, ticking away mercilessly into the time allowed for this visit: he needed an answer today. In two weeks' time the trial would begin, and even now it might be too late.

'When you take the hand of the Devil, it's for life. I never hid my true nature from that little bastard. He knew from the beginning what was expected of him, and then he gets a twinge of conscience and breaks like a dry twig. You know who I am- what I am - and today I need your decision. Are you going to help me?' Adam knew that the choreography was over. His life would now be divided into two stages, the one before this minute, and the one afterwards; he took his last draw on the cigarette, stubbed it out on the silver-coloured ashtray, trembling slightly. 'Yes'. Coughlin sank back into the blue plastic chair, still perfectly composed, his face expressionless. 'There's only one thing I need from you, Adam. Just a small piece of information. I need Melas's e-mail address'.

Adam blurted out a laugh. 'Don't you already have it? He was *your* employee, after all'. The prisoner's demeanour remained unchanged. 'He changed it on the wise advice of our friends at Scotland Yard. And now he's being kept incommunicado in some hotel here in London, perhaps just a few minutes' walk away, in the witness protection programme. But what could he fear from me?' He mockingly turned his hands upwards towards Adam in a gesture both amusing and deeply threatening at the same time. 'I need to contact him, to ask him to think again about cooperating with the Prosecution in this travesty of a case'. The mocking tone had resurfaced. 'Send it here when you have it'. He pushed a torn-off cigarette lid towards Adam upon which was written the e-mail address of one of his most trusted lieutenants; Adam picked up the note and slid it into his wallet.

'So, young man, we've nearly concluded our business. Not wanting to appear indelicate or to change the otherwise courteous tone with which this meeting's proceeded, but can we now turn to the matter of your fee?' 'I want one hundred and fifty thousand pounds paid to my lawyer in Monaco'. Silas smiled; the lawyer was out to punish him, so personal gain was evidently not the driver. But if this was true, what led this successful young man, standing on the threshold of a glittering career, into such a compromise of his professional and personal ethics? Coughlin believed he understood the human psyche with all its ugliness and selfishness, so he was always pleasantly surprised when someone came along who challenged his view of the world. But this was a rare event, an exception which proved the rule. The amount demanded would be nothing more than a drop in the ocean of the wealth the defendant had stashed in accounts around the world. 'That's one hell of a pricey e-mail', he laughed.

'And freedom is priceless too, don't you agree?' responded the lawyer, now feeling at ease with the certainty, the finality, of the new state of affairs. He'd sleep well that night, the decision now made. He stood, shook hands with his new paymaster, and left.

Chapter Eighteen

Thomas bounded up the white concrete steps which led to the lobby of London Commodities Ltd, the privately owned multinational commodities brokerage which had been one of Clements's most lucrative clients for the past five years. The company had a reputation for secrecy, and was suspected in the financial media of having both the power and the willingness to manipulate prices of precious metals, oil and grains via a network of agents spanning the industrialised and developing worlds. The company was owned lock, stock, and barrel by Solomon Silverstein, a reclusive Polish émigré who'd been granted British citizenship in the 1950s. But the reality was that the company was now too large to have total control concentrated in one person's hands, and the owner, now in his late seventies, had to start considering the issue of succession. Silverstein was an Orthodox Jew who refused to allow either the company or the world in general come between himself and his religion. He had married his beloved wife in the 1940s and had never recovered from her death in the early-1990s. He'd always been known for his irascibility and argumentativeness, but these qualities had become more pronounced in the years following his wife's death. His two sons, Nathaniel and Isaac, and daughter, Rebecca, worked in the business, and had borne the full brunt of his frustrations during the past five years. Matters had not been helped by the fact that all three children had rejected the religious conservatism of their father, opting instead for a more liberal Reform Judaism.

The receptionist peered over her half-moon glasses. 'Can I help you?' 'Thomas Stoneacre of Clements Accountants to see Mr. Silverstein'. 'Please take a seat and I'll ring through'. Within seconds a woman in her mid-twenties, dressed as sharp as a pin, appeared and greeted him. 'Mr. Stoneacre, good to see you. I hope your journey was not delayed by the strikes we've been having these past few days. This morning I arrived an hour late. So many trains rushing past, too full to take any more passengers. Please come through: Mr. Silverstein has been looking forward to meeting you'. Ms. Ahava Gold led the accountant down a brightly lit corridor lined with a series of abstract works by modern artists. Thomas instinctively knew that they were originals, all carefully selected by a single mind with a perfect eye for thematic coordination and style. He noted the absence of paintings or photographs of either the founder, his family, or, for that matter, any employees of the business. At the end of the corridor the two came to a nondescript door. 'This is the conference room', whispered the guide. 'The Chairman is waiting for you, so I'll leave you now'. She gently pushed open the door, spoke a few words in Yiddish then ushered Thomas inside.

Solomon Silverstein stood just over five feet five inches in height, with not an ounce of spare flesh on his body. His hair was snow white, as was a small well-groomed beard. He wore a sharp Savile Row suit but beneath this was a simple dark blue waistcoat, immediately apparent as a personal addition to the outfit. A dark red bow tie stood out on a crisp white shirt purchased the previous day from Pink's by one of the dozen secretaries who buzzed around the twelve stories of the office hive, taking and delivering reports and other communications between the company's three hundred and twenty employees. Thomas mused to himself that the multi-millionaire standing before him would not have looked out of place as an assistant in a haberdashery, with a tape measure permanently suspended about his neck. 'Mr. Stoneacre: a pleasure to meet you. I hope I've not kept you waiting too long'. The sprightly company chairman got up from his seat at the far end of the room and in seconds had reached Thomas, greeting him with a firm handshake. From the seating arrangement Thomas noted that this was not a company where gestures were made to political correctness; this was not a circular table around which equals discussed policy, but rather an oblong table presided over by a chairman who sat at its head, fully in charge. 'Please, take a seat. Can I get you a coffee?' Thomas was surprised when the old man himself walked over to an alcove, poured two cups of coffee, and then returned to the table. He proceeded to pour the cream, at his guest's request. There was a natural and unaffected sense of welcoming, of humility, about

Silverstein which Thomas had never previously encountered in meetings with other wealthy clients of the firm.

'You'll already know about the main businesses of London Commodities and the company's organisation, so I'll not take up your time explaining the existing share structure; I'll get straight to the point. My concern is this. I have three children who work for the company, all of whom I love more than life itself. They all have their individual talents, and all have contributed in their unique ways to the betterment of the business. But I'm getting old' (he smiled at Thomas at the understatement) 'and I need to make proper arrangements for the handover when the right time comes'. Thomas replaced the now empty white bone china cup on the delicate saucer before him. 'Well, Mr. Silverstein', 'please, call me Solomon', 'Thank you, Solomon. If I'm to advise on the transition, I'll need information about your objectives. For example, do you wish all of your children to have board appointments? Is one of them to assume the role of chairman or would you prefer an outside appointment? Our firm has an excellent 'headhunter' service. If your children are going to run the company, are they to have equal powers and responsibilities? Family conflicts at board level can destroy a company when these issues are left unresolved before a handover of control by the founder'. He paused, and as Silverstein was merely nodding and not yet responding, he continued: 'Perhaps you'd like to have your children in attendance at this meeting so they'll be apprised of the options for any potential future restructuring of the business? If they are to succeed to the business, then they'd probably appreciate being involved in the planning.'

The chairman smiled and Thomas was immediately aware from the prolonged pause that there were personal issues which would determine the future development of the business which would probably eclipse any practical proposals he might wish to put forward. The client's response was firm and precise, indicating a nature unaccustomed to compromise or discussion. 'My children do not need to be privy to our discussions, sir. I alone make the long-term decisions in the best interests of my company, and I alone bear the ultimate responsibility if these prove to be misconceived. The wellbeing and continuance of the company override any personal considerations'. Thomas now understood in an instant how London Commodities had evolved into a global player in the international commodities business in the space of just a handful of decades.

For the next hour the two men discussed possible strategies for the division of shares in London Commodities between the three children. Whilst Silverstein spoke highly of the personal qualities of his sons, it was apparent he had a low regard for their business acumen. Thomas was surprised at the directness with which he criticised their lack of professional skills. 'My sons are weak and foolish when it comes to dealing with the day-to-day affairs of the company. They don't understand the business world and would destroy the company if they had too much influence on its decision-making processes. They mustn't be given any real power, although of course I'd like them to continue being present at board meetings, as happens now, for the sake of appearances and to keep the family connections strong'. Thomas reflected upon the dichotomy faced by the entrepreneur who on the one hand loved his children and was loved by them in return, but on the other could not entrust the future control of his business to them because of their intellectual flaws. Eventually he was able to propose an acceptable strategy.

'I suggest that your sons continue in their present positions as the Commercial and Marketing Directors. This will give them seats on the board going forward and should go some way towards counterbalancing any disappointment they may feel at being excluded from genuine power within the company. They'll also be given non-voting shareholdings; these will generate dividends should the future profitability of the company warrant a distribution in this way. They'll continue to receive their present salaries, although you may also consider increasing these bearing in mind the greater responsibilities they'll assume following your retirement'. Thomas knew his proposals were subtle, neat and practical but he was also aware that he was yet to address the fundamental issue of the future control and leadership of the business. Was it the chairman's intention to continue running the company from retirement? If so, this could lead to paralysis of the business and postponement of the issue until he eventually died, at which point the struggle for power could be damaging.

'Solomon, I've assumed that the same arrangement will also apply to your daughter, Rebecca, but this still leaves the vital issue of the future day-to-day control of the business unaddressed. I must ask you again to consider an outside appointment to the position of Managing Director of the company. This person could also hold the chairmanship but I'd caution against this for a company of London Commodities's size. If you give us the green light we'll begin the search for suitable candidates. We can have a list ready for your consideration within three months'. Silverstein paused and stretched out his arm, revealing an ancient silver watch. 'Thomas, I need to end our meeting now; the day's getting on and there are matters I must attend to before the close of trading. I appreciate your concern about issues of control following my retirement, which you are quite correct to raise, and we'll have to discuss these later. But before we end there are several important considerations which I must make known to you since they affect all aspects of the strategy I'll adopt'.

Thomas knew that after all the gentle verbal jousting, after all the technical explanations, the client's next few words would be the most important of all those spoken that day. 'Despite my wealth, despite all my worldly goods, I am and always will be a simple Jew trying to make my way in the world. When I die I'll be wrapped in a simple white sheet, laid in a wooden casket and placed in the ground. Kaddish will be recited for me. All that will remain, the only indications of my past existence in this world, will be my children and my company. I am determined that they will prosper and endure. Talmudic law, the law by which I've strived to live my life, requires that Nathaniel, my eldest son, should inherit the business. But pragmatism engendered in a faithful Jew by the closeness of the hour of reconciliation with his Maker is a powerful emotion. Rebecca, the last born, my only daughter, will inherit control of the business.' Thomas wanted to speak, to discuss the implications of the client's revealed intention, but instead felt it appropriate to remain silent. To look into the soul of a client, however fleetingly, was something new, strange and beguiling. Silverstein quickly rose to his feet, collected the cups and replaced them in the alcove. 'We'll continue our discussion another time. It's been a pleasure spending the afternoon with you, and I'm sure we'll be seeing each other again soon. Please be sure to speak with Ms. Gold before you leave'.

Thomas shook the old man's hand, thanking him for the confidence he'd placed in him as his adviser. At the reception desk he was greeted again by the officious but undeniably friendly Ms. Gold. 'Mr. Silverstein asked me to arrange a time convenient to you for dinner. Do you have your diary to hand?' This was unexpected; he'd apparently given instructions for a dinner appointment to be arranged before the meeting had even taken place. Thomas's social engagements were decidedly thin for the coming week, so a date was set with relative ease. The dinner would take place in three days' time, the client stipulating one of the most prestigious (and most expensive) restaurants in Mayfair. He briefly wondered whether his 'client entertainment' account with the firm would extend to the bill - assuming he'd have to pay, of course.

Chapter Nineteen

Saul stepped out of the Hotel de Paris and into the early evening heat haze. His silk purple tie, brilliant white tuxedo and black trousers made him feel at ease with the jetsetters with whom he'd mingled earlier in the lobby. He'd arrived the previous evening, taking the direct flight from London to Nice International Airport, business class. As he'd gazed down on the Alps, sipping chilled Champagne whilst intermittently reading a trashy crime paperback he had bought before boarding, he reflected on the current state of his life. Things were going well, and were hopefully about to get a lot better. But this was not a business trip claimed against expenses; he'd used up several days' annual leave entitlement from the company in order to make it.

As he'd traced bubbles of condensation trickling across the window against a backdrop of fluffy white clouds and looming peaks, he wondered about the specific purpose of his trip. What was it meant to achieve? He knew the general purpose only too well and had no trouble with this. But the detail-this was the unknown factor. As he walked across the Place towards the Café de Paris, the agreed meeting point, he looked up to the surrounding hills dotted with the apartment blocks of residents of Monaco. To any passer-by he blended seamlessly into the affluent picture, but he felt strangely distanced from it all, observing this world as an outsider, as an imposter. One day, though, all of this would be his.

He took a small table outside the Café and within seconds a fleet-footed waiter took his order while he awaited his host for the evening. The exotic creatures of Monaco passed before him as they moved on to concerts, opera, or to the exclusive restaurants they'd haunt until the early hours. He sat and visually imbibed the colours and scents of the evening, taking in snatches of dozens of simultaneous conversations, sometimes in English, but more usually, of course, in French. It would have sufficed to sit there all evening, listening, seeing, thinking, and dreaming. The freshness of the air and the clink of glasses on other tables as guests celebrated birthdays, business successes, or just the pleasure of being alive, pressed home the awareness in Saul of a lifestyle he believed now lay within his grasp. He wanted this, but was unsure of the risks he'd be prepared to take to attain it. He would know by the time he boarded the return flight home.

'Saul, welcome, and so pleased you accepted my little invitation'. Saul snapped out of his daydream and looked up at the young man now standing immediately in front of his table. Nicholas Herschell, Head of Equities Trading at Sheldons, beamed as he shook Adam's hand. He was attired in a white tuxedo, just like Saul, but somehow seemed a natural part of the scenery, more relaxed, perhaps, and more confident of his position in the world, certainly. 'You like the hotel I booked you into?' 'It's fine, thanks, and the Champagne waiting for me on the balcony was much appreciated. With friends like you I don't think I need bother working again'. Herschell laughed as he lit up a cigarette. 'Don't bother working again, Mr. Head of Corporate Finance, and you'll not see friends like me again'. Saul smiled at the openness and sincerity of the comment. It was refreshing not to have to struggle through double-meanings and affectations, as he was accustomed to doing when negotiating with deal-makers from other banks. In his world there was a ritualistic way to conduct oneself, in which every word and action were precisely defined; a careless word could result in extra 'basis points', or hundredths of a single percentage point, being payable by a client, increasing the cost of a syndicated loan by hundreds of thousands of dollars, perhaps more, over a five, ten, or fifteen year period. Herschell's incautiousness therefore appealed to him and was a breath of fresh Riviera air; in many ways it was also a statement of trust, although things said presently and any offers made could always be denied later after the two had returned to London on different flights.

The two sat for the next hour at their table outside the Café du Paris, savouring the famous local delicacy of oysters and drinking their way through the bottle of Champagne the waiter served in a silver ice-packed bucket upon their arrival. A gentle breeze came down from the surrounding hills, pushing at the enormous spoked canvas umbrella slowly turning above their table. Saul knew that his host was one of the 'star performers' at Sheldons Bank, but to a large extent this was due to the efforts of the sales team for which he was responsible. His host's bonus payments were dependent upon the profitability of the team, and this made him a very demanding taskmaster. The cost of his lifestyle had been outstripping his earnings for several months, and he'd become frustrated that Saul hadn't responded to his earlier overtures at the Indian restaurant in Brick Lane. He needed to considerably augment his earnings, and these few days in Monaco were to be his final attempt to bring Saul 'on board'. If he couldn't be persuaded to participate in the conspiracy in the unique and diverting environment of Monaco, then nothing was going to convince him and he was perhaps a man of higher ethical standards than Herschell had originally anticipated. But he wouldn't have incurred the costs of these few days - Saul's flight, the hotel, the entertainment - unless he was confident that success was close at hand. Anyone, the theory went, could be bought; the question was always just a matter of finding the right price.

After the darkness of the late evening had fallen, the two finished their second bottle of Champagne, left the Café, and strolled to the casino which lay in wait just along the front. Saul had played in many London casinos, from the glitzy, chintzy palaces of the West End to the seedier nouveau riche gangster haunts of the East End. They were all too similar, too predictable in their clientele, their atmospheres, and the croupiers who spun the wheels to supplement their modest earnings from a thousand dead-end day jobs. But the Monte Carlo Casino was a different world. As they passed through the marble atrium surrounded with its onyx columns and into the Salle Garnier auditorium, Saul stared up at the red and gold frescoes, bas-reliefs and sculptures which adorned the walls. The colour and vastness of the space spoke of a bygone age, reminding Saul again of the lifestyle to which he aspired.

The impact Herschell desired had been achieved; soon he could start discussing specifics. For the rest of the evening the two moved from gaming room to gaming room, playing the roulette, Chemin de Fer, and shooting craps. Herschell was known to most of the croupiers, who greeted him warmly at the tables they visited. Saul knew his colleague was an 'outright rogue' as the manager of the back office at Sheldons had once called him to his face, but liked him for his lack of affectation and his infectious confidence. After all, their personalities were similar in so many ways. Herschell also had a genuine and instant rapport with everyone they met: croupiers, bar staff, or the anonymous jetsetters who'd previously benefited from his investment recommendations. Occasionally Herschell would leave Saul's side to whisper for a matter of seconds into the ears of beautiful diamond-bedecked women watching the tables from the shadows, prompting them to step forward to toss high value chips across the stacked beige cloth. Sometimes it was just a kiss. He was evidently a well-connected man.

A couple of hours later Herschell suggested that they took their leave. Saul had won a few hundred pounds whilst his friend, who'd been willing to take greater risks, had come away with several thousands. After cashing in their chips, Saul was guided through to the back of the casino and out onto one of the terraces that looked out to the sea. The air was full of the scent of flowers and the moon shimmered on the gentle waves in the distance. Visible in the darkness were the dim white hulls of dozens of yachts of various sizes that floated up and down, the gentle motion assisting the sleep of the multi-millionaires and their families who owned them. Saul stood gazing into the distance, transfixed. 'Chinese walls say that you and I should never talk to each other, at least not in our professional capacities'.

Saul's eyes refocused as he switched his attention from the dreamlike scene to his friend who was starting a new conversation. He knew that this was the opening of 'the pitch', the broaching of the subject that lay at the heart of the invitation to Monaco. He'd decided to work with Herschell after arriving in the Principality the previous day; now it would be entertaining to hear how the Head of Equities approached the simple issue of lawbreaking in the complex context of insider dealing at the bank. 'What I want from you, Saul, is information'. Saul hesitated before replying. 'Assuming I'm willing to work with you, and… let's say for argument's sake that I am, what sort of information do you want, and how do I get it to you bearing in mind that all internal and external calls are recorded, and the Stock Exchange is always looking for unusual movements in share prices prior to important announcements?'

Herschell was pleased; the fish had been landed without much of a struggle. 'You have access to the plans of Sheldons' corporate clients. You know about intended takeovers, proposed mergers, and boardroom reorganisations, long before the Press gets to hear about it. Often your department arranges the financing. We in Equities only get to hear about what you've done after the information's entered into general circulation, so our opportunity to take a share early is almost non-existent. I want to be in before a share price bounces'. 'Okay, I can provide you with this, but obviously I must be getting something out of the arrangement too. Neither you nor I can invest directly because the bank would find out before the deal's even been done. So, what exactly do you propose?'

Herschell explained that he had set up a trust in Monaco a few months earlier. The trustee was a local lawyer whom he trusted implicitly, whilst the main beneficiaries were Herschell and several traders from other financial institutions. Nobody could look behind the trust, and the trust made all investments on behalf of its anonymous beneficiaries. The trustee could be given a general freedom to make investments as he thought appropriate on behalf of the beneficiaries. Alternatively he could be given instructions on an ad hoc basis, combining a general discretion with occasional specific directions from the beneficiaries. Herschell and his accomplices had adopted this latter arrangement; it provided the best of both worlds, enabling them to rely on the trustee's skills and knowledge whilst at the same time allowing intervention in the decision-making process when they wanted specific share purchases to be made. 'I communicate details of the shares to be bought to Dieter Morgenthau. He instructs his contact at Banque Monaco, Pierre Van den Luc, to make the purchase, and nobody back in London is any the wiser. There is no link between Dieter and me for the world to see. The set-up is perfect; the only thing missing is a regular flow of reliable information'. Saul agreed that his next step would be to set up a similar trust and with this in mind, Herschell agreed to introduce him to Dieter Morgenthau the following day. Saul then came to the most important aspect of their future cooperation, at least from his perspective. 'So, I pass the information to you, putting both my job and liberty on the line in the process. What's my return?' 'Two and a half percent of the value of all transactions I initiate on the basis of information supplied by you. Van den Luc will simply credit your trust with the cash after he's made the calculations. As for getting the information to me in the first place, we'll just have to be imaginative'. The arrangement was fine – Saul didn't even feel the need to negotiate, because percentage-wise it offered great possibilities, particularly if Herschell used the information to invest through his trust on behalf of other investors who were not as yet participants in the scheme.

'And if you're ever caught, will you bring me down with you?'
Herschell smiled at the directness of the question. 'You have my word,
for whatever it's worth, that your identity as the provider of the information will remain known only to me. The other beneficiaries will never be
told and if the Serious Fraud Office ever comes knocking on my door,
your name will never be revealed. The SFO doesn't torture people as far
as I know, so I can guarantee my lips will be sealed. But if I get into
trouble, I'll expect you to do whatever you can to help me out – without,
of course, compromising your anonymity'.

Saul wondered whether he could, or should, take the word of someone who was, after all, involved in a conspiracy against his employer and
prepared to profit by illegal means. But sometimes you have to look
someone in the eyes and make a judgment, and all that there is to rely on,
to inform one's decision, is the vagueness of instinct. He hoped his
instinct was good. In the event of the worst case scenario happening, Saul
believed that in this narrowest of slivers of trust Herschell would not
bring him down.

The two shook hands on the agreement, walked back through the
casino and out into the cool fresh air. As they wandered past the flower-
beds and across the carefully tended lawns in front of the casino, Saul felt
a deepening sense of longing for the lifestyle he'd witnessed that day. He
wanted the freedom and the wealth, to be able to visit (and spend lei-
surely lengths of time in) such places, to look up at the stars and dream.
He wanted a yacht moored off the port of Monaco. Wealth would be the
true liberator. At one of the ponds Herschell stopped, kneeled down and
splashed his hands in the cold water. Without looking up at Saul he
spoke in a strong confident tone. 'Of course, you could seal our arrangement now by giving me something to take home with me to London.
What do you say? Is there an investment you'd like to recommend?' Saul
helped Herschell to his feet.

'Buy three month call options on Elma-Hammer Engineering'.
Herschell made no comment. 'Saul, this evening's been a pleasure. I'll
call by your hotel tomorrow at 11.30am, and then we'll move on to a
party. There are some people I'd like you to meet. Sleep well'. Herschell
gradually disappeared into the distance, walking through the lawns that
gently sloped up towards the town. Saul returned to the luxury of his
suite at the Hotel du Paris; there he'd spend the next hour half asleep in

a wide wicker chair on the balcony, the ever-present moonlit sea shimmering in the distance.

The following day Herschell arrived at the hotel at the agreed time, dressed casually in a white flannel jacket and navy trousers, a light blue shirt and a blood red cravat. He was relaxed, as usual, despite the fact that he'd been up late into the night making calls to his contacts in the Far East regarding Elma-Hammer Engineering. He'd been informed that it was a sleepy and unexciting company with a share price that, whilst undervaluing assets, nevertheless reflected general investor disinterest. These days there was very little appetite for these kinds of predictable, safe, 'old economy' companies; the real 'buzz' was to be gained from the high tech stocks that were leapfrogging the wider marketplace. The share price was stable; too stable, in fact, and the possibility of a sudden and unexpected hike in the short term was thought to be remote. So why had Saul made the recommendation? He would think it over during the day, but ultimately his decision on whether or not to buy share options would come down to a matter of blind trust.

They left the hotel and walked to the port, Herschell pointing out architectural features as they went. This was not the time to be talking about Sheldons; it was a morning when the realities of working life were to be suspended, albeit temporarily. Upon arrival at the port Herschell pushed some notes into the hand of a waiting motorboard owner, pointed into the distance, and soon they were speeding out through white crested waves towards a distant horizon dotted with yachts of infinite colours. Saul squinted through his sunglasses in the bright sunlight. It was difficult to hear Herschell's running commentary over the roar of the engine, so instead he simply absorbed the scene, licking the occasional splashes of salty water on his lips as the motorboard smashed through the waves. Eventually the noise of the engine began to lessen as the owner gently reduced speed and their destination came into view. Saul looked up in amazement as the vessel *The Sylvan Princess* loomed before them, its white bow thrusting out of the water like a tower block. Other boats in the vicinity were dwarfed by the giant in their midst.

Saul knew he'd arrived: a new world awaited him. As he and Herschell climbed the ladders suspended over the side he heard music, laughter, and dozens of voices speaking simultaneously in as many separate conversations. The party had already begun. Soon they were mingling with numerous groups spaced across the deck; Herschell, ever the perfect social companion, introduced Saul to bankers, lawyers, film producers and recording artists who were either based in Monaco itself, or in France or Italy. As he looked into the distance and watched the brilliantly coloured sails of smaller yachts racing each other around the Bay, he thought of his friends Thomas and Adam, and sincerely wished they were there to share the atmosphere. It would be difficult to describe these few days in Monaco following his return to London.

As the afternoon progressed Saul was aware he'd not yet met the owner of the yacht, conspicuous by his absence from the festivities. When he asked whether he'd be introduced, Herschell replied that they'd be called to the conference room below deck at the appropriate time, but that for now they would have to 'wait their turn'. An hour later Herschell interrupted a conversation Saul was enduring with a fading but rich French film star; the yacht's billionaire owner (whom Saul suspected to be an 'informal' client of Herschell's) was ready to receive them. Saul suddenly realised he didn't even know the name of the absent host, and indeed nobody that afternoon had either mentioned him or alluded to his existence. He wondered how someone of such wealth and influence could remain so curiously invisible.

Eventually, after passing along several long winding corridors, the two arrived at the conference room below deck. Herschell rapped on the door and then pushed it open. Standing at the end of the room and gazing out at the sea was a man whom Saul guessed to be at least six feet four inches tall, with collar-length black hair, graying at the temples. His complexion had been gently tanned during his time in the Mediterranean, but it was apparent that the natural hue was pale, even grey. Physically he was a powerful man with strong chiseled face and deep-set, cold shark's eyes. Saul's immediate intuitive response was one of considerable unease for reasons he didn't quite understand, or have time to ponder. He guessed that the host was in his late sixties, but as he emerged from the shadow at the far end of the room and the lines on his face became apparent, he added an extra five years to his estimation. He was evidently older than he at first appeared, but his vigour and stature helped him retain a relatively youthful air.

'Saul Quartermain, I'd like to introduce you to the owner of this yacht, the owner of Moscow Alpha Bank and a good friend of mine, Petr

Damyanovitch'. The imposing man stepped forward and began to speak, in perfect English with a faint Russian accent. 'I'm pleased to meet you, Saul. I've heard a lot about you and I'm hoping that we'll soon be working with each other'. Saul took the outstretched hand; it had an iron grip, and whilst he shook it he looked into the grey, impassive eyes which did not smile along with his face. 'It's a pleasure to meet you, sir, and I'm grateful to have been invited here today'. The three then wandered over to the windows and watched the yachts pass by, exchanging some pleasantries but then quickly turning to business. Damyanovitch was keenly interested in Saul's role at Sheldons and in the bank's activities generally, but was curiously reticent about Moscow Alpha's business other than to explain its involvement in the syndicated loans market. The bank was a minor player amongst a group of banks that regularly issued bonds on behalf of multinationals and governments, in particular the Russian government. It was apparent he harboured ambitions for Moscow Alpha to become a syndication 'lead manager' in the not-too-distant future, building greater prestige and taking higher arrangement fees in the process. He was interested to learn whether Saul had any experience in the new markets of Central and Eastern Europe, and Central Asia.

'What do you know about the Russian oil industry, Saul? Do you think it has a future, or is it just a relic from Soviet times?' Saul was on firm ground. 'I've done some business in the oil sector but that was a few years ago and for a small US refinery. I know that Russia has extensive reserves, particularly in Siberia, but due to obsolete pipeline infrastructure it loses… let me see, I think around twenty five percent of pumped oil. It's light-years behind regional competitors, or at least it was when I last did business there'. Damyanovitch was irritated by the brevity and negative honesty of the reply, and his reply was terse. 'Oil and gas account for a quarter of Russian GDP, a half of our export earnings, and a third of government tax revenues. In short, the industry's crucial to the future wellbeing of my country'. Saul listened closely and became aware that this was a business rather than a social meeting. The billionaire's words were those of an impartial economist, a shrewd banker, and yet behind the statistics Saul knew he was in the presence of a dedicated nationalist. 'Russia ranks 7th in world terms of proven oil reserves but has only 5% of world supply compared with 25% for Saudi Arabia, Kuwait and UAE, and Iran on somewhere around 9%. Tell me Saul, do you love your country?' Saul was taken aback by the directness of the question and the subtle, potentially hostile change of direction in the conversation. 'It's a place where I earn a living and which gives me a quality of life which others would envy. But love? That's a different thing. I don't feel an emotional attachment if that's what you mean. Perhaps if war broke out I might think differently. But I don't think this is going to happen, particularly now that the Soviet Union's finally gone'. Herschell winced at the gauche remark; Saul should have suspected that Damyanovitch had had some role in the old regime, even if neither of them had any idea about what that may have been. He decided to break what he sensed was mounting tension in the room. 'Saul thinks of his country as a PLC. Patriotism is just a quaint and alien concept, isn't that right, Saul?' Saul laughed. 'Guilty as charged, with no plea in mitigation'. Damyanovitch smiled but was not to be diverted. 'Nothing is more important than a sense of nationhood, of belonging. It is the nation that endures. Those who know true commitment, those willing to make the ultimate sacrifice when survival is threatened: it is they who bear the heavy weight of destiny upon their shoulders. Russia will be strong again, and oil will make it so. Moscow Alpha will be involved in this process'.

Saul paused before responding. 'I understand, sir. I can't see Sheldons Bank getting involved in the Russian oil sector for the foreseeable future though. It's just too risky, with true ownership of the oil companies hidden behind opaque shareholding structures. With respect, the local mafia is also very active in the sector, and this is sure to put off Western investors'. Damyanovitch hesitated, barely able to control his mounting anger. 'So, Saul... you in the West would prefer to be dependent upon a handful of sheikhs for your energy needs? How they despise your liberal values, your religion, and your secular governments. Yet the West in its infinite wisdom prefers doing business with them rather than us. Why do you think this is so, Saul? Do they think they can control the indolent and corrupt suppliers in the Middle East indefinitely? Or is it instead that they fear domination by a greater, reinvigorated Russia?'

Saul had a choice: either he could bring the conversation to a close with a flippant comment or he could engage and risk alienating his host even more in the process. 'The reasons why the West prefers doing business with the Middle East, particularly the Saudis, are many. First, the costs of getting the oil out of the ground there are the lowest on Earth.

Second, the day-to-day control of the business is, de facto, in the hands of Western engineers, administrators and bankers, particularly Americans. Local autocrats get military protection against interference from their neighbours in return for giving up true control of their resources. Russia, on the other hand, has outdated infrastructure just now. More seriously, from Western companies' points of view, its government combines corruption with nationalism, and is unpredictable as a consequence. Investors don't like unpredictability, and that's why the Russian oil sector is given a wide berth'.

Damyanovitch seemed to take this well, and as he spoke, Saul breathed a small sigh of relief, initially at least. 'I respect your directness, Saul. You are free of the evasiveness and feigned courtesies I've come to expect from Western bankers, diplomats and lawyers. Your analysis is a sound one but, if I may say so, underestimates the ability of individuals to fashion the future. I'll not stand idly by whilst Russia is prevented from achieving her true destiny, taking her rightful place at the head of the table of nations. We'll not be denied our prize by lazy financiers, Middle Eastern despots, or by greedy ill-wishers on our borders. And when we do strike it will be terrible for the world to behold, as it has been before'.

For Herschell the meeting was not going according to plan. He was supposed to introduce Saul to Damyanovitch, they would talk about business, about Sheldons' investment capacities, and a new client would be hooked. But instead there was tension between the two protagonists, and he had become a bystander. 'Gentlemen, it's been instructive to hear your views but the afternoon's passing us by. We're sitting here in the half-light whilst above us the sun shines and Champagne flows. Can I propose a vote? The proposition is that we adjourn above deck and over-indulge in the excellent food, drink and company until we're fit for nothing. How say you?' Damyanovitch relaxed and began to smile again. 'The vote is passed, nem con'. Saul was relieved that levity had re-entered the conversation. The black cloud of Russian anger that had settled in the room appeared to dissipate, although his feeling of unease remained.

Back on deck, the three circulated amongst the guests. Crewmen in immaculate uniforms kept glasses topped up whilst proffering trays of canapés. Herschell moved from group to group, quickly becoming the center of attention. In contrast Damyanovitch avoided the separate gatherings dotted about the deck; his preference was for private one-to-one conversations with individuals who, like him, preferred to stand back from the partygoers. His detachment made him almost invisible, and no-one approached him without his making eye contact first, as though to select them. As the party began to wind down, Saul moved to the yacht's rail to be alone with his thoughts. He gazed out over the glassy deep blue water towards the port, watching as strings of coloured lantern lights began to flicker into life. Suddenly his attention was interrupted; Damyanovitch had appeared alongside and now looked out on the same scene. For some unknown reason Saul looked down at the handrail and was startled by what he saw. He noticed the host's crisp white cuffs with simple, gold cufflinks, but also that half of two fingers of the right hand were missing, as if severed cleanly, chopped with a sharp knife.

'It's a perfect setting, isn't it? So tranquil. An image of opulence. You're thinking you'd like it for yourself, yes?' Saul returned his attention to the port's outline. 'Yes, I want it and I'll have it. I want wealth not just for its own sake, but also for the freedom it brings.' Damyanovitch patted the young man on the back before tucking a card into his top pocket. 'The question is, Saul, are there limits to what you're prepared to do to achieve it? When the time's right and you want to talk again, call me'.

Half an hour later Saul and Herschell thanked the host for his generosity and disembarked into the same motorboard by which they'd arrived, summoned from the shore by a call from Herschell's mobile. As the speedboat headed towards the shore they reviewed the evening and agreed that, broadly speaking, it had been a success. 'The chairman liked you. He showed some emotion during that discussion, even if it was anger, when usually he's as cold as an iceberg; I'm not sure that was a bad thing. You can never tell what he's thinking, and I've known him for quite a while'. Saul asked about the two half-fingers. 'I've never asked and he's never said. I always avoid personal questions. Someone told me he lost them during the War, but he's never mentioned that either. I suggest you keep away from anything to do with his past if you see him again, which I'm sure you will'. The boat glided into port: the two stepped back onto dry land, shook hands and walked off in separate directions. Saul turned back briefly to look at the huge yacht gently rising and falling in the darkness. Momentarily he thought he saw the silhouette of a tall, well-built man staring back at the land. That night, his sleep was broken by strange dreams of unfriendly faces and unknown places.

Chapter Twenty

As Thomas weaved towards his table past the other seated guests in the five-star Mayfair restaurant, he pulled at the cuffs of his white silk shirt, unwrapped from a cellophane envelope in which it had been kept for a special occasion for the past month. Feeling composed, he gave his name to the maitre d' and was taken to the stall reserved by Ms. Ahava Gold on the day of his meeting with Solomon Silverstein. He'd deliberately arrived early to acquaint himself with his surroundings. The restaurant was large, but with ample opportunity for intimacy. Waiters rushed between stalls, scattered like so many little islands, in a well-rehearsed and coordinated choreography. Iced water with a sliver of lemon refreshed him as he sat and waited.

At 8.00pm on the dot, Solomon Silverstein appeared in the restaurant's ante room; to Thomas's surprise he was accompanied, but by whom he did not know. Perhaps it was another board member or a solicitor from the law firm which advised the company on its commercial activities. But the stereotype image held in his mental eye didn't correspond with the person on Solomon's arm; as the pair approached he intuitively knew that the additional guest was the client's daughter Rebecca, the intended inheritor of control of London Commodities Ltd. Thomas stood to his feet and awaited the introduction. 'Thomas, good to see you again. I hope we've not kept you waiting long'. Solomon was smartly but modestly dressed and wore the same skullcap as he had at their earlier meeting. This was the outward sign to the world of his faith, the foundation stone of his soul. His few words of greeting conveyed the sincerity and unaffectedness which had so appealed to Thomas previously. 'I hope you'll not mind, but I've brought a guest with me. It's my pleasure to introduce to you my daughter, my only daughter, Rebecca. Rebecca, allow me to introduce Thomas Stoneacre, the exceptionally talented young man who's been advising me on future arrangements for our company'.

Solomon gestured towards his daughter and then to him. Rebecca Silverstein was beautiful; standing, like her father, not more than five foot five, her auburn hair was tied back, revealing an ivory complexion and striking hazel eyes. She wore a flowing light blue chiffon dress with an unobtrusive but stunning necklace of turquoises set in a gold lattice framework clinging tightly about her long neck. The neckline of her dress was modest, perhaps in deference to her father's orthodox sensitivities. 'I'm so pleased to meet you, Thomas. I've heard so much about you from my father'. He wanted to kiss the additional guest as he would in any other similar situation, but being uncertain of the appropriateness or otherwise of the gesture, decided instead to offer his hand. To his surprise she shook his hand and then kissed him on his cheek. Her face was cool with a subtle fragrance of an expensive Parisian perfume.

The party took up their places at the small table in the stall, engaging in small talk about the humid weather the Capital had been experiencing over the past few days. By the time they ordered, the conversation was already flowing, interspersed with laughter and whispered observations about colleagues at both Clements Accountants and London Commodities. Thomas was soon at ease; Solomon and Rebecca were easy and enjoyable company, and the flickering patterns thrown out by the candle on their table added to the magic of the evening. As they progressed through course after delicious course, it became strikingly obvious why Rebecca rather than the other two sons had been chosen to lead the company after her father's retirement. Her knowledge of the company's businesses was exceptional, as was her ability to explain the financial markets and the commodities futures exchanges on which it traded every second of every day. Her forceful personality, drive and determination shone throughout the evening while her proud father looked on. Thomas had learned an adapted twist on a popular saying from his father many years earlier, that the road to Hell is paved with first impressions; but tonight he felt sure that he was in the presence of genuine people who had not been corrupted in their morality or outlook by the great wealth their company's success had brought them.

None of the party took notice of the time as the evening rushed by, and suddenly he realised that whilst he'd been lost in his thoughts, lulled by the gentle background hum of the remaining guests whispering in other stalls, end of evening stillness had settled over the table. Solomon had not spoken for a while: he sat and looked at his daughter, but his thoughts were elsewhere. His face was shining in the candlelight but now showed a touch of sadness. He returned his gaze to the accountant and then picked up a piece of bread remaining on a side plate from an earlier course. 'In our tradition, Thomas, we call a simple loaf of bread 'Challah'. It used to be part of our custom that after kneading, a small piece of dough would be separated and burned, representing our obligation to the Kohanim or Priests, the descendants of Aaron, brother of Moses. We dip the bread in salt before eating; salt never decays and is symbolic of our eternal covenant with God. Before separating the Challah we offer this prayer; *Baruch atta Ado-noy Elo-hai-nu Melech ha'olam asher kid-e-sha-nu b'mitz-vo-tav v'tzi-vanu li-haf-rish Challah.* Blessed are you, Lord our God, King of the Universe, who has sanctified us with His commandments, and commanded us to separate Challah'. Thomas had not heard Hebrew spoken before, and listened to the melodic tone with which Solomon chanted the ancient prayer. There was a beauty in the simplicity and the gentleness of the words.

'When I break bread with friends I think on these words and remember my childhood in Warsaw'. In the flickering darkness Thomas felt a sense of intimacy, and the opening of a channel to distant places and long-past events. 'I'm honoured, sir, that you share your thoughts with me. I hope one day I'll have the privilege to be counted amongst your friends'. The old man continued: 'Do you know about the Uprisings?' Thomas had to admit that he had only a vague idea about them – at school he'd learned about the War from a very British perspective. He remembered stories about Dunkirk, the Battle of Britain and the Normandy landings, but not much else, and especially not the Eastern European tragedies which tended not to be taught much at all.

Solomon continued: 'On the night of April 18th 1943 my father, mother and I broke bread in our home in Wola, a district in Warsaw. My father recited the prayer of Challah, and after we'd eaten we stood in a candle-lit blacked-out room and just held each other. I remember my mother's heavy breathing in the silence as she tried to hold back her tears. She knew that the following day would probably be our last'. Rebecca, who had said nothing for some time, took her father's hand and held it gently. Nothing was said as he in turn clenched her hand and smiled. 'The following day, April 19th, the Uprising of the Jewish Ghetto of Warsaw began. Before this the Germans had deported 300,000 Jews from the Ghetto, but on the 19th, the Eve of the Passover, they'd decided to deport the remaining 60,000 inhabitants. I remember seeing Mordechai Anielewitz, the main instigator of the Uprising – he was the leader of Zydowska Organizacja Bojowa, the Jewish Fighting Organisation - screaming at a crowd a few days earlier. 'Shall we die like sheep driven to the slaughter, or like lions, proud on our final day of life?' We were certain that the trains that left the city regularly had been taking Jews to their deaths, but fear and hopelessness beget paralysis and a weariness of the soul. We were the last, the final group marked for deportation from the Ghetto, sleepwalking to extinction. How can I explain this to you, Thomas? Everywhere there was fear and bewilderment, nobody knowing what to do. But we all knew that soon enough our dwindling numbers in Warsaw would fall to nothing, as Himmler intended. Mordechai was killed in battle during this first Uprising on May 8th 1943. He was barely 24 years old and with life's table of riches laid out before him. But what's a lifetime of existence compared to death on the battlefield, on the outskirts of humanity where barbarism triumphs over the broken bones of countless thousands of corpses? My friend, I tell you these things so you'll understand what binds my family, my company and me to the past. Time is short, and the decision you must make this night will determine the continuance or destruction of the thread that runs between then and now'. Until then Thomas hadn't realised that there was a purpose to the disclosure of so many fragments of sadness. But now he began to realise that Solomon, one of the firm's most important clients, was about to change their client-advisor relationship.

'Your parents, did they survive?' 'On the first day of the Uprising my mother died lowering me to our fighters from the first floor of a building which had been shelled and was on fire. She'd been searching for children in the block. My last mental image of her was as I looked up from the street, only to see her fall backwards into the flames. The SS Major General, Stroop, had decided to burn every building in the Ghetto to drive out the 'insurgents'. I was taken by the men who caught me as I fell through the air to a bunker in another part of the city. There, my father had been coordinating communications between the fighters, drawing on knowledge he had gained in his pre-war career as an electrical engineer. When they told him his wife was dead he wept in silence. I'd never seen him cry before and never saw him do so again'.

The waiter, who'd been hovering between the remaining dinner parties' tables, appeared again to ask whether Solomon required further coffees. Thomas's attention was temporarily broken by the interruption. The old man smiled at the waiter; 'Thank you sir, but we've had enough. Your attentiveness this evening has been appreciated, and you're a credit to this restaurant'. The waiter thanked him for his words, genuinely appreciative of this first actual praise he'd received from any of the tables served during the evening. Thomas observed the brief exchange with incredulity; in the depths of his anguished recollections, Solomon still had the time, the need, to show respect to someone whom Thomas had not really noticed. The waiter departed, his spirits having been lifted by the personal compliment which would be followed by a generous tip when they left.

'The Ghetto Uprising ended on May 16th 1943. 60,000 Jews had been captured and deported to the death camps. 7,000 Jews died in the fighting, and the remaining Jewish inhabitants of Warsaw were deported in the months that followed. Nazi plans for a Jew-free Warsaw were near realisation, and as a symbol of the victory the Great Synagogue on Tlomacki Street, where I'd received my Bar-Mitzva a year earlier, was reduced to rubble. My father and I, together with a few dozen others, escaped from the centre of the fighting through the sewers. For the next 15 months we travelled through the countryside, given refuge in remote villages by supporters of the Polish Underground Home Army. Those were times of great kindness shown by Gentiles to Jews, even though by so doing they put their own lives and the lives of their families in terrible danger. Each day I live, I recall with gratitude the warmth shown by others in the midst of such brutality. By 1st August 1944 we'd returned to Warsaw where my father fought in the second Warsaw Uprising. He helped set up the underground radio station Blyskawica which communicated information to the fighters of the Home Army, while also keeping alive the flame of struggle in the people. In the first week of August 65,000 of the civilians in the districts captured by the Germans were executed. Between late August and early September over 30,000 civilians in Warsaw were killed; the Germans lost about 4,000. In the months following surrender by the Uprising's leader General Bor Komorowski in October '44, a further 600,000 inhabitants were deported to the death camps, 150,000 sent to forced labour camps in Germany. In January 1945 the Red Army entered Warsaw, ending the war, but beginning an occupation that lasted for the next 45 years'.

Thomas's scant school years knowledge of the Warsaw Uprising had been transformed by this chance to hear personal testimony. 'I can't begin to comprehend the brutality of that time but you, sir, and your father survived it, came out alive to bear witness to what happened. That counts for something'. Rebecca had remained silent whilst her father spoke but now intervened. 'My grandfather didn't survive, and was executed shortly after the surrender. Himmler ordered that all Warsaw inhabitants should be slaughtered and the city raised to the ground as a warning to other European capitals still under occupation'. Solomon turned back to Thomas. 'On October 1st a group of us were travelling for what seemed like miles through the sewer system beneath Warsaw, our main means of moving around. Due to a miscalculation by our group leader we emerged through a manhole cover into a street under German control. The group, twelve men and women, were stood in a line and all shot in the head, one by one. The defiance on my father's face was the last and most precious mental image I hold from that day. Three children, including myself, were taken to the *umslachger* or deportation centre, to be sent from there to the death camp in Gross Rosen in Eastern Germany. The camp was liberated by the Red Army in February '45, but I and another had escaped earlier, on October 18th '44. Escaped is perhaps the wrong word; we were smuggled out by one of the camp's female guards who'd been informed that we and the rest in our barracks were to be gassed the following day. She smuggled in her own children's clothes, we changed into these, and then she simply walked us out of the camp as if we were her own. Why she chose us I never found out, or indeed why we were not stopped at the gates. I guess others were involved in the conspiracy. She saved our lives: one glimmer of light in what must have been a wicked soul'.

'For the next few days we traveled in the back of farm trucks, wagons and lorries through the chaos in that part of Germany, desperate to get home but not really knowing how to do so. Fear and panic was everywhere, but we managed to slip through the Russian lines unmolested - immediately recognisable as victims of the Nazis, our striped uniforms had by extreme paradox saved our lives. Eventually we reached the advancing Americans, and at long last we were safe. Shortly afterwards I became attached as a translator to the occupying British Army in Berlin, and in December 1950 I left for Britain, gaining full citizenship in that year. To complete my story in brief, after several years' employment with a tea, metals, and grains brokerage, where I'd started as an office clerk who spoke broken English to eventually rise to take a seat on the board, I left to set up London Commodities Ltd in 1965. The company is my witness to those years of struggle'.

Thomas stared at the man with snow-white hair sitting in front of him, realising that the events described were not distant recollections but instead horrors as fresh as the day on which they'd taken place. Solomon's driving ambition was in part a product of his desire to give reason to his survival, a need to find justification when those closest to him had been murdered in front of his eyes. His faith had no doubt also been a sustaining force throughout the War and the years of hardship which followed. His determination that this faith, his family, and his company should continue into the future had a clarity, certainty and simplicity for which Thomas had unqualified respect.

'Thomas, do you trust me?' The question was unexpected. Thomas paused, not knowing how to respond. 'How do you mean, sir? I believe the accuracy of the events you describe. You are a witness to these'. 'Do you trust me?' Thomas was aware the evening's earlier atmosphere had changed, and that Solomon had moved from the past into the present in a single leap. His instinct was to become defensive, but he resisted this. 'Are you referring to our business relationship, to our roles as client and professional advisor? It's probably inappropriate for me to say anything at this stage. It's too early to have formed a professional view since I haven't been through your company's accounts yet. My Managing Partner's always advised me that personal and professional instincts should be kept separate'. Thomas hated himself for his evasiveness. 'Do you trust me?' The client asked gently for what the young man knew would be the last time. 'Yes, I trust you'. The old man closed his eyes. 'Thank you'.

After a few seconds' pause, the old man's eyes reopened; he then spoke in a firm and measured way, with neither urgency nor hesitancy. 'Thomas, I've mentioned before that my two sons Nathaniel and Isaac are weak in matters of business, even though they've taken significant roles until recently in the daily management of the company. I of course take full responsibility for having allowed personal preference take precedence over commercial wisdom. Today London Commodities is on the brink of collapse due to foolish decisions they made three months ago, mistakes which were deliberately concealed from Rebecca and me'. Thomas felt a physical reaction as if emersed in a bath of ice water; suddenly he realised he had to awaken from the dulled state into which he'd gently settled during the evening. Now he had to have his professional wits about him and listen closely to what the client was about to explain.

'In an attempt to significantly increase the company's profitability my sons, in concert with a small group of other brokers, embarked upon a strategy to control the price of one of the main commodities in which we are active traders, copper. The strategy failed, leaving us with huge short term borrowings and unhedged positions in the futures markets. The consequences of this have not yet impacted upon the company, and while we're now technically insolvent there is a prospect, as Rebecca will explain, that the company may survive if there's a confluence of events in the way we anticipate'. Thomas stared at him, barely able to respond coherently. 'If I'm to help I need to know the extent of this exposure. As you know, my firm's been engaged to audit the company's activities over the next few weeks. I'm due to start collecting information tomorrow morning in preparation for the full audit. Bearing in mind what you've just told me, I'll need all the paperwork, the details of futures contracts, and so on, if the extent of the company's difficulties is to be properly recorded in the accounts'.

Solomon's daughter, who had listened intently to the discussion without showing any outward sign of concern, now spoke with the same firmness and decisiveness as had her father. 'My brothers' intention was to monopolise both the physicals and futures markets in copper. Regarding the former, through our agents around the world they made substantial purchases of the commodity, stockpiling it in warehouses. The purchases were made with short-term high interest loans the company took out with private banks. Payment of interest has been funded from the company's cash reserves which now stand at virtually nil, plus further loans from finance houses of which the banks are not aware'. Thomas was shocked by the scale of the mismanagement. 'So the company was borrowing to pay interest on its existing borrowings?' 'That is correct. The company continued trading when it knew that it was technically insolvent. In other words, we were trading fraudulently.' Solomon re-entered the discussion. 'The activities in the physicals market alone would have been sufficient to destroy the company, but our exposure was magnified by the strategy simultaneously pursued in the futures markets'. Rebecca's technical knowledge was greater than that of her father's and, accordingly, she could explain more precisely the scale of the company's problems.

'The potential losses for a company left holding a futures contract which nobody wants to buy because the market to which it relates is in freefall, are huge'. Thomas knew that futures and options came in standardised contracts, the majority with fixed dates by which the obligation or entitlement had to be honoured or exercised. 'The futures contracts your brothers bought - when will the company have to honour them?' 'My brothers built up massive long positions which become due over the next two, five and eight months. Nathaniel funded margin calls on the contracts by borrowing from the same banks that funded the purchases of the physicals, but through separate companies which we control. When the contracts fall due, unless we can get out of them, the company will have to take delivery of the copper to which each contract relates: that's the essence of being long. We would then have to sell into a falling market, and that's when we'd suffer unsustainable losses. And because the market's been falling recently, we cannot find buyers at present for our long futures positions. The original plan was that prices would rise because London Commodities would withhold copper supplies from the market; we would have bought the contracts at a low price and sold later, high'.

'The problem for us is that prices have been falling during past weeks, sending the value of our long positions into a tailspin. Our position deteriorates by the day. Nathaniel and Isaac intended repaying the the money borrowed to buy up the long positions using profits on the sales of the contracts they'd make in a rising market. But despite their efforts to manipulate the physicals market through buying up huge quantities of copper, they just couldn't get control of the price'.

Thomas continued to be shocked by the revelations as Rebecca explained the full implications of the failed strategy. 'I can't understand how this situation has come about. Surely you or your father realised that the company's trading strategy could lead to financial disaster?'

Solomon smiled. 'Nathaniel was responsible for the 'front end' of our activities, the purchasing of the futures contracts, Isaac the 'back office', or the documentation of trades on a daily basis. They camouflaged the transactions by setting up a bogus 'client' account. So, it appeared that these positions had not been taken by us - they were not exposures on our own books - but were financial risks held by a third party. We only discovered the truth about the bogus account a week ago. I've allowed my sons to continue in their present positions in title alone, but in reality they no longer have any influence in the company. To fire them would risk attracting attention, when at this stage we need to present a 'business as usual' image'.

Thomas had now composed his thoughts and identified the steps that he, as the company's auditor, would need to take. He would need to try first to restore some sense of professional distance between himself and the client. 'As you know, I'm due to start work with you tomorrow, and the question will be how to reflect in the accounts the extent of the risk the company's burdened with. First we must inform the London Metals Exchange that your futures positions are unhedged. The bogus client account will also have to be disclosed. Second, we'll need to report all risk exposure in a provisional balance sheet my firm will prepare. I have a professional and ethical obligation to ensure that any statements we issue are accurate and not misleading. Third, and perhaps the most difficult for you Solomon, we'll need to consider appointment of outsiders to your board so that both the Exchange as well as the banks retain confidence in the company'

He silently congratulated himself on the practicality of his recommendations. After reflecting upon these proposals, however, and recognising them as futile before they'd even been finished, Solomon responded. 'Thomas, I asked you earlier if you trust me. In two months' time, one month after our accounts have been made public, a major shock originating in South America will shatter the global copper market. One of the principal Chilean producers, F.P. Huerez, will file for protection under the country's bankruptcy laws. The reserves the company has been claiming will be revealed as non-existent, a lie. Its mines will be exhausted within three months, and not in the five years forecast in its last set of accounts'. Thomas decided against asking how the inside information had been obtained. 'If this information is correct, how will it affect your business?' The question was directed at Solomon but answered by Rebecca. 'Industrial users of copper will boost their stock levels as a matter of urgency in anticipation of a shortage as Huerez withdraws as a major supplier to the market. We'll unload stock we currently hold at a significant profit. Loans taken out to make these purchases in the first place will be paid off immediately. We'll close out all our futures positions by selling the contracts to other brokers, realising a massive gain'.

Thomas understood Rebecca's prediction, but didn't see how this could protect the company from the effects of the disclosures which would have to be made in the accounts in a few weeks' time. 'If correct, this information will benefit your company in the medium term but with respect, both of you know that as soon as the current position is reported the banks will panic and demand repayment of all loans. The company will also be suspended by the Exchange. I don't see how this information changes anything from my perspective as company auditor'.

Solomon continued. 'Thomas, the company's survival is now in your hands. I told you about Warsaw: the thread which runs from that time through to this night will either be severed now or continue into the future. Our future will be determined by you'. Thomas stared into Solomon's piercing blue eyes; his decision would have to be made on the basis of emotion, on unqualified trust, rather than on an accountant's dispassionate evaluation of a desperate situation. He spoke calmly, masking the trembling of uncertainty which he felt building inside. 'What do you want me to do?'

'Tomorrow you're due to inspect the company's internal accounts. You'll discover the fictitious client account, since my sons' attempts at concealment were amateur. I ask you now to continue this fiction and not consolidate the risk into the company accounts'. 'And if your information about the Chilean copper producer is wrong, what then?' He already knew the answer to his question. 'You know what will happen. London Commodities will collapse within days. Most of the banks will lose the money they've lent to the company, and some may not survive. Your firm will be sued for professional negligence, and it will lose. You will lose your job, becoming unemployable in your profession. My sons will go to jail. Probably, I will go to jail'. Thomas forced a smile. 'Solomon, I hope you'll accept this criticism in the spirit in which it's made, but your powers of persuasion leave a lot to be desired'. Another day, another week, in which to make the decision wouldn't make a difference; he had to decide that night for there still to be a valid choice of paths. 'I will trust you, Solomon. I will do as you ask. Please don't fail me'. Rebecca placed her hand over Thomas's, but said nothing. 'A Jew's debt to a Gentile has the highest value. I promise I'll not fail you'. The evening drew to a close with this new alliance forged.

The following day Thomas returned to London Commodities Ltd's offices and began work. A few days later he reported back to the Managing Partner at Clements that profits had increased from the previous year and the company was continuing to follow a prudent trading strategy. The bogus account was not even mentioned. The firm duly issued unqualified and glowing accounts within the month. Three weeks later the global copper market experienced its worst crisis for thirty years; one of the largest Chilean producers had filed for bankruptcy protection after dishonestly declaring inaccurate reserves for the past five years. Market expectations were that its ability to supply copper would continue for a further three months, and not the five years forecast in the most recent set of accounts. The value of copper inventories held in warehouses around the globe skyrocketed on the news. Brokers scoured the derivatives market for holders of long positions in copper futures contracts willing to sell to industrial users who were now desperate to hedge against price instability. Market analysts singled out Solomon Silverstein, Chairman of London Commodities, for his farsightedness, his business acumen, and his ability to survive in a volatile and unpredictable world.

Chapter Twenty One

'Mr. Creed, I'm surprised you're making this application, not only because of its lateness, but also bearing in mind the character of the person to whom it relates'. Roger Pitt, the Prosecution solicitor who was attending the private hearing in the judge's chambers and the person whom Adam would later take to dinner at an exclusive restaurant in Mayfair, noted the tone of disapproval. Now he'd pitch in to the conversation which until then had been proceeding entirely between Mr. Justice Maplethorpe and his opponent in the case. 'Your Honour, we firmly oppose this application to move Silas Coughlin from Pentonville Prison to an open prison. Indeed we repeatedly asked Mr. Creed not to proceed with it, but unfortunately to no avail. Given the hopelessness of the application we respectfully request that an order for wasted costs be made'. 'Your Honour, with respect to Mr. Pitt, my client has been subjected to bullying at Pentonville, and we have grounds to believe that his life may be in danger. For this reason alone we make this application, knowing that it will be considered with your customary sense of fairness'.

Mr. Justice Maplethorpe, an old Etonian and a veteran of the Coldstream Guards, paused: it was important to give the impression of dutiful consideration of both arguments. He loathed these late Friday afternoon applications and the lawyers who made them. He looked at Adam and felt intimidated. The prosecuting solicitor was like all the rest in the Crown Prosecution Service who appeared before him: a silly little man, weak in presentation and lacking in either presence or courtesy. But the defendant's solicitor was a different animal; there was something unsettling about him. He also dressed well; never a good sign, often indicating a propensity to appeal against one's ruling. He would need to tread carefully. As he squinted over his glasses he gazed into the young man's piercing grey eyes and disliked him even more. 'Mr. Creed, there's no way on Earth I'm going to allow this application. Quite apart from the serious nature of the offences with which your client's been charged, the police have intimated there's a strong possibility he'd interfere with the legal process. More specifically, he would intimidate witnesses. This application should never have been made, and you must have known it was doomed to fail. The application is dismissed, with a wasted costs order. Good afternoon, gentlemen'.

Roger Pitt nonchalantly replaced the papers into his barely used leather attaché case. This was the first application he'd won all week - and against a solicitor from Roxburgh Thymes! Back at the office he'd feast on this victory for at least another week. 'Well done, Roger. It's not often we lose an application like this, so it's a feather in your cap for sure. I've booked a table at the Hilton for 6.30 this evening. I thought we'd take a taxi direct from here, have some drinks in the bar, and then go in for the meal. Are you still okay for this?' The innocent, naïve Prosecution lawyer hesitated. 'I should get back to work just to drop off these papers and check I'm not needed for anything on Monday morning. But I guess it can wait…. After all, it's Friday and I deserve to celebrate today's success, don't I?'

Adam smiled; he'd known all along that the application would be dismissed, and indeed had not even told the client he was going to make it. What was important was that he and a briefcase full of crucial information guarded by a blissfully innocent Prosecution lawyer would be sharing each other's company for the next few hours. The two lawyers arrived at the hotel at 5.30pm after a twenty-minute taxi journey through Central London at peak rush hour. For the next hour Adam ensured that his guest's glass was constantly refreshed with one of the stronger wines from the hotel's cellar. Pitt was in an optimistic, excited state of mind; after a drought of success in court appearances in recent months, at long last he had something positive to report back to his boss. The two spoke frankly about their respective employers, the relaxed atmosphere encouraging a less inhibited, more critical perspective on Pitt's part. He'd been unable to refuse the 'top ups' his dining partner had been pushing his way as they chatted aimlessly in the bar, and this had loosened his tongue. He wasn't drunk, yet, but when the time arrived for the two to move to their table in the adjoining restaurant he was feeling too free and easy for his own good.

'So why did you go for a career in law, Roger? What attracted you to the CPS instead of private practice? It can't have been the pay!' The inebriated lawyer drained the last drop from his glass but thought it polite to hesitate for a few minutes before reaching for the bottle for a refresher. 'On your second question, I joined the CPS because I just wasn't good enough to survive in private practice. Simple as that. I'm not a good lawyer. I'm below average, maybe not by much, but the managers who appraise me are pretty hopeless too, so they couldn't spot a bad lawyer anyway'. Adam was startled by the admission, even though it merely confirmed what he already felt about state prosecutors generally. 'On your first question as to why a career in law, the answer's also simple. I've believed since I was a child that law brings social progress and justice, so if I could play a part in the legal system, then this would be my contribution. I guess this is my way of trying to do some good in the world'.

He began slurring his words as the wine finally tipped over the boat of his mental faculties, drowning his ability to articulate thoughts with any sense of coherence. Adam listened closely; the person for whom he previously had contempt had a depth to his character belied by the creased suit and lack of presence exhibited at the hearing earlier that day. His struggle to make even a small difference unsettled Adam as he reflected upon his own abandonment of ethical and professional principles. He lacked Pitt's moral clarity on the one hand, and Coughlin's focused amoral purpose and ruthlessness on the other. The two extremes highlighted his existence in a sort of no-man's land of lost conscience. In different circumstances, he thought, they could have been friends.

As they awaited the final course a waiter arrived at the table. 'Mr. Pitt, there's a courier waiting for you in reception. He's here to deliver some papers from a Mr. Watts at your office. Sorry to disturb you, but the package has to be signed for'. The lawyer looked startled; quickly he stood up, straightening his tie and throwing down his napkin as he clumsily pushed back his chair. 'Looks like a weekend court application, and guess who's been lumbered with it? Sorry; unusual for the office to send paperwork this late, but at least it shows the out of hours diary system works. Back soon.' He rushed after the waiter who led him down a flight of stairs, across a crowded lobby, to a reception desk where nobody awaited him. Saul, the mystery courier, had left as soon as the concierge disappeared from view; as far as he was concerned this was just a practical joke played by Adam on a work colleague. In recent weeks he'd felt that his friend was too preoccupied with work, too serious-minded; a light-hearted prank was therefore a good sign.

Adam calmly picked up Pitt's attaché case. It was not locked. Without hesitation he clicked open the clasp, pulled out the manila file he'd seen in the judge's chambers, and quickly started thumbing through its contents. There were dozens of pages of accounts headed with company names he recognised from his previous conferences with Coughlin. There were also letters from the investigating officer, Chief Inspector Ian Slansfield, in which Coughlin's violent antecedents were documented in detail. He'd evidently been trying to secure a conviction for several years, his personal obsession immediately apparent from the tone in his correspondence. There were also sworn affidavits from Andreas Melas giving details of his responsibilities while he was employed as chief accountant to Coughlin's business. But these were not the documents for which Adam was searching. And then he found what he'd been looking for: the single piece of information for which the client was willing to pay £150,000.

The e-mail headed 'Information re intra group dividend payments' contained a list of questions from Pitt's line manager at the CPS, Frank Watts, and was addressed to **AMelas123@abacab.net.** Adam wrote down the address on the taxi receipt he'd been given earlier and then replaced the file as dexterously as he'd withdrawn it. By the time the CPS lawyer returned Adam's mission had been accomplished. The disheveled lawyer slid back into his chair, perplexed rather than irritated. 'That was strange. Someone asked for me at reception but when I got there he'd disappeared. If it was a courier and he was in a hurry, I'm sure he'd have left any papers intended for me. I don't understand it. Perhaps I should give the office a call later'. By now the threads of their earlier conversation had been lost; within quarter of an hour they left and went their separate ways.

The following day Adam sat in front of the computer in his room at Roxburgh Thymes, the cursor hovering over 'send' to the e-mail address Coughlin had provided at their previous meeting. The message contained Andreas Melas's e-mail address and nothing else. He always needed to know all potential consequences of his actions but on this occasion he was unsure. What was the greatest harm if he sent Melas's address to one of Coughlin's henchmen? At worst he would probably just receive a threatening e-mail or an offer of a bribe to withdraw his testimony. He closed his eyes and clicked, sending the address off into the ether. Later that evening, in a dingy two-star hotel on the outskirts of London, Andreas Melas logged onto to the internet in his dimly lit room. He'd just eaten with his two Special Branch minders and was relaxed despite an inner fear that was gathering pace as the date fixed for the trial approached. He was to be the principal witness for the Prosecution but had been promised a new identity and a substantial payment with which to start a new life afterwards. But still, he was afraid.

Suddenly a chat window opened on the computer screen. 'Good evening Andreas. Silas sends his regards'. He froze in terror as a list of names and addresses then scrolled down before him; these were his brothers and sisters, his nieces and nephews, back in Malta, and now they were in terrible danger. The list came to an end with a simple but chilling warning. 'Their lives are in your hands.' The window closed, leaving no evidence of the 'break in'. The Maltese accountant slumped back and switched off the desk light. He knew what had to be done.

Chapter Twenty Two

Adam stood and bowed his head as Mr. Justice Andrew Peterson entered Courtroom Number Three in the case of the Crown versus Silas Coughlin. He'd appeared before Peterson on several previous occasions and knew him to be a judge of exceptional intellectual powers. He was at least six foot four in height, and in the full judicial garb of scarlet robe and purple sash was an impressive presence in the courtroom. Adam glanced around at the principal actors in the play about to commence. Andrew Cannon-Smith QC sat immediately in front of Adam, adjusting his wig before proceedings got underway. There was a sheaf of perfectly organised papers in front of him but by this late stage he had no need to look at them, apart from the occasional glance to remind him of the awfulness of the defendant he now represented. This was a brief he'd mastered several weeks ago although his mind was made up months before then, after his first meeting with the defendant. His face was puce and his gimlet eyes searched around the courtroom for familiar faces. He smiled at the judge: they'd first met eight years ago and had been good friends for the past five. A week earlier they'd taken lunch together, although the impending case had not, of course, been discussed.

Roger Pitt sat to Adam's left, wearing the same suit he'd worn at the previous court appearance. He smiled at Adam and mouthed silently 'good luck'. Adam smiled back: 'You too'. He felt uncomfortable with every aspect of the case, and knew that without a shadow of a doubt he'd perverted the course of justice by passing on the information he'd stolen from Pitt to Coughlin's associate. A conviction for this alone would see him imprisoned for several years, but it was his inability to accurately calculate all the possible consequences of the theft itself that most unsettled him. Usually, he could anticipate the outcome of a case in which he was the representing solicitor, subject of course to the caprices of a jury-based system; but in this he couldn't even be sure how his client would perform.

177

Would he come up to proof or would his latent violence come bursting forth like some oil strike during a rigorous cross-examination?

The Crown had appointed William Harcourt QC to handle the case, a barrister renowned for his abrasive style and formidable knowledge of the finer points of evidence. He now sat in front of Pitt, thumbing through the witness statements to heighten his state of readiness. His determination to succeed in this case would easily eclipse that of Cannon-Smith, whose commitment to the principle of a fair trial was at best questionable and at worst positively hostile. Adam surmised that there'd been some indirect communication by Coughlin with the Prosecution's principal witness but had no way of knowing what form it had taken. Probably a bribe had been offered, but whether this had been accepted was another unknown. Would the jury be influenced by the presence of destitute pensioners sitting in the visitors' gallery, waiting for the justice of a guilty verdict? For a few seconds he placed his head in his hands whilst a torrent of imponderables swirled through his thoughts. He'd not been in this position before, at the mercy of events.

Coughlin sat down in the dock, resentful at being obliged to follow court custom of standing to his feet in respect for the judge. He hated them all. He despised the rituals of the courtroom and the polite chatter between solicitors and barristers who were supposed to be on opposite sides but in truth owed their loyalty to no-one. He mused to himself that in the unlikely event that he was convicted, he'd be taken down to the cells to await return to Pentonville while they headed off to some swanky winebar in the West End to celebrate the outcome, and soon forget all about it. It was all just a game to them, a game in which the reality was that neither the Prosecution nor the Defence ever lost in any true sense of the word. The client always paid, sometimes just with money, more often with his liberty. He smiled as he stared ahead, concealing his hatred from members of the jury now sneaking glances from the other side of the courtroom. He recalled Adam's advice in their meeting in the cells earlier that morning: 'Look straight ahead, don't stare at the jury, and show respect for the court'.

For a moment his mind returned to an earlier court appearance. He was 15 when he first stood before a judge but then it had been for a more 'honest' crime, a stabbing in a rundown backstreet in the East End. He remembered it well: rain splashing on his white face, water forcing its way along clogged gutters, crunching glass underfoot from a broken streetlamp, and blood - lots of blood. He'd stood over the bleeding, squirming body with the flick knife smoking in his hand, but nothing was said. He remembered the silence; neither he nor the victim had made a sound. The truth was that although the local loan shark had told him to 'put the frighteners' on the unemployed middle aged debtor, he'd wanted to finish the job, to plunge the blade in again and again. But it was self-control that night, and a large dose of luck, that had saved him, just, from an even longer period of incarceration.

'I call Chief Inspector Ian Slansfield'. The defendant's inward eye instantly switched from past events to the play now commencing before him. William Harcourt had called his first witness, the Scotland Yard high flier who'd eventually arrested Coughlin after years of dogged pursuit. The tall, impeccably dressed detective entered the witness box and took the familiar oath: his heart was racing. He adjusted his pale blue double-knotted tie, smiled towards the defendant, and awaited Harcourt's questions. 'Chief Inspector Slansfield, could you tell the court how long you've been with Scotland Yard?' 'I joined the Metropolitan Police as a 'bobby on the beat' twenty years ago. I started in Brixton and after ten years transferred over to Scotland Yard'. Harcourt's priority was to establish the witness's credentials with the jury and more importantly, his professional integrity.

After fully apprising the jury of Slansfield's 'impeccable' record, his commitment to the local community and his pursuit of justice and fairness, Harcourt fired his closing shot. 'What would you say are the personal qualities required of a person aspiring to high rank in the police force today, Chief Inspector?' The witness paused, the jury foreman leaned forward, and the defendant closed his eyes. 'I believe that in today's cynical world the police must abide by two fundamental principles: impartiality in the collection of evidence, and absolute adherence to the presumption of innocence until proof of guilt. Public confidence will only be maintained if we observe both the letter and the spirit of these principles'. Harcourt looked at the jury and noted with satisfaction that several members were nodding in concurrence. He'd established the witness's credentials: now, on to the detail of the case. 'Please tell us, Chief Inspector, what you discovered in your investigations about the defendant's role in the Delphi Investment Corporation, and his connection with the Gandalph Trust. What was it that first brought his activities to your attention - that gave you a cause for concern about the financial interests of the investors?'

'For a year we'd been investigating the defendant's activities in connection with a Switzerland-based trust, the Gandalph Trust. We'd received details of complaints via another agency from investors who'd placed their life savings with a UK financial services provider, the Delphi Investment Corporation, only to see their money reduced to virtually nothing overnight, ostensibly because of 'a downturn in the domestic economic climate', or so they were told'. 'What was the true nature of the defendant's association with Gandalph? Delphi must have been authorised by the UK financial services regulator, so why was it permitted to continue trading when its performance was hopeless and its relationship with Gandalph was at the very best questionable, and at worst downright suspect?' The Prosecution witness explained how he came to eventually unravel the full extent of the Gandalf-Delphi relationship. In Companies House he discovered that Gandalph owned seventy five percent of Delphi's share capital, the remainder held by Swiss nominee shareholders. He made several trips to Switzerland, Gandalph's place of incorporation, where he was provided with an avalanche of documentation by the local intelligence agencies. All the shares in Gandalph were in turn owned by a Panama-based corporation, the true ownership of which it had been impossible to ascertain.

'The UK regulator knew of the irregular nature of the relationship between Delphi and Gandalph - we'd specifically warned them about it for a number of months. But Delphi was permitted to continue trading because of the presence of 'noteworthies' on the company's board of directors. Also, the defendant had no direct association with Gandalph that we could prove. Its directors were local Swiss nationals - lawyers and accountants - who ensured that the company complied with legal formalities whilst at the same time implementing the instructions of the true owner, the defendant. Coughlin was not on the board. There was a single shareholder in Gandalph: a Panamanian-registered company'. For the next half hour Harcourt took the jury on a guided tour of exotic offshore tax havens with the aid of a large multi-coloured, multi-arrowed map pinned to an easel in front of them. At each stage the flow of funds was explained simply but damningly by a running commentary provided by Chief Inspector Slansfield. The closing questions for him from the Prosecution were now at hand.

'Chief Inspector, can you explain to the jury what eventually led you to arrest the defendant? You appear to have had substantial proof of his guilt for several months prior to this, so why the delay? His culpability for fraud was staring you in the face and yet you did nothing. Can you explain this?' Slansfield smiled: now he could lodge in the jury's collective mind an unshakable belief that this was a case without a grain of procedural or evidential irregularity. He continued with his perfectly measured and convincing testimony. 'We had to be sure we had the right man. We had to gather the evidence, review it, and where possible identify witnesses who would be willing and unafraid to come forward to testify and prove what we suspected. It was vitally important that this guilty man should not escape conviction on a technicality'.

Mr. Justice Peterson leaned forward, a shaft of light breaking through a stained window at the rear of the court to illuminate his bright red robes. 'Chief Inspector, it is for the jury and not for you to decide issues of guilt or innocence. Your function is to gather in and present the evidence and not to express your personal opinion upon it'. The witness jumped as if stung by the lazy wasp that had hovered above the jury for the past hour, terrorising some of its members whenever its orbit dropped below a certain parallel. 'I apologise, your Lordship. I'm fully aware of my role in this trial. I'll continue to observe the utmost impartiality'. 'Good. I suggest that you do. Now, please continue'.

'Six months ago we obtained a search warrant for the defendant's office. When we searched the premises we found paperwork proving that sums extracted by Gandalph for, and I quote, management charges, marketing support and investment guidance, were not represented by the provision of any actual services to Delphi. They were just a device used to strip out the company's reserves and investors' savings. There were also a number of dividend payments made by Delphi to its Swiss parent, but – and this is very important - these had been paid from capital and not from profits, which were non-existent anyway. The capital base was being stolen via dividend payments made to Gandalph. We know from our Swiss colleagues that as soon as the funds passed across, they were then moved again to Gandalph's Panamanian shareholder, by the same device. By the time we arrested Coughlin, Delphi's bank accounts had been emptied'.

William Harcourt recognised the flaw in the Prosecution's evidence when he'd first read the brief: now he would deal with it head on. 'Chief Inspector, the documentation you describe is indeed crucial, but how could you be sure that the defendant was the mastermind behind this complex relationship between the two companies, and for that matter that the Panamanian shareholder was he? Did any of the documents bear a signature, an imprimatur if you will: something which connected the defendant personally to any of the transactions? And what about control of Gandalph; where was the proof that he was the true owner of the shares? From what you've said, they were properly owned by a Panamanian corporation. So where's the smoking gun?'

This was the difficulty the prosecuting barrister faced: the defendant had signed none of the documents. Slansfield looked towards the dock and then continued. 'During our search we found a share transfer form showing that Gandalph held the Delphi shares as the defendant's nominee; the shares were held on his behalf. We found further documentation showing that Gandalph's shares, the shares held by the Panamanian corporation, were in fact in bearer form. These were pledged as security by the defendant for a loan taken out with a Luxembourg-based private bank. This was the connection, the proof of ownership, which we'd been looking for'.

Harcourt continued, confident that his witness would now deliver the coup de grace. 'Chief Inspector, whilst the defendant's beneficial ownership of Gandalph's shares may have been established, you have still to prove that he has personal responsibility for the transactions which ultimately led to Delphi's demise. That he deliberately transferred investors' money, to use a helpful analogy, from one pocket in his coat, Delphi Investment Corporation, to another pocket in the same coat, Gandalph. Are you able to lift the corporate veil, so to speak, to prove that he, rather than the company itself, was in control of its decision-making processes? Surely it was Delphi's board and not the defendant who controlled the day to day business?' Slansfield recognised the prompt: now was the time to introduce the Prosecution's principal 'inside' witness in the case.

'Fortunately someone came forward, a witness at the heart of the defendant's empire, who gave us the vital information we needed. Andreas Melas, the defendant's personal accountant for over ten years, attended all Delphi's board meetings and had detailed knowledge of the transfers to Gandalph. He took his instructions directly from the defendant and negotiated the terms of the loan with the Luxembourg bank. Mr. Melas's inside knowledge pulled the whole structure together'. 'So, Andreas Melas's evidence was crucial in the decision to make the arrest, would you agree?' 'Yes. His evidence, combined with the evidence we uncovered during our search'.

After a further twenty minutes of technical questioning, William Harcourt concluded the examination-in-chief of one of the two principal witnesses in the case for the Prosecution. As he awaited cross-examination, Chief Inspector Slansfield's thoughts wandered as he reflected upon the previous night's unpleasantness. He'd visited Patricia at 8.00pm prompt, as he'd done Monday and Wednesday nights for the past six months. At 9.00pm he put the usual two fifty pound notes on the pillow as he got dressed and prepared to return to his wife, arriving home again by 10.00pm. Her friends were impressed that the marriage was strong enough to withstand the overtime demands placed upon him by his high position at the Yard. But this was one of the sacrifices that had to be made: a successful career brought heavy responsibilities at the expense of family life, at least in the short term. But last night Patricia (he'd never enquired about her real name) announced that she wanted more from the relationship than he was prepared to give. As far as he was concerned it was merely a commercial transaction, a trade, and she'd been happy with the arrangement until now, or at least had seemed to be. But now she wanted to be treated as a 'companion', to be taken out to wine bars and fancy restaurants and not hidden away in a dingy tenement block on the outskirts of London. Yes, they would need to talk during his next 'visit'.

Cannon-Smith's cross-examination was as limp and soulless as Adam had anticipated. He went through the motions, querying technical aspects of Slansfield's evidence, but as Adam switched his attention across to the jury he knew they were bored. They'd lost interest and the fidgeting, coughing, yawning and blinking dry eyes all pointed towards a lost case. The barrister was not an emotional man; that much was obvious. He was not someone with 'court presence', an ability to hold a jury in the palm of his hand and present key issues in a simple, easily understood form. But in this case his prejudice against the defendant manifested itself in the 'easy ride' he afforded to the Chief Inspector. After half an hour of adding precisely no new insight, the portly, disinterested barrister dismissed the witness. He dabbed his face with a fragrant white handkerchief as he turned to the solicitor with a look of embarrassment and, strangely, brazenness. The reality was that he didn't care; indeed, in a subterranean cavern of his mind he harboured a desire to lose.

Adam knew the outcome of the case would depend upon two factors. First, whether the principal witness for the Prosecution, Andreas Melas, would come up to proof. Second, and perhaps more importantly, whether the defendant would be able to keep his temper, keep his mouth shut, and not frighten the jury with an outburst. It was the latter of the two which was more worrying and, for that reason, the most dangerous to the case. After a further fifteen minutes of re-examination by Harcourt in which Slansfield's credibility was reinforced and minor evidential 'creases' ironed out, the court adjourned for lunch.

The defendant was led out of the dock and returned to the cells. It was only the stenographer, a grey haired sixty-something year old woman who'd worked in the court service for the past twenty years, who noticed on his face the look of a man who knew he couldn't lose. She'd not understood the complicated business of offshore trusts, illegal funds transfers and so on, but she was a shrewd judge of character. That evening her husband would ask her the same question he always asked at the end of a case: did the defendant do it? She would give her answer without hesitation: yes he did but no, he'll not be convicted. As she closed down her steno machine she was sure that, for a fleeting second, he looked at her. She even thought he winked at her. She pulled her jacket about her and shuddered.

Adam stood as Mr. Justice Peterson re-entered the courtroom. For once in his professional life he felt nervous and unprepared. The morning had been a disaster. The first witness for the Prosecution had been impressive and yet his own man, Cannon-Smith, had been almost negligent in his representation of Coughlin's interests. Events were now threatening to spin even further out of control; another well-rehearsed witness would soon take the stand, to be followed by the only witness for the Defence, Coughlin himself. His violent antecedents, his past convictions, would then be rolled out by William Harcourt during cross-examination for the jury to see and be horrified by. Whilst awaiting

Melas's arrival Adam reflected upon his failure to talk Coughlin out of taking the stand. He had a right to remain silent, to force the Prosecution to prove the case against him, and yet he was determined to enter the box and have his say, his rant at the world.

Harcourt slowly stood to his feet, exuding confidence. The time had arrived to call the witness who would crystalise the defendant's guilt in the jurors' minds before they'd even left the courtroom to deliberate. He licked his lips in anticipation. In contrast to the state of heightened expectation inside Courtroom Number Three, Andreas Melas sat outside the closed heavy doors with a sense of dread and resignation. He'd been rolling his pale yellow tie for the past half hour, trembling with fear, knowing that the time was close at hand to bring the sky down upon the proceedings. There would be acrimony, of course, recriminations, and a spitting contempt from Chief Inspector Slansfield. But blood had to be thicker than justice; he thought of his family before he walked into court.

Adam looked at the short, dapper, balding man as he entered the witness box and was afraid. He knew from experience that quiet little men could single-handedly destroy the mightiest of corporations, politicians, or defendants with gently spoken truths delivered to a jury willing to listen. After a few preliminary questions intended to put an obviously nervous witness at ease, William Harcourt turned the focus of his examination-in-chief to the detail of the case. 'Mr. Melas, we've established that you were employed as the chief accountant to the Delphi Investment Corporation since the company's incorporation, and that during this time you were also responsible for oversight of its relationship with its principal shareholder, the Gandalph Trust. Are you able to confirm this to the jury?' 'That is correct. I was privy to all decisions regarding investment of clients' funds, and transfers of moneys to our parent company, Gandalph.' The witness spoke precisely and without nervousness.

Harcourt continued. 'With regard to these transfers, it is the Prosecution's contention that these were part of the defendant's dishonest and fraudulent strategy. Their real purpose was to siphon out investors' monies from Delphi, pass them over to Gandalph, and then out again to Gandalph's sole Panamanian shareholder. It is our contention that the true owner of the shares in Gandalph was, in fact, the defendant himself. You were privy to all of these transfers and indeed your signature appears on all instructions to Delphi's bank. In the statement you made to the police you said, and I quote, 'These transfers were merely a device by which clients' funds could be misappropriated'. Please could you describe the defendant's complicity in this complex series of transactions, better described as a 'scam'?' Harcourt glanced across at the jury; this last word was simple and understandable and would lodge in the mind of the most uneducated of onlookers. The witness hesitated, and then looked straight ahead at the defendant in the dock: Coughlin returned the stare.

'Gandalph had incurred substantial costs in connection with Delphi in terms of administrative support, marketing, and provision of expertise. The payments made by Delphi to Gandalph were not in my view disproportionate to the services rendered'. Harcourt had been relaxed until this point, even nonchalant, but his reaction now was of a man shot. His knowing gaze switched instantly from the jury to the fidgeting witness.

He would try another approach. 'It's been suggested that the Swiss-based shareholder in Delphi, the Gandalph Trust, was in fact the defendant's nominee. The shares were held on behalf of the defendant who in reality owned the company outright. Indeed a blank share transfer form was found during a search of the defendant's business premises, signed by the nominee shareholder, naming the defendant as the future transferee. Gandalph's seventy five percent shareholding enabled funds to be extracted from Delphi via fraudulent transfers. The truth regarding the defendant's ownership of the Gandalph shares is established by the fact that he used them as security for a loan he raised from a Luxembourg-based bank. Who was the true owner of the shares in Gandalph? How did the defendant manage to raise such a large sum of money, five hundred thousand pounds, from the Luxembourg bank with which he didn't even hold an account?'

Harcourt had delicately avoided an allegation of leading the witness, but any barrister other than Cannon-Smith would have objected to such a blatantly prejudicial line of quick-fire questioning. The witness replied with a matter-of-fact delivery and much to the surprise of the Prosecution, proceeded to calmly unpick most of their case. 'All the shares in Gandalph were owned by a Panamanian-registered corporation. As far as I'm aware, this investor had no connection with the defendant and did not at any time work in concert with him. It was an entirely legitimate company and was not the defendant's creature as you suggest. Gandalph's board of directors comprised five independently-minded Swiss nationals: lawyers and accountants. I was responsible for all communications into and out of the defendant's office, and at no time was he in contact with any member of the board. As far as I'm aware the loan from the Luxembourg bank was unsecured, and was not raised by the pledging of any assets by the defendant'.

Mr. Justice Peterson looked at the defendant sitting at ease in the dock and then in turn at his barrister and solicitor. He was searching for a glimmer of guilt, a pricked conscience indicating complicity in the crime now unfolding in his courtroom. But both were sitting bolt upright, incredulous of the testimony now being delivered. No, their surprise was genuine enough, but something in the defendant's demeanour suggested to the judge that he was witnessing a perversion of justice. Harcourt instantly realised that the witness upon whom he'd been relying to deliver the knockout blow had let him down, and in fact undermined his case. The Prosecution case could now only be saved by a ferocious attack on the defendant's character as soon as he set foot into the witness box. He decided to dispense with Melas before he did any further damage. Hopefully Cannon-Smith's cross-examination would be as imprecise and muted as it had been earlier. Harcourt continued. 'Mr. Melas, how would you characterise your relationship with the defendant?' 'We've known each other well for nearly five years, and during this time I've developed a personal and professional respect for him. He is a man guided by a deep understanding of corporate governance and ethics. He's always striven to do what he thinks best for his clients'. Harcourt smiled; this hyperbole alone might well be sufficient to discredit the witness in the eyes of the jury, now completely lost in the proceedings.

What the barrister failed to notice was the look of fear on Melas's face; what he also failed to read in the exaggerated statements was the desperate cry for help of a threatened witness. Instead he concluded that money had changed hands: somehow the defendant had reached out from his prison cell and offered an irresistible bribe. 'If you have such confidence, sir, in the defendant's integrity, how is it that you were able to make a statement to the police in which you said, and I quote, 'Mr. Coughlin is a violent man who has used transfers to fake corporations to defraud his clients'? How do you explain the blank share transfer form which, incidentally, also bears your name as the person who prepared the documentation?'

Mr. Justice Peterson leaned forward. 'Mr. Harcourt, I've afforded you some latitude in your line of questioning, but please remember that the person now giving evidence is a witness called by you. This is your examination- in- chief of your own witness. If you prefer to take a different approach, then you'll know the application that must be made. Please tread with care. Proceed'. The barrister bowed his head in acknowledgement of the criticism, apologised, and then returned to the task in hand. The judge had not exempted the witness from the obligation to answer; at best his replies would damage his credibility should he subsequently be called as a witness by the other side.

'Mr. Melas, I'd be grateful for your answers to these very important questions. Or perhaps you'd prefer clarification as to what I'm looking for? We have plenty of time and as you know, this is not a straightforward case'. The witness drew in his breath, steadied himself, and holding the gold-plated bar that framed the witness box began his reply. 'The statement regarding the defendant's violent nature was written by Chief Inspector Slansfield and not by me. He threatened that if I didn't sign it I'd be charged with criminal conspiracy. The blank share transfer form was fabricated by the Chief Inspector as part of a personal vendetta against the defendant'. There was a collective gasp from the jury. Screams of 'Shame, shame on you' resounded from the visitors' gallery where several elderly (and near-bankrupt) spectators were now in need of assistance from officials.

The general tumult echoed around the courtroom: the presiding judge realised he was in danger of losing control of proceedings. 'Order. Order. *Order!* There will be silence in court or I'll suspend this trial. I'll not have mayhem in this courtroom'. Composing himself, the judge made the only decision that was possible in the circumstances. 'Members of the jury, I apologise for the disorder which has entered this court. This trial will be adjourned until after lunch by which time, hopefully, Prosecution and Defence Counsel will have clarified their thoughts as to how they wish to proceed'. After the usual bow of judge to the court and the court to judge, all parties emerged into the lobby, apart from the defendant who was again returned to the cells.

In a room immediately outside the courtroom William Harcourt, Roger Pitt, and Chief Inspector Slansfield sat around a paper-cup strewn oval table. The atmosphere was one of panic and anger. The barrister decided that it would be politic not to raise the witness's allegations against the Inspector: these were matters for another time and place. For now the focus had to be on the task in hand: preventing the defendant from eluding justice (and prejudicing Harcourt's unbroken record of wins in high profile fraud trials). Slansfield spoke, barely able to contain his fury. 'William, I've worked for too long on this case to let Coughlin slip through my fingers this late in the day. We'll deal with Melas at a later date. How do we proceed now that our principal witness has let us down?' Harcourt was aware of how much was riding on the case. First, there was the Inspector's reputation; a failure in this case would jeopardise his career advancement, at least in the short term, and the flow of high fee prosecution work to Harcourt's chambers in the process. Second, there was the small consideration that a dangerous fraudster would be at large again.

'When the court reconvenes I'll apply for Melas to be made a hostile witness. This is done in the jury's absence. If successful I'll then cross-examine him on his earlier contradictory statements. I might even suggest in open court that Coughlin's agents have got at him, but we'll have to tread carefully when making unsubstantiated allegations. The judge might not like it, and we could be stopped in our tracks. And I've been embarrassed enough during the past half hour'. 'And what about the defendant, what are you going to do with him when he goes into the box?' Harcourt smiled at the prospect of remedying his earlier humiliation. 'I'll cross-examine on his business practices and the offshore companies he set up. He won't be able to get away with denying any knowledge of them. The jurors aren't fools. They'll see through his evasiveness. And when we get to the subject of his previous convictions for fraud and violence- we can cross-examine on these since he'll have impugned the characters of our own witnesses, thrown away his shield as we say-what do you think they're going to conclude? Yes, I'm still optimistic about the outcome of this case'.

In an interview room alongside the cells the defendant and his team were also meeting. Cannon-Smith glowered over his half-moon glasses at

Adam. 'Did you know Melas was going to throw the Prosecution case in the way he did? I've got to tell you right now that I've grave reservations about certain aspects of this case. I'd even go so far to say I suspect a principal witness has been interfered with'. The barrister stared at the solicitor accusingly. This was supposed to have been a straightforward case with a predictable outcome; now there was a danger he'd have to work for his fee. He couldn't bring himself to look at Coughlin, disgusted at the thought that he could yet succeed in derailing the train of justice. 'Gentlemen, I don't think there's mileage in contemplating the reasons for Melas's conversion to supporting our case. What's important is that his testimony no longer supports the other side's contentions. Now they have to rely entirely on that bent Chief Inspector who I'm sure Counsel will wish to recall, am I correct?' The barrister ignored Coughlin's perceptive intervention and continued his rant at Adam. 'You realise they're probably going to apply to make Melas a hostile witness. And if he's been bribed or threatened, you can be damned sure this will come out, and then we'll be facing fresh additional charges. And then there's our man. Do you honestly believe the jury's going to be persuaded by him, particularly with the visitors' gallery packed with his victims? There's also the not-so-small matter of a list of past convictions longer than my arm. ' Coughlin smiled sardonically; 'No offence taken'.

Adam was furious; whatever the allegations against the defendant, Counsel had a duty to represent his interests to the best of his ability. The manner in which he was ignoring their client in this meeting spoke volumes about his unspoken thoughts on the case. But Adam also wondered whether his own earlier interference with the course of justice was perhaps worse than the total lack of professionalism he was now witnessing. Slowly he stubbed out his cigarette, taking the opportunity to compose himself and conceal his anxiety. 'First things first, Andrew. There's no evidence that the Prosecution witness has been interfered with, and it would be unwise for you to express such an opinion outside the confines of this room. Second, the visitors' gallery is packed with victims of the defendant's alleged misconduct; the jury's not yet come to a decision as to guilt or innocence in this case and it's for neither you nor I to second-guess this. Third, the jury's opinion of the defendant is now no longer material since he'll not be giving evidence. He'll not be going into the witness box, and there'll be no cross-examination'.

The barrister looked briefly confused, and then the coin dropped. 'Are you bloody mad? I refuse to make that application. It would be a travesty of justice, assuming of course the judge would allow it, which I'm sure he'll not. No, I'm not going to do it'. The two men had stood up and now squared up to each other across the table. 'Andrew, when the court reconvenes you'll make an application of no case to answer. The judge will allow it - the authorities are overwhelming in support of an application in a case like this. There is no direct evidence of the defendant's involvement in any fraud. The principal witness for the Prosecution has testified that our client behaved with the highest ethics in the running of Delphi. In other words he's now our witness, and this new position will be formalised when the other side applies for him to be adjudged hostile. The Chief Inspector's credibility has been shot to pieces by their own witness. You know as well as I do that he has a personal agenda, a vendetta. In this case the usual criminal standard of proof - beyond reasonable doubt - must apply. No judge would allow such a case to go before a jury when the evidence is so doubtful and patently contaminated'. Cannon-Smith's response betrayed him as a child about to be cheated out of winning a playground game. 'I want a full trial. I demand that the defendant go into the box and answer the charges brought against him! This application will be seen as a discreditable attempt to get him off on a technicality. No, I'm not going to stand for it'.

There was brief, sudden silence in the room as Adam considered his response. Cannon-Smith was a highly experienced criminal advocate, held in high regard by other barristers and solicitors alike; to force a confrontation with him could be damaging for his own career and his partnership prospects at Roxburgh Thymes. He spoke in a measured but resolute tone. 'Andrew, I'm the instructing solicitor in this case and you will do as I say. You'll make an application that there's no case to answer, and you'll make it as soon as the court is recalled. If you refuse to do so, or make it in a halfhearted fashion, I'll sack you, withhold your fee, and report you to the Bar Ethics Committee. You'll also never again be instructed by my firm'. The barrister was dumbstruck; he'd never been spoken to in this way before. He was aware that the client who'd remained seated throughout was now staring at him with hatred in his eyes. 'Okay, Adam, I'll follow your instructions to the letter. I'll make the application. But the consequences which will flow from an acquittal will be terrible for you personally and for others. On your head be it'. He took his leave without a further word. After explaining to Coughlin the nature of the application that would be made, Adam left for a short walk around the court building.

All parties in the case of the Crown versus Silas Coughlin returned to Courtroom Number Three after a two hour recess. Both sides requested that the jury be stood down while legal argument was put to the judge. This was agreed and the visitors' gallery cleared. As directed by the instructing solicitor, Defence Counsel proceeded to make the application that the case be dismissed on the ground of there being no case to answer. As expected, William Harcourt vigorously opposed the move, but the authorities meticulously cited by Cannon-Smith emphatically outweighed those he was able to muster. Mr. Justice Peterson had a reputation for strict adherence to the letter rather than the spirit of the law; Defence had established the ground for the application, Prosecution had failed in their rebuttal, and accordingly the case would not be permitted to proceed further. In his heart he knew that justice had been failed, but a conviction made on such flimsy evidence would be overturned on appeal anyway. Despite Prosecution protestations, reluctantly the judge granted the application. The jurors were recalled; as they resumed their places Silas Coughlin smiled. There were times during this case when he'd feared that his past had finally caught up with him and imprisonment for a lengthy term was inevitable. The months spent on remand at Pentonville had depressed and scared him; he'd contemplated the prospect of his empire crumbling into dust. But now he was about to walk free; he wanted to savour the moment, to revel in the despair of those who'd sought to destroy him. There would indeed be a reckoning.

After some minor procedural matters the judge directed the jury to acquit the defendant, who in turn was told that he was free to leave. Coughlin stepped out from the dock and slowly looked around the courtroom. His demeanour was not that of a man who'd just escaped a jail term of six to eight years; instead he was consumed with anger as he looked with contempt at those who'd choreographed the charade of the past day. He walked over to his solicitor and Counsel, shaking hands with the former but completely ignoring the latter then simply walked towards the open door at the back of the court and disappeared into the fresh air. Cannon-Smith remained silent; a guilty man had walked free, and yet in his heart he recognised he'd failed in fulfilling his professional duties during the case. If it had not been for the intervention of the young, aggressive, impertinent solicitor he'd have gladly seen the defendant lose, and in this way would have failed in his ethical duty to 'do his best'. He resented Adam for shining a bright light upon his own shortcomings, but now was not the time for recriminations.

'Adam, I know we've not seen eye-to-eye today, but I hope we can put this case behind us. Your decision to make the application was the right one, it's just a shame that justice was not best served in the process. Let's just hope that neither of us comes to regret the outcome'. He shook the solicitor's hand, picked up his papers and manila files, and left. Apart from the stenographer and clerk, Adam stood alone in the courtroom. He desperately wanted to rush out, to escape from the scene of the crime, before the ghosts of previous cases in which he'd genuinely fought for justice crowded in to condemn his actions in this sordid farce. As he paused on the steps of the court building, he caught sight of Coughlin walking towards a waiting cab. He then noticed Chief Inspector Slansfield step out from behind a pillar and stride purposefully towards the client. When he reached Coughlin he slowed down and appeared to whisper something as he passed to which the acquitted criminal responded. They both laughed and smiled at each other like old friends. Coughlin climbed into the taxi which proceeded to pull out into the traffic now clogging the city's thoroughfares: the early evening rush hour had begun. The Chief Inspector sprinted off into the distance, catching up with the reporters, jurors and court officials recently disgorged from the court and now drifting off to resume their ordinary lives.

Chapter Twenty Three

Later that evening Saul, Thomas and Adam met at the Café Royale. Saul was exuberant after his trip to Monaco, not noticing the depression hovering like a black cloud over Adam. 'I've got to tell you both - Monaco was everything I thought it would be, and more. The food, the views, the women. And did I tell you about the wealth?' 'Yes', came the response in unison. 'The wealth was just awesome. I'm going to get myself a huge slice of that pie someday soon'. He told them about the party on the yacht, and the nouveau riche with whom he'd mingled and chatted. It was apparent to both Thomas and Adam that their friend had been overwhelmed by the trip. It occurred to both of them that his fascination with the materialism and cultured wealth of Monaco was a product of his upbringing in an environment of financial and emotional insecurity. They knew just about everything of the circumstances of his childhood and accordingly were prepared to give leeway when his sometimes less than edifying preoccupation with wealth came to dominate dinner conversations. After a few glasses of Champagne and several bouts of raucous laughter, the three had, as they often did, re-established the carefree spirit of their university days.

The evening was slipping away but Saul had yet to broach the subject which had arisen during his stay in Monaco. The meeting prior to his departure with the legal advisors recommended by Nicholas Herschell had been successful. The Monaco-based firm had suggested a scheme whereby he could receive payments from the insider dealing arrangement with Herschell without his identity being revealed. But he knew that his sense of fulfillment would be greater if he could share the fruits of his success with his two closest friends. Thomas was hoping to marry Chloe Peyton in the near future and if there was a way to ease the inevitable financial strains of the early years of the marriage then Saul wanted to offer it.

'Now, to business. I've come here tonight with a proposal for my two best friends- one which I think will really interest both of you. As you know, I'm now working in the Corporate Finance Division at Sheldons. Come to think of it, I'm Head of it! Every day I receive information that can drive a client's share price either sky-high or down through the floor. Several months ago someone from Equities approached me. He suggested we exchange information every now and again when this could be, quote, 'mutually advantageous'. That's what the trip to Monaco was all about: to discuss how an arrangement could be set up with him, and what the risks might be'. Adam glanced at Thomas. 'What he's really talking about is insider dealing', and then added with a grin, 'He's looking to draw us into dining at Her Majesty's Pleasure for seven years. Are you going to call hotel security to have him thrown out, or shall I?' 'Gentlemen, gentlemen, gentlemen, let's not be hasty. Let's not get hot under our tight collars until you've heard me out. Indulge me a while'.

Adam relit his cigar, puffing a spiral of pale blue smoke up towards the glittering chandeliers. He'd had a terrible day at court and a proposal of an insane moneymaking scheme offered the sort of light relief he'd come to expect on such occasions. 'Okay we'll hear you out, but tread carefully. I've had a tough day. We're not about to put our liberty at risk by getting drawn in to some harebrained scheme you dreamed up while you were cloud gazing on your way back from sunny Monaco'.

Saul explained that Morgenthau and Luthmann, the Monaco-based law firm, had advised him to set up a trust to build up capital outside the UK. The firm would act as trustee, one of the benefits of the trust being that the identities of its beneficiaries would remain secret. It would be possible for the firm to make investments on behalf of the trust but without any of their names appearing on either the share purchase forms or share certificates. Saul could instruct the firm and it would then make the purchases on behalf of its unnamed beneficiaries. To avoid confusion, Saul would be responsible for all communications with the law firm, although any instructions to buy or sell would require prior written consent of all three beneficiaries. 'I'm sure the question of safeguards wouldn't even cross your minds, and that you'd both be much too polite to raise it even if it did'.

They looked at him with exaggerated scepticism. 'But just the same, I'm more than happy to put your troubled minds at rest with this safeguard suggested by Morgenthau's'. Adam was surprised that the scheme was so well thought out, and even more surprised that several aspects of Saul's plan resembled Silas Coughlin's dealings, which had been intended to 'magic away' the funds of his unsuspecting clients. The similarities unsettled him.

'So, to bring to a close a technical explanation, most of which I suspect has gone over your heads, I'm inviting you to become co-beneficiaries in the trust. The main benefit will be that you can pay money into it and benefit from what I assure you will be its highly successful investment strategy. As payers into the trust your identities will remain undisclosed. You'll also not be taxed on the gains unless of course you bring them back into the UK. Any thoughts?' Thomas was the first to raise the question that had already occurred to Adam. 'Assuming that we all make payments of different amounts into the trust, how will the income be distributed between us?' 'That's an easy one. All income will be divided between the beneficiaries in proportion to their contributions. So the more you have in the fund, the greater the payment to which you'll be entitled. Ownership of the fund will be, to use the legalese, 'joint and several'-it will belong to all of us- but that's for another day. All I want to know is whether you're both in?'

Adam thought back to the earlier agreement with Coughlin. The defendant had promised to make the payment for the e-mail address into any bank account anywhere in the world, but he had only a few simple accounts with high street banks and they would inevitably inform the police if a large deposit was made which could be linked to money laundering. The offshore trust suggested by Saul would provide anonymity and at the same time payments couldn't be traced back to him. Thomas, on the other hand, was very reluctant. Trusts and offshore companies were perfectly legal in themselves; problems arise when they're used for illegal purposes. The slightest suggestion of illegality could result in him being 'struck off' as an accountant. And of course there was also the risk of imprisonment if convicted of insider dealing to balance against the wealth he might obtain if he took the risk. But he also hoped to marry Chloe within the next few months; their combined incomes were too low to afford a good-sized property in London for several years, and this would be something of real importance to her. While he didn't want to drift into criminality, Saul's impish delight in describing the scheme, and of course the importance of their friendship, assuaged his concerns.

'Okay, Saul, I'm in. But let's make every effort to keep out of jail, agreed?' Saul patted Adam on the back. 'Good decision – you're wiser than you look. And what about you, Thomas, are you in too?' The third friend was characteristically hesitant, but swaying as always in favour of joining in. 'Yep, I guess so. But I want all the details, and not just your recollection of what some lawyer told you over a two-hour lunch of Champagne and oysters'. 'You'll get all the documents tomorrow. And I'll get in touch with the lawyers to tell them to go ahead. The trust will be up and running within a few days. We'll call it the Tri-Star Trust, unless of course you can think of a better name'. By the end of the evening Adam had regained his confidence and optimism and shaken off his depressed mood. The Coughlin business was almost forgotten for now. Saul's easy-going nature played off well against Thomas's more serious approach, as it always did. He took pleasure in portraying himself as much more of a rogue than he really was.

The evening also brought home to Adam and Saul the central place which Chloe now occupied in Thomas's life. He spoke of her with total commitment near enough obsession, confessing to having proposed to her a year earlier, recalling that she'd turned him down because she felt 'not ready to settle down'. But he was no quitter, and six months ago she'd accepted his engagement ring. They'd marry in three months' time and then everything would be perfect. Although still mentally preoccupied by the trial's collapse earlier that day and his sense of guilt for its outcome, Adam now turned his thoughts to the stability Thomas's marriage to Chloe would bring. He tried to feel happy for him, but deep in his soul there was a fleeting envy, a fragment of resentment. The real question was whether Chloe was the right person for Thomas. He'd met her several times before and had been fascinated by her. She was vivacious, unpredictable, and ambitious, and yet now seemed prepared to turn away from this, her true nature, for a life of certainty and constancy. It all seemed incongruous to him, a little too forced. He wondered whether their relationship was as ideal and durable as his friend seemed to think. He wondered whether it should be tested.

Later that evening Adam stepped into the taxi waiting outside the hotel, Saul and Thomas preferring to stay a while longer. He was beginning to relax again when suddenly a thought entered his mind like a fox emerging from the blackest night. He'd been invited by Silas Coughlin to join him at his favourite jazz club, 'Annabella's', the following evening, a dingy haunt for small-time criminals and failed musicians. In normal circumstances he'd have preferred to receive the client at his office at Roxburgh-Thymes; there there'd be the safety of colleagues within calling distance. But this was not a meeting at which witnesses were to be present. He was to attend with the sole purpose of providing payment instructions to a villain who'd escaped justice earlier that day, and the whole idea was beginning to scare him. Morally he felt wretched, but the money would at least justify his corruption in a practical sense. By the time he reached his flat his depression had returned: another sleepless night lay ahead.

The following day Adam had conferences with clients but was unable to give the usual meticulous attention to detail they'd come to expect of him. His mind was elsewhere, focused on the meeting with Coughlin due to take place later that evening. At half past eight he left the building and walked out into the cool, damp late evening air. After twenty-five minutes' brisk walking he reached Annabella's, tucked away down a narrow alleyway. A rotund lady of pink neon playing a saxophone flashed above a set of stairs leading down into the darkness. Adam began his descent, and after walking through what seemed like miles of dimly lit corridors he entered the underground cavern. A blue, green and red cellophane filter revolved slowly in front of a dull light bulb in one corner, creating shadows that glided across the floor, disappearing into pockets of darkness. In another corner an old man in a minstrel outfit with shiny green bowler was slumped over a piano, gently fumbling its keys to produce an old jazz melody which Adam vaguely recognised but could not name. He was frightened and his heart raced as he gazed upon the surreal scene before him. 'Adam Creed, welcome, welcome, welcome to Annabella's, one of my favourite haunts. So good to see you could make it'. Coughlin emerged from the darkness, looming ever larger as he approached Adam. 'Please, feel at home. You're my guest for the evening and we've so much to talk about'. The former client shook his lawyer's hand then led him to a small table in the corner opposite the one in which the old, heroin-raddled pianist continued to play. 'He's a great musician, don't you agree? I've known Freddie for years. He's the life and soul of the club - but only after he shoots up first!'

A barman appeared from nowhere to take orders, returning a few minutes later with two stemmed crystal glasses and a bottle of red wine. He filled the glasses without speaking and then left. Coughlin smiled as he sipped. 'This wine's stocked especially for my most valued guests. So many people wanting to spend time with me, but sometimes I just have to say no. For example, Chief Inspector Slansfield liked to while away the hours in my company, but unfortunately always on his terms. Rather a selfish, greedy man, but best forgotten now'. Adam was tense, realising that his host's light humour and relaxed manner belied a darker, malevolent nature. 'So let's talk. I know there's plenty you want to ask me and as you know, I've always told you the truth. I must be one of the most honest clients you've ever had! I owe you so much - after all, without your assistance I'd not be sitting here now. But you didn't come here for my sparkling conversation. Where are the bank details for payment of your fee?' Adam passed over the business card Saul had given him in the Café Royale the previous day. 'I'll contact the lawyer tomorrow and wire our little payment as soon as he's given me the account details. Very neat. A transfer to a Monaco law firm, so there'll be no trace back to you. Now, you have some questions – fire away'.

Adam steadied himself: he didn't want his voice to tremble. 'How did you get Melas to change his story?' Coughlin paused: he was proud of the way he'd utilised technology to sabotage the case against him. 'As you know, Melas was being kept in a safe house under police guard. But when he logged on to the internet, as he did each evening to chat with his family, my associate was waiting for him. You see, that's why we needed his e-mail address, so we'd know exactly when he was on line. My associate opened a chat window, told him we knew where all his family lived back in sunny Malta, and threatened to kill them all unless he sang a different tune in the witness box. Sending him an e-mail would have risked other charges but this route left no evidence. Everyone has a weak point: his was his family. What's yours, Adam?' Adam smiled: 'I have none. I care for no-one and no-one cares for me'.

Coughlin leaned across and patted his hand: 'Ah, you and I, we're alike in so many ways'. 'And would you have had them killed if you'd been convicted?' 'Not all of them of course, but some blood would have been spilt - enough to make him regret it. You see, I gave him financial security - I supported his family when he didn't have the wherewithal to do it himself. I trusted him. And how did he repay me? Betrayal'. He suddenly interrupted himself. 'What's the time?' Adam gazed down in the darkness at his watch. 'It's coming up to nine thirty'. He was surprised by the question - after all, his host was wearing a watch.

'And now, please: your next question.' 'The share transfer form found at your premises - why didn't you hide it away? You must have known that one day the police would get a search warrant and tear your office apart. Wasn't this a little careless?' Coughlin laughed aloud. 'The real transfer form was indeed kept in a safe place: a North London safety deposit company. Haven't you worked it out yet? The one in the office was nothing to do with me'. Adam was confused. 'So Melas created the form without your knowledge?' 'No. Wrong again. Have another try- you're not even warm yet'. The young solicitor was genuinely perplexed. 'I'm sorry but you'll have to help me out, Silas'. 'The form was fabricated by Chief Inspector Slansfield and planted by him in my office. The paperwork relating to the loan from the Luxembourg bank was also forged by him. But he knew I'd not order the bank to waive my right of client secrecy because it'd bring into the open the reality that I controlled Gandalph. A very smart move on his part, don't you think?' Coughlin placed his hand over his mouth in feigned shock. 'I'm so sorry, Adam. Didn't you know? Didn't you guess the truth? My dear little lawyer in pinstripes; how you must be disappointed by the behaviour of all of us'. Coughlin smiled but in his eyes burned an unmistakable hatred; he was opening Adam's mind to a wholly corrupt world he'd never previously known had existed.

'When we left court I saw you peeping from behind a pillar- were you thinking about the possible consequences of your actions, Adam? No matter. You were wondering what passed between Slansfield and me just before I got into the taxi weren't you?' Adam nodded. 'He said to me, and I quote, 'Next time, my friend, the evidence will be watertight. Next time we'll have your fingerprints on everything, I'll see to it myself. I'm going to get you some day soon'. And I replied, and I quote again, 'There won't be a next time. You'll be cold in the ground before the week's out'. We both laughed, just like old sparring partners really. I never did any harm to him, but he was obsessed with me. Don't ask me why. Sometimes it just happens - a P.C. Plod gets it into his thick skull to 'fix' a villain whatever the cost.' Adam interrupted, still naïve as to Coughlin's intentions. 'So what now? Will you report Slansfield? He's perverted the course of justice'. 'What's the time again?' 'Nearly Ten o'clock'. Coughlin's face now contorted with hatred as he spat out his words. 'No, I'm not going to waste time that way, my friend. He crossed the line and now he's going to pay. Tonight he's going to die'.

In another run-down part of the city a plain-clothes policeman gently closed the door of his lover's flat as he left to return to his family. He had placed the two fifty pounds notes on the pillow, as he always did; next time they'd talk about 'deepening their relationship', but, he had decided, tonight it could wait. As he stepped out onto the landing he noticed that the single light bulb had been smashed. In the pitch dark he groped his way towards the stairs. The young man who'd been waiting in the shadows for the past half hour and whose eyes were accustomed to the dark rushed forward, plunging a knife deep into the victim's chest. Chief Inspector Slansfield fell to the ground in a crumpled heap. As the blood trickled down the stairs his last thoughts were of his family; what would they think of the circumstances in which his body would be found?

Adam spoke quietly. 'You bastard. I was invited here tonight to provide you with an alibi, wasn't I?' 'Not quite, since I'm sure I won't be needing one. You see, when a cop of Slansfield's rank is knifed to death sneaking out of a prostitute's flat in the dead of night, you can be sure there's not going to be much of an enquiry afterwards. Too much embarrassment for his family and the Force. No, it'll all be put down to being in the wrong place at the wrong time. Brushed under the carpet. 'An outstanding officer who gave up his life in the course of doing his duty', etc, etc, etc. You must know how these things are, or at least be able to guess'. Adam's sense of complicity in Slansfield's death was beginning to flood through to his consciousness. 'And what about Melas - what are your plans for him?' Coughlin's loathing for his enemies now burst forth, briefly interrupting the pianist's concentration. Now he was screaming with rage. 'He's going to die too, and I wish I could be there to see it. To look into his terrified eyes. Disloyalty is the one sin I can never forgive. I spent months in prison while he was outside, throwing in his lot with Slansfield. Well, it's half past ten and I'm free of one of my persecutors - now for the other'.

In a desolate and deserted part of the city, beneath a disused bridge, a large man held little Andreas Melas in a bear hug. It was important that he be restrained, prevented from lashing out and causing bruising to his body which could look suspicious upon later examination. A noose attached to the bumper of a car parked on the bridge above was slipped around the struggling man's neck. The flash of a torch signaled readiness: the engine started, the rope pulled taught, and the traitor was lifted off the ground. After a few minutes the body was still, spinning slowly in mid air. The rope was detached from the bumper and reattached to the bridge structure. The following day's papers would report the suicide of a guilt-ridden employee who'd falsified evidence at the trial of his employer and former friend, Silas Coughlin.

The giver of the execution order and the paymaster of those who carried it out looked down at his watch and then closed his eyes. 'Thank you Adam. Free at last. Free to live. Free to start again. And I owe it all to you'. 'And what about me, Silas? What about tying up this last loose end?' Adam knew that two people had died that night: he was more afraid now than he'd ever been in his life as he waited for a reply in the half-darkness of the sleazy bar.

'Adam, at no time during my 'stay' at Pentonville did I ever consider harming you, and that's still how I feel. After all, you supported me every step of the way. And your handling of that fuddy duddy barrister; it was, well, masterful. I was so impressed by your manipulation of the legal process. Yes, I'm a great fan of yours and that's no lie. And besides, if your real role in this case ever came out, there'd be consequences for both of us, don't you agree? So we have a shared secret, and anyone who was any the wiser is dead now'. Coughlin laughed as he pulled back Adam's sleeve to reveal his watch. 'If your watch is correct, that is'. Adam stood up. 'Silas, I can't say it's been a pleasure to have represented you, although I've learnt a lot from this case. I've learnt that the smallest of actions can have the greatest of consequences. I look forward to receiving my fee in due course'. Coughlin rose and took hold of Adam's hand in his enormous fist. 'Remember me Adam, and keep in mind that there are always bigger fish in the sea. Don't trouble your conscience about Slansfield and Melas. Forget about them. They had it coming, and I was indeed the bigger fish'. He smiled at the analogy. Adam gently pulled his hand free and then left along the same poorly lit corridors by which he came. As he headed out into the street the strains of the glittering, dispossessed pianist gradually faded away. A cold, heavy rain was falling and a rat gnawed at a sack of rubbish cast into the alleyway by a lazy shopkeeper from a street nearby earlier that day. He stood in the darkness, the pink neon light of the saxophone player flashing intermittently upon his sallow complexion. Tears mingled with the drops now coursing down his face as he contemplated the enormity of what he'd done.

Three days later the Monaco-based law firm Morgenthau and Luthmann received a wire transfer from one of Silas Coughlin's numerous Bermuda-registered corporations. According to the recipient client's instructions, seventy five thousand pounds of the one hundred and fifty thousand pounds transfer was to be paid into the Tri-Star Trust. The law firm was to transfer the balance to an orphanage in East London on behalf of a benefactor who wished to remain anonymous.

Chapter Twenty Four

'Thomas, I respect your professional ethics but if we're going to make a go of Tri-Star, then you're going to have to help me out. You're going to have to get your hands dirty. You must give me information'. Saul was irritated. For the past few months he'd used his inside knowledge of planned mergers and acquisitions, joint ventures and forced disposals for the benefit of the trust set up by Morgenthau and Luthmann in which he, Thomas and Adam were the beneficiaries. All three had made substantial cash contributions to the trust at the time of its setting up, and were now reaping the rewards. It was the height of the 'dot com' boom, and it was difficult for anyone with access to 'price sensitive information' to make a loss, provided of course that they had the contacts and the capital to take advantage. Insider dealing was a crime, of course, but nobody seemed to care. Saul was now working closely with Nicholas Herschell, providing him with a steady stream of confidential information which he then passed on to his most trusted clients. They in turn made purchases or sales of shares in advance of announcements that moved prices in either direction. Herschell's reputation had soared; his bonuses doubling in a matter of months. He'd become one of the bank's 'star traders', and it was prepared to pay any price to hold on to him.

When the subject of payment arose during the Monaco trip, Saul had proposed that Herschell pay a sum representing two and a half percent of transactions resulting from his inside information into the Tri-Star Trust. In the space of six months the Trust trebled its initial worth, its value further increased by the avalanche of purchase instructions Saul had given to Morgenthau and Luthmann to execute anonymously on their behalf. Every month the three conspirators met in a small conference room on the eighth floor of an office block overlooking the City. Saul suggested the location was preferable to meeting in a pub or restaurant where their conversations might be overheard, but, in fact, this room and its vista suited his sense of the theatrical. He reveled in the furtiveness of the situation, the thrill of the chase and the frisson of fear of being caught and exposed as an insider dealer at Sheldons.

'All I'm asking for is information about the cash position at Winterstone Technologies, and whether the company's bankers have made any loan facility available to the board'. Thomas was currently in the middle of Winterstone's annual audit, a client of limited importance to his firm in terms of fees. He was mildly irritated by Saul's assumption that he'd be prepared to cast away his professional standards so casually. 'Tell me again why your client Piedmont Communications needs this information. Why don't they just wait until the accounts are released in three months' time? They'll get everything they need then'. Adam leaned against the room's wall-length window, gazing down upon the ribbon of car lights weaving its way through the darkness of the twisting half lit street below. So many people rushing to get home to their husbands, wives, families, their little houses, their homes. The conventionality and security of their imagined lifestyles briefly unsettled him. 'Don't play games, Thomas. You know why we need the information. Piedmont needs to expand by acquisition of a quoted company. If it's a hostile take-over then all the better - nothing bumps up a share price like fear and loathing between hunter and hunted. If Winterstone's got financial muscle it'll be able to fight off Piedmont'. 'So, you're asking me to break the client's trust as well as my professional ethics. And I nearly forgot, put my job on the line at the same time'.

Saul smiled. 'Yep, I guess that's about it. But here's the good news. If Winterstone's as weak as I think it is, then we'll pile in to its shares before the takeover. And I'll make sure the takeover goes ahead because I'm advising Piedmont on its acquisition strategy, completely impartially of course. As soon as the share price peaks, we'll be out with our profits. Tri-Star will make all the purchases, so no-one will know it's us'. Thomas shook his head in disbelief. 'How did I ever get caught up in your schemes? You're just a couple of gangsters in pinstripe suits, and I'm just an innocent passenger coming along for the ride'. He grinned ruefully, but his levity belied a deeper concern he had about the direction in which his friendship with the other two appeared to be taking him. Adam's attention returned to the street below, his thumbs tucked into his red braces as if about to make a closing speech to a jury. 'Don't be naïve, Thomas. You're going to benefit from this just as much as us. And in any case, why did you think the Tri-Star Trust was set up in the first place? For simple tax evasion to save a few thousand here and there? No, it was to enable us to exploit our skills and knowledge and to build up great mountains of cash. And think of your wife-to-be: if not for yourself, then how about doing it for her?' Thomas snapped back with irritation. 'Leave Chloe out of this. She'd never approve of anything remotely unethical. She's as honest as the day is long'. Adam turned back from the window. 'Are you sure about that? She seems quite an ambitious woman. Ambition can lead to compromise of principles when the right circumstance presents itself. Ultimately it's always just a question of whether a price is worth paying'. The two men stared at each other across the chrome and glass conference table, neither wanting to escalate the exchange into a full-scale confrontation.

Saul intervened, sensing the tension between the two. 'Gentlemen, please. We're not here for emotional navel gazing. All this talk of ethics and honesty is making me feel quite nauseous. Let's conclude our business and adjourn. Now, Thomas, here's the request. Will you provide me with the information I need about Winterstone? I'm not looking for a convoluted answer: a simple 'yes' or 'no' will do'. Thomas paused, wondering what the impact of a refusal would be upon the Trust's future investment strategy. If he refused he suspected Saul would embark upon some other illegal plan, without disclosing it to his co-beneficiaries. An agreement to assist would at least mean he remained 'on the team', able to block any wilder plans in the future. 'Ok, I'll do it. But I'm not happy about it, and don't expect me to do something like this again. The setting up of the Trust was a bit of fun for me and sure, I've bent the rules more than once myself in my job. But never for personal gain'. Fleetingly, he recalled his previous collusion with Solomon Silverstein.

'Good man and a wise decision. If we get it right this time we'll be nearer financial independence before the year's out. One big hit and the Trust's going to be self-financing - there'll no longer be any need for any of us to put more capital in. You're seeing Adam tomorrow; give him the paperwork and he can pass it on to me later this week. I'll give instructions to Morgenthau's early next week, after I've seen the financials and got a handle on the plans of the Piedmont board. I'm meeting with them next week, and by then I'll know whether to recommend a takeover or not. Whatever my advice, I know they'll act on it'.

The following day Thomas met with Adam, as agreed. The solicitor was in the middle of a fraud case at the Old Bailey and had an hour to spare before the court reconvened. They met in the usual place, a Cypriot coffee shop tucked away off the Strand, where privacy was assured. Thomas handed over the Winterstone paperwork in a thin brown envelope, having surreptitiously photocopied the relevant boardroom minutes at the client's offices earlier that day. It was immediately apparent to him that the company was as weak as Saul had suggested, the chairman having announced at the most recent meeting that a request to their bankers for funding had been refused. The company barely held sufficient funds to meet next month's salaries. After a couple of large creamy coffees, they paid the bill then walked out into the noisy, fume-filled street. Like a couple of schoolboys they ate baklava as they made their way through the crowds of people who, after rushed lunches in a thousand sandwich bars across the City, were now jostling and pushing their way back to work.

A few days later, Saul entered the conference room at Piedmont Communications where the board had been convened for his presentation. He was an old hand at this kind of event with a confidence borne of experience and belief in his powers of persuasion. He distributed portfolios to each director containing balance sheets and cashflow forecasts compiled from the information smuggled out by Thomas during the recent audit of the target company, Winterstone Technologies. Saul explained how the business was thinly capitalised with barely sufficient cash to meet its salary commitments from one month to the next. Recently the company's share price had drifted downwards significantly; apart from a recent 'blip' precipitated by a series of unexplained purchases by a Monaco-based trust, there was nothing to suggest there was another potential rival bidder waiting in the wings. The company was a sitting duck.

Piedmont's chairman thumbed through the dossier, paying little attention to Saul's presentation. Franklin Shandlin was physically vast, weighing in at at least twenty stones and standing at just over six feet tall. He wore a smart red dicky bow tie which had become his trademark over the years and although approaching his sixty fifth birthday, black hair dye helped perpetuate the illusion, from a distance at least, that he was still in his late fifties. 'Tell me, Mr. Corporate Finance Man: if the company is in such bad shape why are you recommending that we take it over? Shouldn't we just let it sink and then strip its assets when the liquidator flogs them off on the cheap? I know you're going to gain from the fees you'll charge for financing the takeover- I always take it as a given that banks never lose- but what's in it for us in the medium to long term?' Saul responded authoritatively. 'Mr. Chairman, thank you for the question, raised with your customary directness. Winterstone's share price is currently on the floor. Yes, it has difficulties but these are largely due to lack of short-term cashflow. The fundamentals are in good shape. Specifically, it holds intellectual property rights for a range of internet applications which have been developed in-house. And this brings me to the company's second strength. It has highly innovative employees and even if some leave following acquisition by Piedmont, you'll still have one of the most outstanding workforces in the IT sector'.

Shandlin nodded his head in agreement. 'Okay, I follow what your saying so far and I wouldn't be so impolite as to enquire as to the source of the information you've presented about Winterstone's vulnerabilities. I guess this is what we're paying you for. But I'm not persuaded there's a fit between their activities and ours. There's no point in us taking them over if we both do the same sort of things; this will only lead to unnecessary duplication and competition between divisions for the same business. There's no point in all of us chasing after the same fox'. Saul knew he'd addressed the so-called synergies between the lines of business of the two companies in the thick portfolio submitted to the chairman earlier, but Shandlin was a 'gut instinct' businessman. 'Piedmont specialises in internet infrastructure - servers and customised platforms. Winterstone focuses on development of software applications: things like wireless communications, intranet packages for small to medium size businesses. It's a perfect fit. The combined business will be able to provide customers with the entire package: hardware, customised software, and after-sales technical support which can be the greatest earner of the three. You should diversify your risk and develop a capacity to offer 'bundled products' to a wider range of customers'.

The chairman smiled and closed his eyes, placing both hands behind his little head. Several other directors seated around the table then took the opportunity to question some of the projections contained in the portfolio distributed earlier. But all knew that ultimately the decision would be made by Chairman Shandlin alone; he owned the majority of shares in Piedmont and ran it autocratically. Several board members began discussing possible alternative acquisitions with Saul, but this didn't deter the chairman from interrupting without so much as waiting for a break in the conversation.

'Saul, I like your idea and I'm not inclined to sit around waiting for you to come up with other potential targets. I'm sure the board will come around to my way of thinking'. He glowered at the timid ensemble seated around the table. 'Sometimes I wonder whether I'm the only person in this company with any sense of urgency or awareness of the practicalities of surviving in a competitive world. Now, tell me how you propose we finance the deal'. Saul smiled and explained the planned share purchase: the fish had been hooked. 'We suggest you start making share purchases in the open market next week. There's plenty of stock floating around, and some holders who've already suffered losses will take the opportunity to bail out if there's a slight rise in the price. There's no need to go about this incrementally- just go for a full thirty percent buy-up following which Stock Exchange rules require that you make a formal bid for the company'. 'And what about the cash to make these purchases- where will this come from?' 'We'll provide a short-term loan, repayable as soon as the acquisition's done. A facility fee will be payable up-front and of course will be quite obscene'. Shandlin smiled. 'Naturally. I'd be disappointed if it wasn't. And I guess that if the deal's not done, then you'll screw us again with a penalty fee too?' 'Of course. As you put it so succinctly earlier, the banks never lose. When you have the stake you can then make an offer to the remaining shareholders. I'd suggest pitching it somewhere around five percent over the price prevailing at the time of announcement of the bid, probably escalating to around twelve and a half percent to close the deal. The directors of Winterstone don't hold much stock so shouldn't be able to put up much of a fight'.

Shandlin pushed back his jet-black hair, his mood changing in the blink of an eye from playful engagement to hostility and confrontation. 'I'm not going to buy out those lazy fools who made the mistake of buying shares in a hopeless business in the first place. If I'm paying over the odds I'll be rewarding them for their crap decisions. No, I'll offer five percent below the prevailing price and that's the best I'll be willing to do. As an alternative I'll offer one share in Piedmont for every three Winterstone shares. This'll give them a big enough premium'. Saul successfully concealed his concern at this approach. 'That's an interesting proposal Mr. Chairman, and I'll need to talk it through with my team. The question is going to be whether shareholders will agree to make the switch. But if they take the same view of the greater opportunities that will follow the takeover, then they'll probably come around to it'.

Saul contemplated the gains which the Tri-Star Trust would make if everything went in accordance with Shandlin's plans. They'd already made a good profit, buying the shares at rock bottom a month earlier. Market rumours had gently pushed the price upwards, and they were now sitting on a paper profit of eight percent. When the takeover approach was made in the next few weeks the price would rise again, possibly by a further fifteen percent. Shandlin would then have to raise his game, possibly to a two- for- three shares offer. The Trust would be looking at a gain on its investment of anything up to fifty percent in the space of a few months. It would also be holding a sizeable chunk of stock in the newly invigorated Piedmont Communications. He bit his lip to stop a smile breaking out across his face.

The chairman took off his black thick-framed glasses and replaced them in the steel case resting on the closed portfolio in front of him. His board knew from experience that this was the sign he'd heard enough and his attention was about to wander. 'I think we've come to the end of this meeting, Saul. Thank you for your presentation; we're certainly on the same wavelength and I look forward to receiving the loan paperwork early next week. I'll not make any purchases in the meantime - I'm banking on closing this deal with a single blow, one block purchase of stock that won't disturb the price too much. Everybody around this table will observe total secrecy of today's discussion, so any significant price movements will be down to you and your boys at Sheldons. Be sure that I'll not hesitate to bring in the appropriate authorities if there's any sign of insider dealing before this plan's put into effect'. Saul stood to his feet. 'It's been a pleasure, gentlemen, to have had the privilege to speak with you today. I'm sure that this transaction is just the beginning of what will be a long and fruitful relationship'.

Franklin Shandlin could barely contain his excitement. At three thirty in the morning earlier that day he'd paced up and down the thick Persian carpet in his luxury apartment overlooking the Thames, petrified that he was about to be found out. The months of concealment, of juggling phony balances on hundreds of bank accounts across the world, was beginning to take its toll on his health. But now this Mr. Corporate Finance Man, a City boy still wet behind the ears, was going to save him and his empire.

Chapter Twenty Five

Nicholas Herschell gazed at the Bloomberg screen, wondering when the fireworks would start. A week earlier he'd met Saul at the usual Indian restaurant where he was given the latest 'insider tip'. An engineering company, Goldenhawk Engineering, was soon to announce its success in winning a major bridge-building contract in Croatia financed by the European Bank for Reconstruction and Development. It was a no-risk project: when the news became public the share price was certain to rocket. This was going to be a turkey shoot, and Herschell needed to move quickly. The problem was that this time he'd acted too quickly and carelessly; the usual rules agreed with Saul when they first embarked upon their little arrangement had been broken in his enthusiasm to exploit the information and make an even greater profit. In any event, there'd been no time to take the usual precautions. The announcement was to be made in days but his offshore trust was already heavily committed, lacking the surplus cash needed to take advantage of Saul's inside information.

So Herschell was faced with a dilemma; he had personal cash locked away in a Monaco bank, and the information with which to make a killing in a handful of hours. He had a list of private clients to keep sweet with a constant flow of share recommendations. There was no alternative: he instructed the bank to make the purchases directly on his own behalf, hoping to sell before his name even appeared on the engineering company's share register. His greed had led to complacency. At one o'clock on a wet, miserable Friday afternoon the message flashed up on the Bloomberg screen: 'Goldenhawk triumphs in EBRD bid: Croatian bridge contract confirmed'. He leaned back and closed his eyes, contemplating the penthouse in Paris he'd soon be able to buy outright. Sure enough, within minutes of the announcement the share price leapt, first by ten percent followed by a breather while stags took their profits, then another five percent, then a breather, and within an hour a further jump of twenty percent.

At three o'clock that afternoon Herschell put in a call to his personal portfolio manager. He was satisfied with his thirty five percent return on a one-week investment, and now wanted out of the stock. The manager confirmed that the sale would be made at best price before close of trading. It was a perfect end to an otherwise uneventful week of thin markets and extended lunches. He was pleased; the risk had been worth taking, purchase and sale having been made within such a short space of time that no share certificates would be issued in his name. Provided that nobody looked too closely, and there was no reason why they should, he'd get away it.

Three days after making his presentation at Piedmont's offices, Saul called an 'emergency meeting' of the Tri-Star Trust's beneficiaries. He was convinced the Piedmont hostile takeover of Winterstone would provide a huge profit for the Trust, provided of course that the shares were bought in good time. The only question was the extent of the commitment they should make to the deal. He was impulsive by nature, in contrast to the cautiousness of his co-beneficiaries, his friends being unsurprisingly hesitant about illegal investment and its risks and possible consequences. Over the past year the Trust had gone from strength to strength. The initial cash contributions of the three had almost quadrupled thanks in large part to Saul's financial acumen (and his inside knowledge of deals going through Sheldons). Shandlin was a tyrant but nevertheless had an excellent record in building up Piedmont virtually from scratch. A report by a government department a decade earlier had concluded that he was 'a person unfit to hold the office of director of a public company', but this had merely endeared him to the City sharks to whom the phrase 'business ethics' was an oxymoron. Saul had delayed communicating to Shandlin the decision about funding for the takeover until he'd had the opportunity to discuss his own private agenda with his co-beneficiaries; it was after all he who'd determine Sheldons' decision whether or not to provide the loan.

Saul opened the meeting with his proposal for the purchase of shares in Winterstone. Thomas knew that in passing on the company's confidential board minutes he'd betrayed his professional ethics and more importantly, his moral values. But the deed had been done: now he had to make the best of a bad situation. He'd agree the purchase but at the same time making it crystal clear he was not to be put in such a compromising position again. With his marriage to Chloe now imminent he was no longer willing to play 'fast and loose' with his job or his liberty. In contrast to Thomas, Adam had no hesitation in agreeing the purchase. Insider dealing was not a crime in his eyes but merely the exploiting of information, something which happened every day of the year in countless other walks of life. After a relatively short discussion, Saul summarised their decision. 'It seems we're all agreed that the purchase of shares in Winterstone should go ahead, and without delay. The next question is the size of our commitment. Tri-Star currently holds shares in fifteen companies, and there's no spare cash available. So we need to decide what stock to dispose of. Any thoughts before I explain my own solution?'

For the next half hour Adam and Thomas went through each of Tri-Star's holdings, looking at gains made so far and potential further profit. Saul's contribution to the discussion was slight; instead he sat looking out through the window, pitching in with a contrary argument whenever it looked as if the other two were about to reach a consensus. Thomas was exasperated. 'Okay Saul, you've dismissed all our suggestions, let's hear yours'. Saul smiled: they needed to draw upon his expertise, and they both knew it. 'Here's what I suggest and before you dismiss it out of hand, just think of the potential profit if we get this one right. I propose we sell all existing holdings and switch the cash into Winterstone shares. On my calculation, we'll make at least fifteen percent on the rise following the takeover announcement, and another ten percent if the shares convert on a three for two basis into Piedmont stock. That's a twenty five percent gain tax-free over four to six weeks'.

Thomas spoke, his cautiousness shining through. 'What if Winterstone's share price falls after Shandlin goes public? If he buys a chunk of stock it's going to drive up the price, sure, but if other shareholders think he's going to come in with a very low bid for the company, they'll bail out early and the price will fall. And what do we know about Shandlin anyway? Everyone knows he's a crook. Do we really want to end up with shares in a company run by such a man?' Adam intervened. 'Sorry Thomas, but I'm with Saul on this one. Yes it's a risk, but here's a brilliant short-term opportunity to go in for one stock, make a quick killing, then pull out and diversify again.' Outnumbered and out-argued, Thomas agreed to fall into line despite his concerns about the captain of this new investee company. In anticipation of his co-beneficiaries' agreement, Saul had earlier prepared the paperwork authorising disposal of all existing holdings and the purchase of shares in Winterstone. After all three had signed, Thomas hesitantly, they left to spend the remainder of the evening in a dubious East End nightclub, with Thomas again less enthusiastic about the choice than his two friends.

In the early hours of the following morning an anxious Franklin Shandlin poured himself another gin. As he stood at the open window of his luxury apartment breathing in the cold night air, he reflected upon a series of disastrous personal investments made over the preceding three years. His reputation was founded upon smoke and mirrors, bluster and threats of legal action against anyone getting too close to the truth, but the reality was that he'd been finished financially a year earlier. It was only his will, his sheer physical determination, which kept his creditors at arm's length. But recently they'd been circling ever closer, leading him in desperation to plunder the company he'd built from nothing to its present position of global IT player. He started to cry, grateful no-one was present to witness his moment of weakness. But then recovering his composure, he thought again about the cocky finance man who'd addressed the board a matter of days ago. Or was it a week? He worried he was losing track of time, days and dates. Why hadn't he called? Why hadn't the funding for the takeover come through? He wondered if he should call later that day, but thought better of it lest he appear anxious. Better to feign disinterest, to appear aloof, than to draw attention and put the edifice of his deception at risk of collapse. He felt desperately alone. No, he wouldn't call in the morning, but perhaps the following day? He poured another gin and gazed up at the stars. His youth seemed a thousand lifetimes ago. He wished he could sleep, dream, chase off his demons. He thought about death.

The following day Saul contacted the lawyer Dieter Morgenthau. His instructions were simple: all shares currently held by the Tri-Star Trust were to be disposed of at the best prices obtainable. The proceeds were then to be used to buy as many shares in Winterstone Technologies as possible, at the lowest price. The transactions were to be completed without delay: he was to be notified by e-mail as soon as all had been done. The patrician French lawyer replaced the telephone in its cradle and settled back in his large leather-upholstered chair. Lighting up a small cigar he switched on his computer and quickly assimilated the information scattered around the relevant Bloomberg pages. Taking down the prices at which Winterstone was trading he completed some rough calculations on a large jotter. His client was correct, as he nearly always was: the company was significantly undervalued when the share price was compared with asset value, but he was concerned about the risk the transaction would create for the Trust. Saul had explained that Winterstone shares would convert within the month into Piedmont stock and although the lawyer knew that use of such knowledge was probably insider dealing, he didn't regard one of his functions as being policeman to the financial markets.

The fact remained, though, that he had responsibilities as trustee to the Tri-Star Trust, and these he took seriously. One of these was to protect the Trust's assets and, as such, the interests of the beneficiaries. The switch into Piedmont shares would create a completely undiversified portfolio, exposing the Trust to an unacceptable level of risk. He picked up the telephone again, this time to his friend Pierre Van den Luc at Banque Monaco. The banker's opinion coincided with his own, but the advice he gave to minimise the risk helped assuage his concerns and put his mind at rest. A careful risk-hedging strategy would be put in place to protect the Trust. Later that day Dieter Morgenthau telephoned his client and informed him that the disposals had been made as instructed: the Trust was now comprised entirely of shares in Winterstone Technologies.

'Mr. Shandlin, I have Saul Quartermain of Sheldons Bank on the line'. The chairman's secretary rang through from her desk outside the closed door to the inner sanctum into which nobody entered without prior invitation. 'Put the bastard through' came the booming reply. He caught a reflection of his face in the lid of an open silver cigar box on his desk and not liking what he saw, quickly slammed it shut. The attrition of recent months was beginning to take its toll on his appearance; the internal turmoil was now beginning to trickle outwards. 'Mr. Quartermain, what can I do for you?' His heart was racing. 'It's not so much what you can do for me, Mr. Chairman, it's what I can do for you this fine morning. The good news is that finance for your takeover of Winterstone Technologies has been approved'. Shandlin was elated; he thanked his saviour whilst at the same time maintaining his mildly disinterested tone. Although the bank's support was crucial, it was only the first step on a long road of dealing with the desperate problems besetting and besieging both himself and his company. But at least there was now a glimmer in the darkness; if he could continue with the grand bluff and maintain his reputation intact, he'd be able to implement his real intentions. He collected his coat and left without a word to Ms. Dove, his overworked and underappreciated secretary for the last twenty years. He wanted to be alone, to walk in the fresh air and forget his predicament, albeit for just a handful of minutes. He made his way to a nearby park, longing to sleep.

Chapter Twenty Six

It had been six weeks since Nicholas Herschell 'scooped the pool' with his investment in Goldenhawk Engineering, and two weeks since he signed the papers for the purchase of the penthouse in Paris. He felt on top of the world, in more ways than one; his end-of-year bonus was promising to be the best yet, his private clients now regularly called him at home, and his relationship with Saul Quartermain was proving profitable beyond his wildest dreams. Of course, his opposite number in Corporate Finance had also benefited; a steady flow of payments had gushed into his Monaco-registered trust over the past year. But this was the nature of their understanding, their contract. As he sat in his office and completed the paperwork for the week's sales he began surfing European property websites: he was already contemplating his next purchase. His chain of thought was broken by a knock on his door and a sharp voice he didn't recognise.

'Mr. Herschell, Nicholas Herschell isn't it? I'm Detective Inspector Alex Grey and this is my colleague, Detective Chief Inspector Peter Dorling. We're here on behalf of the Serious Fraud Office. I wonder if you could spare a few minutes of your time? There are some matters we'd like to speak to you about. It won't take long; your bosses have made a conference room available so we'll get some peace and quiet. With a bit of luck they'll put on some tea and biscuits because we're parched!' The words were friendly enough, but the underlying tone distinctly hostile. Herschell stiffened as he looked up at the two intruders from the outside world. Slowly he got to his feet, put on his jacket, and followed them out into the foyer and across into the conference room. Previously he'd only entered the room to argue about the size of his bonus with browbeaten, weak directors; now he was entering for an entirely different but as yet unknown purpose. Perhaps one of his sales team had been stealing from the bank, or passing on confidential information to third parties; in either case he'd be unforgiving. The thought that his own criminality might have been discovered didn't even cross his mind.

Two men faced one man across an eight by five foot single piece of black onyx table. 'Nicholas... you don't mind me calling you Nicholas do you?' Herschell nodded his consent. 'That's my name, so feel free to use it'. 'Thanks. I'll get straight to the point. One of the responsibilities of the SFO is to investigate insider dealing. As I'm sure you know, such activity is a criminal offence and carries a term of imprisonment of up to five years. The reason we have this law is to protect investors and to ensure that persons having access to information not available to the general public don't exploit it for personal gain'. Herschell froze with fear, his mouth so dry that briefly he couldn't respond. Grey turned to his colleague. 'There's also a neat twist to the law. Some say that the user's personal gain is the only factor determining whether or not there's a prosecution, but this isn't the whole picture. Even if someone doesn't use the information, if they pass it on to a third party then an offence is still committed. And would you believe it? Even if that person or the third party makes a loss from using the information, they've *still* committed an offence. Now isn't that a tidy, 'belt and braces' piece of law?' Dorling bared his teeth as he smiled; Herschell recognised the personal antipathy, the brooding resentment and petty jealousy of the fleshy-faced, heavily built men, but still didn't know for certain the reason why he was in the room.

'And now Nicholas, we'll tell you why we are here'. Dorling asserted his authority, and Grey sat back. 'We work closely with the Market Surveillance Unit of the Stock Exchange. The Unit's main function is to look for irregular share transactions in advance of public announcements involving takeovers, mergers, those sorts of things. Two months ago a large purchase of shares was made in an engineering company, Goldenhawk, before an announcement of its successful bid for a construction contract. The company's share price jumped thirty five percent immediately after the announcement and this is what attracted the Unit's attention. It's our belief that the advance share purchase was made by you. Is there anything you'd like to tell us?' Herschell felt a rush of blood to his head and for a few seconds felt nauseous and dizzy. His mouth remained bone dry.

He spoke quietly. 'I have nothing to say. I'll only speak with a solicitor present'. Detective Chief Inspector Dorling paused, his face ashen.

'Nicholas Montague Herschell, I am arresting you on suspicion of insider dealing under section 11 of the Criminal Justice Act 1993. You do not have to say anything but it may harm your defence if you do not mention now something that you later rely on in court. Do you understand?' 'Yes'. 'You will now be taken to a police station to be formally charged'. Nicholas Herschell, Sheldons' star trader, was then quickly handcuffed before he even realised what was happening, led out of the conference room, across the trading floor, and folded into the police car waiting outside. As the car pulled away he closed his eyes, knowing that the world as he knew it was about to crash down around him.

News of Herschell's arrest rushed like wildfire through the bank, its dealers dumbstruck to have seen their Head of Trading led out in handcuffs like a common criminal. The directors were even more concerned. Any potential criminality was the least of their worries; they had to find a replacement for Herschell, now suspended on full pay, while at the same time steadying the nerves of the bank's institutional investors. There was also a risk that a sizeable chunk of the client base could evaporate when it emerged that their principal advisor would soon be making court appearances, presumably in the full glare of the media. Saul had been visiting a private client when his co-conspirator received his visit by the 'Men from the SFO', and was informed of the drama by a spotty-faced junior trader upon his return later that day. His immediate reaction was to head for the toilets to spend the next fifteen minutes locked in a stall, staring down into a white porcelain basin, heaving up most of the lunch he'd taken with his client earlier that day. Never before had he experienced such fear as he contemplated the potential implications of the arrest. Surely it was only a matter of time before Herschell divulged his identity, possibly as part of a bargain to keep himself out of prison? It was he rather than Herschell who had breached the trust of so many of the bank's corporate clients; it was this greater culpability which would inevitably result in a higher term of imprisonment. As he pulled the flush for the fourth time he began seriously considering heading for the airport. He'd leave everything and everyone behind, to start a new life with a new identity in a warmer clime, preferably one without an extradition treaty with the UK. After regaining his composure he returned to his office. He'd been unable to daub off splashes of vomit from his pristine white shirt but provided he kept his jacket buttoned, hopefully nobody would notice. But his bleach white face would have given more than just an inkling of suspicion to anyone familiar with Herschell's arrest now looking for clues of wider involvement amongst the bank's other senior employees.

After being taken to a nearby police station to be fingerprinted, photographed and a DNA swab taken from inside his mouth, the frightened and still lightheaded Herschell was released on police bail. He was to return to the station in a week's time. He walked out into the street, his shirt disheveled and tie hanging at an angle, and headed for the nearest coffee bar. There he sat for an hour trying to rationalise what had happened to him, thoughts and fears flying around the inside of his head like a cloud of black bats in a subterranean cavern.

Chapter Twenty Seven

Petr Damyanovitch sank back into his armchair and gazed out over the city. He slowly rotated the ice cubes in the glass of whisky poured earlier, preferring to remain in the darkness of his luxury hotel suite rather than switching on a light which might otherwise break his chain of thought. He'd flown in by private jet earlier that day, touching down at a small airfield just outside Heathrow. This privileged mode of travel meant he avoided the bureaucracy and suspicions of Customs checks which would otherwise slow his progress to the same hotel he stayed in whenever visiting London. Although he utilised the benefits available to him as a member of the new Russian oligarchy, his mindset and outlook on life remained rooted in another time. Once there had been clarity, a simple balance of power in the world, sustained by the dedication and sacrifices of a generation of committed individuals. In the closing years of the Great Patriotic War, twenty million comrades had paid the ultimate price for the survival of a political system and a guiding set of principles. But the Soviet empire had unraveled with a whimper, leaving confusion, selfishness, and ungrateful microstates jostling for independence at Moscow's expense. But Russia would rise again: this was his mission, his promise.

There were several reasons for Damyanovitch's visit, but his first priority was to meet with his contact at Sheldons Bank, Nicholas Herschell. They'd known each other for several years, the trader having previously stayed at his apartment in Monaco and on his yacht whenever it had anchored in the Bay. For the past couple of years he'd received inside information from the trader in return for this hospitality and, of course, regular payment of a generous 'retainer'. Herschell never questioned why someone whose wealth amounted to hundreds of millions of dollars would be interested in making a few extra millions here and there. The reality was that the grubby insider dealing had been an irrelevance to the oligarch from Moscow, the trivial gains disbursed amongst numerous charities of which he was patron. Of course the information had had some use, passed on to Moscow Alpha Bank's private clients to consolidate Chairman Damyanovitch's reputation as a financier of outstanding acumen.

But the Russian was disinterested in flatteries due to his status at the bank he'd built up from nothing. Instead he'd used Herschell for a purpose of which the trader could only have been completely oblivious, in large part because of his assumption that greed was always the driver behind such arrangements. Herschell provided access to the higher echelons at Sheldons Bank; he provided the introductions and connections to the people Damyanovitch would need when the time was right. Yes, he was the chairman and majority shareholder of a medium size finance house in Moscow, but this brought with it some inevitable and undesirable connotations, the prime one being an assumption that Russian success usually involved association with organised crime and an allegiance to politicians who, having their own geopolitical goals, would from time to time call in favours.

The stigma of corruption and a perceived lack of transparency of true ownership had prevented Russian banks from taking their proper place in the world's financial centres. The credit rating agencies were also more diligent when classifying Russian financial institutions than they were when dealing with equally opaque West European or North American competitors. To add to their difficulties they faced competition for global capital from the financial institutions of the Newly Independent States, supported and encouraged by nationalist governments hateful of their former Russian ruler.

Herschell, then, provided his client with inside information of a wholly different and considerably more useful nature. Moscow Alpha's chairman needed details of co-operative arrangements, where these existed, between Sheldons Bank and competitor financial institutions across Central Asia. Herschell had access to this information, partly by virtue of his seniority but also via his network of contacts in other departments across the bank. He'd acted in all but name as Damyanovitch's spy during the past couple of years, without even realising he was doing so, or questioning the purpose for which the information was required.

Sheldons' white collar criminal was not the only person Damyanovitch had made arrangements to meet that week. It had been a while since his previous meeting with Saul Quartermain at the party on board his yacht in the Bay of Monaco, and contact had been non-existent since then. He knew that Saul was the provider of the inside information to Herschell who then passed it on to him, but this activity was merely a sideshow to what he and his associates back in Moscow had in mind for their 'new friends' in London. Quartermain was a crucial player in the development of Sheldons' corporate strategy, particularly in terms of identifying business they should tender for and which they should avoid in the newly emergent Central Asian markets.

The bank was quickly developing a reputation as a 'bridge' between Western capital and Central Asian sovereign and corporate borrowers. The Head of Corporate Finance at Sheldons had initiated this 'Look East' strategy, and its success had been one of the reasons for his rapid promotion at the bank. Damyanovitch looked out past the towering office blocks and considered the consequences if Saul's insider dealing were ever to become known to his employer. He'd be fired, of course, and prevented from resuming another career in the financial services sector for a considerable period of time. There could be wider repercussions should the bank decide to report him to the appropriate law enforcement agencies. But these were academic considerations; it was vitally important that he retain his position at the bank, and Damyanovitch was prepared to do all that was necessary to ensure it. Fools were, after all, the tools of the wise. But the question for this visit was how to gain Saul's cooperation in the greater plan, how to ensnare him and bind him in so tightly he couldn't refuse any instruction from his new master. The dinner arranged for later that week was intended to resolve these remaining imponderables.

Three days after receiving financial backing from Sheldons Bank, Franklin Shandlin launched his takeover bid for Winterstone Technologies. As Saul had predicted, the target company's share price jumped around fifteen percent as soon as the announcement was made. The bitterness of the struggle which ensued lifted the price further as the Winterstone board savaged their adversary's reputation and his personal qualities. They raised the damning report by the government department which had previously investigated Shandlin's business practices, but this was old news. Everyone knew about his ruthlessness, his willingness to slash workforces and strip out assets from companies he'd acquired over the years. But short-term profits were always guaranteed when Franklin Shandlin's huge physical bulk came looming over the horizon to take over a company struggling with incompetent directors or a tired and demoralised workforce. Within two weeks the acrimonious takeover had been achieved. The Tri-Star Trust made a whopping twenty five percent gain on its shares in Winterstone, but further profit was still there to be made. Shandlin's three-for-one share conversion offer had been rejected; through clenched teeth he was now forced to improve his terms to the three shares Winterstone for two shares Piedmont proposal which Saul had predicted. Tri-Star had seen a fifty percent increase in the financial worth of its holdings but was now sitting on a portfolio comprised entirely of shares in a company controlled by a well known liar and crook. Despite Thomas's initial reservations about the Trust being excessively exposed to one company, the three beneficiaries agreed to maintain the strategy for the time being. With luck they might even double the value of their investment within a matter of months.

Saul gazed around the dealing room as he whispered into the telephone receiver. During the past few days he'd tried to maintain a semblance of normality at the bank despite being deeply concerned about Herschell and whether he'd been persuaded, bribed, or coerced into coming to some sort of agreement with his interrogators. He was completely in the dark, the constant fear being that at any moment a couple of heavies could appear at his desk and march him off to the nearest police station for questioning. He'd not slept properly during the nights since Herschell's arrest and as a result was finding it difficult to stay awake during the day.

'Nicholas, where the hell are you? Nobody knows what's going on. What have you told them?' Herschell gabbled out a few confused sentences and the two agreed to meet later that afternoon at a backstreet coffee shop a suitably safe distance from the bank. To pass the time before then, he'd call Thomas. They made small talk about the arrangements he and Chloe were making for their wedding, now just a few months away. The conversation was trite but despite his very real concern for his own survival, Saul still managed to wonder whether the couple made a suitable match. She was, as Adam accurately described her, a 'high main-tenance woman'. Thomas was a complete contrast; he needed stability and predictability in his working and personal life. His views on marriage were conventional to a fault.

Saul sipped his third cappuccino, promising himself that if Herschell didn't appear within the next fifteen minutes he'd leave. But at the same time he knew he couldn't leave, and that he'd stay until closing time in the hope of speaking to Herschell properly. Eventually, nearly an hour later than agreed, Herschell wandered in, looking nervously around the tables in the manner of a novice spy attending the first rendezvous with his controller. It would have been amusing, Saul thought, but for the fact that the behaviour suggested a mental balance which was already severely out of kilter. 'Hi Nicholas. Over here'. Saul raised his hand, drawing attention to the table at which he sat in one of the darker corners of the coffee bar. Herschell made straight for him, shaking him vigorously by the hand. 'So pleased you could make it, Saul. Thanks for coming and for waiting, but the meeting with my solicitors took longer than expected. Anyway, how are you?'

The days since the arrest had taken their toll; he'd lost the cheeky smile and the glint in his eyes which had endeared him to the nouveau riche in Monaco. Now his complexion was sallow and rough, made worse by the fact that he'd not shaved for the past few days. He was casually dressed but his white shirt had the grimy appearance of not having been changed for a while. 'I'm fine thanks but more importantly, how are you keeping? I've heard rumours on the grapevine but nobody at work really knows what happened. I didn't want to ask too many questions or show too much interest, for obvious reasons. Do you want to talk about it?' Herschell proceeded to pour out the details for the next half hour, Saul for the most part remaining silent and just listening. When he eventually explained that it was his carelessness over Goldenhawk Engineering that had brought about his demise, Saul's reaction was immediate and uncontrolled.

'You stupid, stupid, bastard. After all I told you. After all my warn-ings. You just couldn't resist a quick profit even though you put both of us at risk in the process. I told you never to deal directly in your own name. Only a greedy fool would take such a risk. But you went ahead and did it anyway, you *idiot*. So, are you proud of yourself now?' Herschell drew back from the table, shocked by his co-conspirator's anger. A silence followed as Saul considered the potential implications of Herschell's disclosure. He quickly realised that his position was even more vulnerable than he'd earlier thought. The SFO would already know that Herschell had not acted alone. Saul had been Sheldons' principal advisor to Goldenhawk, so it wouldn't take a super sleuth to follow the short trail to him.

'Nicholas, I'm sorry I lost my temper and if there's anything I can do to help then please, just ask. I've been thinking too much about myself and not enough about your situation. This is a nightmare for you but if I get caught up in this mess too then, well… I guess I'll just have to cross that bridge if and when I come to it'. Saul's stoicism brought a more relaxed atmosphere, and both men now felt more able to speak freely. 'So let's get down to details. What have your solicitors advised? Is there a defence to the charge?' Herschell's despondency was almost tangible. 'There's no defence unless I can prove that my earlier decision to buy the shares was unconnected with the later Goldenhawk announcement. In other words, the share purchase was entirely coincidental. But bearing in mind that we were the company's advisors, this will be impossible to do. The SFO will argue that the 'Chinese Wall' was breached, and I acted on information passed on from another department in Sheldons. And I'm afraid this is where you'll be at risk'. Saul nodded. 'Okay Nicholas, I get the picture. I've got to go now, but let's keep in touch. I really need to know what's happening so please call me every day. Not at work but at home any time after nine at night. Leave a message if I'm not in'.

As the two were leaving, Herschell turned to Saul. 'I nearly forgot: what do you suggest I do about the dinner fixed with Damyanovitch for this Friday? Do you still want to go ahead?' Saul had forgotten about the arrangement. 'I think we should still do it, but you need to speak to him before then. Tell him what's been going on. He's also benefited from the information you've passed on to him, so he'll need to take steps to protect his own position. He's a man of the world so he'll understand. Put him in the picture and then let's all meet up as planned'.

The following day, Herschell called his client. Damyanovitch listened intently as he recounted the events of the past few weeks. He asked a few questions but otherwise appeared unperturbed, as Saul had predicted. His main concern was whether Herschell had been questioned and if so, what had been disclosed. He seemed reassured when Herschell explained that, because he'd been formally charged with insider dealing, he couldn't be questioned any further by the Serious Fraud Office. Instead, both sides now had to wait for a trial date, possibly in six to nine months' time. Rigorous cross-examination by the Prosecution would take place in the Crown Court, assuming the case went 'all the way'. This triggered the Russian's curiosity. 'So what would prevent the case from going - how did you put it - 'all the way'? In what circumstances might the case be dropped?' Herschell replied that he'd had to familiarise himself with legal process in a very short time since his arrest. 'If the Crown Prosecution Service takes the view that the evidence is weak or unsubstantiated by reliable witnesses and there's less than a fifty-fifty chance of a conviction, then at that point they'd drop it. If they come to the view that a prosecution would not be 'in the public interest', then it's the same outcome. But this just isn't going to happen in my case'.

There was a pause on the line. 'And what if they ask you to assist with their wider enquiries? What if they offer you a deal? Would this be a way out?' Herschell hesitated, a delay noted by his client. The reality was that the case wouldn't be dropped; the evidence against him was just too overwhelming. The previous day his solicitor had been blunt. The standing of the City in the eyes of the public had deteriorated sharply in recent years and there was a widely held perception that dealers, traders, financiers- 'the whole bucket of eels,' as a leading redtop newspaper had recently branded them - believed they were above the law, corrupting the financial markets for their own ends. Against this backdrop and a vociferous media campaign for something to be done to 'clean out the stables' (how the redtops loved mixed metaphors when taking the moral high ground), a term of imprisonment was inevitable if convicted.

In fact, Herschell's lawyer had asked him for permission to make an informal approach to the SFO; the strategy was that he'd plead guilty and provide information about his secret clients' dealings in return for a non-custodial sentence. He would of course have a criminal record, but at least he'd stay out of jail. The SFO would save on legal costs and would also be better equipped to go after 'the bigger fish'. The solicitor was awaiting Herschell's decision. 'I don't think the SFO would be interested in doing a deal. There's very little I'd be able to offer them. They couldn't turn down an opportunity to make an example of a City high flier, and

I fit the bill perfectly'. Fleetingly, Damyanovitch reflected upon the thousands of lies he must have been told during his years with the KGB. He instinctively knew when someone was concealing the truth, even on the telephone – the practice of torture over a prolonged period of time develops such a sixth sense - and he knew that the man at the other end of the line was lying to him now or, at best, telling a half-truth. But he'd let it pass for the time being. 'I'm looking forward to seeing you and Saul Quartermain this Friday. Let's hope your situation gets a little better and if there's anything I can do, just call'. Herschell felt reassured; the worst of crises brought forth the best of friends and allies, or so he thought.

By the time Friday arrived, Herschell had made up his mind about his solicitor's proposal. The previous day he'd driven to Brixton prison - it was the prison nearest his apartment - and sat in his car a short distance from the entrance. For an hour he simply watched, his vision partly obscured by heavy rain flooding down the windscreen of his car. It clattered like iron bolts on the soft top of his Convertible, the beautiful pale yellow status symbol soon to be returned now that his career lay in ruins. He watched as dozens of people, their clothes soaked through, traipsed through the front gates to meet brothers, fathers, friends, lovers. The misery of the scene was palpable. Sometimes the human traffic flowed in the opposite direction as inmates at the end of terms of incarceration left for what they hoped would be the last time (but in many cases probably wouldn't be). There were the giveaway signs: the dull clothes, the prison-cell pallor, and small packages of Earthly belongings tucked under arms. Some were met by waiting visitors; others walked out alone. Herschell held his head in his hands and despaired. But the scene had at least clarified his thoughts: he'd take his solicitor's advice, cut a deal with the SFO, and betray anyone and everyone if that was what had to be done to save him from disappearing through a prison gate. Survival of the flesh was more important than saving his conscience or soul, such as they were; he'd surely die if he was forced to enter the frightening world opening up just a hundred feet and a Crown Court conviction away from where he sat.

'How did you come to work at Sheldons, Saul? And to become the youngest ever Head of the Corporate Finance Division so quickly?' Saul had been pleasantly surprised at how smoothly the evening had run. Herschell was extremely nervous and fidgety for the first twenty minutes after his arrival at the hotel, but Damyanovitch had gradually put him at ease with tales of the petty bureaucratic corruptions that prevailed during the final days of the Former Soviet Union. It was small talk of no real relevance to the two younger men, but the charismatic Russian appeared determined that a relaxed atmosphere be established before more pressing issues could be broached. Saul observed him throughout the evening, impressed by a sense of latent strength and power which pervaded everything he said or did, even in miniscule matters such as the use of cutlery, or summoning a waiter.

And yet there was also a vague sense of coldness that transcended the superficiality, rooted in a deeper part of his soul. He would smile but his eyes never changed. He would laugh but this was artificial, as if rehearsed and practiced elsewhere. He seemed to lack human warmth or emotion, yet the façade he presented was for the most part successful in concealing this. 'I started at Sheldons five years ago. It was the first job application I made and after the first interview they were keen to sign me up. I achieved my present position by deception and deviousness, and covert character assassination of all potential rivals. And as for the bad things I've done along the way, well, I just wouldn't like to say'. Saul looked over to Herschell and winked in his usual mischievous way. Damyanovitch smiled, not knowing how to react to such flippancy. These were the dying hours of Saul's youthful innocence and naivety; the terror that lay ahead later that night would close this childish chapter in his life for good. 'Nicholas, you've been quiet for a while. If the SFO offers you a deal, would you take it?' The case had been ever-present throughout the evening, hanging in the air like some black pungent cloud, but until then there'd been an unspoken agreement that it would not be mentioned. Damyanovitch had now broken this agreement. Herschell winced and Saul bowed his head, partly in disappointment with his guest but also in embarrassment for his colleague. This was neither the time nor the place to raise the subject.

'I told you earlier, Petr, I'm too small a fish for the SFO to offer me a deal. No, they'll go ahead with the prosecution and I'll just have to take my chances with the jury'. The Russian looked at him sympathetically. 'But we both know you don't have a hope if this case goes all the way. You are - forgive my bluntness – *guilty*, after all. And it's not just the insider dealing they'll be going for, is it? You were skimming your clients' accounts even before we started our association. Isn't that true?' There was a deathly silence until Saul, temporarily overcome by this new revelation, quietly spoke. 'Is this true, Nicholas? Were you taking clients' money? Please tell me it's not true'. Herschell looked at him, the blood drained from his face.

'Yes, it's true. They were profiting from the information so they were just as guilty. I was just taking a percentage of their illegal gains. And I wasn't the only one to benefit. Part of what I took was paid over to your Tri-Star Trust under our agreement'. Saul was visibly shaken, partly by what the former 'star trader' had confessed, but also because he'd raised their collaboration in front of a stranger. It was obvious that Damyanovitch knew everything already, and probably had done for some time before Herschell's arrest. 'We agreed that the payment was to be calculated on the trading turnover and not on the basis of stolen money. Because that's what it is. Stolen money. There's a world of difference between insider dealing, more or less a victimless crime as I see it, and theft, which is what you've done. And I'm implicated in both. It's only a matter of time before the SFO digs a little deeper, and when they do they'll come looking for me'.

Damyanovitch interjected. 'Gentlemen, let's not get ahead of ourselves. The SFO may drop the case, perhaps because the evidence is insufficient. Perhaps the skimming will not come to light. Who can say? Let's not spoil what's been a pleasant evening with recriminations. Allow me to refresh your glasses, and then we'll leave'. The two men stared at each other whilst the perfectly calm Damyanovitch poured the remains of the bottle of fine Rhone red. The conversation switched to lighter matters, and Saul and the bailed trader drew back from their confrontation. 'So apart from events of the past few weeks, everything's going fine for both of you at the bank, yes?' It was the first time that evening Damyanovitch had attempted anything vaguely amusing. Then suddenly Herschell started to sway, his eyes rolling. Saul caught him seconds before he'd have collapsed, holding him in an upright position as far as he was able to do so. He began to ramble, his words barely comprehendible. 'I don't feel too good. Dizzy ... Get me out of here. I'm burning up'. Damyanovitch called for the bill and after settling they left. By this time Herschell was barely able to navigate around the tables: with his arms around the shoulders of the other two he staggered out into the fresh air.

The Russian looked across at Saul and smiled. 'I guess he just can't take his drink. It's a wise man who knows when he's had enough'. But Saul wasn't so sure his colleague's condition had been caused by the wine. 'Nicholas has always been able to hold his drink. This isn't like him, and he hasn't had more than me tonight anyway. There's got to be something else wrong. Shall we take him to hospital?' By this time Damyanovitch had flagged down a taxi. 'No need. We'll just get him back to his apartment and leave him to sleep it off'. Saul searched Herschell's pockets and after finding his keys and address on a bank statement, gave directions to the driver.

Herschell's apartment was on the twelfth floor of an anonymous block overlooking Regent's Park. The aura of wealth was all-pervading, but a sense of isolation hung in the air too. Each tenant inhabited a private, sanitised world, never needing or wanting to venture forth to make the acquaintance of a neighbour. As the three glided up through the building in the silent, carpeted lift, Saul was anxious without knowing why. Damyanovitch hadn't spoken since exiting the taxi, his brooding expression suggesting his mind was elsewhere. When Saul opened the door to the apartment he was overwhelmed by what greeted him. The walls were adorned with modern art posters illuminated by small spotlights strategically placed across the ceiling. The furniture was minimalist, expensive. Such were the trappings of wealth and crime. After gently lowering Herschell into a large white sofa, his two porters sank into easy chairs either side of him. A few minutes total silence followed, although it seemed like an hour to the younger man. 'You know he'll do a deal with the SFO, don't you?' Damyanovitch had broken the silence with a simple sentence Saul knew to be true. 'But he won't escape prison- he'll just lessen his sentence. And you, Saul? You'll be implicated, betrayed, arrested and destroyed. Are you ready for that?'

The Russian hadn't raised his voice: it was the calmness with which he spoke that chilled Saul. 'But it's not just you who'll be affected. I've invested time and money getting to this point. I've gained respectability through association with this young fool, and this has opened many doors. After he's had his day in court all this effort will have been for nothing. I'll be seen as just another member of the Moscow kleptocracy, not to be trusted or welcomed into the London bond markets. Now, what do you suggest we do about this threat to both our futures?' Saul stared at the man sitting alongside Herschell: he hadn't appreciated the extent of their cooperation. He responded with stoicism. 'I don't want to go to prison, of course I don't, but if this is what's meant to be, then so be it. I'll just have to take the punishment'. Damyanovitch smiled at his naivety. 'Believe me, you won't survive, and neither will your friend. It'll be for more than just a few months. You'll be there for years. If I understand the law rightly, you're guilty of insider dealing, and you're also associated with theft of clients' funds, an even more serious offence. And yes, I know all the dirty secrets. I know about Goldenhawk, Rothersmann Chemicals, Smith LB Containers, Elma-Hammer Engineering, etc, etc, etc. I know everything'. Saul was shocked to hear the roll call of shares he'd traded over the past year. Damyanovitch finally whispered, 'I also know about the Tri-Star Trust'.

'Okay Petr, you know everything. So what? Are you going to tell the SFO? If yes, then just get on with it. If no, and it's some deal you want to do, let's hear it. Just get to the point, please'. Saul was surprised by his own directness, but also petrified that details of his own criminality were so well known to his interrogator. 'Would I be right in thinking you'd prefer our mutual friend was silent? That he didn't do a deal with the SFO or reveal your name? Do you want this?' 'Of course it's what I'd prefer, but we've got to live in the real world. He's already been charged. It's just a matter of time before he talks'. The Russian stood to his feet and began gently tapping Herschell's arm. 'Nicholas, how about some fresh air? Would you like that?' The young man was still semi-conscious but managed to nod his head. 'Saul, give me a hand.' The two assisted Herschell across the room and onto the narrow balcony immediately outside the apartment. A gentle breeze pulled at the long silk curtains through which they passed. It was a perfect night, cool and starlit.

In an instant, Damyanovitch took hold of Herschell, effortlessly lifted him off his feet, and heaved him over the side of the balcony into the darkness below.

Saul screamed at the killer. 'What have you done? What the hell have you done?' In the darkness below he could make out the outline of a broken body. Damyanovitch shoved the trembling Saul against the balcony wall, his face expressionless, his voice perfectly calm. 'I've just saved you from a prison sentence. I killed a fool for a worthy cause - to protect myself, so I can serve my country. What pointless, meaningless lives you people lead. You strive towards nothing other than your own greedy gains. Tonight we've both survived because I did what needed to be done. Just be grateful'. Saul broke free from the Russian's grip. He needed to be practical. 'So what will the police make of this when they find the body? Won't they come looking for us? We were the last people seen with him at the restaurant'. 'As far as they'll be concerned, either he jumped because he was too afraid to face a trial or he fell because he was drunk and didn't know where he was or what he was doing. Everyone saw what state he was in, and the drug I put in his wine won't be detectable by the time they find the body'. Saul was outraged by this new revelation. 'You drugged him? What kind of a man are you? You planned this murder before we even met this evening, didn't you?' 'Of course I planned it. I drugged him because you and I needed to talk, but also because I didn't want a struggle. When the police interview you, you'll say we saw him safely back to his flat. He was very depressed at dinner. He said he couldn't go ahead with a trial. We were worried he was thinking of doing something foolish. We stayed with him a while but then had to leave. Just keep to the story and there'll not be a problem'.

They stepped back into the apartment; after Damyanovitch had hung up Herschell's crumpled jacket they entered the same lift used earlier. As they descended, the Russian turned to Saul. 'Tonight I saved your career and your freedom. Neither was ever going to come cheaply. I'll expect the favour returned when I call for it. We've only just begun our association, our *partnership*, so get used to it.' Saul remained silent. 'I know this night's been difficult but you'll get over it, sooner than you think. A Russian leader once said the death of one person is a tragedy, but the deaths of a million are just a statistic. For you tonight's death is a tragedy. For me it's just a statistic. My friend, don't become another statistic'.

The weeks following Herschell's murder were predictably stressful and terrifying for Saul. The dead trader's tormentors, Detective Inspector Alex Grey and Detective Chief Inspector Peter Dorling, knew that he had not worked alone in his crimes but there was no obvious paper trail linking him to anyone else at the bank. A prevalent culture of petty criminality served only to cloud the wider picture; indeed, it was impossible to rule out with any degree of certainty a large number of employees who may have been the dead trader's co-conspirators. Dorling's efforts were further undermined when, within days of the murder, a national newspaper picked up on the story. Headlines such as 'City fraudster in suicide death leap' had a bandwagon effect. A perception quickly gained ground that this was a relatively straightforward case of suicide by a young, frightened trader facing a term of imprisonment. The investigation quickly ran out of steam, and, reluctantly, the two detectives decided to close the case. Messrs Grey and Dorling instinctively knew that bigger fish had got away on this occasion, but sometimes they had to content themselves with persecuting foot soldiers to signal to the generals where the line was drawn.

The whole episode had severely drained Saul's mental and physical reserves. During the early part of the investigation his dreams had been beset by the same recurring image; every night he would return to the balcony, stretch out his hands to catch hold of the falling trader, but always without success. Damyanovitch's impassive demeanour was always the final image in the nightmare, waking him at a time too late to get back to proper sleep, but too early to rise for the day either. The chairman of Moscow Alpha Bank was interviewed and his testimony squared perfectly with Saul's. He was due to leave for Moscow at the end of the week, but agreed that he'd return at short notice should the police wish it.

The autopsy subsequently confirmed that Herschell had consumed a large amount of alcohol immediately prior to his death: there was no trace of suspicious substances present in his body. The matter was closed to the satisfaction of all concerned, including, of course, Herschell's murderer.

Chapter Twenty Eight

Chloe gently swayed her legs in the warm water as she floated beneath the massive full moon. She'd needed to get away, to have time to plan her career, but also to re-appraise her future with Thomas. She loved him, of course: he gave her a stability and predictability which she found reassuring. He had no burning ambition to change the world or for that matter even to see it, and that had been a characteristic she found attractive in the early days of their relationship. But now she was contemplating her own career prospects on an equal footing with, and occasionally placing them above, her imminent marriage.

For Thomas thoughts of career, ambition, and worldly curiosity didn't even feature as distant pinpricks on his mental horizon. Perhaps he loved her too much. Perhaps he would become overly possessive in the later years of their marriage, restricting the freedom she now took for granted. The previous day, Friday, she'd finished work earlier than usual, at four thirty. That weekend he'd be staying at his family home; she'd declined the invitation to travel with him, ostensibly because there were case files that needed preparation for a tax appeal the following week. Instead she packed a small suitcase and headed off to Heathrow, boarded a plane, arriving in Capri three hours later. As she floated in the darkness, her glistening and relaxed body extended across water still as a millpond, she considered her options. It would be easier, much easier, to succumb to what everyone quite naturally expected of her and simply marry him. But as she gazed up at the stars she knew that this compliance with the expectations of others wouldn't bring her happiness or a proper sense of fulfillment, either on the day of the deception or in a lifetime of regret that would follow. Why, too, should she sacrifice the next five or so years, irreparably damaging her chance of a career in any genuine sense of the word, just to satisfy a man's dream of what married life should be all about?

Earlier that day, sitting at a café table overlooking the harbour front, she'd been joined by local schoolchildren looking to practice English with the late summer tourists. Together they'd watched small boats gently bobbing up and down in the distance while eating ice creams, making them last as long as possible in the heat of the afternoon sun. They'd chatted and laughed with each new mispronounced word or phrase, and for that brief half hour she felt utterly at peace with the world. Nobody knew where she was; was such a need for privacy, secrecy, compatible with the openness expected and deserved in a marriage? She had to end things now. She'd meet him on Monday and tell him she no longer wanted to be married. Not to him, not to anyone. She'd justify her decision, couch it in terms of a need to keep her freedom and continue her career. She expected, with a heavy heart, that he'd pursue her, beg her to change her mind, and in so doing lose her respect. If his self-respect was to remain intact, his romanticised image of her would have to be destroyed. Although this would not be easy to achieve, she knew there was one human failing that Thomas considered reprehensible above all others. There was one unique act that could never be forgiven, and that act was betrayal. A chill breeze gently rippled the cool waters surrounding her: she began powering her way back to the shore. A lone seagull passed effortlessly overhead, and despite its height she could hear the feathery mechanical motion of its wings. As she emerged from the darkness she felt a sense of trepidation, of looming cataclysm. But she also felt more alive, more confident and focused, than at any time during the past year. Wrapped in the light beach robe she'd earlier left folded on the sand, she headed back to the hotel. She would sleep well that night.

Several weeks passed before Saul was capable of focusing properly upon his day-to-day duties at Sheldons. Damyanovitch had been correct in his assertion that Herschell's 'suicide' would bring an end to the police investigation into insider dealing at the bank. The death also led to an extension of his responsibilities at Sheldons and a deepening of the trust and regard with which he was held by the board. He was now temporarily responsible for supervision of the sales team until such time as a permanent replacement for Herschell could be found. His salary was duly increased to reflect these additional duties, but it was the influence that holding the two posts of Head of Corporate Finance and Manager, Equities, afforded over the bank's strategy that significantly enhanced his power and indispensability.

At the same time, though, he found that he had completely lost his appetite for insider dealing: it simply wasn't worth the risk anymore. He'd got away with it once: he'd be slow to return to the game for a while. In any event, the Tri-Star Trust was still totally committed to Franklin Shandlin and his company, Piedmont Communications; there was no spare cash available for other speculative, illegal investments. The company's share price continued drifting upwards in the following months, negating any argument for selling until all gains from the takeover 'bounce' had been realised. In the short term they'd simply 'sit tight' and hold on to the shares.

Although Saul was the person to whom junior and middle management reported on a daily basis, he too was required to make his own reports to the bank's board of directors. It therefore came as no surprise when he received an e-mail from the chairman inviting him to lunch later that week. He wasn't requested to make a formal presentation on any particular issue, and for this reason assumed it was merely the chairman availing himself of an opportunity to exchange ideas, discuss general strategy, and to get to know better a key player in the bank. But by the time the day of the lunch arrived Saul's fears had resurfaced. Perhaps Grey and Dorling had succeeded in finding fresh evidence of his earlier collusion with Herschell and would be waiting in the chairman's room to make an arrest. Perhaps the chairman had come to know about his involvement in the Tri-Star Trust and was about to give him a 'last meal' before dismissing him with immediate effect. Objectively this was unlikely, but Saul was not always thinking rationally these days.

He smiled as he sauntered towards the room, successfully concealing his nervousness. 'Saul, welcome; good to see you'. Paul Phineus had been Sheldons' chairman and chief executive for five years and during his stewardship profitability had increased year on year. During the fifteen years prior to his appointment he'd passed through several other top City financial institutions, holding the post of chief executive in two of them. He had an outstanding intellect and an uncanny ability to predict shifts in currency rates, commodities and stock markets in advance of political events and economic crises. He had the two essential qualities for success in the City: technical foresight, and luck. The two sat down to lunch which included the best wine brought out from the bank's stock only for the highest fee- paying clients. After finishing the main course, the chairman proceeded to the subject which had been preoccupying him for the past week. 'What do you know about Petr Damyanovitch, Saul? Is he the sort of man we should do business with? You're the driver of our Central Asia strategy, so you'll already know the players in these markets. I'm curious to know more about this man and his bank Moscow Alpha - should we get involved with either?'

Saul hesitated; he hadn't realised Damyanovitch was already known to the chairman and was anxious to know how the connection had come about. He tried concealing his interest. 'I can't tell you much about Damyanovitch; I hardly know the man. I know he's the majority share-holder in Moscow Alpha, and I guess that makes him one of Russia's new oligarchs. I'd need to ask some of my contacts what they know about him and the bank. I can find out soon enough whether they're suspected of any of the usual concerns for that part of the world. You know the sorts of things - mafia shareholders, money laundering, non-existent capital bases, etc, etc, etc'. The chairman drew on the cigar he was gently teasing with a match and raised an eyebrow. 'I'm surprised you don't know him well enough to express an opinion. He seems to know *you* very well. He was here a month ago, sitting where you're sitting now, and spoke very highly of you. Was he exaggerating his acquaintance with you? If not, you can be open with me – why the reticence?' Phineus fixed him with a beady eye, gazing through the smoke puffing out from the glowing cigar. 'I'm flat-tered, but apart from a dinner a few months ago we've not met before. I must have made quite an impression, but I have this effect on nearly every-one I meet'. Phineus grinned. 'Naturally. Now, tell me about the bank'. 'Well, purely from memory, it has adequate capital at the very least. It has a conservative lending policy, I think, and keeps a tight rein on its assets-to-liabilities ratio. Historically, bad debts have been almost zero. It's amaz-ing how the prospect of being taken down a Moscow back-alley and beaten up, or having a member of your family kidnapped and held to ransom, focuses the mind of the most recalcitrant of borrowers'. The chairman smiled; he liked Saul's humour and cynicism, even if other board members found it flippant. 'And what about transparency? Do we know who's really behind the bank?' 'Damyanovitch holds most of the shares. The remain-der are held by two other oligarchs from the energy and shipping sectors. But remember, nearly all the Russian oligarchs are in collusion in one way or another with the political forces in the country. They have to be, just to survive and to be allowed to retain their economic power'.

Phineus puffed out several grey-blue smoke rings whilst mulling over Saul's analysis. His guest's instinct interested him, that intangible sixth sense that dowsers use to find water, and farmers to call in cattle on a perfect day, hours before a storm. 'So if there's limited transparency and mafia money everywhere, why have you been driving a strategy to take us deeper into this market? What is it about Central Asia that puts it above China, for example, on your list of new regions for our investment capital?' 'Oh, that's quite simple. Central Asia, particularly the Caspian States, present us with unique opportunities to build up relationships with local banks at the very time their need for capital is at its greatest. If we get in now there's a good chance they'll stay with us when they're on their feet and able to pick and choose their partners. Russia, as we know, is going for free market capitalism in a big way and has to compete for capital with these newly independent countries which it ran until recently. We'll be in there first, reaping the benefits'.

The chairman liked what he heard, but was more circumspect. 'I understand your enthusiasm Saul, but we must be cautious. I agree with you about the opportunities, but we need to take care in choosing the partners we work with. As I mentioned earlier, Damyanovitch came to see me a month ago to discuss a project. He wants us to work together on a bid to lead manage a bond issue by two of the largest energy companies in the region. Moscow Alpha will benefit from our technical know-how and investor base, and we'll gain from their expertise in the local markets and network of political contacts. In fact, one of the reasons I asked you here today was to tell you that he specifically asked that you visit him at the bank's head office to discuss the proposal in more detail. I'd like you to contact him and fix up a meeting for the next few weeks. It'll just be for a few days, and you'll get to know more about the man while you're there. Have you been to Moscow before?' Saul concealed his terror at the prospect of meeting Damyanovitch again, but this time on his home territory, and replied with the calm assurance expected of him. 'I've been to nearly all the former Soviet satellites but never to Russia. Strange really, bearing in mind I've been driving our strategy in that part of the world for the past few years. It'll be interesting to make the trip and get a feel for the opportunities there. If Damyanovitch can open doors for us, and if Moscow Alpha is up to the job, then let's go for it. I'll check my diary but I should be okay to go out next week.'

Chapter Twenty Nine

The Swissair flight from Heathrow to Moscow was perfect in every way. The changeover at Zurich was efficient, leaving Saul with only fifty minutes to fill before boarding the flight onwards to Domodedovo, Moscow. After a total flight time of just under six hours, his plane touched down on Russian soil. During the descent through a cloudless sky, Saul contemplated the prospect of meeting the chairman of Moscow Alpha Bank again. Would they greet each other and discuss the weather as if nothing had happened in London? On his way through customs a pale, unsmiling official superficially searched his small hand luggage. As he strolled along with the English speakers who'd arrived on the same flight and were equally lost, he tried to gain his bearings. Eventually he picked out a slim, smartly dressed young woman in the crowd holding a small placard with his name, misspelled, printed in bright-red ink. He headed towards her and she seemed to recognise him. 'Mr. Quartermain. Welcome to Moscow. It's a pleasure to meet you'. She beamed as she spoke. After the genuine greeting Laura Simenova shook his hand and led him out to a black limousine parked (illegally) two minutes away from the airport's main entrance.

The driver turned and smiled as Saul climbed in. 'Welcome to Moscow, sir. I hope you will be having a good time when you are here'. Sergei Ivanov, Petr Damyanovitch's driver, held out his hand. After placing his luggage in the boot, Ms. Simenova opened the door and slid in alongside Saul. The large leather-upholstered seats seemed to swallow her up, and her relaxed demeanour instantly indicated she was accustomed to a chauffeur-driven lifestyle. During the short journey from the airport into central Moscow Saul's companion chatted, laughed, and teased as if they'd known each other a lifetime. Her lack of affectation, her warmth and gentle inquisitiveness were disarming: Saul's earlier fear of being on the murderer's home ground was temporarily forgotten. As they reached the sprawl of the city outskirts after time on the motorway, he looked out through tinted glass. He was struck by the diversity of Muscovites. There were the usual tourists of course, and young entrepreneurs in sharp suits with mobile phones clamped firmly to their ears, shouting above the cacophony to business partners in other parts of the city. But there were also the old and the infirm, wandering lost along unfriendly sidewalks, proffering sprigs of heather and trinkets to anyone speaking English. These were the casualties of the transition to a market economy.

'We've booked you in at the Metropol Hotel. If you go up to the top floors you'll have a wonderful view of the domes of St. Basil's Cathedral, Red Square and the Kremlin. We'll collect you at 6.30pm.' Half an hour later they arrived at their destination. Saul shook her cool hand and thanked her. 'We'll see you later. We've also arranged a surprise for you. I hope you won't mind that I've arranged for a change of clothing to be left in your room. I knew you'd be traveling light since you're only here a couple of days'. With a frisson of childish excitement in anticipation of the evening's event, Saul stepped out of the car and entered the hotel lobby. At 6.30 pm precisely, Laura and Damyanovitch strolled into the hotel bar where Saul had been listening to a small group of jazz players for the past hour. He'd already had a few glasses of the local beer and was feeling relaxed and slightly light-headed. He gently kissed her in welcome, any inhibition he may have felt for local etiquette weakened by the alcohol. He then shook hands with Damyanovitch. 'Saul, good to see you again. It seems like only yesterday we met in London, but it must be several months ago now'. Saul smiled. 'Four, to be exact. Thanks for asking Paul Phineus to send me; I know there were plenty of others at Sheldons who would've jumped at the opportunity to come. I hope you won't be disappointed'. The Russian smiled broadly. 'Saul, I know you'll not disappoint me. You're the right man for the project I have in mind. The two of us, and of course Sheldons and Moscow Alpha, have a unique opportunity to shape the course of history in this part of the world, and there's nobody I'd rather work with than you. Now, if you're ready, shall we leave? We've something special in store for you'.

Saul was perplexed by Damyanovitch's confidence; how could he be so certain that Sheldons would agree to any joint business venture, despite Moscow Alpha's recent upgrading by the credit rating agencies? The talk of 'shaping history' also perturbed him; he lived entirely for the here and now and was by instinct suspicious of those who entertained such lofty ambitions. Such people were usually either mad, in which case relatively harmless, or genuine and accordingly dangerous and unpredictable. Damyanovitch was the latter. 'I'm pleased Laura managed to get a tuxedo for you; it fits perfectly. But I take the credit for correctly guessing your measurements'. After five minutes' walk, Damyanovitch brought them to a halt on a street corner opening out onto a square behind him. 'Saul, I said we had a treat for you, and here it is'. He moved aside to reveal the stucco'ed façade of a temple-like building with a pale pink exterior which was fronted by elegant colonnades. A circular fountain gushed in front of them, cooling the air, its droplets lifted on a gentle breeze. 'I give you the Bolshoi Theatre, and we have tickets for tonight's performance of Shostakovich's "Lady Macbeth of Mtsensk". Shall we?'

He extended his hand and the three proceeded up the steps and into the hallowed shrine of international ballet and opera. As they ascended the flights of stairs to their box on the second floor, Saul was surprised, impressed, by the many people who greeted Damyanovitch as he passed. Some bowed their heads in respect, but his demeanour never seemed to change. After they'd entered the box Saul looked out over the auditorium. He felt privileged, almost like royalty, as he settled back in one of the best positions in the house, listening to the hubbub in the stalls below and around the dress circles. 'Saul, it'll not be long before the performance gets underway and I hope you won't think me impolite, but there are a few things I need to clarify with you ahead of tomorrow's board meeting. I need to get a picture of Sheldons' activities in this part of the world. Can we talk for a while, even if only in general terms?' 'Feel free to ask anything you like, Petr. I'm as eager as you are to get things moving between Moscow Alpha and Sheldons. For the past few years I've been developing our strategy for Eastern Europe and Central Asia. Your bank is just the sort of local institution we'd like to tie up with, but that of course depends on what sort of business you have in mind'. Below, the orchestra started tuning up; he could see musicians flicking through sheets in the pit's half-light, adjusting strings, applying resin to old bows and gently blowing on an array of burnished wind instruments.

'I need to know which parts of the Caucasus Sheldons is active in. We have an interest in the development of Caspian Sea oil reserves, and because of this I need to know about your links with banks in the region.

Tomorrow all will be explained, but if you can provide an overview from your side beforehand, it would be most helpful to me'. Saul tried refocusing; he'd been asked for very specific, commercially sensitive information albeit concealed in generalised questions. 'Petr, you're asking about confidential matters. I'm sure that if my boss were here tonight we'd be talking about the fabulous interiors of this theatre and the storyline of what we're about to see. Not the bank's secrets. You know the game'. Damyanovitch smiled. 'My friend, you're no insider dealing virgin, as we both know. We've been sharing information for quite a while now through our intermediary. We're about to put in place a mutually beneficial relationship between Moscow Alpha and Sheldons. Please, don't get defensive on me at this early stage. It just doesn't suit you'. Saul laughed even though this was the first time any reference, albeit obliquely, had been made to the late and unlamented Herschell. 'Okay, I think I can give a little without getting into too much ethical trouble. We have relations with Baku Bank of Azerbaijan, Kazakbank, Turkmenbank, and Tblisi Bank of Georgia. We're negotiating with Uzbekbank and should have a tie-up within the next six months. Now, does that help you gain an insight into our strategy for the region?'

The oligarch's attention had noticeably sharpened at the mention of names of financial institutions with which he was fully familiar. Although he already knew that Sheldons was active in the region, the network was more extensive than he'd thought possible. He would press his guest a little further. 'That's very helpful indeed, thank you. Now, what can you tell me about these links? Keeping all this information to yourself, not being able to share it, this must be such a burden. I'd like to share your burden. What would you like to tell me?' Saul didn't see how he could evade the questions, so continued to talk. 'Sheldons has put in place lines of credit to each bank to assist with short term funding needs, and made medium term loans at low interest rates. After all, we've sizeable shareholdings in each bank so we've got a vested interest in seeing them succeed'. Laura had been watching the preparations in the pit below, her eyes sparkling as she gazed at the trickle of latecomers now taking up their seats across the auditorium. The curtain started to rise and the audience fell silent.

'So, Saul, what did you think of 'The Lady'? Was it to your liking, or was it perhaps a little too intense?' As the three descended the stairs they chatted about the performance like old friends. They walked out into the street, the coolness of the night air refreshing after the theatre's heavy atmosphere. It was eleven o'clock but crowds were everywhere, pouring out from smaller theatres and restaurants in the vicinity. Vodka-soaked demobbed soldiers staggered past the new glitterati, seeking out dry doorways for the night. This was a city where the destitute and the nouveau riche lived cheek by jowl but in completely separate worlds. Flashing neon signs and familiar fast food chains trumpeted the arrival of Western consumerism. 'Laura, we've a busy day tomorrow so perhaps now's a good time to bring a fine evening to its end. Saul, I have to tell you that my exceptionally talented personal assistant made all this evening's arrangements. Her organisational skills, her imagination, and her free spirit are very precious to me'. Damyanovitch raised the young woman's hand and placed it against his lips, their eyes meeting for seconds. Saul felt like a spectator, trying to fathom the nature of their relationship. A Mercedes appeared as if from nowhere. Laura turned again to Saul. 'It's been a pleasure to have spent this evening with you, and we'll do the same again soon. I'll not see you tomorrow because I'm traveling to St. Petersburg early in the morning. Sergei will collect you after the meeting with the board and take you to the airport. So I'll wish you a good night's sleep and a safe flight back to London'. She kissed him, entered the waiting car, and disappeared into the night.

'Saul, I know it's late but this is your first time in Moscow and I'd like to show you some of our city's famous landmarks. Would this please you?' The young banker felt alert and energetic. 'I can't think of a better way to end my day here. Please, lead on.' After ten minutes they were standing before two towers straddling two portals. Looking through one of the portals Saul could make out St. Basil's coloured onion domes silhouetted against the night sky. 'This is the Resurrection Gateway. It's a useful metaphor for what's happened to Russia over the past decade. It was taken down in the first place because it blocked the entry of tanks into Red Square during May Day celebrations and their military parades. Now that we've suddenly become a third-rate military power, we don't have a need for those celebrations anymore. Our military pride has gone. We've becoming a nation of black marketeers and second-hand car dealers, and the tragedy is, we've closed our eyes to what's become of us'.

The two men walked through into the vastness of Red Square, St. Basil's Cathedral looming before them. Young and old, rich and poor, the Square was full of people despite the late hour. The Russian stopped and gazed into the distance; his thoughts had returned to another time. 'In 1945 I stood here watching as our victorious army swept into the Square. One of our greatest leaders, General Zhukov, rode a white horse at the head of the procession. We'd come through Hell and triumphed. Those were the greatest of days'. He looked out into the distance again, returning in his mind's eye to that late autumn afternoon a lifetime ago, and for a moment he was gone. Suddenly he seemed to change as he turned his attention to Saul. The emotion which had flickered into his face had disappeared, replaced by his familiar steely countenance.

'Tomorrow you'll meet with the board of Moscow Alpha. They'll explain the contribution we can make to any joint venture with Sheldons Bank but it's our local knowledge and contacts which will be of most interest to you. We work with some of the largest private and publicly quoted companies in the Russian Federation, and have 'favoured status' at the highest levels of government.' Saul smiled. 'With respect, Petr, I know all this from the checks I ran on Moscow Alpha before coming here. This is small talk. What are you really looking for from Sheldons, and where do I fit in with your plans?' The Russian remained impassive. 'I respect your directness Saul, but before I answer your questions, I'll ask a general one of my own first. What do you know about the BTC pipeline?' Saul knew about the Caspian Sea's oil reserves: Sheldons had previously financed several exploration companies in the region. 'You're referring to the Baku-Tbilisi-Ceyhan oil pipeline, not yet built because of the cost of laying pipelines on the Caspian Sea floor between Kazakhstan and Baku. It'll go through several politically unstable regions as far as I understand; Azerbaijan, Chechnya, and Kurdish Iraq.'

'Your knowledge is impressive, as always. Let me add to it. The Americans want a pipeline rising in Azerbaijan's capital Baku, terminating in the Mediterranean at Ceyhan. Oil transit would be through Turkey, which they see as the least unstable country in the region and, of course, the West's ally. This is the BTC option. Russia's neighbours in the Caspian region will do well out of it, but my country will suffer - economically and politically'. Saul was confused: how could a single pipeline present such a threat to an energy superpower like Russia? 'Petr, I don't understand your concern. One pipeline's not going to make a difference. You'll still have the existing network from Soviet times. What does it matter if a new network's constructed alongside it?' Damyanovitch answered directly. 'If our neighbours don't have to use our network to transport their oil, we'll not be able to charge transit fees. And we'll not be able to turn off the flow when we need to apply pressure upon their governments in the future. They'll have broken free of us in more ways than you can imagine. I'll not allow it. I'll not stand idly by as our place in the world is eroded in this way.' His calm, rational resentment was unmistakable. He paused and then smiled, his demeanour changing in an instant. 'But I'm sure you don't want to hear the personal views of 'Chairman Damyanovitch'. Now, to your questions. What do we want from Sheldons, and what will be your role? We want to take advantage of your bank's status in the international capital markets, and your investor base. As for your role, we need someone to act as trusted intermediary between Moscow Alpha and those financial institutions in the Caspian States with which Sheldons already cooperates. You see, they distrust anything that comes out of Russia. We're the old bogeyman, the former ruler trying to restore our power in the region'. The underplay was disingenuous: the former master was still a military power to be reckoned with, a goliath brooding and resentful on its neighbours' borders. 'They'll conclude that if an English bank makes a proposal to them fronted by a slick, handsome, pinstripe-suited gentleman, then even if there's Russian involvement, it's bound to be safe. Your trustworthiness is needed to conceal our interest and our schemes'.

Saul was unsettled by his candour: the Russian clearly regarded him as a useful fool in some greater plan. 'Petr, don't assume that my loyalty can be switched around so easily. You want me to attend Sheldons board meetings and push the envelope on your behalf, without even disclosing it's you I'm representing. You want to conceal your involvement from our partners in the Caspian. Unless you give me a lot more information, quickly, I'll walk away and hang you and Moscow Alpha out to dry'. Damyanovitch hesitated before replying to Saul's bluntness, his threat. 'I'm sorry if I've offended you. Tomorrow should clarify things, but ultimately it will indeed come down to a matter of price. We're both realists so let's have no self-delusion about professional ethics. You need wealth to live life the way you want, on your own terms. You're self-interested, and I understand that - it's not a crime, except when insider dealing is part of the plan. But let's not go back over old ground. My country's future prosperity is my sole concern, and will be until my last breath. You should realise that there's nothing I wouldn't do to achieve my goals. I'm not constrained by moral boundaries and for this reason alone you should fear me'.

Chapter Thirty

The following morning Saul was woken up by a sharp knock at his hotel room door. 'Mr. Saul, your room service. Mr. Saul, you are awake?' He got out of bed, threw on his dressing gown and made his way to the door, yawning and stretching as he went. 'Mr. Saul, good morning. I hope you slept well. Please, may I come in with your breakfast?' In front of him stood an overweight young woman of about twenty-five, wearing a hotel uniform at least one size too small for her ample proportions. She smiled shyly as Saul beckoned her in, walking over to the glass-topped table where she placed the heavy silver tray bearing a luxurious breakfast. 'Will you be seeing the sites of our great city today, Mr. Saul, or perhaps some business meetings?' Without asking permission she pulled the curtain cord, flooding the room in an instant with brilliant sunlight.

Seeing that the guest's eyes had narrowed with the sudden and unex-pected intrusion of the outside world into his cocoon of semi-darkness, Helga Korchikov moved to position herself between Saul and the wall-length window. Her strategy worked and for a moment an interceding body eclipsed the outside sun in its cloudless sky. She chuckled at his discomfort. Saul smiled, amused by her vim and healthy disrespect. As he walked with her to the door he gave her fifty dollars, the biggest tip she'd received since starting at the hotel, and over half her weekly wage. 'Thank you Mr. Saul, thank you so much. You are so kind. I wish you very, very good day. *Dassvedaniyah*'. For the next half hour he made his way through a woven silver basket of croissants and blinis, still hot enough to melt the syrup which smothered them. The silver coffee pot had been filled to the brim, a generosity lacking in most of the West European hotels in which he'd stayed over the past few years. At eight thirty he was sitting in the lobby reading the day's Washington Post, waiting for Sergei Ivanov and his immaculate black Limousine.

Saul had half-expected Moscow Alpha's board to consist of a high proportion of former Party apparatchiks, with basic or non-existent English. Such had been the case with most of the boards he'd attended in those Central European banks with which Sheldons had recently established links. He was used to meeting directors who had no idea of international banking but who'd nevertheless risen to positions of prominence by virtue of political connections and, most likely, bribery. Burdened with these preconceptions, Saul arrived at the bank's head office, his expectations low. It therefore came as a refreshing surprise to find a board dominated by young, seemingly dynamic individuals, experienced through placements with some of the leading financial institutions of Western Europe and the US. Of course there were representatives of the old regime, still Communists to a man, but even they spoke with perfect English, engaging with the younger members as if the age difference just didn't exist. As the meeting got underway Saul was impressed by the enthusiasm of those seated around the table, firing questions at him about Sheldons' Central Asia strategy. At the head of the conference table sat Petr Damyanovitch, occasionally intervening with questions of his own but for the most part leaving his guest's cross-examination to the younger acolytes. To his left was Ivan Chelneko, the principal shareholder in St. Petersburg Shipping; to his right, George Polnikov, chairman of Sovoil, the state-owned energy company. Between them, these three men represented Russia's new oligarch class; they'd seized economic power and now intended to use it.

The two other oligarchs looked on impassively as Damyanovitch opened with pleasantries and emphasised that their bank was prudent and well-run. 'Now we'd like to discuss a proposal we hope you'll take back to London and put before your board. Last night you and I informally discussed the BTC pipeline. This project has been spoken about by energy economists and politicians for years. President Clinton once described it as the 'cornerstone' of US foreign policy in the Caucasus and his successor, George Bush Jr. has taken a similar line. But until now, the economics just didn't add up. The huge investment needed to lay a pipeline across the Caspian Sea floor couldn't be repaid for decades. But the world has changed. Global demand for oil remains insatiable but the regions from which it's supplied remain politically unstable and in the case of our new neighbours, frankly, unreliable. And herein lies the dilemma. Should the industrialised nations simply continue consuming oil at the present rate, keeping their fingers crossed the suppliers will not collapse into anarchy and chaos, or instead start making alternative arrangements? We believe the latter provides the only rational answer, a view shared with our political masters here in Russia, and with our friends in the United States'.

Saul couldn't conceal a smile at the mention of 'friends in the United States'. The world had indeed changed: two formerly sworn enemies were now working together towards common goals. But the phrase also raised a more fundamental question: who exactly were Damyanovitch's 'friends' in the US? 'I'd like to pass over now to our oil analyst Adam Borkowski to give an overview of Caspian Sea oil economics. I'll then follow on with the proposal we'd like you to take back to London'.

The young Russian oil futures trader walked to the front of the room and loaded a presentation into the computer. He proceeded to describe the politics of those countries bordering the Caspian Sea, the so-called littoral states of Azerbaijan, Kazakhstan, Turkmenistan, Iran, and of course Russia. Saul saw past the complicated graphs and charts and understood Damyanovitch's obsession with the region and the proposed pipeline. The Caspian's oil reserves were truly vast; if the benefits were reaped by Russia's neighbours alone, the shift in the balance of power would be seismic. The BTC pipeline would transport oil across to the Turkish port of Ceyhan, but around rather than over Russian territory which would be bypassed entirely. The power to shut off the flow and hold intransigent states to ransom would be lost forever; age-old Russian political power in the region would be consigned to the history books. There was also the practical matter of the loss of huge transit fees to the Russian economy, presently extracted from far-from-willing users of the clapped-out Russian pipeline system. The young oil expert switched off the computer and resumed his seat. Damyanovitch looked around the table and then spoke. 'I thank the board for attending this meeting today. I'll not detain you further so if you'd like to leave now I'll be grateful'. Moscow Alpha's directors dutifully filed out except for the principal shareholders in St. Petersburg Shipping and Sovoil. Damyanovitch had addressed his board with courtesy and respect, but it was apparent that the key players now remained.

Damyanovitch turned to Saul and resumed their conversation. 'Now we can talk freely. However trustworthy one's board, there's always a risk of leaks, particularly when a new project is still in its infancy. And we've not even reached that stage yet.' Chelneko and Polnikov remained silent. 'We have an ambitious project here, and one that will establish Sheldons' dominant position in the Caspian oil sector and at the same time provide Moscow Alpha with access to low-cost Western capital. We want to bid with Sheldons for the mandate to finance one of the major Caspian pipelines, underwritten by a consortium of banks from the littoral states'. Saul was startled by the proposal, not least because of the huge sum of capital which could be involved. He paused to order his thoughts. 'That's certainly an ambitious proposal Petr, but this would be of a size and complexity that we've not dealt with before. Let's say that Moscow Alpha and Sheldons are co-leads of the deal, how many other banks would be in the syndicate? What type of bond issue are you thinking of and where are the investors going to come from? You say that banks in the littoral states will underwrite the issue, but if the project went pear-shaped and they were called upon to honour their commitments – if they went bust in the process, which is likely- then there'd be an economic catastrophe in the region'. Damyanovitch continued. 'The issue would be for three and a half billion dollars and payable over ten years. There'd be five members of the management group, and this is where you'd make your first contribution. You already have links with the major players in Kazakhstan and Azerbaijan. They have their own investors so should be able to sell the bonds locally. The underwriters would be smaller banks in the region. Yes, they'd be taking on a larger amount of risk than they're used to, but they'd be willing to do this if there's a trustworthy foreign bank in charge – and by that I mean your bank'. Saul found that he was attracted by the idea of taking forward associations with the major Central Asian banks he'd nurtured over the past five years.

For the first time Sovoil's chairman spoke. 'Moscow Alpha will propose the issue of commodity-linked bonds. Chairman Damyanovitch will send you details when you're back in London, but the basic idea is that interest payable to investors will be linked to the oil price'. Damyanovitch intervened. 'If I'm right, Sheldons issued a copper bond for a Chilean copper mining company a few years ago. As copper prices went up so did the coupon to bond holders. But if the price of copper fell, the interest payable would also fall. The company was able to survive a downturn in the market because payment costs on its debt fell with the copper price. You see, our oil bond would have the same mechanism'. Saul was familiar with commodity-linked debt and had been the architect behind the Chilean deal to which the chairman referred.

'Let's go over the protection of investors. The role of the underwriters is to pay up if the borrower goes bankrupt or simply can't pay investors what they're entitled to. But you say the underwriters will be Kazakh and Azeri banks. They don't have the capital strength to take on this sort of risk'. Damyanovitch responded to Saul's concern. 'I agree; banks are usually very weak in this part of the world. But we have a solution. If the oil price goes up beyond a pre-specified benchmark, the burden of paying the interest will fall on the syndicate members. The local energy companies building the pipeline won't be able to meet the higher payments, so we'll have to give this fall-back assurance. There'll also be a one-off payment to investors equal to half of the total sum raised as an incentive. The benchmark will be set so high that it will be impossible in real terms that this right will ever be triggered. We'll get a large fee for assuming this risk, even though it will never materialise'.

'There are, presently, several joint ventures between the state-owned oil companies in Kazakhstan and Azerbaijan and Russian companies for the exploitation of Caspian Sea resources, as well as of course their shareholdings in the BTC pipeline. We'll suggest that these state-owned companies transfer their seabed rights to an offshore special purpose holding company as extra security for the issue. When the bonds are eventually paid off the rights will be re-transferred. But if the syndicate is called upon but fails to honour its commitment, then investors will take control of those rights'. Saul was impressed by the plan's creativity, but doubtful of the willingness of politicians in the littoral states to hand over ownership of 'national treasures' to a foreign holding company over which they'd have no control. 'Why would bureaucrats or politicians be willing to collateralise the commitments of their national banks by signing over nationally owned assets? Where's the incentive?' Damyanovitch smiled: this was the simple part of the plan. 'If the pipeline goes ahead it will give them control over their natural resources, and they won't have to continue relying on the Russian network. Today the Russian government could shut off their foreign earnings by simply refusing the transit of their oil and gas over its territory. They know they're exposed to this risk and they don't like it. This is one of the main reasons behind the drive to open up new pipelines from the Caspian Sea westwards to Europe, and eastwards to China and India. Everyone wants to bypass Russian territory'. Damyanovitch's colleagues nodded in agreement.

Saul liked the pipeline project and knew that he was present at a pivotal moment, with the people who instigated and controlled world events. The group adjourned to the chairman's private room concealed behind a nondescript door further along the corridor. It was sparsely furnished and along one wall ran a heavy black cabinet on which were numerous glass 'tombstones' - tokens of the bank's participation in previous syndicated deals. Saul picked up each matchbox-sized block, noting the names of the Russian borrowers. The pop of a Champagne cork drew his attention back to the host. 'I'd like to propose a toast to future cooperation between Sheldons Bank and Moscow Alpha'. Damyanovitch raised his glass. After some further small talk Damyanovitch's co-directors shook hands with Saul and left. Later that day they'd make separate reports to their political masters in the Kremlin, describing in detail what they regarded as a successful first meeting.

The two men stood in silence at a window overlooking a seamier side of the city. It was Damyanovitch who eventually broke the silence. 'Saul, I hope you'll be a reliable advocate for this project when it comes before your board. We've not got long before you leave for your flight- is there anything you'd like to ask me?' Saul paused, reluctant to say something that might spoil an otherwise perfect day. 'I have two questions, Petr. The second you'll no doubt have anticipated, confirming the impression you already have of me. The first is this. If you care so much about your country's power in the world, why support a project which will undermine it?' After a pause he replied. 'You're right of course, Saul. I'd never endanger Russia through either my actions or my omissions. But we shouldn't be afraid to compete with our neighbours and if the outcome of such competition is a more modern, more efficient Russian energy industry, then our participation in this project will have been of benefit'. Saul nodded his understanding of the answer whilst being unconvinced of its sincerity.

'Now, your other question.' Saul smiled. 'Please correct me if I'm mistaken, but you want me to lobby the board secretly on your behalf to persuade them to come in on the project as co-lead managers with Moscow Alpha. Presumably if I have concerns about the risks involved, I should conceal these. If necessary I should withhold information. Lie where appropriate. This brings up a simple question: what's in it for me?' Damyanovitch laughed, patting Saul on the back. 'You're right; it's refreshing to know you're still driven by that most reliable of base instincts, greed. Here's what I offer you. This deal will be for three and a half billion dollars. If you're successful in putting together a syndicate with Sheldons and Moscow Alpha as lead managers, then we'll pay you, personally and secretly, a sum equal to one percent of the amount raised'. Saul gasped. 'You're willing to pay me that much for putting this deal together? What's the catch?' He recalled Herschell's fate and wondered whether his own life would be at risk if he took on the now vacant role of Damyanovitch's 'inside man' at Sheldons. 'No catch. This project is vital to Russia's economic interests, power, and influence in the world. We'll pay any price, make any sacrifice, to achieve our goals. Against this such a payment to you is nothing'.

'And what about my safety? What assurances do you offer?' Damyanovitch returned his gaze to the street below. 'I never give assurances and besides, if I did, would they give you peace of mind? You and I are driven by totally different considerations, so the possibility of a conflict of interest just doesn't arise. Your gain will not be my loss, nor vice versa. But, if you betray my trust then there'll be nowhere to hide'.

Fifteen minutes later they stood outside Moscow Alpha's head office, a good example of now-converted Stalinist Gothic architecture. Saul gazed up at the grey stone arch above the heavy steel doors. He noticed the hammer and sickle carvings, remnants of the pride of the former regime, on the immensely proportioned block. Somehow the Soviet decorations didn't look out of place, evidence of the personal history and mindset of the building's present owner. Forty years earlier the Ministry of Labour had occupied the building. As a young KGB officer Damyanovitch had had occasion to visit the building to take away a low ranking Party official suspected of spying. The man had died during interrogation at the Lubyanka, as had innumerable others, the guilty and the innocent alike. Nobody knew the history, only him and the ghosts that shuffled along the winding corridors at night after the new occupants, the bright young things, had left for wine bars scattered across the city. Damyanovitch opened the door of the waiting Limousine. 'To the hotel first, Mr. Saul, to get your luggage?' 'Yes please, Sergei, and then to the airport'. In a couple of hours Saul was on board the Swissair return flight to London via Zurich. His mission accomplished, he'd catch up on sleep during the flight and in the two days' leave extracted from Paul Phineus at their recent lunch. He closed his eyes and thought of nothing. It was time to dream.

Chapter Thirty One

Two men sat on a bench beside the river, between them a large brown paper bag full of stale bread. They didn't look at each other, and from a distance they appeared not to know each other. It was a perfect day and the sun beamed down from an empty sky. The smaller man took bread from the bag and tossed it onto the water, attracting the attention of ducklings lurking in the coolness of the reeds nearby. The splashing of tiny wings as they half paddled, half flew towards the waiting meal broke the silence. In the near-distance a lone rower powered through the water, the strong swish of oars audible to lethargic onlookers sauntering, jackets over shoulders, through the heat of the midday sun.

'Are you threatening me, Aaron? Please tell me you're not. It'd be a shame for both of us if we were to fall out after so many years of partnership.' The huge, pale faced, sweating man spoke without turning to look at the diminutive onlooker sitting further along the bench. The little man replied, 'I know you've got problems but I'm sure you'll find a way out, just as you've always done. You're a survivor. But what I'm telling you is that we can't help you this time. Tel Aviv was quite definite when I discussed the financials with them yesterday. I'm not threatening you: after three decades of partnership I wouldn't dream, wouldn't dare, to do as much. You and I go back too far to play games with each other, wouldn't you agree?' The large man nodded, drawing a red and white polka-dot handkerchief from his pocket to dab at beads of sweat now trickling down his brow. His face had become contorted as he realised he wasn't persuading the little man of the seriousness of his plight. He felt anger, frustration, and fear. 'Aaron, all I'm asking for is a short-term loan, paid through Switzerland as we've always done. All I need is a hundred million dollars, and that's not a big deal for TA. It'll tide me over through the next creditors' meeting. After I've sold some assets- I've got a buyer lined up for a subsidiary already, by the way- I'll be able to pay you everything back. Right down to the last cent. I'll pay interest on the loan if that's what it'll take. But without this, I'm finished. And then what good will I be to you or TA? I've never bluffed before, and I'm not starting now. So, what's it to be?'

Aaron Goldstein threw the last piece of bread to the ducks now waddling and squawking in the shadow cast by the fat man panting as he sat on the edge of the bench. Some time earlier he'd loosened his tie but still he struggled to catch his breath. The air was hot and thin, playing havoc with his lungs, which were struggling to oxygenate blood forced by an overworked heart around a great bulk of a body. He leaned forward and placed his head in his hands. The little man shook out the remaining crumbs, screwed up the bag, and with a single throw successfully directed it into a nearby litterbin. He smiled at his accuracy; perhaps he should have followed his father's advice and become a basketball player after all. But on reflection he just didn't have the height. And besides, employment with Mossad had enabled him to make an infinitely greater contribution to his nation's wellbeing than would ever have been possible if he'd opted for such a frivolous career instead. He glanced at his watch; there was one final meeting at the embassy for later that day and then he'd be up in the clouds again, flying back to New York and his family.

'I'm going to be candid with you, Franklin. We're not going to bail you out, not this time. You've always served the cause well, and we'll never forget this. We've looked after you when so many of your banker friends didn't want to know. They treated you like a pariah, but we stood by you. We supported you and opened doors to finance when all others were closed. You know this is true. And I've always thought of you as a friend, a brother. I'd never hold back from intervening if your survival was put at risk by something we'd done or omitted to do. But that's the point, isn't it? Your current predicament is because you overstretched yourself. You were greedy, and you expanded your business too quickly. We're not going to bankroll you this time because this is not a mess of our making, it's yours. I'm sorry but the answer is No'. Franklin Shandlin lifted his head from his hands, pushed back his greasy black unkempt hair and raised a heavy body into an upright position. He'd regained his composure despite the justified stubbornness of his controller. His ferocity and renowned pugnacity welled up from within a desperate soul.

'And you know so much about business, of course. You and the schemers and temple traders in Tel Aviv. I built up Piedmont from nothing. It was my will alone that created the most dynamic technology company this country's ever seen. And you talk to me now about overstretching, about expanding too quickly. How dare you question my business judgment when I've achieved so much and you so little'. His voice boomed as he berated the now nervous-looking agent. 'You deign to say I've served the cause well. That understatement offends me. Let's remind ourselves of a few facts. I was the front man for marketing the software your spies stole from US Intelligence and later used to eavesdrop on governments across the world. I sold the system but it was you, Mossad, who reconfigured it to gain 'back door access' into the governments who adopted it. Now you've got information flowing in to TA from dozens of countries, all of it confidential and leaking out, or should I say gushing out, without the slightest knowledge of the owners. You've owed me big time for years, and now I'm calling in the debt'.

Aaron Goldstein brushed a few crumbs from his perfectly pressed trousers as he carefully considered his next words. To continue with outright refusal would risk a scene; his associate's anger was mounting and now secrets that should never see the light of day were being tossed around in a public place like confetti at a windswept wedding. He'd err on the side of caution and give the big man the assurance he was looking for. This was a crisis for others to resolve. 'Okay Franklin, all I can say is that I'll do my best. I don't have the authority to make any commitment here and now. If only it was that simple. I need to get back to Tel Aviv with further information about your predicament and your request to us. And if, as you say, you can repay soon, this should alleviate some of the concerns back home. Try to keep a cool head and don't be panicked by the present situation. You've come through worse. I'll use my influence, for whatever that's worth, to try get you the money you're looking for. No promises though. So, are you happy to proceed on this basis, or would you prefer we stay here a little longer so you can shout at me some more?' Shandlin managed a forced a smile, but he was a frightened man. As such he was both unpredictable and dangerous. Tel Aviv would know what to do: a previously fruitful relationship was now drawing to a close.

'I've got a meeting with those leeches at the banks in three weeks' time. If I've not got the funding by then they're going to tear down the company and I'll be lucky not to go to jail. You see Aaron, I've always sailed close to the wind; you've got to, to run a successful business - but my creditors won't be sympathetic if they think I deliberately set out to defraud them'. 'And did you, Franklin? Did you continue raising fresh loans when you knew there was little prospect of repaying them? If that's the case then what makes you think Tel Aviv would be willing to step in?' Shandlin ignored this line of argument. He stood up, but too quickly; by now his balance and ability to concentrate were beginning to desert him. The cocktail of Halcion and Zanax taken earlier that morning to get him through the day had kicked in and he staggered slightly. 'Just get me the money, get me the bloody money. If I go down I'll take you all with me. I'll sing so loudly in court they'll hear me on the Temple Mount. And more importantly - you tell Tel Aviv this: they'll hear me in Washington too'. He started to move off, swaying slightly as his eyes refocused through the afternoon heat haze. 'Just get me the money, do you hear me? Get me the money. Or I'll tell everything'. His words trailed off, giving way to incoherent mumbling. As Shandlin's great bulk of a body disappeared into the distance Aaron Goldstein looked at his watch and wondered if he'd make the meeting at the embassy. It was no longer important: the priority was to deal with the 'freelance agent' now spinning out of control, and threatening to disclose Mossad's secrets.

Chapter Thirty Two

Saul returned to the office, refreshed and excited after his trip to Moscow. He'd pushed a window of opportunity wide open for Sheldons in Central Asia, co-leading a substantial bond issue in the emerging energy sector. At the same time he was closer now than he'd ever been before in his life to making a large personal fortune in one strike. He briefly checked Bloomberg, noting to his satisfaction that shares in Piedmont had risen during his absence. He wondered whether there was a ceiling to the profit which could be made by Tri-Star on its investment in the company. Before leaving his apartment that morning he'd stood in front of the wall-length mirror carefully knotting his silk red tie, clipping in his simple gold cufflinks before easing in to his Savile Row suit. As he combed his blond hair he smiled as he looked at the reflection, not with vanity, but instead with certainty that his time had come. He arrived at the office at seven o'clock, half an hour earlier than his usual start time. Details of Moscow Alpha's bond issue would be waiting for him, sent by encrypted e-mail; he knew well the importance of fully understanding its terms and implications prior to the meeting with Paul Phineus scheduled for later that day. His vested interest in the project's approval would not, of course, be disclosed - this was a private matter. He'd lobby for it, regardless of its risk, and the only potential obstacle was the chairman and the mousetrap-like mental skills which he would apply in assessing the project's feasibility.

'So Saul, you had a good time in Moscow at our expense. Good food, excellent entertainment. But somewhere in your breathtaking schedule did you manage to discuss business? Please don't let me think I've sanctioned this overindulgence with no prospect of gain on our side'. Phineus sipped from a gold-rimmed bone china coffee cup, eyeing his guest with a mischievous smile. Saul knew he was in a good mood. The previous quarter's figures had been reported earlier that day, showing a fifteen percent increase in profits, half of which were attributable to the efforts of the Corporate Finance Department, of which Saul was the pampered, flattered Head.

'As you'll recall from your earlier meeting with Damyanovitch, Moscow Alpha is looking for a tie-up with Sheldons to take advantage of our investor network and our ability to market complex bonds. He's looking to make a joint bid to finance a new Caspian Sea pipeline. The amount to be raised will be three and a half billion US dollars. But he's proposing a commodity bond, with interest payments linked to the oil price'. The chairman leaned forward. 'Okay, you've got my interest, but the deal's larger than we're used to. Tell me about the fees. How much is in it for us?' 'Sheldons will take a management fee of one and a half percent. We'll also get fifteen percent of the bonds to place with our own investors. Another fifteen percent will go to Moscow Alpha. The remainder will be distributed amongst the management group made up of those banks in Azerbaijan and Kazakhstan with which we already have strong ties'. Phineus leaned back, placing his hands behind his head as he mulled over the proposal. The fee was exceptionally generous, although he needed to know considerably more about the risk Sheldons would be taking.

'What security and other incentives will be given to bond holders? They'll be getting more in interest if the oil price goes up. But what if there's a default? And is there a sweetener we can give them in return for accepting lower interest payments on the bonds?' These were the specific questions Saul dreaded, principally because the answers could undermine the entire proposal. He carefully crafted his response. 'The bonds will be issued by a special purpose vehicle we'll set up in the British Virgin Islands, or possibly the Caymans. The state-owned oil companies of Azerbaijan and Kazakhstan will sign over to the SPV their rights in existing oil pipelines, and also their rights in the Caspian seabed'. The chairman licked his lips: the bond features, and the fees, would give him a seven figure bonus by the end of the year.

'The bond will also include a contingent payment. If the price of oil rises by a specified percentage- we've got in mind a thirty percent increase- then investors will get a one-off payment of half of the bond value, payable by the syndicate. The consortium building the pipeline couldn't meet such a commitment; they just don't have the capital, so we would then take it on instead. We'll use a futures contract traded on the New York

Mercantile Exchange as the benchmark. It'll be one of the longer dated contracts so we're not caught out by very short term volatility- blips in the prices which often affect shorter dated instruments. You know the sort of thing- market panic one day which blows over by the next'. Paul Phineus shook his head: the proposed terms shocked him, and the more he considered the risk to Sheldons the more his usually calm demeanour started to change to an agitated one. 'No, no, no. I'd never get an issue like that approved by the board. The risk would be far too great. If the oil price rises above the 'worst case scenario' you describe, however unlikely that might be, then we'd be killed by the investors. We and the rest of the syndicate would collapse. And then of course they'd seize the oil rights held by the SPV which are, as I understand it, the only national assets these countries possess of any value. Tell me you've thought about this risk, or there's no point in us talking any further'. Saul was taken aback by the chairman's solid dismissiveness. He knew he'd have to argue his case, but before doing that, he had anticipated a more favourable initial response. But if he was going to receive a personal commission of one percent of the project's value he was willing to deploy all his skills of persuasion to get it accepted.

'Paul, the risk we're talking about is purely theoretical. The oil price has never jumped by anywhere near these sorts of percentages. The Saudis have always been ready to increase output to stabilise prices and this will continue to be the case. But we've got to have these features to attract investors'. The chairman regained his composure but was still unsettled. 'Okay Saul, you've given me enough to think about. Let me get back to you later'. The chairman smiled; the commission structure was, as Saul said, 'fantastic', but then so was the risk. The reality was that if this was triggered, the Azeri and Kazakh partners, as well as Moscow Alpha, would stand as much chance of withstanding the financial fallout as a tree sapling in the middle of a hurricane. Local economies would collapse in the wake of such an event. But on the other hand, the deal would propel Sheldons into the super-league of global financial institutions active in the energy sector.

The telephone on Phineus's understated opaque glass desk started to buzz; he rose to his feet and walked over to take the call. The scheduled meeting with Saul had come to an end; he raised his hand, then his thumb, and resumed his telephone conversation. This was the only outward sign, but an important one nonetheless, that Saul had made headway in his campaign to win acceptance for the deal. He left the room, satisfied.

Chapter Thirty Three

Adam kissed his lover's forehead as he reached across for the watch he'd placed on the bedside table the previous night. Her scent was as sweet and fresh as when they'd met at the conference the previous day, and for a while he simply wanted to watch her as she slept. The firm had paid for him to attend a course as part of his 'professional development', held over two days, with participants being put up in one of the best hotels in London. He'd met her the previous day during a workshop, and later they'd had dinner together in one of the hotel's chic in-house restaurants. They'd then adjourned to her room where their love-making continued for most of the night. In the semi-darkness he stared at her perfect face and wondered if he'd see her again, or whether instead this would be just another one night stand. Silas Coughlin had correctly identified the coldness in his soul, branding him an iconoclast who needed to test the law to destruction. Adam had hated him for his perceptiveness: he knew in his heart that the same destructiveness afflicted his associations with friends and lovers alike. Now he lay alongside a truly beautiful woman with whom he could imagine spending a lifetime, and yet the destructive part of his nature militated against such long term emotional commitments.

The following morning the two went down for breakfast. They were fortunate enough to have a table to themselves, most of the other guests having already returned to their rooms. Adam tapped the table with a book of matches imprinted with the hotel's name and bright logo, wondering how to ask if he could see her again. He felt shy, like a schoolboy on a first date. He lit a cigarette and placed the book in his pocket. 'Can I see you again?' Adam interrupted her chain of thought with his gently enquiry. She looked at him directly and smiled at his naivety. She did not answer.

Saul raised a Champagne flute to his two friends as they gazed into the distance, trying to focus through the brilliant heat haze of a perfect early June afternoon. In their top hats and tails and bright coloured cravats they blended into the scene perfectly: impeccably attired representatives of the new social elite, taking their place in a 'classless' social order. Behind them they could hear the approaching avalanche of thuds like an unbroken roll of thunder, but as yet could see nothing. 'I'd like to propose a toast. I give you the Tri-Star Trust; may its successes rise to even greater heights'. Thomas and Adam raised their glasses. Adam responded; 'I propose a vote of thanks to Franklin Shandlin, the old fraudster's done us proud'. 'Franklin Shandlin'. The three then set about the crystal bowl of strawberries bought earlier, the sweetness of the plump fruit immeasurably enhanced by the chilled Champagne still lingering on their palates. 'And now your turn, Thomas. Let's have your toast'. Thomas hesitated then raised his glass. 'I give you love, friendship, and trust'. Saul and Adam raised their glasses, surprised by the uncharacteristic show of emotion. 'The lady's been a bad influence, and that's no mistake'. Saul winked at Thomas and he grinned. 'You're talking about my wife-to-be, so be careful'.

Out of the blue charged the horses, raising applause from the crowd of spectators. It was perfect conditions for the Epsom Derby, the annual event that owed as much to its reputation as a social gathering for the rich and famous as it did to its place in the equestrian calendar. The air was dry and fresh, with no sign of the humidity that had on many previous occasions caused difficulties for the horses that laboured and gasped in the heat. Saul looked on as the spectacle burst into his visual horizon, his eyes widening with excitement. The brilliant colours of the jockeys' chequered shirts, the thundering of hooves and the incomprehensible commentary echoing through a distant tannoy formed a heady mix of impressions. As the competitors charged off into the distance and out of view, the only sounds audible above the crash of horseshoes on firm grass were the swishes, like muffled firecrackers, of riders urging on bearers with flicks of crops on shiny scrupulously brushed rumps. Adam turned to Thomas and above the noise commented that even in this, the sport of kings, cruelty was sometimes justified in the pursuit of winning. He knew that Thomas still harboured grave misgivings about his conduct of the Coughlin trial. In the aftermath of the murders he'd discussed his collusion, his complicity, with his friend, in part to unburden himself, but also with hope of absolution. Neither had been achieved and their friendship had changed, albeit barely perceptibly, as a consequence. Thomas continued gazing into the distance, and replied. 'There's a world of difference between gentle cruelty and killing a horse in the process of winning. We must all pay for the consequences of our actions'.

Saul stared at the two, sensing the changed atmosphere. 'What are you two whispering about? Why the serious faces? Why don't you forget about work for today and relax? This is time out; a celebration of our success in the Tri-Star investment. Of course it's entirely down to my financial acumen, but modesty prevents me, well, you know'. Saul's intervention helped defuse the tension between Adam and Thomas. 'But Saul, don't forget Thomas's contribution. It was he who handed over the inside information you needed. No leaked balance sheets, no leaked board minutes, and you'd never have been able to advise Shandlin on the takeover. So, credit where it's due'. Thomas smiled at the irony; they were both guilty, in Adam's case of a high crime, in his of a misdemeanour. But the consequence was that the Tri-Star Trust had achieved significant profits from the illegal investments they had made; through ownership of one third of the Trust he was now, albeit on paper, a wealthy man. He smiled at the paradox.

For a while Chloe observed the three from the shadow of a nearby grandstand. They looked at ease, laughing and chatting, pointing into the distance at the horse they'd backed but which now cantered in gently along the course, bringing up the rear. She smiled as she gazed upon the scene, momentarily recoiling from following through the plan rehearsed in her mind so many times the night before. Thomas looked happy and at peace with himself; she pitied him, recognising the scale of destruction she was about to inflict upon their relationship. In the corner of his eye Saul noticed a slither of pale blue in the shadow of a nearby spectators' stand. Looking over he was pleased to see Thomas's fiancé whom he'd secretly invited to the event earlier that week. She was radiant, attired as if for the cover of a high society fashion magazine. He watched as she threw back her hair but she didn't appear to be looking at anything, not the riders disappearing into the distance, nor the other spectators floating about her, nor the few horses that had retired prematurely and were now being led back to the paddocks. She seemed distracted, remote. He tapped Thomas's shoulder and pointed in Chloe's direction. As soon as he saw her he beamed with surprise then ran off towards her, his top hat almost toppling but kept in place with his hand. 'Isn't true love a beautiful thing to behold?' Saul joked to Adam. 'Sometimes too saccharine for my liking', his friend replied. Thomas quickly reached the grandstand, now slightly out of breath. 'Chloe, I wasn't expecting you here today. How did you know where we'd be?' He kissed her before she had time to answer. 'Saul called me on Tuesday and asked if I wanted to come. He was persuasive; you know how he can be'. Thomas smiled. 'I couldn't wish for better friends or a more perfect fiancé'. Chloe looked away and then returning to look into his bright excited eyes spoke again, but this time quietly. 'Thomas, we need to talk. It's important.' Her sentence trailed off. 'Can we walk?' He slid his arm around her waist, puzzled by her seriousness. Saul and Adam watched from a distance: everything appeared as it ought to be.

'So Adam, what are you going to do with your profit from Tri-Star after we've cashed in on Piedmont Communications? You're going to be a rich man - we all are - so what are you going to do with your slice of the cake? You'll be rich enough to pack in your job. You'll be able to escape the nine to five routine and live life on your own terms.' Adam paused as he gazed at the horizon, waiting for horses. 'I'd never give up my job, even if I became a 'man of independent means' after selling off the Piedmont shares. The law's what I'm good at and without it I'd just fall apart. It gives my life purpose. Next year I'm going to make partner. If I'm financially independent it'll make a hell of a difference to the way I approach the job. I'll be doing it for the pleasure, for the intellectual challenge, and not because I have to do it'.

Saul was surprised: he'd always thought Adam a 'fellow traveller', a mercenary in a pinstripe suit to whom a job was merely a means to an end. 'I didn't know you had such lofty principles. And here was me thinking you were just another shark circling in the murky waters of the legal profession. It just goes to show how wrong you can be'. Adam smiled but suddenly became aware of raised voices. He squinted, lifting his hand to shield his eyes from the blazing sun immediately overhead. Close to the gleaming white barrier running alongside the racecourse he could make out the profiles of Thomas and Chloe. Both were animated, excited, but despite his efforts he couldn't hear their conversation above the surrounding din of the crowd.

'Why Chloe, why have you done this to me? I gave you everything, I gave you unconditional love, and yet you've come here today to destroy me. I never thought anyone could be so callous. And worst of all, you come here to tell me you've betrayed me. That you've sneaked behind my back and behaved like a whore. I don't know whether to pity you or hate you'. Chloe looked into her fiancé's already reddened, wide eyes, shocked by the anger her confession had provoked. She'd come to the event with the sole purpose of ending the engagement, of changing his opinion of her fundamentally and irrevocably. She wanted him to hate her and in so doing, maintain his self respect. In short time he'd hopefully move on with his life. But the device she'd used to bring the temple down, betrayal, had provoked an unexpected rage. She was frightened. 'Thomas, I'm so, *so* sorry. I'm *really* sorry. But perhaps you just never knew me as well as you thought you did. I've always told you I need to be free. My spirit can't be confined, repressed, in a marriage - not to you, not to anyone. Can't you understand that? You pushed me into this engagement. I asked you to wait but you wouldn't listen.' Thomas grabbed her by both arms. 'If you'd spent more time sorting out your mind instead of always working on your career and going to those bloody conferences, then perhaps you'd appreciate the things that really matter in life. Tell me the name of the bastard you've betrayed me with. I have a right to know. And when I find him I'm going to kill him. *Tell me*'. He started to shake her, shouting and crying at the same time. She struggled to prise herself from his vice-like grip, screaming at him 'It's over, Thomas. It's over'. Bystanders standing near them and walking past had by now started to openly stare at the scene. Saul and Adam continued to watch from a distance, unsure whether or not to intervene.

With one great tug Chloe was free, and in that moment of confusion, a moment in which all sense of bearings was temporarily lost, her only concern was to escape. Confused, she ducked beneath the adjacent white barrier and burst out into freedom. The riders didn't stand a chance. Thomas, Saul and Adam looked on helplessly as a blur of reds, yellows, greens, and whites collided with blue. Three horses crashed into Chloe's body, the first throwing her up into the air like a rag doll, then two more, when she returned to earth with a thud, trampling her prone form. The crowd gasped, and screams echoed down from nearby stands. Several horses continued galloping erratically down the course, their riders desperately trying to bring their steeds to a halt. As the battered body lay still on the dry brown grass, everyone knew that the lady in blue was dead.

Within minutes the local emergency services arrived, but as administering emergency treatment was clearly futile, all they could do was to take away a body. It took all their powers of gentle persuasion to take the lifeless corpse from Thomas, as he cradled her in his arms, sitting weeping in the middle of the now deserted course. As the ambulance glided slowly away into the distance, Thomas looked on at first with bewilderment but then with extreme anger. His two friends stood by his side, neither knowing what to do or say. Eventually Saul broke the silence with softly whispered words. 'Thomas, it's time. Time to leave. There's nothing more any of us can do here. Are you ready to come with us?' Thomas stared at him, unable to find words. Adam looked up at the sky; dark clouds had suddenly appeared as if from nowhere, a warm breeze heralding the imminent arrival of a summer thunder storm. He reached into his top pocket and drew out a half-empty packet of cigarettes; a craving for nicotine always manifested itself at such times of extreme stress. From his other pocket he withdrew a small, brightly coloured book of matches, but in his haste it dropped to the ground. Picking up the book Thomas gazed at the lettering. 'Southcastle Hotel. That's where she went for her last course'. His attention seemed to drift off but after a few seconds his eyes refocused as he looked again at the book, and then at Adam. His eyes now flashed with a hatred neither Adam nor Saul had seen before.

'You bastard. You dirty vicious bastard. It was you, wasn't it? You're the one who's responsible for all this. You're the one who's destroyed everything'. He leapt at Adam, grabbing him by the throat and squeezing as tightly as he could. 'Say it. Admit you're the one. You're a dead man'. As Adam's face turned puce and his eyes started to close Saul rushed to pull the two apart. Thomas's blows rained down into Adam's face as they were separated. 'Enough, Thomas. Enough. Let him answer you. Adam, is this true?' Adam raised a handkerchief to staunch the flow of blood from his nose. 'Yes, it's true. But she was free to decide. It was her decision'. Saul looked at him, dumbstruck; Thomas despised him even more for saying what he knew to be the truth. Regaining his composure but still burning with anger, he raised his finger and pointed at his former friend. 'Everything you love in life, everything that matters to you, I'm going to take away. I'm going to destroy you just as you have destroyed me today'. With that he began walking in the direction of the stands and from there out of the ground. Saul looked at Adam, still unable to comprehend what had happened or what had been confessed. 'This time you've gone too far. Thomas will never get over this, and neither will I. I can't believe you've done what you've done. And for what? Just to tempt her, to test them? Was the destruction of so much really worth it? I need to get away from you. You disgust me'. Saul wandered off into the distance, leaving Adam alone. Suddenly the skies opened; heavy drops of rain began falling, mingling with the spatters of blood now discolouring his brilliant white shirt and disheveled purple cravat. His sense of guilt and self-loathing was infinite. Slowly he began his long and lonely journey home.

Chapter Thirty Four

Franklin Shandlin stood on the deck of his luxury yacht, moored five kilometers off Gibraltar. For a third consecutive night he'd eaten alone. He gazed out into the darkness, feeling more bloated than usual as the vast quantities of food consumed earlier that evening were slowly digested in his gut. When he had left London earlier that week the Piedmont Communications share price had been at an all-time high following a stream of 'buy' recommendations by financial analysts in the major brokerage houses. Of course the majority of these 'City scribblers' had been bought, bribed, by Shandlin; indeed, in a few cases, the reports released to investors had been prepared in-house by the Piedmont marketing team.

But there was another reason why the share price continued to climb. In the months following the takeover of Winterstone Technologies, Shandlin had systematically plundered the company's pension fund, using decades of contributions by its workforce to sustain a share price defying the laws of economic gravity. Shandlin's obsession with the price was for good reason. Huge loans taken out a year earlier had been secured on the company's shares; if these were to fall in value the lenders would demand more security, something the company couldn't provide. The loans would then be called in and the scale of his crimes would be revealed. In a week's time he was due to attend a meeting with the company's creditors; he wondered whether the share price would hold until then. In normal circumstances he'd be anticipating another sleepless night, pacing the deck worrying that he was finally about to be 'rumbled', but tonight he felt calm. The previous day he'd taken a 'shore to ship' call from his Mossad contact, Aaron Goldstein. His spy masters in Tel Aviv had finally sanctioned payment of the one hundred million dollars loan he'd previously demanded in return for his continued silence. Once cleared, the funds would be used to pay off some of the existing loans, and also to make huge purchases of shares in his company via a series of secret offshore trusts. In this way the share price would continue to rise, keeping his creditors happy while also reaffirming his reputation as a brilliant 'captain of industry'.

That night he'd receive a visit from three Mossad agents who'd bring a bankers draft for one hundred million dollars with them. Like so many freelance spies he was a fantasist, and such cloak-and-dagger arrangements were the very stuff of his 'other life'. In anticipation of the meeting most of the crew had been given the night off, disembarking for the bars and nightclubs of Gibraltar several hours earlier. There remained a skeleton crew but since the vessel was on autopilot and the sea as calm as a millpond, they'd retired below deck an hour earlier. Shandlin was now alone, pacing as he eagerly awaited the arrival of his secret service associates and the delivery of the draft. During the day his spirits had lifted a little, as he came to believe that his financial worries could finally be nearing an end.

At quarter to midnight he heard the gentle hum of the engine of an approaching motorboat. As the sound drew nearer he walked to the rail and cast over rope ladders in anticipation of the arrival of his guests. Within minutes, muffled thuds indicated that the boat had come alongside. Shandlin popped the cork of the bottle of Champagne he'd brought on deck to celebrate their arrival as well as the lifeline, the bankers draft, they were bringing with them. He watched the ropes pull taught as the three visitors in wetsuits rapidly ascended the gleaming white hull jutting like a smooth iceberg from the lapping waves beneath. Shandlin held out his hand to greet them. 'Shalom, my friends. Welcome aboard the Golden Wave'. His face was beaming as he awaited the customary Yiddish greeting in return. Two of the three men walked swiftly towards him, still without speaking a word. As Shandlin again extended his hand he was seized around the neck by one of the assailants, the other stepping forward to empty a syringe of nerve agent into a vessel behind his ear. Within seconds the chairman's vast bulk lay motionless on the deck. The third assassin who'd disappeared immediately after coming on board now returned from Shandlin's quarters below deck with his bathrobe and slippers. They quickly set about stripping their victim of his casual clothes and re-dressing him in his sleeping wear. His size made the task difficult: throughout, he was limp and unable to move, but fully conscious of what was being done. After several minutes the three had achieved their objective; the chairman lay like a beached whale, still paralysed. No words had been said during his ordeal, but with the most difficult part of the plan completed, one of the three now kneeled down alongside the victim and spoke. His voice was firm and strangely sympathetic. 'Franklin, can you hear me? If you can, please blink'. Shandlin blinked. 'Tonight you're going to die. I wish your soul peace. You will always be a hero to our people and to the nation you've served. We salute you on this your last of days'.

Shandlin closed his eyes as the three heaved him up from the deck and moved slowly towards the rail. As they stood in the blackness they gently swung the vast body by its arms and legs. After achieving sufficient momentum the motionless but still fully conscious body was cast over the side, landing with a loud splash which, however, was inaudible to the crew sleeping soundly in their bunks below. Caught in a passing current, this curious white-robed semi-submerged island slowly disappeared into the distance. The three Mossad agents pulled up the rope ladders and neatly stowed them in their proper place. Having achieved their assignment they dived from the deck, climbed into the waiting motorboat, and headed back to shore.

Chapter Thirty Five

Thomas arrived back at his flat in the early evening. For a full half hour he sat on the edge of his bed, still wearing his grey suit and, by now, loose yellow cravat. The white carnation was still in the buttonhole, but now it and his previously immaculate white shirt were spattered with drops of Adam's blood. In a dream-like state he surveyed the wreckage that constituted his life and hopes, dropped his head into his hands and wept. The sense of betrayal was overwhelming. So much emotional capital had been invested into the relationship with Chloe, and yet in some fundamental way he'd failed to appreciate her aspirations, to understand her own longings. The infidelity was simply confirmation of this misjudgment. He needed to think, to reflect, on where everything had gone so wrong.

Then he thought of Adam. Everything his former friend had said was true, of course. Chloe would have gone with him voluntarily, albeit for reasons he'd yet to work out. But he also knew Adam's need to test people, systems and beliefs to their limits, and beyond if necessary. In some way he pitied Adam: he always failed to foresee the consequences of his actions. This had been the case in the Coughlin trial; he'd tested the legal system, corrupted it to get his way, but failed to anticipate the murders which followed his client's acquittal. And again with Chloe; he must have foreseen the devastation the infidelity would inflict, but then again, no one could have predicted the terrible chain of events which actually ensued. His tragedy was that he possessed limited foresight, but also a conscience to feel guilt for unintended consequences. But this was not a time for forgiveness. If he'd married Chloe, would Adam have continued with their adulterous affair? In his heart he knew the answer, and as the image of the two lying naked together came into focus in his mind, anger and hatred supplanted his earlier feelings of sorrow and incomprehension.

Quickly, he changed into casual clothes and packed his bags. Transferring a single telephone number from his directory onto a small strip of paper which he placed in the inner pocket of his jacket he left the flat, jumped into his car and headed for the motorway. Within an hour he'd reached his destination. After checking in to a cheap hotel in one of the less salubrious back streets in Brighton he was soon asleep, exhausted. For just a handful of days he'd simply disappear from the face of the Earth. The following morning, after a night of broken dreams filled with recurring images of Chloe's broken body flying through the air, he took early breakfast and left. For the remainder of the day he drifted around the seafront, stopping occasionally for coffee in tacky cafes tucked away down alleyways and side streets. The sea air was bracing, refreshing, and for hours he found he was actually succeeding in barely thinking at all. Perhaps he was still in shock. He'd stay in the town for the next few days, anonymous and incommunicado. That morning he'd contacted Andrew Singer, managing partner at Clements. After explaining how his fiancée had died the previous day in an accident at the racecourse, he'd been granted compassionate leave until the end of the week. As the afternoon slipped away he began to think again about Adam. It was strange that his thoughts kept coming back to his former friend, and not to the woman he thought he had loved. The question couldn't be left unasked: if not with him, then would there still have been betrayal, but simply with another? His accountant's mind hated the lack of clarity, the absence of simple rights and wrongs on either side of a precise balance sheet. Adam had to be punished and this was an immutable reality. He had no respect for moral or professional boundaries, and for this reason alone he was a dangerous man. A failure to respond to what Adam had perpetrated would be to condone it. And a failure to take steps now to force his life into a different direction would also place others at risk in the future. After returning to the hotel he made his way to his room. There, he calmly picked up the telephone and dialed the number he had scribbled on the strip of paper the previous day.

Over the days following the cataclysmic incident at the races Adam tried without success to make contact with Thomas and Saul. Thomas was away from the office on compassionate leave, and nobody knew where he was staying. Saul, on the other hand, was simply refusing to return his calls. He felt alone in the world, with an overwhelming sense of guilt crushing down on him. But somewhere in his soul, buried deep beneath the angst and self-approbation, was a suspicion, a grain of sand in the oyster's flesh, that perhaps he'd done his friend a favour. Perhaps the marriage simply wasn't to be, that she'd wanted out at any cost. If this were the truth then the unpalatable reality would be that she'd used him, knowing that infidelity would be the ultimate sin in her fiancé's eyes. But she was dead, could not be cross-examined, and one of the principal anchors in his life, his friendship with Thomas and Saul, had now broken free, leaving him becalmed and depressed.

The only glimmer of light in the darkness, and it was admittedly a small one in the greater scheme of things at the moment, was that he'd been invited to join the firm's managing partner for lunch, for what he suspected would be a formal offer of partnership. He made his way to the room of the firm's power broker and aggressive managing partner, Nathan Cranmer. 'Adam, good to see you. It's hot weather for June, so if you want to take off your jacket, please do'. The two then sat down to discuss the firm's business informally over lunch. At the end of the meal, as the managing partner raised his coffee cup, he looked directly at Adam and asked a question that struck horror into his heart. 'Tell me about the Coughlin case. Why was it that the Prosecution's principal witness turned hostile at the last minute, and why do you think he went on to kill himself so soon after the trial?' Adam paused whilst trying to construct a rational answer. 'Melas was an unreliable witness. The Prosecution would have found this out if they'd only taken the trouble to question him on his statement in advance of the trial. They should have known there was a risk he wouldn't come up to proof; he'd worked for the defendant for years and was bound to have divided loyalties'.

Cranmer smiled. 'And what about the Prosecution evidence? I mean the bank statements and foreign transfers? I've looked at these myself and it appears they had a watertight case. Do you have an opinion about this evidence?' Adam was becoming unsettled by the specificity of the partner's questions. 'I'll tell you about that evidence. It was forged, fabricated by a Chief Inspector desperate to get a conviction regardless of what he had to do to get it. If Coughlin was guilty, then so was the gatherer of that evidence. A conviction obtained by corrupt practices is not justice in my book. It's the road to a police state'. Cranmer was visibly surprised by Adam's reply. 'This is a serious allegation you're making. Do you have concrete evidence that Slansfield perverted the course of justice? If not, then you'd better keep your mouth shut. If you do, I'd like to know how you came to possess it. And of course we can't ask any questions of the Chief Inspector anyway, because he's dead, isn't he? Murdered, I suspect on your client's orders, within days of the trial. So many deaths. Doesn't it trouble you to have these on your conscience?' With these few words Adam realised his host knew more about the case than he was revealing; the question was, how much did he actually know?

'Why should the deaths be on my conscience? I did my job and won the case. As a lawyer I merely present the facts, I don't make them. It's not for me to second-guess the guilt or innocence of those I represent. And if there's some defect in the legal process, or if the other side's witnesses are not up to proof, then my job's to exploit that, within the letter of the law, of course'. Cranmer remained impassive, concealing his anger at the lawyer's clever evasiveness. 'Adam, you're being much too modest about your complicity in the outcome of the case. Let me tell you what I know: it won't take long. Yesterday afternoon I received a phone call. At first I thought I was speaking to a disgruntled client of yours. He told me you'd passed on personal information about the chief Prosecution witness, Andreas Melas, to the defendant. Specifically, you provided information that enabled the defendant to make direct contact with the witness. He suggested I check the e-mails on your computer. As you'll know, we've the right to do this under the terms of your contract of employment with us. There I found a communication sent a week before the trial, containing Melas's e-mail address. No other words, greeting or sign off. Just his address. I'm sure that if the police check the recipient e-mail address they'd find an accomplice or employee of Mr. Coughlin. What do you think?'

Adam's face paled; his cross-examiner clearly knew the extent of his involvement in the trial's collapse, but what he intended to do with his knowledge was as yet unknown. Denial would be pointless. 'I admit I was involved in the case more than I should have been. And yes, I did provide Coughlin's accomplice with the contact details. But I thought the only consequence would be that the Prosecution would lose one of their witnesses. He'd simply refuse to give evidence, and the case against Coughlin would be weakened. The firm's not an innocent party in all this; we're always being told to 'win at any cost' after all. I was following our firm's policy. As for the deaths, they're a consequence of what I did and I'll have to bear that burden for the rest of my life'. There was a brief silence, and then the managing partner spoke again. 'There's no moral equivalence between the way this firm is run-its ethics and its way of doing business-and what you've done here. To suggest that there is is an insult to everyone who works here. You perverted the course of justice and people died as a direct consequence'.

'We now have to decide the way forward. As I see it, we have two options. First, I can bring in the police and hand over the e-mail, explaining my suspicions as to why the case collapsed. With the barrister's testimony, I think we can be certain you'll be convicted and go down for a minimum of four years, possibly a lot more. Of course the firm's reputation will be damaged in the process, and we'll probably be subject to a Law Society investigation. The confidence our clients have in us will also take a knock, and inevitably we'll lose a few'. Adam looked at the partner; knowing the alternative solution, he'd already accepted his fate. 'And the second option?' 'That you tender your resignation now, with immediate effect. You'll leave these premises at the end of this meeting and never return. You have no need to go back to your room- your personal belongings have already been packed and are awaiting collection at the front desk. We'll not provide a reference but if asked why you resigned, we'll say nothing. After all, by not disclosing what I know to the police I'll also be committing a crime. So what's it to be? Which option do you prefer?'

There was nothing to be gained from feigning any deep reflection: he agreed to resign immediately. To his sadness and disappointment, Cranmer produced a letter of resignation prepared in anticipation of the meeting's outcome. He signed it. As he stood he offered his hand and for seconds the partner hesitated. Eventually he took it. 'You could have been a great lawyer. You could have gone right to the top. But you've been a bloody fool and thrown it all away for a reason I still don't understand. If you learn from this tragedy it'll not have been without purpose. I wish you luck'. He couldn't bring himself to smile. Adam left the room and walked to the front desk to collect his belongings. He then ran down to the underground car park, got into his car, and drove away from his career.

Chapter Thirty Six

It had been four days since Chloe's death and Saul still hadn't spoken to Adam or Thomas. He had no desire to speak to Adam, but Thomas was a different matter. Saul had tried contacting him immediately after returning from the races, but there'd been no reply on his home number and his mobile was switched off. He'd called his office the next day only to be told that Thomas was off work and would not be returning 'for a while'. He was concerned for his friend's mental state, but knew there was nothing he could do until Thomas decided to make contact himself. Until then he'd just have to wait. As he walked to the office at eight o'clock that morning, he stopped at an Italian patisserie to purchase 'essentials' for the day ahead. With a full brown paper bag cradled in his arm he pulled out his pass with his free hand and showed it to the security guard. As the lift ascended he decided that today he'd re-establish contact with Adam. The present crisis was a serious one, but they could survive it and, hopefully, emerge from it with their friendship intact. He closed the door and settled at his desk. As the computer whirred into life he leaned back and slowly began pushing in the first cake, vaguely wondering how much he could force in before reaching gagging point. As the Bloomberg website began loading he read the ticker tape running across the bottom of the screen, as he did at the beginning of each working day to update himself on the world's overnight news. What he read made him freeze in disbelief, the last few inches of the cake still jutting out from his mouth.

'Media tycoon found dead in waters off Gibraltar. Franklin Shandlin falls from yacht: tragic accident or suicide?'

He quickly switched to another page, desperately scanning for the Piedmont quote. Already the price had fallen steeply, dropping twenty five percent on the previous day. The Tri-Star Trust had to dispose of its holding in the company immediately or the gains made on the back of the Winterstone Technologies takeover would be lost. But he also remembered that the terms of the Tri-Star Trust were specific when it came to stock disposals: communications had to be signed by all three beneficiaries and failure to comply would result in the rejection of an instruction by Dieter Morgenthau. He knew from the earlier conversation that Thomas was on compassionate leave, but he must have left a telephone number or an address where he could be contacted in an emergency. He tried remaining calm as he spoke again to Thomas's secretary; after explaining that Thomas had neglected to provide contact details the secretary hung up, mildly intimidated by Saul's abruptness. He closed his eyes, his heart racing. He reached again for the telephone, this time calling through to Adam's office. As he waited for the call to connect he glanced again at the share price: it seemed to be holding, but the earlier twenty five percent drop hadn't been recovered.

'Good morning. Please put me through to Adam Creed'. The secretary paused before responding. 'To whom am I speaking?' 'This is Saul Quartermain, a friend of Adam's, I think we've spoken before'. He recognised her voice as she did his. 'Hello Saul. I'm sorry but I can't help you. I thought you'd know but Adam is no longer with the firm. His employment with us ended last week and I've no idea where he is now'. Saul held the receiver away from his face and looked at it with incredulity. 'What? You must be mistaken. I know nothing about this. Can you check again? Perhaps you're confusing him with someone else who's left'. 'Sorry Saul but there's no mistake. He definitely left last week- I saw him hand in his pass to security. Nathan Cranmer sent around an e-mail informing all staff about it'. Saul was shocked: he had to know the truth. 'Cecile, this is a bolt out of the blue. I need to know - has he been sacked?' There was a pause. 'Yes he was sacked, but I really have no idea why. It must have been for something really serious. You'll have to ask him what the reason was because I haven't a clue'. Saul thanked her for her help, wished her well and then replaced the telephone in its cradle. After several further fruitless attempts to make contact he sat silently and perfectly still, gazing into space. His only hope now was that the share price would rally as soon as investors came to a view that the company was greater than the man who'd run it. For the remainder of the day he kept returning to the Bloomberg page, watching as the Piedmont share price bobbed up and down like a cork on the sea. But apart from the earlier announcement of the death there was nothing further reported in the media. At 6.30 pm he gave up and left. Without his co-beneficiaries' signatures there was nothing he could do.

In his plush office in Monaco, Dieter Morgenthau, the Tri Star Trust trustee, lifted his coffee cup in mock salute as the Piedmont share price collapsed on the screen in front of him. He smiled as he took another few sips, and then spoke aloud as if in the presence of the beneficiaries the protection of whose interests was his sole legal obligation: 'Here's to you, gentlemen. Congratulations on your impressive investment acumen. Perhaps you're just not as smart as you think you are after all'. He then made a call to Pierre Van den Luc, the Trust's banker; for a while they chatted and laughed about the latest rumours doing the rounds in the remarkably close local banking fraternity. Morgenthau then explained the real purpose of the call: the risk management strategy for the Tri-Star Trust put in place many months earlier was to be activated before close of trading that day.

Next day Saul returned to the office, deep black circles beneath his eyes testament to a sleepless night. He switched on the computer and a brief sense of relief set in as it became apparent that the share price had remained unchanged overnight. He sank back into his chair and waited for updates to begin feeding through on the newswires. Within an hour an announcement flashed across the bottom of the screen; Piedmont's Chief Finance Officer had assumed the chairmanship, issuing a statement that it would now be 'business as usual'. Slowly the share price began to recover, and by midday it looked as if the Tri-Star Trust would, incredibly, claw back most of its gains. Saul mustered a nervous smile as he peered at the tickertape: perhaps things would work out after all. After lunch in a local wine bar he sauntered back to the office, his confidence and optimism almost fully restored. As he passed through the dealing room one of the traders shouted after him: 'So what's it like having a dead mega-crook as a client? Franklin Shandlin? More like Franklin Swindling'. The young man laughed and then another trader pitched in. 'You should be grateful you didn't take us into the stock, or else you'd be looking for another job by the end of today. Pity the poor sods who couldn't get out before the news broke'. Saul rushed through to his office. Staring at the tickertape now traversing the Bloomberg page, instantly he knew the game was up, the holdings of the Tri-Star Trust in Piedmont worthless, and his dreams of escaping to an idle life of luxury vanished into the ether. He switched to a more detailed news service.

'Earlier today offices of Piedmont Communications were raided by the Serious Fraud Office. Before his recent death it is believed that Franklin Shandlin, chairman and founder of the company, plundered the pension funds of both his own company and the recently acquired Winterstone Technologies, embezzling cash to prop up Piedmont's share price. The full extent of the fraud is yet to be determined. The overnight share price has collapsed a catastrophic eighty percent on frenzied Far East trading before this morning's suspension. Liquidation is believed to be unavoidable'.

Saul switched off his computer and put on his navy blue jacket. The red silk lining gleamed as it caught a shaft of late afternoon sunlight. Slowly he walked past the traders who were still laughing and calling out sarcastic comments directed at him. He didn't even hear them. As he entered the street he felt light-headed, walking as if in a trance. He needed to find a place, a public place, with plenty of ordinary people talking about ordinary, mundane, insignificant things. He needed to come to terms with the enormity of the change in his financial circumstances. Checking his pockets he realised he'd left the office without money; he then caught sight of a young man begging, standing on the sidewalk with a flat cap in his extended hand. 'Got some change sir? It's a nice day. How about giving me what's in your pocket and making it even better?' Saul smiled. 'I've not got a penny on me, sorry, and today I've lost three million pounds. Can you spare me a couple of quid so I can buy myself a coffee?' The young man reached into his cap and pulled out a handful of change. 'No problem, mate. Have it on me. And remember, laugh and the world laughs with you, cry and you cry alone'. The two men laughed and after shaking his hand, Saul headed off to a nearby coffee house.

PART THREE

Caspian

Chapter Thirty Seven

Saul gazed out at the clouds as Damyanovitch emerged from the cockpit of the private jet holding two flutes and a bottle of Champagne. It was obvious from his demeanour that he was satisfied with the meetings they'd had over the past three days in Astana, Kazakhstan's capital city. They'd given presentations to the boards of the country's leading banks, and received overwhelmingly favourable responses to the Caspian pipeline deal. The three major Kazakh banks had agreed to underwrite part of the risk associated with the project, and underpinning the whole transaction would be a 'special purpose vehicle', or SPV, set up to give reassurance to bondholders. This would hold shares in two major Caspian pipelines, transferred to it by the state-owned energy companies of Azerbaijan and Kazakhstan. Without this additional security the energy ministries in both countries knew it would be impossible to raise the required finance in the international bond markets. At the heart of the entire project were bonds which paid interest linked to movements in the oil price. If the price went up, investors received a higher payout, and, of course, vice versa.

Damyanovitch popped the cork and gently poured the Champagne into both glasses. 'I think we did well Saul, and with the banks and the Ministry for Energy falling into line the project's on course. What did you make of our new Kazakh partners?' Saul sank back into the leather-upholstered seat and gazed out of the window. 'The main problems are that they lack experience and have weak capital bases. If something does happen, if a war breaks out somewhere in the Middle East and there are problems with the bond issue, then the Kazakh banks won't be able to meet their underwriting commitments. And for that matter, neither would Sheldons or Moscow Alpha. We'd all collapse'. Damyanovitch was acutely aware of the risks associated with the project: after all, he was counting on a major disaster bringing about its failure and collapse.

He reflected on the paradox that while Saul's concern was to identify risks and minimise them, by contrast his was to conceal and maximise them. Saul's aim was to avoid chaos, whilst his was to bring it about. 'So, if there are so many risks associated with this project, what do you propose we do to protect ourselves and the other syndicate members?'

Damyanovitch looked at the talented financier sitting opposite, draining the last drops of his third glass of Champagne and beginning to look the worse for it. He was so young, so naïve, yet at the same time possessed knowledge and skills that could destroy the plan which he and his colleagues in the Kremlin and in Washington had been working on so diligently and patiently for the past few years. Saul hiccupped as bubbles rushed up his nose. 'Take my word for it Petr, we'll have to reduce the risk. Not to do so would leave us and our Azeri and Kazakh partners dangerously exposed. And if we all collapse then the investors will seize the Caspian seabed rights held by the SPV. Without their prime national assets, the countries themselves would be plunged into economic chaos. No, we've got to have a risk hedging strategy. Paul Phineus wouldn't agree to anything less'.

The chairman's face whitened with suppressed irritation: he knew he was failing to communicate his real requirements to his fellow passenger. He eyed Saul, now thumbing through a magazine bought before the departure of their private flight. 'Saul, there will be no hedging strategy, no risk containment. You'll not disclose your concerns to either your chairman at Sheldons or to any syndicate member. You'll remain silent when anybody broaches the subject of risk with you. Do you understand?' Saul put down the magazine and tried to construct a coherent response to Damyanovitch's simple but unbelievable instruction, a task made difficult by the amount of alcohol he'd consumed. 'Petr, without these precautionary measures we'll be in grave danger. Do you really want to expose Moscow Alpha to the risks I've described? And if the local Azeri and Kazakh banks collapse, the ensuing economic meltdown across the region could last for years. Is there something I should know?' No reply was forthcoming, so he stood up and walked to the washroom at the rear of the plane. There he splashed cold water over his face and took several deep breaths before re-emerging, refreshed and better able to engage with the chairman.

'So Petr, where were we? I think you were about to reveal the real agenda behind this pipeline deal, in the spirit of openness and trust you've mentioned before. Or was I mistaken? I don't expect to be told everything, but what you said earlier makes me nervous. What's it to be?' Damyanovitch resented being challenged; he was accustomed to unquestioning obedience, previously from his underlings at the KGB and now from employees, managers and directors at Moscow Alpha. He was being pressed by a disrespectful, inebriated young man whose life he could snuff out in an instant. But, he did need his cooperation. He smiled as he reflected on this dependency, and the present state of vulnerability of the plan. Saul looked into his pale, soulless eyes and waited. 'This pipeline project will give us control over the only natural resource of the Caspian that counts, its oil. How we intend achieving this is not a matter you need to know about. If you just follow the simple guidance I give you then you'll become an extremely rich man, and no harm will come to you'. Saul already knew he was being used as a pawn in a much bigger game, but at this point in time it didn't trouble him. He recalled Damyanovitch's previous promise of great wealth, and, not for the first time, set it against the three million pounds lost by the Tri-Star Trust through the collapse of the Piedmont shares six months' earlier. The potential return on this deal would easily eclipse the profit that had slipped through his fingers. Damyanovitch's mention of harm, however, did trouble him. He was unsure whether he'd just been threatened; he decided he probably had.

'Gentlemen, we'll shortly commence our descent into Baku, touching down in about fifteen minutes. Please fasten your seat belts. I can also tell you that the weather on the ground is fine, in fact it's a really hot day at 32C. Please have your papers ready for inspection'. Slowly the jet began its gentle fall through a cloudless sky. Saul blinked at the sun as he gazed out past the wings at the dots of other larger planes hovering higher up, stacked whilst awaiting clearance. Damyanovitch didn't look out through the window, preferring instead to read through the confidential resumes of the bank officials and government apparatchiks they were scheduled to meet over the next few days. He recognised names of low ranking party members from the old regime who had, like himself, somehow managed to reinvent themselves to thrive in the brave new world they'd inherited.

So many people desperate to hide their pasts, to deny previous complicities, but he had the measure of all of them. When their like had been brought before him in chains for interrogation at the Ljubianka, it was often only a threat of violence, an intimation of imminent torture, which focused their minds, encouraging them to offer up anybody, even the innocent, to quicken their release and avoid pain. He thumbed through the pages again, dutifully prepared by his colleagues at the KGB's successor organisation, the FSB. Looking at the CV of the person whom they were scheduled to meet at the Ministry of Energy, he knew the task of obtaining agreement to the project would be a difficult one. Nascent nationalism combined with historic resentment would prove a dangerous and awkward mix in the negotiations. But he'd have their agreement eventually, whatever he had to do to achieve it.

The plane coasted to a halt, and as Saul quickly followed Damyanovitch in disembarking he was struck by a wall of heat rising from the tarmac. The Russian had visited this country on many occasions before, of course, both in his present and previous incarnations. After the two had passed through Customs (using the VIP route appropriate to visitors of such standing, much to Saul's amusement) they proceeded to their hotel in the heart of the city. En route Saul decided to raise a subject that had been troubling him for several months, confident that Damyanovitch would help if minded to do so. 'Petr, I need to ask a favour, not for myself but for a friend who's fallen on hard times'. Saul described how Adam had been a 'rising star' in the law firm which employed him, but had been forced to resign because of a mistake in the conduct of a case. Pressed by Damyanovitch he felt obliged to reveal more than he'd initially intended: after all, it was he who was seeking the favour. Damyanovitch listened intently; from the little which Saul described he recognised in Adam several of his own character traits. 'So tell me Saul, what would you have me do? How can I be of assistance to your friend?' He laughed at Saul's awkwardness at raising a personal matter, but was impressed by his loyalty and willingness to risk embarrassment on behalf of another.

'Adam needs a job, and quickly. If you have contacts, if you can get him back into a law firm, then this will save him. And of course, I'll be very grateful'. Damyanovitch winked at him. 'As soon as I return to Moscow, you can consider it done. I have an old friend in an American law firm with a branch in London. He and I are already working with each other on other matters, so it'll be no problem to put in a word. But it will be for you, and not for him, that I do this favour'.

Chapter Thirty Eight

The following morning Saul was surprised to see Damyanovitch's driver waiting in the hotel lobby. 'Sergei, hello. What are you doing here?' They were shaking hands as Damyanovitch walked in. 'Sergei, welcome to Baku. Did you make the arrangement I instructed yesterday?' He nodded and the three left for the meeting. Sergei Ivanov had flown in to Baku in the early hours the previous morning. At the airport he'd collected a hired Limousine and then driven to the hotel. Within ten minutes the car pulled up outside the vast, beautifully ornate building that was the state-owned oil company SOCAR's head office. In the foyer they were met by a young woman who led them to the conference room, the company's inner sanctum overlooking an extensive inner courtyard around which the building had been constructed. Around a large table sat fifteen people, five of whom were women. Their ages varied considerably: about a third appeared to be in their late fifties, whilst the other two thirds were noticeably younger, in their late thirties or early forties, representing the 'new generation'. These were the decision makers from the country's commercial banks and the Ministry of Energy, but the holder of real power in the room was Artur Kordovski, Director of Strategy at SOCAR. Saul and Damyanovitch took their places, nameplates positioned strategically at the opposite end of the table from the chairman.

After the customary pleasantries the meeting commenced in earnest. Saul was surprised by the aggression with which he and Damyanovitch were cross-examined on the project's terms by the younger board members. Most had evidently read closely the documentation sent by Sheldons in advance of the meeting, and now wanted to discuss the risks identified in the 'small print'. But despite their questioning and concerns, Saul instinctively knew that a majority were in favour of the deal. Only the older directors, former Party apparatchiks who'd sneaked into their positions immediately following the country's independence, showed significant scepticism. But they were the minority: it would be the younger generation who'd seal the deal. Throughout the discussion Kordovski barely spoke, instead jotting down notes on a small pad, occasionally looking up and staring at Damyanovitch. Their eyes would meet but they didn't address each other directly; there was a silent hostility between them even though they'd never met before.

To Saul it was ironic that the person with the greatest influence at the meeting and the greatest bearing upon its outcome had elected to say the least. But this was about to change. 'Gentlemen, ladies, I think this meeting is nearing its conclusion. I believe we all now have a more precise understanding of each other's positions on the project proposed by our friends from Moscow and London. I believe the general view around the table is positive. Would I be correct in this assumption?' The majority of the delegates, predominantly the younger ones, nodded. 'It is for this reason that I must, with regret, express my opposition to this project. I must inform you that I will be advising the SOCAR board in the strongest possible terms to reject entirely the pipeline project as presently structured'. There was a murmur of shocked surprise as the younger representatives evaluated the impact of the announcement upon the prospect for involvement of their own banks in the project. After a pause, Damyanovitch responded. 'May I enquire as to the reason for your opposition? We've spent the past few hours discussing the terms of the bond issue and I thought we'd dealt satisfactorily with all concerns. What are your concerns, Mr. Kordovski?' Saul had never seen the Russian rejected in this way, his authority challenged so openly, so publicly, and without fear or deference on the part of the challenger.

'With respect sir, you didn't deal with the concerns of everyone present. I'll tell you why I don't support this project. As I understand it, SOCAR will transfer its shareholding in the Caspian Pipeline Consortium, as well as its interest in the BTC pipeline currently under construction, to an SPV. The reason for this is to provide security to investors. There is therefore a possibility that our most valued national assets will fall into the hands of foreigners. And of course we'll also lose control of our own oil supplies because we'd be unable to influence the transit tariffs across the network we currently jointly own with others. We'd have to continue using the Russian system, with the potential for 'shut off' at Russian discretion in the future. Would this be a fair assessment of the risk implicit in your project?' Damyanovitch's expression remained impassive but he was surprised that Kordovski had seen through the conspiracy in such a short time and with such clarity. 'We haven't concealed this risk during our discussions here today but as I've also indicated, it can be regarded as an extremely remote possibility. Oil prices have never jumped by the margin required to trigger the additional features in the bond issue'. Kordovski closed the note pad in front of him. 'You may regard it as a remote possibility but I couldn't take such a risk with the future economic wellbeing of my country. The answer is therefore No.' Disregarding the customary shaking of hands and well-wishing among guests, he immediately walked to the door at the opposite end of the room and left.

Damyanovitch was silent during the journey back to the hotel, gazing out of the window as he contemplated the new state of affairs. Without the transfer of the pipeline rights the project's entire purpose, as he saw it, would be defeated. One man, an Azeri nationalist with, he supposed, a hatred of Russia, was putting everything at risk. Eventually Saul broke the silence. 'I know you're disappointed by Kordovski's behaviour at the meeting Petr, but I'm sure the project can still be saved. The majority around the table liked our proposal. Forget about Kordovski'. Damyanovitch turned his gaze to Saul, his eyes refocusing from infinity. 'Transference of their oil rights is vital to our plan. We must have it. We will have it. The rights will be transferred to the SPV and nobody, least of all a bureaucrat from the old days, is going to prevent it'. By the time Sergei Ivanov pulled up outside the hotel Damyanovitch had decided they should remain in Baku for a further day.

As the three sat in the hotel lobby awaiting late afternoon tea Damyanovitch took out his mobile and began tapping in a number. 'Please put me through to Mr. Kordovski if he hasn't already left for the day. My name is Petr Damyanovitch and he may be expecting my call'. Saul heard the name but was confused as to why the chairman was making the call after the humiliation he'd suffered from the Azeri earlier that day. 'Hello Artur, I'm pleased to have caught you this late in the day. I just wanted to thank you for making time to see us earlier today. I'm disappointed things didn't work out as planned, but I respect you for your candour at the meeting. It's refreshing to have a straight answer in business, even if it's not the one you want to hear'. Saul could hear forced laughter at the other end of the line. 'Artur, I won't be returning to Baku for a while, so we were wondering whether you'd join us for an early evening meal tomorrow?' Kordovski loathed the Russian just as he loathed all Russians, and was surprised to hear from him again so soon after his humiliating rejection earlier that day. But the prospect of emphasising his opposition, and, most probably, embarrassing Damyanovitch again, was just too appealing to resist. He'd turn up at the hotel, be taken to an expensive restaurant where he'd be wined and dined at their expense, and then end the evening by rejecting their request again.

He smiled to himself, and after graciously accepting the invitation replaced the telephone. Saul looked at Damyanovitch, unable to conceal his curiosity. 'I thought Kordovski said no to our proposal? And it wasn't a qualified no either. He was adamant that SOCAR wouldn't get involved. So why the invitation to dinner tomorrow?' Damyanovitch smiled enigmatically. 'While we're here in Baku we must make every effort to resolve this impasse. As you said yourself, the majority at the meeting wanted to go ahead, so all we have to do is convince Kordovski of the project's merits. I'm sure we'll be able to change his mind'.

<hr />

'Artur, good to see you again and thanks for accepting our invitation at such short notice. You've already met my colleague from Sheldons, Saul Quartermain, but I'd also like to introduce my assistant at Moscow Alpha, Sergei Ivanov'. The short thin man with a dark complexion made all the more striking by a thick mop of white hair shook hands with Damyanovitch and then with Saul and the driver. 'It's a pleasure to see you again Petr, and I'm pleased you decided to stay an extra day in our beautiful city. Have you been to Baku before?' Damyanovitch smiled at the clumsy attempt to elicit information about his personal history. 'Yes, I've visited the city on several previous occasions, but not recently'.

There was a pause as Kordovski considered the response. 'I've also been to Moscow, but that too was a while ago. You remember those days, when all loyal Soviet citizens made at least one pilgrimage in their lifetime to pay homage at the Mausoleum in Red Square. I remember those days well. Tell me, have they taken Comrade Lenin out of that glass box yet? I've heard that his face is disintegrating, and it's been decided to plant him under the Kremlin's walls at last. Is this true?' Damyanovitch didn't reply.

Saul was becoming aware of the hostility between the two. 'So Artur, you found the hotel easily? Did you come by taxi or drive yourself?' The Azeri nationalist transferred his gaze to the younger man. 'I drove here- this hotel's well known in Baku. I left my car in the hotel car park. I hope this is okay'. Damyanovitch needed to put his opponent at ease and yet the evening had already started with a confrontation. 'There's no problem in leaving your car, but if we don't inform the concierge it'll be towed away. Sergei will let him know. If you could leave your key with him he'll be able to move it if the space is needed by a hotel guest- they take priority over visitors'. Kordovski agreed: 'I'll speak with him on our way out. Shall we leave? Which restaurant have you booked?'

'I've reserved places for us at Scallini's in Bakihanov Street. Unfortunately Sergei is unable to join us, but he'll take us there and collect us later. We'll bring you back to pick up your car'. Ivanov brought the Limousine round to the front of the hotel, and after the three had climbed in he began the short drive to the restaurant.

For the first hour at the Italian restaurant the conversation was light, trivial, and good-humoured. Kordovski spoke with enthusiasm about SOCAR's plans for the future, and of his intention to establish joint ventures with companies in Western Europe, the US, and Japan. There were already such agreements in place with Russian partners, but it was increasingly apparent that his preference was to reduce SOCAR's ties with its former master. Damyanovitch listened intently to his guest, looking for the right moment to raise the project rejected the previous day. He respected Kordovski's knowledge of the global energy sector, but as the evening progressed he was confirmed in his belief that emotional rather than economic reasons lay behind his stubbornness.

'Artur, Saul and I will be returning to Moscow later tonight so I hope you won't mind if I raise again the proposal we put to you yesterday. This evening's been an opportunity for us to get to know each other, and I hope that the favourable impression I now have of you is mutual. I'm sure we could work well with each other in the Caspian project and as you must know, SOCAR's participation is crucial to its success. We need you on board. The temporary transfer of your Caspian seabed rights to the SPV is essential; it underpins the entire deal. Could we discuss it again? Please, what are your objections?' Saul was surprised at the emotional intonation in Damyanovitch's voice. It was as apparent to him as it must have been to their guest that this was an unusual state of affairs: the chairman of Moscow Alpha needed something badly and was frustrated by his lack of progress in achieving it. Kordovski drank the last drop from his coffee cup, replaced it on its saucer, and then replied. 'There are three reasons why I cannot agree to SOCAR's participation, none of which you'll like and none of which can be overcome. Surely better to move on and consider other possibilities, other avenues? Sometimes it's better not to ask, wiser not to know. Let's instead part company as friends, Petr?' They stared at each other across the coffee cup and wine glass-strewn table; Saul realised his attempt to keep the peace that evening had finally failed. He knew Damyanovitch would need to hear Kordovski's reasons even though he probably knew what these were before the white-haired embittered nationalist arrived at their hotel earlier that evening. 'I've never been one to run from the truth, my friend, so please speak frankly. I'm sure I'll not be offended if what you're about to say is objective and rational. Please, go ahead'.

'Well…. If you insist. As I said, you won't like it. First, as I said yesterday, the oil rights that would be transferred to the SPV are essential to my country's economy. To risk losing control of these is a risk we cannot take. It would be irresponsible'. 'And the second reason?' 'The second reason is that I don't believe that Azerbaijan needs Russia anymore. I don't believe we should be entering into more partnerships with Russian energy companies or banks. Of course, we already have some collaboration in Caspian oil field development, but this is a necessity for geopolitical rather business reasons. It's also useful tokenism to show that links are not entirely severed, even though we're moving on to form new partnerships'.

Damyanovitch's suspicions were confirmed; the people behind SOCAR, probably including senior members of the government in Baku, had an agenda to isolate Russia and hasten her economic collapse. 'And what of Russia? Does she just stand on the sidelines and wait for her neighbours to sign agreements to carve up the oil wealth of the Caspian Sea?' Kordovski smiled sardonically. 'Petr, I don't think you're facing up to reality. Regional groups of independent countries are working together on Russia's borders and nothing's going to stop this process, because they – *we* - have a perfect right to do so. We are sovereign nations. Soon Iran will join us, and then Turkey, in exploiting the Caspian oil reserves. Russia's had her day in this part of the world, if you don't mind my being so blunt'.

Damyanovitch started to clap, at first slowly and then faster and faster. 'Well said, Artur. Spoken like a true nationalist. I came here tonight hoping that objectivity would change your mind. But, plainly, you're a man guided by your heart and your bitterness, and not by your business head. Out of curiosity, what's the third reason for your obstinacy?' Kordovski's face reddened with anger at Damyanovitch's condescension; he felt belittled in front of the young man from London, and the need to vent his true feelings now became irresistible. 'The third reason is my loathing for your country and everything it represents, past and present. It used to be run by psychopaths but now it's run by drug dealers and gangsters instead. I spent eight and a half years of my life, *eight and a half of my best years*, as a slave in Siberia. And why was I there? Simply because I'd written poems and leaflets about our history. And my parents? They had been sent into internal exile before. Neither of them survived. And you wonder why I loathe your country so much, and its attempts to interfere with mine? You question me and insist that I state the reasons for my hostility to your devious project? Its only purpose is to destroy the heart of our economy, and you insult me by thinking me too stupid to see it. What kind of a fool do you take me for?'

Damyanovitch gently patted the corners of his mouth with a napkin. 'I think I've heard enough. It's best if we leave now. I'm sorry the burden of resentment weighs so heavily upon your shoulders, but we're all products of the past so I should be more understanding. But I'm not, and there's no point in talking further'. The waiter was summoned and the bill was paid, with a healthy tip for the Azeri waiting staff. The three found Ivanov waiting beside the Limousine parked outside, and warm rain had started to fall. Kordovski took the front seat alongside the driver without hesitation, patting down his suit lapels as he fastened his seatbelt. Damyanovitch and Saul climbed into the darkness behind him, on the back seats.

For the first few minutes no words were spoken as the car gently passed along the deserted streets. It was Damyanovitch who broke the silence. 'Artur, I'll ask you one last time. If you won't support the project, could I ask that you at least defer from blocking it? Could you give way on this one request?' The passenger in front of him turned and replied with unconcealed hatred; 'I've told you, I'll not allow our national assets to be robbed in the way you have in mind. I'll use every fibre of my being to oppose this deal, so don't ask again'. He returned to sullenly staring at the road ahead.

The chairman then spoke the pre-agreed signal words to Ivanov: 'Sergei, take care with your driving'. The following seconds passed as if in slow motion as Saul looked on, paralysed with shock. Damyanovitch reached into his pocket and took out what in the darkness resembled a comb; a click of the mechanism followed as the knife flicked out of its holder. In an instant he reached forward, crooked his arm around Kordovski's head and pulling it back, raised his free hand and slashed the blade across his throat. Blood spurted from the severed artery, spraying across Ivanov and Saul's faces as the victim struggled to break free. Kordovski reached up in horror at the arm gripping him like a vice but his killer was too strong: within twenty seconds he was dead. Saul started to scream incoherently. Damyanovitch let the body crumple back into the seat, returned the blade into its holder and calmly placed it back into his pocket. He turned to the now hysterical passenger and slapped him across the face. 'Be silent! Haven't you seen a man die before? Did you really think I'd let him get in the way? Sometimes bad blood must be spilt.' He leaned forward to speak with Ivanov, who had maintained the same steady speed throughout the murder, entirely unaffected by it. Saul realised he must have witnessed the same violence before, and had known what to expect when he collected them from the restaurant.

'Sergei, take us to the lane we visited last night. Do you have what we need?' The driver didn't even turn around. 'Yes I have it. It's in the boot. We'll be there in a few minutes'. The Limousine soon rolled into an alley-way before coming to a halt. Ivanov climbed out and walked to the back of the car, returning with what looked like a large mail sack. He opened the passenger door and the lifeless body flopped out onto the ground. After dragging it out he pushed it into the mail sack with relative ease. He dragged the bag to the rear of the car and heaved it into the boot. Getting back into the car he turned to Damyanovitch; 'Shall I head for the airport now? We're scheduled to leave in fifty minutes'. Damyanovitch nodded his approval. Saul had been looking on in silent horror and only now was able to speak. He felt too nauseous to wipe away the blood still spattered across his face. 'You're nothing more than a murderer, a cold-blooded murdering bastard. I want nothing more to do with you, you hear? You'll never get away with this this time'. Damyanovitch smiled before replying in a tone so calm and unperturbed it was as if the previous few blood-soaked minutes hadn't even happened. His heartbeat hadn't increased during Kordovski's execution, and his breathing showed no sign of stress or effort. 'Think before you say anything more. Think about all you have to lose if we end things. And I think you'll find I will get away with it. As for Kordovski, he'll be missed for a week or so, but when they find his car in a derelict part of town, the interior scattered with ten thousand dollars in one hundred dollar bills, it'll be assumed there was more to his private life than his colleagues realised. The papers will say he was involved with the local mafia- in fact', he paused to smile at his own preparations, 'I've already paid a local editor to run the story in a few days' time. We have a local man of mine ready to lose this car, too. There's a deep canal he's used before. Thanks to Sergei, everything was arranged well in advance according to my instructions'.

Saul was appalled at the cynical planning by Damyanovitch and his accomplice. He'd believed the evening was about convincing Kordovski of the merits SOCAR would derive from the deal, but its real purpose was to prepare him for execution. Now the person with whom he'd laughed and shared wine just a few hours earlier was dead, tied up in a mail bag specially brought along for the purpose. Within a short time they pulled up alongside the Gulfstream jet on which they'd arrived in Baku, parked in exactly the same part of the landing strip where it had been left earlier. As Saul showered to rid himself of the blood on his skin in a guard's outhouse which Damyanovitch had ushered him into next to the runway, he saw from an open window Ivanov and the captain lifting the heavy mailbag from the Limousine's boot and throwing it like a large sack of potatoes into the cargo hold. The car was handed over by Ivanov to a bulky man in overalls who grinned as he was handed an envelope. Saul and Damyanovitch, by now clean and wearing fresh clothes, then ran back to the plane, its engines being fired up ready for takeoff. Once Ivanov had joined them, the jet was airborne.

Within a few hours the plane began its descent to a private landing strip within the boundaries of Domodedovo airport, Moscow. The journey had passed in complete silence as Damyanovitch read through paperwork generated by the meetings in Astana and Baku. Saul was disinclined to talk for obvious reasons; he was disgusted at what he'd witnessed and queasy at the thought of Kordovski's stone-cold body folded up in a mailbag a few feet beneath where he was sitting. They disembarked, placing their hand luggage on the vacant front passenger seat of the waiting Mercedes. After loading the mailbag into the car's boot Ivanov took the wheel, the captain remaining with the plane to take it the short distance to a nearby hangar. During the short journey to the main airport Damyanovitch spoke to Saul, still silent and by now deeply depressed. 'Saul, our presentations in Astana and Baku were a success and you should be proud of this. When you get back to London you'll tell your chairman that the project is on course. Sheldons should soon receive formal confirmation from the Kazakh and Azeri banks of their willingness to participate in the deal. SOCAR will confirm in due course, after the dust of Kordovski's disappearance has settled. We work well together, and I hope you'll want to continue the relationship. After you get back to London and have had time to think, please let me know whether or not you want to proceed. If not, then no harm done. I hope we'll still be able to part as friends.'

Saul looked at him icily; 'What are you going to do with the body? It's a pity his family won't get the opportunity to bury him, don't you think?' 'You needn't concern yourself with this, but be sure it'll be buried somewhere where no one will find it. Sometimes killing has to be done, for the most noble of causes'.

The car came to a halt outside the airport's main entrance and Ivanov unloaded Saul's luggage. As Saul stepped out Damyanovitch leaned forward and extended his hand. Saul shook it and Moscow Alpha's internationally respected chairman smiled. As Saul made his way into the airport the Russian called after him: 'And don't worry about your friend - he'll be back in work soon'. Within an hour Saul was airborne again. He gazed out into the darkness.

Chapter Thirty Nine

Saul sat on a bench overlooking the Serpentine, struggling to turn the pages of a redtop with one hand and clutching an ice cream cone with the other. It was a glorious day, a week since he had returned from Baku, and he'd neither heard from Damyanovitch nor indeed felt any inclination to make contact with him. He closed his eyes, listening to the cacophony of noises around him. Children playing, dogs barking, birds, water. Hyde Park was one of his favourite places, and his position at the bank meant he could come and go as he liked without being questioned as to where he was going or when he'd be returning. Ultimately it was the department's profit figures alone that mattered, and not his idiosyncrasies or time keeping. Nearby in the shade of leaf-laden ancient trees a group of pensioners acting in unison stretched and pointed into the distance. He loosened his tie and straightened the jacket he'd earlier placed alongside on the bench. In the distance a runner in a scruffy blue tracksuit broke through the glimmer of the early morning heat haze; his hair was unkempt and as he drew nearer, his unshaven face and scuffed, battered trainers indicated to Saul someone of very meager means.

Saul closed the newspaper and placed it on top of his jacket, then sat and waited. The young man was soon standing in front of him. 'Saul, thanks for coming. It's great to see you again. How's work?' 'Adam, it's good to see you too. I'd say you're looking well, but I'd be lying and you'd know it. You look a wreck. If you could look the other way while we're talking just in case there's anyone who knows me nearby, then it'd be much appreciated. After all, one always judges a man by the company he keeps'. Adam could still appreciate his friend's acerbic humour, and laughed. But Saul had become concerned by the spiral of depression into which Adam had descended in the months following his dismissal from his firm. As the managing partner correctly predicted on the day of his 'resignation', it had subsequently proved impossible to get so much as an interview with any law firm, either in London or elsewhere. Nobody wanted to see him, and the prospect of an early return to the profession he loved was diminishing by the day. Saul also suspected that his personal finances had collapsed during recent months; the evidence was overwhelming, from promises to pay 'next time' when they met at restaurants, to his general shabbiness. His physical appearance was also deteriorating; he'd go for days without shaving, sleeping into the early afternoon and then heading to the park to run, trying to stave off the effects of the junk food on which he now survived.

'You said last night you had some news - what is it? Don't keep me in suspense'. 'The news is I've got an interview. I had a call yesterday from a law firm here in London, an American firm. It was the partner who rang. He said he'd heard I was looking for employment and would like me to send over my details. I e-mailed my CV and his secretary called back straight away to say they wanted to see me. I've got an interview the end of this week. It's the first response in six months and although there's no saying they'll give me a job, it's lifted my spirits'. Saul smiled: Damyanovitch had kept his word. 'Strange to get a call out of the blue like that'. Adam hesitated; 'Yes, I suppose it is. But I've sent out so many letters over the past few months it's possible a firm passed on my CV. Saul, I've got to ask a favour, and to tell the truth it's the main reason I asked to see you today. I hate to ask it and wouldn't if there was any alternative, but time's short'. Saul looked at him, hoping he was not about to be asked for something which was beyond his power to deliver. 'OK Adam, ask away. You know I'll help if I can'. After a further pause Adam continued, evidently embarrassed. 'The past few months have been difficult, financially speaking. If Piedmont hadn't collapsed after Shandlin's death I'd have been able to cash in my Tri-Star holding. But it's been one thing after another and I've been getting by on almost nothing. I've had to sell everything just to keep up with my bills. And by everything I mean my suits, ties, jackets - the lot. Could you lend me the money to buy a suit for Friday's interview?' Saul was saddened to see Adam reduced to making such a request; he wondered if his pride would ever recover from the humiliation that had been heaped on him, even if this had been his own fault. 'You and I are going to Savile Row this afternoon to get you suited and booted. Go back to your flat, get washed and shaved, and I'll see you here in three hours' time. And the day I give you a loan will be the day Hell freezes over.' Adam couldn't bring himself to reply. He simply nodded, stood up and ran off into the distance.

Saul returned to Sheldons to delegate the afternoon's work to staff in his department. With five minutes to spare he sent an e-mail to Moscow. The brief e-mail read: 'Re our continuing collaboration, despite reservations the answer is yes. Regards, Saul'. He then left to spend the remainder of the afternoon with Adam at one of the most expensive tailors in Savile Row.

Two days later Adam stood outside the London branch office of the American law firm Druckerstein, Kahn and Nixdorf. He looked down at his perfect suit and straightened his sky blue tie; the gifts from his friend created the image he wished to convey, but in his soul he felt ashamed. He looked around and seeing nobody, vigorously rubbed both sides of his face to put some colour into his grey complexion. He walked into the lobby and introduced himself to the receptionist, a confident, bubbly American woman of fifty or so. 'Mr. Creed, welcome to Druckerstein, Kahn and Nixdorf. Mr. Buckmaster is expecting you. I'll take you through to the conference room. Best of luck for the interview. Give 'em hell'. Alice Penn shook his hand and as she led him through she paused and turning to Adam, surprised him by straightening his tie. In a thousand other situations he would have disapproved of such informality by someone not even met before, but here it seemed just right, a genuine gesture. 'Thank you. I was sure I'd fixed it outside, but this tie's got a life of its own'. 'You're welcome. Now please, Mr. Buckmaster's waiting for you'. She pushed open the door and gestured Adam to enter; he walked in and heard the door click closed behind him.

'Mr. Creed, it's a pleasure to meet you. Thanks for coming along at such short notice'. Adam was greeted by Carter Buckmaster, the London partner of Druckerstein, Kahn and Nixdorf, whose appearance chimed in every way with his Southern drawl. He was at least six foot three, and of a medium build with a ruddy complexion. He had bleach white collar-length hair and a closely cropped white beard, and sported a red polka-dot tie. In any other situation his appearance would have been clichéd, too clichéd, for a lawyer from Tennessee, but in his case it created a perfectly natural, easy image. 'Please, sit yourself down and let's talk. You have a very interesting CV, so we'll talk about that first if that's okay with you. And then I'll tell you about our firm, the work we do, and what we'd require of you should we offer you a position and should, of course, you decide to accept it'. The two lawyers then talked through the CV Adam had e-mailed over a few days earlier. The partner's eye for detail was sharp enough, as he questioned Adam about his work at Roxburgh Thymes, and his general success rate. But in any event the decision to offer the job had been made a week earlier, after he'd been contacted by the close friend he had made all those years ago at the Kennedy-Khrushchev summit in Vienna. He'd been asked to give this young man a job, and was happy to oblige.

The interview was nearing a close; as far as Adam was concerned, if the position were to be offered he'd grasp it with both hands. And then Buckmaster fell silent, as if carefully framing a final, more intrusive question in his mind, the only question which would really matter in the entire interview. Adam waited for the inevitable question: why wasn't he currently in employment? Buckmaster must have concluded even before the interview had been arranged that his previous employer had dismissed him: it was now only a matter of time before the subject was broached. If asked, Adam didn't know even at this late stage in the interview how much of the truth he dared reveal. Buckmaster patted his white beard and then fixing Adam with a different, cold stare he spoke. 'Adam, we've talked a lot about your work at Roxburgh's and the opportunities this firm may be able to offer you. But there's something I must raise with you, a personal matter. I hope you'll not think me presumptuous, but it goes to the heart of this firm'.

Adam held his breath: here was the question he'd been dreading. 'Are you a Christian?' The question was so entirely different from the one he'd been expecting that for a few seconds he was taken aback, not knowing how to reply. 'What do you mean? I'm sorry but I don't understand'. He berated himself for the weakness of his reply. Buckmaster laughed; 'I guess your response is an answer in itself'. His smile disappeared and a serious tone entered his voice. 'I've got to tell you Adam that we're a Christian firm and always have been. All our partners are committed Christians, and we expect our employees to be of faith and to conduct themselves in the same way. We believe this to be a small expectation, but in a world engulfed by violence and blasphemy it's important we do our part to influence the lives of those around us. We're going to offer you a job, but it's vitally important that in due course you make this commitment. Now, if you don't have any further questions, we'll finish here. You'll receive our offer in the next few days. I like you and I know we're going to get on just fine'.

He shook Adam's hand then left, the young lawyer still confused by the direction the interview had taken in its closing minutes. He'd expected to be asked why he'd left his former employer without having a job to go to, but this hadn't been the case; it was as if the decision to offer a position had been made before the interview had even commenced. He left the room to be greeted again by Alice Penn; she'd been hovering around the lobby, wondering why the young man hadn't left the interview room at the same time as the senior partner. 'I was beginning to wonder whether you'd left the building via the window, voluntarily or otherwise. Mr. Buckmaster can be quite brutal in interviews, you know'. Adam laughed and took her hand in both of his in an act of spontaneous informality. 'Alice - may I call you Alice? - it's been a pleasure meeting you here today. I'm pleased to say I got the job, and it was entirely down to my perfectly arranged tie. Without your intervention I'd not have stood a chance'. She smiled. 'I'm delighted for you, Adam. I'm sure this is a new beginning and better times are ahead'. It was the first reference that day, oblique as it was, to his present situation. He thanked her again and with his self-confidence on its way to full restoration, walked outside into a world in which he could hold his head up high once again.

Chapter Forty

'Saul, I've got Mr. Antanis of SOCAR on the line. He says you met during your recent visit to Baku. Shall I put him through?' Saul had become increasingly anxious during recent weeks; the deal had not yet been approved, and the murdered Kordovski's successor had not been appointed. The prospect of complete failure seemed a real possibility, and before the project had even got off the ground. 'Yes, please put him through'. 'Dimitri, good to hear from you again. It seems like we met yesterday but I guess it must be about a month ago now. So how are things at SOCAR? Have you any good news for me? Please don't be offended but we were expecting Mr. Kordovski to make contact with us.' His deceit temporarily appalled him: he knew, of course, that the elderly Kordovski was long dead.

'Saul, you're right, it's been just over a month and I'm sorry nobody's got back to you before now about the pipeline deal. I can't go into details but unfortunately the lead negotiator from our side at the earlier meeting, Artur Kordovski - you may remember that I was his 'acting number two'- is no longer with us, and this is why there's been a delay'. Saul paused to steady his voice. 'I'm sorry to hear that. We got on well with Artur, even though he wasn't keen on our proposal initially. Has he moved to another job?' 'As I say, I don't want to talk about this but perhaps it's only fair to you if I explain a little. In this part of the world, I'm sorry to say, crime and corruption are common. Mr. Kordovski disappeared shortly after our meeting, and there's strong evidence he was involved with the local mafia. It later turned out he had many bank accounts set up in different names. Even his car, when the police found it later, had a large quantity of cash stashed in the boot. It's been very disappointing for me because I trusted him and knew his family. But who can tell what goes on in a man's heart?' Saul was overcome with guilt: to have been an accessory to murder was enough of a crime, but to know that an innocent man's character had been destroyed among those who knew him, and not to speak out, was perhaps almost an equally grave offence.

'Dimitri, I'm sorry to hear that news, especially as I imagine you were close to him. I suppose we must move on. You're calling now to give me the decision of the SOCAR board, right?' 'Yes. I have some good news for you. SOCAR has agreed to the terms of the deal. We'll transfer our shareholding in the Caspian Pipeline Consortium, our stake in the future BTC pipeline, and our oil rights in the Caspian seabed, to the special purpose vehicle. We understand that this will be part of the security offered to investors in the bonds. All dividends payable on our interest in the pipeline will continue to pass through to us, even though our share-holding will be legally owned by the SPV. As for the Azeri banks present at our earlier meeting, they're also coming in. In truth they're eager to participate. They see this project as an opportunity to develop a long-term relationship with Sheldons. So, it's a definite 'yes' from our side. And from what I understand, our opposite number in Kazakhstan has also signed up to the project. Is that right?' 'Yes, you're right, Dimitri. Mr. Damyanovitch and I started our 'road show' in Astana and made the first presentation to the CEOs of the main Kazakh banks as well as board members from your partner in this project, Kazakh Oil. They were all very enthusiastic about the project. The new pipeline will lock in Azerbaijan's and Kazakhstan's control of the Caspian Sea resources, and that's why participation of the leading banks and oil companies of the two countries is so crucial to the success of the venture. And since we're co-lead managers of the deal with Moscow Alpha, the commission we're going to share with them will be pretty impressive. We're not participating for altruistic reasons, as you've probably already guessed!' The two men laughed, agreeing that capitalism had finally reached the countries around the Caspian. The conversation over, Saul leaned back and breathed a deep sigh of relief; the project was back on course, and the outcome of the presentation in SOCAR's head office in Baku, despite the horrible event which had followed it, was now turning out better than he could ever have hoped for.

Chapter Forty One

Carter Buckmaster clambered into a yellow cab outside J.F.K. Airport. It had been a long, tiring flight from London, but his working day was only just beginning. The heat wave which smashed into him as he exited the airport was oppressive, particularly after the light rain and coolness of London the previous day. Although he was a Southerner by birth, and therefore accustomed to a near-tropical climate, the dampness and grey skies of the UK had affected his 'inner barometer', as he liked to inform friends whenever he returned home. The prospect of spending time in New York didn't engender positive thoughts in the lawyer who'd spent most of his flight from London reading the Bible and the commentary provided by his church at his childhood baptism. This was a city of sin and debauchery, a focal point of avarice and sodomy whose very existence disgusted and repelled him. Joe Salvatore stared at him in the mirror, tapping the wheel as he awaited his customer's instructions. 'So where to, sir? Or maybe you'd prefer we just sit here while you think about it? Either way the clock's running'. He spoke with a pure third generation Italian-American accent: confident and brash, with the customary impertinence of a New York cabby kept waiting longer than a handful of seconds. Buckmaster looked at the eyes staring back at him in the mirror. 'Sorry, yes. 33rd Street and 5th, if you'd be so kind'. His Southern drawl and the courtesy of his reply betrayed his origins and the fact that he was a stranger in the city. 'Yessir. Traffic's not so bad, so we should be there in no time. Sorry the air con's not working - it broke this morning. If you want to wind down the window, that's fine'.

As the cab proceeded through the traffic-choked streets, Buckmaster became increasingly uncomfortable. The heat was overwhelming, and even though the windows were open, this merely filled the cab with fumes from the surrounding vehicles. He felt sweat trickling down his back and noticed stains beginning to appear across his shirt. The situation was not helped by Joe insisting on talking at high speed for the journey's duration. Buckmaster's impeccable Southern manners precluded the usual native New Yorker response in such a situation: 'Why don't you just shut your mouth and concentrate on driving?' Eventually they arrived and after paying the fare plus a substantial tip he climbed out onto the sidewalk. 'Thanks, sir. Very generous of you. Have a nice day now'. Buckmaster was relieved to see the cab disappearing into the distance. As he gazed up at the skyscraper towering above him he stood in awe for a few seconds, the two American eagles staring down from above either side of the entrance. He'd seen it before, of course, and traveled the full distance of its one hundred and two floors numerous times throughout his career. But despite this familiarity he always paused in the same spot just to marvel at the enormity, the unparalleled confidence, of the structure poking up through the clouds.

The interior was cool, a sanctuary from the burning heat outside. As he looked around at the 1930s Art Deco he saw again the flagpoles above the entrances to the elevators, his heartbeat quickening (as it always did) at the sight of 'Old Glory' suspended from them. He checked in at Empire State reception then proceeded up the escalator, entered the waiting lift and glided up to the fortieth floor. 'Carter, such a pleasure to see you again. You're looking well. Come in'. The lawyer looked around the large office suite; it was always the spectacular view over the city that caught his attention. As he gazed into the distance his host read his thoughts. 'I never tire of that view and I've been working here for five years now. So high up in the clouds, watching gulls pass by at eye level, looking down on the panorama of this great metropolis of ours. It makes me feel like a king of the world'. Buckmaster smiled and then in his heavy accent responded to the younger man's polished New England tone; 'Let's not ever forget there's only one king of the world'. The young man's casual blasphemy irritated him. 'Of course, Carter. Of course'. Positioned around the suite's perimeter were small tables, each occupied by a single individual. Lincoln Davies gestured towards each of them. 'Carter, you know Henry sitting over there. I think you've met him before. CEO, Montana Standard Oil. And next to him, Andrew Dexter of Salt Lake Energy. Alongside, Peter Tapp of California International Finance. Next to him and showing his usual contempt for the health lobby, Philip Dulamore of Penn Eagle Bank'. The grossly overweight guest drawing on a Castro-style cigar responded with a mock salute. After the nine bankers and oil barons had been introduced, some of whom Buckmaster had previously worked for in a professional capacity, the exuberant Lincoln Davies, CEO of Global Energy Bank, poured his latest guest a glass of iced tea. He knew from previous meetings that he'd not welcome a dram of the Macallan with which the other attendees had been welcomed as they'd trickled in during the past half hour. Buckmaster took a table towards the rear of the room.

'And now gentlemen, seeing as we're done with the pleasantries and introductions, I'd like to proceed to business. I'd like to start by inviting Carter to explain progress to date with our project. So Carter, over to you'. Buckmaster remained seated and after taking a few sips of tea to sooth his dry throat, addressed the assembled multi-millionaires and billionaires. 'I'm pleased to be able to report that everything's going smoothly. A month ago our colleague in Moscow secured the participation of the target Kazakh and Azeri banks in the Caspian deal. Lead managers will be Sheldons and Moscow Alpha, both of which will be destroyed in Phase One of the project in line with our expectations and, of course, those of our Russian colleague. Without his commitment to the project we'd never have got this far'. Lincoln Davies smiled; 'I've never met him but I hear he's been doing a great job. I'd like to propose a round of applause for our absent friend'. Without exception, everyone in the room clapped in agreement. Buckmaster coughed to regain the room's attention.

'As regards the bond issue, the special purpose vehicle that'll sell the bonds has yet to be set up, but this will be a formality. We'll probably incorporate in the British Virgin Islands, our preferred location for avoiding withholding tax. And now, I am pleased to move on to the *particularly* good news. The state-owned companies Kazakh Oil and SOCAR, the joint venture partners in this construction deal, have agreed to transfer their shareholdings in existing pipelines as well as their Caspian seabed rights to the SPV. We argued that without this added security the bonds wouldn't be taken up, the finance wouldn't be raised, and that, therefore, the new pipeline wouldn't go ahead'. Lincoln Davies interrupted in a semi-humorous tone; 'The only buyers of the bonds are sitting here in this room'. Several participants nodded their heads in agreement, whilst the others laughed. 'Carter, what happens after the structure's been set up and the shareholdings transferred?' 'After the bonds have been issued our consortium will become the sole investor, although of course this will happen via an offshore company we'll set up to maintain our anonymity. As soon as the issue's features are triggered by the spike in the oil price, as investors we'll call on syndicate members to meet their underwriting obligations and make the one-off payment which is clearly provided for under the bond terms. The local Azeri and Kazakh banks won't be able to meet this and will collapse. Sheldons has made loans to these banks, so it will crash shortly after that. At that point, the investors, you kind gentlemen here today, will seize the security underpinning this whole deal, taking ownership of the major pipelines and the oilfields of the Caspian Sea'. Philip Dulamore stubbed out his cigar before responding; 'Your Russian friend - how's he going to benefit from all this? It's not that I question your judgment of character, but let's face it, it wasn't much more than a decade ago when the Soviets were our sworn enemies. Have things changed so much that we can now work with a former commie who probably used to hate everything we stand for? Maybe he still does'.

Davies looked at the lawyer and, realising he wasn't about to respond, intervened again. 'Carter, perhaps I should field this one if that's okay with you. First, he has an objective we can all understand. Our Russian friend will take a holding in the offshore company we'll set up and through which we'll buy the bonds. He's got the capital and I believe he's also partly financed by his own government. So although Moscow Alpha as a syndicate member will collapse, he'll personally make a substantial gain in his personal capacity when we take control of the SPV's assets. But, I can also tell you, there's something else which we know to be of equal importance to him. The collapse of the Kazakh and Azeri banks should trigger a meltdown of their respective economies. In the chaos that will follow he intends that Russia will restore its political control in the region. The jewel in the crown, at least as far as we're concerned, is that the US gets shared control of a new oil source, the Caspian Sea. Just think of it, gentlemen: no more reliance on the A-rabs, and control of the price at which the oil's sold to us. A perfect result, don't you agree?'

Poindexter Energy's CEO, Bill Herbert, now spoke up: 'So let me get this right, Lincoln. Those states bordering the Caspian are simply to be destroyed then handed back to Russia after we spent so much of the last ten years trying to set them free? What makes you think our politicians are going to sit idly by as our old enemy steps in to take control again?' Davies smiled at his associate's naivety: 'Thanks Bill. You raise a valid point. I'd never go ahead with such a project without squaring it first with our political masters. Washington's just as concerned about instability in the Caspian region as is Moscow. Militant Islam's already gained a foothold and it's only a matter of time before these governments become hostile not only to Russia but to us. If the cost of achieving stability in the region and reducing our reliance on the A-rabs is the sacrifice of a few countries, then I can tell you now that as far as the President's concerned, it's a price worth paying. He'll simply look the other way, make a few indignant noises, and then wait for the cheap oil to start flowing in. He's a realist - he knows when to play the democracy game and when to step away from the table for a while. He also knows as well as we do that the House of Saud is finished. It's just a matter of time before it collapses under the weight of its own corruption and contradictions. We've seen it all before. Remember the Shah? Remember how everyone believed the Peacock Throne would never fall? But it did, and what a cost we paid. This time we've got a pragmatist in the White House'.

The meeting's host looked up at a row of clocks at the rear of the room, all indicating different global time zones; it was time to demonstrate practicalities. 'Gentlemen, today I wanted to have a 'dry run' to prove the feasibility of one of the core components of our strategy. It's now 4pm here and as you can see, it's 11pm in Riyadh. Please, watch'. He clicked a remote control and a projector threw two images, side by side, onto a large screen. To the left they saw the CNN news channel, and to the right the website of the New York Mercantile Exchange, 'NYMEX', where oil futures contracts are traded. The audience waited as trivial news passed along the bottom of the CNN screen, but then the newscaster tapped his earpiece and spoke somberly. 'We're just getting reports of a series of explosions in the Saudi Arabian capital, Riyadh. We're still awaiting details but it appears there's been a major terrorist offensive across the city. Unconfirmed reports say that casualties appear to be very heavy, with substantial damage to industrial installations'. There followed archive images of the city and previous Saudi rulers, and footage from the air above the city showing plumes of black smoke, while the network lined up interviews with diplomats and officials. Within seconds the NYMEX indices started to react; the prices of short-term oil contracts jumped upwards as the markets assessed the risk of disruption to supplies. As the news on the left became more specific, so the prices on the right jumped to ever-greater heights. But the longer-term contracts barely moved, speculators anticipating limited medium term disruption to the Kingdom's oil production. Lincoln Davies stood in front of the projector; 'Gentlemen, I hope you'll agree that this provides proof that our project will work. A substantial and sustained jump in the oil price, and we're home and dry. The syndicate will never be able to meet its payment obligations and when they fail, as the only investors in the bonds we'll take control of the Caspian seabed and everything under it. This is the neatest deal I've ever had the pleasure and the privilege to be involved in'.

Philip Dulamore lit up another cigar before speaking. 'Two questions, Lincoln. First, how are you going to push up the longer-dated NYMEX contracts? Second, and I feel we do need to know this - were our people behind the attacks today?' Davies hesitated as he ordered his thoughts, and decided to stonewall rather than reveal everything about the wide-ranging strategy now being deployed. 'We're planning for a major crisis in Saudi Arabia, but I hope you'll forgive me if I refrain from providing precise details at this point in time. Suffice to say that one of the effects of our strategy will be an immediate driving-up of the price of long-dated contracts traded on NYMEX. Overnight we'll take control of Kazakh and Azeri rights in the Caspian oilfields, so our energy needs will be unaffected by chaos in the Middle East. I've given this assurance to the President. On your second question, we do not have people in the field. Today's attacks are the responsibility of The War of the Martyrs Army, a terrorist group that's penetrated deep into Saudi military and intelligence services'.

He continued in measured, businesslike tones: 'So how did I know, precisely, when the attacks were going to be launched today? Well, in short, we're financing them. We're working with their leader in exile. We're both committed to tearing down the existing regime; the difference is that we don't care what goes in its place, but they have very specific aims: they want a religious state. They'll get their state and we'll get control of new oil supplies. The global energy map will be redrawn, and we and this great nation of ours will be the beneficiaries'. The meeting soon drew to a close, and the host wished his guests safe journeys to their respective destinations across the city. The participants began leaving, alone and in pairs, for the yellow taxis waiting outside in the late afternoon heat; all were confident that the future was theirs for the taking.

'Carter, thanks for staying behind to talk. Would you like a trip up to the Observatory? On a day like this the views are breathtaking. And of course the air's cleaner up there. Shall we go?' Buckmaster momentarily flinched as the instigator of the countless deaths which had occurred minutes earlier took him by the arm.

'Yes, I'd be happy to'. The two made their way to the elevator and in seconds arrived at the Observation Deck on the eighty-sixth floor. Davies had been correct: the view was indeed breathtaking and momentarily Buckmaster remained silent, wanting nothing more than to stare out at the surrounding landmarks and then ahead into the clear blue sky. He breathed in deeply and recited a prayer in his mind, feeling so close to his Maker. 'A beautiful view isn't it? I try to come up here at least once a week. It's so peaceful. Carter, what is the news about your client, the one who's incarcerated in London? I'm sure I don't need to remind you about his importance to the project. I need to be sure he'll be released as soon as we're ready. Can you give me this assurance?' Buckmaster closed his eyes as a gentle breeze brought temporary relief from the blazing heat of the late afternoon sun. 'Our client's safe and sound. After all, what better protection could there be than that provided by the British government? As soon as we're ready we'll return him to Saudi Arabia to lead the people. And if they decide to reject twenty-first century life in the process, and step backwards to a 'purer' age, then they are free to do so as far as I'm concerned. It's their choice'. The younger man smiled; 'Carter, I hope you're not going to get moralistic on us. Remember, if the oil price is to be permanently shifted we need a mighty big bang in the Kingdom to trigger everything off. Timing will be crucial, so you have to be sure he can be returned when we give you the go-ahead. Who's dealing with things on your side?'

Buckmaster trusted his Russian friend's judgment when it came to selecting the right person for a particular task, and his recent recommendation would prove no exception. 'A lawyer's just joined us who's more than capable of taking on the case. After the bonds have been launched and our consortium's bought up the lot, just give me the signal and we'll move on getting the client freed and back to Saudi'. He then turned to the financier standing beside him, addressing him directly: 'And as for getting moralistic, my friend, I can't envisage a situation when I'd be anything other'. He took out a Bible from his pocket and held it in front of Davies. 'This is all that matters to me. I've built my life around the teachings in this Book. So if being guided by moral considerations is a crime, then I'm guilty as charged'.

Davies hesitated, aware that his attempt at gentle humour had completely missed its mark, misinterpreted by this devoutly Christian man. 'Okay Carter, I didn't mean to question your faith and if I've caused offence then I apologise. All I wanted to confirm was that the London side of the project is in safe hands. But I hope you'll not mind if I ask a personal question, just for my own curiosity. I know what drives the other participants in our project, but I'm still unsure as to why you joined us. Everyone present today is looking for greater wealth than they already have. Greed is such a simple emotion to understand. I'm not ashamed to say that this is entirely the reason for my involvement, as well as of course the thrill of the chase. But you I'm not sure of. Why would someone so committed to his faith be prepared to work alongside such a motley crew of sinners? That's how you must see us, I would have thought?'

Buckmaster took out a handkerchief from an inner pocket to dab at beads of perspiration on his brow. He remembered his son and daughter, two of the finest missionaries his church had ever offered to the world. Their innocence hadn't protected them, blown from the skies by a twenty five year old Saudi fanatic who'd strapped explosives around his waist an hour before boarding the plane, pulling the pin and murdering its hundred and fifty passengers. 'I'll tell you why I'm involved in this project, why I'm absolutely committed to its goals. The Saudi government sits like a spider at the centre of a web of wickedness that covers the world. Wherever Christianity is oppressed, there you'll find Saudi money bankrolling the oppressors. Pull down the government, take away its financial resources, and slowly people will have freedom to worship as they wish. And since our jailed client in London regards misuse of Saudi oil wealth as one of the causes of his country's moral decline, then I guess we share the same view as to what the solution should be. We all want the same outcome, but for entirely different reasons'. A smartly dressed boy of about five or six ran over to where the two men stood and held up a camera to the one resembling his grandfather. 'Excuse me sir, please would you take a picture of us?' He held up a camera to Buckmaster and pointed to where his parents were standing, smiling in the brilliant light. 'It will be my pleasure, young man. And where would you like it to be taken?' Accompanying the child he walked over to the young couple, remembering his own son and daughter still pictured in his mind. The older man then backed away and peered through the camera lens, fixing the family in the frame against the perfect backdrop of the Manhattan skyline. Lincoln Davies looked on, reassured by both the moral and practical certainties of one of his principal co-conspirators. They shook hands, confident and proud in their enterprise.

Chapter Forty Two

Petr Damyanovitch lay on the ground and felt its coldness through his shirt. The air was fresh and clean, unusual for London, he thought, and as he gazed up into the cloudless night sky he breathed in the scents floating up from the street below. In the distance people chattered and laughed as they made their way to nightclubs and restaurants; this was a young person's city at night, the older generation preferring either to move around in the myriad of black cabs forcing their way through the clogged streets, or to stay at home.

'Laura, great to see you again, this time on *my* home ground. How was your flight?' Saul embraced the diminutive, beautiful woman and remembered the evening they'd spent at the Bolshoi Theatre during his visit to Moscow. She kissed him on the cheek. 'Good to see you again too, Saul. The flight was fine thanks, although we were held up outside Heathrow for half an hour. But we landed safely, and that's what counts'. Saul looked around the room packed with guests in dinner jackets and glittering evening dresses; 'This may be the annual dinner of the Anglo-Russian Trade Association, but I'm convinced it's just an excuse for diplomats to get together and discuss the world's problems over Champagne and canapés. Where's Petr?' Laura smiled as she looked into his inquisitive blue eyes. 'He had some calls to make and said he'd join us later. He'll be along soon'.

Saul took her by the arm and for the next half hour introduced her to guests gathered in the large atrium, most of whom he knew through their companies' or governments' business dealings with Sheldons Bank. A string octet in evening dress played in one part of the vast space, while at the opposite end an illuminated fountain bubbled and gushed, cooling the faces of those seated around its perimeter. Laura was relaxed and confident as she mingled with the other guests, conversing in perfect English, and only occasionally lapsing into her mother tongue. 'So tell me Laura, are you having a good time this evening? I can tell they like you, but I'm your companion so I hope I don't stir up petty jealousies'. She laughed at his flattery then turned away to see if the person with whom she'd made the flight from Moscow had arrived yet. He'd still not appeared but she knew it wasn't her place to keep enquiring as to where he was or to leave the function to visit his room. He would arrive in his own good time. 'Tomorrow Petr's meeting our chairman, Paul Phineus. Will you be coming too?' 'Yes. I haven't traveled to London just for the shopping. I'll be overseeing placement of Moscow Alpha's portion of the Caspian bonds with our investors, so I'll need to know how we're going to market them'. She took his hand. 'I'm having a great evening, and you're a perfect host. Could we step outside for some air?' The two made their way to a balcony leading off from the atrium and overlooking gardens, and for a while they simply talked in the coolness of the night.

Within half an hour of taking up his position on the rooftop, Damyanovitch watched a nondescript navy blue Ford saloon enter the street below. It stopped at the designated point immediately outside the hotel opposite, dead on time. All the information provided by New York had been correct; the number plate was as specified, three male passengers sitting in the rear of the car, and a chauffeur was at the wheel. He looked through the sight of the high velocity rifle he'd earlier unzipped from its leather bag, relaxed his body and waited, lining up the cross-hairs against passers-by for practice. After five minutes two men alighted from the car and looked about the street, their hands sufficiently close to their jackets to indicate easily withdrawn small firearms. Still he waited, aligning the hairs just above the car door nearest the pavement across which the principal passenger would shortly scurry. Eventually one of the men tapped on the car roof: this was the moment he'd been waiting for. A man of about six foot five, physically imposing but with a slowness of movement that betrayed his advanced years, stepped out from the car and looked anxiously about the street: General Abdul Ibn Yahyah, Head of Security at the Saudi Arabian Embassy, London, had an appointment to keep. A week earlier contact had been made with their 'mole' in the War of the Martyrs Army. Tantalisingly, he'd indicated he had a list of names of persons employed throughout the security services sympathetic to the group's cause and who were now recruiting converts to their terrorist network. The source was reliable, having previously provided information leading to the torture of suspects, some of whom had even been guilty. Accordingly a request for a meeting had to be taken seriously, even if the location was not as secure as the General would have ideally liked. As soon as he had the list, a new purge could begin.

Damyanovitch lined up the cross-hairs. The weapon felt cold in his hands: he remembered earlier times, his youth, and the struggle of the War years. He pressed his eye to the sight and lined up the head; the trigger was gently squeezed, releasing the mercury-tipped bullet at high velocity. In an instant the General's head exploded, blown clean off his shoulders, leaving no entry wound on a corpse to betray the sniper's location to subsequent forensic investigation. To add to the panic in the street below, and to distract the police who would arrive in minutes, he immediately lined up the General's stunned guards, shooting both in the legs. They collapsed to the ground, bleeding across the pavement, and would be the first priority for the police before fanning out around the scene in a fruitless search for the assassin. Calmly, he replaced the rifle into the leather bag and after zipping it closed hid it beneath the slates of the rain channel identified as suitable for the purpose earlier that day. After dusting himself down he carefully arranged his bow tie, slipped on the black dinner jacket hung from an ancient hook on a rotted doorframe an hour earlier, and bent down to polish away with spit scuffmarks from his gleaming leather shoes.

After passing along winding unlit corridors he eventually came to a lift; in less than a minute he was stepping out into the bright, warm, lobby. The smell of food, alcohol and humans filled his nostrils, and he smiled. As he made his way through the crowd he was delayed and his hand shaken by two or more guests in each of the numerous circles which had formed during the earlier part of the evening. He was happy to stop and talk: he wanted to use this visit to London to renew acquaintances but on a more practical level, they'd provide a useful alibi in the unlikely event of any enquiries from Special Branch over the coming days. Eventually he caught sight of Saul and Laura sitting next to the fountain. Shaking hands and politely accepting business cards from guests as he passed through, he proceeded towards them, mildly concerned that they were so deep in conversation they were unaware of the rest of the gathering, or of his approaching presence. His pace quickened.

'Saul, Laura, a pleasure to see you both here. Sorry I wasn't able to come along earlier. I trust you've been having an enjoyable evening so far? Laura, you've been raising the flag for Moscow Alpha?' The chairman slipped his arm around her waist, but it was a gesture of affection and not a subtle contact between partners who shared a secret passion. She smiled and gazed into his eyes, and although words didn't pass between them, Saul was instantly aware of the depth of their relationship. The chairman turned to him and laughed, reading his thoughts. 'What must you be thinking of us, Saul? We've been ignoring you. I apologise. Tell me about tomorrow. Tell me about your chairman Paul Phineus, and what I should be looking out for in our meeting'. Saul looked at the two again, still not understanding the forces which bound them so closely to each other.

'Phineus is one of the toughest men in the syndicated loans business. He's shrewd when it comes to choosing partners for Sheldons, and since he's come this far with Moscow Alpha on the Caspian deal you can be pretty sure that he's decided you're a safe bet'. Damyanovitch seemed to ignore this reply as he changed tack. 'Saul, I need all information relating to lines of credit Sheldons has in place with the Kazakh and Azeri banks before I leave in two days' time. I also need to know about any cross-held shareholdings. Can you get this for me before I leave?' Saul was surprised by his directness; he also realised for the first time that Laura knew of the extent of their collaboration, otherwise he'd not have made such demands in her presence. Damyanovitch was reading his thoughts again. 'Laura knows we're working with each other, and shares my confidence in you and my respect for you. You're helping Russia rise again, to prosper in the world. Whatever your personal reasons, even if you might sometimes think these are ignoble, they will have a noble outcome. And that's all that matters. That's the paradox'.

Saul looked down at the chandeliers reflected on the surface of his wine and slowly rotated the glass; it was true that he didn't always feel proud of his behaviour, smuggling out confidential information from his office and passing it to others for purposes he didn't even understand. Of course, much more seriously, and imposing a much greater culpability upon him, he'd witnessed two murders and said nothing to anybody about them afterwards. But provided he kept his eye on the prize which was so tantalisingly close, there'd be few requests, however illegal, which he would not now be prepared to entertain. Soon he'd have wealth beyond his dreams, and with it the freedom he craved. Then he could do good things in the world. The ends justified the means. 'I'll have the information by tomorrow. You can have it after your meeting with Phineus. I'll also be there'.

Suddenly he caught sight of several uniformed policemen moving amongst the guests; they appeared to be taking names and writing these down in small notebooks. There was a growing sense of unease amongst the small groups, although few guests showed signs of wanting to leave whilst the night was still young. Eventually one of the policemen reached the fountain where the three were standing. 'Madam, gentlemen, sorry to disturb you but my colleagues and I are here because of an incident outside this hotel earlier this evening. I'm afraid there's been a fatal shooting. We're here to ask all the guests if they noticed anything unusual, either on the way to this function or during it if they had reason to step out into the street for a few minutes. Perhaps you saw a car parked outside that looked out of place, or someone loitering nearby. Even if you think something's insignificant, please tell us anyway. Any piece of information, however small, may help us with our investigation. Unfortunately there were also two other shootings, and because we had to see to the needs of the victims, this delayed our enquiries. Perhaps I could start by taking your names and addresses, if you don't mind'. Laura listened intently, looking at the policeman in amazement; she was accustomed to gangland assassinations in Moscow but didn't expect the same lawlessness in London, a city she had always thought of as safe. Before the policeman left, Damyanovitch asked for his card in the event that they needed to contact him. Saul stared at him and, barely perceptibly, nodded his head. The accused looked back impassively, coldly, and remained silent. Saul knew nothing about the person who'd been murdered: after all, how could he? But instinctively he knew that this was likely to be the work of his guest from Moscow, and his late appearance at the function was all the evidence needed to increase his suspicions. In a state of detachment, he wondered about the victim's identity. How could it be that someone passing along a busy street in the capital could be of such threat to Damyanovitch's plans as to warrant an execution in this way? He'd have liked to ask the chairman how he could kill so casually, and then proceed to socialise, drink wine and eat canapés. But this wasn't possible; he had to content himself that the chairman knew he was aware that the crime had been his.

As Damyanovitch raised his glass, Saul was afraid, conscious of his own complicity in an as yet opaque conspiracy unfolding around him. 'I'd like to propose a toast to my good friend, my associate, Saul Quartermain. May our project succeed and flourish'. Laura lifted her glass. 'To Saul'. The young banker smiled and struck his glass against those of the other two. It was a surreal conclusion to the evening, sharing the company of a beautiful woman and a cold-blooded killer, toasting the future. The irony was that as far as their working relationship was concerned, Saul had no reason to doubt Damyanovitch's honesty; indeed, in many respects he trusted him more than he trusted his own chairman or colleagues at Sheldons. But he also knew that, should he ever step outside the parameters of that working relationship, his life would become seriously imperiled. After a further half hour of pleasant, engaging conversation, Saul took his leave, shaking hands again with Damyanovitch and kissing his assistant on her cool, faintly perfumed cheek. A short distance from the hotel Saul arrived at a cordoned off part of the street; long strips of coloured tape bounded the area, wrapped around lampposts and hastily thrown up barriers like a clumsy attempt by an inebriate at large scale present-wrapping. As he passed by he saw large splashes of blood across the pavement, trickling into the gutter. A motorised street cleaner was approaching; soon the evidence would be hosed away, leaving a shimmering street for the next day's tourists. He walked a little faster.

On the seventh floor of the Crown Prosecution offices at 50 Ludgate Hill in London, the Chief Prosecutor's team assembled for their regular Monday morning review of upcoming trials. After discussing pending prosecutions for burglaries, rapes, batteries and arson, the Chief Prosecutor came to the case now preoccupying both herself and the Home Office, to whose informal pressure she was invariably obliged to bow. She spoke with a clipped urgency uncharacteristic of her usually unflappable manner. 'Thank you all for bringing your case files here today. The review's been useful and we're on course to meeting our targets for this year, even though our overall success rate continues to decline. Now I'd like to discuss a case I've been heavily involved with over the past year, and in which the Home Secretary's been taking a strong interest. As you'll recall, Sheik Hassan Fadlalah has been held in Belmarsh Prison high security wing for a year. He's been charged with terrorist offences but in truth we've delayed going to trial because our evidence has been on the weak side, and few witnesses have been willing to testify. But the civil liberties brigade's now pushing us to get on with things or drop the case and let him go free. I'm circulating extracts from the case file. These *cannot* leave this room'. Ms. Savors passed a dozen manila envelope files around the table. Five minutes' silence followed during which those present quickly perused the paperwork. 'As you'll see from the case notes, MI6 is strongly of the opinion that Fadlalah has been involved in terrorist attacks across the Middle East, specifically in the Gulf States and Saudi Arabia. He's believed to have been responsible for the selection of targets and the financing of assassinations. He's thought to be a high ranking member of Al Qaida, and there's little doubt his Organisation's penetrated deep into the Saudi Arabian intelligence services. He's being held in the UK because of suspicion of involvement in the planning of murders of officials from several Middle Eastern embassies here in London. Evidence supporting our case was weak, but this changed when General Abdul Ibn Yahyah, Head of Security at the Saudi Arabian Embassy here, approached MI5. The General had first-hand knowledge of Fadlalah's involvement in the London attacks and was willing to testify in court, of course in camera, against him. Finally we were ready to go, and looking for a trial date. But last week at about ten o'clock in the evening the General, our key witness, was assassinated in a crowded street in the West End. Realistically, this means that our case against Fadlalah has now collapsed. If our decision to continue to detain is challenged in the courts we'll probably lose'.

The Chief Prosecutor collected in the envelopes and left the room. It was only a matter of time before an illegally detained terrorist walked in the fresh air again, his freedom restored through the assassination of the principal witness in the case against him.

Chapter Forty Three

Saul arrived at Paul Phineus's room the following afternoon but hovered outside, desperately trying to pick up snatches of the conversation taking place inside. He knocked on the door and then pushed it open without waiting for a response. 'Hello again Saul. You're looking well. You've already met my colleague Laura Simenova of course'. Damyanovitch and his assistant stood and shook hands with Saul whilst Paul Phineus remained seated, looking on with his usual Delphic demeanour. 'Petr, Laura: thanks again for your kind invitation to yesterday evening's function'. For the following half hour the discussion focused upon the recent terrorist attacks in the Saudi Kingdom; Phineus was worried about their potential implications for the deal. 'I'll be direct with you, Petr. I saw the market reaction to the Riyadh attacks and it made me nervous. We've got to consider the worst-case scenario-a crisis which sends the oil price through the ceiling and bankrupts all of us-Sheldons, Moscow Alpha, and the local banks we're working with. I'm thinking of postponing the issue'. Damyanovitch paused before replying. 'Paul, I share your concern: the oil markets appear unusually volatile, but like you I've also noted that this hasn't fed through to the longer term futures contracts to which our oil bonds will be linked. If there's any prolonged spike in the oil price, all the major producers will simply step in and increase production. This is how it's always been, and we shouldn't be put off by short term panic in the market'. Paul Phineus relaxed; after weighing up the infinitesimal risk against the potentially enormous profit, he spoke again. 'The main risk in this project, the potential one-off payment to investors, remains of concern, but I agree with you- it would take one hell of a crisis to push up the oil price over the benchmark where this would be triggered. I've worked with the Saudis before- they like market stability as much as we do. If the price shows signs of escalating beyond what's sensible, they can always increase production. And of course there are the Americans.

They can also release some of their vast buffer stocks into the market-place. So, I'm happy to go ahead with the deal. We're still on board!'

Damyanovitch's recommendation of the London branch of the US law firm Druckerstein, Kahn, and Nixdorf to deal with the bond issue's legal technicalities was accepted without question by Phineus. Saul turned to Damyanovitch; 'Petr, I have some paperwork for you. If you wait in the lobby I'll be with you in a few minutes'. Saul headed off to his room, soon re-appearing with a large brown envelope. 'Here's the infor-mation you asked for. It's a list of our contacts with banks in the Caspian states and the lines of credit we've made available to them, as well as our shareholdings. Don't put me in this position again. This is the last time I'll hand over confidential information. Do you understand?' He whis-pered his words; Laura Simenova looked at the two men squaring up to each other, oblivious as to the nature of the conversation. 'You and I know each other well enough now so please, no threatening words. If I need anything again I will ask, and you'll oblige.' Saul looked at Laura and smiled; 'Sometimes you're chairman's too sure of himself, Laura. Perhaps one day I'll surprise him and go against my own predictability. Now wouldn't that put the cat among the pigeons?' Damyanovitch patted him on the back; 'You and I Saul- partners in crime. I never make assumptions when it comes to the people I work with. Now, you keep to your side of our bargain and you'll get everything you're looking for in our arrangement'. Despite everything, despite all he knew, Saul's willing-ness to collaborate with the Russian remained undiminished.

After returning to the hotel Damyanovitch and his assistant stood in the foyer and reviewed the earlier meeting's outcome. She knew he was pleased with what had been achieved. He gently lifted her hand and brushed it against his face. 'The pieces are coming together now, Laura. Sheldons are in. SOCAR and the others will soon transfer their oil rights in the Caspian. And as soon as our American friends deliver on their side of the bargain, we'll be ready'.

Back in his room, Damyanovitch made a call to one of his principal co-conspirators. 'Carter, it's been a while. How are you? Yes, I'm in London, but I'll not be able to call by your office this time. We've had the meeting with Phineus and all went to plan, so we're on course. Moscow Alpha will co-lead the issue with Sheldons, and he's agreed that Druckerstein does the legal work'. Damyanovitch lay back on his bed as he talked with his old Cold War friend; it was a vaguely surreal conversation, combining trivial but genuine enquiries about Buckmaster's family with talk of the specifics of the bond issue which both men hoped would soon plunge the international oil markets into chaos.

Laura Simenova gazed into the distance and watched as the sun gently disappeared below the horizon. They were alone in their own glass bubble, suspended in darkness. The world gently revolved before her; for a few seconds it looked as if several of the more recognisable buildings were ablaze, their outlines stark against the vivid fierce light slowly draining away from them. Saul stood beside her: she could hear his breathing. It had been a perfect evening; first an early West End show, and then a meal in a wine bar tucked away down the warren of side streets which zigzagged throughout 'theatre-land'. Saul was the perfect companion: he knew the history of so many of the landmarks they passed while they casually wandered through the streets, anonymous in the large crowds which moved like shoals of fish through seaways, streets designed for another time and a much smaller population. She turned and kissed him gently. He looked into her excited eyes then took her in his arms, and for a while they stood in silence whilst the world revolved around them.

Eventually he spoke, breaking the silence with a whisper. 'I thought you and Petr were lovers'. She giggled innocently and kissed him again. 'You couldn't be further from the truth. He's my mentor and, yes, my closest friend. All my achievements, my experiences of life, I owe to him, to his generosity of spirit. I love him, but not in the way you're thinking'. Saul was confused by their closeness; how could such a ruthless killer inspire such emotional commitment on the part of this intuitive, highly intelligent, beautiful woman? He could only surmise that she wasn't aware of the blackened wastelands in his soul. He'd witnessed Damyanovitch's calmness as he sliced through Kordovski's throat, holding him like a struggling fish; if she'd ever seen him do such a thing then he doubted she would have spoken of him in this way. The iconic landmark, the London Eye, came to a halt and both knew it was time to leave. Saul accompanied his guest on the taxi journey back to the hotel where she was staying. Initially he attempted to elicit further information about the person who occupied such a prominent position in both their lives, but to no avail. Laura warned him in her friendly, innocent fashion; 'Saul, I've said all I want to say tonight. Please don't press me or I'll just have to say no, and your feelings will be hurt. Talk to me about your friends instead'. He felt he knew Damyanovitch less now than at the beginning of the evening; his preconceptions were too simplistic, too much based on the obviousness of actions rather than an understanding of the emotional forces that drove them. The Russian was not the one-dimensional determined businessman (and assassin) he'd constructed in his mind. Instead his personality was multi-faceted, engendering fear and devotion in equal measure in those around him. The taxi pulled up outside the hotel and Saul leaned across to kiss her goodnight. She took his hand and smiled; 'The evening doesn't have to end here'. She stepped out of the cab and after paying the driver, Saul followed.

At seven o'clock the following morning he held her again, dressed, then headed for the taxi rank outside the hotel. Within an hour he had returned to his flat, showered, and made his way into work. At eight thirty precisely he was sitting at his desk drinking strong coffee and eating a bagel, looking forward to the day ahead. At around the same time Laura sat down to breakfast with her employer. They discussed meetings scheduled for later that day and her mind was as focused and disciplined as usual, but today her smile seemed different.

Chapter Forty Four

Adam stood at the ageing ferry's rail as it slowly glided through still water, the heavy rhythm of its engines reminding everyone who heard it that the vessel's best days were long past. It was a beautiful, fresh late afternoon and about him he could hear ancient languages babbled by toothless widows, seafarers, and traders passing across the watery expanse in search of opportunities in the thriving coastal towns. An old man approached him, smiling and speaking a language that resembled nothing he'd heard before. Eventually, a few words of English. 'Please. Drink for you. Vodka. Good'. He laughed and proffered a small chipped glass towards the foreigner. Adam smiled, momentarily touched to find human generosity in this remotest of places, shown by an ancient man all of whose worldly possessions were probably contained in the leather satchel he carried across his shoulder. He took the glass, saying 'thank you' in several languages, but it was only the Russian version which his fellow traveller understood. He laughed again and repeated Adam's clumsy attempt at articulating the Russian words, bowing his head slightly several times. Adam bowed to him and began drinking the warm liquid; it was gritty, a sediment of impurities having settled at the bottom of the glass, but not wishing to offend he finished the last drop. He passed back the glass to the old man who'd continued speaking in his own language as Adam drank, pointing out into the distance. He knew the foreigner wouldn't understand what he was saying, but attempted communication was preferable to silence and in such places where strangers are thrown together, a gesture of amity. The old man shuffled away along the deck, returning to his equally ancient wife. It was an act of kindness that moved Adam, providing one of the highlights of his trip.

The sun on the water of this vast enclosed sea made him think of life and death, time passing, a journey shared with others. A ship with an unseen captain, pushing through the waters whilst passengers peered into the distance for recognisable landmarks. Further along from where he stood a little girl shook her multi-coloured bag over the rail, emptying its contents of assorted wrappers and partly eaten food onto the water below. Her mother appeared to chastise her; whether for polluting the environment or wasting food, it was impossible to tell. Several gulls swooped onto the waste as it gently floated off into the distance, their massive wings splashing the water, casting up fleeting rainbows. Adam closed his eyes and listened, breathing the salty warm air in deeply. He thought of Chloe and through his mind's eye watched again as her body moved in slow motion upwards through the air, kicked by the hooves of dozens of beautiful horses. He reflected on how the last grains of his soul's innocence had run out that day. A middle-aged man reeled in his fishing line, wrenching from the sea a shimmering, struggling, perfect fish, a gift from the deep. When it had been landed he clubbed it with a small heavy stick and then pushed the still body into a small canvas rucksack. His family in Baku would eat well when the ship docked.

Adam was five hours into the eighteen-hour journey from Aktau, Kazakhstan, to Baku, Azerbaijan, the ferry being the quickest means of transit between the two principal Caspian seaports. Carter Buckmaster laughed when he'd explained to the firm's recently appointed solicitor that he'd soon be doing 'a small amount of traveling' as part of the continuing work on the Caspian pipeline deal. The setting up of the British Virgin Islands-based special purpose vehicle had been completed weeks earlier, and now the substantive part of the deal could begin. The time had arrived for the 'legal consummation' of the agreement, as Saul had so indelicately put it. As legal advisors to the co-lead managers Sheldons and Moscow Alpha, Druckerstein, Kahn and Nixdorf had prepared the documentation, the most important terms of which governed the transfer to the SPV of the ownership of oilfield and pipeline rights in the vast expanse of sea over which he now traveled. The geographical location of these rights took in the second largest oilfield in the world, the Tengiz field in Western Kazakhstan, centred in the swamplands along the northeastern shores of the landlocked Caspian Sea.

At the meeting in KazMunaiGaz's offices in Almaty, Adam encountered hostility from several members of the state-owned company's board. He explained the nature of the documents to be signed and the implications of the transfer of the holdings to the SPV, although it was evident from the chairman's response that these matters had already been dealt with during the earlier visit by Saul and Damyanovitch. Board members had been sceptical about the deal, and strongly objected to the prospect of transferring their most valuable national assets, the nation's rights in the Caspian seabed, to foreigners of unknown identity. Damyanovitch's presence in the background, a known high-ranking official from the former days of Soviet hegemony, only served to perturb them further. But despite these concerns, the transfer agreement had been duly signed by the Energy Minister, who was attending the meeting owing to the national significance of the proposed new pipeline. Photographers from the national media were present, taking pictures as the Minister held the pen above the agreement, smiling broadly. After further pictures, mainly of the Minister shaking hands with Adam, the event was over. Angry board members slowly trickled out from the conference room, the delighted Energy Minister heading for the chauffeur-driven black Limousine waiting outside in the dusty street. The young lawyer then left for the second leg of his trip, to the Azeri capital, Baku.

He returned to the deck having spent several hours sleeping in his dingy, cramped cabin. It was the heat and the airlessness that drove him back, although the constant noise of passengers and crew above and below deck also served to convince him that further sleep would be impossible. He breathed in the cool night air and immediately felt refreshed. As he stared into the distance he could make out the lights of distant vessels; illuminations on bows and sterns made him aware of the sheer size of the ships floating silently through the night around him. The heavy whirring of the ferry's engines gave hope of progress towards a destination, its fragile, ageing body gently rising and falling through the darkness. Some distance off he could hear shouts, laughter and singing of crewmen on invisible tankers and container ships; he recognised none of the words, but the sensation of not being alone in the darkness was strangely reassuring. He gazed up at the stars, so many stars, and thought of ancient mariners passing across this same sea with nothing by which to navigate other than these tiny pinpricks of light fixed in the firmament. Within an hour land was visible in the milky glow of a calm early morning sky. He heard the rush of heavy chains as the ferry dropped anchor, waiting for one of three ships, a medium sized oil tanker and two containers, to leave port and free up a berth. The water was serene, gently lapping about the ferry's bow, and as he looked back he could see a convoy of vessels stretching away towards the horizon, all waiting their turn to dock. After passing through passport control at Baku port he made his way by taxi to the hotel Alice Penn, Druckerstein's receptionist, had arranged for him a week earlier. For the next few hours he slept, crashed out on the large double bed in one of the hotel's best rooms.

Later that morning, after showering and taking a 'continental' breakfast, an unusual combination of coffee, sour cream, croissants and blini (to keep the Russian guests happy) he went to SOCAR's offices to be met by the company's Chief Finance Officer, Dimitri Antanis. The formalities were exactly the same as they'd been at the offices of KazMunaiGaz in Almaty earlier that week. SOCAR's board convened at the agreed time, asked a few questions, and then the chairman and the Energy Minister signed the relevant paperwork. Just as Kazakh oil rights had been signed over to the SPV, now it was the turn of Azeri assets to be offered up as security to investors. Legal ownership of pipeline rights and rights in the Caspian seabed itself were transferred with the flourish of a pen. Unlike the board meeting in Almaty which had been cold and disengaged, the SOCAR board was enthusiastic about the signing ceremony, representing the culmination of protracted negotiations. There were only two people who could have objected to the transfers and neither was in attendance. The body of the first, SOCAR's previous Director of Strategy Artur Kordovski, lay encased in a concrete sarcophagus making up part of a road recently constructed on the outskirts of Moscow. The second potential 'trouble maker', his personal assistant Gregor Halydar, had been dismissed from his job following the discovery of his recently disappeared mentor's involvement with the local mafia. They had worked closely with each other for many years, so the police reasoned that at the very least he must have known of Kordovski's criminal activities, and at worst he'd been an active participant in them. Now he too had disappeared. Suspecting that Kordovski had discussed his concerns with Halydar prior to his murder, Petr Damyanovitch was eager that his associates in Baku find the young man as soon as possible. It was important to tie up loose ends.

Dimitri Antanis looked around the crowded conference room in the heart of the SOCAR building, eventually catching sight of the person with whom he wished to speak. As he breezed past fellow directors and local politicians, he struck his Champagne flute against glasses, toasting the company's and the country's future. He was a 'rising star' in the company, and determined to take credit for the complex capital-raising structure that had now clicked into place with the signing of the transfer agreement. 'Adam, I hope you've had a good trip to our corner of Europe, and thanks for explaining the paperwork to the board. That was helpful, although speaking frankly, few here today have shown much interest in the specifics of the deal. Instead they've preferred to focus on the bigger picture, the raising of finance that'll make our dreams of modernising our pipeline infrastructure a reality'.

Adam was struck by the difference in attitude between the young Antanis and the elderly chairman of KazMunaiGaz whom he'd met earlier that week. The person in front of him, in a perfectly cut designer suit, was self-assured and confident in his understanding of the agreements he and his political masters had just signed. He was a young man in a hurry: eager to impress but lacking the worldly-wise cynicism needed to navigate the cross-currents of the complex conspiracies and trade-offs at the heart of the region's politics. By contrast, the chairman he'd previously met was astute and intuitive; his principal concern was to avoid the embrace of the bear on the border from whose clutches his country had only recently escaped. He continued in his effort to engage with the impressive lawyer from London; 'We're happy for your firm to finalise all the legal work on our side of the deal. Druckerstein's been with this project from the start, so it's only right that you get the credit. Now, on to a more enjoyable subject. Tell me what you think of our beautiful Azeri women!' Adam replied with humorous but sufficiently diplomatic observations to dispel any lingering preconception his host may have had about corporate lawyers being 'cold fish' as he'd characterised them at the meeting earlier that day. He then shook hands with the young Azeri, said his goodbyes to the remaining officials, and headed back to the hotel.

'Mr. Adam, Mr. Adam, I have letter waiting for you here. Handed to me earlier. Please, I fetch it for you'. Adam was surprised when the concierge called after him as he made his way to the lift; he returned to the desk where the permanently smiling young man handed him a small white envelope with his full name carefully handwritten upon it. The concierge leaned over the desk, hoping to catch a glimpse of its contents. His inquisitiveness amused Adam; he smiled as he tucked it into his pocket without opening it, and then proceeded on his way up to his room on the fifth floor. Once there he tore open the envelope: the message inside was written in crisp black ink but didn't bear a signature. 'Mr. Creed: shall we speak of your complicity in the theft of a nation's assets? Do you really know who you work for? Please meet me. Ten o'clock tonight, 30 Kunayev Street. Come alone'. Adam read the note impassively; usually he disregarded unsolicited mail, particularly when left at hotel desks without a name or contact number. But the reference to a nation's assets and 'who he worked for' instantly caught his attention and lingered in his mind. He felt mildly threatened at being targeted in this way, but there was no alternative: if he wanted to know more he'd have to turn up at the address at the designated time.

After an hour's sleep, he put on his nondescript overcoat then walked out of the hotel and into the taxi waiting outside. He passed a small piece of paper bearing the stipulated address to the driver who appeared confused, but after pointing at the address for confirmation and seeing his passenger nod his head, he drove off into the night. Ten minutes later the taxi passed through Fountain Square and entered a maze of unlit side streets running parallel to it. Soon the driver had left behind the sanitised open spaces of the Square with its familiar department store names and modern streetlamps; they'd now entered a darker world where graceful buildings from a bygone era stood incongruously alongside the ugly, dated architecture of the 'brave new world' ushered in by the Communists. Eventually the driver entered a near-derelict street, and stopping outside a dilapidated building he pointed at Adam's slip of paper. 'We here, sir. You go in?' Now Adam understood the driver's earlier confusion; the building was a ruin, its roof long having collapsed and fallen through the upper floor, its front door hanging by its hinges.

As Adam stepped out of the car the driver peered up at him; 'Sir, you be careful. This dangerous place. Not nice people here'. His anxiety was palpable, and within seconds Adam was watching the taillights disappearing into the darkness. He gazed up at the ruin in front of him and, surprised by his lack of fear, pushed open the front door and entered. As he walked across a mosaic floor strewn with rubbish, broken glass and fallen masonry he looked around to find himself in a large room, partially illuminated by the moon peeping in through gaping holes in the floors and ceiling above. Suddenly he heard a splintering of glass under foot and turning to his left he saw a figure pass through one of the distant doorways and into the room. Now he felt a belated rush of fear and a cold prickly sensation across his scalp as he stood perfectly still, waiting for the silence to be broken.

'Mr. Creed, thank you for coming, and alone. Apart from the taxi driver, does anyone know where you are?' The stranger spoke in a reedy tone which only served to further unsettle Adam. 'Nobody knows I'm here, but the driver's employed by the hotel and I'm sure he'll be back there by now'. As he spoke the words he realised the futility of the pretence that he was in some way protected, that there was someone somewhere who'd come looking for him if he went missing. Out of the darkness the man spoke again; 'Not easily frightened, coming here alone tonight. Are you afraid now?' Adam swallowed hard and his heart raced. 'No sir, I'm not. What will be will be. I was interested in hearing what you have to say. And, after all, I'm not the one hiding in the shadows'. His host laughed, a weak, reedy laugh. 'Well said. But be sure, you should be afraid, not of me but of those who give you your instructions, who use you to play their games. Do you know who you really work for, or doesn't it even matter? What do you know of the so-called special purpose vehicle your firm's set up as part of the deal that brings you to my...this country?'

Adam paused, not wanting to antagonise his host. By now his eyes were accustomed to the dark and he could make out the outline of the person standing in the shadows; he was tall, certainly taller than Adam, but not well built, wiry. His voice, though weak, had an undertone of menace. 'I'm sorry but I'll not discuss this confidential information. It would be breaking a client's trust. I don't even know who I'm speaking to. I'd never discuss anything specific with a complete stranger standing in the darkness'. 'Don't be clever, young man. I've not got time for games'. The stranger spoke from the shadows, anger creeping into his voice. 'I'll tell you what I know. This vehicle now holds Azeri and Kazakh oil rights in the Caspian seabed. What I don't know is who's going to buy the bonds financing the arrangement. You can give me this information.' Adam was shocked by the stranger's detailed knowledge of the deal that had only been agreed with the signing of the paperwork earlier that day, but he also knew that if he continued refusing to engage with the stranger it could be a terrible missed opportunity; after all, he also had his own concerns about the deal.

'You're right about transfer of the oil rights. The bonds will be placed in the primary market in the usual way, distributed by the co-leads Sheldons and Moscow Alpha and the other syndicate members. There's no way of knowing who the buyers of the bonds will be. Now please, it would help if I knew who I'm talking to. Are you willing to give, or are you here just to take?' The stranger hesitated and then stepped out from the darkness, but still remaining at the periphery of the room. 'My name is Gregor Halydar, former assistant to Artur Kordovski'. A shaft of moonlight caught his face and Adam saw he was unshaven, and his cheeks were sunken in a sharp, pointed face. He decided to raise his immediate concern head-on; 'I've heard of you and Mr. Kordovski. Is it true your boss was working for the local mafia and he's disappeared because he fell out with them? And you: I've heard you were an accomplice in his crimes and that's why SOCAR fired you. Are these things true?' Halydar replied, abruptly. 'Artur Kordovski was one of the most principled, honest people I've ever known. A true nationalist, and my friend. He despised the mafia for their corrupting influence on our country and was the last person on Earth who'd have worked for them. No, the people manipulating you and driving this treacherous pipeline deal murdered him. He was killed because he opposed the theft of our country's assets by Russian gangsters. As for me, I was his accomplice in as much as I also fought against your clients' plans to steal our oil rights in the Caspian. By refusing to keep quiet I've put my own life in danger, and now I am forced to move about this city at night, sleeping in its filth by day'. He fell silent, listening for movement elsewhere in the derelict building. Adam instinctively knew that what he was being told was the truth, and that a desperate man was reaching out to him: now he'd ask his own questions.

'Mr. Halydar, you still haven't told me who's behind this conspiracy, assuming there is such a conspiracy. This project may be entirely innocent, but if what you suspect is true, what would you have me do about it?' Halydar replied without hesitation, an overwhelming sense of urgency now clearly noticeable in his voice. 'There is a conspiracy. I know it and my former boss paid with his life because he knew it too. As to who's behind it, I can't say with any certainty. They've been skillful in hiding their identity, but I'm convinced Moscow Alpha's involved in some way. You must discover the truth. Start by finding out who'll buy the oil bonds. Ask questions. Disclose information to those who have powers to investigate. Forget about your code of ethics - the future of independent nations is at stake. I must go now. I'll be in contact again soon'. He sounded frightened as he started edging his way back to the doorway through which he'd passed into the room. And then he was gone.

As Adam emerged into the street Halydar headed away in the opposite direction to the car he'd parked behind the building earlier that evening. As Adam waited for a passing taxi, a distance away Halydar inserted a key into the ignition. With a click of the remote control device the explosives detonated, ripping through the car and blasting the roof into space. The resulting inferno blew out the windows, scattering bits of molten glass and debris in all directions. Damyanovitch's Baku associates had been shadowing him for most of the day, waiting for the right time: that time had now arrived.

Hearing the explosion Adam ran down a narrow passageway linking the street he had reached to the rear of the building; as he drew nearer to the burning wreckage engulfed in smoke, he could make out a blackened form rocking back and forward with the ferocity of the flames. There was nothing he could do so he quickly returned to the street, running into the distance with no sense of place or direction.

Chapter Forty Five

The day after returning from Azerbaijan, Adam attended a 'debriefing' with Carter Buckmaster. The trips to Almaty and Baku had been successful in the sense that all objectives had been accomplished. The British Virgin Islands-registered company set up by Buckmaster now had full legal ownership of the Kazakh and Azeri pipelines and Caspian seabed rights; national treasures upon which the futures of the two states depended had been transferred beyond the jurisdictions of their national courts. Now they were owned by a five thousand dollar 'off the shelf' company based in an island state tax haven which few in the local populations of either country would even have heard of. 'So Adam, did you manage to see the sights in Almaty and Baku, or was it all work, work, work? Surely even a workaholic like you takes time off once in a while?' But the young lawyer had returned to London with fundamental concerns about the project. For months he had worked dispassionately, not remotely interested in stepping back and looking at the project in its wider geopolitical context. But the meeting in Almaty at which KazMunaiGaz's chairman expressed misgivings about the deal had whetted his curiosity. Nothing more- just a slight suspicion that all was not as it seemed to be. Gregor Halydar's murder had disturbed him profoundly: suddenly he was aware that the project had far wider implications and that there were people behind it manipulating it, who wished to conceal their identities and, most importantly of all, their real purpose. He hated the thought of being used as a tool in the plots of others, a useful fool. On the return flight home he made a promise to himself to discover the true purpose of the structure he'd spent the past few months setting up in good faith. He decided against discussing his concerns with the firm's senior partner: until he had absolute proof of a conspiracy he would keep his thoughts to himself. As he contemplated these thoughts he had an oblique and fleeting sense of self-doubt: perhaps he was completely wrong.

Later that day Adam met Saul in Hyde Park, the usual meeting place when there was a crisis to deal with or something urgent to discuss. The two walked beside the Serpentine, late morning clouds having chased away most of the tourists. 'So you visited the places in Baku I told you about? I'd go back again tomorrow if I could, but my next trip's a return visit to Moscow. Baku will have to wait…. What's on your mind, though?' For the next twenty minutes the lawyer recounted his conversation with KazMunaiGaz's chairman and his suspicion that there was a hidden agenda behind the pipeline deal. Saul stared across the river; large drops of rain were now crashing into the gently moving water, throwing out ever increasing circles across its surface. He said nothing whilst reflecting upon his friend's concerns. 'Now let me get this right. You believed the chairman when he said there's a conspiracy, but you haven't a clue who the conspirators could be. You think there's some ulterior purpose behind the setting up of the SPV, but you don't have any idea what that purpose could be. But SOCAR's chairman was more than happy with the arrangement, as were the energy ministers of both countries. It's all rather vague, don't you agree?'

Adam spoke more determinedly; 'I know it sounds vague, but there's something I haven't told you. In Baku I met a former employee at SOCAR. He said his boss had been murdered. He was terrified. He was absolutely certain there was a conspiracy behind the deal, and within minutes of my meeting him he was dead too. Murdered. I saw his body, incinerated in a car explosion. He was killed because he knew too much'. Saul's face turned deathly white as he stared at Adam. There was only one person likely to have organised such a murder and although Saul knew of his obsession to see the project proceed, even to the point of murdering anyone posing a threat to it, he was unaware of a conspiracy with a wider political motive. He'd always assumed Damyanovitch was driven simply by the prospect of vast financial gain. But now he was in too deep to extricate himself, far too much of an implicated co-conspirator to take his knowledge to the police; and in any event, who'd believe him? Damyanovitch was a pillar of the international financial community, he was only a deal broker, a petty criminal who'd lost a fortune through badly planned insider dealing.

'Adam, I hear what you're saying and I share your concerns. But I'll remind you of some basic realities. A few months ago, you remember, we walked beside this river. Your career was in ruins. You had nothing left. Remember your despair. Remember what it was like being penniless. Now, if you discuss your concerns with anyone else, if you make allegations that are entirely without proof, then you risk falling back into the pit you've only just escaped from. As for me, my freedom won't be achieved through chasing shadows. I came so close to having it all before, having the world in my hands, when the Tri-Star Trust was at its peak. And then it was all lost. Now I have a second chance and I'm going to grab it. I'll have my place in the sun - I deserve it. I'm telling you Adam, no matter what the full story is – and I promise, I don't know what it is either – please keep out of this. Do your lawyer's job and keep your mouth shut. There's too much at stake, too much to lose, just because you're suffering a spasm of conscience'. Adam was shocked by the response; Saul had always been carefree, flippant, never too serious and sometimes too trivial for his own good, but something had changed. He seemed agitated, restless, and evasive.

It was helpful to be reminded of the months of unemployment he had just escaped from; it was true that nothing should be done to prejudice his newfound security. 'You know something, Saul, don't you? You know what this is all about. Are you going to tell me?' His tone was confrontational, accusatory. Saul hesitated and then spoke, coldly. 'Yes, I know some of it but not all of it. I can't tell you anything. To do so would put you in danger, and I'm not willing to do that. Just do your job and let me do mine'. Adam nodded. 'OK, we'll let it pass. I'm here if you need me. You know what you're doing, you know the risks. But I saw someone murdered just a few days ago and this makes me concerned for you. Just look out for yourself, do you hear?' Saul smiled his usual, recognisable cheeky smile. 'I always look out for myself. You know me; it's all just a game'. They walked a little further before eventually heading off in separate directions. As Saul strolled off into the distance Adam heard his parting words: 'Just do your job, Mr. Big Shot Lawyer. Do you hear me? Just do your job'.

Chapter Forty Six

In the days following the mild confrontation with Adam, Saul's suspicions deepened. He realised that whilst he knew everything about the deal's structure, he knew nothing about its 'big picture'. Russia, manifested in the person of Petr Damyanovitch, brooded on the borders of the Caspian states, resentful of their freedom from their former colonial and ideological master. Like Gulliver, the country had become enmeshed in a web of agreements and regional treaties constraining her from exercising the power she once wielded so freely. Late one Friday afternoon, just as he was winding down for a restful weekend, he received an e-mail from Damyanovitch, sent from his yacht moored in a New York harbour. He needed copies of the SOCAR and KazMunaiGaz agreements couriered in advance of a meeting to be held with investors later that week. Saul smiled to himself; the Russian oligarch's absence from Moscow presented the perfect opportunity to learn more about Moscow Alpha and its charismatic chairman. Within an hour of convincing Paul Phineus that they 'really needed to check out the trading systems and governance structure' of their co-lead manager, he'd booked his flight to Moscow.

Late the following day he arrived at Domodedovo Airport, and after passing quickly through Customs he was met by his lover, Laura Simenova. They embraced and kissed as other travellers streamed around them on either side, forming their own island, oblivious to the world moving chaotically about them. 'It's so lovely to see you again Saul, and at such short notice. But I told you yesterday, Petr's not in Moscow. He's in New York, meeting with investors.' She looked quizzically at him as they ran to her car, parked nearby on 'no waiting' lines, and drove to the now familiar hotel. As Saul checked in, Laura watched from where she'd parked immediately outside the hotel's gleaming chrome and glass-fronted lobby. She smiled whilst observing his gestures as he teased the twenty-something year old clerk who remembered him, and his large tip, from his previous stay. She couldn't hear their words but could see from her blushes that he was innocently but expertly flirting. He had a natural ability to put people at ease, in part because of his physical presence but also his openness and absence of 'English reserve'. He collected his key then walked out, climbing into the car alongside her. 'Petr's going to be out of the country for a few days, so if you've come wanting something signed, or to make changes to the agreement between Sheldons and Moscow Alpha, then you'll return to London a disappointed man. I just don't have the authority'. Saul laughed. 'If the only thing I do while I'm here is spend time with you, how could I ever be disappointed?' He leaned across and kissed her, continuing his charm offensive, but she was determined to have an answer. 'Tell me now Saul, what's the real reason for your visit?' He paused, and sighed: 'OK, if you insist. Sheldons and Moscow Alpha haven't worked with each other before, as you know, and yet we're co-leading a bond issue with you. It's one of the biggest we've undertaken in this part of the world. Paul Phineus thinks we need to check up on MA's admin systems and its capital strength to play its part in the deal. We'll also be relying on you to keep a tight rein on the local Azeri and Kazakh banks in the management group, so we need to satisfy ourselves about your oversight and control systems. This isn't to doubt MA's abilities; it's just Paul being as cautious as always. So our next stop should be your head office, don't you agree?'

Soon Laura was driving her bright yellow Lada into the packed underground car park beneath the Moscow Alpha building. The two entered the brightly lit, silent lift and within seconds stepped out onto the ground floor of the refurbished former government building. After being greeted by the armed security guard standing at the front desk they took a lift to the fifth floor. As they walked through the swipe-card controlled doors Saul instantly recognised the sights and sounds, the sense of excitement and chaos of a typical trading floor. He looked around and although the number of dealing desks was half that of Sheldons, the rough ages of the dealers, their attire and their aggressive outbursts were all remarkably similar. A young dealer in a loosened tie with shirttails flapping strolled past them; she greeted him in English, in deference to her guest. 'Morning, Laura. How are things going with the Avorovitch mandate bid?' Laura smiled. 'It's going fine and we'll have an answer by the end of the week. Looks like we'll be in for fifty million dollars. Are you sure you'll be able to shift the paper?' The young dealer responded postively, his accent heavily Russian but with American intonation, reflecting three years with Chase Manhattan, New York. Laura then introduced Alexei Rauskovitch, Deputy Head of Trading, to Saul. After answering a few questions on trading systems, the young trader disappeared back onto the floor.

'So Saul, your first impressions? What did you make of him?' Saul looked out across the floor, watching Rauskovitch listening in to the calls of his traders, writing bond prices on whiteboards, and shouting for prices on new issues. 'He's certainly enthusiastic and he knows his stuff. Now, tell me if I've got this right. He's the Deputy Head of Trading, yes? And he reports to you as Head of Trading. But he seems to be running the show, so why isn't he in charge of it? No criticism of you, but if you're away from the office so often, shouldn't he be 'top dog'?' Laura paused before responding; 'Petr's instinctively cautious and for him, trust is everything. You're right, Alexei should be Head of Trading, but for Petr all that matters is having someone who'll not let him down or deceive him in overall charge'. Saul frowned as he considered her reply. 'So what you're saying is that the control structure in Moscow Alpha is not based on merit alone, but rather on the chairman's personal preferences and instinct. You know this is the best way to lose staff, don't you? How are you going to hang on to people like Rauskovitch, ambitious high-flyers, when they know their aspirations are capped by the chairman's personal likes and dislikes?'

She blushed, embarrassed to be confronted with the truth in such a blunt way. 'All that you say is right, but you've got to understand that in Russia today everyone's out for themselves. In such an environment trust takes on a particular importance, a higher value. Petr places trust above all other considerations. Alexei's paid well, very well, but if this isn't enough then eventually he'll go, and we accept this. But to put him in a higher position in the bank when there's no personal connection between him and the chairman would be to trust an outsider, and this is something Petr's not willing to do'. Saul looked at her directly, his piercing blue eyes temporarily holding her attention to the exclusion of all else around her. 'And what's the personal connection between you and the chairman?' He asked his question softly: not wanting to answer, she turned away. 'Let me show you the new issues desk. When we're involved in an issue, either as co-lead or part of the management group, it all starts here'.

She led him to a small island at the rear of the floor where five people sat gazing at Bloomberg screens. Scattered around the table were small cubic chunks of perspex and glass recording the bank's participation in previous bond issues, syndicated loans, commercial paper programmes and other financial arrangements. Each of them held details of the transaction - the company name, the amount raised and in the case of bond issues, the coupon and maturity date. 'The new issues desk is vitally important for us. They run the book for bonds we're allocated and keep a tight rein on what the sales team can put out into the market. If we're involved in advising a client on the pricing of a new issue, they'll watch the secondary market to see where comparable bonds are trading. They nearly always get the price right: not too high to put off investors but not too low to give them an instant profit.'

During the short time spent on the trading floor Saul had been impressed by the dynamism and technical competence of the team Damyanovitch had assembled. Co-ordination between the sales team and traders was as good as that in any of the medium size London-based financial institutions. On his return to London he'd report to Paul Phineus that Moscow Alpha's systems were perfectly capable of discharging their obligations as co-lead in the Caspian deal. But he was troubled by Damyanovitch's personal control over apparently all aspects of the bank's activities. Ultimately the chairman was not accountable to anyone; the bank lacked an effective board of independently-minded directors tasked with questioning his decisions or scrutinising his errors. 'Laura, just one final question. Who supervises the back office here? Who's responsible for the paperwork, for recording trades, setting up new client accounts and so on? Every bank's got to have paper trails of all the transactions passing through it. In Sheldons the back office guys jealously guard their independence and I'm sure it's the case for you here too. I'd like to meet the head of the back office, so please, lead on'. Laura started to laugh, oblivious to the seriousness of what she was about to confess. 'Saul, I'm head of the back office. We don't need someone else recording trades - I'm the head of the team, so it's much easier for me to do the paperwork myself'. Saul was astonished; 'Are you telling me that the head of trading is also responsible for the back office? You're joking, right?' Laura realised she'd misjudged the seriousness of his question. 'I've told you before Saul, Petr only appoints people he trusts to senior positions. Because he trusts me implicitly he gave me responsibility for both sides of the bank's activities: the front and back offices. I hope this isn't going to be a problem between us'.

Saul paused, wondering whether he could or should report this revelation back to Phineus, risking jeopardising the entire project if he did so. 'The whole point about having separate control over front and back offices is that if there's an error or fraud in trading, then this will be detected in the paperwork prepared by a separate pair of hands. It's all about oversight and independent scrutiny. Your system fails to deliver on this'. Embarrassed by this gaping hole in the bank's internal governance, Laura tried to muster a response; 'It's not the problem you think it is. I'm not going to forge paperwork or trades. I'd never deceive Petr'. Saul shrugged his shoulders and smiled, then took her hand. 'Nobody's saying you'd ever deceive the chairman. That's not the point. What would concern my chairman if he knew - which he won't - is that there's a potential for wrongdoing. A possibility that trades could be faked, clients' funds misapplied, and so on. You see, when people get desperate, when traders make mistakes they don't want brought out into the light of day, they'll resort to anything to hide what they've done. That's why front and back offices have always got to be separate. Do you see my point?' She nodded her head.

'If Paul Phineus knew about this he'd suspend the deal or jettison it altogether. I want to go now, before you tell me about some other dinosaur-size skeleton you've got in your cupboard here'. She laughed: 'There are none that I know of, and if there are, they'll be mouse-size anyway'. He looked at her sceptically but he'd broken too many of his own bank's rules, as well as a raft of criminal laws, to become sanctimonious about this procedural failing at a Russian bank. And in any event, knowledge of this significant chink in Damyanovitch's armour could prove useful; he had a little more leverage now, should he need it in the future.

⁂

'This, my friend, is the Kuskovo Estate or to give it its correct name, the Summer Entertainment Country House of Earl Sheremetyev'. Saul gazed at the vast palace in front of him, surrounded by stretches of glistening water and perfectly maintained pavilions dotted into the distance. 'Now do you want to talk business, or should I tell you about this beautiful estate instead?' He kissed her; 'Let's do both. Let's walk'. He slipped his arm around her waist. They soon arrived at the estate's 'French' park, and as they walked through its pavilions she explained the theme behind each of its numerous marble statues. As they paused beside one of the park's many ponds he kissed her again: the time had arrived to broach the subject that had weighed on his mind almost from the first day they'd met. 'Laura, I know I've asked this question before but I've got to ask it again. I hope there's enough trust between us now for you to feel able to answer this time. What brought you and Petr together? What holds you together? You said you're not lovers, so what's left? I want to commit to you, but this is getting in the way.'

She hesitated, staring into the distance. 'You ask a lot, Saul. More than you realise. You're asking about something Petr and I have always kept secret. We're not lovers, as I've told you before. I am his adopted daughter. There - you have your answer'. Of all the possible explanations this was one which hadn't even entered his mind; he had to know more. 'Are your mother or father still alive? How old were you when you were adopted? If I'm asking too much then don't answer. I'll understand. I'm genuinely interested though'. She looked at him, her demeanour serene. 'No, it's not a problem. I'll answer; I want to answer. I've never spoken about this with anyone before, and the secrecy became a burden years ago. Petr adopted me when I was five, so I have very little recollection of my parents. Funny how childhood events stay with you, like fragments of dreams. They're not necessarily good or bad, but they're just things you remember. I remember holding my mother's and father's hands on a hot summer's afternoon, jazz playing in a large crowded square. That's probably why I'm addicted to American jazz: I associate it with that summer. There was excitement in the air, a feeling of elation, and my parents were part of it. There was colour everywhere, clothes, posters, and young men and women speaking in raised voices to groups of people around the square. I remember people clapping. That was August 20th 1968 in the place of my birth - in Prague, in what was then Czechoslovakia. It was the Prague Spring, Dubcek was First Secretary of the Czech Communist Party, and the world was changing. I've since learned that my parents were part of a movement pushing for political reform and 'Socialism with a human face', as everyone was calling it. But on the night of the 20th the Warsaw Pact countries, led by the USSR, invaded, smashed the uprising, and arrested its supporters. Dubcek was taken to Moscow, eventually returning to Prague a broken man. The revolution was over and the repression which followed it went on for years afterwards'.

Saul stared at her in stunned silence; 'So you're not Russian? I thought you were born in Moscow'. She smiled; 'No, I was born in Prague. I am Czech by birth, Russian by adoption. On the terrible night of the 20th my parents were amongst the first to die. I actually remember wandering around Wenceslas Square that day; I was five and lost, and so, so scared. Nobody could help me, everyone too worried about their own survival. There were soldiers and tanks everywhere. I remember it all vividly. The day passed and I had nothing to eat or drink. It was beginning to get dark. All I could hear were screams in the distance. Lots of shooting. And then suddenly an enormous man in a greatcoat walked out of the darkness and scooped me up in his arms. He looked noble in all the chaos. I learnt later that he was a high-ranking officer in the KGB. He was Petr Damyanovitch. My last recollection of that day is being driven in a military car and then taken up, high into the air in a helicopter. I was taken to his house in Moscow and didn't go back to Prague until five years ago. Petr officially adopted me on my eighth birthday'.

The afternoon had passed and early evening shadows were creeping out from behind ancient trees and statues, silent witnesses to a bygone era of decadence. The air was heavy as clouds raced across the sky, heralding the imminent arrival of a summer storm. The two headed back to the palace; Laura was determined that Saul should pass through some of its vast halls before leaving. As they proceeded through the building they passed other visitors, principally Russian tourists eager to rediscover their country's past. Laura greeted each of them, invariably in Russian but occasionally in Polish, Czech, or German. Eventually they came to the Dance Hall, ornate and impressive. They were alone, the voices of other tourists barely audible in other parts of the Palace. Saul turned to her and spoke, the hall's acoustics magnifying his words. 'You must have hated him whilst you were growing up, despised him for stealing you away from your family, your home, and your country. And yet you have a deep affection for him now. You told me before that you love him, but then I didn't understand why. Now I do. When did your feelings for him change?' She looked out through the large windows, watching flashes of lightening fork across the darkened sky. His curiosity amused her, his teasing out of her long-suppressed feelings in this way invigorating and almost cathartic.

'I've never despised Petr, not even during the days, weeks and months after I was taken to Russia. Yes, it was different living in his house. I was used to living with two parents and he lived alone. But I never wanted for anything. Of course I missed my parents, but I guess at that age, children are resilient and maybe quite surprisingly able to adapt to changed circumstances. My childhood was perfect. Petr saw to it that I received the very best education, and because of his rank in the KGB he traveled a lot, and I went with him. I saw the world. I trusted him completely. If he'd left me where he found me in Wenceslas Square I probably wouldn't have survived. I'd have ended up in an orphan's institution. He saved me from all of that'.

Saul felt privileged to be entrusted with these secrets and unspoken understandings previously shared only between Laura and Damyanovitch. He knew more, much more, about her now that she'd revealed how the Russian had first entered her life. Paradoxically, he felt he knew Damyanovitch less, much less, than before. It had been difficult enough reconciling his appreciation of culture and art evidenced during their visit to Baku with his ability to murder opponents with cold precision. But his saving of Laura when it would have been easier to leave her on the streets in Prague demonstrated a morality Saul simply couldn't reconcile with what he already knew of the man. The more he learnt of Damyanovitch, the greater his confusion grew at the contradictions which appeared to exist in his soul.

The summer storm dissipated as quickly as it had arrived. The two lovers emerged from the coolness of the near-empty palace and made their way to the car parked nearby. He turned to her and after gently kissing her, whispered, 'Thank you'. They drove back to the hotel, passing through puddles of rainwater spilled across the roads during the earlier storm.

Chapter Forty Seven

Carter Buckmaster pressed the button for the stored number for New York and waited for the line to connect. 'Good morning Lincoln. How's life in the Big Apple? I'm calling with news I'm sure will make you smile.' 'Hi Carter. Life's good here, although the heatwave's showing no sign of breaking. So what's the news? Is everything going to plan?' Buckmaster replied in his Southern drawl, which as ever managed to be simultaneously courteous and formal. In truth, he didn't like Lincoln Davies; never had done. He didn't like the inherited wealth he represented, passed down from traitors who'd brought to an end the dream of a Republic of the South. Where he'd spent his childhood and high school years in Raymond, Mississippi, resentment for Grand Gulf, Vicksburg, and the Union death camps of Rock Island and Ft. Delaware - the 'Andersonville of the North' - was passed down through family lines like heirlooms. He loathed the liberal values of the New York elite, corrupting the young with their secularism and superficial distractions.

'Everything's going like clockwork. Legal ownership of the Caspian seabed rights has been transferred to the British Virgin Islands-registered company, so they're beyond Azeri and Kazakh jurisdiction. Now it's over to you. I take it the consortium will be buying the bonds through an offshore front company, to keep your identities out of the frame? When will the funds be available?' 'We'll make the transfer to the shell company's account as soon as the bond subscription's open. Until then we'll keep our powder dry. I'll let you know as soon as the funds are transferred over. Speak to you soon'. It was now six o'clock in the evening and Buckmaster was about to leave for a function at the US Embassy in Kensington. A retired liberal judge from the Supreme Court was to address an audience of London lawyers on the history of Southern States' civil rights legislation. The lawyer from the Deep South was determined to attend to question her from a conservative perspective, seeing an opportunity to attack values with which he'd never agreed. He looked around Adam's door and wished him goodnight. 'Have a good evening, Carter, and let me know how the presentation goes. I've heard the judge is usually controversial, so don't get too worked up by what she has to say'. 'I'll try not to, but as you know, liberals and secularists are my two worst bugbears, so there's no saying what'll happen if she goes too far'. The two laughed, and after locking his office door Buckmaster left for the night.

Adam continued working for a further couple of hours, partly because a commercial lease had to be drafted within the next few days but mainly because it was only then that the last remaining person on his floor of the building left for the evening. He put on his coat and made his way to the lift. Walking through the lobby, he said goodnight to George the security guard, then made his way out into the street. After a few minutes waiting in the darkness he returned, but this time acting as though he was in a flustered state. 'Hi again, George. I've been such a fool. I've left my keys in the office. I remember pulling the door closed so it'll be locked. Could I borrow your keys just so I can go up and get them?' The guard didn't hesitate in handing over the bunch. 'Thanks. Back soon'. Adam returned to the lift, gliding silently up to the fourth floor. After several attempts he found the correct key to Buckmaster's room: after looking in both directions along the corridor, he entered. Quickly he made his way to the cabinet into which he'd seen the partner place the Caspian file earlier that day; it was locked and none of the keys on the guard's chain would fit. He tried several other cabinets but encountered the same problem. Buckmaster was evidently a cautious man; all files and paperwork had been locked away and all Adam could find on his desk was a large leather-bound jotter. He sat behind the desk, thinking fast, contemplating what to do next.

On the ground floor Carter Buckmaster strode through the lobby, not in the mood for small talk with the guard. George knew him well; he'd been interviewed by him for the job, and for this reason alone the ritual of signing in and explaining the purpose of his presence in the building at this hour could be dispensed with. Buckmaster was angry: the judge at the Embassy had humiliated him in front of an audience of British and American lawyers and the only response he'd been able to make was to march out before the close of her presentation. The elderly judge had strongly and, it seemed to the audience, successfully asserted that it was the Religious Right and not secularism or liberalism that posed the greatest threat to constitutional freedoms in her country. When he'd taken her to task she dismissed his interjection by offering him up to the audience as a caricature of both Southern illiberality, and opposition to abortion rights established in Roe versus Wade (he proudly accepted the second allegation). It was only after storming out that he regretted not standing firm and fighting his corner. Instead of having wasted the entire evening, returning to his modest but comfortable apartment over-looking the Thames so hotheaded as not to be able to sleep, he decided to return to the office to wind down by making a few calls and collecting some paperwork, and then to travel home with work rather than enmity on his mind.

Adam heard the lift approaching and in a panic quickly stepped into one of the room's large fitted wall cabinets, pulling the door closed behind him. He waited in the darkness, peeping through cracks between the wall-length doors. Buckmaster burst through the door, throwing his coat at the stand next to his desk, and missing. He collapsed into his chair, switched on the small desk lamp, and for several minutes Adam watched, standing stock still, as the white-haired man sat with his head tilted back, motionless. Suddenly he appeared to spring back to life, reaching for the telephone with one hand while thumbing through his personal directory with the other.

'Petr, are you well? Sorry to be calling this late but I spoke with Lincoln earlier today and we need some information from your side before going ahead with the bond issue. Can we talk?' There followed some small talk about the weather and the judge's presentation he had just attended, and its moral paucity, but it was not what was said but rather the tone of the conversation that so obviously betrayed their rela-tionship as close friends. Buckmaster was at ease, laughing and arguing with the person at the other end of the line. And then the conversation reverted to the seriousness with which it had started. 'Petr, we need to know, just for the sake of our friend Mr. Phineus, where the bonds are to be placed. Of course we'll be buying them through an offshore company to keep all our names off the register, but we've got to have details of the buyer; by that I mean the company we'll be using. Lincoln needs to know the company's account details so he can make the transfer. He's paranoid about keeping all our identities concealed, so there mustn't be any bank transfer trail. Nobody must know we're the buyers of the Caspian bonds. I guess funds will be deposited in a New York account, as we've always done, but I've got to have the account holder's name'. Damyanovitch started to reply but was interrupted. 'Hold on while I get a pen. Nothing to write on here.... Okay, go ahead'. The Russian gave him the name of the company through which the Caspian bond purchases were to be made and its account with a reputable New York bank to which funds should be transferred. 'That's fine, Petr, just fine. All that needs to be done now is the transfer. Then we'll be free to go ahead with the oil-linked bonds. One step at a time'.

There followed a few minutes' technical discussion about the structuring of the deal; as Adam stood absolutely still in the darkness his legs were beginning to ache, slowly going to sleep. He continued peering through the gap, desperate that Buckmaster should end the conversation and leave, this time for the night. 'I think I've got all I need, thanks Petr'. He sighed, and put one arm behind his head and one foot up on his desk. He listened to the voice on the other end of the line, and sighed again, nodding as he spoke. 'We're so close to finally achieving all we set out for. Lincoln and his backers will be delighted with the oil rights, as they should be, and this time they'll control the price the oil's sold at. The White House will at long last break free of dependency on Middle East despots. And, you and your friends in the Kremlin will get nothing less than ownership of the Sea itself. As for me, I'm more than happy with a world in which my faith can flourish, no longer oppressed by terrorists bankrolled by Riyadh. We've all got so much to gain, and the world will be a better place for our success'.

Adam listened intently: what shocked him most about the conversation was the scale of the conspiracy and the realisation he'd been thoroughly used by the senior partner. It was now apparent that the real drivers of the Caspian pipeline project included politicians at the highest levels in both the US and Russia, their identities hidden behind a maze of interlocking shell corporations. But he was as much in the dark as to the mechanics of the conspiracy as he'd been before the conversation began. He desperately needed more information, and continued to strain to listen as best he could.

Buckmaster sighed and it was a melancholic sound. 'Petr, I know we've talked about it before, many times before, but the prospects of the loss of life and the economic chaos we're going to bring about still troubles me. If it wasn't for my faith I simply couldn't go ahead with it; I just don't have either Lincoln's mercenary view of the world or your nationalistic zeal. It's only in the sure knowledge that what I do is for the greater good that I can keep going. But it's not been easy'. There was a pause whilst Buckmaster listened to attempted reassurance. 'Thank you Petr, that's kind of you to say so. But unfortunately it will not be you who decides whether I've been a spiritual man or not…. And, yes, I'll certainly pass on your best wishes when I next speak to your godchildren. Sleep well'. Adam watched with dismay as the meticulous lawyer tore off the page upon which he'd been writing, folded it neatly, and placed it in his pocket. He then went to one of the cabinets, unlocked it, withdrew a file, and locked it again. After several more minutes' browsing its contents he placed it in his attaché case, picked up his coat, now a creased bundle on the floor, switched off his desk lamp and headed off down the corridor.

At last Adam was alone. After waiting a further five minutes he crept out, walking quickly over to the senior partner's desk. Gazing down upon the jotter he was initially disappointed to see that it was completely blank. Delicately, he ran his fingers over the surface of the jotter's top page, barely touching it, and allowed himself a smile. Detaching it carefully from the rest of the pad, he folded it and placed it in his inner pocket. 'Sorry for the delay, George. Got caught up with an American client on the phone. Knew I shouldn't have picked it up- not at this time of night'. He handed over the bunch of keys and walked out into the cool evening air. Later that night in his apartment he sat for an hour filing down the lead of a chunky-nibbed pencil he'd brought away with him from the office. He then gently dusted the large sheet of heavy paper with the fine silver-grey dust, sprinkled from a bushy artist's paintbrush. Slowly words began to emerge from the blank sheet, and then an account number, then dates and dollar amounts. As he sat at the kitchen table he raised his wine glass to Carter Buckmaster; his characteristically heavy-handed writing style, combined with the temper he was in after his humiliation at the Embassy, had created deep indentations beneath the page torn from the pad. Adam stared at the scribblings: he now had the information he needed.

Blue Sea Holdings NV. He smiled with pride at his success. NV-Naamloze Vennootschap. So, gentlemen, he thought, your front company's incorporated in the Netherlands Antilles. That's *so* predictable.

In the Saudi Arabian Stock Exchange building in Riyadh the young male stockbroker held up his security pass in front of the armed guards. They recognised him: he'd worked there for the past three years, and they greeted him as they did each day. He wished them a pleasant day then passed along the lobby to the lifts. Everything looked the same: he was smartly attired in the usual conservative dark pinstripe suit, had the same wire-framed glasses, and his shoes were as polished and unscuffed as the day he'd bought them. But if they'd looked a little closer they'd have noticed something different: his eyes were just a little wider; a few beads of sweat glistened on his wide brow, but he didn't bother to take out a handkerchief with which to dab them. There was not a movement of a muscle in his face whereas usually he smiled, the creases indicating that this was a man who laughed, cried, and took pleasure in the company of others. As he walked across the highly polished floor his heels sounded a slow, echoing series of clicks as leather came into contact with stone. In his mind he continued reciting the verses learnt in his childhood: the time had come to strike a blow against the Infidel, to frighten the Kingdom's rulers by showing that nothing was safe anymore. As he reached into his attaché case he came to the end of the final verse. Slowly but without a shadow of doubt he took the loose wire between his thumb and forefinger and brushed it against the exposed trigger. In a second his body joined with the elements: fire, air, water, earth. In an instant, nothing of him remained. The explosion immediately devastated the lobby, sending bodies flying in all directions. Shards of glass made a swishing noise as they tore through the air at the speed of bullets. A fireball burst through the lift doors, traveling up the shafts. Alarms and screams filled the air as water gushed from broken fire prevention systems in the ripped-open ceilings above. Everywhere terror and chaos ensued as people ran for the bomb-blasted entrance, desperate to escape and save themselves.

In a darkened room on the fortieth floor of the Empire State Building, Lincoln Davies sat back and watched the images and real-time graphs scrolling across the huge screens in the conference room. As the Saudi Stock Market Index plummeted down to levels not previously witnessed by seasoned traders, his attention turned to the NYMEX oil indices. He smiled approvingly as the prices of short dated contracts hurtled upwards as dealers irrationally contemplated reduced Saudi supplies to the market. But such short-term panic was rarely sustainable or of any serious consequence; market stability would return soon enough. Of more significance, however, he noticed that the longer-dated contracts were also starting to shift: not to the same extent, but sufficiently to suggest the markets were beginning to assess and rationalise more fundamental threats to the House of Saud. He tapped his fingers on the table in front of him, disappointed that the evidence of disruption in the longer-term end of the oil futures market had not been greater. But it was a start and a useful rehearsal. Half an hour later his secretary put him through to his private bank in Switzerland. After a brief conversation he sanctioned a transfer to the account of the Panama-based front company also held at the bank, as he did each month. Within a few days the funds would reach the intended recipients in Riyadh, the War of the Martyrs Army, and a further spate of attacks could then commence. The groundwork had been done.

PART FOUR

———

Reconciliation

Chapter Forty Eight

Thomas ambled around the exhibition hall, occasionally stopping to look at the stall map he'd been given on his arrival. About three hundred companies were packed into a space which had the dimensions and atmosphere of a large aircraft hangar. All were of different sizes, from niche suppliers of precision engineered products, to computer assisted designers, to construction companies who were only interested in high value infrastructure projects. The single common factor was their involvement, directly or indirectly, in the global energy business. Thomas recognised the names of many of the exhibitors: several from the UK, a small number from Japan and a greater number from the European Union, particularly Germany and France. But by far the greatest presence was from the United States. Everyone wanted to give him their latest brochures and open invitations to visit should he be in their country in the near future. The air in the confined space was surprisingly cool, aided by the enormous air conditioners whirring in the roof high above. This was in contrast to the fierce heat outside, and the humidity which left shirts soaking with sweat.

In attending the international exhibition, Thomas had wanted to raise Northern Engineering Group's profile in the oil sector, principally through 'networking'. Although the company had undertaken a number of foreign assignments during recent years, the truth was that these had been small-scale. In terms of size he placed the company in the top thirty percent of those exhibiting, a realisation which boosted his confidence when promoting its capabilities to other businesses the overwhelming majority of which had never heard of Northern Engineering. Wherever he looked there was activity: contracts (or at least verbal agreements) were being agreed with handshakes, and some attendees were receiving demonstrations from manufacturers. This was what he'd missed most in his previous career in accountancy with Clements; these people were real 'movers and shakers', producing innovative and real products, whereas before he'd been just a watcher, recording the profits and losses of others in neat balance sheets. Now, though, he too was a decision-maker.

After strolling around several large islands in the centre of the vast floor Thomas came to the stall of one of the largest American pipeline construction companies. He smiled as he watched the company representative, a big, bold, loud man, deal with several potential customers all at the same time. Thomas reflected that if the world belonged to the brash, the strident and the overconfident, then it would be the Americans who'd inherit it. 'Good afternoon, Sir. Thanks for dropping by. Are you in the industry, or just here out of curiosity? Please, take one of our brochures. Here's my card'. The industrialist shook Thomas's hand. 'I'm in the industry; have been for more years than I'd care to remember. I'm here to see what the competition's up to'. Andrew Ginsberg, the CEO of a Texas-based conglomerate, Fordham Energy, took Thomas's card and read it with genuine interest. 'Hmmm, Northern Engineering Group. An English company. Can't say I've heard of you but that's not to say you're not a fine firm. Back home I know all the companies in my line of business and have a fair idea of everyone who works for them, from CEO down to post boy. But outside the States my ignorance is deeper, wider, and higher than I'd ever admit in front of my shareholders. We're an international company with a redneck at the helm. Quite a paradox, don't you agree?' Thomas instantly liked the man, as his self-effacing easy-going manner set him apart from many of the other exhibitors. 'Why don't I talk you through what we do at Fordham, then you can tell me about your company. Who knows, if there's 'synergy' as those management-speak geeks call it, then maybe we could do some business in the future. What do you say?' Thomas laughed; 'That'll be just fine. So, you first, please, Sir'. The American multi-millionaire picked up an enormous sandwich and took a gigantic bite, drawing his hand across his mouth afterwards. 'Sorry about this, but I've been stood here most of the day and I've been refuelling as and when I get the chance. Can I offer you a bite?' He held out the sandwich mischievously, almost certain it would be declined. 'Thanks, don't mind if I do'. Thomas sank his teeth into the offering, tearing off a piece almost too big to chew. Ginsberg roared with laughter; 'At long last! An Englishman who isn't too proud to share another man's lunch in full public view'.

For the next quarter hour Ginsberg talked about his company, contracts won and the projects he had managed, barely pausing for breath. Thomas was fascinated, at times overwhelmed by his knowledge, experience, and break-neck humour. 'Okay, Thomas, I've said enough. Now it's your turn. Tell me about Northern Engineering. Any interesting projects you're working on?' Thomas explained the company's history, and how his father had expanded its activities into the international pipeline technical support business. Recently, for example, they'd won a contract to build a series of control stations for a new oil pipeline linking the Azeri and Kazakh fields in the Caspian Sea to new markets. Ginsberg listened intently. 'I heard there was a new pipeline planned for the region, but I didn't know the project had progressed as far as that. From what you've said it'll skirt around Russian territory but I never thought those guys in the Kremlin would ever agree to it or allow it. Nobody will want to use their Transneft system now: they'll be losing a fortune in transit fees. It's rather strange don't you agree?' The American was anxious for an explanation. 'So what are you saying, Andrew? That I should go back to the Azeri-Kazakh joint venture partners managing the project and ask if they've obtained prior permission from their Russian neighbour? Do you think there's more risk in this project than meets the eye?' Ginsburg responded and his tone was serious. 'I think there could be. It's possible an agreement's been made, but I haven't heard about it – have you? Let me make some calls and get back to you. Are you staying here for the next few days, until the exhibition closes? Tell me your hotel and I'll call you tomorrow. We can meet up for coffee. By then I should have some answers'.

It was now late afternoon and Thomas was tired, hot and breathless with the heat that had seeped in from the furnace-like streets outside. He said goodbye to Ginsburg and left for his hotel to sleep for the next couple of hours. Later that evening he would return to a conference room annexed to the exhibition hall for a presentation listed in the programme as 'Managing risk in the global oil business.' He anticipated a dry talk but nevertheless one which could potentially be useful, and for this reason alone his conscientious nature felt that it was worthy of attendance. The programme indicated that the speaker was 'to be announced': as his head hit the pillow he was depressed at the prospect of an abstract presentation by some American academic, but he could always leave early, he thought.

After packing away his brochures Andrew Ginsberg walked into the street and held up his enormous hand. A taxi appeared as if from nowhere, and the soaking American folded himself into its air-conditioned back seat. Fifteen minutes later Ginsberg arrived back at his hotel, hot, bothered, and desperate for a double whisky. The day had been a success, and he'd received nearly a dozen sales leads. He was an 'old hand' in the industry, priding himself on being able to pick up the telephone any time of the day or night and discuss a deal with any one of hundreds of contacts across dozens of countries. For the following half hour he sat at the hotel bar, eyes closed, gently rotating ice cubes around a crystal glass of whisky, frequently topped up by the barman. Suitably refreshed he returned to his penthouse suite on the top floor. After tearing off his tie and stripping to the waist he began thumbing his way through the leather-bound directory of contacts he kept with him wherever he went in the world. For him the night was still young: he knew he'd have to make at least twenty international calls, most of which to countries which were at least a few hours ahead. He needed information, and quickly. He started dialing.

By the time Thomas left the hotel for the exhibition centre the burning sun had disappeared below the horizon, lighting up an evening sky of dappled blue, white, and orange. He paused to breath in the cool night air, listening to the call to prayer from a distant minaret. As he drew near to the hall he was relieved to see that other delegates were also dressed casually and comfortably. The thought of sitting through a tiresome talk on the oil futures markets in a heavy dark suit had dampened his spirits, and so at the last minute he'd put on a casual pair of white trousers, a light blue shirt (without a tie) and a blue linen jacket. If everyone else turned up in white tuxedos, it would be they and not he who'd feel the oppressive heat in the airless confines of the conference room. He walked into the large room, took his seat and waited for the speaker to appear at the podium. As the speaker walked across the stage, he looked up and his heart jumped when he recognised the familiar face from his days in London. She straightened the microphone and began to speak.

'Ladies and gentlemen, friends. My name is Rebecca Silverstein, Chief Executive Officer of London Commodities Limited. We're based in London, and are represented in a further twelve countries including the US, Japan, and Poland, which is our hub in Central Europe. Before coming here this evening I looked through the list of attendees and was delighted to discover that we've previously worked with a great many of you. For those of you who've used our services you probably don't recognise me as your point of contact with the company. My father, Solomon Silverstein, established the company in the early 1950s and only recently stepped down from the post of CEO. I was reassured when he said that although he was moving into semi-retirement he still wanted to participate in the company, albeit at arm's length. We agreed he should stay on as President. It's a privilege for me to continue to be advised and guided by someone with such vast experience but who is also so special to me. Like any father and daughter we have our disagreements, of course; it's not easy having someone looking over your shoulder and saying 'I'd never have done what you've just done' or 'I think this could be done in a better way' but if the truth be known, he's usually right'.

The audience immediately warmed to the beautiful, fascinating young woman at the podium. Her confidence seized the attention of everyone in the room, and as Thomas looked at her from the semi-darkness of the back row he recalled their previous meeting, a lifetime ago, at Silverstein's office in Central London. Then, the company had been on the point of complete collapse, the true extent of its unrealised losses concealed from the markets by the sleight of hand and bravado of its founder, the remarkable, charismatic Solomon Silverstein. Thomas recalled the meeting in the company's boardroom when the chairman had asked him in his capacity as auditor to the company to conceal the true scale of the potential losses; in effect, to prepare an unlawful set of accounts. No bribe or promise of reward had been offered in return for the commission of this crime. He remembered looking into the old man's piercing pale blue eyes and knowing somewhere deep in his soul that there was nothing to be afraid of, and that he should oblige the request. The company had survived and prospered, but that night he'd dined with Silverstein and his daughter had been the last time he'd seen either of them. Neither had contacted him afterwards to thank him: there was no need to, their gratitude transcending simple words or gestures. As people of honour, their indebtedness to him for the trust he'd unconditionally confided in them as strangers would, he thought, endure for the rest of their lives. He looked at her in the distance, a shimmering, beautiful enigma, and smiled.

'At London Commodities we have a saying: that every new oil pipeline eventually ends in Turkey. It's a little simplistic, perhaps, but when one considers the impact the BTC project will have on the Turkish port of Ceyhan, the fulcrum of the international energy industry on the Mediterranean, it becomes easier to understand why we have this belief. Because of its key geographical location, Turkey has a fantastic future ahead of it in the international energy business, and I'm sure that this is one of the reasons why so many of you have attended this exhibition. It's a great pleasure to be here in Istanbul this week, meeting with people who share my confidence in Turkey's future.' London Commodities' new CEO then proceeded to discuss in detail the risk hedging contracts in use in the international energy futures markets. When the final slide had been displayed she opened the floor to the audience. The response was enthusiastic and her mental agility in dealing with questions fired in quick succession was impressive. 'Ladies and gentlemen, I'm afraid the clock is against us. It's been a pleasure to have addressed you tonight, and hopefully I'll meet some of you again soon. I'll take one final question'.

Thomas stood to his feet, moving out of the shadows. 'Thomas Stoneacre, Northern Engineering Group. Ms. Silverstein, I'd like to thank you for an excellent presentation. Please could you explain how the futures markets have reacted to recent political unrest in Saudi Arabia.' She looked towards the rear of the room: her heart missed a beat when she caught sight of the familiar face. 'That's an interesting question and I'll answer it shortly. But first ladies and gentlemen, contrary to established etiquette at events such as this I'd like to say a few words about the questioner. I knew Thomas Stoneacre when he and I worked in London several years ago. He was an accountant with a large firm; I assume you've left it for pastures new? - and I was Managing Director at London Commodities. I just want to say that in addition to being one of the finest, most honourable men I've ever met it's also a privilege, an honour, to call him a friend'. There was a pause in the room, a silence whilst the audience considered how to react to this most personal of statements. Several delegates turned to look for the young man standing behind them. And then there was a spontaneous outburst of applause, in part for the speaker for having flouted convention but mainly for Thomas, a man whom they now knew to be someone of principle and as such, to be of high value in a cynical world. After answering his question she brought the evening to a close. The room quickly emptied as delegates made their way out to awaiting taxis.

'Thomas, it's been a while'. She took his hands in hers and kissed him on his cheek. He smiled: she was just as beautiful as he remembered her from the last time they'd met. 'Yes, it has. How's your father? I haven't spoken to him since the three of us met that evening. Is he still in London? It can't have been easy giving up the reins of power, after running the company for so long'. She looked into his eyes: somehow he'd lost the sparkle of innocence she saw in him when they first met, the earlier youthful excitement in his face now partially given way to world-weary lines. 'My father is fine, thank you for asking. But the evening's late and I know the exhibition organisers want to arrange the hall for tomorrow. I want to spend time with you, Thomas, time to talk and not be rushed. Can we meet in the morning, if you haven't made other arrangements?' If he'd had any other plans, which he didn't anyway, he'd simply have cancelled them, and in his enthusiasm he told her just that. 'Great. Let's meet at nine thirty at the Sultanahmet Meydani. If you're coming by taxi, just ask for the Hippodrome. We'll have the morning together, and it'll be a pleasure to take you around one of Istanbul's treasures at the same time. So, until tomorrow'. She kissed him again and left without looking back.

Thomas returned to his hotel by taxi, arriving at eleven o'clock. The lobby clerk handed him a note: Andrew Ginsberg had telephoned a few hours earlier and he should call him regardless of the time he checked in. Thomas collected his room key and headed for his room. Without pausing to take off his jacket he rang the number left by Ginsberg, mildly intrigued by the message's sense of urgency. 'Hello, please put me through to Andrew Ginsberg. It's Thomas Stoneacre. I'm returning his call'. He waited to be put through to the penthouse suite, it being hotel policy to first ask guests of Ginsberg's status whether they wished to receive a call from a particular person. 'Hi Thomas, how did the presentation go?' Thomas provided a brief overview of what had been discussed, but decided against mentioning that he knew the speaker. 'I really wanted to get there but just had too many calls to make. Seems like I've been round the world in the last few hours, but it's been worth it. I need to speak with you urgently. What about tomorrow afternoon?' Thomas anticipated that his arrangement with Rebecca would end by midday: a later meeting wouldn't present a difficulty. Ginsberg gave him the name and address of a coffee house where they should meet and then hung up. Tired, but elated at seeing Rebecca again, he slept well that night.

Chapter Forty Nine

The following morning Thomas took the tram to the location Rebecca had suggested, and arrived a quarter of an hour early. As he stood in the Sultanahmet Meydani he gazed at the exotic architecture dominating the square. The Blue Mosque with its enormous dome towered in front of him, surrounded by its six minarets. As he watched tourists entering and leaving the mosque, Rebecca pulled up in a taxi, precisely on time. 'Thomas, I hope I haven't kept you waiting long. I can see you've been admiring this beautiful building. This is what I had in mind as a meeting place yesterday evening. Shall we?' She pointed towards the mosque's entrance; he noticed the modesty of her attire as she'd alighted from the taxi, and now he understood the reason. As they approached the doorway she pulled a light scarf over her hair but her face and occasionally mischievous eyes remained visible. The two removed their shoes and walked into the vast building. Thomas was immediately awed by the breathtaking beauty and scale of its interior. Light poured in through the stained glass windows high up in the dome, casting beams which danced around the walls and floors. For a short time its profound atmosphere of peace and otherworldliness transfixed him: he refrained from speaking as he stared up into the dome, almost too high for it to be seen. He remembered Chloe and wanted to cry, but drove out thoughts of the past by surveying the richness of the imagery and colours around him. The scene was too much to be accommodated as a whole by human eyes, and the most he could do was pick out vaguely recognised features and forms.

'The Blue Mosque was built during the first two decades of the seventeenth century by the architect Sedefhar Mehmet Aga for Sultan Ahmet the First, after whom the square where we met is named. Its real name is the Sultanahmet Camii: it was called the Blue Mosque by Europeans because of the blue Iznik tiles which you can see throughout its interior. Maybe you know that Islam forbids the use of plant or animal images in holy places, and that's why geometric designs are used here. As we walk around, look for floral patterns in the tiles - you're unlikely to find anything similar in any other mosque in the Muslim world'. Thomas saw the enthusiasm in her large brown eyes and couldn't prevent his thought from escaping. 'You know so much about this place. A paradox?' She smiled, immediately understanding his comment. 'Yes, if you mean that a Jewess should know so much and care so much for Islamic history and architecture. We are two great religions which have been divided by age-old misunderstandings. But, we're united by a shared appreciation of beauty and heritage'. For the following half hour they walked around the building, inspired by the visual imagination of its architect and his successors and only very occasionally communicating, in whispers. The atmosphere was cool and fresh throughout, created and sustained by a vast pool beneath the mosque. Suspended from the ceilings, huge candle-bearing chandeliers brought light to arabesques painted in the domes and higher places. Separately and silently both visitors reflected upon the nature of infinity and the continuity of the soul; over four hundred years later the architect's dream continued to resonate.

It seemed inappropriate to discuss business or plans for their respective companies while they were inside the mosque; whether out of deference to the faithful who worshipped despite the presence of tourists, or from a desire for simple peaceful reflection, Thomas and Rebecca agreed by their silence rather than by words to defer such discussions until later. As they passed out into the adjoining courtyard the brightness of the morning sunlight forced them to close their eyes and then blink repeatedly whilst adjusting to the new surroundings. They paused at an ancient sundial; originally intended to advise the faithful on prayer times, its function was now more decorative than practical.

'You asked about my father yesterday and whether he's still in London. As I mentioned in the presentation, he's stepped down as the company's CEO but continues as President, so his experience is still there for me to draw upon when I need it. I'm in contact with him every day, partly because I welcome his guidance but also because I can't imagine a day going by without us speaking to each other. He's left London now. After retiring from the day-to-day business of running the company he returned to Israel to live out the years remaining to him; this was always his ambition. His home's in Tel Aviv now and he's not been back to

London for several years. I've been out to stay with him many times, but he's just not willing to come back with me, even for a few weeks. He wants to die in Israel, and one of his main worries is that he'll come back to London or some other place in Europe, and it'll be at that time that he'll be called. So he doesn't travel; it's that important to him'. Thomas remembered from meeting with Rebecca's father that he was an Orthodox Jew, although willing to compromise when confronted with practical realities. 'So is he happy with life? How does he cope without the day to day buzz, the excitement of business?' She looked at him mischievously, teasingly. 'You ask a lot of questions, don't you? He says he doesn't miss 'the buzz' as you call it. He was getting tired of the long days, the back-to-back meetings, the constant demands of regulators for records, audit trails, and the like. He felt his spiritual needs were being neglected, and at his age he'd become increasingly conscious of those needs. But as to whether he's happy with his life; well, he's never known happiness or peace of mind. The past casts long shadows, and he's never been able to escape the darkness'.

The conversation switched to talk of their companies, their hopes for the future, and the new possibilities presented by the emerging markets of Central Asia. Northern Engineering's anticipated involvement in the Caspian project excited her. London Commodities was already courting several large petrochemical companies in Kyrgyzstan, Tajikistan, and Turkmenistan, but she believed that developments in the Caspian Sea oilfields offered the greatest opportunities for her company. They sat down on a bench to let the sun's heat warm their faces. Thomas couldn't resist asking more about her father. 'Rebecca, you said your father's never been truly happy, that he's never been able to escape the past. I remember him speaking about the war years, but that was a lifetime ago. His life since then has been a series of successes - an amazing business, a loving family. What more could a man want?' She looked at him but didn't smile, uncertain whether she wished to continue the conversation.

'I said the past casts long shadows. You'll remember that night years ago when we asked our favour of you, how my father described his experience in the Warsaw Ghetto. How he saw his parents die. How death and violence and starvation were all he knew during those childhood years. How could a child remain sane living in such a nightmare? But worse was to come. After the Ghetto's destruction he and many others were moved out to the death camps. But he survived Gross Rosen Concentration Camp, and the randomness of the violence and the murder. How can I begin to fathom the depths to which his soul must have sank? These experiences would have broken the will to live in any man, but an unshakeable faith and overwhelming desire to see the Nazis destroyed sustained him through the darkness. These events were more terrible than words could ever describe but they were not the reason why a lifetime of unhappiness and spiritual turmoil were to follow. Yes they marked his soul, stole his innocence, but like so many others caught up in the terror, he would have rebuilt his life afterwards as best he could. But for him a greater darkness came in another place'. She paused whilst a call to prayer sung by the muezzin from a distant minaret echoed across the city. Thomas bowed his head, comprehending the dreadful contrast between the desolation and hopelessness described by Rebecca and the peace and sanctity of the place in which they now sat like casual tourists. 'Why, then? Please, will you trust me?' He knew he was trespassing on an older sorrow, that he had no right to ask about something so private, so terrible to reveal. But for some reason, he needed to know. She continued, but without looking at him.

'My father and another inmate, his name was Aaron Hoch, escaped from Gross Rosen in late October '44. The end of the war was at hand, there was chaos everywhere, and the guards were more concerned about their own survival than fulfilling their duties. Soldiers were deserting every day, leaving weak points around the perimeter fences. They knew the Russians would soon arrive. If they and their families were still there at that time, they'd be killed. The Americans eventually liberated the camp in April '45. After escaping, my father and Aaron were desperate to return to Poland and after weeks of moving through the countryside, always at night, stealing food from farms and washing in streams, they reached a small East Prussian village called Nemmersdorf. That was a day before the killings. They arrived at night and broke into the church where they hid in one of the crypts. They were tired, cold, hungry, and needed somewhere dry and warm to stay for a few days until they were ready to move on. And then the Russians arrived'.

She paused, the effort of recounting her father's experience emotionally draining. 'My father told me that as they hid in the church all they could hear for hour after hour were screams, gun shots and tanks. They knew something terrible was happening, but out of fear for their lives they remained in the crypt. Eventually there was a lull in the shooting. Thinking it no longer safe to remain in the crypt, and wanting to find out what had been happening outside, they emerged into the church. But it was full of worshippers - young men and women, old people, children. Some were crying, others praying out aloud. Some were standing, most were kneeling. They walked into the aisle but nobody even looked at them. And then the door flew open. Nobody turned to look but my father and Aaron moved to hide behind a pillar. My father's recollection of what happened next is as precise and terrible now as if it happened yesterday. A young man walked in - he couldn't have been older than about sixteen, apparently, and he was wearing a Red Army uniform. He loaded a magazine into a rifle and as the pin clicked everyone turned. There was silence as he looked at them and they at him and then people started screaming, others crossing themselves. In the next few seconds he walked the full length of the aisle, spraying everyone with bullets. He even paused to reload. The blood, the carnage, it was all seen by my father, looking out from behind the pillar. And when he'd finished he sat in the front pew, making a gap for himself by pushing bodies to either side.

There was nowhere to run so my father and Aaron came out from their hiding place and walked towards him. They were all much the same age, my father maybe a few years older. It was their striped concentration camp uniforms that saved them because his immediate reaction was to aim his gun at them. They held up their hands. My father explained in Russian where they'd come from, where they wanted to get to. After murdering dozens of innocent villagers, he simply embraced my father. He gave his name and rank and the town in Russia where he came from. My father remembers everything. His face was filthy, gaunt, his eyes were staring, and as they shook hands my father noticed part of his fingers were missing, probably lost through frostbite. The soldier must have advanced through the Soviet Union with the Red Army, pushing the Germans out ahead of them, for months on end. They embraced again, and then my father and Aaron were free to leave the church.

Walking out of Nemmersdorf was like walking out of Hell. Bodies were stacked in piles every few steps they took along the roadside. Men, women, children, like heaps of rag dolls. Naked bodies were nailed to barn doors, in cruciform. He saw them. Bodies lay in roads, flattened to pulp by tanks deliberately driven over them. But despite all this anarchy and murder around them, they walked out of the village unmolested. My father puts it down to Providence, but I think it was more to do with the uniforms they were still wearing. The Russians knew they were not combatants and after all, they must have looked like helpless children. Within a couple of weeks of travelling west they reached the US Army. I've never been sure how this happened, but I think it was in Nuremburg, or somewhere north of there, days after the troops arrived. As for what happened next, it's not important. Aaron Hoch went to Israel, fought with the Irgun, and was there at the founding of the Jewish State. He never left the country again, and is still alive. He and my father renewed their friendship, albeit much later. As for my father, with his language skills he got a job as a translator with the British Army in Berlin and was granted full British citizenship in 1950.'

Thomas was confused: Solomon survived the war, moved to the UK and established a successful business, and yet the sadness in her voice was unmistakable. He looked at her and she read his thoughts. 'So having survived and with such great achievements later, you're wondering why it was that a lifetime of sadness followed? Of course he'd seen death before: he was in the Ghetto and then Gross Rosen. But it was the massacre in the church that destroyed him. I've spoken to him often about it but I confess I still don't fully understand. Perhaps at the core of his grief is a feeling he should have done something to stop the killings. A belief that if only he'd stepped forward out of the shadows and somehow interposed himself between the gun and the worshippers then perhaps he could have stopped what happened. Yes, he'd have died in the process, but he believes it would have been a spiritual way in which to leave life. I think he regretted it afterwards-each day he lived afterwards- not having died at that point in time. It was the intended moment for him, for his death, but he'd thwarted the divine plan because of his cowardice. Well, that's how he sees it anyway.'

'But there was another reason why the experience was so profound. He knew the worshippers in the church were innocent civilians, praying for spiritual salvation. They were not soldiers. And yet he remembers his first emotion when the shooting started - he felt elation, even though that was quickly displaced by horror and disgust. Perhaps this was because of what he'd seen; the way the Germans had acted in Poland and in the camp. But he knows he took pleasure in the slaughter of innocents, even if for just a grain of sand in the hourglass. His sense of shame has never passed, and nobody in this world can give the peace or forgiveness he craves and to which he is so entitled'. She placed her face in her hands and for seconds there was silence. And then she looked up and smiled a beautiful enigmatic smile. Her dark hair shone in the bright sunlight as her large innocent eyes stared into his.

'I've told you today of things I never speak about. Personal, private thoughts shared between father and daughter. This is how much I trust you. When we asked you to trust us, to save our business from ruin, and ourselves from certain imprisonment, you did so without hesitation and without a thought for the risks you ran. We'll never forget what you did for us, Thomas. Our covenant is that if ever you need us, if you ever need help, call on us. This is our promise. Be sure, such a time always comes'. She placed her hand on his: it was cool and dry. 'I think we should go now. You have things to do and I have prospective clients to see. I'm glad we've had this time together, here in this beautiful place. My father will be delighted when I tell him of our chance encounter at the exhibition, although he's always believed that fate has a way of bringing people together. Remember what I've said. Remember my promise. I know in my soul this will not be the last time we meet'. They walked out from the mosque's grounds and back into the square, speaking of everything and nothing. Their optimism for the future burnt brightly in the heat of the midday sun.

Chapter Fifty

Thomas sat at a table outside one of the older coffee houses in Istanbul which had been suggested by Andrew Ginsberg for their meeting. He watched young women walking past, some wearing black yashmaks, others cool summer dresses. In Istanbul today the struggle between secularism and religiosity, Western liberalism and Eastern orthodoxy, was waged on a daily basis. 'Thomas, thanks for coming. Sorry I'm late. There were just a few calls I had to make before seeing you and the international clock was against me. Friendship's sure tested when you put through a call to someone at three o'clock in the morning, setting off a row with a wife who's also woken up'. He laughed as he shook Thomas's hand. They ordered, and soon two glasses of strong Turkish coffee were placed on the table in front of them, together with a small dish of Lokum, syrupy confectionery. Ginsberg popped a sweet into his mouth and Thomas did the same; they sat and watched the world go by, basking in the dry early afternoon heat haze, as the American proceeded to the purpose of the meeting.

'Thomas, I spent most of last night and this morning ringing around my contacts in the American and European oil companies working in the Caspian Sea. It was when you told me that your company's involved in a contract in the region as sub-contractor to a new pipeline project that my interest really got fired up. You see, I've been trying to get Fordham Energy into the Caspian for years, but without success. And yet, with respect, your company seemed to have just walked in and picked up a contract with no trouble at all. What I also couldn't understand was why Russia has accepted construction of a new pipeline that she'll not control and that'll skirt her borders. It just didn't ring true. Of course I knew about plans for the pipeline, but I didn't realise they'd progressed so far'. Thomas summoned the waiter: they were ready for more coffee. 'Andrew, I have to confess that my company was invited to tender by a close friend who's involved in the financing of the deal. I can't deny that my personal contact smoothed the way. There were no backhanders or anything like that, though, and our costings were as competitive as any other company would have quoted'. Ginsberg smiled. 'No need to get defensive, my friend. I've spent my life doing the same. Good luck to you for using your contacts. But anyway, last night I called a few of my contacts at the state-owned oil companies in Azerbaijan and Kazakhstan. I couldn't find out all the details of the project because it's been dealt with by the 'higher ups', but, from what I was told, the whole deal stinks. Basically the companies have put up security for a bond issue that just simply wasn't necessary. The whole project could have been financed by a simple loan backed up by security-a charge- over future oil cashflows through the pipeline given to the lenders. There was never any need to put up their oil rights in the Caspian fields as security. Meanwhile the Russians are waiting in the wings. Their silence, their lack of any opposition to the construction of a rival pipeline, speaks volumes, don't you agree?' Thomas took a large sip of steaming coffee, considering Ginsberg's concerns. 'Okay Andrew, let's say your concerns are well founded. Let's say there's a conspiracy behind the deal, because that's what you're implying, I think? Where do we go from here? Do you have any practical suggestions?' Ginsberg was eager to explain his solution. 'I've spoken with my friends back in the US: people in the major energy banks I've known and worked with for decades. Presently there's a syndicate of banks that's going to raise the finance for the construction group. There are a good handful of local banks, but the main drivers are a UK bank called Sheldons, and a Russian bank, Moscow Alpha. They're the ones who are going to get the huge management fees for the deal, not the local banks. My friends and I want to put in a rival bid to finance the deal, and we won't ask for a transfer of oil rights in the Caspian seabed as security. We'll just take a charge over future cashflows. It's a much safer proposition, and for us it'd be the opportunity to break into the Caspian market that I've been waiting years for'.

Thomas recognised the Texan's enthusiasm, but was concerned about the ramifications of undoing the existing arrangements so late in the day, and with so many parties affected. 'It sounds do-able, but there's one other problem, a personal issue. My friend, the one who got me the contract in the first place, works for one of the two lead managers on the deal, Sheldons Bank. I couldn't take business away from him and steal it from under his nose. To do so would be to go against everything I believe in, and against a very old friendship. If there's a possibility he'll lose out if the business goes elsewhere, then my answer is going to have to be no.' Ginsberg looked at him, wondering if this was simply youthful naivety or some more profound character weakness. 'How well do you know your friend?' 'I've known him for most of my adult life'. 'Let me ask you a blunt question. Would he be willing to take a sweetener? A payment to assuage any hurt to his pride that might result from the loss of the mandate?' Thomas smiled: Ginsberg had by chance stumbled upon the measure of the man. 'He's the most loyal friend I've ever known. He's committed to his job and has risen fast in the bank on merit. But to answer your question - yes, he'd take a bribe. It's perhaps his only character flaw. But you'll have to go through me to propose it because approaching him directly wouldn't work'. Ginsberg leaned across the cafe table and offered his hand. 'So we're agreed then. I'll get back to my friends and tell them to go ahead and get a group together. I'll get in contact again with the guys in Baku and Astana and ask them to take soundings of their boards to see if they're open to a fresh bid for the financing. I know some of them have been real worried about offering up their Caspian oil rights as security, so they shouldn't take much convincing. You speak with your guy at Sheldons. If it's just a matter of 'how much', if he gives us a figure that'd compensate him for any loss, then I'll have something to think about. Let's meet here again tomorrow afternoon, three thirty, to finalise things. It'll be the final day of the exhibition so I'll be leaving Istanbul immediately after we've talked. If we get this one right, there'll be plenty of other projects for us in the Caspian'.

Ginsberg returned to his hotel suite and began calling the bankers with whom he'd spoken the previous night. Most were enthusiastic, the prospect of high management and underwriting fees drawing them in like bees to a honey pot. And behind each person contacted by Ginsberg were networks of links with other banks, all of whom also had to be engaged in the discussions. But the more extensive a network, the greater the risk of leakage of confidential information. Ginsberg's calls proved no exception. 'Mr. Ginsberg, I have a call for you. A Mr. Lincoln Davies of Global Energy Bank, New York. He says you don't know him but he really needs to speak with you'. Ginsberg lay back on his bed. 'Okay, put him through'.

He knew the call would be in connection with the Caspian syndicate he'd been putting together for the past couple of days, and was intrigued to be contacted by someone with whom he'd not even spoken and about whose company, unusually, he knew absolutely nothing. 'Good evening Mr. Ginsberg, and sorry to be calling you so late. You don't know me but my name's Lincoln Davies, CEO of Global Energy Bank. I hope you won't think me impolite, but I've heard along the grapevine that you're looking to submit a bid to finance a Caspian pipeline project in which I have an interest. Is this correct?' Ginsberg was mildly irritated to be questioned in such an intrusive and direct fashion, particularly when dressed up in mock politeness by someone whom he'd never met before. 'I'm afraid sir I do find your question impolite, but I'll answer it nonetheless. Yes, I'm looking to put a syndicate together and yes, we're going to bid to finance the project. Now it's late so I'll say goodnight to you and end this call'. Davies continued, but this time his tone hinted at anger. 'You know of course that the financial arrangements have already been agreed. That a syndicate's been formed and the Azeri and Kazakh state companies have agreed to all its terms. It'd sure be a shame if Fordham Energy disturbed things this late in the day'. His tone reverted to type: polite and respectful. 'I'm sure that if you want to be in on the deal it's perfectly possible and could be done in a way which keeps everyone happy. Would you be open-minded enough to talk about some possibilities?'

Ginsberg was now sitting upright on the edge of his large four-poster bed. 'Mr. Davies, as far as I'm aware your company isn't even involved in the deal. I know you're not one of the lead managers and I'm pretty sure you're not in the management group either. So, really, this is none of your business and I don't know why you're taking such an interest in what I'm planning to do or not do. As for open-mindedness I've got this aplenty. But I never take an offering from a plate put in front of me by a stranger. No, I'm not prepared to discuss 'possibilities' or anything else'. By now he was gripping the telephone, speaking loudly into the mouthpiece. 'Well Mr. Ginsberg, I'm real sorry that you're taking such an uncompromising approach. Real sorry. Is there nothing I can offer you to back off? Any way I can persuade you to step away from things I don't think you understand?' Unwisely he'd lit the blue touch paper: Ginsberg's torrent of expletives could be heard along the corridor, his rage lasting a full ten uninterrupted seconds. When he was done he slammed down the telephone, picking up a handkerchief to dab his by now bright-red face. He laughed to have been so easily and quickly provoked into losing his temper by a complete stranger. On the fortieth floor of the Empire State Building in New York Lincoln Davies still held the receiver despite the disconnection tone. For several minutes he sat in silence tapping the cold black earpiece against his lips, contemplating the possible unraveling of the project and what he could do to avoid it. Everything was so nearly in place. He replaced the telephone in its cradle then picked it up again. After punching in a string of numbers he waited for the call to connect.

'Hello again, Carter. I'm afraid we have a problem'. He kept the conversation short, but by the end of it Carter Buckmaster was under no illusion about the threat they faced. If Ginsberg's alternative financing proposal was to be accepted there'd be no bond issue on their terms, the special purpose vehicle would be shut down overnight, and they'd never get control of the Azeri and Kazakh Caspian oil rights. The whole deal would fall apart. 'Get on the phone to your friend in Moscow. Ask him if he's got anyone in Istanbul who can help us out. We've got to move fast on this Carter, or there'll have been a hell of a lot of time and money thrown down the drain. And your personal agenda in all of this will be up in flames too. Get back to me after you've spoken to him'. Within minutes a further call was in progress between London and Moscow. Petr Damyanovitch instantly recognised the threat to the project but knew his capacity to do anything about it, at least at such short notice, was non-existent. There'd once been a time that if he wanted something done anywhere in the world, he'd simply make a call from the Ljubianca to the local KGB station and order it done. But now, despite his network of contacts in embassies across the world, he was no longer part of the Service, and unable to issue orders which were to be obeyed without question. 'Carter, I've nobody in Istanbul who can deal with this. If I had a few days there'd be no difficulty, but we don't have the luxury of time. I've only one solution and it will be unpalatable for you. You must go to Belmarsh prison and speak with your client. Explain the situation. If anyone has contacts in Istanbul it'll be him. But you'll need to do this immediately, before everything starts to run out of control. Can you do that for us all?'

Within the hour, Buckmaster passed through the security gates of Belmarsh prison, ostensibly to take further instructions from one of the firm's more newsworthy clients. As he sat in the small conference room listening to the client whispering in Arabic on the mobile smuggled in in his attaché case, he became despondent. He couldn't understand the conversation or the instructions being given, and this unsettled him. Of greater concern, he didn't trust the client to the extent that both Lincoln Davies and Damyanovitch were able to. But, like them, the client potentially also had a prize to win, in his case, a Kingdom; he wasn't about to tolerate a threat to the project at this late stage in proceedings. With the call ended, Buckmaster took back the mobile. The client gave no explanation as to what had been arranged, the solicitor knowing that to ask him to do so would simply be ignored. They shook hands and the lawyer left.

The following day, after wandering around the exhibition floor for the last time, Thomas left for his meeting with Andrew Ginsberg. A gentle breeze dissipated the midday heat as he walked past coffee houses where old men with parchment-dry brown skin puffed on hookahs, playing backgammon in the afternoon sun. Soon he reached the designated place. After tapping the birdcages hanging from the ceiling, disturbing the imprisoned green and yellow canaries, he sat down at the table they'd used the previous day. He relaxed as he waited, sipping a strong, sweet Turkish coffee. Within five minutes he saw Andrew Ginsberg's portly outline appear at the end of the street. He'd thrown his jacket over his shoulder, revealing a white shirt and wide red braces holding up pinstriped trousers struggling at the seams. He quickened his pace when he saw Thomas, lifting his hand in greeting. Suddenly a motorcycle roared into view, appearing as if out of thin air. Two men sat astride it, helmets concealing their faces. As they drew alongside Ginsberg the rear passenger held on with one arm to the driver then lifted the other, holding what looked to bystanders to be a short black stick with a handle. The Uzi machine gun fired off an intense burst of bullets, all of which hit the intended target. Within seconds they'd disappeared into the distant heat haze.

Ginsberg stared down at the stripe of red blotches flowering across his pristine white shirt, linking up the braces on either side. Hopelessly he placed his hands over them then fell to the ground, flat on his face, dead. A police car soon drew up, its siren wailing pointlessly. An ambulance then followed. Thomas, now sitting in the gutter alongside the laid-out Ginsberg, gave a statement as to what he'd seen, in what capacity he knew the victim, and where he was staying in Istanbul. His state of shock was evident to the policeman taking the statement, well aware of the premium fanatics in his country now attached to the murder of foreigners, particularly those from the United States. Realising that the young man was in no fit state to find his way back to the hotel, he offered to take him there himself, and was gladly accepted. That evening a little-known terrorist group, believed by commentators to be an offshoot of the more widely known Saudi Arabia-based War of the Martyrs Army, contacted a local newspaper. The communiqué was stark: 'Let the execution of the American today be a warning to all foreigners. Leave our holy places. Cease the slaughter of our innocents. Our jihad has only just begun'. The following day, Thomas flew out of Istanbul on Turkish Airlines. He'd spend most of the four-hour return flight to Heathrow staring out of the window into oblivion, unable to block out the image of Ginsberg's execution from his mind's eye. The Texan industrialist's alternative plan for the Caspian project had, of course, died with him.

Chapter Fifty One

Saul picked up the telephone after the fifth ring. He was about to leave for the evening and according to his usual rule of thumb, if the call stopped before four it was unimportant, but anything after four was potentially urgent and couldn't be ignored. 'Saul Quartermain speaking'. He immediately recognised the caller, smiled and sat down again. 'Laura, great to hear your voice. Make me happy and tell me you're here in London just to see me. That you want to spend the night with me and nothing else matters'. She laughed. 'No, sorry Saul. I'm still in Moscow, working late as usual, looking out through the window into the black night while the rain pours down. Now, don't you wish you were here?' 'Funnily enough, yes I do. But you're not calling to tell me about the weather. What's the problem? Is everything okay with the Caspian deal? We're getting close to launch date for the bonds, and as far as I know everything's in place and as it should be'. Laura hesitated; she'd not yet discussed her concerns with Damyanovitch, principally because she didn't want to embarrass herself should they prove to be unfounded. 'Everything appears okay but there are still a few things that trouble me about the deal. I'm concerned about the risk that we as lead managers are taking on when the oil price is just bouncing around all over the place. Our commitment under the terms is much more likely to be called upon now than was the case a few months ago. What do you think we should do?'

Saul had also been watching the oil futures market at NYMEX for the past few weeks and was well aware of its increasing volatility, but it was the prospect of the vast payoff he'd receive when the whole deal came together which kept his mouth firmly shut. He also knew Damyanovitch well enough to conclude he'd be aware of the state of the market, but for some unknown reason it didn't seem to trouble him. And if Moscow Alpha were to be destroyed as a consequence, then this too would have been anticipated and planned by him. It would, he thought, somehow be deliberate. He picked up a pen and started to scribble on his desk jotter. Oil price crashes through the threshold. Syndicate unable to make triggered bond payment. Syndicate collapses. Who wins?

'Laura, you'd better speak with Petr, but I'm sure he knows about the state of the market anyway. Tell him and then at least you'll know you've done all you should do.' His scribbling on the jotter had by now extended into a series of arrows and cashflows representing the financial structure of the project, as far as he knew it. He looked at the diagram and for the first time became aware of how little he knew about its investors, its weak points, or the offshore companies through which a large part of the funds would pass. He was running like a blinkered horse along a racetrack, oblivious to events taking place off-course and spurred on by a single voice in the crowd: the voice of a man who he knew little about, except that he'd stop at nothing, not even murder, to achieve his goals. 'I miss you, Saul. When are you coming back to Moscow? Make it soon.' She regretted her emotional openness as soon as the words passed her lips. She continued, quickly back onto topic. 'Why don't you talk about our concerns with Petr? It may be better coming from you, as an outsider, rather than me. He's coming to London again at the end of the week, to finalise things with your chairman'. They agreed to talk again after he'd spoken to Damyanovitch about the risks he and Laura had discussed but which, somehow, he knew the Russian would already be fully aware of.

Saul stepped out of the office just in time to catch a passing black cab. The rain thundered onto the windows, still steamed up from the previous occupants. 'Evening sir. Where to?' 'The Ritz, please, and take your time. I'm early and I need to think. You know how it is'. The driver nodded. 'No problem, sir. I'll go the long way round, that's if the cost doesn't matter'. He laughed, and Saul responded; 'It doesn't matter at all.' He then sat back in the darkness and contemplated Laura's warnings. She was right, of course: there were too many imponderables connected with the project, wheels within wheels and hidden agendas he found unsettling but which until the past few days he'd chosen to ignore. It seemed he was the only person in the world who knew the true Petr Damyanovitch. He'd seen him calmly take Nicholas Herschell by the scruff of the neck and throw him from the twelfth floor of an apartment block. And yet, immediately after the murder, he'd seen a demeanour of tranquility and guiltlessness. Then there was Kordovski, his throat sliced for having the temerity to turn down Damyanovitch's requests. The assassination of the Saudi military official was a killing he hadn't witnessed but instinctively knew to be the work of the man exchanging pleasantries with trade attachés and ambassadors within minutes of pulling the trigger. The murder of the other SOCAR employee, Gregor Halydar, during Adam's visit to Baku was more problematic. He had no grounds to suspect Damyanovitch and indeed it may have been just as the local press reported, a falling out between a corrupt employee and the local mafia. But somehow, and with not a shred of evidence, he knew the chairman had been responsible.

He closed his eyes, wondering if he was falling victim to paranoia then gazed out through the window, following the widening then narrowing streams of raindrops with his fingers. The street was full of movement, chaos, and splashing as the rich and the poor, the old and the young, the honest and the dishonest, darted from doorway to doorway in vain attempt to keep at least part of their bodies dry. He wondered if he'd already sold his soul to the Devil. 'I'm ready for the Ritz now. As quick as you can, please'. Twenty minutes later the taxi pulled up outside the hotel. Saul paid the fare, doubling it with a tip, and got out. As he walked away, the driver leaned out of the window: he never missed an opportunity to dispense homespun philosophy. 'Thanks for the tip sir, and have a good night. Hope you've got your thoughts in order. Life's what you make of it - be true to yourself and you'll be fine'. At the press of a button the electric window closed leaving Saul standing on the pavement, raindrops falling from the end of his nose, watching the red tail-lights disappear into the darkness.

After drying his face with a warm hand towel provided by the concierge who'd watched as he stepped out from the taxi, Saul strolled through to the dining area. His guest had already arrived, inconspicuously observing the other diners at tables nearby. 'Thomas, how are you? I hope you didn't have too much trouble getting past the concierge but places like this are usually careful about who they let in, although apparently not this evening!' Thomas stood up from the table and grasped Saul's hand: he'd missed him and whilst the trip to London presented an opportunity to revisit old haunts, nevertheless he'd come for a different purpose. 'Saul, it's been too long. Good to see you again'. Saul responded warmly; 'And to see you too, Thomas. How's business? Congratulations on winning the pipeline contract. I'm sure it'll be the making of both you and your company'. The two sat down; after passing their orders to the waiter, they turned to the Caspian project.

'I was grateful to you, Saul, for supporting our bid behind the scenes. Once again I'm indebted to you, so all I can say is thanks'. 'Don't mention it. You won the contract on your company's merits. All I did was open the door; your company's record speaks for itself. But I hope you've not come all the way to London just to thank me for pulling strings... which I promise you I didn't do. When we spoke earlier this week you seemed worried. Is everything going okay with your business? Is there something you want my help with?' Thomas explained what had happened during his visit to Istanbul. He described his meeting with Andrew Ginsberg and how, after making his own enquiries into the financing arrangement for the Caspian project, he'd been firmly of the opinion that the deal's structure was 'the worst solution possible'. Saul listened but appeared remote: his thoughts were obviously elsewhere. 'Okay, so let's say your American guy is right and the deal's bad. Why doesn't he simply put together a syndicate of US banks and bid for the mandate? Tell him to have the courage of his convictions and throw his hat into the ring'. Thomas paused as Saul looked at him quizzically. 'He would, and he was about to, but now he can't, because he's dead, and this is why I'm here tonight. You were right to say that I was worried when we spoke a few days ago. It had been a few days since I saw Andrew Ginsberg mown down with a machine gun in a crowded street, just as we were supposed to meet to discuss a rival bid to yours. He was walking towards me, and then.... well, he was murdered in front of my eyes and I know that if I'd been standing with him at the time, I'd have been killed too'.

'The police told me it was a terrorist attack, Americans aren't welcome in Muslim countries these days, and so on, but this doesn't ring true. He was singled out: it was a hit. There were plenty of other American tourists in the street but they weren't touched. I've been thinking this over a lot, and the conclusion I've come to is that what led to his murder was him drawing attention to himself by ringing around banks looking for partners for a rival bid. And if this is true, then it means that someone from your side was involved, directly or indirectly, in the killing. This is why I had to see you. This is why I think Sheldons and my company should withdraw from the project. However attractive the profit, if the price is risking our lives then it can't be worth it'. Saul was shaken by Thomas's revelations, his face becoming paler as he spoke of his rational suspicions with an accountant's deliberate, cautious manner. Here was another execution, another murder connected with the project, and yet once again he had nothing more than an unsubstantiated belief that Damyanovitch had been the directing mind behind it.

Thomas interrupted his train of thought. 'Are you okay? The colour's drained from your face. Do you want some water?' 'No thanks, I'm fine. It's just a little too humid tonight. Perhaps the rain's building up to a storm. Now, about Ginsberg's assassination in Istanbul. You've not mentioned any concrete evidence proving it had anything to do with the Caspian deal. It may have been an unfortunate terrorist attack, just as the police said it was. Here's what I suggest. Neither Northern Engineering nor Sheldons should withdraw, at least not until I've made my own enquiries. Let's not do anything rash. Would you be happy with this way forward?' Thomas nodded in agreement, although he was hoping for a more decisive course of action on Saul's part. 'Okay I'll wait until then, but please keep me in the picture. Call me, and often. I'll be frank with you Saul, if I feel I'm being kept in the dark I'll pull out my company and the construction consortium will have to find another sub-contractor at short notice. Alright?'

Chapter Fifty Two

Sergei Ivanov looked in the rear view mirror for a fleeting glance at his employer. He'd sat in silence for the entire journey from their five star hotel in Central London to the appointed airfield, his mind tightly focused on other matters. 'Mr. Damyanovitch, sir. We'll be arriving in about five minutes. How many people will be participating?' Momentarily his employer frowned at the intrusion: his thoughts were elsewhere, in another place, another time, pulling a heavy church door closed against the cold night air. 'About thirty, divided between twelve baskets, or so the organisers tell me. We'll be going up with Saul Quartermain. Make sure we don't take any others. You know what I'm expecting of you, so it's important we're alone'. 'I understand. There'll be just the three of us. It's a perfect day with just enough upward currents, so we should be away quickly enough. And Saul's boss - he'll be in one of the others?' 'That's right. Just make sure he doesn't come in with us'. The hired navy Jaguar purred into the vast open green space: Damyanovitch stepped out into the sunlight and looked around. As far as the eye could see, flames rushed across the ground, puffing air into what looked like vast half-inflated multi-coloured caterpillars.

Soon Paul Phineus was walking purposefully towards them, his hand extended. 'Petr, it's great you could make it. Thanks for coming to support this charity. Have you been up in a hot air balloon before?' Damyanovitch smiled, his apparent amusement genuine and unforced. 'No, I've never been ballooning before. It'll be an entirely new experience for me, although my assistant used to be in the Soviet Air Force, so he'll not have a problem with the mechanism once he's been shown what to do. You've been up in hot air balloons before anyway, haven't you?' Ivanov nodded but didn't speak. 'How many participants are you expecting, and how many balloons are going up?' Phineus waved his arm across the field's expanse. 'There'll be ten balloons in total, each taking three passengers and of course an operator. The flight's going to be about an hour. If your assistant goes over to the organiser's tent he can collect the map and be shown how the gas mechanism works. I'd like to have gone up with you but I believe you're already taking Saul and with your assistant there won't be any more room. In any case I suppose I should be traveling in the same balloon as my wife! Anyway, may the best man win.' He shook hands with Damyanovitch and Ivanov then returned to supervising the inflating of a balloon proudly emblazoned with the Sheldons name and corporate insignia.

As Saul pulled into the crowded field in his Mercedes SL Convertible he smiled at the sight of the enormous balloons gently hovering above the ground, pegged to Earth by ropes which restrained them from floating up to their freedom. He squinted as he gazed around, recognising familiar faces from banks and finance houses with whom he'd worked in recent years. Although intended as a day when the raising of money for charity took precedence, nevertheless the event inevitably provided an opportunity for 'profile raising and brand reinforcement', as marketing managers had informed their chief executives now strutting about the field, barking instructions to underlings. He caught sight of the Sheldons balloon, beneath which stood Paul Phineus, hands on hips, striking a proud but slightly pompous pose. Upon seeing Saul he waved: a single extension of the arm identical to Nixon's gesture minutes before taking off in disgrace for the last time from the White House lawn. Saul returned the greeting. Suddenly he became aware of two men walking towards him from the near side of the field. Damyanovitch's face was impassive as he greeted him even though a smile quickly appeared. 'Hello again Saul. Good to see you, but at a charity event? Surely not your natural hunting ground?' Saul's blood ran cold; the last time he'd seen Ivanov he was unloading a dead body shoved into a sack from a private jet in Moscow. 'What's he doing here? Surely there aren't any more bodies to be disposed of?' Damyanovitch tutted and wagged his finger. 'Where are your manners, Saul? Surely you can extend the basic courtesy for which you English are so renowned? Sergei piloted my jet earlier this week. Or would you have expected me to come in on British Airways, economy class?' Saul smiled at the thought, relaxed, and then shook Ivanov's hand. 'Hello again, Sergei. Sorry for my abruptness. I shouldn't take out my distaste for your employer's actions on you. It wouldn't be fair. I hope you'll have a pleasant time here today'. Damyanovitch turned away; irritated by Saul's condemnation, he nevertheless appreciated that he was on the young man's 'home turf' and shouldn't respond, even if he wanted to. 'Paul Phineus asked us to take you in our basket because he'll be traveling with his wife, and with one of the organisers with him to handle the heater there's no room for another passenger. That's okay with you, yes?' Saul responded laconically; 'I guess I don't have a choice, so it'll have to be'.

Saul stared into the distance: as far as his eyes could see the horizon was dotted with beautiful, enormous bulb-like shapes floating at varying altitudes through the ether. Occasionally he could hear laughter, sometimes raucous singing, but for the most part there was silence except for the gentle creaking of the solid whicker basket in which they were suspended so far above the Earth. Ivanov had taken off his jacket and shirt beneath which he wore a singlet. His thick-set build and pronounced musclature would easily have qualified him as a 'strongman' in a traveling circus. Saul looked on as he dexterously managed the opening and closing of the gas flame which shot up at irregular intervals into the mountain of orange, blue, and yellow silk towering above their heads. For a while Saul tried to engage Damyanovitch in conversation about the Caspian deal, subtly raising his concerns about the risks associated with the project, but the chairman was disinterested, almost monosyllabic in his responses. It was obvious he had no intention of entering into a discussion of any sort, however cursory or superficial. Saul's frustration at his lack of progress was compensated in part as he looked out over the breathtaking green countryside views of fields, rivers and patches of woods, with occasional houses dotted around them.

Twenty minutes into the flight Damyanovitch poured out three glasses of iced tea, passing around croissants packed in a small satchel brought by Ivanov. Soon the huge brightly coloured balloons were disappearing into the distance, fragments of laughter borne on the wind becoming less frequent. With new flame puffing out from the propane cylinder the balloon slowly drifted to a higher atmosphere; the three now looked down on broken clouds slowly passing beneath them. Damyanovitch redistributed several bags of ballast, grouping them on one side of the basket so that it listed slightly but noticeably away from where the three were standing. Saul briefly held on to the basket's edge whilst regaining his balance. 'Petr, is that wise? The ballast is there to keep the basket balanced. I don't think it's a good idea to be altering things now'. In a matter of seconds Ivanov turned to Saul, gripped him by his safety harness which had been unclipped at Damyanovitch's suggestion from the basket's framework twenty minutes after takeoff, and threw him over the side, holding him, at the last moment, in mid-air. As he struggled to grab hold of the basket's edge Ivanov held him out further, careful to avoid his flailing arms. The new weight imbalance was offset by the redeployment of ballast, but still Saul's struggling and panic caused the basket to list dangerously. 'Shall I let him go now, Mr. Damyanovitch? He's lighter than I thought'. 'Hold him a little longer, Sergei. I'll tell you when I'm ready'.

Terrified, and realising the hopelessness of his position, Saul ceased struggling, becoming completely still. As he stared up at the basket he listened with terror to the casual conversation taking place between its two occupants. He yelled up at his prospective executioner. 'Damyanovitch, you bastard. I did everything you asked. I've given you the Caspian deal on a plate. You said I'd not be harmed, you lying bastard! I hope you rot in Hell!' The chairman walked over to the basket's edge and looked down at Saul. He was impressed by the vituperation of someone so close to death: it would have been easier and more usual if he'd begged or bargained to save his life. 'I told you you'd be safe if you followed instructions. But no, you had to go asking questions, trying to work things out that don't concern you. And with the risk you'd speak to Phineus, that's when your fate was sealed. I was going to make you a millionaire several times over, but that wasn't enough for you. I thought I knew your price, but I was wrong. It's time for you to have an accident'.

Saul knew his final seconds were close at hand: should he prepare himself and say a prayer, or instead try to change the course of events? 'If I die there'll be nobody to stop the Ginsberg bid going ahead', he cried at the top of his voice, his body straining and the wind tugging at him. 'You may have had him killed in Istanbul, but you were too late. He'd already put a rival syndicate together before you got to him. Moscow

Alpha's going to be blown out of the water and all your dreams with it'. It was a bluff of course, but Damyanovitch's shock at hearing Ginsberg's name was sufficient for him to stay Ivanov's hand. How could he possibly know about Istanbul? Only he, Lincoln Davies and Carter Buckmaster had been privy to the planning of the execution, along with Buckmaster's imprisoned client of course. This was worrying. 'What do you know about Andrew Ginsberg? What rival syndicate?' He realised the pointlessness of his questions as soon as he spoke the words. Saul said nothing, gently swaying his legs in the cold air. Damyanovitch had to think quickly. He began to clap his hands. 'Well played, Saul. Well played. If I let you live today, against my better judgment, I want your word on three things, as far as it's worth anything'. He leaned over the edge of the basket, his face not showing a flicker of emotion. 'First, you'll not discuss your concerns with Paul Phineus. Do you agree?' Saul called up: 'Yes, I agree'. 'Second, you'll obstruct any rival bid that may be made by Ginsburg's associates. Agreed?' 'Agreed'. 'And last, you'll stay away from Laura Simenova. You're a bad influence, filling her head with doubts and questions. Agreed?' 'Yes, agreed'. Both knew he was lying on this last promise: it would have to be dealt with some other time. 'OK Sergei, pull him in'.

Effortlessly, Ivanov lifted Saul back from over the edge, lowering him gently back into the basket. Saul's immediate thought was to strike Damyanovitch, to hit him full in the face. But the urge for self-preservation prevailed and instead he simply re-attached his harness to the basket's structure without speaking a word. After a few minutes' silence Damyanovitch spoke again, his tone light and amicable as if nothing had happened. 'So my friend, tell me what you know about Andrew Ginsberg. Where did you hear about him? Did you ever meet him?' Saul started to laugh; minutes earlier he'd faced imminent death, and yet now he was being asked to give up the information that had saved him from certain execution. 'Petr, do you take me for a fool? Until we're back on the ground I'm saying nothing. Nothing at all'. Damyanovitch looked irritated that his request should be dismissed so peremptorily, but in the circumstances realised he shouldn't be surprised. As Ivanov altered the gas jet the balloon slowly began its descent. Within fifteen minutes it landed heavily on the perimeter of the red and white circle painted in the destination field by the event's organisers. Saul swiftly alighted, his face white with rage. As he stood outside the basket Paul Phineus walked up and shook his hand. 'We thought you'd got lost. What took you so long?' Saul forced a smile; 'A little trouble with the cylinder nozzle. Too little flame, according to Sergei. Did you have a good trip?' Phineus nodded his head enthusiastically. 'I think I could take this up as a hobby, that's if my wife will let me. I'm afraid she didn't take to it as much as I did'. Saul saw a green-faced, frightened woman behind Phineus, leaning against the basket of her balloon and taking deep breaths of air. Damyanovitch joined them, small-talking with Phineus. As Saul started to walk away Damyanovitch called after him; 'Don't forget, we must speak about our late friend from Texas some time'. The young man turned and pointed at him with barely concealed anger. 'You can go to Hell'. He walked to his car where he sat motionless holding the wheel for several minutes, then sped off into the distance, leaving Damyanovitch amused and Phineus perplexed.

Chapter Fifty Three

Adam slipped an arm around his companion's waist, turned to her and kissed her passionately. She giggled then pushed his fedora down over his eyes. 'You haven't lost your touch, Adam, although it's been a long while since you last showed such affection. But if it's a way of changing the subject, then I'm afraid it'll not work. You're a lawyer, I'm a lawyer, and we both know how to play these games. So I'll ask again. Why were you sacked, fired, given the push, whatever you want to call it, from Roxburgh's?' Adam tilted his head back and closed his eyes, basking in the bright, warm sun. 'Can't we just walk a while? Talk about old times? Hold hands in coffee shops and watch the world go by? You were always too cynical for your own good. Can't you accept that I've come all this way just to see you and catch up on how you're doing?' She kissed him and took his hand. 'With you Adam, it's impossible to be too cynical. There's always a hidden agenda. Always something going on behind those pale eyes of yours. Perhaps that's why I was first attracted to you - you know, I think I was even infatuated with you - when I joined Roxburgh's as a trainee. You were so sophisticated, so aloof. I have to admit, you drove me crazy from the very first day I worked with you. But I'm nothing if not a practical woman who knows when she's about to be used, so let's get down to business. Why are you here, and what's it got to do with me?'

Adam and Clarissa Forsyth continued along the twisting side streets of Willemstad, looking like a couple of lovers to casual observers, possibly even newlyweds lost in each other's company to the exclusion of everything else. But the reality was more prosaic. A lifetime earlier she'd joined Roxburgh's as a trainee solicitor, and Adam was appointed by the firm as her supervisor. Within weeks both had given in to a mutual attraction, which on her part started the first day of commencing her training. From Adam's perspective it had been 'a little bit of fun', as he explained to Saul and Thomas at the time. They were both consenting adults, and he wondered what she'd be willing to do to quicken her progress within the firm. But after a while he'd felt some affection for her, possibly because she wasn't looking to make career progress from their relationship; instead, she obviously just genuinely liked him. But in due course he decided the relationship couldn't continue, principally because it was making ever increasing demands upon his time. Initially the rejection was met with hostility and resentment: she felt she'd been used, and said so in no uncertain terms, although she also knew in her heart that the courtesy and respect he'd shown during their time together was a good defence against the charge. Despite the ending of their relationship they'd managed to establish a good friendship, and it was an emotional upheaval for him when she announced on completion of her articles that she'd be leaving to take up a post as legal counselor to one of the largest private banks in Curacao. They stayed in contact over the years, albeit sporadically, with emails and the occasional birthday card.

Adam gazed at the gabled buildings with their pastel-coloured frontages. She'd made a wise decision to leave London for the more tranquil, but equally intellectually demanding, environment of Curacao, one of the global centres of offshore tax planning, trusts, and of course private banking. She read his thoughts. 'The island's sometimes called the Amsterdam of the Caribbean. Beautiful, isn't it? So many beaches, festivals, and a perfect climate. And since I was made Head of Legal at First Curacao Bank I set my own hours and there are none of those tedious timesheets to fill in at the end of each day. I'm answerable only to the board and they're pretty hands-off. Jealous? Now, are you going to tell me why you were fired, and why you're here?' They arrived at the Queen Emma pontoon bridge linking Punda with Otrobanda, and as they waited for it to swing closed again after opening for passing ships, he looked at her and wondered how much he could reveal, and whether he'd be putting her life in danger by discussing the Caspian project. The image of a charred Halydar rocking backward and forward in his bombed-out car in Baku passed across his mind, like a lonely cloud caught by the trade winds in the perfectly blue sky above the island.

'Okay Clarissa, here's the deal. I'll tell you why I left Roxburgh's if you give me a lawyer's oath that you'll honour the request I'll make of you in return. Do you want to play?' She laughed at his sudden seriousness.

'You've not been here long enough to have got a touch of the sun, so that's not an excuse. Do you really think I'd give an open-ended undertaking like that? Say yes in advance to a request that hasn't been made yet?' He kissed her again. 'Yep, that's about it. What do you say?' She loved his teasing, and couldn't resist the dare. 'Okay I accept, but on condition that, after you've made your request, I can make one of my own. Deal?'

Adam smiled; 'It's a deal. I was fired from Roxburgh's, as you've rightly heard on the grapevine. I was involved in a criminal case, defending a violent fraudster. I interfered with the main Prosecution witness, passed on confidential information to the defendant, and stole evidence from the Crown Prosecution Service solicitor. We won the case but when my senior partner found out what I'd done he didn't really have any other option but to get rid of me. Now I'm with a US firm based in London, Druckerstein, Kahn and Nixdorf, and I'm still acting for villains and the mafia. It's a commercial case I'm working on that's brought me here to Curacao. And of course I wanted to see you again'. Clarissa stared at him in amazement. Even during her time at Roxburgh's she knew he was a man determined to win whatever the cost, but his admission as to the lengths he'd gone just to win a case he'd been defending surprised her. 'Well, well, well, Adam Creed, you really excelled yourself that time. No half measures. You took the whole rulebook, all of our professional ethics, and flung the lot out the window. I don't know whether to admire you for your brazen flouting of the rules or shake my head and wag my finger. But knowing you as I do, it probably brought you unhappiness - winning at the expense of your professional pride?'

She knew him so well that her assessment was an accurate one even without knowing the full facts. 'Now it's your turn, Adam. What do you want from me, and what really brings you to Curacao?' Adam explained his involvement with the Caspian deal. He knew there was a conspiracy but had yet to determine the identities of its participants or their objectives. She listened closely and without comment. At First Curacao Bank she was responsible for compliance with international anti-money laundering regulations, and liaised regularly with the Curacao local law enforcement agencies; accordingly, she was very familiar with complex transnational schemes designed to use the bank for illegal purposes. If she recommended rejection of every vaguely suspicious corporate structure referred to her by the board, then a considerable amount of the bank's work and fees would simply move elsewhere. Suspicion alone, she'd once been told by the chairman, was not enough reason to decline a client's instructions. Adam continued to explain his concerns.

'First Curacao recently opened an account for a Curacao-based company, Blue Sea Holdings NV. The company will be buying up the entire Caspian oil bond issue at a cost of around three and a half billion dollars. I want to know where the money's coming from and the name of the account's administrator or in other words, who controls it. I need to know who's putting up the money, and only you can find this out. Would you do this for me?'

Clarissa paused outside a crowded coffee shop, formerly the home of a seventeenth century Dutch slave owner, with its original gables still intact, its murky history now concealed beneath a light pastel blue paint. 'You're asking me to ignore my duty of secrecy. I'd be putting my job at risk too. You know all this but still you ask. Unbelievable'. He grasped her hand. 'This is really, *really* important or I wouldn't ask you. I've got to have this information'. She responded abruptly. 'But even if you know where the money's come from, you still won't know who's behind Blue Sea Holdings. You know that with a NV company the shareholders remain anonymous. That's the whole point of setting up companies here in Curacao. Your managing partner…what's his name… Buckmaster; he's been administering the company's affairs through your firm's representative office here in Willemstad. But from what you've said, he's part of the conspiracy and there's no chance of you getting any information out of him. And the Willemstad office will be unlikely to give you what you want because Buckmaster will have given strict instructions that he, and he alone, deals with the company's affairs. Unless…' She looked at him, read his thoughts and gasped. 'No Adam, you can't. It's too dangerous. Tell me I'm wrong and I've misread you, at least this time. You wouldn't dare!'

He looked at her impassively. 'Oh, but I would. I have no choice. I'm going to break into the firm's office and find out who owns the company. When I have this information I'll know what to do. Or I'll know there's nothing I can do. Either way, without it I'll remain in the dark'. She saw the same determination in his eyes which had attracted her so much when she'd first started as a trainee at Roxburgh's. Whether or not she supported him, she knew he'd go ahead with his plan regardless. 'Okay, I'll get you the information you need. I'll get the statements for Blue Sea and take copies for you. We'll meet again tomorrow, late afternoon. But when you're done with the photocopies, promise me you'll destroy them. There's only one place where they could have come from and I don't want to lose my job over this. Agreed?' He nodded his acceptance. 'Now Clarissa, you said you wanted to make the last request in our... negotiations? Now's your turn again. And your request is?' She smiled again: the tension of the previous half hour's discussion suddenly dissipated, now that the deal had been done. 'That you'll stay the night with me, of course. Just for old times'. He laughed: 'For you, Clarissa, it'll be a pleasure'.

For the remainder of the afternoon the two drifted around Old Willemstad, Adam captivated by the buildings which blended the formalism and tidiness of their Dutch heritage with the warmth and colour of the Caribbean world. Everywhere the streets were full of tourists, lawyers, and bankers, all instantly distinguishable by the subject-matter of their conversations, and local residents and owners of dozens of small cafes and restaurants jostling with each other to win passing trade. Later that evening they met as arranged at the Bistro Le Clochard, one of the finest restaurants on the island, located with a perfect vantage point of the Rif Fortress. As they sat watching cruise ships pass by and the bright coloured lights of Punda illuminating the night sky, they talked about the past, and their hopes for the future. Clarissa acknowledged that she'd become the archetypal career woman, if ever there was such a thing. Her hopes for the future were limitless. She hoped soon to be appointed to the board of First Curacao, but it was the chairmanship of one of the island's larger American banks which was her ultimate goal. Adam gazed at her as she spoke of her ambitions; she'd lost none of the joi de vivre which he'd found so attractive when she was his understudy at Roxburgh's all that time ago. When she pressed him about his own career and personal goals, he was evasive. The debacle of the Coughlin case had taken its toll, and although the confidence was still there, it was perhaps no longer over-confidence, tempered by what she could only assume was experience of life's harsh realities and the conflict between personal ethics and his drive for professional advancement and gain. They talked and laughed, consumed the most exquisite of meals and drank fine wines, oblivious to the passing hours. At midnight they left and returned to Adam's hotel. The night ahead was theirs: he would honour the earlier agreement with pleasure.

The following day the Head of Legal at First Curacao instructed one of her assistants to bring details of an account recently opened by a Curacao-incorporated company, Blue Sea Holdings. As with all new business she needed to satisfy herself regarding the identities of its owners, ensuring it didn't raise concerns about potential money-laundering. She looked at the balance on the account and the recent history of transactions and was shocked. After taking photocopies of the statements she spent the remainder of the morning completing a report for the board. At midday she left to meet Adam at the location agreed the previous evening.

Clarissa walked along the short stretch of white sand to where Adam sat beneath a pale yellow beach umbrella. She'd taken off her sandals and held them in her right hand, her thin attaché case in the other. Adam only became aware of her presence when she was standing directly alongside him, his attention transfixed by the small fishing boats bobbing up and down in the water five minutes' strong swim away from the shore. He was feeling relaxed, forgetting his worries and plans momentarily as he sipped a fruit punch whilst watching the world go by, his already darkening skin glistening in the afternoon heat haze. She bent down and kissed him, prompting him to re-engage with reality. 'Hi Clarissa. Have you had a productive morning? This place is sheer bliss. I think I might stay forever. But only with you.' She laughed at his familiar flirtatiousness; 'Of course, Adam, at least until someone younger comes along'.

He quickly moved the conversation to business. 'Did you get the information?' He peered at her expectantly over his Ray Bans. She drew up a wicker chair and pulled out the photocopies from her case. 'One billion US dollars were transferred into the account of Blue Sea Holdings two weeks ago. But here's the interesting part. The money came from five different sources, all of them leading US oil companies. The person with authority over the account is a Mr. Lincoln Davies, the CEO of Global Energy Bank, New York, and one of the five contributors to the account'. Adam gazed out at the turquoise sea, disappointed not to hear of an association of any Russian bank with the account. But, if a US-based group of financiers was covertly taking up the bond issue, then this in itself was evidence of a conspiracy. She smiled, aware of his half-satisfaction with what she'd disclosed. 'Now Adam, if you want the really interesting information, then what are you going to give in exchange?' He laughed at the tease, took off his sunglasses and looked her straight in the eyes. 'If you're free tonight, after I've burgled my employer's office, then how about a reprise of last night?' Her heartbeat quickened but at the same time she was taken aback by the brazenness of his intention to commit a crime. She continued. 'A further two and a half billion dollars was deposited into the account a week later. One billion came from the same five sources, the other one and a half from Moscow Alpha, the transfer authorised by its chairman, Petr Damyanovitch'. At long last, Adam had the connection he'd been looking for. Now his attention was focused, his mental faculties sharpened. 'Why do you think they've transferred the other two and a half billion? What could its purpose be?' Clarissa sipped from the large glass of fruit punch he'd placed on the table in front of her. 'If you want my opinion, as someone more than a little familiar with attempts by investors to conceal their identities, it's this. I think the total capital's going to be used to take up the bonds that'll be issued to finance the Caspian project. Sheldons and Moscow Alpha are the lead managers, but neither bank will want to hold on to the paper for long. They'll sell on the primary market as soon as the trading price of the new issue has stabilised. The other local Azeri and Kazakh banks in the management group will also want to unload their commitments as soon as possible. The end result will be that Blue Sea Holdings will hold all the bonds issued. And if the oil price rockets and the syndicate can't meet its new obligations then the Caspian oil fields will pass to this group of American investors, and of course the Russian participant'.

Adam now understood the vulnerability of the special purpose vehicle which he had set up. But he was still confused about Moscow Alpha's role in the conspiracy. 'If Moscow Alpha is lead managing the issue, are you saying that it will be selling the bonds to itself, because it's provided part of the funds to Blue Sea Holdings that'll be used to buy the bonds? I don't understand'.

Clarissa used her finger to draw a diagram in the sand, showing the respective positions of all participants in the project. 'Moscow Alpha will not own the bonds: the bank's simply providing finance to Blue Sea to enable it to make the purchase. The bonds won't be registered in Moscow Alpha's name, but in Blue Sea's. As for the one and a half billion dollars provided by Moscow Alpha, I checked the bank's details with Standard and Poor's and Moody's. If the ratings agencies are right, then the bank has transferred nearly its entire capital base to Blue Sea Holdings. The bank's been left almost a shell after the transfer. Technically speaking it may already be insolvent, although it appears to have enough working capital to continue day-to-day trading. But that's just a façade. If investors call upon the bank's commitment under the bond issue, it'll collapse. There'll be no money to meet their claims. At that point the investors, and by that I mean the group behind Blue Sea, will seize the SPV's assets. Moscow Alpha may try calling in the money transferred to Blue Sea but my guess is that the transfer was never formally authorised anyway. If that's the case then the money's simply been stolen, transferred without authority by someone high up in the bank'.

Adam's eyes widened as she talked. 'By the time the liquidators track down the money it'll be too late: the bank will have collapsed. What we need to know is the identity of the owners of Blue Sea Holdings. Then we'll know who'll be left holding the Caspian oil rights when the whole project crashes. So now everything hinges on what you find out tonight. Given my interest in the complex scheme I've uncovered today, perhaps I should come along just to hold the ladder'. Adam smiled; in other circumstances he'd have laughed, but he knew that at least one person in Baku had already been killed for getting too close to the truth, and he was already concerned for his own safety as well as for Saul's. For the remainder of the afternoon the two simply sat in the sun, occasionally strolling along the shoreline arm in arm, cooling their feet in the water.

⸙

Adam stood back in the doorway of the building adjacent to the small, unobtrusive office of Druckerstein, Kahn, and Nixdorf, Willemstad. The twisting side street was silent, apart from a handful of brightly dressed young couples waiting eagerly in the darkness. They'd arrived early, determined to take up positions along the most sought-after vantage points. He looked at his watch: like them, he would have to wait. He looked determinedly across at the office, having already identified the weakest point for a forced entry. The frontage was that of an original Dutch colonial trader's house but the nature of the business conducted within was unmistakable. The small brass plaque affixed to the door listed names of the local partners: this could only be the representative office of a foreign law firm. In the distance he could hear music, noise, shouting, laughing, singing, at first barely audible but quickly mounting to fill the narrow streets.

A river of colour flowed into view. First there were women dressed in elaborate multicoloured costumes with enormous headdresses from which huge bright red feathers shot up into the night sky. They were followed by young men in harlequin outfits spangled with red, gold, and metallic blue diamonds, and highwaymen masks. As they progressed past the cheering crowds, they danced rhythmically to the beat of the music booming behind them. Adam looked across to the people on the opposite side of the street; they cheered, enthralled with the procession, the Marcha Despedida or 'Farewell March' held each year as one of Curacao's main carnivals. Within minutes the street was crammed with lithe dancers and floats bedecked with flowers and images from the surrounding Caribbean islands. The air was full of noise, heat, colours, and symbols of ancient rituals, their roots long forgotten, summoned up like spirits from the depths of the island. Youth in all its brazenness and exuberance fizzed and burned brightly in the darkness.

Adam disappeared into the alleyway which ran alongside the office, where the side entrance was. Taking the small, heavy hammer he had bought earlier that day from one of the few hardware stores in Otrobanda, he aimed a blow at the lowest of the large panes of glass in the door. It shattered into a thousand shards, triggering an alarm inaudible above the cacophony which was causing the very walls in the street to vibrate. Lying on his back he slithered through the smashed section, taking care to avoid glass fragments scattered across the floor. A single cut, a solitary drop of blood, would be of great help to the island police who'd investigate the scene of the crime the following day. Soon his eyes were accustomed to the darkness, assisted by beams of coloured lights passing through into the office from the carnival in the street. He could hear a noise sounding like the chirping of a thousand grasshoppers as enthusiastic carnival participants blew repeatedly upon dozens of shiny new steel whistles. As he passed through the small lobby area into the main room of the office he took a small key ring torch from his pocket. He knew what he was looking for, and immediately made his way to the filing cabinets lining the wall on one side of the room. If they were locked, he'd force them open with the hammer's claw. As he half-heartedly pulled on the handle of one of the drawers marked 'A-E', anticipating it to be locked, he let out a whispered 'bingo' as, contrary to expectation, it glided open with minimal effort. He began thumbing through the files and quickly came to Blue Sea Holdings. Attached to the front of the file was a note in bold black letters: 'To be billed to client through Carter Buckmaster, London Office'. It was immediately apparent that the senior partner was the firm's sole point of contact with the client, and that any enquiries had to be referred to him and not handled by anyone else. He felt emboldened as he opened the file, taking pleasure in breaking Buckmaster's jealously guarded proprietorship of all aspects of the client's affairs. Inside the file he found several documents including the certificate of incorporation, memorandum and articles of association, and details of the company's registered office address. There was also a list of the company's nominee directors: local accountants who in the course of their business made their names available to companies looking to keep the identities of their true controllers secret.

But it was the final form in the bundle which seized his attention. Although three and a half billion dollars had recently passed through the company's bank account at First Curacao, the company itself had been incorporated with a mere five thousand shares of a face value of one dollar each, divided equally between two shareholders, Lincoln Davies, of a New York address, and Petr Damyanovitch, of a Moscow address. As he stood in the darkness Adam pieced together the information with that provided by Clarissa. Petr Damyanovitch had transferred such a huge proportion of Moscow Alpha's capital base that the slightest crisis would inevitably result in the bank's collapse. The reality was that Moscow Alpha's capital had passed into Damyanovitch's personal control, to be used as and when Blue Sea Holdings, the shell company over which he shared joint control with his American partner, required. He was impressed by the scale of the fraud; what he'd found confirmed Clarissa's appraisal of the scheme, that Damyanovitch would deliberately destroy the bank of which he was chairman, as well as the smaller local Azeri and Kazakh banks involved in the management group. But the beauty of the deception was that Damyanovitch, as joint shareholder in Blue Sea, would be one of the principal investors who'd end up with control of the Caspian Sea oil rights, along with the American who no doubt represented other undisclosed interests.

As he closed the file he realised that for the conspiracy to work it would be essential too that Sheldons Bank be destroyed in the process. If Moscow Alpha and the other minor banks collapsed, all of their obligations under the issue would simply pass to the survivor under the usual joint and several liability rule accepted by participants on signing up to the syndicate. Inevitably, therefore, Sheldons would collapse soon afterwards, and the shadow investors would then pounce on the special purpose vehicle holding the Caspian rights. But if any of the banks was able to meet the syndicate's obligations, there'd be no entitlement to seize those rights. He was well aware that Saul had always been partial to petty criminality, but the scale of this conspiracy placed it firmly outside anything he would be willing to be associated with. Or did it? Adam recalled Saul's evasiveness when previously pressed about Buckmaster. Perhaps he knew more about the conspiracy than he was willing to admit, or, alternatively, he might be shutting his eyes to its violent realities. If this was true then there had to be a pay-off, some remuneration for looking the other way and remaining silent whilst others set about achieving their goals. He began to wonder if he knew his friend at all.

The break-in had furnished Adam with most of the information he needed, justifying his trip to Curacao. He now knew that the secret investors in the oil bonds would be Damyanovitch, Davies, and their associates. And yet there still remained a crucial question. If they were to take control of the oil rights held by the SPV, there would have to be a seismic shift in oil prices that would reverberate in the futures markets. What was that event to be? Were they planning something? Speculators and oil consumers would have to flood into the market, desperately buying up the futures contract to which the bonds were linked, before there was any prospect of the investors' rights being triggered. But what would cause such panic? He knew the answer wouldn't be found in Druckerstein's representative office on the island, and felt frustrated. He switched off his torch and made his way back to the side entrance. Within seconds he was back among the crowds in the street, watching the carnival procession still passing by. Quickly, he made his way to the car hired earlier that day, parked a safe distance away. Soon he was sitting in the hotel bar again, discussing the fruits of his criminality with Clarissa. For a while they discussed the facts they now knew about the conspiracy, hypothesising about the possible objectives of the true owners of the shares in Blue Sea Holdings. But for most of the evening they talked of other things: of hopes, friends, sailing boats and oceans. There was a magic between them, a closeness, although both knew this might be their last evening together, perhaps for a while, perhaps forever. In the early hours the two lovers bid good night to the barman and left.

The following morning Clarissa drove Adam to Willemstad Airport, disappointed that he was leaving so soon but grateful for the time they'd spent together. Although she'd become a successful lawyer since leaving London, regularly mixing with the island's great and the good, she was lonely. Her time with Adam had been intellectually stimulating, dangerously exciting and passionate, leaving her acutely aware of the emotional deficit in her present life. Sometimes the glass was half empty, sometimes half full; as long as she was happy for most of the time, the darker moments of loneliness would be counterbalanced by successes in other spheres. As they stood outside the Airport Adam held her again. 'Thank you Clarissa, for everything'. She smiled; 'Any time you need more information about the Blue Sea account, just let me know. I'll be in touch as soon as there are any further transfers'. He kissed her. 'I didn't mean that. Thank you for loving me. Thank you for finding my better side and being happy just to be with me'. 'It was always there, Adam, it just needed the magic of the island to bring it out'. They held each other for a final time and then parted.

After checking in and presenting his passport Adam headed for one of the customs-free shops inside the airport. There he bought a small but expensive blue porcelain bottle of eau de toilette. This would suffice for Alice Penn when he returned to the office the following Monday. When requesting annual leave a couple of weeks' earlier he'd lied about his destination, telling Buckmaster he'd be traveling to a remote part of Jamaica where old friends had offered him a free stay at their holiday home. To mention Curacao would have triggered the senior partner's suspicion, heightened considerably by the subsequent break-in at the firm's local office. But if he was told a lie, albeit unknowingly, by a trusted third party - the delightful, reliable, Ms. Penn- then it was much more likely he'd believe it than if it had come from Adam directly. The holiday in Jamaica had really 'recharged his batteries', he'd tell her, his suntanned skin testament to hours spent on beaches, swimming in the perfect blue sea. Over the tannoy he heard the call for passengers to board. He held his shirtsleeve to his face and slowly inhaled the lingering trace of Clarissa's perfume. He'd be thinking of her long after the plane touched down fourteen and a half hours later on a wet, shiny, windswept apron at Heathrow.

Chapter Fifty Four

Lincoln Davies sat and waited, and while he did so, he speculated about the conversations that must have taken place around the table over the years. The crisis in the oil markets during the Iraqi invasion of Kuwait in 1991. The second Iraqi War, the toppling of Saddam and the years of political instability in the region which had followed. For policy makers in successive administrations, such events which threatened the economic prosperity of the American Empire had to be anticipated and a range of economic and military options made available to the President. As far back as Roosevelt, contingency plans had been made for the military occupation of Saudi Arabia and the annexation of the Kingdom's oil fields. But during recent years, dozens of new strategies had emerged from the 'sand pits', the secret workshops held regularly at the Department of Energy. Here, representatives from government and the oil companies came together to discuss scenarios in which global energy supplies were threatened, and how the US should react through diplomatic and military means. Of course the Saudi oil fields annexation option remained at the core of thinking, principally for historical reasons, but the assumption that the government in Riyadh would continue to survive with the Infidel so conspicuous on its territory had recently been called into question. Sand pit strategies now envisaged a popular and widespread insurgency, militants supplied with weaponry by neighbouring states, mainly Iran and Syria, leading to the collapse of the House of Saud within a matter of a few years, or even a few months. US troops would be sucked into a quagmire in which policing of hundreds of miles of pipelines and oilfield stations would become highly problematic.

To fight a new Middle East version of the Vietnam debacle whilst at the same time trying to administer the entire domestic Saudi oil industry was now viewed by many as the least tenable, the least realistic, policy option. Lincoln Davies had participated in most of the sand pits during recent years, chairing several of them. He was privy to current thinking in the White House, concurring with the Department of Energy's publicly stated objective to find and secure alternative oil supplies. But it was the radical strategy proposed by Davies and his associates which had gained the most attention recently at the Department, and with it, the tacit support of the hawks advising the Administration. It was in order to discuss progress on the strategy that Lincoln Davies now sat in the conference room at 1000 Independence Avenue, Washington DC, awaiting the Secretary of State's arrival. No other officials would be present and no minutes taken: this would be a meeting that never took place.

'Lincoln, good to see you here in Washington again. But it looks like you've brought wet weather with you, just as you did last time. A pity that this morning I ignored my wife's advice to bring an umbrella. She can always sense rain in the air'. The short, bespectacled middle-aged Secretary, Quentin Slaney, sat at a right angle next to Davies: to take a chair on the opposite side of the table would have been too formal, requiring raised voices to communicate, increasing the risk of being overheard by some official loitering outside in the corridor. 'Sorry about the rain, Quentin. When I left New York yesterday afternoon it was hot and muggy, so I'm mighty grateful for the freshness of the air here today. With all this talk of climate change who knows- perhaps soon enough we'll be baking all year round wherever we are in this great country of ours'. Slaney decided to bring the small talk to a close. 'Now, what news do you bring today? What can I report back to the President?' Davies smiled: on the previous occasion they'd met in the same room he'd been forced to admit to slow progress, principally because of opposition to his plans mounted behind the scenes by a senior board member at SOCAR, the state-owned Azeri oil company. But this obstacle had been removed: now the project was moving ahead in leaps and bounds.

'Kazakh and Azeri oilfield rights in the Caspian seabed have now been successfully transferred to the special purpose vehicle, as we've previously discussed. As soon as my consortium takes ownership of these assets, we'll have control of new oil supplies which won't be exhausted for decades. The US will no longer be dependent upon Middle Eastern producers. With our Russian partner we'll also fix the price at which the oil's sold to us, since it'll have to pass through the existing Transneft pipelines, and we'll cooperate with the Kremlin in setting the tariffs. We'll also obstruct any further discussions between Kazakhstan and Iran over division of ownership rights in the Caspian; they've still not been able to agree a legal regime but they're getting close to it. With US-Russian control of a large portion of Kazakh assets, we'll put forward proposals via the Baku government that'll never be acceptable to Tehran'.

Slaney found the summary amusing: 'So we're working in partnership with our old enemy, Russia, to quarantine a new enemy, Iran. Just how reliable is our Russian partner?' 'Without Russian involvement in this project we'd never have got anywhere. Mr. Damyanovitch of Moscow Alpha Bank represents the Kremlin's interests, at arm's length of course, to avoid embarrassment. Come to think of it, the relationship mirrors that which my company has with you, as representative of our government'. Slaney frowned momentarily at the comparison, then composed himself and continued to listen as before. 'As soon as the Caspian oil bonds are issued we'll buy up everything that comes to market. If all goes to plan afterwards, the Caspian seabed rights will fall into our hands. As for Russia, the nationalist aspirations of her neighbours will be extinguished. There'll be a wave of regional bank failures as a consequence of what we're planning. With the economic turmoil that'll follow Russia will be invited back in to save the day. With economic dependence comes political control'.

Slaney looked concerned; 'So you're saying we'll be sacrificing the democracies of the region, returning them to the Russian fold? This has been alluded to before and as I have already said, I'm not sure I like this. It reminds me of the zones of influence diplomacy I thought we'd left behind at the end of the Cold War'. Davies looked at him directly; 'When Middle Eastern oil supplies start to run down, and they will do and soon, we'll look back on these sacrifices and congratulate ourselves for having had the prescience, the courage, to have made them'. Slaney was a shrewd politician but was startled by the cold logic with which his guest now confronted him. 'OK, I accept your reasoning, but I, or the President, may have further questions. Now, tell me about Saudi Arabia. What do you know about the recent bombings, the political rallies and protests?' Davies laughed. 'What do I know about them? Everything, of course. After all, my associates and I are funding them. This Administration, like its predecessor, is of the view that the Saudi monarchy cannot survive in the medium term. The House of Saud is finished and the President knows it. But the man who'll lead the revolution, he'll be our man. We've been financing the leader-in-waiting for years. Whenever he curses us, casts us as the Great Satan, it'll simply be gestures for his people – he needs to set himself up this way to gain popular and radical support.

He'll supply our oil needs on our terms once he's in, though, because we'll have put him there in the first place. If any details of our collaboration ever came out, he'd be a dead man. That's the stick we hold over him. As for the carrot, we're handing him a kingdom to rule in line with his religious principles. So one crumbling kingdom collapses, making way for the next. It'll no doubt be a radical-fundamentalist government, but one which gives us what we want, guaranteed'.

Slaney recalled that nearly every scenario considered in recent sand pit sessions had assumed the Saudi government's demise in the not too distant future. Davies's intention to tear down the present regime and collude in the installation of its ostensibly independent radical successor was audacious but politically, highly dangerous. 'So where's your man now, Lincoln? I'm not going to ask how you're planning to bring the present regime crashing down. It's important that I, as a representative of the Administration, am able to plead ignorance if this grand scheme fails and I end up before a Senate Committee Inquiry. The fact that I know you and your associates are behind the current wave of bombings across the Kingdom has already prejudiced this defence, but no matter. Where is he?' Davies smiled mischievously. 'He's safely under lock and key, courtesy of the British government. When we're ready he'll be freed, but in the meantime we'll continue to shake the House of Saud to its foundations. I'll keep you informed'. 'And presumably when the Saudi government falls, at that point the Caspian side of the project comes into effect?' Davies paused: politicians as a breed could never be trusted, and he wondered whether he'd already disclosed too much to the Secretary of State. 'Yes, the crisis will panic the oil markets. This will come about by means you don't need to know about, but ownership of the Caspian Sea reserves will fall into our hands like a ripe apple dropping from a tree. And you'll achieve one of the Administration's principal foreign policy goals: Iran will be banished from the region permanently.' Slaney looked at his guest and smiled. Sitting alongside him was one of the most ruthless, focused men he'd ever encountered: a New England-born, Harvard-educated, rich-as-Croesus son of a bitch who was also, thankfully, *their* son of a bitch. The meeting at an end, the two shook hands. Davies left via the same inconspicuous side entrance by which he'd entered the building: there was no security pass to be returned, and no time of departure to be recorded for this most invisible of visitors to the Department of Energy.

Chapter Fifty Five

The two men walked along the path following the course of the Thames, the full moon illuminating small empty boats bobbing up and down, anchored in the still water. A bright yellow plastic 'kiss me quick' hat afforded a temporary landing pad for a seagull; it surveyed the day's flotsam and jetsam for scraps of food to take back to its hungry brood on the roof of a nearby multi-story car park. As the garish souvenir slipped beneath the water the gull took off again, its wings illuminated by laser beams from a wedding nearby. Eventually the walkers came to a halt at a bench with perfect view of the Houses of Parliament across the river, and for a while no words were spoken as they waited for the trickle of night shift workers and lovers to pass by. Distant laughter, music and drunken, out-of-tune singing briefly distracted the younger man's attention as he tried to compose his thoughts, to catch the questions fluttering haphazardly in his head like butterflies in a bell jar. He was afraid, and fear disrupted his mental processes.

'It's a pleasure being here with you again Saul, especially since our last meeting didn't end on a good note. I'm glad you're willing to put all that behind us. I always gain so much from your company, and our association has delivered such benefits for both of us. I hope it will continue to do so. But as you know, I'm a busy man and I need to get back to my hotel. So young man, what's on your mind? Why have you invited me to this place?' Saul looked across at Damyanovitch: his smile was forced and devoid of emotion, his face pallid, the shadows beneath his eyes made more prominent by the full moon overhead. He decided to confront the Russian with what he knew instead of continuing the façade of politeness he was by now finding irritating. After all, this was the man who'd been within seconds of ordering his execution a matter of weeks earlier, perfectly happy to throw him to his death from a great height. 'Without my participation in your plan, Petr, without my complicity, you and your associates wouldn't be where you are now. And yet you've never trusted me, at least not to any extent that matters. You've never told me what the Caspian project's all about. It's never been just about the money; you're already wealthy beyond most people's wildest dreams. It's not about power; you have this as well. In three days' time you and I will meet again at the pre-launch ceremony, hours before the bonds you've so assiduously planned for, killed for, hit the primary market. They'll all be there. People from the Azeri and Kazakh state oil companies, government officials, diplomats, my chairman. And I'll be among them, having been, with you of course, one of the main drivers in putting the deal together. But the funny thing is that my understanding of its real purpose seems to have diminished rather than deepened over the past few months. Now, at the end of all the negotiations, planning, liaising with lawyers, accountants, other syndicate members, I sit here tonight realising I know almost nothing at all. Is this satisfactory bearing in mind I'm responsible for coordinating everything on behalf of Sheldons, and we're your co-lead managers in the bond issue? When are you planning to tell me what this is really all about?'

Damyanovitch paused whilst reflecting upon the question; at a different time this kind of voiced enquiry, this impertinence, would have led to the demise of the questioner, to his death or, if he was lucky, depending on how you looked at it, his 'disappearance' to a forced labour camp on the outer fringes of the Soviet Empire. 'You ask a lot of questions, Saul. Why do you persist in doing this? Your simple goal is the pursuit of wealth, and your willingness to disregard ethics getting in the way of achieving it was what originally convinced me that we could work with each other. Please don't take this as a criticism - I never make personal judgments because we're all flawed creatures, after all. But now, *again,* you're straying into matters which don't concern you. Haven't I warned you about this already? I promised that within a month of the bonds being issued and the capital raised, I'd pay you a vast amount of money. That was our agreement and it still stands, and you're nearer now to what you've always wanted than you've ever been before in your life. Soon you'll be a millionaire many times over. Isn't this enough? I've also allowed you to live when my instinct told me to do otherwise. So, I must advise you for the last time: just take the money and be on your way. Don't trouble your mind trying to work out the machinations and intrigues of others. You'll not find answers'. From any other person the response would have been patronising, but from a man incapable of the absurdity of personal slight it was merely a statement of reality. Saul suddenly felt the urge to provoke him. For a moment he wondered if the Russian was capable of emotion or whether instead, somewhere in his dark and distant past, he'd been so brutalised that the recognisable qualities of humanity had simply eroded to nothing. The calmness with which he'd executed Nicholas Herschell and sliced the throat of Kordovski in Baku supported this premise.

'Did you order Andrew Ginsberg's murder in Istanbul? Did you arrange the bombing of Gregor Halydar's car in Baku? Is it true that Moscow Alpha is technically insolvent, and that its entire capital base has vanished to who knows where? I have a right to answers'. He looked at Damyanovitch: it was the first time he'd seen any display of emotion in his face, temporarily unable to disguise his surprise at the extent of his associate's knowledge of the project's intricacies. His instinctive reaction was to have Saul taken to a location where he could be interrogated as to the true extent of his knowledge, and from which sources, from which disloyal people, he'd obtained it. But this wasn't Moscow, and there was no place or team at his disposal equipped with the KGB standards of operation which would be needed to do things properly. On the other hand, he had made precautionary arrangements in advance, to cover the eventuality of a last minute withdrawal by the young man. He'd assumed, almost from their first encounter, that Saul was a one-dimensional individual whose simple goal in life, wealth, could be relied upon in the planning and execution of a project like this. He'd play his part, take his payment, and then simply disappear to some sun-soaked island on the other side of the world. But in recent weeks this assumption was exhibiting fault lines, like the creaks in the fabric of a house built in an earthquake zone. If Saul's character flaws could no longer be relied upon at this late stage in the game, the consequences could be severe if he was not managed correctly.

He stared into Saul's eyes, his emotionless demeanour restored. 'You have no right to answers. I hired you to do as I asked, not to question me. How dare you presume to question me? But to satisfy your curiosity, yes, Moscow Alpha is now insolvent. There is good reason for this, I can assure you – reason which justifies taking such drastic steps. I created the bank, it is mine, and I will dispose of it as I see fit. I accept that I am responsible for all those I employ. No one there will go hungry; I will see to it that they survive and prosper. When it does finally collapse, Sheldons will also be destroyed in the aftermath. I am afraid I cannot also look after all those at your London bank. Without Moscow Alpha, Sheldons alone will be responsible for meeting investors' claims, and will break in the process. The other Kazakh and Azeri players in the syndicate will also be destroyed in the firestorm. But then my associates and I will take control of the Caspian seabed rights, leaving my country's enemies with nothing but bread and water to live on. This pipeline project was doomed from the very beginning, not by chance or coincidence, but by design. You are an accessory to its imminent destruction but don't be ashamed- in the process you'll have played your part in the beginning of the restoration of an empire'. Saul shivered in fear at what Damyanovitch told him, shocked by the enormity of his revelation. A global financial crisis was soon to begin in which regional banking systems would collapse and a sea's riches would be stolen. Instinctively he felt little loyalty to Sheldons, but the prospect of being a collaborator in the destruction of so many livelihoods including those of entire nations, then silently slipping away with a handful of millions as a payoff, pushed an immediate sense of guilt into his heart like the thrust of a dagger. Momentarily, he contemplated the possibility that, perhaps, he had a personal morality after all.

'Tell me about Ginsberg and Halydar. Were you behind their deaths?' Damyanovitch paused; 'Halydar yes and directly. Ginsberg was another's handiwork, although of course I was involved, in an advisory capacity. They both threatened the success of the project and, with it, my country's future. Only once in my life have I killed without justification and that was a long time ago. It is my one and only regret'. He regained his focus. 'Both of them were put down like stray dogs. Now you know everything. Are you happy or does this new knowledge trouble you? What price do I now ask of you? How to guarantee your silence at this late hour in our partnership, that's the question'. He looked at Saul and smiled.

'Stand up, please'. Saul was puzzled by the simple command: his heartbeat raced as he contemplated imminent death, and the possible manner of his execution; Damyanovitch was, after all, an innovative assassin. He stood and waited. 'Now, please see'. Saul looked down and saw a small red spot picking out the fabric weave of his jacket. 'You're looking at the infrared marker of a sniper's rifle. Your assassin is standing beneath the bridge on the opposite side of the river, waiting for me to raise my hand, to signal I've no further use for you. Shall I end your life here and now? It would put right my previous indecision, don't you agree?' Saul turned to him calmly, suddenly reassured by realisation that for some reason he still wanted him alive, or alternatively feared the ramifications should his accomplice be found dead in suspicious circumstances. If he was of no further use or if Damyanovitch believed his death would pass unnoticed, then the sniper's bullet would already have found him, within days of the Caspian oil rights passing to the SPV. He began to believe that Damyanovitch was bluffing. 'Kill me now Petr, and Phineus will suspend the project. He's a cautious man - you've worked with him and know this. And what of the boards of the Kazakh and Azeri banks, the other junior syndicate members? They've only dealt with me, never with you. You're Russian, and we both know the resentment there is against Russia in that part of the world. Moscow Alpha may be the co-lead manager in this issue, but as far as they're concerned it's a British deal. And after all, that's why you invited us to join you in the first place; you knew a solely Russian bid to manage the issue would never have had any chance of succeeding. If they get so much as a whisper of a suspicion that the Old Enemy is running things, they'll pull out of the deal. You see, Petr, you're just not trusted by your neighbours. And, with justification, I must say.' The red dot remained, the cross hairs of the telescopic lens perfectly aligned on the target. Sergei Ivanov continued gently holding his forefinger across the cold trigger, his rifle perfectly balanced atop a half-collapsed wall beneath the bridge.

Damyanovitch was in unfamiliar territory: trying to remain threatening when both he and Saul knew that unless he was willing to risk everything, there was indeed little he could do to bring the young financier to heel. He paused in the darkness, stepping out of the orbit of light cast by the mock-Victorian street lamp. In his mind he searched for his protagonist's weak point: something or someone whom he cared about and against whom a real threat of violence could be made. From his jacket's inner pocket he withdrew an object, six inches of steel which glinted in the moonlight. He pressed the button and the full blade sprung out. Saul recognised the sound, the distinctive gliding of metal against metal that he'd last heard in Baku, seconds before SOCAR's Azeri nationalist director had had his throat slashed. He stepped back, afraid that his bluff was about to be called. 'Do you recognise this?' He pointed the blade at him threateningly. 'Kordovski was the last person to feel it cold against his throat. Do you remember the blood? A bullet in the chest is a quick and easy way to go, but to be left bleeding to death, now that's a different matter. Are you so sure of yourself now?' Saul froze in terror as the Russian advanced towards him. 'I'll use this - on you or any of your friends, anyone you care for. Your lawyer friend for example - should I start with him? Perhaps tomorrow, he could be killed in a dark alley by attackers who make off with his wallet. So many possibilities. Give me your promise, *now*, or die. Lie to me and the next death will be your responsibility'.

Suddenly out of the darkness loomed the substantial frame of PC Stephen Goodland, a trainee who'd joined the Metropolitan Police Force three months earlier. He'd heard nothing of the previous conversation, only the commotion of raised voices, but he knew from the silhouettes and the glint of a blade that one man was threatening another with a knife and that an assault was underway. 'Put down the weapon sir. Put it down on the ground and step away. Do it now'. Damyanovitch immediately switched his attention to the policeman, angered by the abrupt intrusion. Saul stepped back in terror: the collision of worlds, the one in which he and Damyanovitch haggled over the future of nations and the one of thugs and random street crime in which the young policeman lived, had suddenly brought unpredictability and a greater danger to the situation. Damyanovitch looked at Saul and spoke, ignoring the policeman's presence. 'Let this be a warning to you, Saul. Watch and see what I'm capable of. Witness what happens and then think of your friend'.

The policeman looked momentarily perplexed: he expected his authority to be respected but here it was being ignored. He shouted again; 'I told you to put down the knife. Do as I say'. Damyanovitch ignored the repeated order and spoke gently to Saul. 'This is for you'. He turned to the policeman and raised his left hand: the assassin below the bridge recognised the signal, lined up the new target, and squeezed the trigger. The bullet struck PC Goodland in the chest: mercury-tipped, it tore through his body and out the other side, embedding itself in the wall behind. The victim fell to the ground like a boxer's punch bag falling with the slashing of the rope by which it is suspended. He was killed instantly. Damyanovitch spoke again. 'Now, is this what you want for your friend? What's your answer?' Saul's mouth was dry with fear: the casual wasting of an innocent life profoundly shocked him. 'I'll do whatever you want me to do. Just give me the money when it's done'. Damyanovitch knew he couldn't be trusted, and wondered whether he should kill him there and then and be done with it. But on a balance he decided to let him live, Saul's earlier warning of the consequences of his death in suspicious circumstances swaying a very close decision. 'I'll take that as a promise you'll continue as agreed, keep the syndicate together and your mouth shut. But remember, I can have you or anybody you care about killed, anytime and anywhere, in the blink of an eye. I'll be watching.' He replaced the flick knife into his pocket, straightened his tie, and disappeared into the darkness. Within fifteen minutes he would arrive at a party hosted at the Georgian embassy; there he'd mingle with diplomats and high-level civil servants, his carefully practiced charm an inspiration to those advocating greater rapprochement with the new Russian Democracy. The Soviet Empire was dead: now was the time to build bridges.

Saul stood in a state of dazed disbelief at what he'd witnessed. He'd long known that Damyanovitch wouldn't hesitate to kill when he perceived his interests to be at risk, but tonight he'd had executed a random British policeman, a representative of the law, in the very heart of the capital. It was evidence of the Russian's simple but absolute belief in his ability to slaughter anyone in any place, with total impunity. He stood with his hands by his sides, the victim's glassy eyes like fish eyes staring back at him out of a strangely sad face. His attention was drawn back towards the dark and brooding bridge in the distance: perhaps the sniper was still watching him, marking his target through a rifle sight. His heartbeat began to race again. He started to walk away from the scene, at first briskly but then bursting into a run. After ten minutes he arrived at a tube station, his clothes soaking with sweat. There he bought a ticket, boarded a train and headed back to his apartment. He made a call. 'Hi Adam. You and I need to talk, but in person. What about tomorrow?' Saul sat in the darkness; he still had the terrible sensation of being watched, that somewhere in the distance a sniper was waiting for a signal. Adam had been working on a complex but particularly dry leasing agreement, and welcomed a distraction. 'Are you okay? You sound out of breath. Where do you want to meet - your office?' Saul paused before replying, trying to think of a safe venue. In recent days he'd come to believe that his office was bugged, although he realised this might simply indicate his deepening paranoia. 'What about the office where we used to meet to discuss investment strategy for Tri-Star? Back in the good old days – remember?' Adam laughed. 'Okay, you book the room and I'll see you there, half seven, just as it used to be.' Saul then made a further call to Northern Engineering during which his powers of persuasion and concealment were tested to the limit. After extracting an agreement to his simple request, and exploiting the trust implicit in friendship, he ended the call.

Chapter Fifty Six

Solomon Silverstein made his way across the vast plaza, the brilliant sunlight casting his long thin shadow across the huge blocks that made up the square. He walked past tourists corralled into groups by guides reciting a historical narrative learned by rote, the clicking of dozens of cameras like a swarm of cicada on a hot day. Young people smiled as he passed and he smiled back. To them he was an old man, deserving of respect; to him they were the future, every life and every soul beautiful and of infinite value in the Universe. His face was deeply lined, hardened by crueler years, but to the young he appeared unmistakably kind and gentle. Soon he arrived at his destination: the Western Wall built by Herod the Great loomed upwards into the perfect blue sky. The old man pulled his tallit, his large blue and white prayer shawl, about his shoulders, fastened tefillin, the phylacteries, around his forehead and wrist, and commenced the Mincha, the afternoon prayer. As he'd grown old, his devotion to the rituals of his faith had deepened. Now, as he entered his final years he appreciated the guidance they'd provided throughout his life, learned first through the teachings of his parents and then at the synagogue. During his early years he'd considered training as a Rabbi, but then the War intervened and changed everything. And then came life's distractions: materialism, and the burning need to be safe and secure after the earlier privations, uncertainties, and barbarities. Although he'd later accumulate riches beyond the dreams of most men, all he ever truly valued, all that ever mattered, was his faith, his family, and the sanctity of the human soul. He bowed his head and started to pray.

With the incantation of Kaddish, he ended the afternoon's prayer. As he stood in the late afternoon heat haze, the Temple Mount towering above, he reflected again upon his past life. Each day since the end of the War he'd offered up silent gratitude for his survival when the lives of so many he loved had been viciously and prematurely extinguished. He began his daily prayer of Shehecheyanu. *Barukh atah Adonai, Elohaynu, melekh ha-olam, she-hekheeyanu v'keeymanu v'heegeeyanu la-zman ha-zeh. (Blessed are you, Lord, our God, King of the Universe, who has kept us alive, sustained us, and enabled us to reach this season).* He prayed for those he loved and those he'd never known who died in the camps. He prayed for his family. He prayed for Israel. Then he took a piece of paper from his pocket and pushed it between the ancient stones in front of him: on it was written a simple prayer, a blessing for the souls of the innocents of Nemmersdorf.

He closed his eyes, drawn again to a church in darkness. He waited for the sound as a door slammed shut. He listened for the gunfire. To save a life is to save the Universe; that night he'd failed even to try to stop the slaughter. But what could he have done? How could he have stopped a soldier intent on wreaking death and destruction? His was the burden of guilt of the witness who walks away from an atrocity, wondering forever afterwards why he'd survived and wishing at times that he hadn't. He remembered the emptiness in the young killer's eyes and his determined, detached demeanour. Frustration and rage forced their way into his consciousness as they always did during these unguarded moments, recently too frequent, when his thoughts took flight like a kite on a windswept hillside. He turned away from the Wall and started to walk: the purity of thought required for prayer had passed, and the anger now in his heart demanded his withdrawal. As he left the plaza he thought of his daughter, his limitless love for her driving out the blackness of the past from his mind. He'd speak with her later that evening, ostensibly to receive her report on a recent business trip to Istanbul. It would have been an unqualified success, of course, he thought: her technical acumen and charisma impressing even the dourest of potential clients, as they always did. But the true reason why he so looked forward to receiving the call was simply to hear her voice again, to argue with her, to laugh with her; being a father was the greatest success, the greatest blessing that life had bestowed upon him.

Chapter Fifty Seven

Saul waited in the darkness at the large oval table: the room was empty. He gazed out across the city, watching the near-unbroken snakes of car lights twisting through the dark streets below, the neon signs blinking in a myriad of colours to a transitory population that never slept. He remembered the last time he'd been in the anonymous conference room with his two friends, when they'd argued over the merits of increasing their investment in Franklin Shandlin's company. He'd been upbeat about the tycoon's plans for the future, and it was his counsel which prevailed. This had, of course, turned out to be one of the greatest mistakes of his life, a miscalculation that had lost the three friends millions. And, yet, there'd never been a word of personal reproach from either Adam or Thomas. They'd never criticised him afterwards, accepting that responsibility was joint and several – the burden was not his alone.

At seven thirty precisely, Adam strolled into the room in 'work garb': a pinstripe suit, crisp white shirt, and striking red tie. 'Well this is déjà vu. How are things at Sheldons? Must be something important to summon me back to this place of past crimes, haunted by ghosts I'd rather not think about. So, what's the news?' He pulled up a chair and stubbed out his half-finished cigarette. He was his usual amusing, sometimes caustic self, but beneath the bravado Saul knew he was unsettled by the venue. Although the reference to ghosts was lighthearted enough, Saul knew the room would indeed have reminded the proud lawyer of his past mistakes. But his selection of the meeting place had been deliberate.

'Last night Damyanovitch killed again, but this time he did it as a direct warning to me rather than an execution for some practical purpose. He said if I did anything that put the Caspian deal at risk then not only would I get the same as the poor bastard who got shot, but he'd see to it that you'd also be lined up in the cross hairs. I've got to tell you now, Adam, that if we continue digging around or do anything to obstruct him, then we're both likely to get killed. If you want to keep going then that's fine with me. If you want to pull out now, then that's also fine. It'd be much easier to just let him follow through with his plan - he's worked long enough for it and he's not going to give up without a bloodbath - and just take the money and run. It's going to be a big payoff and of course I'll share it with you. We get rich and stay alive. He may be a cold blooded killer but as I've said before, I still think he's a man of his word. If we don't get in his way, then we'll be left alone. But it's up to you. Tell me what you think, and then I'll do the same. You first'.

Adam walked over to the wall-length window; for a few minutes he stared out into the darkness, the neon lights flashing on his eyes. Saul sat and waited, not attempting to guess at the thoughts passing through his friend's complicated, brilliant mind. Eventually he turned to Saul and spoke softly. 'And if he has his way, what will the consequences be?' Saul responded in a matter-of-fact tone. 'All the banks involved in the deal will collapse, including Moscow Alpha and Sheldons. The special purpose vehicle that you set up will be destroyed and its assets seized by the investors who we now know, after your visit to Curacao, comprise Damyanovitch and his associates. They'll then control a large chunk of the natural resources of the two states involved, Azerbaijan and Kazakhstan; they'll have the oil and gas rights in the Caspian Sea. The whole region will go into economic meltdown and at that point they'd be 'rescued' in some way by their former colonial master, Russia. No doubt there'll be other consequences, but these are the ones I'm sure of'. Adam reflected upon his own complicity in Damyanovitch's conspiracy, and how he'd been played for a fool by the Russian and the senior partner at Druckerstein's, Carter Buckmaster. His mind flashed back to an earlier time when a guilty client, Silas Coughlin, had done the same to him. He vividly recalled how his own arrogance and willingness to bend the law had led to several deaths following the client's acquittal. He remembered his guilt and desolation at his final meeting with the client, and how he'd later wept for the loss of innocence: he'd been to blame for the deaths. Now history was threatening to repeat itself, but on a far greater scale. He paused before continuing.

'What's left of my soul, Saul, is not for sale. Not at any price. I'll not fall into line, not on this one. At some point in time the compromising has to stop. That time is now, whatever the consequences, whatever the risks'. Saul couldn't prevent himself from smiling: they'd both reached the same decision, albeit by different routes and for different reasons. 'Bloody hell, Adam, you're beginning to frighten me. I'm coming close to thinking you may have a conscience after all, when all along I thought we were both the same, cold heartless chancers. How could I have been so wrong? You'll be sponsoring homes for orphans next.' The humour soon passed; both knew they were selecting by far the least sensible option, taking the fool's road, and that their lives would be placed in grave danger as a result. But the decision was made; now was not the time to be giving voice to each other's fears, to slowly sink into a mire of self-doubt. They shook hands, confident in facing the task ahead.

A mechanical sound from outside the room drew Adam's attention. The lift had begun gliding up the shaft from the ground floor, and yet it was eight o'clock and the building was supposed to be empty. 'That's the lift - you weren't expecting anyone else tonight, were you? If not, then maybe we should get out of here?' Saul appeared relaxed and this reassured him; he walked to the end of the conference table, taking a chair in the penumbra cast by a desk lamp. Approaching footsteps made him momentarily anxious again. Saul spoke quietly but determinedly;'Adam, Damyanovitch is the most ruthless, well-resourced opponent you'll ever meet. If we're going to bring things crashing down on him and the people he's working with we'll need help from wherever we can get it. Alone we'll just not be able to do it. Before you say anything to our guest, think carefully. This is all I ask'. Suddenly the door opened and the new arrival strode in. 'Saul, what the hell's this all about? You call me and beg me to get down here a day earlier than I planned, to meet you in a place I'd rather not go. You'd better have a good reason'.

Thomas remembered the building's layout as if he'd walked out yesterday. The smell in the room was the same: a mixture of stale coffee odour and cheap polish used by the cleaners who filtered through the rooms in a twilight-world after the tenants had left for the night. He walked towards the conference table, his hand outstretched to Saul. 'But I guess a day early isn't a problem. Good to see you'. Saul stood but didn't respond. By now Thomas's eyes had become accustomed to the semi-darkness, dimly illuminated by a desk lamp in a distant corner of the room. Neon lights of pink, red, green and white continued intruding sporadically from the outside world: shadows cast across flock-wallpapered walls, dancing like feint ghosts, disappearing when the external sources of their existence blinked for milliseconds. He became aware of another person in the room sitting sufficiently close to the lamp for his silhouette to be immediately recognisable. Thomas spoke quietly: despite the darkness Saul saw the shock in his face. 'What are you doing here? I said I never wanted to see you again. After everything you did. Have you no shame?' There was no anger in his voice, only a vague sadness as the coincidence of seeing both men again and in the same room used during the earlier years of their careers brought thoughts, cross currents of youth and loss, flooding up from the depths of his soul. He turned to Saul, but now with unmistakable malevolence. 'And you Saul, you tricked me into coming here tonight. You know I would never have come if I knew *he* was going to be here too. Is this some sort of game, to open up the past for your amusement?' He paused, unsure how to react to the utter unexpectedness of the situation. 'I think I'd better go'.

Saul hadn't underestimated the task he'd set himself: he knew the resentment on both sides would probably be as fresh as it had been on the day their friendship had collapsed under the terrible weight of Chloe's death. But he hoped against his better judgment that a reunion on familiar territory could start a process of reconciliation.

'Thomas, if you leave now you can say goodbye to your company. It'll be destroyed within months. The Caspian pipeline will not go ahead, and you'll never get back the money you've already borrowed from the banks and paid to your sub-contractors. And you can say goodbye to that person over there, sitting in the dark and also deceived into being here tonight. He didn't know you'd been invited as well. If he did he wouldn't have turned up either. Antipathy works both ways. But if threats which have been made are carried out, then we'll both be dead soon enough'. Thomas turned to him, shocked. 'What the hell are you talking about? My company's never been in a stronger position than it is now. The pipeline deal you lined us up with is going to be the making of the business. And as for threats, you were always prone to exaggeration. As for him, there was a time not too long ago when I'd have pulled the trigger myself, so why should I care now?' He couldn't bring himself to address Adam directly.

Saul continued, coolly. 'As you expected, the killing of Andrew Ginsburg in Istanbul wasn't the work of terrorists - it was done to the order of a man you're going to meet in two days' time here in London. The guy who's put this entire project together: Petr Damyanovitch. He kills without remorse and will stop at nothing to achieve his goals. He'll kill you too if he thinks it necessary. All I ask is that you listen to what we have to say. And then it's up to you. So what's it to be? Walk out and stumble blindly into the future, or sit and talk?' Thomas paused at the door, his hand already around the handle. A storm of conflicting emotions raged through his mind. He was angry at having been tricked into turning up at this room, of all possible locations, to meet the only person in the world whom he'd ever wanted to kill with his bare hands. But in the depths of his soul, for the first time he felt a trace of a desire to forgive. 'Okay, I'll hear what you have to say. Lie to me or embellish the facts and I'll know. You're putting a lot at stake, so tread carefully'. Saul smiled: 'A wise decision. But nothing's possible until you two resolve your differences. So, it's time for me to leave. Talk, argue, shout at each other, but sort things out. I'll wait outside in the street and will be back in fifteen minutes. That's how long you've got. Fifteen minutes. And if you haven't resolved things by then, well, defenestration can be pretty ugly you know'.

After Saul's departure the two remained at opposite ends of the room, standing in the semi-darkness. It was Thomas who eventually broke the silence: he spoke quietly but the accusatory tone was unmistakable. 'You hurt me, *damaged* me more than you'll ever know. You took away the only person I ever loved. You betrayed me'. A terrible remorse welled up in the lawyer as he heard the simple words of truth. 'I know I did and I'm sorrier than words could ever express. I was arrogant and a fool. If I could turn back the clock I would. But if you're willing to forgive me - I know you can't forget - then perhaps there's a way forward. What can I say, Thomas? I was in the wrong, and will have to live with what happened for the rest of my life'. Thomas reflected on his words, but knew he also had to be honest with himself. Unfairly, perhaps, he'd blamed Adam for everything when he knew the truth to be more complex: guilt should have been apportioned equally between the three of them. He walked to the end of the room and momentarily Adam tensed, preparing to defend himself. He held out his hand. 'I can't deny that I wanted to kill you. I was so angry. I still am. But.... I'm sorry too, Adam. If I'm to be true to myself I must acknowledge that you're not solely to blame for what happened. If you too can forgive me for the hardship I caused you then yes, I think we can move forward'. Adam nodded in agreement: they shook hands and a friendship was, to an extent anyway, restored.

Saul pushed open the door, momentarily anxious as to what might greet him. 'Time's up, gentlemen. So, have you settled things? Please tell me my efforts and petty deceptions haven't been in vain'. Thomas laughed ruefully and Saul instantly knew his goal had been achieved. 'Yes Saul, we've settled things and perhaps we should thank you for your good offices. But then to do so would risk puffing up your ego more than it already is, if that's possible'. Adam interjected; 'Tell me Saul, is there anyone you know who actually trusts you? More to the point, do you trust yourself?' Saul hesitated; 'Yes, I do know someone who trusts me implicitly and for your information loves me too. As to your other question no, I've never trusted myself and in this regard I'm an excellent judge of character'. The three sat down at the table, and discussed what each knew of the Caspian deal until well into the early hours of the following morning. Slowly the jigsaw was pieced together. Saul had the greatest insight into their principal adversary's personality and ruthlessness. Adam's understanding of legal aspects of the venture and Thomas's awareness of the practicalities of the energy business brought technical specificity and depth, confirming in Saul's mind the rightness of his strategy of bringing the two together.

By three o'clock in the morning they were each fully apprised of all aspects of the project and the risks they'd face in challenging Damyanovitch's plans. Determined but also anxious as to what lay ahead, the three left the room, never to return, and headed off into the night.

Chapter Fifty Eight

Petr Damyanovitch smiled politely as the trade attaché from the Kazakhstan embassy berated him for Russian interference in the internal politics of her neighbours. At the far end of the conference room in one of the most expensive hotels in London he noticed three men walk in from the outside lobby. He watched as they handed over their invitations at the door, suddenly feeling the need to end the conversation in which he'd been trapped for the past quarter hour. 'Mr. Dragovitch, I'm not a representative of the Russian government. I'm here tonight representing one of the banks which is participating in the Caspian pipeline project being celebrated this evening. Hopefully, in good time, it will meet the energy needs of Kazakhstan and Azerbaijan. And if in some small way I can assist our neighbours in their journey along the road to economic independence, then I'll welcome the opportunity to do so.' He made no attempt to conceal his sarcasm: to be insulted at such an event, to have his government criticised in such an open and disrespectful fashion, was beneath contempt. He smiled at the short, fat diplomat in front of him who spoke again, now angered even more by his thinly disguised dismissiveness.

'You and your friends in Moscow had better get accustomed to the new world order. We're no longer your slaves - we are free and independent nations'. His face was red with rage as he waved his short podgy finger in Damyanovitch's face. In the past, in the ordered and rigid USSR, he'd have been carted off by the secret police, ending his years somewhere in the gulag archipelago. Damyanovitch reached across and with a movement of his hand brushed away a petal of the carnation the angry man wore in his lapel buttonhole. The attaché was momentarily afraid, waiting for a blow to the head or some other act of violence by this significantly broader and taller embodiment of the old regime. Damyanovitch looked down into the frightened man's wide brown eyes and whispered malevolently in the language of the former oppressor; 'You, sir, have had too much to drink. I suggest you step outside to take some air then come back with a calmer temperament. This is supposed to be your country's night, a celebration of your acceptance into the world of the international moneymen. Let's not extinguish your newfound national pride too early, embarrassed by a drunk with a loose tongue'. He raised his hand again, this time ostensibly to straighten his opponent's cravat. The precise blow shattered the carnation, sending the remaining petals tumbling down the attaché's bursting tuxedo and onto the red carpet.

He looked around the room for the three men who'd earlier caught his attention: seeing them congregated around Paul Phineus, he made his way towards them. 'Paul, a pleasure to see you here tonight. Just fourteen hours to go before we finally taste the fruits of our endeavours.' Paul Phineus shook Damyanovitch's hand; for the past six months he'd worked closely with him in putting together the syndicate that was to issue, place and underwrite the Caspian bonds and had come to trust his technical competence. He was entirely unaware of Damyanovitch's past, his previous high rank in the KGB, and the violence and terror he'd witnessed and perpetrated in that role and, indeed, in the years since leaving it. 'Greetings, Petr. Welcome. Tonight will be the crowning glory of our efforts - a celebration of one of the biggest bond issues ever made in the Caspian energy sector. Here we have representatives from all the Azeri and Kazakh banks involved in the deal. We have diplomats from over a dozen Central Asian countries. What a gathering! I've been in this business for more years than I'd like to say, but putting together this deal with you has been one of my proudest achievements.' Damyanovitch smiled as he listened to the chairman, excited like a child in a sweetshop, then turned to Saul and offered his hand. Taking it, Saul smiled, and briefly it was as though only the two of them stood in the vast, lavish conference room. 'Saul, it's a pleasure to see my partner in crime again. But aren't you going to introduce me to your two guests?' His courteousness was impeccable: his interest in those with whom he came into contact, whether an ambassador at a glitzy event such as this or an illiterate taxi driver in the backstreets of Baku, always seemed genuine. Saul looked at him and reflected upon the contradiction; this was someone who'd threatened his life so very recently but now stood before him engaging in lighthearted conversation as if somehow they'd always been the best of friends. There was a dichotomy at the core of his soul: the ability to appreciate cultural things, to engage enthusiastically with complete strangers, sitting easily, almost naturally, with his ability to kill without hesitation, without a frisson of remorse. Fleetingly he wondered whether the Russian was in fact a true sociopath, or even, indeed, a psychopath.

'Petr Damyanovitch, Chairman of Moscow Alpha Bank, I'm pleased to introduce to you Mr. Adam Creed, solicitor with Druckerstein, Kahn and Nixdorf, the principal legal advisor to the Caspian pipeline deal'. The two shook hands. 'Adam, I've heard so much about you. Thanks for doing such excellent work on the project's legalities. The setting up of the special purpose vehicle was fundamental to the financing, and I know from my conversations with Paul that he was very impressed with the way you handled it. Your presentations in Astana and Baku helped overcome the concerns of a few key sceptics in this project, so we're also grateful for your persuasiveness'. Adam responded but the coldness in his eyes betrayed a wariness about the man he knew had made indirect threats to his life should the deal not proceed as planned. 'You're very kind Petr, but I was only providing a service my firm will be more than happy to charge substantial fees for. We lawyers are such a terrible breed – we're an organised conspiracy against business and the public alike'. Paul Phineus interjected: 'You're so right on that one, Adam. Your fees on this deal shook me to the core, and my board was none too happy either. But you get what you pay for, and the structure you've set up perfectly implements our strategy. So from that point of view, your charges are well-deserved'.

Adam continued; 'As for the sceptics, I'm sure you also played your part in removing them from the picture. I'm sure you're also a very persuasive man'. Damyanovitch stared at him, unsure as to how to respond. The alluding to the murders, obliquely and with enough delicacy and innocence so as not to draw Phineus's curiosity, vaguely irritated him. 'Yes Adam, I played my part, and I'm sure we'll continue working well with each other. From what little I know of you, hearsay of course from your friend here, I believe we have similar natures in many ways. We're both willing to make sacrifices when the need arises. Would that be a fair assessment?' Saul interjected, 'And now I'd like to introduce to you Thomas Stoneacre of Northern Engineering. The company was successful in bidding for a significant part of the construction work on the Caspian project, so it'll be him and his associates who'll actually be getting the whole damn' thing built'. Damyanovitch shook Thomas's hand. The innocence in his eyes instantly indicated they had very little in common. 'A pleasure to meet you, Thomas. I'm sure your involvement in the project will guarantee its success, and will be the start of even greater things for you and your company'. 'Pleased to meet you, Petr. I'm flattered by your confidence'. Thomas looked at Damyanovitch, fully aware of the threat he posed both to the project and to his own company and safety. But an innocent, almost naïve expression concealed his thoughts, and his anger at being drawn into a conspiracy in which the survival of his business was now at risk.

'Petr, I'm disappointed you're not accompanied tonight by Laura Simenova, your Head of Corporate Finance and Trading. We've struck up an excellent working relationship in recent months. I'd even say we have affection for each other if that's possible in this cynical world of ours.' Saul smiled innocently, and Damyanovitch's irritation was barely concealed. 'Laura's currently on secondment with the Saint Petersburg Stock Exchange, harmonising its rules with those of the European and North American exchanges'. He turned to Phineus; 'I hope Saul understands the risks of mixing work with pleasure; sometimes it can be quite dangerous for all concerned'. With mock seriousness he returned his gaze to Saul; 'I hope your intentions towards my most valued employee are honourable. Are they?' After hesitating Saul responded in kind; 'Being honourable is the last thing anyone could accuse me of. I'm sure Miss Simenova would see straight through me. She could spot an imposter, a dangerous man, a mile off, couldn't she?' Damyanovitch ignored the reply, returning his attention to Sheldons' chairman. 'Paul, I've come to London solely for this function but late tomorrow afternoon I leave for New York and I'll be there for the next few days. It's been a privilege working with you on this project and I hope to see you in Moscow soon'. Phineus returned the compliment, assuring Damyanovitch he'd make the journey in the very near future.

For a while, the small group of tuxedoed guests continued with friendly chatter before dividing to take their places at the dining tables according to the plan pinned to a board. Phineus and Damyanovitch moved to the front of the vast room where they'd been seated together by the event's organisers; Saul, Thomas and Adam made their way to a table towards the rear. Before the arrival of a small army of waiters Damyanovitch looked across the room at Saul and for several seconds they simply stared at each other, oblivious to the insignificant conversations proceeding around them. He smiled and then raising the long stemmed glass in front of him, he silently toasted his associate. Nobody around the table noticed the gesture and nobody, not even Thomas or Adam seated either side of him, saw the response. Saul smiled in return at the man whom he admired, hated, feared, and yet now felt he understood to a degree: he raised his glass and returned the toast.

While Saul and Thomas engaged in polite conversation with other guests, Adam sat in silence between the two, slowly rotating the last few drops of wine around his glass. Suddenly and with uncharacteristic spontaneity he pushed back his chair and headed for one of the exits at the side of the hall; he was mildly irritated by the small talk and more importantly, needed a cigarette. As he stepped out onto the veranda overlooking the hotel's immaculate lawns, the night air cooled his face, making him aware of the heat in the room he'd left behind. In the distance he caught sight of two men strolling off into the darkness, their destination a discreet and unused folly. He recognised one of them as a low ranking trade attaché from the Ukrainian embassy, the other a mid-ranking official from the British Department of Trade. They were laughing as they disappeared from view, their whispering borne on a breeze which appeared from nowhere and dissipated just as quickly. He continued watching as another man emerged from the shadow of a nearby colonnade then headed off in the same direction. His smart appearance, his perfect dinner jacket and purple cravat, ensured he didn't look out of place, blending into the background. And yet the miniature digital camera he withdrew from his pocket as he walked briskly away betrayed his true profession. The honey trap carefully laid weeks' earlier had been sprung; photographs taken through an inconspicuous opening into the folly would ensure that the Eton-then-Oxford educated civil servant, soon to be promoted to the Foreign Office, would be a guilt-ridden betrayer of his country for years to come. The spy disappeared from view: with the benefit of technology the incriminating images would reach his controller a few thousand miles away before the night was out. Adam looked on impassively from his vantage point on the veranda; he realised exactly what was unfolding but had no sympathy for the 'high flier', soon to become the victim of a sting. He could easily step over the low wall in front of him, breeze down the emerald green lawns, and break the sequence of events. The sound of a stranger would deter the young civil servant from continuing with his assignation but in another place, another time, he'd probably continue along his path to self-destruction. He tilted his head back, exhaling a luminous blue smoke ring that gently twisted and diffused as it ascended into the darkness. Gazing up into the star-pocked night sky he stared at the brilliant moon, momentarily entranced by its brightness, its stillness.

The drone of background chatter floated out from the open French windows. Suddenly the moon disappeared into the palm of a fist that folded about it; Adam turned, startled by the realisation he was no longer alone. Damyanovitch smiled to see his surprise, amused as Adam tried regaining his composure. 'How long have you been standing there? Shouldn't you be back in the hall, pressing the flesh?' They were alone and he felt in danger. Damyanovitch dropped his fist and ignored the accusatory question, gazing out across the lawns. 'So, you decided not to do anything - not to save that little moth from the spider's web? Does that make you a weak bystander or perhaps worse, a willing accomplice?' Adam gasped, shocked that his thoughts had been read so accurately by this stranger. 'I've never been a bystander so I guess I'll have to be hanged for the greater crime. I take it the game of entrapment playing out there in the dark is your work? I thought blackmail had gone out of fashion in your kind of circles in recent years.'

The Russian appreciated his directness. 'Twenty, thirty years ago yes, it would have been my work for the organisation which I served, body and soul. Life was simpler then. But now we pursue our goals through different, subtler methods. Sorry to disabuse you, but the clumsy though effective ensnarement has nothing to do with me. No, I'm afraid it's your friends from the other side of the Pond who set this one up. Washington loves leverage at the margins in trade negotiations and foreign policy forays when those *dreadful* Europeans just won't come around to its way of thinking. A British civil servant in a strategic post who is susceptible to gentle, irresistible pressure at the right time will be worth his weight in gold. Nothing beats blackmail for concentrating the mind. And what better than the fear of being found out?'

Adam shivered as he contemplated the ease with which individuals like this hapless civil servant could be manipulated and then destroyed.

'Mr. Damyanovitch… is it true you threatened Saul that if he inter-feres with your plans, whatever they may be, you'd kill me? Tomorrow the Caspian bond issue is launched - does this success mean the threat of execution no longer hangs over my head?' Damyanovitch gave his reply with simple certainty; 'Tomorrow's launch is only the beginning; it's not an end in itself, as you well know. Anybody who gets in the way, anybody who interferes in the course of events, will be removed. If my words appear brutal I don't apologise. I cannot. Your life and those of your friends will remain perfectly safe provided none of you stray into matters which do not concern you. Do you understand?' Adam was stunned by his coldness, the absence of emotion in his eyes. Before him stood a man unconstrained by the normal boundaries of human behaviour or morality, willing to kill again and again if the goals he pursued so selflessly were threatened. He nodded his head, too intimidated to speak. 'That's good. Now, recently your friend Saul's become quite mercurial. It seems the prospect of wealth beyond his dreams is no longer sufficient to focus his thoughts, but since his role will soon come to an end, this isn't a problem. He's done all I asked, and I'll honour my side of our bargain. Soon he'll make way for another, someone who'll change the world, who'll help break its order. You are that person'.

Adam stared at him in disbelief. 'Do you think we're all just fools for you to manipulate? I've no desire to change the world - to 'break its order' as you put it.' As the words tumbled from his mouth the iconoclast within him stirred: fleetingly, he recognised his own hypocrisy. Damyanovitch knew the protestation was disingenuous. 'You'll not be asked to do anything. You'll not be asked to put yourself in any compro-mising position or any situation where your life would be at risk'. Adam found himself listening intently: his initial hostility was beginning to dissipate. 'Quarter of an hour ago you took a decision that could change the course of history; you could have intervened to save a little man from blackmail and yet you chose to do nothing. To look the other way whilst others got on with the job they came here to do. That in itself was decid-ing on a course of action'. Suddenly a single muted chime from Adam's inner pocket diverted his attention; he reached inside for his mobile, intrigued as to who could be sending a text at such a late hour. 'Excuse me Petr, but when it comes to clients I'm always at their beck and call'.

Damyanovitch smiled, amused by his own instinctive curiosity. Adam turned away and opened the text message from Curacao.

Instrctns recvd from BlueSeaHoldgs. US$Three and a hlf bn to be used to buy Casp bonds tomrw. I luv u, damn u!

Adam made no attempt to conceal his pleasure at hearing from his former lover, his distraction briefly unsettling the Russian. He closed the mobile; 'Nothing important, just a client at a loose end'. Damyanovitch knew he was lying, but continued. 'There'll come a time, Adam, soon, when you'll have the opportunity to influence the future of nations. A single event will present itself - you'll recognise it when it does. When it arrives, I simply ask that you play your part, and look away while others achieve their goals. The same sum as that payable to your friend will also be transferred to your nominated account, anywhere in the world. Like him you'll never have to work again. And you'll keep your life'. Spoken by anyone else in the world this final 'inducement' would have resembled the thuggish threat of an uneducated dockyard labourer, but from Damyanovitch it was a simple statement of fact. 'You presume a lot about me, Petr. Perhaps I'm not as superficial as you seem to think.'

The two men who'd passed before them earlier came back into view. The civil servant was straightening his tie, whispering to the young East European who laughed at their shared secret. They greeted the watchers on the veranda, the young high flier blissfully oblivious of the dark world soon to engulf him. Damyanovitch waited until the two had disappeared before articulating thoughts passing through Adam's head; 'A moment's pleasure, a lifetime's regret. And you did nothing'. He tutted in mock disapproval. 'I know you very well, Adam. I know how you betrayed your profession. I know about the Coughlin trial. I know about your betrayal of a friend's trust. To entice away a lover and then watch the destruction of their plans for a lifetime's happiness; well, you must have a cold heart indeed. And why did you do these things? To test to breaking point the values of the system your profession props up out of self-interest rather than the morality it professes to uphold. To challenge the resolve of those who cheat and lie to themselves to believe love exists when in truth it never did'. The harshness of his words and their soullessness overwhelmed Adam, reeling at the extent to which his accuser understood his inner darkness. 'Your friend disclosed these secrets to me as part of an earlier bargain. In return for pulling you out from the pit of despair into which you'd fallen. Yes, I engineered your present employment with Druckerstein's. I demanded to be told everything. Your friend's commitment to you is absolute; it's a weakness that was just waiting to be exploited. Disclosure was the price he was willing to pay to save you'. Damyanovitch's tone softened as he continued pursuit of his quarry.

'When the time comes, you'll know what to do. It's a law of nature that some people are destined to break down the order of things, and others to build on the ruins left behind. Don't be afraid of your strengths. Follow your instincts. Now, it's time to go. Shall we?' He gestured towards the open French windows.

Chapter Fifty Nine

The pre-launch celebration over, Adam, Saul and Thomas left for a taxi waiting outside the hotel. As the taxi weaved its way through the night, the conversation was of trivial things, a vague paranoia dampening any enthusiasm the three might have had to discuss private matters in public places, even in the rear of a London cab. Eventually they pulled up outside the modern steel and glass exterior of Sheldons Bank; after paying the driver his fare and tip the three headed inside, into the chairman's inner sanctum. Saul was confident that Phineus wouldn't be returning that night and besides, it was the only room in the building where alcohol was kept. For the next hour they sat around the conference table discussing possible strategies. Adam's disclosure of the information texted from Curacao earlier that evening didn't surprise Saul. He knew from Adam's discoveries on his earlier trip to the Caribbean that a vast pool of capital had been accumulated offshore, but now he was certain of its intended purpose. He also knew that after the Caspian bonds had been bought the next morning, Moscow Alpha would become truly insolvent, its capital base 'magicked away', soon to be converted into assets owned by Blue Sea Holdings which would be difficult to trace. The only remaining imponderable was how Damyanovitch and his associates were planning to drive up the oil price and, with it, the futures market into a sustained panic, triggering their right to seize the Caspian seabed rights.

Thomas watched as the other two discussed, agreed and disagreed, about the true nature of the structure they'd put in place for the Caspian deal. Eventually he interrupted, driven to near distraction by the debate. 'So guys, I'd love to sit here all night listening to you arguing over the details of the deal you've put together, but it'd be better if we could find a way out of this mess. As I see it, the battleground's the oil price - when it rises above the trigger level he's home and dry. But we just don't know how he's going to panic the markets to set everything off in the first place. And none of the syndicate's members, including Sheldons, has sufficient capital to stabilise the oil price if there is a panic. Is this a fair summary of where we're at?' There was a pause as Saul and Adam considered his unexpected interruption; 'Yes, you've got it about right'. Saul's response, short and monotone, conveyed his sudden realisation of the hopelessness of their position. 'Then it looks as if he's going to win, thanks to both of you. And when he and his associates take over the Caspian oilfields, perfectly legally, and all the local banks involved in the deal have collapsed, the economic chaos is going to be quite something. Is this the end game?' Saul folded his arms and pressed his face into them; 'I think we're very close to that'.

Adam idly looked up at a portrait of Nick Leeson, kept in a prominent position at Paul Phineus's insistence. Here was the man who 'broke the bank' of Barings, providing a permanent warning of the effects of unhedged risk to the highly conservative, prudent chairman. 'Remind us, Saul, about how Leeson destroyed Barings Bank. I'm unfamiliar with the detail'. Saul looked up, distracted by what appeared an irrelevant question. 'Well, Leeson's trading strategy was flawed because he didn't hedge his positions. The problem with derivatives, for example futures and options whose value fluctuates in line with currencies, interest rates or commodities, is that enormous profits can be equally matched by sometimes unlimited losses. In a nutshell Leeson was 'long' - he'd bought futures contracts expecting them to increase in value in a market that instead went on to fall sharply. He miscalculated, and when an earthquake hit Japan in 1995 the Nikkei went into freefall. So, the value of what he was holding collapsed as well. You see, he was trading contracts whose value depended on the future direction of the index. He just got it wrong'. Adam paused before asking the question which had already occurred to Thomas. 'So, how did he get away with it, this disastrous trading strategy? Wasn't he supervised properly?' 'Well, that's the crux of the whole thing. Leeson got away with it because he controlled both the front and back office. This meant that not only was he in charge of daily trading but he also controlled the paperwork for each transaction. When he knew things were getting out of control on the trading side, and that he was making unrealised losses which were piling up by the day, he fabricated the paperwork because he also controlled the administrative side of the business. He also had the benefit of control of the notorious 'five eights' account, originally set up as a very short term errors account. He hid unrealised trading losses there because he controlled the Barings Singapore back office. His deception led the bank into believing the enormous losses were being built up by a client, when in actual fact they were being made by the bank itself, the real owner of the trades parked in the five eights account. Leeson ended up in prison in Singapore, as you might remember, but some say he was foolish rather than dishonest, and he's out again now. Basically, a lack of supervision and hopeless internal reporting systems allowed him to do the damage in the first place'.

Thomas listened closely to Saul's account of the Barings failure; now he wondered if there was anything they could learn from it to overcome their present difficulties. 'If the syndicate can meet its payment obligations following an oil price rise, then presumably Damyanovitch won't be able to take control of the Caspian seabed rights. Is there any way you could get Paul Phineus to hedge Sheldons' risk of oil price rises with an offsetting position in the futures market?' Saul hesitated whilst he considered Thomas's suggestion. 'He'd never buy it. As far as he's concerned the chance of the oil price jumping above the trigger level is almost non-existent. The cost of hedging against the risk would be an unjustified expense, and an unnecessary insurance. When, and not if, the oil price goes through the ceiling, Sheldons will be completely unprotected; the bank will be destroyed as sure as Barings was'.

A heavy despondency filled the room, but it was Thomas who eventually broke the gloom, unconcerned about the usefulness or otherwise of his suggestion. 'So if Sheldons isn't going to help, then what are the chances of Moscow Alpha surviving? We know from Adam's Curacao contact that technically the bank's already insolvent, but it has to have some residual working capital just to meet short term day-to-day costs. If Moscow Alpha survives and meets the syndicate's commitments then he and his associates can't seize the Caspian seabed rights. Saul, do you have any contacts in the bank's front or back office who'd be willing to help us?' Saul's face turned deathly pale: Thomas's question stunned him into realising what should have been obvious all along. 'Unfortunately I do. Yes, I have a contact at Moscow Alpha, and I know who controls both their front and back offices. It's the same person'. Saying nothing further, he left.

Chapter Sixty

Adam looked through the glass portal into a brightly lit, sparsely furnished room. In the centre he could see a man kneeling, his forehead pressed to the ground. He could hear no sound. 'Sorry to keep you waiting sir, but you know how it is with human rights these days.' Adam didn't reply, irritated that the short fat guard should presume he shared his prejudices. He peered again through the glass; wire mesh obscured his view, so he squinted and brought his face closer. As condensation began clouding the glass he wiped away the droplets with his suit sleeve, gently tapping it in the process. The occupant looked up, apparently disturbed from concentration by the barely perceptible smudging sound. With a quick movement he stood to his full height; rising from the black rectangular mat he turned towards the door and smiled. The guard spoke again; 'Okay Mr. Creed, you can go in now. I'll be out here if you need me'. Adam turned the handle and entered. 'Mr. Creed, you are most welcome. I hope I've not kept you waiting long. If I have, please accept my apologies'. The client proffered his hand and Adam shook it. 'Mr. Fadlalah, it's a pleasure to meet you, and I apologise too if I disturbed your prayers'.

Contrary to his vague preconceptions, Adam's client was a well-groomed, handsome man, dark-skinned, with a closely-cropped black beard and piercing brown eyes. Although about the same height as him, he was evidently physically more robust, stronger, than his legal advisor. His demeanour and tone of voice were delicate, understated, but sufficiently forceful to intimate an underlying spiritual steeliness.

'So we open our first meeting with apologies on both sides, Adam. May I call you Adam? But such superficial equality is misleading, wouldn't you agree? After all, I'm nothing more than a humble prisoner. But bricks and bars hold only the body, not the soul, and with your intercession I trust that both shall be free soon enough'. He laughed, his self-deprecation deliberately intended to place the young lawyer at ease. 'Please, shall we sit and talk?' He gestured towards two basic metal-frame chairs. As he looked at the young lawyer he recalled his previous meeting a few weeks earlier with the significantly more hardened, more ideologically recognisable managing partner at Druckerstein, Kahn, and Nixdorf, Carter Buckmaster. The older man, his face puce with fear or embarrassment (or both) had paced anxiously around the room, constantly peering through the glass portal to confirm the whereabouts of the indolent security guard tasked with overseeing meetings between lawyers and 'high risk' prisoners. Using the mobile smuggled in by the lawyer, he'd put through a call to his acolyte in Istanbul. The order had been a simple one: the Texan industrialist attending a conference at the specified hotel, his identity carefully described, was to be executed without delay. Of course Buckmaster hadn't understood the conversation, but he knew its general purpose. Fadlalah knew there was another agenda quite different to his own which was driving the American oilmen and financiers to contact him for his help, but ultimately he couldn't care less about it. If the price of sweeping away a corrupt monarchy and driving out the Infidel from the Holy Places was the signing of a few preferential oil supply agreements, then this was a price he was willing to pay. When he'd subtly raised the possibility of an alternative agenda near the close of their previous meeting, minutes after ordering the death of the American in Istanbul, he'd been scornfully reproached by the lawyer; 'You, Mr. Fadlalah, are simply a cog, a very small part of a machine much greater than yourself'. He'd replied quietly; 'Yes sir, but remember, great wheels depend upon the smallest of cogs if they are to turn'.

'Hassan, as you know, you're being held here in Belmarsh under the provisions of United Kingdom anti-terrorist laws which allow imprisonment without trial where the Home Secretary deems this necessary for public safety. You were previously offered deportation to Saudi Arabia but you refused this, your reason being that you were afraid you would be detained upon arrival and face probable torture and execution. The reason you've not been afforded a proper trial is because the Home Office has evidence against you that it would not wish to enter the public domain. This may be telephone intercepts, evidence of informants or spies, or witnesses whose cross-examination in open court could put the lives of intelligence officers in the field at risk'. Fadlalah looked at Adam impassively and then interjected; 'So I've been deprived of my right to a fair trial on the say-so of a politician. Are you saying that human rights are not absolute, that some people are less deserving of them than others?' Adam smiled at the client's feigned innocence. 'No, Hassan, human rights are not absolute and never have been. You and people like you depend upon flaws in the legal process that allow you to be at liberty. I've seen the evidence against you and it's overwhelming. But on the basis of a higher religious law I'm sure you could put forward an arguable defence. Mine is man-made law, and I have no doubt that you would argue yours to be spiritual and of greater validity. But we're not here today to debate the difference. May I continue?'

Fadlalah was surprised by Adam's directness: he was accustomed to lawyers and bureaucrats keeping their opinions unspoken, but here was someone willing without hesitation to dispense with the customary hypocrisy. 'I respect your candour, Adam, and your willingness to speak your mind. Here I have no problem with it, just between you and I, but if you speak in the same terms elsewhere there'll be consequences'. He gently moved his forefinger from side to side in an unmistakable gesture of warning. Adam continued in his detached lawyerly tone, but felt threatened. 'Your right of appeal lies to the Special Immigration Appeals Commission: we'll need to use a recognised advocate, but this won't be a problem. I've come here today at the request of my managing partner Carter Buckmaster. I know you've already met him. We need to go over the evidence against you, or, at least, that which you think may still remain after the assassination of the Home Office's principal witness. But I think you know about this too, don't you?' The Arab considered feigning ignorance but, realising that this would invite further rebuke, thought better of it. 'Yes, I know about General Yahyah's death. He was a liar and a traitor, an apostate; his execution was a cause of great celebration. He was prepared to betray his faith and serve a corrupt monarchy, a puppet regime, and because of that, he died'. He made no attempt to conceal his loathing for the General and his triumphant, righteous demeanour unambiguously signaled his pride and complicity in the killing. At an earlier meeting he'd explained to Buckmaster the danger posed to their plan by the corrupt General, but as to the identity of whoever pulled the trigger, shooting the dog in a London street as the decadent glitterati passed by, he had no knowledge. The assassin, whoever he was, was a man with a talent: someone who had, by his action, laid up riches in the next life.

Adam ignored the outburst. 'Your case will be dealt with in three week's time. As far as I'm aware the entire case against you rested upon General Yahyah's testimony, and with him dead his evidence cannot be properly questioned, although of course there's still his written testimony against you. But in a case like this I'm confident the Tribunal will conclude that this isn't enough on its own, not without corroborating evidence at any rate. So, is there anything else I need to know about?' Fadlalah looked at him, wary of making further unprompted, personal remarks. 'There is no other evidence. There may be statements extracted under torture from my brothers back in the Kingdom, but I don't think any fair tribunal in your country would let the Home Office use these. People have a habit of confessing to anything, condemning anyone, if they're hung upside down and beaten for long enough, don't you agree?' He smiled but as he spoke his own torture scars, both mental and physical, ached. In the late 1990s he had been detained for six months in Ha'ir prison at the 'pleasure' of the al-Mabahith, the Saudi secret police. Before being released without charge, he had endured weeks of relentless interrogation at the hands of sadists; although his body had been broken, his faith had remained steadfast.

'You're right, of course. Evidence obtained under torture is regarded as unreliable here, and for this reason the Tribunal's likely to order your release. If that's the outcome of the hearing, then I presume you'll want to stay in the UK? If you return to Saudi Arabia it's unlikely you'll be greeted with open arms. Wouldn't they imprison you again?' Fadlalah smiled sardonically, reassured by the lawyer's obvious total ignorance of the plan in which he was to play such an important part. 'I've no intention of remaining in the UK, my friend. I'll be returning to my own country as soon as the time's right'. Adam was taken aback by his reply; reaching into his pocket, he took out a packet of cigarettes and after offering one to his client, which was refused, he lit up. 'And when will the time be right? If you're going to stay here for any length of time we'll need to make arrangements for your accommodation. You'll not be free to come and go as you please - you're simply too dangerous for that. Of course, any attempt by the Saudi authorities to extradite you would be unsuccessful, for obvious reasons, so that should give you some peace of mind'.

Fadlalah hesitated before replying. 'I'll return soon enough, but I'm unable to give a precise date. We must in any case wait until the Tribunal's made its decision. So if there's nothing further to discuss we should say goodbye for now. Thank you for your directness.' Adam smiled, mildly irritated that the client had deliberately withheld crucial information throughout the meeting. As the lawyer headed towards the door the client spoke, quietly; 'Tell me Adam, is there anything you believe in? Do you have any faith? Or are you really as empty of principles as you'd like people to think?' Adam turned and smiled: this was a personal intrusion which suggested his own curiosity was reciprocated and was therefore equally capable of frustration. 'What do I believe in? That man steers his own destiny. That history is like a coral comprising billions of small actions of little people forced to act in unexpected situations. That all human actions and reactions are essentially unpredictable, that nothing is pre-ordained. Does this answer your question?' Fadlalah walked to his prayer mat, picked it up and started to roll it, neatly and tightly. 'It does, thank you. We are each other's antithesis. In my world you would be condemned as a blasphemer. In so-called modern Saudi Arabia your words would warrant forty lashes in the public square, and I doubt it would stop there. I wonder which of us is right?' Adam paused, unwilling to be interrogated further; he'd rebuff the client's attempts to engage him in debate intended to turn a questioning finger at himself. 'I'll be in touch again when I know the outcome of the Tribunal's deliberations. Try to keep out of trouble until then'. His final words, spoken in humour, were misjudged and perceived instead as advice to a common criminal. He left the small airless room; within minutes his client had returned to his sparse cell, to wait like a genie in a bottle.

Almost as soon as Adam was back in his office, Carter Buckmaster strode in. For the past half hour he'd been in his room with the door locked, tracing with his finger faces on a photograph which was kept shut away in a drawer in his desk when colleagues or clients were present. In desperate grief, he had, as he often did, silently mouthed the names of his two children: missionaries blown out of the skies five years earlier. Today was the anniversary of their pointless deaths. 'So, Adam, you saw our client, Mr. Fadlalah, this morning. Did the bastard have anything new to say? Is there any outstanding evidence he knows of that the Home Office will use when the case goes before the Tribunal?' Adam was startled: he'd not heard the senior partner swear before, nor had he seen such loathing in his eyes. 'No, Carter, there's no other evidence so we'll probably have our way at the Tribunal. I'd say he'll walk free in three weeks' time. Do you mind if I ask a personal question? Why the hostility towards him? I neither like nor trust him but at the end of the day he's just another client.' Buckmaster stepped closer, looking down at Adam as he reclined in his chair.

'People like Fadlalah rot the souls of anyone with whom they come into contact. I despise him and the wickedness of his interpretation of the magnificent faith he professes to serve. My soul weeps that we should take on such a monster as a client'. His southern drawl was pronounced, heightened with emotion. 'But Carter, if you feel such antipathy towards him, why did you agree for the firm to take him on in the first place? It'd be difficult, but I could still find a way for us to drop him even this late in the engagement'. The tension in Buckmaster's voice lessened: he'd vented his personal feelings in front of a colleague and already regretted it. 'No, Adam, that'll not be necessary. He's just a means to an end, a way of achieving a greater purpose. Sometimes we have to work with baser tools to create a better world. We will continue working for Fadlalah, as we should. My personal feelings are irrelevant'. Adam continued. 'He says that after he's released he's going to return to Saudi Arabia. I just can't understand this. The government there will order his arrest as soon as the plane touches down. Am I missing something here?' Buckmaster stared at him and for a few seconds said nothing. 'He'll go back as soon after his release as we deem practicable'. He spoke with absolute certainty. 'And as for the Saudi government ordering his arrest, perhaps you're making an assumption which shouldn't be made'. Adam leaned forward, experiencing the unique sensation of the lawyer whose cross-examination of a witness is about to yield crucial evidence or even better, a confession. The elderly lawyer drew back, suddenly aware of the mild, silk-gloved interrogation. 'Just make the arrangements with the special advocate. Under no circumstance is any application to be made to bring forward the hearing. Do you understand?' Adam nodded: his attempt at eliciting further information had failed. Buckmaster returned to his room and within five minutes had sent e-mails to Lincoln Davies in New York and Petr Damyanovitch in Moscow. Now they had a definite date for Fadlalah's return.

Within an hour of reading Buckmaster's e-mail Lincoln Davies made a dozen calls to numbers previously supplied by Fadlalah. All were to mobiles whose owners were in the oil-rich cities of the Eastern Province of Saudi Arabia. For those recipients driven by financial as opposed to fanatical considerations, Davies gave assurances that the usual bank transfers would reach their offshore accounts before the week was out. He sat back and gazed out over the Manhattan skyline: the calls had, of necessity, been short, but there'd been so many to make and now his throat was dry. Co-ordination of murder and mayhem across such a wide geographical area had been quite demanding upon the cultured voice of the pillar of the New York financial establishment. He sipped a lemon tea and waited for the night. Hours later the attacks started. The first wave struck in Dammam, Dhahran, and the centre for commerce in the region, the seaport of Al-Khobar. The second wave followed an hour later, hitting Jubail and the home of the largest oil and gas plants in the Kingdom, Abqaiq. The King Fahd Causeway was later rocked by a series of explosions, catching many expatriates and young Saudis heading across the link for the nightclubs and wine bars of the Kingdom's more liberal neighbour, Bahrain. Fatalities across the region were in the low hundreds, injuries considerably higher. Damage to the region's pipeline infrastructure had been visible but largely superficial.

Contingency plans made by the Saudi state authorities during recent years clicked into place, and within hours oil output, pumping and transportation had returned to pre-attack levels. The speed with which production had been restored impressed the international oil markets, the attacks widely described as tick-bites on an elephant. But markets are seldom driven by economics alone; as research departments in the leading international banks assessed the political implications, the picture became more opaque. The unanimous opinion was that the government in Riyadh was experiencing a challenge to its authority which could persist, and in time prove a catalyst for more fundamental change. The Kingdom's problems were seen as deep-seated: a disaffected male youth angered by unemployment and declining living standards, a hostile and conspiratorial religious hierarchy, and a royal elite comprising thousands of princes covertly plotting for their own selfish agendas. But these realities were survivable: all were factions at odds with each other, and none were deemed strong enough to seize control of the levers of power. No figurehead had yet emerged around which all the forces of opposition could coalesce.

Lincoln Davies stared until his eyes grew sore at the ever-changing indices on his Bloomberg screen. The New York Mercantile Exchange was showing 'minor alarm' at news from the Middle East; short term futures prices wobbled slightly but showed none of the signs of the nervous breakdown, the erratic volatility, that followed the Iraqi invasion of Kuwait in 1991. But it was not the short-term indicators which preoccupied him: instead he watched closely the longer-term futures contracts, straws in the wind evidencing wider fears over instability in world oil supplies. He smiled as prices crept slowly but surely upwards. Soon their associate, detained in a London prison for now, would be free; upon his return to the Kingdom he'd seize power, wreaking chaos in the markets as hedgers and speculators flooded in to the longer term NYMEX contracts to fix their costs. And then the trigger mechanism in the Caspian bonds would be activated, shattering banks and with them the governments who had supped with the Devil in this deal. He switched off his computer: everything was going to plan.

Chapter Sixty One

Saul stood in the brilliant sunlight, blinking up at the huge rostral column towering in front of him. At the column's summit he could make out the still functional gas torch, previously used when the column and its partner nearby were deployed as lighthouses for the original harbour. The mock Grecian temple behind the column stood proudly in the midday sun, its gleaming façade witness to rediscovered confidence and wealth in the old imperial capital, St. Petersburg. He walked past the column and made his way for the cool shade cast by the ornate building; as he gazed up at the statue of Neptune across the upper part of the building's frontage, he looked again at the vast expanse of water behind him. This was a city with a history steeped in maritime commerce, the symbols of its former life emblazoned across its architecture. He watched the crowds moving in and out of the building: mostly young men of his age, mobile phones pressed to ears, exuding youthful vitality. Reaching the shade, he concealed himself behind one of the plain white columns; there he would wait, gazing out across the water.

And then she appeared, emerging from the shade of the building's grand entrance, blinking as she passed out into strong sunlight. He smiled as he watched her walk briskly between the columns, a small leather attaché case in one hand and a large red file in the other. Oblivious to the presence of the tall stranger standing just outside her field of vision, she walked briskly towards a row of cars parked haphazardly nearby. He recognised the familiar yellow vehicle: if he didn't move quickly he was going to miss her, defeating the purpose of the previous day's travel. He placed his thumb and forefinger to his lips and produced a loud wolf-whistle. She stopped and turned abruptly, annoyed. On seeing Saul emerge into full view she ran to him, holding him in a display of affection rarely seen at the Stock Exchange. She stepped back after realising there were witnesses to this emotional outburst, some of whom she'd been working with for the past few weeks. She looked around, blushing with embarrassment as a small group of young traders clapped and laughed. She turned away from them and kissed him again.

'What are you doing here? You should have let me know you were coming. I've missed you'. He smiled as he looked into her excited eyes; 'I've missed you too. It was a last minute decision and as far as Paul Phineus is concerned, I'm here to "explore lending opportunities to the St. Petersburg city authority". But, of course, it was really to see you that I've made the trip. Everything else is just an excuse. Now kiss me again, and take me somewhere I haven't been before'. She laughed and did as instructed. 'What do you think of our Exchange? I've been here for a week and love it. They've got a fully-fledged derivatives trading floor and the stocks of the majors are also traded. If I were asked to set up a representative office for Moscow Alpha here I wouldn't refuse. Perhaps I'll suggest it to Petr. What do you think?' Saul hesitated: the mention of the name of the man who was intent on destroying not just Moscow Alpha and Sheldons, but also sparking an economic crisis across the region, made him shiver. 'I'm sure Petr would give your suggestion the consideration it deserves. Now, shall we go?'

Later, as they strolled through the thoroughfares of the Alexander Garden, Saul's remoteness and distraction became more apparent. She knew he wanted to talk but was reluctant to press him: he'd speak when he was ready. As they paused to admire the work of a street artist, she lifted his hand and kissed it; 'Saul, we've been walking for half an hour but your mind's a million miles away. I know you want to tell me something and I'm happy to wait. But wouldn't it be easier if you tell me now?' They continued walking. 'Tell me Laura, how well do you think you know me?' It was an unexpected question. 'I think I know you well enough, Saul: certainly intimately'. He smiled at her directness. 'No, Laura, I'm not talking about that. Could there be any secrets you don't know about, or do I appear open and straightforward? Which is it?' She was becoming unsettled. 'Few people are completely transparent. We all have our private places - things we'd rather not disclose. That's human nature. What's on your mind?' He hesitated; 'If I told you that last year I watched a work colleague - almost a friend but not quite - being thrown to his death from a balcony after being drugged so he wouldn't put up a struggle, and then I said nothing to anybody, not even the police, what would you say?' She stopped and stared at him, shocked by what he'd said; he continued looking ahead. 'I'd have to know why you did nothing. Why you didn't intervene to save him. Why you didn't report it to the police. You're not telling me enough to decide either way'. 'I didn't do anything because I was so stunned to witness something so unexpected, so totally out of character with what I knew of the killer. I was also terrified. And why didn't I say anything later? Because I had a financial interest in the situation and I didn't want to put it at risk, and because I was, and still am, scared'.

His confession shocked her. He continued, but there was no emotion in his voice. 'Let me take you somewhere else. I'm sitting in the back of a car. There are three other passengers, including the driver. The passenger alongside me takes hold of the man in front of him, pulls him back and cuts his throat. He bleeds to death in seconds. I see it all. I'm spattered with the dead man's blood. I do nothing. Later, I keep silent. Am I as guilty as the murderer, even though I didn't take part in the killing or have any idea beforehand about what was going to happen?' They could hear music nearby as they approached an impromptu small-band jazz concert, common in the parks and gardens around St. Petersburg. 'If what you say is true then you're not an innocent party. Your sin is passive rather than active. But you must bear some of the guilt'. He looked at her, his face ashen. 'And does this make you think any less of me?' She looked away as she answered. 'I don't know what to say or think. My feelings for you haven't changed, although they may do, but my thoughts have. My brain tells me what you've done was wrong and I should condemn you for it. But my heart doesn't change so easily. I know you well and in spite of what you've told me, I'm certain you're a good person, even if maybe you are weaker, more naïve, more foolish than I would have guessed. Knowing you've done wrong is half the journey- not even acknowledging it is the real sin. You'll just have to give me time'.

They arrived at the source of the music: four elderly men played on trumpets, a double bass, and a miniature drum kit while a large, middle aged blousy woman sang out with gravel voice, in true American Deep South style. The music was rhythmic and captivating. A large group of young people had gathered; some were dancing, others tapping feet, all were immersed in the atmosphere. The older bystanders looked on with pleasure, relishing the freedom now which had been denied to them in the Soviet years. Saul and Laura stood and watched the band, their impassive expressions in stark contrast to the smiles on faces about them as others laughed, sang and clapped in the hot afternoon sun.

Saul felt his heart beat faster: he knew he'd shocked her with his confession but the worst of what he'd come to say, the terrible truth he'd traveled thousands of miles to tell her, was still held back. He knew that to utter the handful of words would risk destroying their relationship, which was perhaps already damaged. But, to pull back now would be an act of cowardice: he had to continue, and suffer the consequences. He moved closer to her: he'd have to raise his voice to be heard above the cacophony and raucous, earthy crooning of the hearty singer. 'You've not asked me the question, Laura. The most important question. Do you want to ask it?' She turned to him, frightened but without knowing why. 'Who were the killers?' He grabbed both her arms and held them tightly. 'It was one person, Laura. One person killed them both. It was Petr'. She stared at him in horror, trying to comprehend the awfulness of what had been said. She started to struggle, desperately pulling her arms from his tight grip. 'You're lying. Without him I wouldn't be alive today. Why are you lying to me?' She screamed her accusatory words in anger and fear: she hated him for what he'd said but also knew deep in her innermost being that he was probably telling the truth. Even as her words burst forth she knew they were said more in irrational denial than from any certainty that the messenger was wrong, or lying.

Realising that the crowd had switched its attention away from the band, now concerned for the distressed young woman's safety, Saul released her. Two of the band's members were now playing out of tune as they tried catching fragments of the argument taking place before their eyes. As Laura escaped, running off along the path, Saul smiled at the audience; 'Lovers' row. Sorry'. Nobody understood his words. He followed after her, first at a brisk walk but then at a run. Eventually he caught up with her, catching her again by the arm, but this time gently. 'I'm sorry, Laura, so sorry. I know how much he means to you. You asked me why, so I'll tell you. He's a cold-blooded killer for the highest of principles but the basest of reasoning. He's a nationalist, pure and simple. He puts this country at the core of his soul and above all other considerations. Anything that puts its future at risk has to be destroyed. He thinks in absolute terms, in black and white, right and wrong. And once you have such a mindset, you can justify anything to yourself, including murder many times over'.

She looked at him, now more in confusion than anger. In too many of his words she recognised personality traits of the man she'd relied on and trusted and who'd cared for her for nearly her entire life. Eventually she responded but this time in a measured, considered tone. 'I know he cares for his country; he always has done. But why would he kill anybody? How did they pose such a threat to drive him to do such things? I don't understand. I need more than words - I need *proof* of what you say. And even if it's true, what would you have me do about it?' The wildness of her initial reaction had subsided: Saul knew she was receptive to an explanation, even if that was one she'd never accept at face value. 'The killings are linked to the Caspian deal. Petr and his associates - I have no idea who they are - aim to destroy all the banks involved in the syndicate, smash the special purpose vehicle at the heart of the financing, and seize control of the Caspian seabed rights. Once this is done the economies of Azerbaijan and Kazakhstan will falter, particularly when their major banks fail and their national assets fall into foreigners' hands. Russia will 'rescue' them, probably at the request of newly installed puppet governments, restoring her power in the region. So it's not just about oil. It's also about resuming colonial control over ruined neighbours'.

Laura had been involved with the Caspian project from the very beginning, taking instructions from Damyanovitch and liaising with syndicate members and the lawyers in London: she immediately followed the logic of Saul's explanation. He continued. 'You ask for proof and it's right you should do so. To break the SPV it's crucial that the banks in the syndicate collapse first. Moscow Alpha is already insolvent because its entire capital base has been siphoned off by Petr to a Curacao-based shell company. Just a small crisis and the bank will fail. I'm sure you'll know how to check this out for yourself'. Laura was shaking; if what he said was true, a deception of enormous proportions had been perpetrated on the bank's employees, and of course on herself, by her adoptive father, the very person responsible for safeguarding their futures and livelihoods. 'As for those he has killed, I can't lead you by the hand to bodies in shallow graves. I can't show you a blood-stained knife in a desk drawer; this would be too simple, too incautious on his part. No, I'm afraid you'll have to ask him, if my words alone are not enough. He's a pitiless killer, but he's never lied to me. The more I've spent time in his company, the more I've realised he's a deadly paradox –a complex, principled man who's willing to go to any lengths, and to commit any atrocity, to have his way, to fix a new world order as he wishes it to be'.

They continued past ornate fountains and gilded statues which echoed the Romanovs and the pre-Revolution wealth of the old Russian aristocracy. She spoke again, without turning to him as they walked. 'If all you say is true, you must have some thoughts as to what we.. I.. should do about it. Perhaps there is nothing to be done, and we should let fate take its course'. Her mental faculties were sharp, demanding and precise: when problems were presented to her she wanted solutions, and not just explanations of causes. 'Laura, you're in charge of both the front and back office at Moscow Alpha. I want you to set up dozens of fake accounts. You'll put in place a risk management strategy so that when the crisis he's looking to create kicks off, the bank will have a fully protected position. And because the strategy will be run on behalf of the bank through bogus non-existent clients, he won't be able to shut it down easily. He won't know the genuine clients from the fake ones. Hopefully you've enough working capital left to do this, and your control of the back office certainly allows you to create huge numbers of fake paper trails'.

She stopped walking and turned to him; 'So you're suggesting that I betray his trust. That I break Russian securities laws and use the bank's working capital on behalf of clients who simply don't exist. I understand the strategy. It's the deception and illegality that makes me wonder if you've ever known me at all. I need time to think and make my own enquiries back at the bank. As for us, I hope you realise that this might change things, Saul. My heart tells me we might still have a future but my head's not so sure. I need to be away from you for a while. Please, don't try to get in touch. I'll contact you when I'm ready'. They arrived in silence back at the bright yellow car parked a short distance from the park. As she opened the door he kissed her again, but this time she didn't reciprocate. As the car gently pulled away she didn't look back, leaving Saul to make his own way to his hotel. He'd leave for London the following day, hours before Damyanovitch returned from the US. He had come to St. Petersburg with a strategy for defeating Damyanovitch and saving Moscow Alpha along the way, but instead he'd underestimated Laura's independence of mind and spirit, and her commitment to the man who'd saved her when the world had turned its back on the Prague Spring decades earlier. As he returned to the hotel in a rickety, ancient Mercedes taxi he closed his eyes, contemplating the implications of his potential miscalculation.

Chapter Sixty Two

Abdul Khalid gazed up into the star-studded night sky, its awesome blackness uncontaminated by light pollution from the nearest towns, too distant to be heard. He'd been waiting for an hour but didn't mind: he had all the time in the world, his spirit was at peace and his purpose, a noble one. He was Bedu and nothing pleased him more than being alone with his thoughts, his *misbaha* or prayer beads, and a water skin. He poured its sweet content down his dry throat, offering up a simple prayer of gratitude learnt verbatim in his childhood. Educated at Harvard Law School followed by secondments in several of the Kingdom's embassies in Europe, he'd experienced the delights and dazzling fruits of modernity in all its forms. To the secular observer he represented the emergence of a nomadic culture into the bright light of enlightenment and reason, and yet at heart he remained utterly committed to the old, traditional ways. Indeed, the sinful pleasures and worldly corruptions which his fellow countrymen indulged in, cast adrift from their faith, confirmed in his mind the rightness and righteousness of his own belief, and the need to stand firm when all around him were colluding in the coruscation of their souls.

As he stood in his simple robes gently exhausting the water bottle, he reflected on the irony of his existence and the path that had brought him to this point in his destiny. He had walked over gold and diamonds, the baubles of modern life with its false promises and fake values, to stand here tonight gazing up into infinity, preparing to play some small part in the ending of a failed new world and the rebirth of an older one. Suddenly in the distance he heard the 'phut phut' of the engine of some ancient vehicle struggling through the arid, choking sands. Quickly he made his way back to his jeep and reaching in, withdrew the Uzi: slotting into a belt beneath his robes it was easily concealed, hanging sufficiently free for rapid deployment should the rendezvous not go to plan. The tricks of the desert acoustics outside Riyadh had led him to believe that the vehicle was closer than was the case; he waited for several more minutes, calm as he peered into the darkness. When the vehicle eventually lumbered into view it was as old as it had sounded: slowly, it reversed alongside the jeep. A young man energetically jumped out, but instead of greeting the waiting Khalid he dropped to the ground, effortlessly sliding beneath his truck like a sand snake. A few seconds later, after carefully opening a wire mesh cage fixed beneath the crankshaft, he re-emerged, this time holding a large metallic case. This was the cargo so eagerly anticipated by the silent watcher.

He handed over the nondescript container, embraced the recipient and then returned to the truck. And then he was gone; not a word had passed between them and although they'd never met before, nor were likely to again, their affection for each other was the same as that shared by brothers, united as they were by a common purpose and shared values. Khalid momentarily stared at the suitcase and then gently lowered it into the rear of the jeep. He knew nothing of its history nor did he need to, but its successful delivery represented a triumph of international cooperation on a scale which would have surprised him. A month earlier its contents had been bought from the local mafia in Minsk, Belarus; negotiations over price, quantity and delivery had been conducted by a 'freelance' on behalf of Petr Damyanovitch. But the finance had been provided from a different source; an American called Lincoln Davies had arranged the mechanics of the deal, the setting up of the bogus Swiss account through which the only currency which counted in that part of the world, US dollars, could be channelled. This was strictly a cash sale, free of paper trails. The case had made its way across the Black Sea then down through the Ukraine, transported at each stage along a network of ex-KGB contacts which Moscow Alpha's chairman had sustained and then reinvigorated following the collapse of the Soviet Union. But allegiance and loyalty were founded not upon fear as they had been in the old days; instead they now depended on material wealth, and a loathing of the new world order. The former KGB boss could always be trusted when it came to payment for services rendered but if future 'business' was not to be prejudiced, questions as to the nature of the cargo were not, of course, welcome.

Transportation through Turkey and then across Iranian territory could have proven more problematic; Damyanovitch's contacts in these countries were threadbare, and certainly not sufficiently reliable for a task of this magnitude. It was at this later stage that Fadlalah's network came into its own, supplying devotees willing to sacrifice their own lives (and of course the lives of others) if he were to ask. Andrew Ginsberg had been assassinated by one of their number, machine-gunned down in Istanbul. Damyanovitch's agents had served him well but were driven more by promise of financial gain than by ideological goals; in contrast, Fadlalah's followers were true believers, committed to a cause that transcended material considerations. And now the case had reached its final destination, without further diversions or interruptions to its journey. It had all happened like clockwork, Khalid reflected as he turned the ignition key. It had to be destiny. He smiled as he gently pressed the jeep's accelerator, pulling off along the baked dry dirt track. Soon he'd be back in Riyadh, cradling his newborn baby, feeling his sleeping wife's heartbeat next to his as he held her close to him in the darkness.

Chapter Sixty Three

Laura Simenova returned to the St. Petersburg Stock Exchange to collect her belongings and delegate some unfinished work. She was still in a state of shock following Saul's disclosures and confessions earlier that day but managed to conceal this from those who were now embracing her and wishing her well for the future. She shook hands with the chairman, expressing her regret at being unable to continue at the Exchange for the final fortnight of the secondment. He embraced her in a display of unguarded affection, and she smiled warmly despite her inner turmoil. He then produced a keepsake of her time at the Exchange: a framed bearer bond issued in 1915 by the Tsarist government to finance the disastrous closing years of the First World War. She kissed him and left. She then returned to the apartment the bank had rented for the duration of her secondment, and within an hour had packed all her belongings, loaded them into her car, and started off along the motorway.

Usually night driving would require background music, perhaps a local American-style radio station or a compilation tape sent by friends in London. But tonight was different: she needed silence to think, to retrace paths through the past as a bystander to events, going over past conversations again and again, reinterpreting silences, looking for clues as to the true nature of the man who had dominated and shaped her life. Could Saul be right? Could she have been completely wrong? Driving through the darkness, she realised how little she knew about her guardian and mentor, and wondered why she'd never felt the need to know more about him, about his history, about his hopes in life, if indeed he had any. Perhaps she was in awe of him, and had never quite dared to ask. He was the most successful person she knew, by far the wealthiest, and the respect he commanded at the highest levels of Russian society should, she thought, be sufficient achievement for any man. He had a reputation, as Saul had correctly identified, for speaking the truth, for refusing to indulge in obfuscation even when to do so would be an easier path, when he was challenged by corrupt politicians or obstructive regulators. But this was only one part of his personality: now, suddenly, she felt she needed to know everything.

At three o'clock on a cold morning she entered Moscow's outskirts, passing through block after block of the seedy, battery-hen complexes of 'Khrushchevski' flats, built cheaply in the brief political thaw after Stalin's death, which still towered bleakly and menacingly around the capital. Instead of going straight to her own apartment, she headed directly for the office, wondering which guard had been allocated the night shift. If it was Sergei Brezhnev, then all was well: a friendly but indolent and borderline obese young man, he probably wouldn't even record her out-of-hours visit in the log book. But if Vladimir Fyodorov was at the front desk then it would be different; a late middle-aged former low-ranking party official, he was obsessive in enforcing safety protocols, demanding the showing of passes by out-of-hours visitors, regardless of their rank or position in the bank's hierarchy. In contrast to his younger colleague he'd ensure the preciseness of the entry made in the security log. She pulled up outside the entrance; reaching into the glove compartment she withdrew a small package, climbed out and gently pushed the car door closed. After swiping her electronic pass the door clicked open: she passed through into the dimly lit lobby. 'Good morning Sergei. How are you today?' The short fat man, his hands spread across his stomach, dropped his feet to the floor, straightening his tie in a futile attempt to look the part. 'I'm fine Ms. Simenova, just fine. You're working late tonight, or should I say early this morning? I thought you were in St. Petersburg for another couple of weeks?' 'Yes, I've come back early. And it just so happens I've brought you something from my trip'. She placed the package in front of him: as he tore at the paper his eyes widened. 'Just some liqueur chocolates. St. Petersburg's finest.' He smiled as he pushed the log book to one side, no new entry having been made. 'Thanks Ms. Simenova, thanks a lot! Will you be here long?' He was desperate to see her move into the building. 'Just half an hour or so. If I need you I'll call through'. As soon as she'd entered the lift the box was torn asunder.

She immediately made her way to the internal auditor's room; after rifling through the files kept in a fireproof but unlocked cabinet she came to the paperwork she was looking for. The accounts had been signed off a month earlier and according to the external auditors the bank had exceeded the capital adequacy rules set by the Basle Committee, the international 'think tank' responsible for standards across the banking industry. The bank's capital reserves, held in virtually risk-free, easily realisable assets including US Treasury bonds and their Japanese, German and British equivalents, were strong relative to liabilities. The capital base was, according to the auditors, 'sufficiently robust to withstand external shocks or unexpected demands by depositors'. The report was excellent but suffered from one fatal flaw: it was retrospective. What it failed to reveal were decisions taken by the board since it had been signed off by the auditors.

She switched on the internal auditor's computer, clicking through to a file named 'Capital account activities: disposals and purchases'. The evidence flickered onto the screen. Page after page of the foreign government bonds which the bank had previously held, still listed in the external auditor's report as comprising the 'impressive' capital base, and by the side of each listed the date of disposal, all within days of the accounts being signed off. What had been a prudently managed, well-capitalised bank one day had become a bankrupt shell the next, with barely sufficient resources to sustain its day-to-day working capital requirements. She sank back into the internal auditor's chair, her emotions swirling before settling into a single, condensed feeling, not of anger or confusion, but of terrible disappointment. She returned her attention to the screen. The assets had indeed been stripped and Saul had been dreadfully correct, but now she needed to discover the destination of the funds released by the disposals. She picked up the trail quickly enough: the funds had transferred across to a Netherlands-Antilles-based bank, First Curacao Bank, and into the account of a locally-registered company, Blue Sea Holdings. She smiled, instinctively knowing the company was a shell corporation set up with dummy directors, guarding the identities of its foreign shareholders. The transfer was recorded as a loan in Moscow Alpha's accounts, and this angered her. The bogus transaction lacked subtlety or sophistication: what sort of a bank would lend its entire capital base to a thousand dollar Curacao-based company in the near-certainty that it would never be repaid?

But Saul had made other, more serious allegations, not verifiable through balance sheets and impersonal account numbers trailing their truths across a computer screen. She knew she'd have to wait, but as she gazed out into the darkness, watching the first fingers of gentle weak light fumble across the still sleeping city, somehow she already knew the answer.

Chapter Sixty Four

Laura's face came into Damyanovitch's view, previously obscured by the vast umbrella which kept her protected from the heavy rain which was falling vertically from the weeping sky. His mind refocused on the present as he proceeded down the steps from his private jet, surprised to see her standing on the tarmac, exposed to the elements. Usually she'd wait in the terminal lounge or in the privacy of the chauffeured limousine he always arranged ahead during a return flight. 'Laura! This is a pleasant surprise'. He gently kissed both sides of her face, his lips cold, his skin damp with the rain. 'But why the urgency? What brings you out here, standing in the cold and rain?' She looked into his pale grey eyes; they were smiling but for the first time in her life as she gazed through the windows to his soul, she realised there was nothing behind them, no warmth, no emotion. Her response was measured and calm. 'Why are you destroying Moscow Alpha? Why have you bankrupted my future and those of everyone else working there?'

He hesitated, caught off guard; 'Are you questioning me? Questioning my decisions on all of our best interests? If you are, I'll answer, and answer truthfully. But some questions are best left unasked. What's your wish? To open doors to truths you may not like, or keep them closed and make for warmer, drier places? Think carefully before you answer'. For the first time in their relationship she felt afraid. 'Tell me why the bank has to be destroyed. And what of me? What of everyone else who works for you? Are we to be so casually sacrificed?' He stepped out from the protection of her vast umbrella, standing again under the deluge: she'd given the answer he anticipated. 'Moscow Alpha has to be sacrificed, for good reasons and a good purpose. Its continued existence and that of the other banks in the Caspian syndicate protects the SPV. They shield it from the claims of investors. They shield it from me. And when the syndicate's been destroyed, and then the SPV, there'll be a deathblow to Russia's enemies; one from which they'll never recover. The prize for Russia will be control of the Caspian Sea and *all* its oil wealth. But of immeasurably greater importance, our rightful place in the world will be restored, untroubled by petty nationalism on our borders'.

She stared at him: he appeared invigorated by the rain cascading down on him. 'And what of us? What of those who'll lose their livelihoods?' She felt it right to raise this practicality. 'No-one will suffer. Everyone will be paid off, with more than they could ever have hoped for. My commitment to my employees is absolute. And you? I'll look after you, just as I've always done. Your career will flourish, nurtured and guided by me'. His determination to continue controlling and directing her life unsettled her, but now she needed to know the whole truth. 'Saul says you've killed people. Is he telling the truth? How many?' He stepped forward and embraced her, holding her fast like a madman holds a rag doll. He whispered, his lips almost touching her ear; 'Throughout my life, hundreds have died at my hands. During the War and in the years afterwards. Your friend speaks the truth'. She remained perfectly still, staring into the distance, too frightened to turn towards him. She could hear his breathing regular and strong, audible above the cacophony of the pouring rain. He released her and stepped away again. 'Now you know the truth, what will you do, my little Laura? Which path will you take? Stay with me. We're too essential in each other's lives for you not to'. He smiled again and placed a finger to her lips. Saul had previously used the same gesture, invariably in the course of an argument, but his had been sensuous, simple, and passionate. The man who touched her now stirred fear: she felt ice against her mouth but it was the absence of human warmth, the lack of emotion, which took her breath away. 'Don't betray me, Laura. This is all I ask. We'll talk again soon'. He turned away, paused, and then walked off into the distance, leaving her with heavy raindrops still thundering down on her huge black umbrella. Sergei Ivanov stood in the doorway looking down on the scene playing out just beyond hearing range, wondering what had passed between the two. He watched as one of his masters, the one he'd served the longest but to whom he owed no particularly greater loyalty, disappeared into the rain. He returned to the cockpit: there he would pass the time preparing his report, the regular update to be submitted electronically later that evening to his other masters in the Kremlin.

Saul had been at his desk for half an hour, trying to focus on the day's work while his thoughts were in an entirely different place. He felt helpless, powerless to do anything to delay, never mind prevent, Damyanovitch's plan from reaching its destructive conclusion. He'd monitored the NYMEX website for the past few days, and the movement in long term oil futures contracts was unmistakable; everything was shifting upwards as refineries looked to protect prices of their supplies over the coming months, expecting 'choppy waters ahead'. Despondent, and with a sense of utter resignation he placed his head in his hands: for the first time in his life he didn't know what to do next. Suddenly the door flew open and a red-faced, angry Paul Phineus marched into the room. 'What the hell's going on at NYMEX? I've never seen such volatility. Oil futures prices are all over the place and if things go on like this, we're going to be in trouble on the Caspian deal. Do you hear me? *Big* trouble. Once the benchmark rate's been passed, the bond holders will fall on us and the rest of the syndicate like a pack of wild dogs. All we need now is a crisis to hit the headlines and we'll be holed below the water line'.

Saul had seen the chairman under pressure before but this was different: this time there was desperation in his voice. He ran his hand through his hair, pushing it off his face: he looked tired and worried. 'So Saul, I need your suggestions as to what we can do to protect ourselves. Any sparkling ideas I may not have thought of?' Saul hesitated; Phineus was angry, his precise, calculating mind having failed to anticipate the panic trickling into the oil markets like small rushes of sea water through cracks in the hull of some immense tanker. 'What about selling the futures contract? Sheldons could take a few strategic short positions, intimating to the market that whatever the increases in demand in the short term, we're expecting the price to fall in the medium term. It's a risk, of course, because we'd be selling something we don't hold, but if the price comes down in the meantime, we'd be buying low and selling high'. Phineus smiled before dismissing both the solution and its advocate. 'Don't be so bloody stupid. I don't pay you to be bloody stupid, do I? You know very well that the syndicate pledged in the Caspian bond covenants that we'll not manipulate the price of the NYMEX contract by making sales or purchases on our own account. After all, the investors are hoping prices will rise - the additional payout under the bond's terms is dependent on it. The bond trustee would see through what we're doing straight away and then start legal proceedings against us on behalf of the investors. We'd have an injunction slapped on us in hours. And in the meantime of course, we'd just add to panic in the market. The lead manager making secret interventions just to keep the oil futures price down - it doesn't really inspire confidence, does it? Sheldons is heading for disaster, and we won't be the only ones to go down. You'd better get some ideas together fast'.

Lincoln Davies stared out from the fortieth floor of the Empire State Building across a sunlit New York. He pressed his palms against the vast window: it was hot to the touch and for a brief moment, as he looked across the restless city between his spread fingers, it appeared as if the world below was securely in his grasp. He walked back to his desk and picked up the telephone: his secretary had placed the call. 'Andrew, hello. It's been a while'. After exchanging the customary pleasantries with his contact at the Wall Street Communiqué, he turned to the purpose of the call. 'Andrew, I've invited some friends from the Hill for a weekend on the yacht off Cape Cod, end of next month. Families are invited, of course. Just an opportunity for some R&R, but also to talk politics, the world economy, and so on. No formal agenda. There'll be a few senators and congressmen who'll be able to provide some pretty interesting insights. I'd like you and Alice to come, and the boys. So, can you make it?' Andrew Getts could barely conceal his enthusiasm; his recent appointment as Editor-in-Chief (thanks to a few strings pulled at board level by Davies) gave him access to politicians and bankers who made the world go around, and invitations to functions he could only have dreamt of a matter of a few years earlier. He knew he owed it all to Lincoln Davies. Of course he'd be available.

'The second reason for my call, Andrew, is slightly more delicate. I'd never dream of interfering with the content of The Communiqué and of course everyone respects its editorial integrity and independence. But that said, I'd really appreciate it if you would, column space permitting, deal with a subject that's been troubling me lately. As you know, the oil market's been wobbling a hell of a lot lately and there's no sign of this changing anytime soon. A while back, a syndicate of Central Asian banks, joint lead-managed by a Russian bank and an English bank, got together to finance construction of a huge oil pipeline in the Caspian region. The bonds issued to finance the deal have an embedded trigger, activated when the price of a NYMEX oil futures contract passes above a pre-set benchmark. At that point the syndicate must make an additional substantial payment to investors. Now, if you're ready for this, here's the slant for the article in the WSC'.

Getts listened intently as his caller continued. 'With the rise in oil prices the risk of the trigger going off has increased but the banks making up the syndicate just don't have the capital to make the payment if this happens. If the oil price jumps any further these banks will collapse, and when they do they'll take down with them their US and Japanese lenders and shareholders. You could put it across in terms of how a crisis in one part of the world, in this instance the Caspian, can be transmitted elsewhere, mainly through loan default and bank failures, and in that way can reach the US and Japan. A butterfly opens its wings in the Amazon, and there's an earthquake on the opposite side of the world, that sort of thing. What do you think?' Getts paused; he liked the idea of an article dealing with a 'hot topic' such as energy finance, but was concerned about possible negative consequences for the parties involved in the deal. 'Tell me Lincoln, do you think we should name names? Give details of the syndicate members and which US banks have made loans to them? Couldn't it damage them if the markets realise that they're more exposed than anyone had first thought?' Davies responded, but this time he wasn't making a subtle request; 'I'll give you the names, Andrew. I want the banks identified, as well as their US lenders. I want the full article in print by the end of this week. You'll do it, won't you?' Getts knew that Davies's influence at board level at the Communiqué meant that such occasional requests were better complied with than challenged, even though he was plainly being used to some extent. 'Of course I'll do it, Lincoln. This is just the sort of topic the WSC should be dealing with. Give me all the details, the names and so on, and I'll get it out ASAP. I'll give you sight of the copy before we go to print. Is that okay?' Davies smiled: 'I'll e-mail everything across right now. I'm looking forward to seeing you and the family next month. My secretary will be in touch. Send the copy as soon as it's ready'. Five minutes later he made another call, this time to Switzerland. With a bank transfer duly authorised, a further wave of terrorist attacks and explosions would soon break out across the increasingly fragile Kingdom of Saudi Arabia.

PART FIVE

Redemption

Chapter Sixty Five

Adam strolled into the lobby of Druckerstein, Kahn, and Nixdorf, silhouetted against the brightness of the early morning sun as he passed through into the shade and coolness of the building. Alice Penn smiled as he ambled alongside her desk: his little acts of generosity, gifts brought back for her whenever he traveled abroad, his genuine concern for her wellbeing, set him apart from the other fee earners. 'Good morning Adam, how are you today?' 'Fine thanks Alice, but on a day like today I can think of other places I'd rather be'. 'Surely not. Mr. Buckmaster wants to see you and it's urgent. I know he's got a business trip lined up, a pretty spectacular one too. Your tie could do with straightening'. He smiled and tightened the knot: 'What would I do without you?' He headed off in the direction of the senior partner's room.

'Hi Adam. I hope you're well. Pleased we can sit and talk on this beautiful morning. What do you know about the Rub Al Khali?' The red-faced lawyer from Tennessee smiled across the solid oak desk; mistakenly, he thought he'd raised a subject about which the young lawyer would know little or nothing. Adam responded with characteristic confidence; 'The Rub al Khali, otherwise known as the Empty Quarter. It's an area of desert in the south-eastern part of Saudi Arabia, renowned for its desolation and, of course, its vast oil reserves. The biggest find to date is the Shaybah field, its capacity estimated to be around...' Buckmaster had heard enough; 'Okay Adam, I get the picture. You're very well informed on this subject, just as you are on so many others. I thought it might be an opportunity to catch you out, but evidently I was wrong. Six months ago a consortium of international oil companies won a tender to develop Shaybah's capacity through construction of a new pipeline linking the field to Abqaiq, Saudi's nearest gathering centre. Our firm was appointed by the Saudi Government to prepare the Memorandums of

Understanding between the Kingdom and the consortium - a prestigious appointment I'm sure you'd agree'. Adam nodded.

'We recently concluded final terms of the agreement with the consortium, acting on behalf of the Saudi Ministry of Energy. I've done all the work myself; I hope you won't accuse me of the sin of pride for saying so, but there wasn't anyone else in the firm technically equipped to deal with it'. Adam smiled: Buckmaster's legal mind was the sharpest he'd ever encountered and yet he was modest to a fault. 'So, the work done, the invoice submitted, all that remains is the fanfare of trumpets. And that's where you come in. To celebrate the conclusion of negotiations a signing ceremony is to be held in Shaybah. It'll be attended by representatives of the participating oil companies, of course. The Crown Prince and at least half the Cabinet will also be there. You, sir, will attend on behalf of Druckerstein, Kahn and Nixdorf. You'll oversee the final signing of the multi-party agreement, and will sign on behalf of this firm. What do you say?'

Adam sat back, his heart racing with childlike excitement. 'I don't know what to say, Carter. This is an honour and I'm grateful to you. The only thing I'd like to ask; I must ask. Why aren't you attending the ceremony yourself? It's your success after all. Why me, and not you? I hardly deserve it - you've done the work, after all'. Buckmaster paused: briefly there was an uncomfortable silence in the room. 'Didn't your parents ever tell you not to look a gift horse in the mouth? I offer you this and instead of thanking me and being on your way, you question me. A strange way of expressing gratitude, don't you think?' Adam was startled by Buckmaster's reaction; 'I didn't get to know my parents all that well so they never imparted that sort of wisdom to me. You see, they deserted me just before my fifth birthday. Dropped me like a sack of rubbish on the steps of an orphanage then left the country. Weak people, both of them. I think my question's a fair one in the circumstances. But if you don't want to answer then that's fine. I'll just say thank you and as you suggest, be on my way'. He smiled, but his tone was confrontational. Buckmaster stared at him, taken aback by the disclosure of such a deeply buried secret from his past. He continued, deciding that such openness warranted a response in kind. 'My faith is all that matters to me and there it's banned. Outlawed. Anyone who converts to it can be put to death for apostasy. And all the time the regime lavishes the people's wealth upon itself, fomenting intolerance between the great religions. They were the pay-masters of the terrorists who blasted my son and daughter out of the skies. I'll never set foot in that country. To work for them is one thing – I am acting in a professional capacity on behalf of this firm. But to feign friendship and respect at an event like this would be something else. That would be the essence of hypocrisy'.

The two stared at each other across the desk, each stunned by what the other had revealed. Buckmaster broke the silence; he smiled again, the other side of his nature, the amicable and jovial spirit re-asserting itself over the hate-filled darkness that bubbled like a pool of black pitch at the core of his soul. 'So young man, what's it to be? A trip to the Desert Kingdom your rivals here at the firm would kill for, or should I look for someone else?' Adam relaxed; 'You've got a deal, Carter. It'll be a pleasure to represent the firm at the signing.' 'You'll fly to Riyadh and from there you'll take an internal flight to Shaybah. It has its own airport, built by Amoco in fact, to get personnel into and out of the field. Given the current state of unrest in the Kingdom and the Crown Prince attending the event, with bombs going off everywhere, security's going to be very tight and on high alert. We've already received our security pass from the Saudi Embassy here in London. At Shaybah you'll be collected by a Saudi lawyer I've been working with, Abdul Khalid. You'll attend the event together. You'll leave the day after tomorrow, and the ceremony's on Thursday. I know it's short notice but nobody at the Saudi end is happy with long lead ins to any event; they just give the terrorists time to make their plans. Speak with Alice - she's already made the arrangements'.

A couple of days had passed since Paul Phineus's outburst, but since then the oil price appeared to have stabilised. It was five o'clock in the afternoon and Saul felt drained, his eyes sore from monitoring the NYMEX website for straws in the wind indicating the direction of the market. Suddenly there was a tap-tap at the door: Paul Phineus entered, this time obviously a very frightened man. His face was grey, his shirt and tie were disheveled, and without uttering a word he walked over to Saul's desk and threw a folded open newspaper in front of him. Saul tried picking out words from the page of the Wall Street Communiqué which had evidently caused such distress to the chairman, but without success. Phineus spoke with a raised voice near to a rant; 'If this doesn't break the back of the Caspian deal, then nothing will. It's all here. Every member of the syndicate's named, including us and Moscow Alpha. And do you know what they're suggesting? That somehow we're all facing collapse because of volatility in the oil market and the fact that we've linked coupon payments to fluctuations on NYMEX. They say, and I quote, 'Here we have a group of banks playing with complex derivatives, not understanding the grave consequences that can follow if the worst case scenario actually happens. If it does, bondholders are going to have a field day. It will be a turkey shoot. Perhaps it's time for lenders to re-appraise their positions before everything hits the fan and banks start collapsing". Phineus paused for breath. 'This article's malicious, deliberately intended to cause panic at a time when we're at our most vulnerable'. He collapsed into the chair opposite, his eyes narrow with anger. 'Tomorrow there's going to be one hell of a crisis. Lines of credit will be withdrawn; there's no doubt about this. And when I look at some of the junior members of the syndicate, at our Azeri and Kazakh partners amongst others, there's no way they've enough capital to survive such a sudden, rushed withdrawal of foreign loans. They'll just collapse. And as you'll recall, liability's joint and several in this deal, so if one member collapses, its burden divides equally among those who are still standing. The Communiqué's analysis is correct in that the risk of the syndicate falling apart increases each time the market goes up a dollar. We're on the brink, and if there's one more push we'll all topple over'.

The following day Phineus's worst fears for his bank were realised. Overnight, emergency meetings of the boards of three leading US financial institutions were convened and the decisions arrived at the same: lines of credit were to be withdrawn from the Kazakh and Azeri banks named in the WSC, at least until the 'dust had settled'. Japanese investors followed suit within hours, selling off shareholdings built up during the years since the countries had achieved independence. By the late morning, shares in two Kazakh and three Azeri banks were in freefall. By late afternoon, CNN was showing clips of bank offices besieged by local depositors desperate to withdraw their money: the panic had begun. Saul watched the tickertape running along the bottom of the screen like a farmer watching dust and debris scooped up in the distance, heralding the imminent arrival of a hurricane. He felt a lightheaded detachment as the full extent of the crisis loomed ever greater over the financial markets; this was something he'd helped to bring about, colluding with a murderous nationalist bent on revenge and economic ruination of his country's neighbours.

Phineus suddenly re-appeared, standing in the doorway with his hands in his pockets. He spoke quietly, his earlier panic having given way to subdued resignation. 'You know what's happening? The syndicate's coming apart at the seams. Soon it will only be Sheldons and Moscow Alpha still standing, bearing the full weight of this bloody Caspian deal. Another five percent rise on NYMEX and we're all finished. I'm addressing the board tomorrow. Where the hell's Damyanovitch? He's not returning my calls'. His voice trailed off and he slipped away again, not waiting for a reply. Saul looked at the NYMEX website again. Phineus was correct: a further five percent rise and investors' rights would be triggered, bringing a payout obligation down upon the bank which it hadn't a hope in hell of being able to meet. They were approaching the end game, a game Damyanovitch and his associates were on course to winning. Depressed, he wondered if things could get any worse.

Chapter Sixty Six

Laura Simenova rubbed her reddened eyes before pressing the green button on the photocopier for the final time. For the past couple of hours she'd darted between her office and the central administration room at Moscow Alpha clutching bundles of papers and files; to an onlooker it would have appeared as if she was going about her usual daily business, albeit rather frantically, although it may have seemed odd that she rather than her secretary was spending so much time on such basic work. The truth was a different matter. Previous instructions received from clients over recent weeks and months had been 'cannibalised', headed notepaper guillotined and then pasted onto paper containing new orders faked by Laura. The newly created falsified orders had been photocopied and then passed through to the dealers for execution. The margins payable on transactions were credited to the clients' accounts with Moscow Alpha, via transfers from the bank's own working capital account.

Dozens of additional fictitious clients had also been set up and orders placed in their names. Funding of these transactions was recorded as 'not yet paid', financed through short term loans made by Moscow Alpha. The paperwork for these was distributed throughout the bank: to the traders in the front office, and then to the back office where paper trails were meticulously kept, paradoxically by the perpetrator of the fictional trades, Laura herself. A number of the transactions were also quite genuine; Laura had her own private clients who were perfectly happy to act upon her personal recommendations while at the same time agreeing not to disclose the source of that advice to the dealers whom they instructed. In this way it had become impossible to determine which were genuine transactions and which bogus. And since the person overseeing the back office as well as certain crucial aspects of the front office had manufactured much of the documentary evidence from which an accurate paper trail could be constructed, it would be impossible for either the internal or external auditors to get at the real truth. Just as in the Barings Bank collapse, the situation had now arisen in which the bank itself was the client, trading in many of the transactions on its own behalf and not on behalf of the clients which it believed, at least on paper, that it was representing.

By the end of the afternoon she'd accomplished all she'd set out to achieve. Returning to her room she pushed the door closed and sank into her chair. For the past few hours her heart had not missed a beat: such was the intensity of her concentration on the job in hand that there was no time for nervousness which could be noticed by colleagues further along the corridor. There was neither time for self-doubt nor for contemplating the magnitude of the web of deception she was spinning throughout the bank. But now, as she sat alone, she reflected upon the extent of the crime she was committing, towering over the manipulation of invoices and the setting up of bogus accounts. She'd committed the ultimate crime, the only one which her guardian could never forgive - betrayal. Fear rushed through her body, her mental processes firing frantically before returning to some sense of control as she contemplated what his reaction might be. She feared for her life. An hour later she locked her office door, said goodnight to Brezhnev, the lazy security guard, and passed out into the street. The Moscow Alpha building had been constructed during the 1950s, near the height of the Cold War; as such it was built to last, to survive attacks of a conventional rather than nuclear nature which most in the Politburo at that time believed to be imminent. It was impossible for Laura to make personal calls, particularly overseas calls, using the internal telephone network: there was too much risk of being monitored, old habits possibly persisting amongst the lower ranks at the bank. But to make a mobile phone call was also problematic: network signals were simply unable to penetrate the concrete and steel infrastructure originally intended to protect against all but the most direct of hits. As she stood in the street she switched on her mobile and dialed, long-distance. Her message was brief, the anguish and sense of guilt now enveloping her like a fog. 'It's me. I've done what you asked, but I can't talk now. Tomorrow'. She ended the call without waiting for a response, and headed for home.

'Laura, are you there? Speak to me'. The line was dead and Saul's attempt to reconnect was met with a robotic message: the mobile was switched off and he should try again later. It was six o'clock and he hoped to leave within the next quarter hour, sneaking past Phineus's half-open door like a prisoner making a bid for freedom. It would be nine o'clock in Moscow; he thought of her alone in some side street near the bank and worried for her safety. He looked again at the NYMEX website; speculators had driven up the futures contract price another couple of percent during the day, hoping to make quick profits in the chaos. The market was experiencing a crisis that would in time become the stuff of legend, as huge flows of capital ebbed and flowed through its clearing systems. As Saul passed by the chairman's office, he glanced around the slightly ajar door; Phineus was sitting with head in hands, an image of despair, waiting for the storm to break. His Head of Corporate Finance slipped away into the coolness of the early evening.

In the Empire State Building, Lincoln Davies glided up in the lift to the fortieth floor and entered his office. Settling back at his substantial desk, he took a few sips of coffee from the delicate white bone china cup, and then switched on his computer. The NYMEX website was bookmarked as a favourite: he clicked the cursor over the link and waited. It had been a lifetime since he last felt such a rush of excitement, not since his early years as a twenty-something year old oilfield financier when a client made a 'lucky strike'. Of course there'd always been the family wealth to fall back on, but he'd made his way in the world on his own merit, and was proud that no strings were pulled to assist his career advancement. He gazed at the screen and for a moment was confused; despite the new wave of bombings which had taken place across Riyadh overnight, the benchmark futures price was still bobbing around at fairly stable levels. The trigger price had not been breached: the holders of the Caspian bonds - he and his associates - would have to stay patient and continue to wait. He put down the coffee cup: why wasn't the market responding as it should? The absence of any sign of panic unsettled him.

He picked up the telephone and within minutes had all the information he required, although this only served to deepen his confusion. A couple of dozen companies, nearly all of them offshore with concealed true ownership, had entered the market and were selling the contracts, settling the market as to the availability of future oil supplies. The chaos he'd hoped for had simply not materialised. But there was something else he simply couldn't get his mind around: a handful of the sellers were located in Eastern Europe, and orders had seemingly been placed on their behalf by Moscow Alpha Bank. Damyanovitch needed a sky-high price, just as he did if ultimately they were to seize control of the Caspian seabed rights; so why would the bank place orders that would have exactly the opposite effect, satiating market demand instead of frightening it? Although he knew it was still early morning London-time, he didn't care; woken from a deep sleep to which he wouldn't be able to return, Carter Buckmaster was informed precisely and succinctly of the nature of the problem and the need for urgency. Davies would call the Russian himself but the nature of the enquiry couldn't be dressed up in polite discourse: this was a task best suited for the mutually trusted go-between. Five minutes later, Buckmaster was explaining his conversation with Lincoln Davies to his friend in Moscow. He was startled to learn that Moscow Alpha's chairman knew nothing of the stream of transactions placed by the bank on behalf of its own clients over the past twenty-four hours. He would not have believed anyone else, but he'd never known Damyanovitch to lie and had no reason to think he was doing so now. Gently urging his friend to resolve the matter before it became a crisis, he wished him goodnight and ended the call.

Damyanovitch glanced coldly as he passed the security guard and then proceeded to the internal auditor's room where he would spend the next half hour rummaging through the neat files kept in one of the fire-proof but unlocked cabinets. Everything appeared in order. All the relevant paperwork was present: Moscow Alpha had indeed been putting dozens of transactions through to NYMEX brokers on behalf of its clients, and the paper trail of instructions was there in black and white. But there were also a number of client names he didn't recognise: small to medium sized companies registered offshore, in Panama, the British Virgin Islands and the Cayman Islands, where concealment of true ownership was guaranteed. At eight thirty precisely, Mikhail Astov arrived, visibly shocked to see the chairman in his room, browsing through the files scattered across his desk. Customary politeness was dispensed with. 'Mikhail, we have a problem. Your files are showing transactions passed through to NYMEX brokers on behalf of our clients, but I have no knowledge of these. I don't even recognise many of the names. I want you to check through all client transactions for the past few days and bring me a consolidated report on our NYMEX activities. Do a random sample and contact a few clients. Use any pretext - a paperwork enquiry or whatever but check whether or not the transaction is genuine. I want the report by midday, do you understand?'

Damyanovitch returned to his room and immediately put in a call to London. 'Carter, about our conversation last night. I've got one of our people tracing all NYMEX trades put through by Moscow Alpha. He'll report back to me within a few hours. It could be a simple coincidence; the oil market's in chaos, just as we expected, so it's possible some of our better-informed clients are just speculating against future price movements. But I'm surprised Lincoln's concerned. These new transactions may have stabilised the market, but it's just postponing the inevitable. Provided your young lawyer Adam Creed does what's expected of him, in less than forty-eight hours the market's going to have the massive crisis we've been planning for'.

At one o'clock the bank's internal auditor entered the chairman's room to deliver his report. He was afraid, not so much as to what he'd found but of what the chairman's reaction would be. He started to speak, quietly and with a slight, anxiety-induced stutter. 'Mr. Damyanovitch, I've completed the task you set me this morning and although the findings need further enquiry, it appears that Moscow Alpha has been party to a series of fake trades'. The chairman looked up at him from the paperwork on his desk, his demeanour remaining impassive. 'I contacted a number of our clients who placed orders through us with brokers on NYMEX. These transactions were perfectly genuine, although the clients refused to discuss why they'd made them, and upon whose advice they acted. But there were a larger number of clients who had no knowledge of transactions executed by us on their behalf. These transactions - the client orders and subsequent paperwork - have all been falsified although by whom and for what reason I cannot begin to speculate. As for the clients you didn't recognise, most of these are offshore and I've no way of knowing whether they're genuine or not. Contact information is not on file'. Damyanovitch stared at him, but still without a flicker of emotion in his face.

'So Mikhail, if some of these transactions are bogus, where has the money come from to make the margin payments with NYMEX? How long before you can tell me the exact scale of this deception?' Astov's face turned white. 'The transactions were funded by short-term loans credited to their accounts held with Moscow Alpha. We are providing the funds. It will take me at least five days to check through every client file to identify those transactions which are genuine and those which are not, those which are real clients and those which I suspect don't even exist. With regard to these bogus clients, this means that some of the transactions are in reality being placed by Moscow Alpha in its own name, albeit behind fictitious clients'. Damyanovitch closed his eyes and for a minute which seemed an hour to Astov, there was silence in the room. Eventually, he spoke. 'Thank you Mikhail for the work you've done. Return to your room and continue with the audit. Borrow staff from other departments if need be. I need this done urgently. Do not discuss this with anyone, either at the bank or outside. Report back to me when you've completed your work. Now go'. Duly dismissed Astov scuttled out of the room.

Damyanovitch leaned back and closed his eyes again. He prided himself on knowing the details of every transaction, however small, which passed through the bank, and yet over the past few days a series of large orders had been placed with NYMEX about which he knew absolutely nothing. Worse still, the bank appeared to be the victim of a highly organised conspiracy designed to strike at the very foundations of the Caspian project. Whoever was responsible must have extensive knowledge of all aspects of the conspiracy, and this unsettled and irritated him. He contemplated whether his co-conspirators in the Kremlin could be responsible; were they now turning against him? He quickly dismissed the idea: they had too much to gain from his success. Who had the means, the motive, and the will? Suddenly his eyes opened wide, startled by the image that had burst into his mind: he saw Laura's beautiful face. His blood ran cold, his anger unfocused, spinning like a compass in a magnetic storm. His thoughts then immediately turned to Saul.

Hassan Fadlalah stood as a free man at the front of a small windowless room in a nondescript mosque, tucked away down a side street in one of the poorer parts of East London. He looked at the young people standing in front of him, his hands outstretched in gratitude. There was silence: all arrangements had been made and everything that needed to be said had been said. These were the dedicated true believers who'd follow him back as soon as the essential spark of the revolution had been ignited. After months of incarceration in Belmarsh prison sharing the air with kafirs, taking meals in their presence, he'd emerged uncontaminated by the experience, thanks in no small measure to good legal representation. He smiled at his followers: their fanaticism would embolden and energise the covert network of supporters so painstakingly put in place across the Kingdom during the past year. He spoke softly; 'Brothers, I am honoured by your presence. My gratitude is boundless for the safety and comfort you have afforded me since my release. The hour of liberation of our country from the rulers grown fat and indolent on the bounty sprung from the soil, the black gold, is close at hand. We must have courage and believe in Providence. Our destiny cannot and will not be denied. Soon, my brothers, these puppets of the Americans, these supporters of the Zionist Entity, will be slaughtered like sheep. Across the Kingdom the dispossessed and the abused, those who have witnessed the desecration of the holy sites by the presence of the Infidel, will rise up. Under our leadership they will purge away the stain of the Unbelievers from our sacred land. The regime, its supporters and supplicants, will be cast like dust before our mighty and unstoppable storm of anger. Rivers across our land will run red with their blood. Their bones will bleach white in the noonday sun and then fall to dust. My return is hours away. Even now as we wait in this soulless land of debauchery a mighty weapon is ready for use against our enemies. With their sacrifice a new dawn breaks'.

Slowly, he moved through the gathered audience. No words were spoken, but as he gazed into each man's eyes it felt as though he reached down into the depths of his soul, fathoming its commitment, its desire for martyrdom. If the price to pay to cleanse a corrupted Kingdom was compromise with the Infidel, supplying oil to the Old Enemy, the Great Satan, at preferential rates after he and his government took control, then this would be a price worth paying. As one they fell to their knees and prayed. He then left the room for the last time, to Heathrow and then on to Muscat: there he'd await the signal from a loyal acolyte. If all went to plan he'd board the next plane, returning to Riyadh two hours later. And unlike his ignominious flight into exile five years earlier, this time he'd return to the Kingdom in triumph, to tumultuous crowds, to lead it out of its chaos and decadence, out of its darkness.

Chapter Sixty Seven

During the flight from Riyadh to Dammam, Adam dozed. Sufficient effort had been made to engage in polite conversation with his fellow travellers, all connected with the signing ceremony, during the long flight to Riyadh: now he needed rest in preparation for the ceremony, and no longer cared whether they liked him or not. Upon arrival at the Sheraton Dammam Hotel and Towers he slept soundly in his room until he was woken the following morning by a tap tap at the door as room service arrived with a breakfast of croissants, assorted fruits, tea and coffee. He felt like a king as he sat out on the veranda, looking out on a perfect day, not a cloud to be seen in a vast pale blue sky. Within an hour, the party vacated the hotel and boarded a private Aramco jet used to ferry company employees from Dammam across to Shaybah. Adam looked around at the bleary-eyed washed out faces, still hung over from the bottles of whisky smuggled into the hotel and drunk during the small hours. The jet moved through the thin air, flimsy like a paper dart, occasionally dipping below the horizon then shooting up again at a forty-five degree angle (he wondered whether this was to avoid targeting with a missile from the ground below). He gazed out of the small portal upon the most beautiful, endless landscape of desolation he'd ever seen. Below them was the desert, the largest on Earth, rolling on like a vast rust-coloured ocean, its outlines of dunes crashing and flowing like enormous waves. He stared down upon a scene that exceeded his dreams of infinity, pin-pricked by atoms of humanity as Bedouin caravans passed across its face as they'd done for over a thousand years and would probably continue to do until the end of time.

The Empty Quarter, the Rub Al Khali, magnified his expectations; arid and endless, barren and scorched for millennia by a fierce sun, this place had previously been avoided by international capital, reluctant to send its servants into an unwinnable conflict with the elements. But technological innovation had pushed back nature's boundaries: now the Arab traders and Bedouin tribesmen had company in this desolate world of sand, a place hostile to mankind. Thirty million cubic tonnes were excavated during its development: the Shaybah oilfield represented one of the largest projects in the global energy industry for two decades. Now in the great desiccated wilderness, roads had been built, a 'dormitory town' to accommodate just under a thousand of Saudi Aramco's ex-pat employees and, of course, an airport. All constructed in the space of eighteen months. As the jet gently coasted to a halt on the apron, Adam looked out across the tarmac. The airport gleamed in the sun, a triumph of the West's ceaseless quest for profit, achieved through a Saudi-American joint venture.

But here also was a symbol of a new invasion, its missionaries resented by the indigenous nomadic communities threatened by their encroachment, and antagonised by the Infidel in their midst. The early morning air was fresh, warmed by a dry heat passing in from the surrounding desert. A gadfly teased at Adam's face but with an effortless sweep of his hand it was gone.

'Adam, how are you getting to the signing ceremony? Are you coming with us? Don't worry, we won't take offence if you're tired of our company. You've got your reputation to look after and piling out of some clapped out van with us, well, it could be left in tatters before you've had chance to give out your first business card'. Red Patrick, chief engineer to Saudi Aramco and self-appointed leader of the group, gestured exaggeratedly towards a large, white air-conditioned transit van stationed nearby. The other passengers had already disembarked from the jet and were now snaking in a line towards it. Although the pavilion for the signing ceremony was a matter of fifteen minutes drive away, the prospect of passing more time in a confined space with Patrick and his still mildly inebriated associates didn't quite appeal to Adam. 'Thanks Red, but I've got to wait here for the local lawyer who's been working on the project. Now, how do you feel about having two lawyers on board? Perhaps we could all get to know each other better. You know, talk about tax planning, wills, anybody about to get divorced? That sort of thing. What do you say?' The burly Irish American laughed: 'Thanks but no thanks. You've said enough. Lawyers, taxes and death - I do my best to avoid all of them. We'll not be offended if you make your own way there. See you later'. He pulled closed the sliding door; within seconds the van disappeared in a cloud of sand thrown up from well-worn tyres, raucous laughter emanating out through its wide-open windows.

Adam remained alone on the apron. Drawing in the fresh, warm, sweet air he closed his eyes, straining to discern each separate sound of the desert, some of which travelled by a trick of the atmosphere from a great distance away. Five Bedouin on camels passed nearby: he watched as they slowly progressed across the tarmac. They moved in silence, the only sound to be heard the occasional braying of the 'ships of the desert' as they were gently swatted with sticks to urge them forward. Their riders, the nomadic tribesmen passing through to who knows where, were entirely anonymous, their faces concealed behind headdresses, ghutra, that served to protect them from the sandstorms they were always guarding against. The colours of their simple attire were striking, contrasting with the uniformity of the rusty landscape that stretched beyond the power of the human eye. Beneath dark cloaks they wore thawbs, ankle-length flowing outfits made of large squares of orange, red, and yellow silk, sewn together on the most basic of technology in some village clinging to shifting sands, surrounding some distant oasis, hemmed at the sleeves with small silver bells. He watched as the caravan slowly passed before him, certain he could hear movement of water in half-empty animal skin bottles slung either side of each camel. The clothing, wool upon silk, made no noise, the only audible sound the occasional swish of camel tails flicking at persistent flies. His senses, particularly his hearing, were heightened to new levels; as he stood beneath a blazing sun he was aware of his heartbeat, his mortality, of whispers of infinity in the vastness of the world of sand about him.

Suddenly in the distance he could hear a vehicle approaching; he peered at the horizon and saw a jeep trundling towards him. Within seconds it stopped alongside and a handsome, smartly dressed man stepped out with his hand extended. 'Adam, delighted to meet you. I've heard so much about you from Mr. Buckmaster. He speaks very highly of you'. Adam shook the hand, mildly irritated that the senior partner had been discussing him with a person who was, at least to Adam anyway, a complete stranger. 'You must be Abdul Khalid, yes?' 'Yes, I've been working with Carter for the past year on the Shaybah oilfield project. Such a pity he was unable to come to the signing ceremony, but I'm sure you'll be a fine representative'. His tone was friendly, with an occasional Americanised lilt, the result of several years' study at Harvard Law School. But those days of fornication, drunkenness and arrogance were long passed: he was now a spiritually pure being. Adam looked at him as he smiled; his beaming white teeth, dark brown excited eyes, simple charcoal grey suit with a loose scarlet tie, were the archetypal trademarks of an exuberant ambitious young lawyer, a product of the modern world. And yet there was something in his demeanour, a hostile remoteness as barely discernible as grains of sand on the wind, at variance with the image he was projecting. Adam was mildly confused but, shrugging off his uneasiness, he climbed into the Bedouin lawyer's vehicle and fastened the seat belt.

During the short journey the conversation was relaxed but, for reasons he didn't understand, Adam remained apprehensive. Khalid refused to be drawn on any matter of consequence; the recent terrorist attacks in Riyadh were the actions of a 'handful of hotheads': the government was doing 'a fine job' and had the right solutions to the nation's problems: foreigners were to be welcomed and not frightened off. His responses to Adam's questions were vague and at times flippant; on the occasions when he switched his attention from the road ahead to his passenger, the insincerity in his eyes was unmistakable. By the time the two lawyers reached the roadblock ahead of the cordoned off area where the signing ceremony was to be held, conversation had faded away. The barrier itself was impressive: three solid white and red horizontal poles stretching across the full length of the road. At first sight, security looked efficient and intimidating; at least half a dozen machine gun-wielding soldiers stood behind the barrier, with a further dozen looking on at a short distance. Adam stepped out of the jeep and was immediately approached by a soldier, the stripes and decorations on his uniform indicating him to be of a higher rank than the others. He spoke perfect English, asking politely but firmly to be shown the appropriate pass papers. Adam produced the documentation provided by Alice Penn before he left London, carefully couriered to the office by the Saudi Arabian Embassy in Knightsbridge. The General scrutinised the information then unclipped a walkie-talkie from his belt. The ensuing conversation was in Arabic but Adam realised the veracity of the pass was being checked with a third party, together with confirmation of his credentials. He felt unsettled, aware that several of the younger soldiers had already half-trained their weapons on him, ostensibly still pointing them at the ground but now at the ready, fingers on triggers, prepared for the slightest irregular movement.

The General handed back the papers, not a trace of a smile on his face. 'Your papers are in order, Mr. Creed. But do you have papers for the person over there, your driver, as well?' Adam paused: he'd assumed that Khalid had his own pass. 'No, Sir, I believe Mr. Khalid is traveling to the ceremony on this pass. He's the local representative of Druckerstein, Kahn, and Nixdorf, so we assumed the same pass would cover him. Is there a problem?' General Hak now faced a dilemma: Adam's paperwork was in order but to let through someone who lacked a similar invitation was an irregularity which according to the strict letter of his instructions he shouldn't permit. But, to let one party through and to deny the other would be to risk accusations of bureaucratic inefficiency, and the driver, after all, was a representative of an important firm, according to Mr. Creed. He walked over to the vehicle and for several minutes questioned the driver, requiring him to produce an identity card and other information, including evidence of his license to practice as a lawyer in the Kingdom. Duly satisfied with his enquiries the General waived the ceremony attendees through. Khalid gazed into the rear view mirror as they slowly pulled away, the white and red barrier swiftly lowered again as soon as they'd passed. He smiled: the last remaining obstacle to his martyrdom was now disappearing out of sight.

A few minutes later Khalid unexpectedly brought the vehicle to a halt at the roadside. 'Adam, I hope you don't mind but I need to make a short call. I'll be done in a minute and then we can make our way to the ceremony. We have plenty of time'. He took out a mobile from a compartment beneath the dashboard and although the conversation that followed was in Arabic, it was spoken in a hushed and slightly hurried tone. 'Dear brother, I was not stopped at the road barrier. As you rightly predicted, the English lawyer's pass was sufficient. Now we make our way to the ceremony. The timer was set an hour before collecting him. In two hours' time, our mighty weapon will light the sky. Nothing can stop us now. Blessed am I to serve, to have this opportunity to sacrifice my worthless life. Remember me and keep me in your heart until we embrace again in the next life'.

He restarted the engine but now there was no need for trivial conversation with his passenger: his thoughts were on higher things.

Chapter Sixty Eight

Laura stepped out through the narrow fire escape entrance onto the flat roof of the Moscow Alpha building. For a few seconds she stood motionless, looking around for any sign of movement, any indication that there might be someone else present on the grey plateau which was shining with small puddles of the previous night's rainfall. Apart from several large heating vents there was little opportunity for concealment; she was alone. Now she'd try again to get a signal on her mobile. If successful she would call Saul, as she'd been trying to do for the past hour in the privacy of her room, a room with walls too thick to be penetrated by flimsy mobile signals. She walked over to the waist-height wall running around the full perimeter of the space, the only barrier between her and the great drop to the ground below. Placing the mobile on the wall while it struggled to connect to a network, she leaned over cautiously and gazed down at the people moving about the streets below, soaking up the warmth of the midday sun. Then she became aware of another person's presence on the rooftop; Petr Damyanovitch was making his way towards her across the vast grey expanse. He appeared at ease, smiling as his eyes met hers. He'd left his jacket in his office: attired in silk white shirt, gold cufflinks and pressed navy trousers, he was the epitome of Moscow's nouveau riche, the elite of its banking community. She gazed at him, her feelings numb: he was a figure of physical strength, raw power and charisma. He came to a halt a few steps in front of her, the usual gentle embrace dispensed with. He spoke softly, disarmingly.

'My beautiful Laura, what have you been doing while I've been away? Something you're ashamed of, perhaps? But no need to worry - I'm sure we can work things out. Do you want to tell me what you've done?' His earlier smile had vanished; now he looked at her impassively, not a trace of emotion in either his demeanour or voice. She hesitated before replying; by now he was likely to know that a series of transactions had been placed with NYMEX brokers by Moscow Alpha on behalf of its clients, but neither he nor the internal auditor would have had time to determine the scale and details of the deception or the client accounts through which the orders had been placed. 'You have betrayed this bank and everyone who works here. You've got to be stopped. I'm going to stop you. The trades I've put through to NYMEX will rally confidence in the market. But even if I fail and this bank collapses, at least I'll have done my best to halt the criminal ambitions of others'. He looked at her and smiled, and then pointed at his wrist watch. 'In one hour from now, my dear, clever Laura, the oil markets will be dealt a blow of such magnitude they will take more than just a few months to recover from the shock. As you have correctly worked out… or have been told, my associates and I need to push NYMEX into a crisis, a crisis sufficient to drive up the prices of a handful of futures contracts. Your strategy's been working, causing considerable embarrassment to me. But no matter; in an hour's time half the Saudi Arabian government as well as the Crown Prince will be *removed*, made possible by your lover's lawyer friend. And what will be the effect of this 'terrorist outrage' on the markets, I wonder? So you see, Laura, you're simply too late'.

She stared at him, momentarily too shocked to respond. 'I used to respect you, to love you - how could I have been so wrong? You've wealth beyond the dreams of most, so what's all this for? How has life come to mean so little to you, that it is so cheap that innocents can be coldly executed, and in such numbers? You have the mentality of an abattoir butcher. I just don't understand you, and now I know I probably never did'. He took a step towards her but she moved away. His voice started to rise. 'You condemn me with words like 'betrayal', 'the cheapness of life', 'cold executions'. You speak about things you know nothing about, raising questions from the perspective of your simple, sheltered existence. The years of your life are still only counted on pairs of hands; you know nothing of time or history or struggles for survival. I've stood in pits filled with corpses and pools of blood - the remains of those murdered as the Nazis retreated from this land. I've witnessed killing on an industrial scale, images and horrors burned upon my soul that could never trespass into your gentle dreams. As Comrade Stalin once said, a single death is a tragedy, a million deaths just a statistic. And so it is with those people you now concern yourself with. What is the value of a handful of lives when placed in the scales against the survival of this nation and its future generations? They are like feathers weighed against iron bars'.

'I do what I do not for personal gain - wealth and material comforts are nothing to me and never have been. Instead I do it for this blood-soaked land, once again under siege. In an hour from now a so-called 'dirty bomb' will detonate in an inconsequential desert town that few people in Russia or the West will even have heard of, and when it does many will die. I bear no hatred towards them, but a noble cause requires their sacrifice. The earth will be scorched and laid barren for a mile. The chain of events that will follow will save our nation and silence the enemies at our borders. Now, you tell me, is this not a price worth paying? A handful of deaths of complete strangers against the nation's survival?'

His tone was confident and persuasive: his reasoning was brutal and callous. She struggled to find words, her throat constricted by fear and an anger blowing up like an unexpected summer storm. The true scale of the conspiracy he'd so painstakingly plotted now loomed fully into view; everyone, including herself, had been manipulated, deceived, and their expertise and loyalties, their beliefs that they were somehow contributing to the economic improvement of the wider region, applied towards wholly different purposes. Eventually she found her voice, her throat dry. 'What you say disgusts me. What you intend to do can never be justified, not on moral grounds nor for any misplaced belief that somehow it's being done to save the nation. And even if it is, even if this country's under attack as you seem to think it is, to kill innocents to protect it cannot be the answer. Yours is not an honest war, a fight in the open, it's a subterfuge, a sly undermining of nations that have rightly broken free of our rule. Your willingness to sacrifice people who have nothing to do with your conflict is the highest form of cowardice'.

She trembled as the last few words tumbled from her mouth. In a second he stepped forward, gripped her arms and pressed her against the wall, holding her so her feet were raised off the ground. His complexion was deathly white. She knew, in her panic, that he was contemplating whether her life should be spared. His words were measured: 'How dare you use the word cowardice in my presence- I, who fought in a war of barbarity... the likes of which the world has never known, before or since. I've given everything for my country, sacrificed my soul. Your ingratitude takes my breath away. I've given you so much, and you thank me with betrayal. You know nothing of war, of struggle and sacrifice. You know little of me. Now, give me the names of the fake accounts you've set up. Give them to me now'.

His words were threatening, pulsing with rage contained like a tightly compressed spring. She stared into his cold, emotionless eyes, knowing her death was imminent. 'I'll not tell you, Petr. Small deeds can save the world, and mine may just do this. Do what you will to me'. He looked at her and the image of a blood-stained child lying on the stone floor of a church in Nemmersdorf flashed before him. Momentarily he closed his eyes, observing himself lifting the body, shaking it gently to see whether life was still present. He was sure for a moment that he could smell the cordite of the weapon he had used that day. It was the only act in his entire life which he regretted. He set her down; as she stumbled away from the wall the mobile that had successfully found a signal shortly after his arrival on the rooftop was sent spinning through the air, crashing to the ground below. He spoke again, but this time with a fleeting but discernible sadness; 'You mustn't betray me, Laura. Respect the way I see the world, even if you don't accept it. I saved you in Prague for a reason. You are my atonement. Don't become my error now'. Knowing she'd escaped execution for a reason she didn't understand, she ran to the fire escape, quickly descended the emergency staircase, and disappeared into the early afternoon crowd.

Saul had listened with mounting fear to the conversation between Laura and Damyanovitch. He knew there was nothing he could do to influence its outcome, to protect her or even to let his adversary know that there was a witness to what might be about to take place, albeit at the end of a telephone sitting in an office over a thousand miles away. Suddenly the line went dead as the mobile fell through the air, smashing into the ground below. He screamed Laura's name into the mouth piece but there was no reply. Frantically he dialed her number, but each time there came the same message: 'Sorry, number unavailable. Please try again later'. His blood ran cold. He'd witnessed Damyanovitch's use of brute force before: he feared Laura had met the same fate as the others he had seen executed. He replaced the telephone and struggled to organise his thoughts. Recalling the earlier conversation, he instantly realised he had all the information he required; the missing piece of the jigsaw was in place. He now knew how Damyanovitch and his co-conspirators intended to crash the oil markets: an assassination of a gathering of Saudi Arabia's political elite in some little-known town would precipitate a crisis that would resonate in the derivatives market, forcing up NYMEX to previously unknown levels. He remembered, too, Damyanovitch's reference to his 'lawyer friend', and realised the great danger now facing Adam. He looked at the small onyx clock on his desk; the bomb would detonate within the hour and the conversation had ended five minutes' earlier. Time was slipping away: he was desperate as the inevitability of Damyanovitch's success sharpened into focus. Quickly he grabbed the telephone and pressed the speed dial for his friend's mobile; there was no signal and the voicemail had been switched off. With the panic of a drowning man clutching at straws, he continued dialing.

Chapter Sixty Nine

Adam gazed up at the lights, suspended like enormous bunches of grapes in the Bedouin marquee. Outside the sun burned fiercely but the thickness of the structure's material fostered an early evening darkness, only dimly illuminated by the lamps. It was all symbolism, of course: an attempt by government officials who'd arranged the signing at Shaybah to summon up an atmosphere of earlier times when the nation's forefathers had roamed the desert, their homes rolled up and stored on the backs of camels. But everyone attending the ceremony appreciated the gesture, the huge marquee towering above them, and the intricacy of the weave of enormous carpets laid throughout the enclosed space. The signing of the multi-party agreement had proceeded exactly to plan; the representatives of each oil company involved in the development of the Shaybah field placed the required signatures on each page of the leatherbound tome and then stepped aside, leaving the limelight for the Crown Prince and the Minister for Energy. Other Saudi state officials looked on from a respectful distance. Some of their number viewed the signing with trepidation: was it wise to invite the Unbeliever onto their land for new exploitation, during such times of heightened social and political unrest? But this was neither the time nor the place to display ambivalence; instead they simply looked on and smiled. Adam signed the agreement on behalf of Druckerstein, Kahn, and Nixdorf, legal advisors to the project, and as he did so his heartbeat rushed with pride and excitement. It was, as Carter Buckmaster correctly observed, the apex of his career, of his life, to date.

The formalities completed, the celebration began. Huge platters of food were brought into the marquee by a dozen young men dressed in white tunics fastened with wide scarlet waistbands. They bowed as they passed before the Crown Prince, and then disappeared as quickly as they'd arrived. Adam made his way to the tables groaning under the weight of food stacked upon them; not having eaten for several hours, he feasted on the array of meats, dates, and vegetable dishes. Although not one for small talk, this day he took pleasure in mingling with the oil company representatives and Saudi officials. He was relaxed and the good humour of the event's participants, the trivial conversations with real power players, and the laughter with people he'd never met before, all contributed to the magic of the occasion. He felt that finally, his life was beginning to take shape. He was happy, and the unusualness of the emotion delighted and disappointed at the same time: disappointment that it had eluded him for so long without his even knowing it was missing.

As the event drew to a close the Minister for Energy approached: they shook hands. He stood at least six inches taller than Adam in his full-length white thobe, partially covered beneath the mishlah, his head covered by a ghutrah held in place by a black circular cord, and with a ceremonial dagger by his side he looked majestic, noble. He thanked Adam and the absent Carter Buckmaster for their work in preparing the agreement and liaising between the government and the project's participants. It was a 'work of art, splendidly prepared', and a tribute to the firm's technical expertise. On discovering that it was Adam's first time in Saudi Arabia, he enquired about his initial impressions of the Kingdom. The young lawyer's response was diplomatic enough, couched in compliments and vague observations. They smiled at each other, both aware that there were areas, particularly the prevailing political situation, into which foreigners were precluded by custom and politeness from trespassing. But that didn't seem to matter; the more they talked, the greater a mutual respect and amity was evident between them.

Eventually the event drew to a close and it was time for participants to leave. The Minister shook Adam's hand and thanked him again. Unexpectedly, he turned away and made a beckoning gesture towards the furthermost end of the marquee. A large man, evidently a soldier or guard, moved forward and out from behind him stepped two children; they ran across the carpeted space and shyly took their father's hands. 'Adam, I'd like to introduce you to my children, Haitham and Azhaar. Children, this gentleman is a lawyer from England. I respect him very much and hope that he and I will become friends. Next time he visits our country I've invited him to stay with us in our home. Now, please, shake his hand'. The two children, neither older than five or six, shook Adam's hand. It was a gesture on the Minister's part that touched Adam, standing on its head his previous misconception of a conservative political elite too aloof to welcome the non-believer from a foreign land. After further goodbyes to the remaining Saudi officials, Adam walked out from the marquee into the heat of the late afternoon sun.

Shielded beneath his raised hand, his eyes began to focus in the strong daylight. He looked on impassively as a procession of older German, British and Japanese vehicles pulled away into the distance: minor officials and state-authorised reporters were looking to get away before the later congestion of government ministers and their outriders. His mobile began to ring; the voice he heard was as welcome as it was unexpected but there was a sense of panic about it, a rush of near-garbled words that at first he couldn't associate with the speaker. 'Slowly Saul, slowly. I can't hear what you're saying. What are you calling me for? You know I'm not even in the UK. Remember - you took me to the airport; have you forgotten already?' Adam laughed nervously as he tried to calm his friend, but instinctively he knew that something terrible had happened or was about to happen; only a crisis could precipitate such desperation in a man capable of keeping his head in the severest of situations. 'Adam, listen to me carefully because we don't have much time. Remember how we decided before you left that Damyanovitch would only be successful in destroying the Caspian deal if the oil markets were hit by some sort of catastrophe, but we couldn't work out what this could be? Earlier today I found out how he's going to do it. When you got to Shaybah airport, how did you get from there to the ceremony? Were you collected by someone?'

Adam looked at the parking area temporarily set up for attendees; it was packed with limousines, Mercedes and Rolls Royces but, standing on its own was the vehicle in which he'd traveled from the airport. At its wheel he could make out the silhouette of Abdul Khalid sitting so still he wouldn't be noticed by anyone passing through the car park. 'Yes, I was collected by a local lawyer, someone who worked with Buckmaster on the Shaybah agreement. Why do you ask?' He was becoming irritated and frightened at the same time by the direction in which he instinctively knew Saul's warning was heading. 'Adam, he's brought a dirty bomb with him. It'll be in the car. In ten minutes from now, if

Damyanovitch's timing is correct, the bomb's going to go off, killing everyone in a one mile radius. Warn others if you can but you've got to get away now. Get into a car, *any* car, and just drive as fast and as far as you can. You've still got time to put enough distance between yourself and the centre of the blast. Can you do it? Call me as soon as you're at a safe distance'. The line went dead, leaving Adam in a state of shock at what he'd been told. For a few moments his mind went blank, unable to grasp the enormity of the danger he now faced or what action he should take to evade it, to save his life.

Suddenly a mocking voice startled him out of his fear-induced trance. 'Adam, what the hell are you doing standing here all alone? You've not been thrown out, have you? For being disrespectful, maybe? Making a pass at a beautiful woman? You lawyers are all the same. Tell us. We can keep a secret'. He looked up to see Red Patrick, Chief Engineer to Saudi Aramco, grinning at him from the open window of the transit van used to ferry his 'opposite numbers' from the other oil companies from Shaybah airport to the ceremony. 'Get in the van. We'll give you a lift. Nobody's going to get you away from here faster or to the airport in quicker time. So what do you say? Are you with us?' Adam stared at him: his only means of escape was in front of him, and was perfectly timed. And then he remembered Damyanovitch's words: history was sometimes made by those looking the other way and letting events unfold when they could intervene and simply choose not to. Was this what the Russian had meant? Was this the scenario he envisaged? Damyanovitch was right: he could simply get into the van and with Red Patrick's foot firmly down on the accelerator he'd reach a safe distance in minutes. He could leave behind those who would inevitably die and nobody would know of his moral culpability. But, *he* would know.

'Thanks Red, but I was warned years ago not to get into cars with strangers or in the case of your passengers, strange people. I'll pass. Thanks anyway'. Patrick made an exaggerated salute, climbed into the van, and disappeared in a cloud of dust. Adam sauntered over to where Abdul Khalid was parked, his heart beating so frantically his head began to ache. He looked in through the window; the young, lean man had his eyes closed as he contemplated his last few minutes on Earth and his imminent arrival into the afterlife. He jumped when he heard the door open, startled at having further interaction with a human at this late stage in the plan. Adam slipped into the passenger seat, stretching his arm behind the young Bedouin. 'Abdul, I just wanted to see you before leaving to thank you for collecting me from the airport. It was a pleasure traveling with you'. Khalid relaxed and smiled; there was no threat to the schedule. With lightening movement, Adam caught hold of the back of his head and slammed his face into the windscreen. As he rocked back in shock the attack was repeated but this time the young man's body slumped to one side, now unconscious.

Leaning across, Adam opened the driver's door and pushed Khalid out onto the temporary gravel where he landed limply in a heap. Sliding across behind the wheel, he turned the key: the engine roared into life. Within seconds he was speeding away, flying over sand dunes, watching the small encampment and its central towering marquee diminish in his rear view mirror before disappearing altogether. As he pressed down on the accelerator he smiled as he recalled the faces of the Minister's children. They would live to see another day: they were the hope for the future. Ten minutes later and after checking the distance traveled, he stopped the jeep and stepped out. Now it was safe. He gazed at the vast stretches of undulating nothingness surrounding him; there was absolute silence and once again he could hear his heart beating. But this time it was gentle and regular, free from doubt or fear. An eagle circled above at low altitude; he could hear its wings moving effortlessly as it floated by on a passing current of warm air. For the first time in his life he felt completely at peace with the world and with himself. His career, the wealth, the striving to succeed, were nothing, and led nowhere but towards vague dissatisfaction. Damyanovitch was right: he would change the course of history, not by looking away while others achieved their goals, but instead by intervening, by stepping forward to change an otherwise inevitable course of events. He thought of the people in his life who loved him and whom he loved in return: he had been successful after all. He smiled and as he reached into his pocket for a cigarette, the bomb detonated. The flash of light as he left the world was visible a mile away.

Chapter Seventy

Hassan Fadlalah relaxed back in his economy class seat on the flight from Muscat to Riyadh, waiting for the two hour journey to end. He had waited in Muscat for the signal from his acolyte Abdul Khalid and when he received the call, his heart had leapt. Nothing could have stopped the young Bedouin lawyer; he'd successfully passed through the security checkpoint, navigated his way through the lines of soldiers, and delivered the bomb on time and entirely according to schedule. His martyrdom was assured: he'd be remembered the length and breadth of the soon-to-be-reborn Arabian lands. As the plane circled above Riyadh, stacked with other flights delayed by the uncertainty raging on the ground below, he contemplated the first decrees he would make upon assuming power. The Infidel would be expelled, of course, banished from the holy sites, never to return. But then there would be the liberals to deal with: the enemies within, those advocating a more 'flexible' interpretation of the sacred texts. They would be executed in the days to follow: the shedding of blood of the corrupt and the apostates would cleanse the land.

Soon, rumours started circulating among the cabin crew and then through to the passengers that a bomb had indeed exploded in the Shaybah oilfield region, a dirty bomb that had taken out a whole square mile of land. The state-controlled media was maintaining a news black-out about the explosion, but since at least half the government and the Crown Prince were attending a ceremony in the region at the time, it had to be concluded that they'd been the object of the terrorist outrage and that they had likely perished in the aftermath. But in the fog of war, truth is often the first casualty, and now was no exception; the government had survived the attack, saved by the self-sacrifice of an English lawyer. Now it was poised to launch its counteroffensive. Abdul Khalid had been captured within minutes of the flash that followed the detonation, wandering around the makeshift car park in a concussed state. The threat of incarceration was not what had persuaded him to disclose all he knew, nor even the threat of summary execution which was, after all, what he would have wanted. Instead it was the threat to torture his family in front of his eyes and then imprison them forever in a prison in the middle of nowhere. He quickly revealed that Fadlalah was soon to arrive from Muscat, that for the past year he'd fomented unrest across the Kingdom in collusion with foreign associates, and that he intended a coup d'etat following the demise of the government in the Shaybah explosion. The hapless Khalid was then taken away to a local prison to await the date for his trial and inevitable execution.

Fadlalah's flight coasted to a halt on the tarmac after finally receiving clearance to land from the control tower, its civilian management now replaced by Saudi Intelligence. He looked out through the portal, surprised not to see signs of his supporters running in near-ecstasy towards the plane: wasn't this how all revolutions started? As he stepped out onto the gantry he looked into the distance in horror as police and soldiers swarmed out from the terminal building, machine guns trailed on the plane. Passengers who'd already disembarked lay prostrate around the apron, obeying orders barked at them from megaphones nearby. The air was filled with deafening sirens and alarms; several armoured personnel carriers lumbered towards the plane, weaponry at the ready. As he continued his descent down the steps he placed his hands behind his head, utterly confused as to how his plan that had been working like clockwork could fall apart at the last moment in such spectacular fashion. As he lay on the ground, his face pressed to the tarmac, he realised his critical error: if only he'd been able to take some small weapon on board, a handgun or even a simple knife, but this would have been impossible given the high state of alert at boarding points for the Kingdom. He'd have raised the gun, if he had had one, on exiting the plane, the gesture guaranteeing his death in a hail of bullets. But instead he'd been captured: a fate much, much worse than death. And now he'd be frog-marched away for interrogation, held in a cage like an animal, put on display to heighten his public humiliation and prove the futility of his cause. He wondered if he'd survive, or be imprisoned, probably forever, or whether his followers would continue his struggle and release him at some later time, succeeding where he had failed. But deep in his soul he knew what would happen. Within the hour he was taken to a high security interrogation centre on the outskirts of Riyadh: a non-descript building squatting in the suburbs, the inhabitants of the surrounding houses oblivious of the activities taking place inside. In different circumstances he'd have been subjected to 'torture lite' first: verbal threats, random acts of physical violence, and sleep deprivation. Threats to his family could also be included, assuming they could quickly be found and detained. But these were not 'usual' times: the regime needed answers quickly and didn't have the luxury of a prolonged period of questioning. 'Torture lite', therefore, had to be dispensed with: absolute brutality was to be the starting point and where to go from there, well, they'd cross that bridge if and when they got to it. The regime's survival was at a higher risk now than at any other time in its recent history: savagery was justified.

Within twenty-four hours, Saudi Intelligence knew the identities of most of those within the country's borders who would have assumed power alongside Fadlalah if his plan had been successful. As for the foreigners involved in the plot, the depth and extent of the conspiracy had been truly shocking, involving nationals of the country the regime believed it could count upon in times of crisis. The information on Lincoln Davies's involvement, as a super-wealthy individual looking to accrete to himself even greater capital through oil deals struck with Fadlalah once he was in power, was received with no surprise. Mercenaries such as he were by and large predictable, their needs and ambitions simple enough. But given his connections within the American political establishment, it had to be concluded that government officials were involved in the planning too; even if they had simply turned a blind eye to what he and his co-conspirators were up to, they were still equally culpable. Was the House of Saud being deserted by its most important ally at its greatest hour of need?

In the weeks that followed, after the inevitable hoo-hah over human rights abuses during the purges had abated, approaches would be made through the Kingdom's embassy in Washington. If the allegation of collusion, whether it had been tacit, passive, active or otherwise, was not dealt with to their satisfaction, then a rebalancing of Saudi foreign policy would be likely. Perhaps the European Union could be a 'new friend'; after all, it needed their oil, and was usually willing to look the other way when human rights conflicted with its own longer term economic interests. The American lawyer, Buckmaster, was a different matter, driven by a dogma which made compromise a near-impossibility. To Saudi Intelligence it was ironic that a fundamentalist Christian could collude with a fundamentalist Islamist to make cause against a perceived common enemy. In time he'd be dealt with, but for now the regime remained hamstrung by diplomatic considerations that made direct action problematic. But the lawyer's hatred for the Kingdom's ruling elite meant he couldn't be ignored: he'd find other ways to strike at them again, and probably in the not too distant future. His name would be omitted entirely from discussions soon to take place at diplomatic level in Washington; they'd resolve their irreconcilable differences with him at a time of their choosing. Twenty-five hours after his arrest Fadlalah was dead: tortured to death, his battered body stretched out on the floor of the same cell in which, by unhappy coincidence, his brother had died some years earlier.

Lincoln Davies looked sullenly and dejectedly at his computer screen. For a moment his eyes widened, encouraged by the real time news tripping ticker tape-style across the bottom of the page; finally, after all his efforts, the NYMEX trigger price would soon be breached. But one of the principal objectives of the wider strategy had been the installation in Riyadh of a Fadlalah-led theocratic government; on this they had completely failed. Fadlalah was dead and cheap oil was no longer on the agenda, at least not from that part of the world anyway. Later he was scheduled to attend his weekly meeting at the Department of Energy where he would deliver his off-the-record oral report, but its contents would be a curate's egg. On the minus side, the regime in Riyadh had survived; their man had not seized power and what he'd disclosed under torture was anyone's guess. But on the plus side, Davies and his associates would soon take control of a major part of the Caspian Sea oil and gas reserves, ensuring security of supply to the US at favourable prices well into the future. So, he would argue, things weren't all bad: there was still much to play for. But as he gazed at the constantly changing prices, he knew the entire project remained highly vulnerable. If the market held its nerve then the trigger level wouldn't be breached, the syndicate would survive, the SPV would remain intact, and the oil rights underpinning the deal would not pass into their hands. He crossed his fingers and hoped for the worst.

In an oak-paneled conference room at the office of the Monaco-based law firm of Morgenthau and Luthmann, Dieter Morgenthau, the senior partner and head of the Private Client Department, settled back into his leather chair and looked over his half-moon glasses at the new trainee with mild disappointment. He'd undertaken his day's tasks with diligence and enthusiasm, but this was not the cause of his principal's despondency; instead, the cause was the news he now brought to their end-of-day feedback meeting. 'So, Alex, today you've done your business press review? And in last week's Financial Times there was a death reported. Read it to me again, please'. Alex Pfeffer picked up the newspaper cutting and read it out carefully. 'Adam Creed, of London-based law firm Druckerstein, Kahn, and Nixdorf, died yesterday in an explosion at the Saudi Arabian oil complex at Shaybah. Initial reports indicate suspicious circumstances surrounding the death, although details remain sketchy. Mr. Creed died leaving no dependants. A spokesperson for the firm, Ms. Alice Penn, said he will be sadly missed'. Morgenthau looked again at the young man; 'Well done for finding this piece of information. It would probably have gone unnoticed if it hadn't been for your excellent recollection of the names of our private clients. And if you hadn't spotted it we'd have continued managing his business, in complete ignorance. Eventually we'd have landed in big trouble. Of course I'm saddened by his death, although I can't say I knew him personally. The practical consequence is that we'll no longer be able to charge fees for our work - it all comes to an end now. Here's what I want you to do. Prepare a letter for me to send to the appropriate people - you'll find both of their names on file. We need to inform them of the change of circumstances of the Tri-Star Trust, and about what happens next. I want this matter wrapped up as quickly as possible. Now, unless there's something else you want to discuss, I think we'll finish for today. Well done again'.

Chapter Seventy One

Saul walked towards Thomas across a windswept London Bridge. Workers and tourists in waterproof jackets and clinging to umbrellas rushed to the safety of their offices, hotels, and dimly-lit coffee shops. He looked out of place in his dark-brown oilskin coat and wide-brimmed hat, without an umbrella. Always the most sensible of the three, Thomas was better prepared, a black dome towering over him, buffeted in the wind, but keeping out every droplet falling from the sad, grey London sky. They came to a halt, facing each other: this was the place where Saul requested they meet in their brief telephone conversation the previous day. 'Adam's dead'. Thomas simply nodded, acknowledging his devastating words. The two set off for a nearby coffee shop, eager to get out of the rain. There they would share their thoughts in a place of noise, life and laughter, surrounded by tourists, students and down and outs, certain the conversation would be neither heard nor understood by anyone. For a while they sat in silence. Eventually Thomas spoke again, this time about practicalities. 'What news on the Caspian deal? Is everything safe now?' Saul stared at him; suddenly he appreciated there would be victims further afield after Damyanovitch's goals had been realised. 'Everything's hopeless. Everything's lost. The oil markets are in chaos and the others in the syndicate, all the Azeri and Kazakh banks, have collapsed. If NYMEX goes up any further then Sheldons and Moscow Alpha will be called upon, and as we're the only banks still standing the entire payment burden's going to fall on us. Moscow Alpha's technically insolvent, just a shell. And since we don't have the capital to meet investor demands we'll go bankrupt too. Then there'll be nothing to stop him. It's so perfect, don't you think?'

There was an unfamiliar despair in his voice; he seemed resigned to Damyanovitch's imminent victory. 'And the supreme irony is that as soon as he's got what he wants, I'll get millions of dollars paid into an account of my choosing anywhere in the world. Blood money for playing my part, for helping set everything up, for standing by and saying nothing while he killed everyone who got in his way. I feel guilty, to the depths of my soul.' Thomas's need for practical solutions reasserted itself; 'You've got to keep focused, Saul. Think. Even at this late stage there must be a way to derail the conspiracy. Is there a point where he's vulnerable?' Saul sighed. 'Most of the volatility in the oil markets is in response to the attempted assassination of the Saudi government. If they'd gone then there'd be no hope of the market calming itself in the short term. But they've survived and, as soon as they restore order, round up their opponents, the markets will settle down. I think that'll be quite soon so if we get through the next few days, if some short term stability returns, then I think we could stop him. But the NYMEX benchmark is now within touching distance - just one more push and Damyanovitch and his associates' rights will be triggered. The problem is, Sheldons doesn't have the resources to keep the market stable and in any case Paul Phineus would never allow it. So just one more fit of panic in the markets and we're done for'.

Thomas snapped at him, angered by his uncharacteristic defeatism; 'So, if we can get the futures contract price down, then we can stop him, yes?' 'Yes, that's the way it is. But you've not heard what I've been saying. It's not easy by any means. We don't have sufficient capital to do it'. With nothing decided and Saul's despondency deepening, they left. As they stood in the café's doorway watching a child in bright yellow boots jumping through the puddles on an uneven pavement, Thomas turned to Saul and smiled; 'Remember Saul, the show's not over...' He left without finishing his sentence. As he disappeared into the distance, Saul added under his breath, 'until the fat lady sings...'

Saul returned to the office, unable to see the slightest glimmer of hope in the situation. Soon he'd receive a payment from Damyanovitch that would set him up for life; he'd never need to work again, and could walk away from Sheldons and leave it to its demise. But his imminent freedom from 'wage slavery' and a new phony lifestyle of fast cars and yachts, beautiful women and glamorous hotels on the French Riviera, didn't even register in his mental processes. As he passed through the dealing room he looked around; young men and women were laughing, shouting down telephones at dealers in other banks, eating sushi brought in by a local delivery company. None were aware of the bank's imminent collapse- how could they be?- or his role in bringing it about. He felt desperately guilty as he snatched fleeting glances at their youthful, enthusiastic faces. Though not religious, he thought of Judas clutching a handful of silver pieces.

He walked to his room, closed the door and sat at his large desk, head in hands. Suddenly there was a gentle tap at the door: Paul Phineus entered, smartly attired with a demeanour Saul couldn't immediately decipher. 'Hi Saul, I just thought I'd drop by to give you an update on the Caspian deal, although you've probably been keeping yourself up to speed on the NYMEX website anyway'. He was remarkably relaxed given that he must have known the bank was now well and truly in the danger zone after further rises in futures prices overnight. 'Today I was asked to address the Sheldons board. I reported that the triggering of investors' rights is now imminent and that in all likelihood this bank will be unable to meet its commitments. We're now just hours away from collapse. And then investors will move against the SPV to take control of the Caspian Sea oilfields, which I'm beginning to think was the plan all along. But I've got no proof and it doesn't matter to me anymore'. Saul stared at him, knowing what was coming next. 'At this morning's meeting I explained the situation. Members of the board then asked me to submit my resignation with immediate effect or be sacked on the spot if I didn't. Of course I obliged. So, I'm now going back to my room to collect my belongings and I'll be gone within the hour. Not an honourable way to end twenty five years in banking, but sometimes when you're faced with an irresistible force it's best to just lie down rather than be torn down. I suggest you start looking for a new job elsewhere, because by my reckoning, this bank's not going to be standing by the end of the week. It's been a pleasure working with you, and I wish you all the best for the future'. He shook Saul's hand and left. They would never see each other again.

Chapter Seventy Two

After his meeting with Saul, Thomas went straight to Heathrow. Three hours later, after one of the most intrusive and time-consuming check-ins he'd ever experienced, he boarded the plane. The problem, or more specifically the cause for suspicion at security, was that he had no luggage to speak of: no suitcases, no additional clothing, not even a toothbrush. He did, however, have his passport, still in his wallet after his previous trip to Istanbul. Just under seven hours' later and after a short stopover in Zurich, he reached his destination. After satisfying Immigration Control officials that he was on a short business trip and providing the name and address of the person he'd come to visit, he was allowed to leave the airport. As the taxi pulled away from Ben Gurion he breathed a tense sigh; everything depended on this one visit, time was of the essence, and any delay would be most unwelcome. Within half an hour the taxi pulled up outside the Tel Aviv Hilton, where a deep sleep awaited him. After buying a fresh shirt the next morning, he returned to the hotel, showered, and then made his way to the place designated for the meeting. He'd called his host before setting off for Heathrow to confirm whether or not he'd be available at such short notice; although years had passed since their last meeting, in that brief conversation they'd spoken as old friends. The firmness of voice was the same as Thomas remembered, conveying the natural confidence of a man accustomed to giving orders. But the affection was immediate and unambiguous; theirs was a friendship founded upon mutual respect and a single favour granted a long time ago.

Thomas gazed out from the Observatory on the forty-ninth floor of the Round Building at the Azrieli Centre. In the far distance he followed the coastline stretching from Ashkelon in the south to Hadera in the north, embraced by the beautiful, deep blue sea glimmering in the early morning heat haze. Looking through a tourist telescope he could make out several container ships on the horizon, awaiting clearance to deliver their cargoes. The air was fresh and cool, the aspect from the highest building in the Middle East breathtaking. He'd deliberately arrived half an hour early: he needed time to think, to prepare the words of the single request he'd make of the man shortly to join him on this platform in the sky. But after struggling to string together the vital sentences he realised that this was a time when to rehearse would be to weaken: instead, he'd speak from the heart. He tried to relax, returning his attention to the vessels in the distance leaving white trails of foam as they powered effortlessly through the water.

'Thomas, what a pleasure to see you again! What do you think? An amazing view of this beautiful country of ours, isn't it? I hope my invitation to meet here hasn't inconvenienced you but I thought you would be impressed'. Thomas immediately recognised the voice; turning, he held out his hand to Solomon Silverstein but instead of taking it in his own, the old man embraced him. 'You look older, my friend. I think you've developed worry lines since we last met. But that was a long time ago, and I expect the cares of the world weigh more heavily upon you now than in those earlier days at Clements. My daughter told me a while ago that you left the firm to work in your family's engineering business. A wise decision. Nobody achieves true success serving someone else. You've got to be your own master'. For a while the old man directed Thomas's attention to point after point along the distant horizon, discussing modern and ancient history with knowledge and understanding that would have been a credit to the most seasoned tourist guide. He spoke from his soul with an intensity of emotion handed down through the millennia, bred in the essence of the nation of which he was evidently so proud. At the same time, Thomas recognised the humility that had struck him at their first encounter in London. Courteous as always, he waited for the appropriate moment to broach the subject which had brought him to Israel with such urgency. Suddenly he realised that his host was no longer speaking; there was a silence, friendly rather than awkward or hostile, and he didn't even know for how long it had been so. He'd been listening intently one minute but in the next his concentration had evaporated, taken away in a miasma of thoughts of failure, defeat and loss.

The old man smiled then spoke quietly. 'My friend, you came here for a reason, an urgent reason. Why wait any longer to tell me of it? What is it you want of me?' Thomas looked into his knowing eyes: it was now or never. 'Solomon, I've come here to ask a favour of you but I just don't know how to put it. My situation is desperate and I can't see a way out, not without the help of someone with the power, the will and the resources to intervene. There is an oil futures contract traded on the New York Mercantile Exchange whose price has jumped sharply in recent days. I need the price to come down, for reasons I'll explain later; there is no time just now. The present chaos on NYMEX is a consequence of a criminal conspiracy which will permanently change the balance of power in the international oil market if it's successful. The independence of new nations will also be swept away by it. I came to Israel to ask you to intervene in the market, to use the resources of London Commodities to drive down the price of this contract. Can you help?' Solomon looked at him, his demeanour unperturbed despite the potential implications of what Thomas had asked of him. He paused before responding.

'You're asking me to use the company's capital to sell the contract in a rising market? To short the market? You know, of course, the amount of capital we'd have to commit to affect the price - we'd have to use nearly every last dollar we hold to do that. And even then, if the price continues to rise we'd eventually be forced to buy high and sell low. That would be our contractual obligation - to make delivery at the future date according to the agreement. You understand that?' Thomas nodded, and Solomon continued, in a neutral tone. 'The potential losses could be ruinous for London Commodities. On the other hand, if the price falls in the meantime we'd buy low and sell at the higher price, and make huge profits, but that's not the point. You're asking me to gamble everything, to risk the bankruptcy of the business that took me decades to build up and which I hope eventually to pass on to my children, yes?' He waited for Thomas to correct his interpretation of the request.

The young man said nothing and Solomon laughed. 'So apart from this small favour, is there anything significant you want to ask of me? You came all this way just to make this one request? I'd have expected at least another five - a bundle of requests to make the journey worthwhile'. Thomas didn't attempt to force a smile: his host had starkly and succinctly identified the risks implicit in his request. The old man gazed out to the horizon, collecting his thoughts. 'Thomas, when you and I first met at my office in London, years ago, I asked a favour of you. Perhaps if I'd kept a tighter rein on my sons, what happened wouldn't have happened in the first place, but that's another story. Fathers often believe in their sons more than they should, more than is wise. I've no doubt that had you denied my request my sons would have been arrested, tried and imprisoned. And, of course, my reputation and my daughter's future would have been beyond saving. You, a Gentile, took a huge risk for me, a Jew, a complete stranger, facing ruin. I promised you then that if you ever needed my help in the future, you only had to ask. Well, Thomas, better that I walk in rags through the streets, give up the last of my earthly belongings, than betray a trust and abandon you now. Yes, I will do what you ask of me. Now, let's talk practicalities'.

For the next half hour the two discussed the strategy which would have to be followed if the market was to be moved in the direction Thomas required. Despite the scale of the undertaking and the potentially fatal strain it could place upon the resources of London Commodities, Solomon was calm and good-humoured. His knowledge of the practices, risks and mores of the energy futures markets was supremely impressive, gained through decades of participation which had begun as a trader after the War. Thomas watched as he sketched a trading strategy on the back of an envelope withdrawn from a pocket in his simple jacket. His eyes were wide with excitement, constantly peering at the young accountant over his silver-rimmed pince-nez glasses when he felt an explanation was required. But both knew that in attempting to beat the market it was likely, perhaps inevitable, that the company would be snapped like the dry branch of an ancient tree in a hurricane.

'So we're agreed on how we should proceed, my friend. Today you've invited me to contemplate the prospect of destruction in material terms of everything I've ever achieved, and yet I've not felt so alive in years. I'm looking forward to the fight and it will be interesting to see if we can disprove, just for once, the old adage…' Thomas completed the sentence: 'you can't beat the market'. The strategy agreed, the two descended from the Tower, leaving behind its near-mystical prospect upon a beautiful, ancient, troubled land rolling out to the furthermost boundaries of the imagination.

Chapter Seventy Three

A short taxi ride took Thomas and Solomon to Dizengoff Square, Tel Aviv's restaurant quarter. As they passed Agam's modernistic fountain in the centre of the square, its huge multi-coloured structure resembling the fan-like divisions of an old slide projector, Thomas smiled; earlier he'd looked out from the Azrieli Tower across an ancient landscape but now he was at the heart of a modern, vibrant city where Sephardic Jews mingled with camera-toting tourists and secular Jewish teenagers in military fatigues. Their taxi stopped outside one of the city's famous fish restaurants. Solomon settled the fare and after displaying his papers to the soldier standing outside, he led Thomas through the discreet entrance and into the lobby. 'I hope you won't mind if we wait here instead of going straight through to our table, but I'm hoping a colleague will join us shortly. I was only able to ask at very short notice so I'm not sure if we'll be in luck'. He suddenly smiled as he looked towards the door; 'Yes, there'll be three of us for lunch. I believe you've met before'. Thomas followed his gaze and was delighted to see the newly arrived guest. Rebecca, as beautiful as he remembered her in Istanbul, walked towards them and after gently embracing her father she turned and delicately kissed Thomas. 'Thomas, I'm so pleased to see you again and at long last on my own home ground. How did Istanbul go? A great success for you, I hope. It was such a pity we both had to rush off but hopefully you'll be staying with us for longer this time'. The affection between the three was obvious, founded upon trust, respect and an indefinable magical ingredient so fundamental to the most enduring of friendships. They passed through to the main restaurant area, Solomon's 'personal connection' with the owners, as he mischievously put it, ensuring they had a table separated off from the rest, in a private alcove to the side of the main room.

After light conversation over a succession of courses which included some of the freshest fish Thomas had ever eaten, Solomon's tone, until then warm and humorous, changed. He looked to Rebecca: now he was serious, almost grave, his eyes fixed upon hers. He spoke and his words were firm and precise. Thomas looked at them and felt like a bystander, almost as if he wasn't present. 'My daughter, this man comes to us with a request. He needs our help at a desperate hour and just as he obliged us in our time of trouble before, it is my wish to help him now. It's possible we'll lose everything - our business, our wealth, and our homes. But without honour these things are nothing. I gave him my word before and I'd rather give up my life than renege on it now. I love you so much. I must know if you'll support me in the crucial and perhaps ruinous decision I'm about to make'. She smiled, lifted his hand and kissed it. 'Father, I'll support you until time runs out. If this decision is one you have to make and the sky falls in as a consequence, I'll be there with you when it happens, just as you've always been there for me. Please, tell him he has our agreement'.

He looked into her eyes; her resilience, toughness, confidence, and most important of all, her love for him, reminded him so much of her mother, his long-deceased wife who nevertheless visited him daily in his thoughts. He returned his attention to Thomas: the number around the table was three again. 'My friend, you have our support in this your time of need. Be guided by my daughter. She has the sharpest of minds and an understanding of the markets I've yet to see equalled. Now I'd like to propose a toast, after which perhaps you'll propose one yourself. I invite you, Thomas, our friend, and you, Rebecca my beautiful daughter, to raise your glasses to friendship'. The three raised their glasses and repeated the words in unison. 'To friendship'. Thomas lifted his glass again. 'I propose a toast to the now inevitable defeat of the man who's brought us together again in determination and opposition. I propose a toast to Petr Damyanovitch'. Solomon's hold of his glass suddenly failed, letting it fall to the ground where it smashed into a thousand shards. His face turned deathly white, his eyes closing tight shut. He was a vision of turmoil at the mention of a name which he had not heard for over half a century but which had brought such sadness and suffering to his dreams and waking hours in the intervening years. Rebecca rushed to his side: waiters ran towards the table fearing for the elderly guest's health. Politely, calmly, he waved them away: after reassurance that he was physically well, she returned to her position at the table, seated at his side. Distraught, he looked at both of them in turn and then spoke, his tone that of a man who asks a question but already knows the terrible answer.

'It has to be a shared name. It *must* be someone else. Tell me it's another person. This has to be a terrible coincidence'. He placed his hand on the table, spreading out the fingers. 'Tell me one thing. What can you tell me about his hand?' Thomas paused, his accountant's eye for detail searching through his stored mental images of Damyanovitch. And then he remembered. 'Two of the fingers, I think on his right hand - half of each is missing. But how do you know? Is it important?' The old man froze, staring at Thomas in disbelief. Eventually and with unmistakable sadness, he continued. 'Yes, it's important. There is only one man I've ever known who went by that name and with that disfigurement. A man who was... and is.... terrible for his crimes, steeped in the blood of innocents'. He paused, and for a moment Thomas thought he saw a tear in his eye. 'The man is a killer, a murderer without conscience. In front of my eyes he slaughtered men, women, and children. Slaughtered them like animals in an abattoir, without mercy. And you speak this name now: you bring it into daylight when it should be mentioned only in dark places. You bring the past's sadness and guilt back to me today'.

Thomas was extremely shaken. He knew from Saul that Damyanovitch was capable of calculated acts of brutality, but Solomon was talking about crimes of an entirely different magnitude. Both he and Rebecca struggled to understand the silver thread of coincidence that ran between the two men, unable to guess at how they could know each other. Thomas broke the silence. 'If I could have avoided causing such sadness to you in this way then I would have done so. His name disturbs you, for reasons I daren't ask. But he's the reason we're sitting here today. He is the cause of the turmoil in the markets, and the man at the head of the conspiracy. I know of his killings but neither I, nor my friend Saul Quartermain, have had either the evidence or the courage to report them to higher authorities. Saul was caught up in his web, first when he was promised great wealth and then by threats of death if he didn't remain silent. You see, every man has his price'.

Solomon was visibly shocked. 'You know about Nemmersdorf? How could you know? Only three people left the church that night: myself, Aaron Hoch, and him. My friend and I never spoke of it afterwards, not to each other or to anybody else. Nobody was told. And he would never have said anything: confession is an alien concept to such a man. How do you know? Tell me now'. His voice was rising; Thomas now realised they were speaking at cross purposes, describing different events. 'I know nothing of Nemmersdorf. No, I'm talking about crimes I know he's guilty of, but committed in other places. I've no reason to doubt what you say is true, but why didn't you report these killings to the local police in Nemmersdorf? I can't remember reading anything about such an atrocity. How is it that a crime of such magnitude went unreported? I don't understand'. Solomon nodded as he came to understand the reason for the confusion between them. Thomas had taken his words to refer to crimes committed in Nemmersdorf during the recent past, assuming that they coincided with other atrocities which Damyanovitch was evidently also guilty of; the confusion was simply but crucially a matter of timing. Nemmersdorf had been decades ago but for him it was a place he had visited in his nightmares, ever since. Thomas listened as he described the events of the night he first encountered Damyanovitch. Before that night the small village of Nemmersdorf had existed in obscurity for centuries, an innocent backwater in what was then East Prussia, then later part of the USSR. But then the Russians arrived, carving its bloodstained name into the brutal annals of the Second World War. The War ended, Germany was defeated, and everyone went home. Nemmersdorf was forgotten; none of its German inhabitants remained, and victors seldom face retribution for crimes against the vanquished. On the Allies' side, the side of the angels, the number of those escaping justice dwarfed that of their defeated counterparts; now they returned home to be feted as heroes and showered with medals. Nobody would answer for Nemmersdorf or for the millions of innocent Germans ethnically cleansed from 1945 onwards from lands that had been their home for generations.

For Solomon the destructiveness of a desire for retribution without justice manifested itself in all its ugliness in a little German church in an unimportant village in October 1944. He recounted how a young man entered a holy place with a bloodlust in his heart. As he explained how bodies had fallen row after row, he began to weep. But he had to continue: this was his catharsis. 'The air was blue with smoke, the moans of the dying rising to the rafters. Nobody was spared. I was a witness that night but, in not intervening, part of my soul died'. He paused, the anguish almost too terrible to bear. 'And then he arrived at the front of the church. Nobody was upright, nobody alive, all caught by the indiscriminate bullets. I watched from behind a pillar, trembling with fear. He lifted up the body of a child and shook it, as if trying to make a broken toy work again. And when there was no response, no sign of life, he cradled it in his arms before letting it slump to the ground. It was the one sign of humanity I saw in him. And when I gasped in horror, that's when he saw us, hiding in the shadows. He demanded to know who we were, where we'd come from. I told him we were Jews escaped from Gross Rosen, that we were exhausted and had come into the church to rest and hide. He embraced us then offered his hand - I took it, and as I did so he gave his name. I remember his words precisely. "I am Petr Damyanovitch of the 11th Guards Army of the 3rd Belorussian Front of the Red Army of the Soviet Union. I greet you as comrades. Long live our Leader. Long live the Revolution". We left, grateful to still be alive. We never saw him again'.

He gazed at Thomas and then Rebecca, confused, questioning, sorrowful. 'Is it too late for justice? Must the innocent remain forgotten and the guilty be allowed to go free? When will I be free of these images of Hell? When will my guilt be washed away?' His daughter took his hand again and spoke gently. 'There is a time for everything, father. A time when truth escapes into sunlight. A time when we must forgive ourselves for our own human failings. Now we must deal with the crisis in hand. If we strike now and use our resources as Thomas wishes, then we'll deprive him of the prize he's desperate to win, the goal he's spent so much time and effort pursuing. He's so close to success: to have the cup snatched away from his lips this late in the day may be punishment enough. He's in the twilight years of his life, so he'll know it's too late to start again. Failure will be a bitter draught and he'll have to drink it, and drink deeply'. Solomon smiled; 'Your words, as ever, are wise and yes, he'll hopefully be deprived of his goal, and we'll work with Thomas to achieve this. But for me it will never be anywhere near enough. Denying him riches cannot free me, cleanse me of my guilt. Now I know he is still alive, it has to be more'.

The three left the restaurant for London Commodities' office in Tel Aviv. In truth although the company's headquarters was based in the UK, real power resided in Israel, in the hands of its elderly President and majority shareholder. Rebecca Silverstein ran the company from London as its Chief Executive Officer: she was its public face. But it was also accepted, sometimes reluctantly, by the company's board that long-term strategy and priorities were decided elsewhere, in private discussions between a father and his daughter, to which no one else was privy. London Commodities was an international business with offices stretching across the globe, but in essence it was a simple family-run business in terms of ownership and control. For the remainder of the day, e-mails and faxes were sent from Tel Aviv out across the company's vast network of branches and subsidiaries, instructing the liquidation of easily realisable assets such as UK gilts, US treasuries, and 'JGB's' or Japanese Government Bonds. Faced with problems realising the less liquid investments it held, an alternative strategy was adopted. The company simply borrowed from banks with which it already had lines of credit, raising funds on the security of its portfolio of assets. By the close of the day, after frenetic transactions across multiple time zones, London Commodities' liquidity was vast. Cash had been drawn in from the furthermost corners of its empire, now available for use in a single focused transaction on a scale to rock the foundations of an entire market. NYMEX was the target, a sandcastle awaiting the imminent arrival of a tidal wave.

The following morning and after a restless night, Thomas returned to the nondescript office of London Commodities, Tel Aviv. The three sat around the small table in the chairman's room; everything was in place, and the time for taking the final decision had arrived. Solomon Silverstein spoke. 'Thomas, when you came to me earlier it was to ask that the resources of London Commodities be used to change the direction of a futures contract traded on NYMEX. My view as well as that of my energy research team is that market confidence will be restored soon. Saudi Arabia may be ruled by despots but after Fadlalah's death and the purging of his supporters, it's a more secure regime now than it was a few months ago. Its medium term survival may be questionable, but for our purposes it means that NYMEX prices generally are probably higher than they should be. Today London Commodities will 'borrow,' if you will, futures positions held by NYMEX brokers and sell them into the market, with the aim of repurchasing them at a later agreed date when we have to return them. Now this strategy will have two consequences, if the laws of market psychology hold true. First, by selling now something we don't yet own, going 'short', this will bring new supply of the contracts into the market. The second consequence is less guaranteed but of more profound significance to us. If the market sees a company of our size following this strategy, the interpretation of our action will be that we're expecting prices to fall. We have to be expecting this. That's how profits are made, and that's how the market works'.

He smiled; it was on such simple principles that his billion dollar global trading empire had been founded. Rebecca laughed, temporarily lightening the seriousness of the moment. 'I hope you'll forgive Solomon for explaining things I know you already understand. Thomas, the reason we've had to liquidate most of our assets is to provide against potential risks. If the market falls as we expect and hope it will, then we'll be able to buy the contracts at lower prices and return them to the brokers. Sell high now and buy low later, as Solomon says. But if the market continues to go up we'll end up having to buy at prices higher than we've sold at now. Our possible losses could be enormous if a wide margin opens up between the two. The risk is that if prices increase by just a few percent between now and then our positions will become uncoverable. London Commodities would then go under, and market turmoil would increase significantly. Then your opponents will win the day, making even bigger profits on the long positions we know they've been building up in the NYMEX contracts. Their holdings must be huge by now and if the price falls, they'll be the ones who'll catch a cold'.

Her father interjected; 'You see my friend, we can't both be right. It's going to be either them or us to take the full impact when the market eventually comes back into balance. But we can talk details for hours and still be no further forward. The question's now a simple one - are we ready to strike?' Thomas looked ashen: ultimately this had to be his decision. 'Yes Solomon, if it has to be done, then it's best done now'. Rebecca walked over to her desk; after delivering simple instructions to the fore-warned Head of Trading who was awaiting her call in London, she returned. The blue touch paper had been lit: the question was, who would win and who would lose, now that the game was on?

Thomas, Solomon and Rebecca left the office, the purpose of the morning's short meeting achieved. Soon the NYMEX brokers would be placing orders on behalf of a new player in the market; a giant, secretive financial institution was about to enter with a perception as to its future direction that went against the prevailing wisdom, against the herd instinct and against the panic which had been bubbling under in recent days. If market participants thought the strategy was wrong and based upon some miscalculation, then prices would continue to soar. But if, instead, it was believed that some adjustment was now overdue, that perhaps it was time for reflection and calm, then prices would start to fall, slowly at first, then rapidly if a trend developed. And with each percentage point of fall, the prospect of Damyanovitch's dreams being realised would slip further away.

Their taxi pulled up outside the British Embassy for an audience granted the previous day. Solomon and the Ambassador were old friends: setting up a meeting at such short notice would have eluded the most prominent of businessman or politician but for him, the President of one of Israel's foremost financial institutions, the Embassy's door was always open. Time being of the essence, Solomon made his simple request. The Ambassador's shock at his words was palpable; carefully he explained the impossibility of what had been asked of him, the diplomatic furore that would inevitably follow, and the million and one reasons why it would be doomed to fail. But he knew his friend was a determined man, and that his mind was made up: he smiled and gave way. He'd accede to Solomon Silverstein's request, even if a diplomatic Pandora's Box would be opened in the process. The three thanked the Ambassador for his time and left. Within an hour they were aboard an El Al flight for London, heading for the centre of the storm. As soon as the Ambassador was alone he reflected upon what he'd been asked to do; he reached for the telephone on his desk. In the space of an hour he made several calls: it was vital to adhere to the correct protocols and see that the necessary paperwork was completed. His final call was to New Scotland Yard, London; detectives would be waiting for Solomon as soon as his flight touched down at Heathrow.

Chapter Seventy Four

Lincoln Davies looked at the ticker tape passing across the computer screen, first in mild disbelief and then with a more intense and mounting panic. There had to be a reporting error, but a click through to the NYMEX real time website confirmed the worst: oil futures prices were falling across the board, gradually reversing the steady rise over the past few days. He had been trading in the commodities markets for over a decade, first as a grain futures speculator and then as a market maker in oil derivatives, and was familiar with their capacity for unpredictability and short-term erratic, groundless swings. But today's shift went against all conventional wisdom; turmoil in Saudi Arabia looked set to continue, and his efforts and those of his associates to drive up the market had been bearing fruit in recent weeks. Now the market was heading south and there was no obvious reason for the overnight change in sentiment. With eyes still on the webpage he reached for the telephone; pressing a speed dial button put him through to his principal contact at NYMEX. 'Frank, I guess you've been expecting this call. I'll get straight to the point. What the hell's going on? You know I'm holding huge long positions and every percentage point fall loses me millions, and yet you didn't call. I've had to call you. Just tell me - why's the market falling? There's no comforting news coming out of the Mid East; last I heard there's still chaos, panic and murder everywhere. Players like me as well as the refineries - we've all been going long. And yet the market's drifting downwards. What's it all about?'

Usually Davies exemplified New England 'old money' courtesy, but now there was anger in his voice. Tacit criticism of his fair-weather informant at NYMEX didn't help. Frank Slapij recounted information he'd gleaned from other brokers, but this was unreliable, sketchy hearsay. His efforts to find out more about the giant which was now pushing the market in a new direction, any information to do with its intentions and, more importantly, its financial resources, had been fruitless. Eventually, a name had emerged. After a shower of expletives and personal attacks on the broker's competence or lack of it, Davies decided there was no further purpose to the conversation. 'I suggest you get on with doing what I pay you to do. Find out about this company, London Commodities. Who the hell are they? Just try to tell me something. Ring me back within the hour, and it'd better be good. Otherwise you'd better start looking for another job, but I can tell you now, it'll not be in this market again'. He slammed down the telephone. Slapij was left holding the receiver; he smiled, amused by the way dockside obscenities had been delivered in the most cultured of Harvard-educated accents. But the threat, he knew, was not an empty one: he began making his calls.

Precisely on the hour the telephone on Davies's desk rang: it was Slapij. This time the information was more detailed but he had nothing to report about the company's resource base. London Commodities was a highly secretive privately-held UK-based company with representative offices in all the major capitals of the world. It had a reputation for ignoring short term market trends and, unfortunately for Davies, its hunches usually proved correct. It had links with Israel's business and political circles, and this seemed to be one of the factors encouraging other speculators on NYMEX to follow the company's lead. If any organisation knew anything about the Byzantine world of Saudi politics and knew with any degree of certainty the likelihood of the survival of the House of Saud, it would be Israeli Intelligence, Mossad. By comparison, the US's home-grown agencies, principally the CIA and its associated 'think tanks', were rank amateurs. And if Mossad knew anything for sure, it would be quickly communicated to the country's informal financial backers. London Commodities, the market believed, clearly fell within this category and accordingly any strategy it appeared to be pursuing was to be taken very seriously. 'Lincoln, this downturn may only be a short-term market reaction to some candyfloss rumours. But if it's not, then I'm afraid you'll have to start liquidating your positions and fast, even if this means taking a loss. Bailing out of a collapsing market is always difficult. As an alternative, why not try getting together with London Commodities? Strike a deal. Contact their head office in London, talk to them, find out what they want, and see if they're willing to negotiate. That would be my advice to you. You've got nothing to lose'. Davies regained his composure: there was a problem, it could be dealt with, and emotional outbursts just wouldn't help. 'Thanks Frank, and sorry for my temper earlier. I've got a lot to lose. If you hear anything meantime, I'll be grateful if you could get back to me'. He was still angry but had to conceal it; after all, if the market came to think that his own company was in financial difficulties, that he himself was wobbling, then the wolves would begin to gather.

⁕

General Salman Rahman, Head of the Saudi Counter-Insurgency Unit, leaned across the table in a windowless room. He sat in the heart of the Ministry for Internal Security building in downtown Riyadh. For the past hour he'd explained to the Minister the measures he'd implemented to quash the insurgency sweeping through the Kingdom's principal cities. Torture had been routine but low-level in most cases. Shootings on sight had been commonplace; there was nothing one could do with bad blood other than purge it completely. He agreed with the Minister's observation that the court system, a reliable component of the state apparatus, made the outcomes of future trials fairly predictable; but in the meantime potential martyrs would have to be held in Saudi jails, doing their utmost to rally the disaffected, the young, and the militants. The Minister, the General respectfully suggested, should accept his advice: given the present chaos, it was better to circumvent the system altogether and accept the principle and practice of state-sanctioned summary executions. In this way the Government would avoid lengthy and distracting appeals, however token these may be, which would attract publicity generated by foreign human rights activists. The Minister sighed; yes, the killings should continue, at least until hard-line opponents were either dead or, at the very least, in exile. And then there'd be the time and stability to enter into dialogue with the moderates. Both knew in their hearts that such a time would never arrive.

'Now General Rahman, we come, of course, to the matter of the attempted coup which as we know, was led by Hassan Fadlalah but financed and coordinated elsewhere. Where are we on this?' Rahman thumbed through the file he'd brought to the meeting: the record of the last strangled gasps of Fadlalah before his death. 'As you know Minister, Fadlalah intended to lead a new, illegitimate government himself, had his terrorist plans been realised. But we also know there were wealthy individuals in other countries who bankrolled and protected him and his supporters in the Kingdom. To a large extent they were successful in this strategy; the riots they whipped up, combined with the bomb attacks in our cities, stretched the resources of my department close to breaking point. We now have a name for the coordinator of the foreign involvement - an American called Lincoln Davies. This man is exceptionally wealthy and has powerful political connections in the White House. I'm afraid there's little we can do about him other than to make complaints through the appropriate informal diplomatic channels. I suspect the US Administration will be keen to avoid the embarrassment of this becoming public, so perhaps we should just leave the matter in their hands'. The Minister nodded in agreement; the Embassy in Washington would be made aware of Davies's involvement, and their concerns and strong protest would be expressed at the next scheduled meeting between the Ambassador and the Secretary of State. Diplomatic exchanges rarely achieved satisfactory results for either side, but if the Administration agreed to rein in this errant billionaire, this at least would be a reasonable outcome. The fact that the Saudis knew that this highly placed American had been supporting an attempted coup might also come in very useful as leverage in future deal brokering on other subjects.

The General turned a few more pages. 'Minister, we also have another name: a London-based American lawyer, Carter Buckmaster. This man has been acting as go-between between Fadlalah and Davies but his political protection is, as far as we're aware, non-existent. There's no doubt he visited Fadlalah during his time in Belmarsh Prison, gave him advice, and smuggled in a mobile phone on several occasions'. The Minister looked surprised at this; 'So in other words, he enabled the prisoner to make contact with his followers here, presumably to counsel and encourage them about bombings and assassination targets, yes? You're saying this man, Buckmaster, played an active part in the recent murders of our citizens, government officials and members of the military? I don't understand. Is he a Zionist?' The General smiled, a sinister grin rarely seen outside the interrogation rooms. 'No Minister, he's not a Zionist. Nor is he a wealthy man or a seeker of wealth. Mr. Buckmaster is a Christian fundamentalist who hates everything we stand for. From what Fadlalah told us during questioning he blames us for most of the suffering and conflict in the world. He's the sort of man who'll come back again and again until a fatal blow is delivered against us. In this regard, our assessment would be that he's a significantly more dangerous opponent than Lincoln Davies'.

The Minister frowned; the General was evidently concerned about this man but the possibility of retaliation via diplomatic channels seemed remote. 'So what do you suggest, General? That we wait until he next visits this country then arrest him at the airport? Wouldn't that just spark a diplomatic incident? Where is he now? Can we extradite him to face charges here?' The General murmured: 'He's in London so there's no prospect of extradition. As we know, many of our enemies shelter in that city, exploiting human rights laws. If we can't even get our own criminals sent back, there's no prospect of getting hold of a US citizen'. 'So what's your solution?' Salman Rahman looked at him but said nothing. Suddenly the Minister understood the single thought passing through the General's mind, and was shocked. Stepping away from the table, he pointed his finger accusingly. 'Have you gone mad? I could never agree to that- state-sanctioned assassination of a non-Saudi citizen, and on a friendly country's soil. Do you understand the consequences if it were discovered that we'd been involved? We'd become a pariah state overnight. Our enemies in the foreign media would be delighted; it would confirm everyone's prejudices about us. We'd be ordered to scale back our embassy staff in both Washington and London, and the Europeans would follow suit soon afterwards. You've just not thought this through.' The General stood up, angered by the Minister's disrespect; his voice began to rise. 'I'll tell you what I know, sir. For the past few months I've been fighting an insurgency that's had the makings of a civil war in all but name. And now, you suggest I worry about diplomatic etiquette when dealing with the very people - foreigners or otherwise, it doesn't matter a damn to me - who've brought about this crisis. I'm not going to hold back when it comes to protecting our country and our way of life. I'll use any means to smash our enemies, whether they are at home or abroad. This man Buckmaster deserves to die. Now, are you going to get in the way of justice being served against an enemy of our state?' The Minister was shocked by the outburst, aware at the same time that the regime he served was both buttressed and protected by the military on whose behalf the General spoke. He knew he had to back down for now, to give way to the General's proposed course of action despite its potentially destructive ramifications. 'It seems your mind's made up, General Rahman, and there's little I can say to dissuade you. I suppose that if I will the ends, I must also will the means. Do what you must, but please, I don't wish to know anything about it. I'll not specifically authorise anything; just tell me when it's done'. Exhausted by the confrontation and fearful for the future, he left.

———⊶⊷———

Carter Buckmaster approached Ms. Penn at reception, carrying his attaché case, as he strolled out of the office early. He put his finger to his lips. 'Don't tell the others- I don't want to cause unrest in the ranks'. She smiled: 'I'll not tell a soul, Mr. Buckmaster. Have a pleasant evening'. 'You too, Ms. Penn, you too'. He leaned across the desk and gently kissed her on the side of her face, his lips barely making contact. The middle-aged woman, worldly-wise and newly invigorated by divorce from her feckless husband who was still living in the US, smiled and blushed. She knew it was an impulsive act on his part, wholly innocent and without ulterior motive. It was something he'd never done before and would never do again. She'd remember the kiss until the day she died.

Buckmaster made his way to the nearby multi-storey car park, considering his options for the evening ahead. He would return to his flat and then head for the local park later, where an open-air opera was being performed by a local company; he relished the thought of music and colour beneath a starlit sky. He would be able to relax and think his own thoughts, however melancholic those might be. He climbed into his car and turned the ignition key. The explosion that followed was heard several streets away; it would be hours later before the fire service and police, arriving at the scene within minutes, were able to disentangle the owner's remains from the wreckage, and later again before his identity could be determined. The national news agencies, taking a lead from their state-owned Saudi Arabian counterparts, quickly put the assassination down to a revenge attack by a London-based splinter group of supporters of Hassan Fadlalah, the recently executed Saudi dissident for whom Buckmaster's firm had acted in the past. But the minor official in the trade attaché's office at the Saudi Arabian Embassy, the resident high-ranking officer in Saudi Intelligence and an expert in explosives, knew otherwise.

Chapter Seventy Five

Seventy five miles south east of Baku, in the Zafar-Mashal block of the Azerbaijan sector of the Caspian Sea, semi submersible drilling rig DSS-20 bobbed up and down in the darkness. Waves as high as two-storey houses lashed across her pontoons and columns, the calmness of the earlier part of the day given way in the blink of an eye to angry swirls of deep, dark waters that tugged and pulled at the legs of the monster trespasser. The rig was robust, of course: a technological marvel sent in by the Great Powers to plunder the black gold, including Azerbaijan herself who'd kept back fifty percent of the field's ownership. On deck Captain Aliyev strutted and screamed at the sky like a madman, even though it had been weeks since a drop of vodka passed his lips. A dozen or so of the thirty crew on board braved the elements on deck, and to them his exuberance was infectious; they too gathered around, holding hands for safety but also to dance as one across the deck sodden with salt water. Bottles of coca cola were shared between them, the usually hard-drinking sailors wary of the stronger stuff given the violence of nature around them.

Aliyev continued laughing, occasionally pulling a crewman over to dance with him in the circle. He planned to retire within a year, and today Mother Nature had blessed him with her bounty. Today had been the best day of his life, one of the handful he'd really always remember and whisper about as his children and grandchildren gathered about him as he lay on his deathbed, twenty five years later. Today drilling rig DSS-20 had struck oil in the Zafar-Mashal block, a find likely to be so big that it would eventually dwarf all the previous finds in the area. And he had been the captain when it happened; he had been in charge when the seabed cracked and the inky, thick treasure burst forth towards the hammer smashing down through the waves above, crunching all the way through the Earth's ancient crust. He embraced his comrades and started to cry through sheer elation. After today, the foreign conglomerates would be happier; their investments in the Caspian would now bear fruit into the dimly lit future. And their immediate master, the state-owned company SOCAR, would also be happy; proof was there for all to see, as they'd always said it would be, that this was the new Klondike after all. But most importantly of all, at least for the men and women who'd risked their lives to make it all possible, they'd be heroes to their country and to their families not seen for months but thought of every waking hour. Soon they'd be home again, home with those they loved.

News of the Zafar-Mashal strike flashed with instant efficiency through the international energy community. As the potential impact of the find was assessed and its implications for future energy supplies disseminated, market participants breathed a collective sigh of relief. Now there was an alternative to the Middle Eastern producers which could well be on-stream in the very near future: more reliable, and not racked by secular-religious schizophrenia or political ambivalence towards foreign direct investment. But in any case the Saudi regime had survived; it had seen off its most dangerous opponent, so supplies were assured from that part of the world as well, at least for the time being. Fear, combined with a herd instinct, is a far greater driver of markets than cool consideration of economic realities, as NYMEX had shown for the past few weeks. As frayed nerves began to settle, calmness breezed through the market. Refineries and speculators who'd gone long during recent weeks, buying up futures contracts to hedge against unquantifiable risk, now began unloading, and at speed. Analysts now urged clients to 'go naked': not to bother taking any positions in the futures markets and simply to brave the calmer fluctuations of the open marketplace. With order restored, the value of the long futures positions held by Lincoln Davies and his associates dropped like a stone, the price collapsing well beneath the trigger level fixed in the terms of the Caspian bonds. Investors' rights would not arise, at least not for now, and not without a fresh period of market upheaval. The Caspian seabed rights, long craved by Damyanovitch and held by a special purpose vehicle constructed by two now dead lawyers, were safe.

Chapter Seventy Six

Lincoln Davies made his way by taxi to his regular weekly meeting at the Department of Energy, 1000 Independence Avenue in Washington. He would have preferred to call off the meeting, having nothing but unfavourable news to report to the Secretary of State, Quentin Slaney. The as yet unrealised losses mounting up in the vast NYMEX positions he'd accumulated over recent weeks also meant that his time would be better spent at his office, on the telephone, cajoling and threatening the weaker members of the conspiracy who were anxious at the slide in the market and the corresponding deterioration in their own positions. But the enquiry as to whether the Secretary of State would be willing to postpone had been met with outright refusal; it was evident that Davies's strategy was failing, and Slaney was duty-bound to interrogate him as to what steps he intended to take to remedy the situation.

As Davies waited in the large conference room, he sweated, dabbing a handkerchief about his brow and face. But this wasn't due to the temperature - the air conditioning was perfect - but instead a fear of the barrage of criticism he knew he'd soon endure was causing him to perspire profusely. 'Lincoln, a pleasure to see you again, and apologies I couldn't accommodate your request for a postponement. I think you'll agree we've all got to keep a tight rein on matters of timing these days'. The infinitely polite but notoriously unforgiving Secretary of State shook his hand. There was a violent schizophrenia at the core of his personality which Davies had heard about but not as yet witnessed personally; he wondered if today it would be his turn to experience the ambitious and aggressive young man's wrath. They began as usual with small talk: prospects for the Party at the next Congressional elections, basketball (for which Davies had no interest or knowledge to engage properly on the subject), and the state of the global oil markets.

The younger man then turned to the meeting's real purpose; he spoke with an unmistakable frisson of threat, even menace, in his voice. 'Now this next subject's one that's really been preoccupying me the last few days. Let me see if I've got it right. When you first came to me it was with a handful of promises that you and your associates would deliver on if this Administration and I gave you a free hand. The present Saudi regime would be given a fatal push and then be replaced with a fundamentalist government, apparently hostile but which, beneath the surface, would deliver oil supplies to us at preferential rates. You also assured us that you'd take control of the oil rights in the Caspian seabed without a single shot being fired, and that US supplies from the area would be guaranteed well into the future. All that you required was that we looked the other way while you got on with things. That we didn't ask too many questions. Gave diplomatic cover where needed. That sort of thing. Now correct me if I'm wrong about this, Lincoln, but you've failed to deliver either of these promises. Is that accurate?'

Davies shifted awkwardly in his chair: he was being treated like a naughty schoolboy. 'Our Caspian strategy depended upon a substantial rise in prices on the New York Mercantile Exchange. This was happening as we had predicted, but then, due to unforeseeable events, the market settled and prices have been falling ever since'. The Secretary of State remained calm, impassive. 'Fadlalah, your man, is dead, so there's precisely zero prospect of you delivering on the first promise. On your other promise, your success depends entirely on unlocking the SPV that holds the Caspian oil rights, am I correct? And you simply don't have the key. Let me turn to another matter that's concerning me. Yesterday I received a copy of a private letter delivered to the President by the Saudi Ambassador here in Washington. It complains that certain US citizens led by a prominent US businessman - and I should be clear about this - you're named by them... they say these people have conspired to bring down the Saudi Government'. Davies was visibly shaken: he'd spent most of his business life in the shadows, hiding behind an opaque network of offshore shell companies, but now he was the subject of official communications between governments. He felt uncomfortably exposed.

'Now, earlier, I implied that a distinction exists between the Administration and myself, although of course I'm part of the Administration. This is because the President gave me a 'carte blanche' for action. He didn't want to know the details so that should any of this come out, he could justifiably claim ignorance as his defence - that he hadn't been informed by those further down the tree. Blame rogue elements in the CIA, Saudi extremists living in exile, that sort of thing. He was entirely in agreement with the general thrust of the plan but didn't want to know how we were going to achieve it. But this letter changes things. He has now instructed me to ask you- to *order* you- to desist with the present strategy with immediate effect. So, what I'm requiring you to do now is give up on your attempts to manipulate NYMEX. You've failed up until now and there's no reason to think you're suddenly going to start succeeding in the near future. You'll also scale back efforts to destabilise the economies of those states adjoining the Caspian Sea. Politically, the Administration's priorities have changed; now we're looking to establish an economic bulwark against Russia, right up against her borders, and your goals no longer coincide with ours. So Lincoln, do you understand what you've got to do, or do I have to go over it with you again, in more detail?'

Davies paused; gazing down at his perfectly polished shoes, he contemplated whether to fight or take flight, to stay or passively take his leave. He loathed democracy and the hypocrisy and expediency of its third-rate servants. He responded, his voice measured and succinct. 'There are those who look to change the world, Mr. Secretary, and those who sit back and watch it being changed. I am in the former category while, with respect, I have to say that you, as well as your master in the White House, are in the latter. You're nothing but a coward, selling out your country, giving up while the game's still being played, just because the going got a little tough. And he's the same, Sir - a man with no principles, no guts. What hope can we have for this nation's future when it's in the hands of shysters such as you?' The younger man leapt to his feet, his face reddening with rage; his words frothed out in anger. 'You dare to come here today and speak to me like this? You'll do as I say. We are the masters and this is a democracy. When we say 'jump' you, and people like you, say 'how high'. The only reason we're backing away from you is because you failed. Do you understand? *Failed*. Now, are you going to follow my instructions? If not, you can damn well get out of this office because we'll be wasting our time speaking any further'. He then spoke quietly, in stark contrast to the preceding deafening rant. 'Be sure to understand, Lincoln, that the President will not allow another set of Plumbers to come before a Congressional Committee. You'll recall where that ended. No, there'll be no parting salute on the White House lawn, not this time. So what's it to be?' Davies stood up, shocked by the analogy; Watergate had been very different, of course, although then, as now, a President's complicity lay at the end of a sequence of murky operations and apparently unconnected incidents. Davies's contempt for the Commander-in-Chief was sustained. 'Mr. Secretary, I'll continue going about my business and no, I'll not stop just because you're getting a fit of the jitters. Now get out of my way - I've got work to do'. The Secretary of State stood aside; within seconds Lincoln Davies re-emerged into the still stifling mid-afternoon heat. It would be a further quarter of an hour before the pre-arranged taxi arrived: the driver, not tipped earlier, had decided to keep him waiting.

Back in the safety of his office, Davies poured a large whisky, sipped it, and waited for his anger to subside. After several minutes with his eyes shut and his brain buzzing, he picked up the telephone and began dialing. 'Hello, Petr? I'm calling you because we've got problems, as I'm sure you realise if you've been following NYMEX. I know it's always suited us to communicate through Carter but now Fadlalah's assassins have got him, we've got no choice but to collaborate more closely. When the Saudis killed Fadlalah they cut off the Hydra's head, and now London's infested with his fanatical supporters. I guess Carter was an easy target'. Damyanovitch was stunned; he knew nothing of Buckmaster's death, but was aware of how horribly wrong everything had gone in Shaybah. Now his close friend from the Cold War days was dead: it looked as if everything was rapidly unraveling. 'I hadn't heard about Carter's death. He was a friend... but now's not the time for reflection. What do you propose we do to put our strategy back on course, before it's too late?'

The edge of panic in Davies's voice was unmistakable. 'In the past few days there's been another reason, quite apart from the recent oil strike in the Caspian, for the market's cooling. A company called London Commodities- I'd never heard of them until I spoke with my broker- has come late into NYMEX, taking absolutely huge short positions. This signalled to the market that they know something important about the Saudi political situation, or Mid East oil output, perhaps some impending announcement of a new find, and futures prices are going to tumble as a result. The company's got close ties with the Israeli political establishment, so the assumption is that they should know. Going short now suggests they expect to buy at a much lower price later. That's how the game goes. They've got vast financial clout and inside information - the perfect combination. You've got to get to them, get them to unwind their short positions and switch strategy. It'll look like they've made a mistake, so this should unsettle the market again'. Damyanovitch waited, but Davies failed to address the obvious question. 'Lincoln, why should they change now? The market's falling so they're already deep in profit territory. They can only make more by just holding their existing positions. What are we going to put on the table?'

Davies snapped his reply, irritated that his co-conspirator seemed to be expecting him to take the lead. 'Offer them anything, Petr. My positions on NYMEX are killing me; we've got to do something and quickly. If the prices don't head north soon, you can say goodbye to breaking up the SPV and any hope we had of taking control of the Caspian oil rights. I suggest you speak with the president of the company. I don't know who the hell he is, nobody does, but we must be able to find out, and invite him in on our project. I'm sure we can come to an arrangement for an equal share-out, if they're willing to play. You'll just have to speak to him and negotiate in the old-fashioned American way. Everybody's got a price, it's just a matter of finding out what it is'.

With military precision, Damyanovitch's personal secretary set to work. First, she tracked down the address in Central London where London Commodities had its registered office, and then made telephone contact with the personal assistant to the president. A meeting was arranged at short notice. To Damyanovitch's irritation it was apparent that they'd been expecting his call, and had already set out a range of dates and times from which he was invited to choose. Perhaps the company's willingness to talk was indicative of an eagerness to negotiate, and yet something didn't seem quite right: everything was too organised, and they were being too accommodating. After all, they'd know he was the one who needed to plead and ask for favours: they needed nothing, and their position was one of absolute strength. London Commodities was already sitting on vast unrealised profits on its short positions on NYMEX, and these could only increase with the passing of time and the further drifting downwards of prices. But this was not the time to contemplate hidden agendas; the situation was deteriorating by the hour and the company had the resources and the influence on NYMEX to put the project back on track. Sergei Ivanov was instructed to ready the private jet. Within an hour Damyanovitch arrived at the private airfield alongside Moscow Domodedovo airport; half an hour later he was airbound to Heathrow.

Armand Hunter sat calmly on the bench at 34th Herald Square subway. With his eyes fixed firmly upon the previous day's Wall Street Journal, a loose fitting, expensive Italian designer suit concealing the taut muscles of his abdomen, he was the epitome of the successful New York professional. And that was the image he was keen to put out. He pushed his fake spectacles back up onto the bridge of his nose and waited. An hour and a half earlier he'd slouched around his small rented apartment in a seedy block in the Bronx in just a vest and shorts, chewing his way through pastrami on rye, contemplating which distant part of the country he'd move to after the day's work had been done. He despised the heat. But now he had a job to do; he watched the crowd pushing and shoving at the doors of each train coming in, but didn't move. To a naive onlooker he was obviously waiting for the crush to subside, passing the time perusing his vast stockholdings in the WSJ. But a more intuitive watcher with time to stand at a distance and observe would have perceived the unmistakable body language of a predator: pretending to be looking in one direction while in truth keeping his attention focused elsewhere, scrutinising the passing herd forcing its way through the system like wildebeest, looking for a victim.

An equally impressively attired man appeared on the platform, his disdain for common humanity evident as he tried in vain to maintain a distance, perhaps just a hand's width, between himself and the crowd milling about him. He was about the same age as the man now folding away his newspaper, but in terms of physique there was no comparison. He pushed his way to the front of the crowd until he stood at the platform's edge, staking out his claim to the ground below and the air above into which nobody would be allowed to trespass. The immeasurably stronger onlooker had by now also propelled himself through the crowd, manhandling out of his path the young and the old alike. Eventually he reached his goal, standing immediately behind the arrogant man refusing to allow into his space those people whose presence might, paradoxically, have protected him. He stood alone, unshielded, gazing up the tracks with unconcealed irritation. What was the cause of the delay? Why had so many people been allowed on to the platform at the same time? He swore this would be the last time he'd use public transport, just as he'd sworn last time, and the time before that. But now he was determined to get into the next train come hell or high water: he moved closer to the edge. And then it came: the gust of air heralding an imminent arrival. As the train glided out of the darkness and into full view the familiar surge forward happened. The bespectacled, well dressed man gripped Lincoln Davies by both arms: raising his knee he pushed at the back of his legs so he buckled like a dropped sack of potatoes, suspended by the arms now held so tightly he couldn't move. As the train rushed in the assassin threw his victim forward, just in time as it seared and sparked along the metal rails. Brakes screeched, filling the air with pungent odour, but it was all too late: nothing could stop the unstoppable iron fist punching its way right through the warm flesh. The lifeless body was pushed along the tracks, mangled beneath the front of the train, to the opposite end of the platform; the walls echoed with screams of shock and terror as the herd stampeded to get away from the scene.

Armand Hunter melted away with the crowd. There was no reason to remain behind: he knew he'd delivered on his assignment, so it was time to leave. Within a day he'd be lying on a beach, sipping cocktails, watching the world go by. His fee would be paid before the week was out, invoiced by a Delaware-registered energy consultancy for a report snappily titled 'The Kyoto Protocol failures: carbon emissions trading - what future now?' He knew nothing about Kyoto but the report would hold up to the closest of inspection by government spending watchdogs; after all, it had been written by the Secretary of State at the Department for Energy himself, although of course his name would be absent from it. A fee of one hundred thousand taxpayer dollars was hardly disproportionate when buying such expertise. Hunter smiled as he wandered out of the subway and into the bright light of day. The job had almost been a pleasure; it was so much easier dealing with government officials, particularly directly with a Secretary of State, compared with earlier 'Black Bag' days when the simplest of coverts had to be approved along an opaque chain of command. Hopefully there'd be more assignments like this in the not-too-distant future; he looked forward to a fruitful and deepening relationship.

The decision to terminate Lincoln Davies had been made even before his arrival for the previous meeting with the Secretary of State. If he'd been passive and accommodating, agreeing to sail off into the sunset for a year's trip around the world in his luxury yacht there was a chance that perhaps, just perhaps, he might have been reprieved. But his aggressiveness and absolute unwillingness to compromise had sealed his fate. There was also a touch of madness in his disrespectfulness. He'd never have held up in front of any future Congressional Inquiry hearing: he'd have lost his temper and then it would all have come out. The President's claim to be ignorant of detail would have saved him, at least in the short term, but probably destroyed any future prospect of re-election. And for Slaney himself it would have been prison. Government investigators have a habit of pulling at loose threads, trying to find where they truly begin and end; who would have thought, after all, that the arrest of low level burglars at the Watergate hotel, the media-dubbed 'Plumbers', would lead to the resignation of a President and the washing away of a Republican Administration by a Democrat tidal wave? This young, ambitious, amoral Secretary of State was not about to let history repeat itself; Davies was now safely dead and soon enough the trail would be, like him, stone cold.

Chapter Seventy Seven

Damyanovitch's plane coasted to a halt on the small airfield outside Heathrow. He and the pilot proceeded through Immigration Control with barely a question asked. This was after all one of the principal benefits of 'dual residence' status in the United Kingdom notwithstanding the reality of spending the overwhelming part of one's time outside the country: one could pass through with minimal fuss, enquiry or paperwork. There had been other considerations too, persuading him of the wisdom of compromising his Russian status in this way: having a bolthold should the government in Moscow become hostile to a loyal servant; tax benefits; and ease of opening foreign bank accounts without the stigma of applying from a Russian domicile. The two men headed for the pre-booked hotel. After a meal and brief rest it was time for the chairman of Moscow Alpha Bank to make his way to the office of London Commodities for a rendezvous with a nemesis he didn't even know existed. As the taxi weaved its way through the choking traffic he made several attempts to contact his associate in New York; there was no reply, only a diversion to voicemail. He was unwilling by instinct to leave a message. Lincoln Davies never had his phone switched off: he wondered if there was a problem.

As he entered the discreet modern building he looked around and was impressed; its simple, modest décor reflected a corporate mind evidently unconcerned with impression management and puffed-up image. He stopped at the central desk and was mildly perturbed by the security guard's familiarity; he immediately recognised Damyanovitch's name and the room to which he should be directed without even needing to glance down at the register in front of him. He wasn't even signed in, being instead waved through to the lift and instructed to travel up to the seventh floor. He knocked firmly on the door of the room he had been directed to, but there was no reply from within; pushing at the door he entered an empty room, taking his place at the end of a long chrome and glass table. There he sat and waited, irritated that nobody had had the courtesy or business etiquette to be there to meet him. Apart from one glass and a carafe of water, the table was bare. No name plates, no files, no paper pad or pens. The door at the opposite end of the room opened and an old man walked in. He said nothing, but instead took his place at the head of the table, not even passing down to shake his guest's hand. His attire was simple: corduroy trousers, a charcoal grey jacket which didn't match, white shirt and red bow tie. On his head was a discreet black velvet kippah skullcap. Rather than the head of a multi-billion dollar commodities business, he epitomised a Jewish tailor or a simple tradesman from early twentieth century Warsaw.

Damyanovitch stared at the old man: there was something familiar, something that stirred him, troubled him at the core of his being, but he didn't know its cause. Still the old man hadn't spoken; he just sat there, his fingers calmly interlinked, and gazed at his guest. Unsettled by the silence, Damyanovitch spoke. 'Mr. President: I take it you are the President of London Commodities? I've come here today in my capacity of Chairman of Moscow Alpha Bank and as the representative of a consortium of businessmen with interests in the international oil business. As I'm sure you're aware, we've been pursuing a strategy in recent months that's involved taking substantial long positions in a particular futures contract traded on NYMEX. During the past few days this strategy has been put at risk by the large short positions your company has been taking on the Exchange in the same futures contract in which we're interested. I'm here today to negotiate with you to resolve this apparent conflict of objectives'. He thought he saw a slight nod, and briefly encouraged, added 'So, shall we discuss possible terms? What would it take to persuade you to liquidate your existing positions?'

Silverstein listened intently, not to the words, but to the intonations of the voice which was uttering them. It was as powerful and confident as it had been the last time they'd met; unaffected by the passing of so many years. Still without uttering a word, he stood up and walked towards the monster he now recognised: but he had to be sure. Misreading his host's purpose, Damyanovitch extended his hand: if they were to shake now, better this late than not at all. Silverstein took it but instead of shaking it, he gripped it and held it up, unfolding the fingers. He nodded when he saw the two half-digits: now, no doubt remained in his mind. 'My name is Solomon Silverstein. I am a Jew escaped from the Gross Rosen Death Camp. I've come here to hide, for safety. Please, spare my life'. He stared deeply into his visitor's eyes now, and Damyanovitch's eyes in response widened in horror as his past instantly reared up in all its awfulness. With a dreadful, crystal clarity the image of a child burst onto his mind's eye, now even sharper and even more terrible than it had ever been before in his frequent dreams, and in its intrusions into his moments of quiet reflection. He was holding the child, listening to it draw its final breaths, its death brought about by the one act in his life, the single act of savagery, which he regretted and which had haunted him ever since. The old man continued. 'I am a Jew who speaks for the innocents of Nemmersdorf. You are here to answer for the guilt of Nemmersdorf. You should have killed me that night. I am a witness'.

Damyanovitch momentarily faltered; overwhelmed by the shock of the situation, he placed his hand on the conference table to steady himself. 'That was then….it was the War. I cannot be summoned back into the past, not now, and not by you'. He stared back at the old man then spoke with unmistakable hostility. 'I raised myself above the heaps of bodies of those who deserved to die, and at my hands. I came through it all with my innocence and clarity of purpose intact. But then fate brought me to Nemmersdorf, and all was lost.' He trembled with rage, but the anger was not for his accuser: it was for another. 'One single death, one life taken in error, and the lives of those also there that night; I have been damned by the lifetime of regret which followed. You, a Jew, will know that to save a life is to save the world, but to take the life of an innocent is to destroy it. If I could be hanged a thousand times for that child, and for them, it would not be enough. Is the guilt I've borne for a lifetime, this tonne of iron that crushes down upon my soul in my every waking hour, to be my only punishment? I weep for the feebleness of justice'.

The internal door through which the old man had entered opened again. Four men walked in: one in a suit and the others in police uniform. The British Ambassador in Tel Aviv, enraged to learn of the wartime massacre on holy ground, had done his work well; all the appropriate documentation had been speedily filed with the Attorney General back in London, and the Metropolitan Police had been informed. Silverstein looked to them and nodded; the suited man approached Damyanovitch.

'Sir, please confirm your name to be Petr Damyanovitch'. He looked at the policemen standing nearby. 'Yes, that is my name'. 'Please also confirm that you are Petr Damyanovitch, a veteran of the 11th Guards Army of the 3rd Belorussian Front of the Armed Forces of the Former Soviet Union'. He'd not heard these words for a lifetime: he felt proud again. 'Yes, I am he'. The suited man paused and then continued in an officious voice; 'Petr Damyanovitch, I am arresting you pursuant to powers vested in me under the War Crimes Act, 1991 on suspicion that you did, on or about the twenty first day of October 1944, commit a war crime in the German village of Nemmersdorf. You do not have to say anything but if you choose not to raise matters now that you subsequently come to rely on in court, this may be used in evidence against you. Do you understand this warning, and the charge on which you are now being arrested?'

Damyanovitch's power to reason was slipping away: he wondered whether he was in some terrible dream. He tried to answer but his mind was confused; for the first time in his life he was deeply afraid. 'You can't arrest me. I am a Russian citizen. I am not British. You have no authority to do this. I will leave now and you would be unwise to stop me. I demand to be taken to the Russian Embassy'. The Chief Inspector from Scotland Yard spoke again, addressing each of the defences raised by the prisoner; 'Sir, the War Crimes Act applies to British citizens and to those persons who have become resident in the United Kingdom at any time since 1990. You come within this latter category. The Act applies to crimes committed on German territory, and to territory controlled by the German Army between 1939 and 1945. Your crime was committed in Nemmersdorf during this time, and as such is eligible for prosecution under the Act. You will now be taken from here to a local police station to be formally charged. You will not be permitted to travel to the Russian Embassy, and should now consider yourself formally under arrest. You'll be allowed to see your own solicitor, or to have one appointed for you, in due course'. In handcuffs, Damyanovitch was then led outside to be transported to Paddington Green Police Station for processing prior to transference to a secure prison. They pushed his head down as they steered him into the back seat of a waiting police car. For so proud a man, this was the ultimate humiliation.

Solomon Silverstein sat alone in the deserted conference room. He felt a burden of sadness for those who had died around him in Gross

Rosen: so many killed, so many family lines torn up and destroyed, leaving no trace at all of their existence. For them there were no descendants, nobody to mourn them or light candles for their souls. His thoughts turned again to that night in the small church and the atrocity he had witnessed. They had been innocents too, or at worst passive collaborators, terrorised by a regime that had drifted in like an all-enveloping fog off the sea. He wanted to weep for all of them, equally. Thomas and Rebecca now appeared at his side, having observed his wish not to be present when he confronted the tormentor of his dreams. He held their hands and smiled. Realising the significance of the moment, Thomas spoke; 'Well done Solomon. Damyanovitch's Day of Judgment is closer now than it's ever been before. If he's never called to account for those things I know he's done in recent months, at least now he'll be tried for his earlier crime'. Rebecca kissed him and spoke quietly; 'Father, I'm proud of you'.

But he was sanguine: he knew the odds were stacked against a conviction. 'The chances are, I'm sorry to say, he'll escape justice. Juries are often sceptical about the accuracy of recollections of aged witnesses and this case, if and when it gets to court, will probably be no exception. But this is not the point. This man will be brought down low when word of what he's done reaches the ears of those who have, until now, respected him. He'll be an outcast, shunned in his remaining years. I will have my testimony heard. I will not be silent to accommodate the political expediencies of others. Nemmersdorf will never be forgotten'. He turned to Thomas and smiled: it was time to talk of the present. 'Tell me young man, what news of our endeavours in the oil market? Have you destroyed my company yet, or do you need a little more time?' The three of them laughed; his wit had returned. 'Sir, I have only good news for you. As you'll recall, we went short on NYMEX, going completely against market sentiment. But with the collapse in futures prices and the restoration of calm, we'll now be able to buy up the contracts when the time arrives at far lower prices, making a substantial profit.' Solomon looked at him teasingly: 'You mean we've sold high now, but will buy back low later? Seems a well-thought out strategy. But if the market had continued to rise, what would have been the outcome then, I wonder?' Thomas shrugged his shoulders: 'Who can say, Solomon, who can say?'

Several days later, as Damyanovitch left the preliminary magistrates court hearing, walking towards the white van that would take him to a secure prison pending trial, a younger man looked down from the roof-top of a nearby building. Sergei Ivanov had two masters: the one now trapped in the British legal system like a bee in treacle, and the other in the Kremlin. He picked up his rifle and carefully aligned the target in the cross hairs. A glint of sunlight flashed off the sight: Damyanovitch looked up and recognising the distant silhouette, turned face-on. It was his final wish that the shot should be a clean one: he would accommodate his executioner. He knew his life had run its course: there was nothing left worth struggling for. Ivanov looked again through the sight: the line of fire was now perfect. Whispering the words 'Thank you', he pulled the trigger. He'd loved and respected the war hero but there were other con-siderations to think of. Russia, now a user of diplomatic means in the pursuit of global ambitions, could not afford to be embarrassed by links to a plot to destabilise her neighbours; for a greater purpose, it was time for Damyanovitch to take his last breath. The target's head exploded: it was a perfect hit. There would be no trial.

Chapter Seventy Eight

Thomas and Saul left their favourite Italian restaurant and sauntered back to Sheldons head office. They had been trying to celebrate the bank's survival but instead were subdued as they contemplated the death and destruction which had recently taken place around them. They talked of a friend lost: they would miss him. Briefly, Saul alluded to the millions of dollars he would no longer be receiving now that Damyanovitch was dead and the conspiracy in ruins. But it didn't matter anyway: it would have been blood money which, in retrospect at least, he felt he could never have accepted. He had rediscovered his conscience. For Thomas, the position was worse. The first instalment on the bank loan he'd raised to finance subcontractors on the Caspian pipeline contract was due within days, and he wouldn't be able to pay it: he was about to lose everything he had. As they entered Saul's room they noticed a large white envelope on his desk. It was correctly addressed, marked 'Strictly Private and Confidential: For the Attention of Saul Quartermain Only'. Thomas sat down whilst Saul wandered over to the window, carefully opening his mail with a gold paperknife. Thomas watched as his demeanour changed from studiousness to confusion and then to elation, all in the space of seconds. He read the letter aloud:

'Dear Mr. Quartermain,

You will recall that several years ago you and your associates, Mr. Thomas Stoneacre and Mr. Adam Creed, requested that Morgenthau and Luthmann, Attorneys, act for you in the administration of an offshore trust, the Tri-Star Trust. You will also recall that, pursuant to your instructions, we invested the entirety of the Trust's funds in one company, Piedmont Communications. In observance of our legal duties as Trustee we advised you a year after making the investment that continued holding of the stock was inadvisable. Despite this warning you declined our advice. However, as Trustee we were also empowered, and legally obliged, to 'take such measures as deemed necessary' to protect the Trust's capital. In exercising this power, and bearing in mind your instruction to continue holding the stock, we took the precautionary step of hedging the value of the Trust's portfolio through appropriate use of share options. You will recall that the stock's value subsequently collapsed; however, our hedging strategy ensured that the Trust was in fact entirely protected against this. Although the stock became worthless, this loss was offset by the gain made on the options the Trust was by now holding. In lieu of any further instructions from you, we decided to make such further investments as we deemed fit, exercising our power to do so under the Trust's terms.

Recently and with great sadness I read of Mr. Creed's death. The Tri-Star Trust's ownership was 'joint and several'; in other words, if one beneficiary should die, his share in the Trust accrues automatically and in equal shares to the surviving beneficiaries. You and Mr. Stoneacre have now succeeded to Mr. Creed's share. I am writing to you now to enquire as to whether you wish to maintain the Tri-Star Trust in existence or whether instead you and Mr. Stoneacre would prefer it to be wound up and its capital distributed between you. As of the close of play today the value of the Trust is approximately $9,000,000 (nine million US Dollars). I therefore await your instructions.

With sincere regards,
Dieter Morgenthau.'

Saul finished reading the letter and for several moments they stood looking at each other in stunned disbelief. It was Saul who started to laugh first and then Thomas, until they could be heard several rooms away along the corridor. Thomas's business would be saved: he now had the money for the first loan repayment. For Saul, his unwillingness to reach accord with Damyanovitch and instead sabotage his plans had lost him the promised 'success fee', but now he'd fulfilled his goal, albeit by a more circuitous route. As they celebrated, the telephone rang. Saul lifted the receiver and immediately recognised Laura's voice. 'Hi Saul, how's

London today? I miss you.' He smiled and his heart raced to hear her again. 'I had to call you because I've got some news. I hope it's not going to change things between us. Today Petr's will was read by the lawyers. All his shares, including his majority stake in Moscow Alpha, have been left to me. It's going to be a challenge pulling it back from the brink, but you're now talking to the bank's new Chairperson. You will still love me, won't you?'